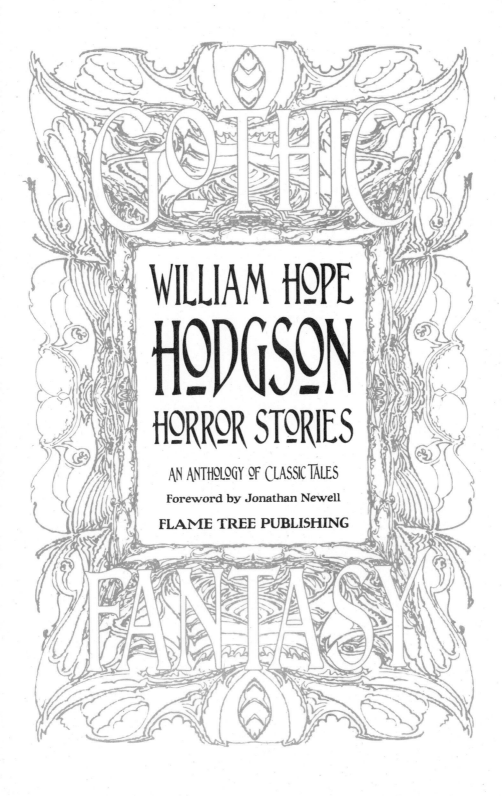

GOTHIC

WILLIAM HOPE

HODGSON

HORROR STORIES

AN ANTHOLOGY OF CLASSIC TALES

Foreword by Jonathan Newell

FLAME TREE PUBLISHING

FANTASY

This is a FLAME TREE Book

Publisher & Creative Director: Nick Wells
Senior Project Editor: Gillian Whitaker

FLAME TREE PUBLISHING
6 Melbray Mews, Fulham,
London SW6 3NS, United Kingdom
www.flametreepublishing.com

First published 2024

24 26 28 27 25
1 3 5 7 9 10 8 6 4 2

ISBN: 978-1-80417-796-9
Special ISBN: 978-1-80417-904-8

The cover image is created by Flame Tree Studio based on artwork by Slava Gerj, Gabor Ruszkai and FraVal Imaging.

A copy of the CIP data for this book is available from the British Library.

Printed and bound in China

GOTHIC

WILLIAM HOPE

HODGSON

HORROR STORIES

AN ANTHOLOGY OF CLASSIC TALES

Foreword by Jonathan Newell

FLAME TREE PUBLISHING

FANTASY

Contents

Carnacki Tales

Dangers at Sea

The Boats of the 'Glen Carrig'

The Weird and Strange

GOTHIC FANTASY

Foreword: William Hope Hodgson Horror Stories

DECADES BEFORE the cephalopodic horror of H.P. Lovecraft's Cthulhu and its many-tendrilled ilk became synonymous with weird fiction, a host of tentacular monsters, interdimensional invaders, fungus-ridden ghouls, and similar cosmic nightmares crawled, slithered, and shambled through the works of William Hope Hodgson. A bodybuilder, a sailor, and a war-hero as well as a writer, Hodgson lived a life of adventure, desperation, and danger – a life, as it were, on the borderland. His fiction is riddled with liminal zones: mysterious thresholds, tenebrous abysses, otherworldly doorways, myriad portals through time, space, and reality. Perhaps none recur with such force and frequency as the sea, whose depths reputedly held for Hodgson an intense and long-abiding dread, becoming the dwelling-place of some of his most memorable and macabre creations. During the same decades that Sigmund Freud was theorizing the murky recesses of the unconscious, the way our psychic past might haunt and bedevil us, Hodgson was transforming his seafaring experiences into the stuff of modern horror, finding in the fathomless dark an uncanny universe teeming with manifestations of our deepest, most primeval fears. In stories like 'The Derelict', the sea becomes a cauldron of metamorphosis and terror, transfiguring the detritus of human enterprise into forms alien and grotesque, decay giving way to loathsome life; in 'From the Tideless Sea' it appears as a wreck-clotted cemetery, an entropic wasteland every bit as grotesque and bleakly evocative as the poetic desolation of T.S. Eliot or W.B. Yeats.

Hodgson lived at a point of social and technological transition, his life spanning the twilight of the Victorian era through to the apocalypse of the First World War. It is no coincidence that his work seems preoccupied with decline and ruination, fascinated with science, and possessed by a rapt, sometimes horrified vision of the future. Much as the hypochondriac Hodgson habitually gargled, washed his hands after so much as handling an article of mail, foreswore the abomination of public toilet seats, and pursued an exacting regimen of exercise, fitness, and nutrition, so do his characters relentlessly attempt to forestall the incursion of unclean powers, what he memorably calls 'the ab-human', a term which scholars and writers from Kelly Hurley to China Miéville have used to describe the sense of encroaching meaninglessness and fragmentation pervading modernity. Thomas Carnacki, Hodgson's legendary 'ghost-finder', keeps otherworldly invaders at bay with the aid of his Electric Pentacle, a synthesis of occult and scientific technology; a shipwrecked couple obsessively prune their bodies of infectious mycelial growth in 'The Voice in the Night', cleansing them with carbolic soap; beleaguered sailors set up canvas shields in *The Boats of the 'Glen Carrig'*, hoping to deter such monstrosities as 'a many-flapped thing shaped as it might be, out of raw beef', writhing, yowling trees which 'bleed like any live creature', a reeking horror with a 'white demoniac face, human save that the mouth and nose had greatly the appearance of a beak', and a parade of tentacled interlopers lurking in the weed-choked nightmare-ocean of the Sargasso Sea. We can trace, in these meagre, frequently insufficient *cordons sanitaires* against the supernatural, something of the desperation of Hodgson's time – the increasingly panicked efforts to contain the seething anxieties of late-Victorian and Edwardian society, whose cataclysmic eruptions would eventually claim the life of Hodgson himself on the battlefields of Belgium.

Many of Hodgson's stories were critically well-received, recognized by his contemporaries for the vast scope of their imagination, their deft command of suspense, and their capacity to unsettle and disturb; a faux-warning prefaced his Carnacki story 'The Whistling Room', included in this collection, with the claim that his works had produced 'a widespread epidemic of Nervous Prostration'. Nonetheless, he remained a relatively marginal figure for much of the twentieth century and saw only modest financial success from his literary work during his own lifetime. Over recent decades, however, reviving interest in the weird, both scholarly and popular, has begun to lift Hodgson from the depths of unjust obscurity. You will find here both horrors and wonders, abject revulsion and numinous awe. On the surface the tales in this collection are pulp adventure at its finest. Beneath that surface roil the incomprehensible and inhuman forces of a world still being born.

Jonathan Newell

Publisher's Note

FOR OUR LATEST classic single-author collection, William Hope Hodgson seemed a clear candidate. Now chiefly remembered for his ingenious horror, he remains unmatched in his depiction of the sea, with all the mysteries, peril and unsettling terrors to be found there. In journeying through this anthology it will become apparent just how influential Hodgson's tales have been in his own day as well as ours. Along with H.P. Lovecraft, Algernon Blackwood and Arthur Machen, he helped define a particularly weird strain of horror, effectively creating his own mythos with his Sargasso Sea stories and earning Lovecraft's praise with his ability to hint at 'the nearness of nameless forces'. Not forgetting, too, the popular series featuring Carnacki, the occult detective, which forms the first thematic category of this book.

Following the Carnacki tales, we've devoted a whole section to Hodgson's nautical works, after which we've included in full his first novel, *The Boats of the 'Glen Carrig'*. The final group of stories gathers together those that suggest an even more otherworldly and fantastical, frightening realm beyond comprehension, such as 'The Voice in the Night' and an extract from his second novel *The House on the Borderland*. Onc late Carnacki tale appears not in our Carnacki section, but as the final story of the book, and part of the Weird and Strange: hopefully readers will agree that the fascinating monstrosity of The Hog is a suitable note on which to end. Two recommended reads are also provided at the end of each story for the reader's interest, in what we hope proves an enjoyable collection of Hodgson's best horror fiction.

GOTHIC

WILLIAM HOPE
HODGSON
HORROR STORIES

AN ANTHOLOGY OF CLASSIC TALES

Foreword by Jonathan Newell

FLAME TREE PUBLISHING

FANTASY

Carnacki Tales

The Gateway of the Monster

IN RESPONSE to Carnacki's usual card of invitation to have dinner and listen to a story, I arrived promptly at 427, Cheyne Walk, to find the three others who were always invited to these happy little times, there before me. Five minutes later, Carnacki, Arkright, Jessop, Taylor and I were all engaged in the 'pleasant occupation' of dining.

"You've not been long away, this time," I remarked as I finished my soup; forgetting momentarily, Carnacki's dislike of being asked even to skirt the borders of his story until such time as he was ready. Then he would not stint words.

"That's all," he replied with brevity; and I changed the subject, remarking that I had been buying a new gun, to which piece of news he gave an intelligent nod, and a smile which I think showed a genuinely good-humoured appreciation of my intentional changing of the conversation.

"As Dodgson was remarking just now, I've only been away a short time, and for a very good reason too – I've only been away a short distance. The exact locality I am afraid I must not tell you; but it is less than twenty miles from here; though, except for changing a name, that won't spoil the story. And it is a story too! One of the most extraordinary things I have ever run against.

"I received a letter a fortnight ago from a man I must call Anderson, asking for an appointment. I arranged a time, and when he came, I found that he wished me to investigate, and see whether I could not clear up a long standing and well – too well – authenticated case of what he termed 'haunting'. He gave me very full particulars, and finally, as the thing seemed to present something unique, I decided to take it up.

"Two days later, I drove to the house, late in the afternoon. I found it a very old place, standing quite alone in its own grounds. Anderson had left a letter with the butler, I found, pleading excuses for his absence, and leaving the whole house at my disposal for my investigations. The butler evidently knew the object of my visit, and I questioned him pretty thoroughly during dinner, which I had in rather lonely state. He is an old and privileged servant, and had the history of the Grey Room exact in detail. From him I learned more particulars regarding two things that Anderson had mentioned in but a casual manner. The first was that the door of the Grey Room would be heard in the dead of night to open, and slam heavily, and this even though the butler knew it was locked, and the key on the bunch in his pantry. The second was that the bedclothes would always be found torn off the bed, and hurled in a heap into a corner.

"But it was the door slamming that chiefly bothered the old butler. Many and many a time, he told me, had he lain awake and just got shivering with fright, listening; for sometimes the door would be slammed time after time – thud! thud! thud! – so that sleep was impossible.

"From Anderson, I knew already that the room had a history extending back over a hundred and fifty years. Three people had been strangled in it – an ancestor of his and his wife and child. This is authentic, as I had taken very great pains to discover, so that you can imagine it was with a feeling that I had a striking case to investigate, that I went upstairs after dinner to have a look at the Grey Room.

"Peter, the old butler, was in rather a state about my going, and assured me with much solemnity that in all the twenty years of his service, no one had ever entered that room after nightfall. He begged me, in quite a fatherly way, to wait till the morning, when there would be no danger, and then he could accompany me himself.

"Of course, I smiled a little at him, and told him not to bother. I explained that I should do no more than look around a bit, and perhaps affix a few seals. He need not fear; I was used to that sort of thing. But he shook his head, when I said that.

"'There isn't many ghosts like ours, sir,' he assured me, with mournful pride. And, by Jove! he was right, as you will see.

"I took a couple of candles, and Peter followed, with his bunch of keys. He unlocked the door; but would not come inside with me. He was evidently in a fright, and renewed his request, that I would put off my examination, until daylight. Of course, I laughed at him again, and told him he could stand sentry at the door, and catch anything that came out.

"'It never comes outside, sir,' he said, in his funny, old, solemn manner. Somehow he managed to make me feel as if I were going to have the 'creeps' right away. Anyway, it was one to him, you know.

"I left him there, and examined the room. It is a big apartment, and well furnished in the grand style, with a huge four-poster, which stands with its head to the end wall. There were two candles on the mantelpiece and two on each of the three tables that were in the room. I lit the lot, and after that the room felt a little less inhumanly dreary; though, mind you, it was quite fresh, and well kept in every way.

"After I had taken a good look round I sealed lengths of baby ribbon across the windows, along the walls, over the pictures, and over the fireplace and the wall-closets. All the time, as I worked, the butler stood just without the door, and I could not persuade him to enter; though I jested with him a little, as I stretched the ribbons, and went here and there about my work. Every now and again, he would say: 'You'll excuse me, I'm sure, sir; but I do wish you would come out, sir. I'm fair in a quake for you.'

"I told him he need not wait; but he was loyal enough in his way to what he considered his duty. He said he could not go away and leave me all alone there. He apologised; but made it very clear that I did not realise the danger of the room; and I could see, generally, that he was in a pretty frightened state. All the same, I had to make the room so that I should know if anything material entered it; so I asked him not to bother me, unless he really heard something. He was beginning to get on my nerves, and the 'feel' of the room was bad enough, without making it any nastier.

"For a time further, I worked, stretching ribbons across the floor, and sealing them, so that the merest touch would have broken them, were anyone to venture into the room in the dark with the intention of playing the fool. All this had taken me far longer than I had anticipated; and, suddenly, I heard a clock strike eleven. I had taken off my coat soon after commencing work; now, however, as I had practically made an end of all that I intended to do, I walked across to the settee, and picked it up. I was in the act of getting into it when the old butler's voice (he had not said a word for the last hour) came sharp and frightened: 'Come out, sir, quick! There's something going to happen!' Jove! but I jumped, and then, in the same moment, one of the candles on the table to the left of the bed went out. Now whether it was the wind, or what, I do not know; but just for a moment, I was enough startled to make a run for the door;

though I am glad to say that I pulled, up before I reached it. I simply could not bunk out, with the butler standing there, after having, as it were, read him a sort of lesson on 'bein' brave, y'know'. So I just turned right round, picked up the two candles off the mantelpiece, and walked across to the table near the bed. Well, I saw nothing. I blew out the candle that was still alight; then I went to those on the two other tables, and blew them out. Then, outside of the door, the old man called again: 'Oh! sir, do be told! Do be told!'

"'All right, Peter,' I said, and, by Jove, my voice was not as steady as I should have liked! I made for the door, and had a bit of work, not to start running. I took some thundering long strides, as you can imagine. Near the door, I had a sudden feeling that there was a cold wind in the room. It was almost as if the window had been suddenly opened a little. I got to the door and the old butler gave back a step, in a sort of instinctive way. 'Collar the candles, Peter!' I said, pretty sharply, and shoved them into his hands. I turned, and caught the handle, and slammed the door shut, with a crash. Somehow, do you know, as I did so, I thought I felt something pull back on it; but it must have been only fancy. I turned the key in the lock, and then again, double-locking the door. I felt easier then, and set-to and sealed the door. In addition, I put my card over the keyhole, and sealed it there; after which I pocketed the key, and went downstairs – with Peter; who was nervous and silent, leading the way. Poor old beggar! It had not struck me until that moment that he had been enduring a considerable strain during the last two or three hours.

"About midnight, I went to bed. My room lay at the end of the corridor upon which opens the door of the Grey Room. I counted the doors between it and mine, and found that five rooms lay between. And I am sure you can understand that I was not sorry. Then, just as I was beginning to undress, an idea came to me, and I took my candle and sealing-wax, and sealed the doors of all the five rooms. If any door slammed in the night, I should know just which one.

"I returned to my room, locked the door, and went to bed. I was waked suddenly from a deep sleep by a loud crash somewhere out in the passage. I sat up in bed and listened, but heard nothing. Then I lit my candle. I was in the very act of lighting it when there came the bang of a door being violently slammed, along the corridor. I jumped out of bed, and got my revolver. I unlocked my door, and went out into the passage, holding my candle high, and keeping the pistol ready. Then a queer thing happened. I could not go a step towards the Grey Room. You all know I am not really a cowardly chap. I've gone into too many cases connected with ghostly things, to be accused of that; but I tell you I funked it; simply funked it, just like any blessed kid. There was something precious unholy in the air that night. I backed into my bedroom, and shut and locked the door. Then I sat on the bed all night, and listened to the dismal thudding of a door up the corridor. The sound seemed to echo through all the house.

"Daylight came at last, and I washed and dressed. The door had not slammed for about an hour, and I was getting back my nerve again. I felt ashamed of myself; though in some ways it was silly, for when you're meddling with that sort of thing, your nerve is bound to go, sometimes. And you just have to sit quiet and call yourself a coward until daylight. Sometimes it is more than just cowardice, I fancy. I believe at times it is something warning you, and fighting *for* you. But, all the same, I always feel mean and miserable, after a time like that.

"When the day came properly, I opened my door, and, keeping my revolver handy, went quietly along the passage. I had to pass the head of the stairs, on the way, and who should

I see coming up, but the old butler, carrying a cup of coffee. He had merely tucked his nightshirt into his trousers, and he had an old pair of carpet slippers on.

"'Hello, Peter!' I said, feeling suddenly cheerful; for I was as glad as any lost child to have a live human being close to me. 'Where are you off to with the refreshments?'

"The old man gave a start, and slopped some of the coffee. He stared up at me and I could see that he looked white and done-up. He came on up the stairs and held out the little tray to me. 'I'm very thankful indeed, Sir, to see you safe and well,' he said. 'I feared, one time, you might risk going into the Grey Room, Sir. I've lain awake all night, with the sound of the Door. And when it came light, I thought I'd make you a cup of coffee. I knew you would want to look at the seals, and somehow it seems safer if there's two, Sir.'

"'Peter,' I said, 'you're a brick. This is very thoughtful of you.' And I drank the coffee. 'Come along,' I told him, and handed him back the tray. 'I'm going to have a look at what the Brutes have been up to. I simply hadn't the pluck to in the night.'

"'I'm very thankful, Sir,' he replied. 'Flesh and blood can do nothing, Sir, against devils; and that's what's in the Grey Room after dark.'

"I examined the seals on all the doors, as I went along, and found them right; but when I got to the Grey Room, the seal was broken; though the card, over the keyhole, was untouched. I ripped it off, and unlocked the door, and went in, rather cautiously, as you can imagine; but the whole room was empty of anything to frighten one, and there was heaps of light. I examined all my seals, and not a single one was disturbed. The old butler had followed me in, and, suddenly, he called out:'The bedclothes, Sir!'

"I ran up to the bed, and looked over; and, surely, they were lying in the corner to the left of the bed. Jove! you can imagine how queer I felt. Something *had* been in the room. I stared for a while, from the bed, to the clothes on the floor. I had a feeling that I did not want to touch either. Old Peter, though, did not seem to be affected that way. He went over to the bed-coverings, and was going to pick them up, as, doubtless, he had done every day these twenty years back; but I stopped him. I wanted nothing touched, until I had finished my examination. This, I must have spent a full hour over, and then I let Peter straighten up the bed; after which we went out and I locked the door; for the room was getting on my nerves.

"I had a short walk, and then breakfast; after which I felt more my own man, and so returned to the Grey Room, and, with Peter's help, and one of the maids, I had everything taken out except the bed, even the very pictures. I examined the walls, floor and ceiling then, with probe, hammer and magnifying glass; but found nothing suspicious. And I can assure you, I began to realise, in very truth, that some incredible thing had been loose in the room during the past night. I sealed up everything again, and went out, locking and sealing the door, as before.

"After dinner that night, Peter and I unpacked some of my stuff, and I fixed up my camera and flashlight opposite to the door of the Grey Room, with a string from the trigger of the flashlight to the door. Then, you see, if the door were really opened, the flashlight would blare out, and there would be, possibly, a very queer picture to examine in the morning. The last thing I did, before leaving, was to uncap the lens; and after that I went off to my bedroom, and to bed; for I intended to be up at midnight; and to ensure this, I set my little alarm to call me; also I left my candle burning.

"The clock woke me at twelve, and I got up and into my dressing-gown and slippers. I shoved my revolver into my right side-pocket, and opened my door. Then, I lit my dark-room lamp, and withdrew the slide, so that it would give a clear light. I carried it up the corridor, about thirty feet, and put it down on the floor, with the open side away from me, so that it would show me anything that might approach along the dark passage. Then I went back, and sat in the doorway of my room, with my revolver handy, staring up the passage towards the place where I knew my camera stood outside the door of the Grey Room.

"I should think I had watched for about an hour and a half, when, suddenly, I heard a faint noise, away up the corridor. I was immediately conscious of a queer prickling sensation about the back of my head, and my hands began to sweat a little. The following instant, the whole end of the passage flicked into sight in the abrupt glare of the flashlight. Then came the succeeding darkness, and I peered nervously up the corridor, listening tensely, and trying to find what lay beyond the faint glow of my dark-lamp, which now seemed ridiculously dim by contrast with the tremendous blaze of the flash-powder.... And then, as I stooped forward, staring and listening, there came the crashing thud of the door of the Grey Room. The sound seemed to fill the whole of the large corridor, and go echoing hollowly through the house. I tell you, I felt horrible – as if my bones were water. Simply beastly. Jove! how I did stare, and how I listened. And then it came again – thud, thud, thud, and then a silence that was almost worse than the noise of the door; for I kept fancying that some brutal thing was stealing upon me along the corridor. And then, suddenly, my lamp was put out, and I could not see a yard before me. I realised all at once that I was doing a very silly thing, sitting there, and I jumped up. Even as I did so, I *thought* I heard a sound in the passage, and quite *near* me. I made one backward spring into my room, and slammed and locked the door. I sat on my bed, and stared at the door. I had my revolver in my hand; but it seemed an abominably useless thing. I felt that there was something the other side of that door. For some unknown reason I *knew* it was pressed up against the door, and it was soft. That was just what I thought. Most extraordinary thing to think.

"Presently I got hold of myself a bit, and marked out a pentacle hurriedly with chalk on the polished floor; and there I sat in it almost until dawn. And all the time, away up the corridor, the door of the Grey Room thudded at solemn and horrid intervals. It was a miserable, brutal night.

"When the day began to break, the thudding of the door came gradually to an end, and, at last, I got hold of my courage, and went along the corridor, in the half light, to cap the lens of my camera. I can tell you, it took some doing; but if I had not done so my photograph would have been spoilt, and I was tremendously keen to save it. I got back to my room, and then set-to and rubbed out the five-pointed star in which I had been sitting.

"Half an hour later there was a tap at my door. It was Peter with my coffee. When I had drunk it, we both went along to the Grey Room. As we went, I had a look at the seals on the other doors, but they were untouched. The seal on the door of the Grey Room was broken, as also was the string from the trigger of the flashlight; but the card over the keyhole was still there. I ripped it off and opened the door. Nothing unusual was to be seen until we came to the bed; then I saw that, as on the previous day, the bedclothes had been torn off, and hurled into the left-hand corner, exactly where I had seen them before. I felt very queer; but I did not forget to look at all the seals, only to find that not one had been broken.

"Then I turned and looked at old Peter, and he looked at me, nodding his head.

"'Let's get out of here!' I said. 'It's no place for any living human to enter, without proper protection.'

"We went out then, and I locked and sealed the door, again.

"After breakfast, I developed the negative; but it showed only the door of the Grey Room, half opened. Then I left the house, as I wanted to get certain matters and implements that might be necessary to life; perhaps to the spirit; for I intended to spend the coming night in the Grey Room.

"I got back in a cab, about half-past-five, with my apparatus, and this, Peter and I carried up to the Grey Room, where I piled it carefully in the centre of the floor. When everything was in the room, including a cat which I had brought, I locked and sealed the door, and went towards my bedroom, telling Peter I should not be down to dinner. He said, 'Yes, sir,' and went downstairs, thinking that I was going to turn in, which was what I wanted him to believe, as I knew he would have worried both me and himself, if he had known what I intended.

"But I merely got my camera and flashlight from my bedroom, and hurried back to the Grey Room. I locked and sealed myself in, and set to work, for I had a lot to do before it got dark.

"First I cleared away all the ribbons across the floor; then I carried the cat – still fastened in its basket – over towards the far wall, and left it. I returned then to the centre of the room, and measured out a space twenty-one feet in diameter, which I swept with a 'broom of hyssop'. About this I drew a circle of chalk, taking care never to step over the circle. Beyond this I smudged, with a bunch of garlic, a broad belt right around the chalked circle, and when this was complete, I took from among my stores in the centre a small jar of a certain water. I broke away the parchment and withdrew the stopper. Then, dipping my left forefinger in the little jar, I went round the circle again, making upon the floor, just within the line of chalk, the Second Sign of the Saaamaaa Ritual, and joining each Sign most carefully with the left-handed crescent. I can tell you, I felt easier when this was done and the 'water-circle' complete. Then, I unpacked some more of the stuff that I had brought, and placed a lighted candle in the 'valley' of each Crescent. After that, I drew a Pentacle, so that each of the five points of the defensive star touched the chalk circle. In the five points of the star I placed five portions of bread, each wrapped in linen, and in the five 'vales', five opened jars of the water I had used to make the 'water circle'. And now I had my first protective barrier complete.

"Now, anyone, except you who know something of my methods of investigation, might consider all this a piece of useless and foolish superstition; but you all remember the Black Veil case, in which I believe my life was saved by a very similar form of protection, whilst Aster, who sneered at it, and would not come inside, died. I got the idea from the Sigsand MS., written, so far as I can make out, in the fourteenth century. At first, naturally, I imagined it was just an expression of the superstition of his time; and it was not until a year later that it occurred to me to test his 'Defence', which I did, as I've just said, in that horrible Black Veil business. You know how *that* turned out. Later, I used it several times, and always I came through safe, until that Moving Fur case. It was only a partial 'Defence' there and I nearly died in the pentacle. After that I came across Professor Garder's 'Experiments with a Medium', When they surrounded the Medium with a current, in vacuum, he lost his power – almost as if it cut him off from the Immaterial. That made me think a lot; and that is how I came to make the Electric Pentacle, which is a most marvellous 'Defence' against certain manifestations. I used the shape of the defensive star for this protection, because I have, personally, no doubt at all but that there is some extraordinary virtue in the old magic figure. Curious thing for a Twentieth Century man to admit, is it not? But then, as you all know, I never did, and never will, allow myself to be blinded by a little cheap laughter. I ask questions, and keep my eyes open!

"In this last case I had little doubt that I had run up against a supernatural monster, and I meant to take every possible care; for the danger is abominable.

"I turned to now to fit the Electric Pentacle, setting it so that each of its 'points' and 'vales' coincided exactly with the 'points' and 'vales' of the drawn pentagram upon the floor. Then I connected up the battery, and the next instant the pale blue glare from the intertwining vacuum tubes shone out.

"I glanced about me then, with something of a sigh of relief, and realised suddenly that the dusk was upon me, for the window was grey and unfriendly. Then round at the big, empty room, over the double barrier of electric and candle light. I had an abrupt, extraordinary sense of weirdness thrust upon me in the air, you know; as it were, a sense of something inhuman impending. The room was full of the stench of bruised garlic, a smell I hate.

"I turned now to my camera, and saw that it and the flashlight were in order. Then I tested my revolver, carefully; though I had little thought that it would be needed. Yet, to what extent materialisation of an abnatural creature is possible, given favourable conditions, no one can say, and I had no idea what horrible thing I was going to see, or feel the presence of. I might, in the end, have to fight with a materialised monster. I did not know, and could only be prepared. You see, I never forgot that three people had been strangled in the bed close to me, and the fierce slamming of the door I had heard myself. I had no doubt that I was investigating a dangerous and ugly case.

"By this time the night had come; though the room was very light with the burning candles; and I found myself glancing behind me, constantly, and then all round the room. It was nervy work waiting for that thing to come. Then, suddenly, I was aware of a little, cold wind sweeping over me, coming from behind. I gave one great nerve-thrill, and a prickly feeling went all over the back of my head. Then I hove myself round with a sort of stiff jerk, and stared straight against that queer wind. It seemed to come from the corner of the room to the left of the bed – the place where both times I had found the heap of tossed bedclothes. Yet, I could see nothing unusual; no opening – nothing…!

"Abruptly I was aware that the candles were all a-flicker in that unnatural wind…. I believe I just squatted there and stared in a horribly frightened, wooden way for some minutes. I shall never be able to let you know how disgustingly horrible it was sitting in that vile, cold wind! And then, flick! flick! all the candles round the outer barrier went out; and there was I, locked and sealed in that room, and with no light beyond the weakish blue glare of the Electric Pentacle.

"A time of abominable tenseness passed, and still that wind blew upon me; and then, suddenly, I knew that something stirred in the corner to the left of the bed. I was made conscious of it, rather by some inward, unused sense, than by either sight or sound; for the pale, short-radius glare of the Pentacle gave but a very poor light for seeing by. Yet, as I stared, something began slowly to grow upon my sight – a moving shadow, a little darker than the surrounding shadows. I lost the thing amid the vagueness, and for a moment or two I glanced swiftly from side to side, with a fresh, new sense of impending danger. Then my attention was directed to the bed. All the coverings were being drawn steadily off, with a hateful, stealthy sort of motion. I heard the slow, dragging slither of the clothes; but I could see nothing of the thing that pulled. I was aware in a funny, subconscious, introspective fashion that the 'creep' had come upon me; yet I was cooler mentally than I had been for some minutes; sufficiently so to feel that my hands were sweating coldly, and to shift my revolver, half-consciously, whilst I rubbed my right hand dry upon my knee; though never, for an instant, taking my gaze or my attention from those moving clothes.

"The faint noises from the bed ceased once, and there was a most intense silence, with only the sound of the blood beating in my head. Yet, immediately afterwards, I heard again the slurring of the bedclothes being dragged off the bed. In the midst of my nervous tension I remembered the camera, and reached round for it; but without looking away from the bed. And then, you know, all in a moment, the whole of the bed-coverings were torn off with extraordinary violence, and I heard the flump they made as they were hurled into the corner.

"There was a time of absolute quietness then for perhaps a couple of minutes; and you can imagine how horrible I felt. The bedclothes had been thrown with such savageness! And then again, the brutal unnaturalness of the thing that had just been done before me!

"Abruptly, over by the door, I heard a faint noise – a sort of crickling sound and then a pitter or two upon the floor. A great nervous thrill swept over me, seeming to run up my spine and over the back of my head; for the seal that secured the door had just been broken. Something was there. I could not see the door; at least, I mean to say that it was impossible to say how much I actually saw, and how much my imagination supplied. I made it out only as a continuation of the grey walls.... And then it seemed to me that something dark and indistinct moved and wavered there among the shadows.

"Abruptly, I was aware that the door was opening, and with an effort I reached again for my camera; but before I could aim it the door was slammed with a terrific crash that filled the whole room with a sort of hollow thunder. I jumped, like a frightened child. There seemed such a power behind the noise; as though a vast, wanton Force were 'out'. Can you understand?

"The door was not touched again; but, directly afterwards, I heard the basket, in which the cat lay, creak. I tell you, I fairly pringled all along my back. I knew that I was going to learn definitely whether what was abroad was dangerous to Life. From the cat there rose suddenly a hideous caterwaul, that ceased abruptly, and then – too late – I snapped on the flashlight. In the great glare, I saw that the basket had been overturned, and the lid was wrenched open, with the cat lying half in, and half out upon the floor. I saw nothing else, but I was full of the knowledge that I was in the presence of some Being or Thing that had power to destroy.

"During the next two or three minutes, there was an odd, noticeable quietness in the room, and you must remember I was half-blinded, for the time, because of the flashlight; so that the whole place seemed to be pitchy dark just beyond the shine of the Pentacle. I tell you it was most horrible. I just knelt there in the star, and whirled round, trying to see whether anything was coming at me.

"My power of sight came gradually, and I got a little hold of myself; and abruptly I saw the thing I was looking for, close to the 'water-circle.' It was big and indistinct, and wavered curiously, as though the shadow of a vast spider hung suspended in the air, just beyond the barrier. It passed swiftly round the circle, and seemed to probe ever towards me; but only to draw back with extraordinary jerky movements, as might a living person if they touched the hot bar of a grate.

"Round and round it moved, and round and round I turned. Then, just opposite to one of the 'vales' in the pentacles, it seemed to pause, as though preliminary to a tremendous effort. It retired almost beyond the glow of the vacuum light, and then came straight towards me, appearing to gather form and solidity as it came. There seemed a vast, malign determination behind the movement, that must succeed. I was on my knees, and I jerked

THE GATEWAY OF THE MONSTER

THE GATEWAY OF THE MONSTER

back, falling on to my left hand and hip, in a wild endeavour to get back from the advancing thing. With my right hand I was grabbing madly for my revolver, which I had let slip. The brutal thing came with one great sweep straight over the garlic and the 'water-circle', almost to the vale of the pentacle. I believe I yelled. Then, just as suddenly as it had swept over, it seemed to be hurled back by some mighty, invisible force.

"It must have been some moments before I realised that I was safe; and then I got myself together in the middle of the pentacles, feeling horribly gone and shaken, and glancing round and round the barrier; but the thing had vanished. Yet I had learnt something, for I knew now that the Grey Room was haunted by a monstrous hand.

"Suddenly, as I crouched there, I saw what had so nearly given the monster an opening through the barrier. In my movements within the pentacle I must have touched one of the jars of water; for just where the thing had made its attack the jar that guarded the 'deep' of the 'vale' had been moved to one side, and this had left one of the 'five doorways' unguarded. I put it back, quickly, and felt almost safe again, for I had found the cause and the 'defence' was still good. And I began to hope again that I should see the morning come in. When I saw that thing so nearly succeed, I'd had an awful, weak, overwhelming feeling that the 'barriers' could never bring me safe through the night against such a Force. You can understand?

"For a long time I could not see the hand; but, presently, I thought I saw, once or twice, an odd wavering, over among the shadows near the door. A little later, as though in a sudden fit of malignant rage, the dead body of the cat was picked up, and beaten with dull, sickening blows against the solid floor. That made me feel rather queer.

"A minute afterwards, the door was opened and slammed twice with tremendous force. The next instant the thing made one swift, vicious dart at me, from out of the shadows. Instinctively I started sideways from it, and so plucked my hand from upon the Electric Pentacle, where – for a wickedly careless moment – I had placed it. The monster was hurled off from the neighbourhood of the pentacles; though – owing to my inconceivable foolishness – it had been enabled for a second time to pass the outer barriers. I can tell you, I shook for a time, with sheer funk. I moved right to the centre of the pentacles again, and knelt there, making myself as small and compact as possible.

"As I knelt, there came to me presently, a vague wonder at the two 'accidents' which had so nearly allowed the brute to get at me. Was I being *influenced* to unconscious voluntary actions that endangered me? The thought took hold of me, and I watched my every movement. Abruptly, I stretched a tired leg, and knocked over one of the jars of water. Some was spilled; but because of my suspicious watchfulness, I had it upright and back within the vale while yet some of the water remained. Even as I did so, the vast, black, half-materialised hand beat up at me out of the shadows, and seemed to leap almost into my face; so nearly did it approach; but for the third time it was thrown back by some altogether enormous, over-mastering force. Yet, apart from the dazed fright in which it left me, I had for a moment that feeling of spiritual sickness, as if some delicate, beautiful, inward grace had suffered, which is felt only upon the too near approach of the abhuman, and is more dreadful, in a strange way, than any physical pain that can be suffered. I knew by this, more of the extent and closeness of the danger; and for a long time I was simply cowed by the butt-headed brutality of that Force upon my spirit. I can put it no other way.

"I knelt again in the centre of the pentacles, watching myself with more fear, almost, than the monster; for I knew now that, unless I guarded myself from every sudden impulse that came to me, I might simply work my own destruction. Do you see how horrible it all was?

"I spent the rest of the night in a haze of sick fright, and so tense that I could not make a single movement naturally. I was in such fear that any desire for action that came to me might be prompted by the Influence that I knew was at work on me. And outside of the barrier that ghastly thing went round and round, grabbing and grabbing in the air at me. Twice more was the body of the dead cat molested. The second time, I heard every bone in its body scrunch and crack. And all the time the horrible wind was blowing upon me from the corner of the room to the left of the bed.

"Then, just as the first touch of dawn came into the sky, that unnatural wind ceased, in a single moment; and I could see no sign of the hand. The dawn came slowly, and presently the wan light filled all the room, and made the pale glare of the Electric Pentacle look more unearthly. Yet, it was not until the day had fully come, that I made any attempt to leave the barrier, for I did not know but that there was some method abroad, in the sudden stopping of that wind, to entice me from the pentacles.

"At last, when the dawn was strong and bright, I took one last look round, and ran for the door. I got it unlocked, in a nervous, clumsy fashion; then locked it hurriedly, and went to my bedroom, where I lay on the bed, and tried to steady my nerves. Peter came, presently, with the coffee, and when I had drunk it, I told him I meant to have a sleep, as I had been up all night. He took the tray, and went out quietly; and after I had locked my door I turned in properly, and at last got to sleep.

"I woke about midday, and after some lunch, went up to the Grey Room. I switched off the current from the Pentacle, which I had left on in my hurry; also, I removed the body of the cat. You can understand I did not want anyone to see the poor brute. After that, I made a very careful search of the corner where the bedclothes had been thrown. I made several holes, and probed, but found nothing. Then it occurred to me to try with my instrument under the skirting. I did so, and heard my wire ring on metal. I turned the hook-end that way, and fished for the thing. At the second go, I got it. It was a small object, and I took it to the window. I found it to be a curious ring, made of some greyish metal. The curious thing about it was that it was made in the form of a pentagon; that is, the same shape as the inside of the magic pentacle, but without the 'mounts' which form the points of the defensive star. It was free from all chasing or engraving.

"You will understand that I was excited, when I tell you that I felt sure I held in my hand the famous Luck Ring of the Anderson family; which, indeed, was of all things the one most intimately connected with the history of the haunting. This ring was handed on from father to son through generations, and always – in obedience to some ancient family tradition – each son had to promise never to wear the ring. The ring, I may say, was brought home by one of the Crusaders, under very peculiar circumstances; but the story is too long to go into here.

"It appears that young Sir Hulbert, an ancestor of Anderson's, made a bet, in drink, you know, that he would wear the ring that night. He did so, and in the morning his wife and child were found strangled in the bed, in the very room in which I stood. Many people, it would seem, thought young Sir Hulbert was guilty of having done the thing in drunken anger; and he, in an attempt to prove his innocence, slept a second night in the room. He also was strangled. Since, as you may imagine, no one has spent a night in the Grey Room, until I did so. The ring had been lost so long, that it had become almost a myth; and it was most extraordinary to stand there, with the actual thing in my hand, as you can understand.

"It was whilst I stood there, looking at the ring, that I got an idea. Supposing that it were, in a way, a doorway – You see what I mean? A sort of gap in the world-hedge. It was a queer idea, I know, and probably was not my own, but came to me from the Outside. You see, the wind had come from that part of the room where the ring lay. I thought a lot about it. Then the shape – the inside of a pentacle. It had no 'mounts', and without mounts, as the Sigsand MS. has it: 'Thee mownts wych are thee Five Hills of safetie. To lack is to gyve pow'r to thee daemon; and surlie to fayvor thee Evill Thynge.' You see, the very shape of the ring was significant; and I determined to test it.

"I unmade my pentacle, for it must be made afresh *and around* the one to be protected. Then I went out and locked the door; after which I left the house, to get certain matters, for neither 'yarbs nor fyre nor water' must be used a second time. I returned about seven-thirty, and as soon as the things I had brought had been carried up to the Grey Room, I dismissed Peter for the night, just as I had done the evening before. When he had gone downstairs, I let myself into the room and locked and sealed the door. I went to the place in the centre of the room where all the stuff had been packed, and set to work with all my speed to construct a barrier about me and the ring.

"I do not remember whether I explained to you. But I had reasoned that if the ring were in any way a 'medium of admission', and it were enclosed with me in the Electric Pentacle' it would be, to express it loosely, insulated. Do you see? The Force, which had visible expression as a Hand, would have to stay beyond the Barrier which separates the Ab from the Normal; for the 'gateway' would be removed from accessibility.

"As I was saying, I worked with all my speed to get the barrier completed about me and the ring, for it was already later than I cared to be in that room 'unprotected'. Also, I had a feeling that there would be a vast effort made that night to regain the use of the ring. For I had the strongest conviction that the ring was a necessity to materialisation. You will see whether I was right.

"I completed the barriers in about an hour, and you can imagine something of the relief I felt when I saw the pale glare of the Electric Pentacle once more all about me. From then, onwards, for about two hours, I sat quietly, facing the corner from which the wind came. About eleven o'clock a queer knowledge came that something was near to me; yet nothing happened for a whole hour after that. Then, suddenly, I felt the cold, queer wind begin to blow upon me. To my astonishment, it seemed now to come from behind me, and I whipped round, with a hideous quake of fear. The wind met me in the face. It was blowing up from the floor close to me. I stared down, in a sickening maze of new frights. What on earth had I done now! The ring was there, close beside me, where I had put it. Suddenly, as I stared, bewildered, I was aware that there was something queer about the ring – funny shadowy movements and convolutions. I looked at them, stupidly. And then, abruptly, I knew that the wind was blowing up at me from the ring. A queer indistinct smoke became visible to me, seeming to pour upwards through the ring, and mix with the moving shadows. Suddenly, I realised that I was in more than any mortal danger; for the convoluting shadows about the ring were taking shape, and the death-hand was forming *within* the Pentacle. My goodness! do you realise it! I had brought the 'gateway' into the pentacles, and the brute was coming through – pouring into the material world, as gas might pour out from the mouth of a pipe.

"I should think that I knelt for a moment in a sort of stunned fright. Then, with a mad, awkward movement, I snatched at the ring, intending to hurl it out of the Pentacle. Yet it eluded me, as though some invisible, living thing jerked it hither and thither. At last, I gripped it; yet, in the same instant, it was torn from my grasp with incredible and brutal force. A great, black shadow covered it, and rose into the air, and came at me. I saw that it was the Hand, vast and nearly perfect in form. I gave one crazy yell, and jumped over the Pentacle and the ring of burning candles, and ran despairingly for the door. I fumbled idiotically and ineffectually with the key, and all the time I stared, with a fear that was like insanity, towards the Barriers. The hand was plunging towards me; yet, even as it had been unable to pass into the pentacle when the ring was without, so, now that the ring was within, it had no power to pass out. The monster was chained, as surely as any beast would be, were chains rivetted upon it.

"Even then, I got a flash of this knowledge; but I was too utterly shaken with fright, to reason; and the instant I managed to get the key turned, I sprang into the passage, and slammed the door with a crash. I locked it, and got to my room, somehow; for I was trembling so that I could hardly stand, as you can imagine. I locked myself in, and managed to get the candle lit; then I lay down on the bed, and kept quiet for an hour or two, and so I got steadied.

"I got a little sleep, later; but woke when Peter brought my coffee. When I had drunk it I felt altogether better, and took the old man along with me whilst I had a look into the Grey Room. I opened the door, and peeped in. The candles were still burning, wan against the daylight; and behind them was the pale, glowing star of the Electric Pentacle. And there in the middle was the ring… the gateway of the monster, lying demure and ordinary.

"Nothing in the room was touched, and I knew that the brute had never managed to cross the Pentacles. Then I went out, and locked the door.

"After a sleep of some hours, I left the house. I returned in the afternoon in a cab. I had with me an oxy-hydrogen jet, and two cylinders, containing the gases. I carried the things to the Grey Room, and there, in the centre of the Electric Pentacle, I erected the little furnace. Five minutes later the Luck Ring, once the 'luck', but now the 'bane', of the Anderson family, was no more than a little solid splash of hot metal."

Carnacki felt in his pocket, and pulled out something wrapped in tissue paper. He passed it to me. I opened it and found a small circle of greyish metal, something like lead, only harder and rather brighter.

"Well?" I asked, at length, after examining it and handing it round to the others. "Did that stop the haunting?"

Carnacki nodded. "Yes," he said. "I slept three nights in the Grey Room, before I left. Old Peter nearly fainted when he knew that I meant to; but by the third night he seemed to realise that the house was just safe and ordinary. And, you know, I believe, in his heart, he hardly approved."

Carnacki stood up and began to shake hands. "Out you go!" he said, genially. And, presently, we went, pondering to our various homes.

If you enjoyed this, you might also like…
The Whistling Room, see page 37
The Hog, see page 402

The House Among the Laurels

"THIS IS A CURIOUS YARN that I am going to tell you," said Carnacki, as after a quiet little dinner we made ourselves comfortable in his cosy dining room.

"I have just got back from the West of Ireland," he continued. "Wentworth, a friend of mine, has lately had rather an unexpected legacy, in the shape of a large estate and manor, about a mile and a half outside of the village of Korunton. This place is named Gannington Manor, and has been empty a great number of years; as you will find is almost always the case with Houses reputed to be haunted, as it is usually termed.

"It seems that when Wentworth went over to take possession, he found the place in very poor repair, and the estate totally uncared for, and, as I know, looking very desolate and lonesome generally. He went through the big house by himself, and he admitted to me that it had an uncomfortable feeling about it; but, of course, that might be nothing more than the natural dismalness of a big, empty house, which has been long uninhabited, and through which you are wandering alone.

"When he had finished his look 'round, he went down to the village, meaning to see the one-time Agent of the Estate, and arrange for someone to go in as caretaker. The Agent, who proved by the way to be a Scotchman, was very willing to take up the management of the Estate once more; but he assured Wentworth that they would get no one to go in as caretaker; and that his – the Agent's – advice was to have the house pulled down, and a new one built.

"This, naturally, astonished my friend, and, as they went down to the village, he managed to get a sort of explanation from the man. It seems that there had been always curious stories told about the place, which in the early days was called Landru Castle, and that within the last seven years there had been two extraordinary deaths there. In each case they had been tramps, who were ignorant of the reputation of the house, and had probably thought the big empty place suitable for a night's free lodging. There had been absolutely no signs of violence to indicate the method by which death was caused, and on each occasion the body had been found in the great entrance hall.

"By this time they had reached the inn where Wentworth had put up, and he told the Agent that he would prove that it was all rubbish about the haunting, by staying a night or two in the Manor himself. The death of the tramps was certainly curious; but did not prove that any supernatural agency had been at work. They were but isolated accidents, spread over a large number of years by the memory of the villagers, which was natural enough in a little place like Korunton. Tramps had to die some time, and in some place, and it proved nothing that two, out of possibly hundreds who had slept in the empty house, had happened to take the opportunity to die under shelter.

"But the Agent took his remark very seriously, and both he and Dennis the landlord of the inn, tried their best to persuade him not to go. For his 'sowl's sake', Irish Dennis begged him to do no such thing; and because of his 'life's sake', the Scotchman was equally in earnest.

"It was late afternoon at the time, and as Wentworth told me, it was warm and bright, and it seemed such utter rot to hear those two talking seriously about the impossible. He felt full of pluck, and he made up his mind he would smash the story of the haunting, at once by staying that very night, in the Manor. He made this quite clear to them, and told them that it would be more to the point and to their credit, if they offered to come up along with him, and keep him company. But poor old Dennis was quite shocked, I believe, at the suggestion; and though Tabbit, the Agent, took it more quietly, he was very solemn about it.

"It seems that Wentworth did go; and though, as he said to me, when the evening began to come on, it seemed a very different sort of thing to tackle.

"A whole crowd of the villagers assembled to see him off; for by this time they all knew of his intention. Wentworth had his gun with him, and a big packet of candles; and he made it clear to them all that it would not be wise for anyone to play any tricks; as he intended to shoot 'at sight'. And then, you know, he got a hint of how serious they considered the whole thing; for one of them came up to him, leading a great bullmastiff, and offered it to him, to take to keep him company. Wentworth patted his gun; but the old man who owned the dog shook his head and explained that the brute might warn him in sufficient time for him to get away from the castle. For it was obvious that he did not consider the gun would prove of any use.

"Wentworth took the dog, and thanked the man. He told me that, already, he was beginning to wish that he had not said definitely that he would go; but, as it was, he was simply forced to. He went through the crowd of men, and found suddenly that they had all turned in a body and were keeping him company. They stayed with him all the way to the Manor, and then went right over the whole place with him.

"It was still daylight when this was finished; though turning to dusk; and, for a while, the men stood about, hesitating, as if they felt ashamed to go away and leave Wentworth there all alone. He told me that, by this time, he would gladly have given fifty pounds to be going back with them. And then, abruptly, an idea came to him. He suggested that they should stay with him, and keep him company through the night. For a time they refused, and tried to persuade him to go back with them; but finally he made a proposition that got home to them all. He planned that they should all go back to the inn, and there get a couple of dozen bottles of whisky, a donkey-load of turf and wood, and some more candles. Then they would come back, and make a great fire in the big fireplace, light all the candles, and put them 'round the place, open the whisky and make a night of it. And, by Jove! He got them to agree.

"They set off back, and were soon at the inn, and here, whilst the donkey was being loaded, and the candles and whisky distributed, Dennis was doing his best to keep Wentworth from going back; but he was a sensible man in his way, for when he found that it was no use, he stopped. You see, he did not want to frighten the others from accompanying Wentworth.

"'I tell ye, sorr,' he told him, ''tis of no use at all, thryin' ter reclaim ther castle. 'Tis curst with innocent blood, an' ye'll be betther pullin' it down, an' buildin' a fine new wan. But if ye be intendin' to shtay this night, kape the big dhoor open whide, an' watch for the bhlood-dhrip. If so much as a single dhrip falls, don't shtay though all the gold in the worrld was offered ye.'

"Wentworth asked him what he meant by the blood-drip.

"'Shure,' he said, ''tis the bhlood av thim as ould Black Mick 'way back in the ould days kilt in their shlape. 'Twas a feud as he pretendid to patch up, an' he invited thim – the O'Haras they was – siventy av thim. An' he fed thim, an' shpoke soft to thim, an' thim thrustin' him, sthayed to shlape with him. Thin, he an' thim with him, stharted in an' mhurdered thim wan an' all as they slep'. 'Tis from me father's grandfather ye have the sthory. An' sence thin 'tis death to any, so they say, to pass the night in the castle whin the bhlood-dhrip comes. 'Twill put out candle an' fire, an' thin in the darkness the Virgin Herself would be powerless to protect ye.'

"Wentworth told me he laughed at this; chiefly because, as he put it: – 'One always must laugh at that sort of yarn, however it makes you feel inside.' He asked old Dennis whether he expected him to believe it.

"'Yes, sorr,' said Dennis, 'I do mane ye to b'lieve it; an' please God, if ye'll b'lieve, ye may be back safe befor' mornin'.' The man's serious simplicity took hold of Wentworth, and he held out his hand. But, for all that, he went; and I must admire his pluck.

"There were now about forty men, and when they got back to the Manor – or castle as the villagers always call it – they were not long in getting a big fire going, and lighted candles all 'round the great hall. They had all brought sticks; so that they would have been a pretty formidable lot to tackle by anything simply physical; and, of course, Wentworth had his gun. He kept the whisky in his own charge; for he intended to keep them sober; but he gave them a good strong tot all 'round first, so as to make things seem cheerful; and to get them yearning. If you once let a crowd of men like that grow silent, they begin to think, and then to fancy things.

"The big entrance door had been left wide open, by his orders; which shows that he had taken some notice of Dennis. It was a quiet night, so this did not matter, for the lights kept steady, and all went on in a jolly sort of fashion for about three hours. He had opened a second lot of bottles, and everyone was feeling cheerful; so much so that one of the men called out aloud to the ghosts to come out and show themselves. And then, you know a very extraordinary thing happened; for the ponderous main door swung quietly and steadily to, as though pushed by an invisible hand, and shut with a sharp click.

"Wentworth stared, feeling suddenly rather chilly. Then he remembered the men, and looked 'round at them. Several had ceased their talk, and were staring in a frightened way at the big door; but the great number had never noticed, and were talking and yarning. He reached for his gun, and the following instant the great bullmastiff set up a tremendous barking, which drew the attention of the whole company.

"The hall I should tell you is oblong. The south wall is all windows; but the north and east have rows of doors, leading into the house, whilst the west wall is occupied by the great entrance. The rows of doors leading into the house were all closed, and it was towards one of these in the north wall that the big dog ran; yet he would not go very close; and suddenly the door began to move slowly open, until the blackness of the passage beyond was shown. The dog came back among the men, whimpering, and for a minute there was an absolute silence.

"Then Wentworth went out from the men a little, and aimed his gun at the doorway.

"'Whoever is there, come out, or I shall fire,' he shouted; but nothing came, and he blazed forth both barrels into the dark. As though the report had been a signal, all the doors along the north and east walls moved slowly open, and Wentworth and his men were staring, frightened into the black shapes of the empty doorways.

"Wentworth loaded his gun quickly, and called to the dog; but the brute was burrowing away in among the men; and this fear on the dog's part frightened Wentworth more, he told me, than anything. Then something else happened. Three of the candles over in the corner of the hall went out; and immediately about half a dozen in different parts of the place. More candles were put out, and the hall had become quite dark in the corners.

"The men were all standing now, holding their clubs, and crowded together. And no one said a word. Wentworth told me he felt positively ill with fright. I know the feeling. Then, suddenly, something splashed on to the back of his left hand. He lifted it, and looked. It was covered with a great splash of red that dripped from his fingers. An old Irishman near to him, saw it, and croaked out in a quavering voice: – 'The bhlood-dhrip!' When the old man called out, they all looked, and in the same instant others felt it upon them. There were frightened cries of: 'The bhlood-dhrip! The bhlood-dhrip!' And then, about a dozen candles went out simultaneously, and the hall was suddenly dark. The dog let out a great, mournful howl, and there was a horrible little silence, with everyone standing rigid. Then the tension broke, and there was a mad rush for the main door. They wrenched it open, and tumbled out into the dark; but something slammed it with a crash after them, and shut the dog in; for Wentworth heard it howling as they raced down the drive. Yet no one had the pluck to go back to let it out, which does not surprise me.

"Wentworth sent for me the following day. He had heard of me in connection with that Steeple Monster Case. I arrived by the night mail, and put up with Wentworth at the inn. The next day we went up to the old Manor, which certainly lies in rather a wilderness; though what struck me most was the extraordinary number of laurel bushes about the house. The place was smothered with them; so that the house seemed to be growing up out of a sea of green laurel. These, and the grim, ancient look of the old building, made the place look a bit dank and ghostly, even by daylight.

"The hall was a big place, and well lit by daylight; for which I was not sorry. You see, I had been rather wound-up by Wentworth's yarn. We found one rather funny thing, and that was the great bullmastiff, lying stiff with its neck broken. This made me feel very serious; for it showed that whether the cause was supernatural or not, there was present in the house some force exceedingly dangerous to life.

"Later, whilst Wentworth stood guard with his shotgun, I made an examination of the hall. The bottles and mugs from which the men had drunk their whisky were scattered about; and all over the place were the candles, stuck upright in their own grease. But in the somewhat brief and general search, I found nothing; and decided to begin my usual exact examination of every square foot of the place – not only of the hall, in this case, but of the whole interior of the castle.

"I spent three uncomfortable weeks, searching; but without result of any kind. And, you know, the care I take at this period is extreme; for I have solved hundreds of cases of so-called 'hauntings' at this early stage, simply by the most minute investigation, and the keeping of a perfectly open mind. But, as I have said, I found nothing. During the whole of the examination, I got Wentworth to stand guard with his loaded shotgun; and I was very particular that we were never caught there after dusk.

"I decided now to make the experiment of staying a night in the great hall, of course 'protected'. I spoke about it to Wentworth; but his own attempt had made him so nervous that he begged me to do no such thing. However, I thought it well worth the risk, and I managed in the end to persuade him to be present.

"With this in view, I went to the neighbouring town of Gaunt, and by an arrangement with the Chief Constable I obtained the services of six policemen with their rifles. The arrangement was unofficial, of course, and the men were allowed to volunteer, with a promise of payment.

"When the constables arrived early that evening at the inn, I gave them a good feed; and after that we all set out for the Manor. We had four donkeys with us, loaded with fuel and other matters; also two great boarhounds, which one of the police led. When we reached the house, I set the men to unload the donkeys; whilst Wentworth and I set-to and sealed all the doors, except the main entrance, with tape and wax; for if the doors were really opened, I was going to be sure of the fact. I was going to run no risk of being deceived by ghostly hallucination, or mesmeric influence.

"By the time that this was done, the policemen had unloaded the donkeys, and were waiting, looking about them, curiously. I set two of them to lay a fire in the big grate, and the others I used as I required them. I took one of the boarhounds to the end of the hall furthest from the entrance, and there I drove a staple into the floor, to which I tied the dog with a short tether. Then, 'round him, I drew upon the floor the figure of a Pentacle, in chalk. Outside of the Pentacle, I made a circle with garlic. I did exactly the same thing with the other hound; but over more in the northeast corner of the big hall, where the two rows of doors make the angle.

"When this was done, I cleared the whole centre of the hall, and put one of the policemen to sweep it; after which I had all my apparatus carried into the cleared space. Then I went over to the main door and hooked it open, so that the hook would have to be lifted out of the hasp, before the door could be closed. After that, I placed lighted candles before each of the sealed doors, and one in each corner of the big room; and then I lit the fire. When I saw that it was properly alight, I got all the men together, by the pile of things in the centre of the room, and took their pipes from them; for, as the Sigsand MS. has it: 'Theyre must noe lyght come from wythin the barryier.' And I was going to make sure.

"I got my tape measure then, and measured out a circle thirty-three feet in diameter, and immediately chalked it out. The police and Wentworth were tremendously interested, and I took the opportunity to warn them that this was no piece of silly mumming on my part; but done with a definite intention of erecting a barrier between us and any ab-human thing that the night might show to us. I warned them that, as they valued their lives, and more than their lives it might be, no one must on any account whatsoever pass beyond the limits of the barrier that I was making.

"After I had drawn the circle, I took a bunch of the garlic, and smudged it right 'round the chalk circle, a little outside of it. When this was complete, I called for candles from my stock of material. I set the police to lighting them, and as they were lit, I took them, and sealed them down on the floor, just within the chalk circle, five inches apart. As each candle measured approximately one inch in diameter, it took sixty-six candles to complete the circle; and I need hardly say that every number and measurement has a significance.

"Then, from candle to candle I took a 'gayrd' of human hair, entwining it alternately to the left and to the right, until the circle was completed, and the ends of the hair shod with silver, and pressed into the wax of the sixty-sixth candle.

"It had now been dark some time, and I made haste to get the 'Defence' complete. To this end, I got the men well together, and began to fit the Electric Pentacle right around us, so that the five points of the Defensive Star came just within the Hair Circle. This did not take me long, and a minute later I had connected up the batteries, and the weak blue glare of the intertwining vacuum tubes shone all around us. I felt happier then; for this Pentacle is, as you all know, a wonderful 'Defence'. I have told you before, how the idea came to me, after reading Professor Garder's 'Experiments with a Medium'. He found that a current, of a certain number of vibrations, *in vacuo,* 'insulated' the medium. It is difficult to suggest an explanation non-technically, and if you are really interested you should read Carder's lecture on 'Astral Vibrations Compared with Matero-involuted Vibrations below the Six-Billion Limit.'

"As I stood up from my work, I could hear outside in the night a constant drip from the laurels, which as I have said, come right up around the house, very thick. By the sound, I knew that a 'soft' rain had set in; and there was absolutely no wind, as I could tell by the steady flames of the candles.

"I stood a moment or two, listening, and then one of the men touched my arm, and asked me in a low voice, what they should do. By his tone, I could tell that he was feeling something of the strangeness of it all; and the other men, including Wentworth, were so quiet that I was afraid they were beginning to get shaky.

"I set-to, then, and arranged them with their backs to one common centre; so that they were sitting flat upon the floor, with their feet radiating outward. Then, by compass, I laid their legs to the eight chief points, and afterward I drew a circle with chalk around them; and opposite to their feet, I made the Eight Signs of the Saaamaaa Ritual. The eighth place was, of course, empty; but ready for me to occupy at any moment; for I had omitted to make the Sealing Sign to that point, until I had finished all my preparations, and could enter the Inner Star.

"I took a last look 'round the great hall, and saw that the two big hounds were lying quietly, with their noses between their paws. The fire was big and cheerful, and the candles before the two rows of doors, burnt steadily, as well as the solitary ones in the corners. Then I went 'round the little star of men, and warned them not to be frightened whatever happened; but to trust to the 'Defence'; and to let nothing tempt or drive them to cross the Barriers. Also, I told them to watch their movements, and to keep their feet strictly to their places. For the rest, there was to be no shooting, unless I gave the word.

"And now at last, I went to my place, and, sitting down, made the Eighth sign just beyond my feet. Then I arranged my camera and flashlight handy, and examined my revolver.

"Wentworth sat behind the First Sign, and as the numbering went 'round reversed, that put him next to me on my left. I asked him, in a low voice, how he felt; and he told me, rather nervous; but that he felt confidence in my knowledge and was resolved to go through with the matter, whatever happened.

"We settled down to wait. There was no talking, except that, once or twice, the police bent towards one another, and whispered odd remarks concerning the hall, that appeared queerly audible in the intense silence. But in a while there was not even a whisper from anyone, and only the monotonous drip, drip of the quiet rain without the great entrance, and the low, dull sound of the fire in the big fireplace.

"It was a queer group that we made sitting there, back to back, with our legs starred outward; and all around us the strange blue glow of the Pentacle, and beyond that the brilliant shining of the great ring of lighted candles. Outside of the glare of the candles, the large empty hall looked a little gloomy, by contrast, except where the lights shone before the sealed doors, and the blaze of the big fire made a good honest mass of flame. And the feeling of mystery! Can you picture it all?

"It might have been an hour later that it came to me suddenly that I was aware of an extraordinary sense of dreeness, as it were, come into the air of the place. Not the nervous feeling of mystery that had been with us all the time; but a new feeling, as if there were something going to happen any moment.

"Abruptly, there came a slight noise from the east end of the hall, and I felt the star of men move suddenly. 'Steady! Keep steady!' I shouted, and they quietened. I looked up the hall, and saw that the dogs were upon their feet, and staring in an extraordinary fashion towards the great entrance. I turned and stared, also, and felt the men move as they craned their heads to look. Suddenly, the dogs set up a tremendous barking, and I glanced across to them, and found they were still 'pointing' for the big doorway. They ceased their noise just as quickly, and seemed to be listening. In the same instant, I heard a faint chink of metal to my left, that set me staring at the hook which held the great door wide. It moved, even as I looked. Some invisible thing was meddling with it. A queer, sickening thrill went through me, and I felt all the men about me, stiffen and go rigid with intensity. I had a certainty of something impending: as it might be the impression of an invisible, but overwhelming, Presence. The hall was full of a queer silence, and not a sound came from the dogs. *Then I saw the hook slowly raised from out of its hasp, without any visible thing touching it.* Then a sudden power of movement came to me. I raised my camera, with the flashlight fixed, and snapped it at the door. There came the great blare of the flashlight, and a simultaneous roar of barking from the two dogs.

"The intensity of the flash made all the place seem dark for some moments, and in that time of darkness, I heard a jingle in the direction of the door, and strained to look. The effect of the bright light passed, and I could see clearly again. The great entrance door was being slowly closed. It shut with a sharp snick, and there followed a long silence, broken only by the whimpering of the dogs.

"I turned suddenly, and looked at Wentworth. He was looking at me.

"'Just as it did before,' he whispered.

"'Most extraordinary,' I said, and he nodded and looked 'round, nervously.

"The policemen were pretty quiet, and I judged that they were feeling rather worse than Wentworth; though, for that matter, you must not think that I was altogether natural; yet I have seen so much that is extraordinary, that I daresay I can keep my nerves steady longer than most people.

"I looked over my shoulder at the men, and cautioned them, in a low voice, not to move outside of the Barriers, *whatever happened*; not even though the house should seem to be rocking and about to tumble on to them; for well I knew what some of the great Forces are capable of doing. Yet, unless it should prove to be one of the cases of the more terrible Saiitii Manifestation, we were almost certain of safety, so long as we kept to our order within the Pentacle.

"Perhaps an hour and a half passed, quietly, except when, once in a way, the dogs would whine distressfully. Presently, however, they ceased even from this, and I could see them lying on the floor with their paws over their noses, in a most peculiar fashion, and shivering visibly. The sight made me feel more serious, as you can understand.

"Suddenly, the candle in the corner furthest from the main door, went out. An instant later, Wentworth jerked my arm, and I saw that the candle before one of the sealed doors had been put out. I held my camera ready. Then, one after another, every candle about the hall was put out, and with such speed and irregularity, that I could never catch one in the actual act of being extinguished. Yet, for all that, I took a flashlight of the hall in general.

"There was a time in which I sat half-blinded by the great glare of the flash, and I blamed myself for not having remembered to bring a pair of smoked goggles, which I have sometimes used at these times. I had felt the men jump, at the sudden light, and I called out loud to them to sit quiet, and to keep their feet exactly to their proper places. My voice, as you can imagine, sounded rather horrid and frightening in the great room, and altogether it was a beastly moment.

"Then, I was able to see again, and I stared here and there about the hall; but there was nothing showing unusual; only, of course, it was dark now over in the corners.

"Suddenly, I saw that the great fire was blackening. It was going out visibly, as I looked. If I said that some monstrous, invisible, impossible creature sucked the life from it, I could best explain the way the light and flame went out of it. It was most extraordinary to watch. In the time that I watched it, every vestige of fire was gone from it, and there was no light outside of the ring of candles around the Pentacle.

"The deliberateness of the thing troubled me more than I can make clear to you. It conveyed to me such a sense of a calm Deliberate Force present in the hall: The steadfast intention to 'make a darkness' was horrible. The *extent* of the Power to affect the Material was horrible. The extent of the Power to affect the Material was now the one constant, anxious questioning in my brain. You can understand?

"Behind me, I heard the policemen moving again, and I knew that they were getting thoroughly frightened. I turned half 'round, and told them, quietly but plainly, that they were safe only so long as they stayed within the Pentacle, in the position in which I had put them. If they once broke, and went outside of the Barrier, no knowledge of mine could state the full extent of the dreadfulness of the danger.

"I steadied them up, by this quiet, straight reminder; but if they had known, as I knew, that there is no certainty in any 'Protection', they would have suffered a great deal more, and probably have broken the 'Defence', and made a mad, foolish run for an impossible safety.

"Another hour passed, after this, in an absolute quietness. I had a sense of awful strain and oppression, as though I were a little spirit in the company of some invisible, brooding monster of the unseen world, who, as yet, was scarcely conscious of us. I leant across to Wentworth, and asked him in a whisper whether he had a feeling as if something were in the room. He looked very pale, and his eyes kept always on the move. He glanced just once at me, and nodded; then stared away 'round the hall again. And when I came to think, I was doing the same thing.

"Abruptly, as though a hundred unseen hands had snuffed them, every candle in the Barrier went dead out, and we were left in a darkness that seemed, for a little, absolute; for the light from the Pentacle was too weak and pale to penetrate far across the great hall.

"I tell you, for a moment, I just sat there as though I had been frozen solid. I felt the 'creep' go all over me, and seem to stop in my brain. I felt all at once to be given a power of hearing that was far beyond the normal. I could hear my own heart thudding most extraordinarily loud. I began, however, to feel better, after a while; but I simply had not the pluck to move. You can understand?

"Presently, I began to get my courage back. I gripped at my camera and flashlight, and waited. My hands were simply soaked with sweat. I glanced once at Wentworth. I could see him only dimly. His shoulders were hunched a little, his head forward; but though it was motionless, I knew that his eyes were not. It is queer how one knows that sort of thing at times. The police were just as silent. And thus a while passed.

"A sudden sound broke across the silence. From two sides of the room there came faint noises. I recognised them at once, as the breaking of the sealing-wax. *The sealed doors were opening.* I raised the camera and flashlight, and it was a peculiar mixture of fear and courage that helped me to press the button. As the great flare of light lit up the hall I felt the men all about me jump. The darkness fell like a clap of thunder, if you can understand, and seemed tenfold. Yet, in the moment of brightness, I had seen that all the sealed doors were wide open.

"Suddenly, all around us, there sounded a drip, drip, drip, upon the floor of the great hall. I thrilled with a queer, realising emotion, and a sense of a very real and present danger – *imminent*. The 'blood-drip' had commenced. And the grim question was now whether the Barriers could save us from whatever had come into the huge room.

"Through some awful minutes the 'blood-drip' continued to fall in an increasing rain; and presently some began to fall within the Barriers. I saw several great drops splash and star upon the pale glowing intertwining tubes of the Electric Pentacle; but, strangely enough, I could not trace that any fell among us. Beyond the strange horrible noise of the 'drip', there was no other sound. And then, abruptly, from the boarhound over in the far corner, there came a terrible yelling howl of agony, followed instantly by a sickening, breaking noise, and an immediate silence. If you have ever, when out shooting, broken a rabbit's neck, you will know the sound – in miniature! Like lightning, the thought sprang into my brain: – *It has crossed the Pentacle.* For you will remember that I had made one about each of the dogs. I thought instantly, with a sick apprehension, of our own Barriers. There was something in the hall with us that had passed the Barrier of the Pentacle about one of the dogs. In the awful succeeding silence, I positively quivered. And suddenly, one of the men behind me, gave out a scream, like any woman, and bolted for the door. He fumbled, and had it open in a moment. I yelled to the others not to move; but they followed like sheep, and I heard them kick the candles flying, in their panic. One of them stepped on the Electric Pentacle, and smashed it, and there was an utter darkness. In an instant, I realised that I was defenceless against the powers of the Unknown World, and with one savage leap I was out of the useless Barriers, and instantly through the great doorway, and into the night. I believe I yelled with sheer funk.

"The men were a little ahead of me, and I never ceased running, and neither did they. Sometimes, I glanced back over my shoulder; and I kept glancing into the laurels which grew all along the drive. The beastly things kept rustling, rustling in a hollow sort of way, as though something were keeping parallel with me, among them. The rain had stopped, and a dismal little wind kept moaning through the grounds. It was disgusting.

"I caught Wentworth and the police at the lodge gate. We got outside, and ran all the way to the village. We found old Dennis up, waiting for us, and half the villagers to keep him company. He told us that he had known in his 'sowl' that we should come back, that is, if we came back at all; which is not a bad rendering of his remark.

"Fortunately, I had brought my camera away from the house – possibly because the strap had happened to be over my head. Yet, I did not go straight away to develop; but sat with the rest of the bar, where we talked for some hours, trying to be coherent about the whole horrible business.

"Later, however, I went up to my room, and proceeded with my photography. I was steadier now, and it was just possible, so I hoped, that the negatives might show something.

"On two of the plates, I found nothing unusual: but on the third, which was the first one that I snapped, I saw something that made me quite excited. I examined it very carefully with a magnifying glass; then I put it to wash, and slipped a pair of rubber overshoes over my boots.

"The negative had showed me something very extraordinary, and I had made up my mind to test the truth of what it seemed to indicate, without losing another moment. It was no use telling anything to Wentworth and the police, until I was certain; and, also, I believed that I stood a greater chance to succeed by myself; though, for that matter, I do not suppose anything would have taken them up to the Manor again that night.

"I took my revolver, and went quietly downstairs, and into the dark. The rain had commenced again; but that did not bother me. I walked hard. When I came to the lodge gates, a sudden, queer instinct stopped me from going through, and I climbed the wall into the park. I kept away from the drive, and approached the building through the dismal, dripping laurels. You can imagine how beastly it was. Every time a leaf rustled, I jumped.

"I made my way 'round to the back of the big house, and got in through a little window which I had taken note of during my search; for, of course, I knew the whole place from roof to cellars. I went silently up the kitchen stairs, fairly quivering with funk; and at the top, I went to the left, and then into a long corridor that opened, through one of the doorways we had sealed, into the big hall. I looked up it, and saw a faint flicker of light away at the end; and I tiptoed silently towards it, holding my revolver ready. As I came near to the open door, I heard men's voices, and then a burst of laughing. I went on, until I could see into the hall. There were several men there, all in a group. They were well dressed, and one, at least, I saw was armed. They were examining my 'Barriers' against the Supernatural, with a good deal of unkind laughter. I never felt such a fool in my life.

"It was plain to me that they were a gang of men who had made use of the empty Manor, perhaps for years, for some purpose of their own; and now that Wentworth was attempting to take possession, they were acting up the traditions of the place, with the view of driving him away, and keeping so useful a place still at their disposal. But what they were, I mean whether coiners, thieves, inventors, or what, I could not imagine.

"Presently, they left the Pentacle, and gathered 'round the living boarhound, which seemed curiously quiet, as though it were half-drugged. There was some talk as to whether to let the poor brute live, or not; but finally they decided it would be good policy to kill it. I saw two of them force a twisted loop of rope into its mouth, and the two bights of the loop were brought together at the back of the hound's neck. Then a third man thrust a thick walking-stick through the two loops. The two men with the rope, stooped to hold the dog, so that I could not see what was done; but the poor beast gave a sudden awful howl, and immediately there was a repetition of the uncomfortable breaking sound, I had heard earlier in the night, as you will remember.

"The men stood up, and left the dog lying there, quiet enough now, as you may suppose. For my part, I fully appreciated the calculated remorselessness which had decided upon the animal's death, and the cold determination with which it had been afterward executed so neatly. I guessed that a man who might get into the 'light' of those particular men, would be likely to come to quite as uncomfortable an ending.

"A minute later, one of the men called out to the rest that they should 'shift the wires'. One of the men came towards the doorway of the corridor in which I stood, and I ran quickly back into the darkness of the upper end. I saw the man reach up, and take something from the top of the door, and I heard the slight, ringing jangle of steel wire.

"When he had gone, I ran back again, and saw the men passing, one after another, through an opening in the stairs, formed by one of the marble steps being raised. When the last man had vanished, the slab that made the step was shut down, and there was not a sign of the secret door. It was the seventh step from the bottom, as I took care to count: and a splendid idea; for it was so solid that it did not ring hollow, even to a fairly heavy hammer, as I found later.

"There is little more to tell. I got out of the house as quickly and quietly as possible, and back to the inn. The police came without any coaxing, when they knew the 'ghosts' were normal flesh and blood. We entered the park and the Manor in the same way that I had done. Yet, when we tried to open the step, we failed, and had finally to smash it. This must have warned the haunters; for when we descended to a secret room which we found at the end of a long and narrow passage in the thickness of the walls, we found no one.

"The police were horribly disgusted, as you can imagine; but for my part, I did not care either way. I had 'laid the ghost', as you might say, and that was what I set out to do. I was not particularly afraid of being laughed at by the others; for they had all been thoroughly 'taken in'; and in the end, I had scored, without their help.

"We searched right through the secret ways, and found that there was an exit, at the end of a long tunnel, which opened in the side of a well, out in the grounds. The ceiling of the hall was hollow, and reached by a little secret stairway inside of the big staircase. The 'blood-drip' was merely coloured water, dropped through the minute crevices of the ornamented ceiling. How the candles and the fire were put out, I do not know; for the haunters certainly did not act quite up to tradition, which held that the lights were put out by the 'blood-drip'. Perhaps it was too difficult to direct the fluid, without positively squirting it, which might have given the whole thing away. The candles and the fire may possibly have been extinguished by the agency of carbonic acid gas; but how suspended, I have no idea.

"The secret hiding paces were, of course, ancient. There was also, did I tell you? A bell which they had rigged up to ring, when anyone entered the gates at the end of the drive. If I had not climbed the wall, I should have found nothing for my pains; for the bell would have warned them had I gone in through the gateway."

"What was on the negative?" I asked, with much curiosity.

"A picture of the fine wire with which they were grappling for the hook that held the entrance door open. They were doing it from one of the crevices in the ceiling. They had evidently made no preparations for lifting the hook. I suppose they never thought that anyone would make use of it, and so they had to improvise a grapple. The wire was too fine to be seen by the amount of light we had in the hall; but the flashlight 'picked it out'. Do you see?

"The opening of the inner doors was managed by wires, as you will have guessed, which they unshipped after use, or else I should soon have found them, when I made my search.

"I think I have now explained everything. The hound was killed, of course, by the men direct. You see, they made the place as dark as possible, first. Of course, if I had managed to take a flashlight just at that instant, the whole secret of the haunting would have been exposed. But Fate just ordered it the other way."

"And the tramps?" I asked.

"Oh, you mean the two tramps who were found dead in the Manor," said Carnacki. "Well, of course it is impossible to be sure, one way or the other. Perhaps they happened to find out something, and were given a hypodermic. Or it is just as probable that they had come to the time of their dying, and just died naturally. It is conceivable that a great many tramps had slept in the old house, at one time or another."

Carnacki stood up, and knocked out his pipe. We rose also, and went for our coats and hats.

"Out you go!" said Carnacki, genially, using the recognised formula. And we went out on to the Embankment, and presently through the darkness to our various homes.

If you enjoyed this, you might also like...
The Mystery of the Derelict, see page 138
The Thing Invisible, see page 78

The Whistling Room

CARNACKI shook a friendly fist at me as I entered, late. Then he opened the door into the dining room, and ushered the four of us – Jessop, Arkright, Taylor and myself – in to dinner.

We dined well, as usual, and, equally as usual, Carnacki was pretty silent during the meal. At the end, we took our wine and cigars to our usual positions, and Carnacki – having got himself comfortable in his big chair – began without any preliminary:

"I have just got back from Ireland, again," he said. "And I thought you chaps would be interested to hear my news. Besides, I fancy I shall see the thing clearer, after I have told it all out straight. I must tell you this, though, at the beginning – up to the present moment, I have been utterly and completely 'stumped'. I have tumbled upon one of the most peculiar cases of 'haunting' – or devilment of some sort – that I have come against. Now listen.

"I have been spending the last few weeks at Iastrae Castle, about twenty miles northeast of Galway. I got a letter about a month ago from a Mr. Sid K. Tassoc, who it seemed had bought the place lately, and moved in, only to find that he had bought a very peculiar piece of property.

"When I got there, he met me at the station, driving a jaunting car, and drove me up to the castle, which, by the way, he called a 'house shanty'. I found that he was 'pigging it' there with his boy brother and another American, who seemed to be half-servant and half-companion. It seems that all the servants had left the place, in a body, as you might say, and now they were managing among themselves, assisted by some day-help.

"The three of them got together a scratch feed, and Tassoc told me all about the trouble whilst we were at table. It is most extraordinary, and different from anything that I have had to do with; though that Buzzing Case was very queer, too.

"Tassoc began right in the middle of his story. 'We've got a room in this shanty,' he said, 'which has got a most infernal whistling in it; sort of haunting it. The thing starts any time; you never know when, and it goes on until it frightens you. All the servants have gone, as you know. It's not ordinary whistling, and it isn't the wind. Wait till you hear it.'

"'We're all carrying guns,' said the boy; and slapped his coat pocket.

"'As bad as that?' I said; and the older boy nodded. 'It may be soft,' he replied; 'but wait till you've heard it. Sometimes I think it's some infernal thing, and the next moment, I'm just as sure that someone's playing a trick on me.'

"'Why?' I asked. 'What is to be gained?'

"'You mean,' he said, 'that people usually have some good reason for playing tricks as elaborate as this. Well, I'll tell you. There's a lady in this province, by the name of Miss Donnehue, who's going to be my wife, this day two months. She's more beautiful than they make them, and so far as I can see, I've just stuck my head into an Irish hornet's nest. There's about a score of hot young Irishmen been courting her these two years gone, and now that I'm come along and cut them out, they feel raw against me. Do you begin to understand the possibilities?'

"'Yes,' I said. 'Perhaps I do in a vague sort of way; but I don't see how all this affects the room?'

"'Like this,' he said. 'When I'd fixed it up with Miss Donnehue, I looked out for a place, and bought this little house shanty. Afterward, I told her – one evening during dinner, that I'd decided to tie up here. And then she asked me whether I wasn't afraid of the whistling room. I told her it must have been thrown in gratis, as I'd heard nothing about it. There were some of her men friends present, and I saw a smile go 'round. I found out, after a bit of questioning, that several people have bought this place during the last twenty-odd years. And it was always on the market again, after a trial.

"'Well, the chaps started to bait me a bit, and offered to take bets after dinner that I'd not stay six months in the place. I looked once or twice to Miss Donnehue, so as to be sure I was 'getting the note' of the talkee-talkee; but I could see that she didn't take it as a joke, at all. Partly, I think, because there was a bit of a sneer in the way the men were tackling me, and partly because she really believes there is something in this yarn of the Whistling Room.

"'However, after dinner, I did what I could to even things up with the others. I nailed all their bets, and screwed them down hard and safe. I guess some of them are going to be hard hit, unless I lose; which I don't mean to. Well, there you have practically the whole yarn.'

"'Not quite,' I told him. 'All that I know, is that you have bought a castle with a room in it that is in some way 'queer', and that you've been doing some betting. Also, I know that your servants have got frightened and run away. Tell me something about the whistling?'

"'Oh, that!' said Tassoc; 'that started the second night we were in. I'd had a good look 'round the room, in the daytime, as you can understand; for the talk up at Arlestrae – Miss Donnehue's place – had made me wonder a bit. But it seems just as usual as some of the other rooms in the old wing, only perhaps a bit more lonesome. But that may be only because of the talk about it, you know.

"'The whistling started about ten o'clock, on the second night, as I said. Tom and I were in the library, when we heard an awfully queer whistling, coming along the East Corridor – the room is in the East Wing, you know.

"'That's that blessed ghost!' I said to Tom, and we collared the lamps off the table, and went up to have a look. I tell you, even as we dug along the corridor, it took me a bit in the throat, it was so beastly queer. It was a sort of tune, in a way; but more as if a devil or some rotten thing were laughing at you, and going to get 'round at your back. That's how it makes you feel.

"'When we got to the door, we didn't wait; but rushed it open; and then I tell you the sound of the thing fairly hit me in the face. Tom said he got it the same way – sort of felt stunned and bewildered. We looked all 'round, and soon got so nervous, we just cleared out, and I locked the door.

"'We came down here, and had a stiff peg each. Then we got fit again, and began to think we'd been nicely had. So we took sticks, and went out into the grounds, thinking after all it must be some of these confounded Irishmen working the ghost-trick on us. But there was not a leg stirring.

"'We went back into the house, and walked over it, and then paid another visit to the room. But we simply couldn't stand it. We fairly ran out, and locked the door again. I don't know how to put it into words; but I had a feeling of being up against something that was rottenly dangerous. You know! We've carried our guns ever since.

"'Of course, we had a real turn out of the room next day, and the whole house place; and we even hunted 'round the grounds; but there was nothing queer. And now I don't know what to think; except that the sensible part of me tells me that it's some plan of these Wild Irishmen to try to take a rise out of me.'

"'Done anything since?' I asked him.

"'Yes,' he said – 'watched outside of the door of the room at nights, and chased 'round the grounds, and sounded the walls and floor of the room. We've done everything we could think of; and it's beginning to get on our nerves; so we sent for you.'

"By this, we had finished eating. As we rose from the table, Tassoc suddenly called out: 'Ssh! Hark!'

"We were instantly silent, listening. Then I heard it, an extraordinary hooning whistle, monstrous and inhuman, coming from far away through corridors to my right.

"'By G—d!' said Tassoc; 'and it's scarcely dark yet! Collar those candles, both of you, and come along.'

"In a few moments, we were all out of the door and racing up the stairs. Tassoc turned into a long corridor, and we followed, shielding our candles as we ran. The sound seemed to fill all the passage as we drew near, until I had the feeling that the whole air throbbed under the power of some wanton Immense Force – a sense of an actual taint, as you might say, of monstrosity all about us.

"Tassoc unlocked the door; then, giving it a push with his foot, jumped back, and drew his revolver. As the door flew open, the sound beat out at us, with an effect impossible to explain to one who has not heard it – with a certain, horrible personal note in it; as if in there in the darkness you could picture the room rocking and creaking in a mad, vile glee to its own filthy piping and whistling and hooning. To stand there and listen, was to be stunned by Realisation. It was as if someone showed you the mouth of a vast pit suddenly, and said: That's Hell. And you knew that they had spoken the truth. Do you get it, even a little bit?

"I stepped back a pace into the room, and held the candle over my head, and looked quickly 'round. Tassoc and his brother joined me, and the man came up at the back, and we all held our candles high. I was deafened with the shrill, piping hoon of the whistling; and then, clear in my ear, something seemed to be saying to me: 'Get out of here – quick! Quick! Quick!'

"As you chaps know, I never neglect that sort of thing. Sometimes it may be nothing but nerves; but as you will remember, it was just such a warning that saved me in the 'Grey Dog' Case, and in the 'Yellow Finger' Experiments; as well as other times. Well, I turned sharp 'round to the others: 'Out!' I said. 'For God's sake, *out* quick.' And in an instant I had them into the passage.

"There came an extraordinary yelling scream into the hideous whistling, and then, like a clap of thunder, an utter silence. I slammed the door, and locked it. Then, taking the key, I looked 'round at the others. They were pretty white, and I imagine I must have looked that way too. And there we stood a moment, silent.

"'Come down out of this, and have some whisky,' said Tassoc, at last, in a voice he tried to make ordinary; and he led the way. I was the back man, and I know we all kept looking over our shoulders. When we got downstairs, Tassoc passed the bottle 'round. He took a drink, himself, and slapped his glass down on to the table. Then sat down with a thud.

"'That's a lovely thing to have in the house with you, isn't it!' he said. And directly afterward: 'What on earth made you hustle us all out like that, Carnacki?'

"'Something seemed to be telling me to get out, quick,' I said. 'Sounds a bit silly, superstitious, I know; but when you are meddling with this sort of thing, you've got to take notice of queer fancies, and risk being laughed at.'

"I told him then about the 'Grey Dog' business, and he nodded a lot to that. 'Of course,' I said, 'this may be nothing more than those would-be rivals of yours playing some funny game; but, personally, though I'm going to keep an open mind, I feel that there is something beastly and dangerous about this thing.'

"We talked for a while longer, and then Tassoc suggested billiards, which we played in a pretty half-hearted fashion, and all the time cocking an ear to the door, as you might say, for sounds; but none came, and later, after coffee, he suggested early bed, and a thorough overhaul of the room on the morrow.

"My bedroom was in the newer part of the castle, and the door opened into the picture gallery. At the East end of the gallery was the entrance to the corridor of the East Wing; this was shut off from the gallery by two old and heavy oak doors, which looked rather odd and quaint beside the more modern doors of the various rooms.

"When I reached my room, I did not go to bed; but began to unpack my instrument trunk, of which I had retained the key. I intended to take one or two preliminary steps at once, in my investigation of the extraordinary whistling.

"Presently, when the castle had settled into quietness, I slipped out of my room, and across to the entrance of the great corridor. I opened one of the low, squat doors, and threw the beam of my pocket searchlight down the passage. It was empty, and I went through the doorway, and pushed-to the oak behind me. Then along the great passageway, throwing my light before and behind, and keeping my revolver handy.

"I had hung a 'protection belt' of garlic 'round my neck, and the smell of it seemed to fill the corridor and give me assurance; for, as you all know, it is a wonderful 'protection' against the more usual Aeiirii forms of semi-materialisation, by which I supposed the whistling might be produced; though, at that period of my investigation, I was quite prepared to find it due to some perfectly natural cause; for it is astonishing the enormous number of cases that prove to have nothing abnormal in them.

"In addition to wearing the necklet, I had plugged my ears loosely with garlic, and as I did not intend to stay more than a few minutes in the room, I hoped to be safe.

"When I reached the door, and put my hand into my pocket for the key, I had a sudden feeling of sickening funk. But I was not going to back out, if I could help it. I unlocked the door and turned the handle. Then I gave the door a sharp push with my foot, as Tassoc had done, and drew my revolver, though I did not expect to have any use for it, really.

"I shone the searchlight all 'round the room, and then stepped inside, with a disgustingly horrible feeling of walking slap into a waiting Danger. I stood a few seconds, waiting, and nothing happened, and the empty room showed bare from corner to corner. And then, you know, I realised that the room was full of an abominable silence; can you understand that? A sort of purposeful silence, just as sickening as any of the filthy noises the Things have power to make. Do you remember what I told you about that 'Silent Garden' business? Well, this room had just that same *malevolent* silence – the beastly quietness of a thing that is looking at you and not seeable itself, and thinks that it has got you. Oh, I recognised it instantly, and I whipped the top off my lantern, so as to have light over the *whole* room.

"Then I set-to, working like fury, and keeping my glance all about me. I sealed the two windows with lengths of human hair, right across, and sealed them at every frame. As I worked, a queer, scarcely perceptible tenseness stole into the air of the place, and the silence seemed, if you can understand me, to grow more solid. I knew then that I had no business there without 'full protection'; for I was practically certain that this was no mere Aeiirii development; but one of the worst forms, as the Saiitii; like that 'Grunting Man' case – you know.

"I finished the window, and hurried over to the great fireplace. This is a huge affair, and has a queer gallows-iron, I think they are called, projecting from the back of the arch. I sealed the opening with seven human hairs – the seventh crossing the six others.

"Then, just as I was making an end, a low, mocking whistle grew in the room. A cold, nervous pricking went up my spine, and 'round my forehead from the back. The hideous sound filled all the room with an extraordinary, grotesque parody of human whistling, too gigantic to be human – as if something gargantuan and monstrous made the sounds softly. As I stood there a last moment, pressing down the final seal, I had no doubt but that I had come across one of those rare and horrible cases of the *Inanimate* reproducing the functions of the *Animate*, I made a grab for my lamp, and went quickly to the door, looking over my shoulder, and listening for the thing that I expected. It came, just as I got my hand upon the handle – a squeal of incredible, malevolent anger, piercing through the low hooning of the whistling. I dashed out, slamming the door and locking it. I leant a little against the opposite wall of the corridor, feeling rather funny; for it had been a narrow squeak.... 'Theyr be noe sayfetie to be gained bye gayrds of holieness when the monyster hath pow'r to speak throe woode and stoene.' So runs the passage in the Sigsand MS., and I proved it in that 'Nodding Door' business. There is no protection against this particular form of monster, except, possibly, for a fractional period of time; for it can reproduce itself in, or take to its purpose, the very protective material which you may use, and has the power to *'forme* wythine the pentycle'; though not immediately. There is, of course, the possibility of the Unknown Last Line of the Saaamaaa Ritual being uttered; but it is too uncertain to count upon, and the danger is too hideous; and even then it has no power to protect for more than 'maybee fyve beats of the harte', as the Sigsand has it.

"Inside of the room, there was now a constant, meditative, hooning whistling; but presently this ceased, and the silence seemed worse; for there is such a sense of hidden mischief in a silence.

"After a little, I sealed the door with crossed hairs, and then cleared off down the great passage, and so to bed.

"For a long time I lay awake; but managed eventually to get some sleep. Yet, about two o'clock I was waked by the hooning whistling of the room coming to me, even through the closed doors. The sound was tremendous, and seemed to beat through the whole house with a presiding sense of terror. As if (I remember thinking) some monstrous giant had been holding mad carnival with itself at the end of that great passage.

"I got up and sat on the edge of the bed, wondering whether to go along and have a look at the seal; and suddenly there came a thump on my door, and Tassoc walked in, with his dressing gown over his pyjamas.

"'I thought it would have waked you, so I came along to have a talk,' he said. '*I* can't sleep. Beautiful! Isn't it!'

"'Extraordinary!' I said, and tossed him my case.

"He lit a cigarette, and we sat and talked for about an hour; and all the time that noise went on, down at the end of the big corridor.

"Suddenly, Tassoc stood up:

"'Let's take our guns, and go and examine the brute,' he said, and turned towards the door.

"'No!' I said. 'By Jove – *no!* I can't say anything definite, yet; but I believe that room is about as dangerous as it well can be.'

"'Haunted – *really* haunted?' he asked, keenly and without any of his frequent banter.

"I told him, of course, that I could not say a definite *yes* or *no* to such a question; but that I hoped to be able to make a statement, soon. Then I gave him a little lecture on the False Re-Materialisation of the Animate-Force through the Inanimate-Inert. He began then to see the particular way in the room might be dangerous, if it were really the subject of a manifestation.

"About an hour later, the whistling ceased quite suddenly, and Tassoc went off again to bed. I went back to mine, also, and eventually got another spell of sleep.

"In the morning, I went along to the room. I found the seals on the door intact. Then I went in. The window seals and the hair were all right; but the seventh hair across the great fireplace was broken. This set me thinking. I knew that it might, very possibly, have snapped, through my having tensioned it too highly; but then, again, it might have been broken by something else. Yet, it was scarcely possible that a man, for instance, could have passed between the six unbroken hairs; for no one would ever have noticed them, entering the room that way, you see; but just walked through them, ignorant of their very existence.

"I removed the other hairs, and the seals. Then I looked up the chimney. It went up straight, and I could see blue sky at the top. It was a big, open flue, and free from any suggestion of hiding places, or corners. Yet, of course, I did not trust to any such casual examination, and after breakfast, I put on my overalls, and climbed to the very top, sounding all the way; but I found nothing.

"Then I came down, and went over the whole of the room – floor, ceiling, and walls, mapping them out in six-inch squares, and sounding with both hammer and probe. But there was nothing abnormal.

"Afterward, I made a three-weeks search of the whole castle, in the same thorough way; but found nothing. I went even further, then; for at night, when the whistling commenced, I made a microphone test. You see, if the whistling were mechanically produced, this test would have made evident to me the working of the machinery, if there were any such concealed within the walls. It certainly was an up-to-date method of examination, as you must allow.

"Of course, I did not think that any of Tassoc's rivals had fixed up any mechanical contrivance; but I thought it just possible that there had been some such thing for producing the whistling, made away back in the years, perhaps with the intention of giving the room a reputation that would ensure its being free of inquisitive folk. You see what I mean? Well, of course, it was just possible, if this were the case, that someone knew the secret of the machinery, and was utilising the knowledge to play this devil of a prank on Tassoc. The microphone test of the walls would certainly have made this known to me, as I have said; but there was nothing of the sort in the castle; so that I had practically no doubt at all now, but that it was a genuine case of what is popularly termed 'haunting'.

"All this time, every night, and sometimes most of each night, the hooning whistling of the Room was intolerable. It was as if an intelligence there knew that steps were being taken against it, and piped and hooned in a sort of mad, mocking contempt. I tell you, it was as extraordinary as it was horrible. Time after time, I went along – tiptoeing noiselessly on stockinged feet – to the sealed door (for I always kept the Room sealed). I went at all hours of the night, and often the whistling, inside, would seem to change to a brutally malignant note, as though the half-animate monster saw me plainly through the shut door. And all the time the shrieking, hooning whistling would fill the whole corridor, so that I used to feel a precious lonely chap, messing about there with one of Hell's mysteries.

"And every morning, I would enter the room, and examine the different hairs and seals. You see, after the first week, I had stretched parallel hairs all along the walls of the room, and along the ceiling; but over the floor, which was of polished stone, I had set out little, colourless wafers, tacky-side uppermost. Each wafer was numbered, and they were arranged after a definite plan, so that I should be able to trace the exact movements of any living thing that went across the floor.

"You will see that no material being or creature could possibly have entered that room, without leaving many signs to tell me about it. But nothing was ever disturbed, and I began to think that I should have to risk an attempt to stay the night in the room, in the Electric Pentacle. Yet, mind you, I knew that it would be a crazy thing to do; but I was getting stumped, and ready to do anything.

"Once, about midnight, I did break the seal on the door, and have a quick look in; but, I tell you, the whole Room gave one mad yell, and seemed to come towards me in a great belly of shadows, as if the walls had bellied in towards me. Of course, that must have been fancy. Anyway, the yell was sufficient, and I slammed the door, and locked it, feeling a bit weak down my spine. You know the feeling.

"And then, when I had got to that state of readiness for anything, I made something of a discovery. It was about one in the morning, and I was walking slowly 'round the castle, keeping in the soft grass. I had come under the shadow of the East Front, and far above me, I could hear the vile, hooning whistle of the Room, up in the darkness of the unlit wing. Then, suddenly, a little in front of me, I heard a man's voice, speaking low, but evidently in glee:

"'By George! You Chaps; but I wouldn't care to bring a wife home in that!' it said, in the tone of the cultured Irish.

"Someone started to reply; but there came a sharp exclamation, and then a rush, and I heard footsteps running in all directions. Evidently, the men had spotted me.

"For a few seconds, I stood there, feeling an awful ass. After all, *they* were at the bottom of the haunting! Do you see what a big fool it made me seem? I had no doubt but that they were some of Tassoc's rivals; and here I had been feeling in every bone that I had hit a real, bad, genuine Case! And then, you know, there came the memory of hundreds of details, that made me just as much in doubt again. Anyway, whether it was natural, or ab-natural, there was a great deal yet to be cleared up.

"I told Tassoc, next morning, what I had discovered, and through the whole of every night, for five nights, we kept a close watch 'round the East Wing; but there was never a sign of anyone prowling about; and all the time, almost from evening to dawn, that grotesque whistling would hoon incredibly, far above us in the darkness.

"On the morning after the fifth night, I received a wire from here, which brought me home by the next boat. I explained to Tassoc that I was simply bound to come away for a few days; but told him to keep up the watch 'round the castle. One thing I was very careful to do, and that was to make him absolutely promise never to go into the Room, between sunset and sunrise. I made it clear to him that we knew nothing definite yet, one way or the other; and if the room were what I had first thought it to be, it might be a lot better for him to die first, than enter it after dark.

"When I got here, and had finished my business, I thought you chaps would be interested; and also I wanted to get it all spread out clear in my mind; so I rung you up. I am going over again tomorrow, and when I get back, I ought to have something pretty extraordinary to tell you. By the way, there is a curious thing I forgot to tell you. I tried to get a phonographic record of the whistling; but it simply produced no impression on the wax at all. That is one of the things that has made me feel queer, I can tell you. Another extraordinary thing is that the microphone will not magnify the sound – will not even transmit it; seems to take no account of it, and acts as if it were nonexistent. I am absolutely and utterly stumped, up to the present. I am a wee bit curious to see whether any of your dear clever heads can make daylight of it. *I* cannot – not yet."

He rose to his feet.

"Goodnight, all," he said, and began to usher us out abruptly, but without offence, into the night.

A fortnight later, he dropped each of us a card, and you can imagine that I was not late this time. When we arrived, Carnacki took us straight into dinner, and when we had finished, and all made ourselves comfortable, he began again, where he had left off:

"Now just listen quietly; for I have got something pretty queer to tell you. I got back late at night, and I had to walk up to the castle, as I had not warned them that I was coming. It was bright moonlight; so that the walk was rather a pleasure, than otherwise. When I got there, the whole place was in darkness, and I thought I would take a walk 'round outside, to see whether Tassoc or his brother was keeping watch. But I could not find them anywhere, and concluded that they had got tired of it, and gone off to bed.

"As I returned across the front of the East Wing, I caught the hooning whistling of the Room, coming down strangely through the stillness of the night. It had a queer note in it, I remember – low and constant, queerly meditative. I looked up at the window, bright in the moonlight, and got a sudden thought to bring a ladder from the stable yard, and try to get a look into the Room, through the window.

"With this notion, I hunted 'round at the back of the castle, among the straggle of offices, and presently found a long, fairly light ladder; though it was heavy enough for one, goodness knows! And I thought at first that I should never get it reared. I managed at last, and let the ends rest very quietly against the wall, a little below the sill of the larger window. Then, going silently, I went up the ladder. Presently, I had my face above the sill and was looking in alone with the moonlight.

"Of course, the queer whistling sounded louder up there; but it still conveyed that peculiar sense of something whistling quietly to itself – can you understand? Though, for all the meditative lowness of the note, the horrible, gargantuan quality was distinct – a mighty parody of the human, as if I stood there and listened to the whistling from the lips of a monster with a man's soul.

"And then, you know, I saw something. The floor in the middle of the huge, empty room, was puckered upward in the centre into a strange soft-looking mound, parted at the top into an ever-changing hole, that pulsated to that great, gentle hooning. At times, as I watched, I saw the heaving of the indented mound, gap across with a queer, inward suction, as with the drawing of an enormous breath; then the thing would dilate and pout once more to the incredible melody. And suddenly, as I stared, dumb, it came to me that the thing was living. I was looking at two enormous, blackened lips, blistered and brutal, there in the pale moonlight....

"Abruptly, they bulged out to a vast, pouting mound of force and sound, stiffened and swollen, and hugely massive and clean-cut in the moon-beams. And a great sweat lay heavy on the vast upper-lip. In the same moment of time, the whistling had burst into a mad screaming note, that seemed to stun me, even where I stood, outside of the window. And then, the following moment, I was staring blankly at the solid, undisturbed floor of the room – smooth, polished stone flooring, from wall to wall; and there was an absolute silence.

"You can picture me staring into the quiet Room, and knowing what I knew. I felt like a sick, frightened kid, and wanted to slide *quietly* down the ladder, and run away. But in that very instant, I heard Tassoc's voice calling to me from within the Room, for help, *help*. My God! But I got such an awful dazed feeling; and I had a vague, bewildered notion that, after all, it was the Irishmen who had got him in there, and were taking it out of him. And then the call came again, and I burst the window, and jumped in to help him. I had a confused idea that the call had come from within the shadow of the great fireplace, and I raced across to it; but there was no one there.

"'Tassoc!' I shouted, and my voice went empty-sounding 'round the great apartment; and then, in a flash, *I knew that Tassoc had never called*. I whirled 'round, sick with fear, towards the window, and as I did so, a frightful, exultant whistling scream burst through the Room. On my left, the end wall had bellied in towards me, in a pair of gargantuan lips, black and utterly monstrous, to within a yard of my face. I fumbled for a mad instant at my revolver; not for *it*, but myself; for the danger was a thousand times worse than death. And then, suddenly, the Unknown Last Line of the Saaamaaa Ritual was whispered quite audibly in the room. Instantly, the thing happened that I have known once before. There came a sense as of dust falling continually and monotonously, and I knew that my life hung uncertain and suspended for a flash, in a brief, reeling vertigo of unseeable things. Then *that* ended, and I knew that I might live. My soul and body blended again, and life and power came to me. I dashed furiously at the window, and hurled myself out head-foremost; for I can tell you that I had stopped being afraid of death. I crashed down on to the ladder, and slithered, grabbing and grabbing; and so came some way or other alive to the bottom. And there I sat in the soft, wet grass, with the moonlight all about me; and far above, through the broken window of the Room, there was a low whistling.

"That is the chief of it. I was not hurt, and I went 'round to the front, and knocked Tassoc up. When they let me in, we had a long yarn, over some good whisky – for I was shaken to pieces – and I explained things as much as I could, I told Tassoc that the room would have to come down, and every fragment of it burned in a blast-furnace, erected within a pentacle. He nodded. There was nothing to say. Then I went to bed.

"We turned a small army on to the work, and within ten days, that lovely thing had gone up in smoke, and what was left was calcined, and clean.

"It was when the workmen were stripping the panelling, that I got hold of a sound notion of the beginnings of that beastly development. Over the great fireplace, after the great oak panels had been torn down, I found that there was let into the masonry a scrollwork of stone, with on it an old inscription, in ancient Celtic, that here in this room was burned Dian Tiansay, Jester of King Alzof, who made the Song of Foolishness upon King Ernore of the Seventh Castle.

"When I got the translation clear, I gave it to Tassoc. He was tremendously excited; for he knew the old tale, and took me down to the library to look at an old parchment that gave the story in detail. Afterward, I found that the incident was well known about the countryside; but always regarded more as a legend than as history. And no one seemed ever to have dreamt that the old East Wing of Iastrae Castle was the remains of the ancient Seventh Castle.

"From the old parchment, I gathered that there had been a pretty dirty job done, away back in the years. It seems that King Alzof and King Ernore had been enemies by birthright, as you might say truly; but that nothing more than a little raiding had occurred on either side for years, until Dian Tiansay made the Song of Foolishness upon King Ernore, and sang it before King Alzof; and so greatly was it appreciated that King Alzof gave the jester one of his ladies, to wife.

"Presently, all the people of the land had come to know the song, and so it came at last to King Ernore, who was so angered that he made war upon his old enemy, and took and burned him and his castle; but Dian Tiansay, the jester, he brought with him to his own place, and having torn his tongue out because of the song which he had made and sung, he imprisoned him in the Room in the East Wing (which was evidently used for unpleasant purposes), and the jester's wife he kept for himself, having a fancy for her prettiness.

"But one night, Dian Tiansay's wife was not to be found, and in the morning they discovered her lying dead in her husband's arms, and he sitting, whistling the Song of Foolishness, for he had no longer the power to sing it.

"Then they roasted Dian Tiansay, in the great fireplace – probably from that selfsame 'galley-iron' which I have already mentioned. And until he died, Dian Tiansay ceased not to whistle the Song of Foolishness, which he could no longer sing. But afterward, 'in that room' there was often heard at night the sound of something whistling; and there 'grew a power in that room', so that none dared to sleep in it. And presently, it would seem, the King went to another castle; for the whistling troubled him.

"There you have it all. Of course, that is only a rough rendering of the translation of the parchment. But it sounds extraordinarily quaint. Don't you think so?"

"Yes," I said, answering for the lot. "But how did the thing grow to such a tremendous manifestation?"

"One of those cases of continuity of thought producing a positive action upon the immediate surrounding material," replied Carnacki. "The development must have been going forward through centuries, to have produced such a monstrosity. It was a true instance of Saiitii manifestation, which I can best explain by likening it to a living spiritual fungus, which involves the very structure of the aether-fiber itself, and, of course, in so doing, acquires an essential control over the 'material substance' involved in it. It is impossible to make it plainer in a few words."

"What broke the seventh hair?" asked Taylor.

But Carnacki did not know. He thought it was probably nothing but being too severely tensioned. He also explained that they found out that the men who had run away had not been up to mischief; but had come over secretly, merely to hear the whistling, which, indeed, had suddenly become the talk of the whole countryside.

"One other thing," said Arkright, "have you any idea what governs the use of the Unknown Last Line of the Saaamaaa Ritual? I know, of course, that it was used by the Ab-human Priests in the Incantation of Raaaee; but what used it on your behalf, and what made it?"

"You had better read Harzan's Monograph, and my Addenda to it, on Astral and Astral Co-ordination and Interference," said Carnacki. "It is an extraordinary subject, and I can only say here that the human vibration may not be insulated from the astral (as is always believed to be the case, in interferences by the Ab-human), without immediate action being taken by those Forces which govern the spinning of the outer circle. In other words, it is being proved, time after time, that there is some inscrutable Protective Force constantly intervening between the human soul (not the body, mind you) and the Outer Monstrosities. Am I clear?"

"Yes, I think so," I replied. "And you believe that the Room had become the material expression of the ancient Jester – that his soul, rotten with hatred, had bred into a monster – eh?" I asked.

"Yes," said Carnacki, nodding, "I think you've put my thought rather neatly. It is a queer coincidence that Miss Donnehue is supposed to be descended (so I have heard since) from the same King Ernore. It makes one think some curious thoughts, doesn't it? The marriage coming on, and the Room waking to fresh life. If she had gone into that room, ever…eh? *It* had waited a long time. Sins of the fathers. Yes, I've thought of that. They're to be married next week, and I am to be best man, which is a thing I hate. And he won his bets, rather! Just think, *if* ever she had gone into that room. Pretty horrible, eh?"

He nodded his head, grimly, and we four nodded back. Then he rose and took us collectively to the door, and presently thrust us forth in friendly fashion on the Embankment and into the fresh night air.

"Goodnight," we all called back, and went to our various homes. If she had, eh? If she had? That is what I kept thinking.

If you enjoyed this, you might also like…

The Searcher of the End House, see page 63
The Gateway of the Monster, see page 13

The Horse of the Invisible

WHEN I REACHED 427, Cheyne Walk, Chelsea, I found Carnacki sitting alone. As I came into the room, he rose with a perceptibly stiff movement, and extended his left hand. His face seemed to be badly scarred and bruised, and his right hand was bandaged. He shook hands and offered me his paper, which I refused. Then he passed me a handful of photographs, and returned to his reading.

Now, that is just Carnacki. Not a word had come from him, and not a question from me. He would tell us all about it later. I spent about half an hour, looking at the photographs, which were chiefly 'snaps' (some by flashlight) of an extraordinarily pretty girl; though in some of the photographs it was wonderful that her prettiness was so evident, for so frightened and startled was her expression, that it was difficult not to believe that she had been photographed in the presence of some imminent and overwhelming danger.

The bulk of the photographs were of interiors of different rooms and passages, and in every one the girl might be seen, either full length in the distance, or closer, with, perhaps, only a hand or arm, or portion of the head or dress included in the photograph. All of these had evidently been taken with some definite aim, that did not have for its first purpose the picturing of the girl, but obviously of her surroundings; and they made me very curious, as you can imagine.

Near the bottom of the pile, however, I came upon something *definitely* extraordinary. It was a photograph of the girl, standing abrupt and clear in the great blaze of a flashlight, as was plain to be seen. Her face was turned a little upward, as if she had been frightened suddenly by some noise. Directly above her, as though half-formed and coming down out of the shadows, was the shape of a single, enormous hoof.

I examined this photograph for a long time, without understanding it more than that it had probably to do with some queer Case in which Carnacki was interested.

When Jessop, Arkwright, and Taylor came in, Carnacki quietly held out his hand for the photographs, which I returned in the same spirit, and afterwards we all went in to dinner. When we had spent a quiet but profitable hour at the table, we pulled our chairs round, and made ourselves snug; and Carnacki began:

"I've been North," he said, speaking slowly and painfully, between puffs at his pipe. "Up to Hisgins of East Lancashire. It has been a pretty strange business all round, as I fancy you chaps will think, when I have finished. I knew, before I went, something about the 'horse story', as I have heard it called; but I never thought of it as coming my way, somehow. Also I know *now* that I never considered it seriously – in spite of my rule always to keep an open mind. Funny creatures, we humans!

"Well, I got a wire, asking for an appointment, which of course told me that there was some trouble. On the date I fixed, old Captain Hisgins himself came up to see me. He told me a great many new details about the horse story; though, naturally, I had always known the main points, and understood that if the first child were a girl, that girl would be haunted by the Horse, during her courtship.

"It is, as you can see, an extraordinary story, and though I have always known about it, I have never thought it to be anything more than old-time legend, as I have already hinted. You see, for seven generations the Hisgins family have had men children for their first-born, and even the Hisgins themselves have long considered the tale to be little more than a myth.

"To come to the present, the eldest child of the reigning family, is a girl, and she has been often teased and warned in jest by her friends and relations that she is the first girl to be the eldest for seven generations, and that she would have to keep her men friends at arm's length, or go into a nunnery, if she hoped to escape the haunting. And this, I think, shows us how thoroughly the tale had grown to be considered as nothing worthy of the least serious thought. Don't you think so?

"Two months ago, Miss Hisgins became engaged to Beaumont, a young Naval Officer, and on the evening of the very day of the engagement, before it was even formally announced, a most extraordinary thing happened, which resulted in Captain Hisgins making the appointment, and my ultimately going down to their place to look into the thing.

"From the old family records and papers that were trusted to me, I found that there could be no possible doubt that prior to something like a hundred and fifty years ago there were some very extraordinary and disagreeable coincidences, to put the thing in the least emotional way. In the whole of the two centuries prior to that date, there were five first-born girls, out of a total of seven generations of the family. Each of these girls grew up to Maidenhood, and each became engaged, and each one died during the period of engagement, two by suicide, one by falling from a window, one from a 'broken heart' (presumably heart failure, owing to sudden shock through fright). The fifth girl was killed one evening in the park round the house; but just how, there seemed to be no exact knowledge; only that there was an impression that she had been kicked by a horse. She was dead, when found.

"Now, you see, all of these deaths might be attributed in a way – even the suicides – to natural causes, I mean, as distinct from supernatural. You see? Yet, in every case, the maidens had undoubtedly suffered some extraordinary and terrifying experiences during their various courtships, for in all of the records there was mention either of the neighing of an unseen horse, or of the sounds of an invisible horse galloping, as well as many other peculiar and quite inexplicable manifestations. You begin to understand now, I think, just how extraordinary a business it was that I was asked to look into.

"I gathered from the records that the haunting of the girls was so constant and horrible that two of the girls' lovers fairly ran away from their lady-loves. And I think it was this, more than anything else, that made me feel that there had been something more in it, than a mere succession of uncomfortable coincidences.

"I got hold of these facts, before I had been many hours in the house; and after this I went pretty carefully into the details of the things that happened on the night of Miss Hisgins' engagement to Beaumont. It seems that as the two of them were going through the big lower corridor, just after dusk and before the lamps had been lighted, there had been a sudden, horrible neighing in the corridor, close to them. Immediately afterwards, Beaumont received a tremendous blow or kick, which broke his right forearm. Then the rest of the family came running, to know what was wrong, and the servants. Lights were brought, and the corridor and, afterwards, the whole house searched; but nothing unusual was found.

"You can imagine the excitement in the house, and the half-incredulous, half-believing talk about the old legend. Later on, in the middle of the night, the old Captain was awakened by the sound of a great horse galloping round and round the house.

"Several times after this, both Beaumont and the girl said that they had heard the sounds of hoofs near to them, after dusk, in several of the rooms and corridors.

"Three nights later, Beaumont was awakened by a strange neighing in the night-time, seeming to come from the direction of his sweetheart's bedroom. He ran hurriedly for her father, and the two of them raced to her room. They found her awake, and ill with sheer terror, having been awakened by the neighing, seemingly close to her bed.

"The night before I arrived, there had been a fresh happening, and they were all in a frightfully nervy state, as you can imagine.

"I spent most of the first day, as I have hinted, in getting hold of details; but after dinner, I slacked off, and played billiards all the evening with Beaumont and Miss Hisgins. We stopped about ten o'clock, and had coffee, and I got Beaumont to give me full particulars about the thing that happened the night before.

"He and Miss Hisgins had been sitting quietly in her aunt's boudoir, whilst the old lady chaperoned them, behind a book. It was growing dusk, and the lamp was at her end of the table. The rest of the house was not yet lit, as the evening had come earlier than usual.

"Well, it seems that the door into the hall was open, and suddenly the girl said: 'S'ush! what's that?'

"They both listened, and then Beaumont heard it – the sound of a horse, outside the front door.

"'Your father?' he suggested; but she reminded him that her father was not riding.

"Of course, they were both ready to feel queer, as you can suppose; but Beaumont made an effort to shake this off, and went into the hall to see whether anyone was at the entrance. It was pretty dark in the hall, and he could see the glass panels of the inner draught-door, clear-cut in the darkness of the hall. He walked over to the glass, and looked through into the drive beyond; but there was nothing in sight.

"He felt nervous and puzzled, and opened the inner door and went out on to the carriage-circle. Almost directly afterwards, the great hall door swung to with a crash behind him. He told me that he had a sudden awful feeling of having been trapped in some way – that is how he put it. He whirled round, and gripped the door handle; but something seemed to be holding it with a vast grip on the other side. Then, before it could be fixed in his mind that this was so, he was able to turn the handle, and open the door.

"He paused a moment in the doorway, and peered into the hall; for he had hardly steadied his mind sufficiently to know whether he was really frightened or not. Then he heard his sweetheart blow him a kiss out of the greyness of the big, unlit hall, and he knew that she had followed him, from the boudoir. He blew her a kiss back, and stepped inside the doorway, meaning to go to her. And then, suddenly, in a flash of sickening knowledge, he knew that it was not his sweetheart who had blown him that kiss. He knew that something was trying to tempt him alone into the darkness, and that the girl had never left the boudoir. He jumped back, and in the same instant of time, he heard the kiss again, nearer to him. He called out at the top of his voice: – 'Mary, stay in the boudoir. Don't move out of the boudoir until I come to you.' He heard her call something in reply, from the boudoir, and then he had struck a clump of a dozen, or so, matches, and was holding them above his head, and looking round the hall. There was no one in it; but even as the matches burned out, there came the sounds of a great horse galloping down the empty drive.

"Now, you see, both he and the girl had heard the sounds of the horse galloping; but when I questioned more closely, I found that the aunt had heard nothing; though, it is true, she is a bit deaf, and she was further back in the room. Of course, both he and Miss Hisgins had been in an extremely nervous state, and ready to hear anything. The door might have been slammed by a sudden puff of wind, owing to some inner door being opened; and as for the grip on the handle, that may have been nothing more than the sneck catching.

"With regard to the kisses and the sounds of the horse galloping, I pointed out that these might have seemed ordinary enough sounds, if they had been only cool enough to reason. As I told him, and as he knew, the sounds of a horse galloping, carry a long way on the wind; so that what he had heard might have been nothing more than a horse being ridden, some distance away. And as for the kiss, plenty of quiet noises – the rustle of a paper or a leaf – have a somewhat similar sound, especially if one is in an overstrung condition, and imagining things.

"I was preaching this little sermon on common sense, versus hysteria, as we put out the lights and left the billiard room. But neither Beaumont nor Miss Hisgins would agree that there had been any fancy on their parts.

"We had come out of the billiard-room, by this, and were going along the passage; and I was still doing my best to make both of them see the ordinary, commonplace possibilities of the happening, when what killed my pig, as the saying goes, was the sound of a hoof in the dark billiard room, we had just left.

"I felt the 'creep' come on me in a flash, up my spine and over the back of my head. Miss Hisgins whooped like a child with whooping-cough, and ran up the passage, giving little gasping screams. Beaumont, however, ripped round on his heels, and jumped back a couple of yards. I gave back too, a bit, as you can understand.

"'There it is,' he said, in a low, breathless voice. 'Perhaps you'll believe now.'

"'There's certainly something,' I whispered back, and never taking my gaze off the closed door of the billiard-room.

"'H'sh!' he muttered, 'There it is again.'

"There was a sound like a great horse pacing round and round the billiard room, with slow, deliberate steps. A horrible cold fright took me, so that it seemed impossible to take a full breath, you know the feeling; and then I know we must have walked backwards, for we found ourselves suddenly at the opening of the long passage.

"We stopped there, and listened. The sounds went on steadily with a horrible sort of deliberateness; as if the brute were taking a sort of malicious gusto in walking about all over the room in which we had just been. Do you understand just what I mean?

"Then there was a pause, and a long time of absolute quiet, except for an excited whispering from some of the people down in the big hall. The sound came plainly up the wide stair-way. I fancy they were gathered round Miss Hisgins, with some notion of protecting her.

"I should think Beaumont and I stood there, at the end of the passage, for about five minutes, listening for any noise in the billiard-room. Then I realised what a horrible funk I was in, and I said to him: – 'I'm going to see what's there.'

"'So'm I,' he answered. He was pretty white; but he had heaps of pluck. I told him to wait one instant, and I made a dash into my bedroom, and got my camera and flashlight. I slipped my revolver into my right-hand pocket and a knuckle-duster over my left fist, where it was ready, and yet would not stop me from being able to work my flashlight.

"Then I ran back to Beaumont. He held out his right hand, to show me that he had his pistol, and I nodded; but whispered to him not to be too quick to shoot, as there might be some silly practical joking at work, after all. He had got a lamp from a bracket in the upper hall, which he was holding in the crook of his damaged arm, so that we had a good light. Then we went down the passage, towards the billiard-room; and you can imagine that we were a pretty nervous couple.

"All this time, there had not been a sound; but abruptly when we were within perhaps a couple of yards of the door, we heard the sudden clumping of a hoof on the solid parquet-floor of the billiard room. In the instant afterwards, it seemed to me that the whole place shook beneath the ponderous hoof-falls of some huge thing, coming towards the door. Both Beaumont and I gave back a pace or two, and then realised, and hung on to our courage, as you might say, and waited. The great tread came right up to the door and then stopped, and there was an instant of absolute silence, except that, so far as I was concerned, the pulse in my throat and temples almost deafened me.

"I daresay we waited quite half a minute, and then came the further restless clumping of a great hoof. Immediately afterwards, the sounds came right on, as if some invisible thing passed through the closed door, and the passage, and I know that I spread myself stiff against the wall. The clungk, clunck, clungk, clunck, of the great hoof-falls passed right between us, and slowly and with deadly deliberateness, down the passage. I heard them through a haze of blood-beats in my ears and temples, and my body extraordinarily rigid and pringling and breathless. I stood for a little time like this, my head turned, so that I should see up the passage. I was conscious only that there was a hideous danger abroad. Do you understand?

"And then, suddenly, my pluck came back to me. I was aware that the noise of the hoof-beats sounded near the other end of the passage. I twisted quickly, and got my camera to bear, and snapped the flashlight. Immediately afterwards, Beaumont let fly a storm of shots down the passage, and began to run, shouting: – 'It's after Mary. Run! Run!'

"He rushed down the passage, and I after him. We came out on the main landing and heard the sound of a hoof on the stairs, and after that, nothing. And from thence, onwards, nothing.

"Down, below us in the big hall, I could see a number of the household round Miss Hisgins, who seemed to have fainted; and there were several of the servants clumped together a little way off, staring up at the main landing, and no one saying a single word. And about some twenty steps up the stairs was old Captain Hisgins with a drawn sword in his hand, where he had halted just below the last hoof-sound. I think I never saw anything finer than the old man standing there between his daughter and that infernal thing.

"I daresay you can understand the queer feeling of horror I had at passing that place on the stairs where the sounds had ceased. It was as if the monster were still standing there, invisible. And the peculiar thing was that we never heard another sound of the hoof, either up or down the stairs.

"After they had taken Miss Hisgins to her room, I sent word that I should follow so soon as they were ready for me. And, presently, when a message came to tell me that I could come any time, I asked her father to give me a hand with my instrument box, and between us we carried it into the girl's bedroom. I had the bed pulled well out into the middle of the room; after which I erected the electric pentacle round the bed. Then I directed that lamps should be placed round the room, but that on no account must any light be made within the pentacle, neither must anyone pass in or out. The girl's mother

I had placed within the pentacle and directed that her maid should sit without, ready to carry any message, so as to make sure that Mrs. Hisgins did not have to leave the pentacle. I suggested also, that the girl's father should stay the night in the room, and that he had better be armed.

"When I left the room, I found Beaumont waiting outside the door, in a miserable state of anxiety. I told him what I had done, and explained to him that Miss Hisgins was probably perfectly safe within the 'protection'; but that, in addition to her father remaining the night in the room, I intended to stand guard at the door. I told him that I should like him to keep me company, for I knew that he could never sleep, and I should not be sorry to have a companion. Also, I wanted to have him under my own observation; for there was no doubt but that he was actually in greater danger than the girl. At least, that was my opinion; and is still, as I think you will agree later.

"I asked him whether he would object to my drawing a pentacle round him, for the night, and got him to agree; but I saw that he did not know whether to be superstitious about it, or to regard it more as a piece of foolish mumming; but he took it seriously enough, when I gave him some particulars about the Black Veil case, when young Aster died. You remember, he said it was a piece of silly superstition, and stayed outside. Poor devil!

"As it chanced, the night passed quietly enough, until a little while before dawn when we both heard the sounds of a great horse galloping round and round the house, just as old Captain Hisgins had described it. You can imagine how queer it made me feel, and directly afterwards, I heard someone stir within the room. I knocked at the door; for I was uneasy, and the Captain came. I asked whether everything was right; to which he replied yes, and immediately asked me whether I had heard the sounds of the galloping; so that I knew he had heard them also. I suggested that it might be well to leave the bedroom door open a little, until the dawn came in, as there was certainly something abroad. This was done, and he went back into the room, to be near his wife and daughter.

"I had better say here, that I was doubtful whether there was any value in the 'defence' about Miss Hisgins; for what I term the 'personal-sounds' of the manifestation were so extraordinarily material, that I was inclined to parallel the case with that of Hartford's, where the hand of the child kept materialising within the pentacle, and patting the floor. As you will remember, that was a hideous business.

"Yet, as it chanced, nothing further happened; and so soon as daylight had fully come, we all went off to bed.

"Beaumont knocked me up about midday, and I went down and made breakfast into lunch. Miss Hisgins was there, and seemed in very fair spirits, considering. She told me that I had made her feel almost safe, for the first time for days. She told me also that her cousin, Harry Parsket, was coming down from London, and she knew that he would do anything to help fight the ghost. And after that she and Beaumont went out into the grounds, to have a little time together.

"I had a walk in the grounds myself, and went round the house, but saw no traces of hoof-marks; and after that, I spent the rest of the day, making an examination of the house; but found nothing.

"I made an end of my search, before dark, and went to my room to dress for dinner. When I got down, the cousin had just arrived; and I found him one of the nicest men I have met for a long time. A chap with a tremendous amount of pluck, and the particular kind of man I like to have with me, in a bad case like the one I was on.

"I could see that what puzzled him most was our belief in the genuineness of the haunting; and I found myself almost wanting something to happen, just to show him how true it was. As it chanced, something did happen, with a vengeance.

"Beaumont and Miss Hisgins had gone out for a stroll in the dusk, and Captain Hisgins asked me to come into his study for a short chat whilst Parsket went upstairs with his traps, for he had no man with him.

"I had a long conversation with the old Captain, in which I pointed out that the 'haunting' had evidently no particular connection with the house, but only with the girl herself, and that the sooner she was married, the better, as it would give Beaumont a right to be with her at all times; and further than this, it might be that the manifestations would cease, if the marriage were actually performed. The old man nodded agreement to this, especially to the first part, and reminded me that three of the girls who were said to have been 'haunted' had been sent away from home, and met their deaths whilst away. And then in the midst of our talk there came a pretty frightening interruption; for all at once the old butler rushed into the room, most extraordinarily pale:

"'Miss Mary, Sir! Miss Mary, Sir!' he gasped out, using the old name. 'She's screaming… out in the Park, Sir! And they say they can hear the Horse—'

"The Captain made one dive for a rack of arms, and snatched down his old sword, and ran out, drawing it as he ran. I dashed out and up the stairs, snatched my camera-flashlight and a heavy revolver, gave one yell at Parsket's door: – 'The Horse!' and was down and into the grounds.

"Out in the darkness there was a confused shouting, and I caught the sounds of shooting, away out among the scattered trees. And then, from a patch of blackness to my left, there burst suddenly an infernal gobbling sort of neighing. Instantly I whipped round and snapped off the flashlight. The great blare of the light blazed out momentarily, showing me the leaves of a big tree close at hand, quivering in the night breeze; but there had been nothing else; and then the ten-fold blackness came down upon me, and I heard Parsket shouting a little way back to know whether I had seen anything.

"The next instant he was beside me, and I felt safer for his company; for there was some incredible thing near to us, and I was momentarily blind, because of the brightness of the flashlight. 'What was it? What was it?' he kept repeating in an excited voice. And all the time I was staring into the darkness and answering, mechanically, 'I don't know. I don't know.' There was a burst of shouting somewhere ahead, and then a shot. We ran towards the sounds, yelling to the people not to shoot; for in the darkness and panic there was this danger also. Then there came two of the gamekeepers, racing hard up the drive, with lanterns and their guns; and immediately afterwards a row of lights dancing towards us from the house, carried by some of the men-servants.

"As the lights came up, I saw we had come close to Beaumont. He was standing over Miss Hisgins, and he had his revolver in his right hand. Then I saw his face, and there was a great wound across his forehead. By him was the Captain, turning his naked sword this way and that, and peering into the darkness; and a little behind him stood the old butler, a battle-axe from one of the arm-stands in the hall, in his hands. Yet there was nothing strange to be seen anywhere.

"We got the girl into the house, and left her with her mother and Beaumont, whilst a groom rode for a doctor. And then the rest of us, with four other keepers, all armed with guns and carrying lanterns, searched round the home-park. But we found nothing.

"When we got back, we found that the Doctor had been. He had bound up Beaumont's wound, which, luckily, was not deep, and ordered Miss Hisgins straight to bed. I went upstairs with the Captain and found Beaumont on guard outside the girl's door. I asked him how he felt; and then, so soon as they were ready for us, Captain Hisgins and I went into the bedroom and fixed the pentacle again round the bed. They had already got lamps about the room; and after I had set the same order of watching, as on the previous night, I joined Beaumont, outside of the door.

"Parsket had come up while I had been in the bedroom, and between us we got some idea from Beaumont as to what had happened out in the Park. It seems that they were coming home after their stroll, from the direction of the West Lodge; when, suddenly, Miss Hisgins said, 'Hush!' and came to a standstill. He stopped, and listened; but heard nothing for a little. Then he caught it – the sound of a horse, seemingly a long way off, galloping towards them over the grass. He told the girl that it was nothing, and started to hurry her towards the house, but she was not deceived, of course. In less than a minute, they heard it quite close to them in the dark, and they began to run. Then Miss Hisgins caught her foot, and fell. She began to scream, and that is what the butler heard. As Beaumont lifted the girl, he heard the hoofs come thudding right at him. He stood over her, and fired all five chambers of his revolver at the sounds. He told us that he was sure he saw something that looked like an enormous horse's head, right upon him, in the light of the last flash of his pistol. Immediately afterwards, he was struck a tremendous blow, which knocked him down; and then the Captain and the butler came running up, shouting. The rest, of course, we knew.

"About ten o'clock, the butler brought us up a tray; for which I was very glad; as the night before I had got rather hungry. I warned Beaumont, however, to be very particular not to drink any spirits, and I also made him give me his pipe and matches. At midnight, I drew a pentacle round him, and Parsket and I sat one on each side of him; but outside of the pentacle; for I had no fear that there would be any manifestation made against anyone, except Beaumont or Miss Hisgins.

"After that, we kept pretty quiet. The passage was lit by a big lamp at each end; so that we had plenty of light; and we were all armed. Beaumont and I with revolvers, and Parsket with a shotgun. In addition to my weapon, I had my camera and flashlight.

"Now and again we talked in whispers; and twice the Captain came out of the bedroom to have a word with us. About half past one, we had all grown very silent; and suddenly, about twenty minutes later, I held up my hand, silently; for there seemed to me to be a sound of galloping, out in the night. I knocked on the bedroom door, for the Captain to open it, and when he came, I whispered to him that we thought we heard the Horse. For some time we stayed, listening, and both Parsket and the Captain thought they heard it; but now I was not so sure, neither was Beaumont. Yet afterwards, I thought I heard it again.

"I told Captain Hisgins I thought he had better go back into the bedroom, and leave the door a little open, and this he did. But from that time onward, we heard nothing; and presently the dawn came in, and we all went very thankfully to bed.

"When I was called at lunch-time, I had a little surprise; for Captain Hisgins told me that they had held a family council, and had decided to take my advice, and have the marriage without a day's more delay than possible. Beaumont was already on his way to London to get a special licence, and they hoped to have the wedding the next day.

"This pleased me; for it seemed the sanest thing to be done, in the extraordinary circumstances; and meanwhile I should continue my investigations; but until the marriage was accomplished, my chief thought was to keep Miss Hisgins near to me.

"After lunch, I thought I would take a few experimental photographs of Miss Hisgins and her *surroundings*. Sometimes the camera sees things that would seem very strange to normal human eyesight. You see what I mean? With this intention, and partly to make an excuse to keep her in my company as much as possible, I asked Miss Hisgins to join me in my experiments. She seemed glad to do this, and I spent several hours with her, wandering all over the house, from room to room; and whenever the impulse came, I took a flashlight of her and the room or corridor in which we chanced to be at the moment.

"After we had gone right through the house in this fashion, I asked her whether she felt sufficiently brave to repeat the experiments in the cellars. She said, yes; and so I rooted out Captain Hisgins and Parsket; for I was not going to take her down even into what you might call artificial darkness, without help and companionship at hand.

"When we were ready, we went down into the wine cellar, Captain Hisgins carrying a shot-gun, and Parsket a specially-prepared background and a lantern. I got the girl to stand in the middle of the cellar, whilst Parsket and the Captain held out the background behind her. Then I fired off the flashlight, and we went into the next cellar, where we repeated the experiment.

"Then, in the third cellar, a tremendous, pitch-dark place, something extraordinary and horrible manifested itself. I had stationed Miss Hisgins in the centre of the place, with her father and Parsket holding the background, as before. When all was ready, and just as I pressed the trigger of the 'flash', there came in the cellar that dreadful, gobbling neighing, that I had heard out in the Park. It seemed to come from somewhere above the girl; and in the glare of the sudden light, I saw that she was staring tensely upward at no visible thing. And then in the succeeding comparative darkness, I was shouting to the Captain and Parsket to run Miss Hisgins out into the daylight.

"This was done, instantly; and I shut and locked the door, afterwards making the First and the Eighth signs of the Saaamaaa Ritual opposite to each post, and connecting them across the threshold with a triple line. In the meanwhile, Parsket and Captain Hisgins carried the girl to her mother, and left her there, in a half-fainting condition; whilst I stayed on guard outside of the cellar door, feeling pretty horrible, for I knew that there was some disgusting thing inside; and along with this feeling there was a sense of half-ashamedness, rather miserable you know, because I had exposed Miss Hisgins to this danger.

"I had got the Captain's shot-gun, and when he and Parsket came down again, they were each carrying guns and lanterns. I could not possibly tell you the utter relief of spirit and body that came to me, when I heard them coming; but just try to imagine what it was like, standing outside of that cellar. Can you?

"I remember noticing, just before I went to unlock the door, how white and ghastly Parsket looked and the old Captain was grey-looking; and I wondered whether my face was like theirs. And this, you know, had its own distinct effect upon my nerves; for it seemed to bring the beastliness of the thing bash down on me in a fresh way. I know it was only sheer will power that carried me up to the door and made me turn the key.

"I paused one little moment, and then with a nervy jerk, sent the door wide open, and held my lantern over my head. Parsket and the Captain came one on each side of me, and held up their lanterns; but the place was absolutely empty. Of course, I did not trust to a casual look of this kind; but spent several hours, with the help of the two others in sounding every square foot of the floor, ceiling, and walls. Yet, in the end, I had to admit that the place itself was absolutely normal; and so in the end we came away none the wiser. But I sealed the door, and outside, opposite each door-post, I made the First and Last Signs of the Saaamaaa Ritual, joining them, as before, with a triple line. Can you imagine what it was like, searching that cellar?

THE HORSE OF THE INVISIBLE

"When we got upstairs, I inquired very anxiously how Miss Hisgins was, and the girl came out herself to tell me that she was all right and that I was not to trouble about her, or blame myself, as I told her I had been doing. I felt happier then, and went off to dress for dinner; and after that was done with, Parsket and I went off to one of the bath-rooms to develop the negatives that I had been taking. Yet none of the plates had anything to tell me, until we came to the one that was taken in the cellar. Parsket was developing, and I had taken a batch of the fixed plates out into the lamplight to examine them.

"I had just gone carefully through the lot, when I heard a shout from Parsket, and when I ran to him, he was looking at a partly-developed negative, which he was holding up to the red lamp. It showed the girl plainly, looking upward, as I had seen her; but the thing that astonished me, was the shadow of an enormous hoof, right above her, as if it were coming down upon her out of the shadows. And, you know, I had run her bang into that danger. That was the thought that was chief in my mind.

"As soon as the developing was complete, I fixed the plate, and examined it carefully in a good light. There was no doubt about it at all; the thing above Miss Hisgins was an enormous, shadowy hoof. Yet I was no nearer to coming to any definite knowledge; and the only thing I could do was to warn Parsket to say nothing about it to the girl; for it would only increase her fright; but I showed the thing to her father, for I considered it right that he should know.

"That night, we took the same precautions for Miss Hisgins' safety, as on the two previous nights; and Parsket kept me company; yet the dawn came in without anything unusual having happened, and I went off to bed.

"When I got down to lunch, I learnt that Beaumont had wired to say that he would be in soon after four; also that a message had been sent to the Rector. And it was generally plain that the ladies of the house were in a tremendous fluster.

"Beaumont's train was late, and he did not get home until five, but even then the Rector had not put in an appearance; and the butler came in to say that the coachman had returned without him, as he had been called away unexpectedly. Twice more during the evening the carriage was sent down; but the clergyman had not returned; and we had to delay the marriage until the next day.

"That night, I arranged the 'Defence' round the girl's bed, and the Captain and his wife sat up with her, as before. Beaumont, as I expected, insisted on keeping watch with me, and he seemed in a curiously frightened mood; not for himself, you know; but for Miss Hisgins. He had a horrible feeling, he told me, that there would be a final, dreadful attempt on his sweetheart, that night. This, of course, I told him was nothing but nerves; yet, really, it made me feel very anxious; for I have seen too much, not to know that under such circumstances, a premonitory conviction of impending danger, is not necessarily to be put down entirely to nerves. In fact, Beaumont was so simply and earnestly convinced that the night would bring some extraordinary manifestation, that I got Parsket to rig up a long cord from the wire of the butler's bell, to come along the passage handy. To the butler himself, I gave directions not to undress and to give the same order to two of the footmen. If I rang, he was to come instantly, with the footmen, carrying lanterns; and the lanterns were to be kept ready lit all night. If, for any reason, the bell did not ring, and I blew my whistle, he was to take that as a signal in the place of the bell.

"After I had arranged all these minor details, I drew a pentacle about Beaumont, and warned him very particularly to stay within it, whatever happened. And when this was done, there was nothing to do but wait, and pray that the night would go as quietly as the night before.

"We scarcely talked at all, and by about one a.m. we were all very tense and nervous; so that, at last, Parsket got up and began to walk up and down the corridor, to steady himself a bit. Presently, I slipped off my pumps, and joined him and we walked up and down, whispering occasionally, for something over an hour, until in turning I caught my foot in the bell-cord, and went down on my face; but without hurting myself or making a noise.

"When I got up, Parsket nudged me.

"'Did you notice that the bell never rang?' he whispered.

"'Jove!' I said, 'you're right.'

"'Wait a minute,' he answered. 'I'll bet it's only a kink somewhere in the cord.' He left his gun, and slipped along the passage, and taking the top lamp, tip-toed away into the house, carrying Beaumont's revolver ready in his right hand. He was a plucky chap, as I think you will admit.

"Suddenly, Beaumont motioned to me for absolute quiet. Directly afterwards, I heard the thing for which he listened – the sound of a horse galloping, out in the night. I think that I may say, I fairly shivered. The sound died away, and left a horrible, desolate, eerie feeling, in the air, you know. I put my hand out to the bell-cord, hoping that Parsket had got it clear. Then I waited, glancing before and behind. Perhaps two minutes passed, full of what seemed like an almost unearthly quiet. And then, suddenly, down the corridor, at the lighted end, there sounded the clumping of a great hoof; and instantly the lamp was thrown down with a tremendous crash, and we were in the dark. I tugged hard on the cord, and blew the whistle; then I raised my snapshot, and fired the flashlight. The corridor blazed into brilliant light; but there was nothing; and then the darkness fell like thunder. I heard the Captain at the bedroom door, and shouted to him to bring out a lamp, *quick;* but instead, something started to kick the door, and I heard the Captain shouting within the bedroom, and then the screaming of the women. I had a sudden horrible fear that the monster had got into the bedroom; but in the same instant, from up the corridor, there came abruptly the vile, gobbling neighing that we had heard in the park and the cellar. I blew the whistle again, and groped blindly for the bell-cord, shouting to Beaumont to stay in the pentacle, whatever happened. I yelled again to the Captain to bring out a lamp, and there came a smashing sound against the bedroom door. Then I had my matches in my hand, to get some light before that incredible, unseen Monster was upon us.

"The match scraped on the box, and flared up, dully; and in the same instant, I heard a faint sound behind me. I whipped round, in a kind of mad terror, and saw something, in the light of the match – a monstrous horse-head, close to Beaumont.

"'Look out, Beaumont!' I shouted in a sort of scream. 'It's behind you!'

"The match went out, abruptly, and instantly there came the huge bang of Parsket's double-barrel (both barrels at once), fired (evidently single-handed by Beaumont) close to my ear, as it seemed. I caught a momentary glimpse of the great head, in the flash, and of an enormous hoof amid the belch of fire and smoke, seeming to be descending upon Beaumont. In the same instant, I fired three chambers of my revolver. There was the sound of a dull blow, and then that horrible, gobbling neigh, broke out close to me. I fired twice at the sound. Immediately afterwards, Something struck me, and I was knocked backwards. I got on to my knees, and shouted for help, at the top of my voice. I heard the women screaming behind the closed door of the bedroom, and was dully aware that the door was being smashed from the inside; and directly afterwards I knew that Beaumont was struggling with some hideous thing, near to me. For an instant, I held back, stupidly, paralysed with funk; and then, blindly, and in a sort of rigid chill of goose-flesh, I went to help him, shouting his name. I can tell you, I did not feel much of a hero. There came a little, choking scream, out of the darkness; and at that, I jumped forward into the dark. I gripped a vast, furry ear. Then something struck me another great blow, knocking me sick. I hit back, weak and blind, and gripped with my other hand at the incredible thing. Abruptly, I was dimly aware of a tremendous crash behind me, and a great burst of light. There were other lights in the passage, and a noise of feet and shouting. My hand-grips were torn from the thing they held; I shut my eyes stupidly, and heard a loud yell above me; and then a heavy blow, like a butcher chopping meat; and something fell upon me.

"I was helped to my knees by the Captain and the butler. On the floor lay an enormous horse-head, out of which protruded a man's trunk and legs. On the wrists were fixed great hoofs. It was the monster. The Captain cut something with the sword that he held in his hand, and stooped and lifted off the mask; for that is what it was. I saw the face then of the man who had worn it. It was Parsket. He had a bad wound across the forehead, where the Captain's sword had hit through the mask. I looked bewilderedly from him to Beaumont, who was sitting up, leaning against the wall of the corridor. Then I stared at Parsket, again.

"'By Jove!' I said at last, and then I was quiet; for I was so ashamed for the man. You can understand, can't you. And he was opening his eyes. And, you know, I had grown so to like the man.

"And then, you know, just as Parsket was getting back his wits, and looking from one to the other of us, and beginning to remember, there happened a strange and incredible thing. For from the end of the corridor, there sounded, suddenly, the clamping of a great hoof. I looked that way, and then instantly at Parsket, and saw a horrible fear in his face and eyes. He wrenched himself round, weakly, and stared in mad terror up the corridor to where the sound had been; and the rest of us stared, all in a frozen group. I remember hearing vaguely, half sobs and whispers from Miss Hisgins' bedroom, all the while that I stared, frightenedly, up the corridor.

"The silence lasted several seconds; and then, abruptly, there came again the clumping of the great hoof, away up at the end of the corridor. And immediately afterwards, the clungk, clunck – clungk, clunck, of mighty hoofs coming down the passage, towards us.

"Even then, you know, most of us thought it was some mechanism of Parsket's still at work; and we were in the queerest mixture of fright and doubt. I think everyone looked at Parsket. And suddenly the Captain shouted out:

"'Stop this damned fooling at once. Haven't you done enough!'

"For my part, you know, I was frightened; for I had a *sense* that there was something horrible and wrong. And then Parsket managed to gasp out:

"'It's not me! My God! It's not me! My God! It's not me.'

"And then, you know, it seemed to come home to everyone in an instant that there was really some dreadful thing coming down the passage. There was a mad rush up the passage, and even old Captain Hisgins gave back with the butler and the footmen. Beaumont fainted outright, as I found afterwards; for he had been badly mauled. I just flattened back against the wall, kneeling, as I was, too stupid and dazed even to run. And almost in the same instant the ponderous hoof-falls sounded close to me, and seeming to shake the solid floor, as they passed. Abruptly the great sounds ceased, and I knew in a sort of sick fashion that the thing had halted opposite to the open door of the girl's bedroom. And then, you know, I was aware that Parsket was standing rocking in the doorway, with his arms spread across, so as to fill the doorway with his body. Parsket showed extraordinarily pale, and the blood was running down his face from the wound in his forehead; and then I noticed that he seemed to be looking at something in the passage with a peculiar, desperate, fixed gaze. But, there was really nothing to be seen. And suddenly the clungk, clunck, clungk, clunck, recommenced, and passed onward down the passage. And in the same moment, Parsket pitched forward out of the doorway on to his face.

"There were shouts from the huddle of men down the passage, and the two footmen and the butler simply ran, carrying their lanterns, but the Captain went against the side-wall with his back and put the lamp he was carrying over his head. The dull tread of the Horse went past him, and left him unharmed; and I heard the monstrous hoof-falls going away and away through the quiet house; and after that a dead silence.

"Then the Captain moved, and came towards us, very slow and shaky, and with an extraordinarily grey face.

"I crept towards Parsket, and the Captain came to help me. We turned him over; and, you know, I knew in a moment that he was dead; but you can imagine what a feeling it sent through me.

"I looked at the Captain and suddenly he said:

"'That— That— That—,' and I know that he was trying to tell me that Parsket had stood between his daughter and whatever it was that had gone down the passage. I stood up, and steadied him; though I was not very steady myself. And suddenly, his face began to work, and he went down on to his knees by Parsket and cried like some shaken child. And then, you know, I knew that the women were in the doorway of the bedroom and I turned away and left him to them, whilst I went over to Beaumont.

"That is practically the whole story; and the only thing that is left to me is to try to explain some of the puzzling parts, here and there.

"Perhaps you have seen that Parsket was in love with Miss Hisgins; and this fact is the key to a good deal that was extraordinary. He was doubtless responsible for some portions of the 'haunting'; in fact I think for nearly everything; but, you know, I can prove nothing, and what I have to tell you is chiefly the result of deduction.

"In the first place, it is obvious that Parsket's intention was to frighten Beaumont away; and when he found that he could not do this, I think he grew so desperate that he really intended to kill him. I hate to say this; but the facts force me to think so.

"It is quite certain that Parsket was the person who broke Beaumont's arm. He knew all the details of the so-called 'Horse Legend', and got the idea to work upon the old story, for his own end. He evidently had some method of slipping in and out of the house, probably through one of the many French windows, or possibly he had a key to one or two of the garden doors; and when he was supposed to be away, he was really coming down, on the quiet, and hiding somewhere in the neighbourhood.

"The incident of the kiss in the dark hall, I put down to sheer nervous imaginings on the part of Beaumont and Miss Hisgins; yet, I must say that the sound of the horse outside of the front door, is a little difficult to explain away. But I am still inclined to keep to my first idea on this point, that there was nothing really unnatural about it.

"The hoof-sounds in the billiard-room and down the passage, were done by Parsket, from the floor below, by pomping against the panelled ceiling with a block of wood tied to one of the window-hooks. I proved this, by an examination, which showed the dints in the woodwork.

"The sounds of the horse galloping round the house, was also done by Parsket, who must have had a horse tied up in the plantation, nearby, unless, indeed, he made the sounds himself; but I do not see how he could have gone fast enough to produce the illusion, you see?

"The gobbling neighing in the park was a ventriloquial achievement on the part of Parsket; and the attack out there on Beaumont was also by him; so that when I thought he was in his bedroom, he must have been outside all the time, and joined me after I ran out of the front door. This is probable, I mean that Parsket was the cause, for if it had been something more serious, he would certainly have given up his foolishness, knowing that there was no longer any need for it. I cannot imagine how he escaped being shot, both then, and in the last mad action, of which I have just told you. He was enormously without fear of any kind for himself, as you can see.

"The time when Parsket was with us, when we thought we heard the Horse galloping round the house, we must have been deceived. No one was very *sure*, except, of course, Parsket, who would naturally encourage the belief.

"The neighing in the cellar, is where I consider there came the first suspicion into Parsket's mind that there was something more at work than his sham-haunting. The neighing was done by him, in the same way that he did it in the park; when I remember how ghastly he looked, I feel sure that the sounds must have had some infernal quality added to them, which frightened the man himself. Yet, later, he would persuade himself that he had been getting fanciful. Of course, I must not forget that the effect upon Miss Hisgins must have made him feel pretty miserable.

"Then, about the clergyman being called away, we found afterwards that it was a bogus errand, or rather, call; and it is obvious that Parsket was at the bottom of this, so as to get a few more hours in which to achieve his end; and what that was, a very little imagination will show you; for he had found that Beaumont would not be frightened away. You see what I mean?

"Then, there is no doubt at all but that Parsket left the cord to the butler's bell in a tangle, or hitched somewhere, so as to give him an excuse to slip away naturally to clear it. This also gave him the opportunity to remove one of the passage lamps. Then he had only to smash the other, and the passage was in utter darkness, for him to make the attempt on Beaumont.

"In the same way, it was he who locked the door of the bedroom, and took the key (it was in his pocket). This prevented the Captain from bringing a light, and coming to the rescue. But Captain Hisgins broke down the door, with the heavy fender-curb; and it was his smashing the door that had sounded so confusing and frightening in the darkness of the passage.

"The photograph of the monstrous hoof above Miss Hisgins in the cellar, is one of the things that I am less sure about. It might have been faked by Parsket, whilst I was out of the room, and this would have been easy enough, to anyone who knew how. But, you know, it does not look like a fake. Yet, there is as much evidence of probability that it was faked, as against; and the thing is too vague for an examination to help to a definite decision; so that I will express no opinion, one way or the other. It is certainly a horrible photograph.

"And now I come to that last, dreadful thing. There has been no further manifestation of anything abnormal; so that there is an extraordinary uncertainty in my conclusions. If we had not heard those last sounds, and if Parsket had not shown that enormous sense of fear, the whole of this case could be explained away in the way in which I have shown. And, in fact, as you have seen, I am of the opinion that almost all of it can be cleared up; but I see no way of going past the thing we heard at the last, and the fear that Parsket showed.

"His death— No, that proves nothing. At the inquest it was described somewhat untechnically as due to heart-spasm. That is normal enough, and leaves us quite in the dark as to whether he died because he stood between the girl and some incredible monster.

"The look on Parsket's face, and the thing he called out, when he heard the great hoof-sounds coming down the passage, seem to show that he had the sudden realisation of what before then may have been nothing more than a horrible suspicion. And his fear and appreciation of some tremendous danger approaching was probably more keenly real even than mine. And then he did the one fine, great thing!"

"And the cause?" I said. "What caused it?"

Carnacki shook his head.

"God knows," he answered, with a peculiar sincere reverence. "If that thing was what it seemed to be, one might suggest an explanation, which would not offend one's reason, but which may be utterly wrong. Yet I have thought, though it would take a long lecture on Thought Induction to get you to appreciate my reasons, that Parsket had produced what I might term a kind of 'induced haunting', a kind of induced simulation of his mental conceptions, due to his desperate thoughts and broodings. It is impossible to make it clearer, in a few words."

"But the old story!" I said. "Why may not there have been something in *that?*"

"There may have been something in it," said Carnacki, quietly. "But I do not think it had anything to do with *this*. I have not clearly thought out my reasons, yet; but later I may be able to tell you why I think so."

"And the marriage? And the cellar – was there anything found there?" asked Taylor.

"Yes, the marriage was performed that day, in spite of the tragedy," Carnacki told us. "It was the wisest thing to do – considering the things that I cannot explain. Yes, I had the floor of that big cellar up; for I had a feeling I might find something there to give me some light. But there was nothing.

"You know, the whole thing is tremendous and extraordinary. I shall never forget the look on Parsket's face. And afterwards the disgusting sounds of those great hoofs going away through the quiet house."

Carnacki stood up:

"Out you go!" he said in friendly fashion, using the recognised formula.

And we went presently out into the quiet of the Embankment, and so to our homes.

If you enjoyed this, you might also like...

The Sea Horses, see page 184
The House Among the Laurels, see page 25

The Searcher of the End House

IT WAS STILL EVENING, as I remember, and the four of us, Jessop, Arkright, Taylor and I, looked disappointedly at Carnacki, where he sat silent in his great chair.

We had come in response to the usual card of invitation, which – as you know – we have come to consider as a sure prelude to a good story; and now, after telling us the short incident of the Three Straw Platters, he had lapsed into a contented silence, and the night not half gone, as I have hinted.

However, as it chanced, some pitying fate jogged Carnacki's elbow, or his memory, and he began again, in his queer level way:

"The 'Straw Platters' business reminds me of the 'Searcher' Case, which I have sometimes thought might interest you. It was some time ago, in fact a deuce of a long time ago, that the thing happened; and my experience of what I might term 'curious' things was very small at that time.

"I was living with my mother when it occurred, in a small house just outside of Appledorn, on the South Coast. The house was the last of a row of detached cottage villas, each house standing in its own garden; and very dainty little places they were, very old, and most of them smothered in roses; and all with those quaint old leaded windows, and doors of genuine oak. You must try to picture them for the sake of their complete niceness.

"Now I must remind you at the beginning that my mother and I had lived in that little house for two years; and in the whole of that time there had not been a single peculiar happening to worry us.

"And then, something happened.

"It was about two o'clock one morning, as I was finishing some letters, that I heard the door of my mother's bedroom open, and she came to the top of the stairs, and knocked on the banisters.

"'All right, dear,' I called; for I suppose she was merely reminding me that I should have been in bed long ago; then I heard her go back to her room, and I hurried my work, for fear she should lie awake, until she heard me safe up to my room.

"When I was finished, I lit my candle, put out the lamp, and went upstairs. As I came opposite the door of my mother's room, I saw that it was open, called goodnight to her, very softly, and asked whether I should close the door. As there was no answer, I knew that she had dropped off to sleep again, and I closed the door very gently, and turned into my room, just across the passage. As I did so, I experienced a momentary, half-aware sense of a faint, peculiar, disagreeable odour in the passage; but it was not until the following night that I *realised* I had noticed a smell that offended me. You follow me? It is so often like that – one suddenly knows a thing that really recorded itself on one's consciousness, perhaps a year before.

"The next morning at breakfast, I mentioned casually to my mother that she had 'dropped off', and I had shut the door for her. To my surprise, she assured me she had never been out of her room. I reminded her about the two raps she had given upon the banister; but she still was certain I must be mistaken; and in the end I teased her, saying she had grown so accustomed to my bad habit of sitting up late, that she had come to call me in her sleep. Of course, she denied this, and I let the matter drop; but I was more than a little puzzled, and did not know whether to believe my own explanation, or to take the mater's, which was to put the noises down to the mice, and the open door to the fact that she couldn't have properly latched it, when she went to bed. I suppose, away in the subconscious part of me, I had a stirring of less reasonable thoughts; but certainly, I had no real uneasiness at that time.

"The next night there came a further development. About two thirty a.m., I heard my mother's door open, just as on the previous night, and immediately afterward she rapped sharply, on the banister, as it seemed to me. I stopped my work and called up that I would not be long. As she made no reply, and I did not hear her go back to bed, I had a quick sense of wonder whether she might not be doing it in her sleep, after all, just as I had said.

"With the thought, I stood up, and taking the lamp from the table, began to go towards the door, which was open into the passage. It was then I got a sudden nasty sort of thrill; for it came to me, all at once, that my mother never knocked, when I sat up too late; she always called. You will understand I was not really frightened in any way; only vaguely uneasy, and pretty sure she must really be doing the thing in her sleep.

"I went quickly up the stairs, and when I came to the top, my mother was not there; but her door was open. I had a bewildered sense though believing she must have gone quietly back to bed, without my hearing her. I entered her room and found her sleeping quietly and naturally; for the vague sense of trouble in me was sufficiently strong to make me go over to look at her.

"When I was sure that she was perfectly right in every way, I was still a little bothered; but much more inclined to think my suspicion correct and that she had gone quietly back to bed in her sleep, without knowing what she had been doing. This was the most reasonable thing to think, as you must see.

"And then it came to me, suddenly, that vague, queer, mildewy smell in the room; and it was in that instant I became aware I had smelt the same strange, uncertain smell the night before in the passage.

"I was definitely uneasy now, and began to search my mother's room; though with no aim or clear thought of anything, except to assure myself that there was nothing in the room. All the time, you know, I never *expected really* to find anything; only my uneasiness had to be assured.

"In the middle of my search my mother woke up, and of course I had to explain. I told her about her door opening, and the knocks on the banister, and that I had come up and found her asleep. I said nothing about the smell, which was not very distinct; but told her that the thing happening twice had made me a bit nervous, and possibly fanciful, and I thought I would take a look 'round, just to feel satisfied.

"I have thought since that the reason I made no mention of the smell, was not only that I did not want to frighten my mother, for I was scarcely that myself; but because I had only a vague half-knowledge that I associated the smell with fancies too indefinite and peculiar to bear talking about. You will understand that I am able *now* to analyse and put the thing into words; but *then* I did not even know my chief reason for saying nothing; let alone appreciate its possible significance.

"It was my mother, after all, who put part of my vague sensations into words:

"'What a disagreeable smell!' she exclaimed, and was silent a moment, looking at me. Then: 'You feel there's something wrong?' still looking at me, very quietly but with a little, nervous note of questioning expectancy.

"'I don't know,' I said. 'I can't understand it, unless you've really been walking about in your sleep.'

"'The smell,' she said.

"'Yes,' I replied. 'That's what puzzles me too. I'll take a walk through the house; but I don't suppose it's anything.'

"I lit her candle, and taking the lamp, I went through the other bedrooms, and afterward all over the house, including the three underground cellars, which was a little trying to the nerves, seeing that I was more nervous than I would admit.

"Then I went back to my mother, and told her there was really nothing to bother about; and, you know, in the end, we talked ourselves into believing it was nothing. My mother would not agree that she might have been sleepwalking; but she was ready to put the door opening down to the fault of the latch, which certainly snicked very lightly. As for the knocks, they might be the old warped woodwork of the house cracking a bit, or a mouse rattling a piece of loose plaster. The smell was more difficult to explain; but finally we agreed that it might easily be the queer night smell of the moist earth, coming in through the open window of my mother's room, from the back garden, or – for that matter – from the little churchyard beyond the big wall at the bottom of the garden.

"And so we quietened down, and finally I went to bed, and to sleep.

"I think this is certainly a lesson on the way we humans can delude ourselves; for there was not one of these explanations that my reason could really accept. Try to imagine yourself in the same circumstances, and you will see how absurd our attempts to explain the happenings really were.

"In the morning, when I came down to breakfast, we talked it all over again, and whilst we agreed that it was strange, we also agreed that we had begun to imagine funny things in the backs of our minds, which now we felt half ashamed to admit. This is very strange when you come to look into it; but very human.

"And then that night again my mother's door was slammed once more just after midnight. I caught up the lamp, and when I reached her door, I found it shut. I opened it quickly, and went in, to find my mother lying with her eyes open, and rather nervous; having been waked by the bang of the door. But what upset me more than anything, was the fact that there was a disgusting smell in the passage and in her room.

"Whilst I was asking her whether she was all right, a door slammed twice downstairs; and you can imagine how it made me feel. My mother and I looked at one another; and then I lit her candle, and taking the poker from the fender, went downstairs with the lamp, beginning to feel really nervous. The cumulative effect of so many queer happenings was getting hold of me; and all the *apparently* reasonable explanations seemed futile.

"The horrible smell seemed to be very strong in the downstairs passage; also in the front room and the cellars; but chiefly in the passage. I made a very thorough search of the house, and when I had finished, I knew that all the lower windows and doors were properly shut and fastened, and that there was no living thing in the house, beyond our two selves. Then I went up to my mother's room again, and we talked the thing over for an hour or more, and in the end came to the conclusion that we might, after all, be reading too much into a number of little things; but, you know, inside of us, we did not believe this.

"Later, when we had talked ourselves into a more comfortable state of mind, I said good night, and went off to bed; and presently managed to get to sleep.

"In the early hours of the morning, whilst it was still dark, I was waked by a loud noise. I sat up in bed, and listened. And from downstairs, I heard: bang, bang, bang, one door after another being slammed; at least, that is the impression the sounds gave to me.

"I jumped out of bed, with the tingle and shiver of sudden fright on me; and at the same moment, as I lit my candle, my door was pushed slowly open; I had left it unlatched, so as not to feel that my mother was quite shut off from me.

"'Who's there?' I shouted out, in a voice twice as deep as my natural one, and with a queer breathlessness, that sudden fright so often gives one. 'Who's there?'

"Then I heard my mother saying:

"'It's me, Thomas. Whatever is happening downstairs?'

"She was in the room by this, and I saw she had her bedroom poker in one hand, and her candle in the other. I could have smiled at her, had it not been for the extraordinary sounds downstairs.

"I got into my slippers, and reached down an old sword bayonet from the wall; then I picked up my candle, and begged my mother not to come; but I knew it would be little use, if she had made up her mind; and she had, with the result that she acted as a sort of rearguard for me, during our search. I know, in some ways, I was very glad to have her with me, as you will understand.

"By this time, the door slamming had ceased, and there seemed, probably because of the contrast, to be an appalling silence in the house. However, I led the way, holding my candle high, and keeping the sword bayonet very handy. Downstairs we found all the doors wide open; although the outer doors and the windows were closed all right. I began to wonder whether the noises had been made by the doors after all. Of one thing only were we sure, and that was, there was no living thing in the house, beside ourselves, while everywhere throughout the house, there was the taint of that disgusting odour.

"Of course it was absurd to try to make believe any longer. There was something strange about the house; and as soon as it was daylight, I set my mother to packing; and soon after breakfast, I saw her off by train.

"Then I set to work to try to clear up the mystery. I went first to the landlord, and told him all the circumstances. From him, I found that twelve or fifteen years back, the house had got rather a curious name from three or four tenants; with the result that it had remained empty a long while; in the end he had let it at a low rent to a Captain Tobias, on the one condition that he should hold his tongue, if he saw anything peculiar. The landlord's idea – as he told me frankly – was to free the house from these tales of 'something queer', by keeping a tenant in it, and then to sell it for the best price he could get.

"However, when Captain Tobias left, after a ten years' tenancy, there was no longer any talk about the house; so when I offered to take it on a five years' lease, he had jumped at the offer. This was the whole story; so he gave me to understand. When I pressed him for details of the supposed peculiar happenings in the house, all those years back, he said the tenants had talked about a woman who always moved about the house at night. Some tenants never saw anything; but others would not stay out the first month's tenancy.

"One thing the landlord was particular to point out, that no tenant had ever complained about knockings, or door slamming. As for the smell, he seemed positively indignant about it; but why, I don't suppose he knew himself, except that he probably had some vague feeling that it was an indirect accusation on my part that the drains were not right.

"In the end, I suggested that he should come down and spend the night with me. He agreed at once, especially as I told him I intended to keep the whole business quiet, and try to get to the bottom of the curious affair; for he was anxious to keep the rumour of the haunting from getting about.

"About three o'clock that afternoon, he came down, and we made a thorough search of the house, which, however, revealed nothing unusual. Afterward, the landlord made one or two tests, which showed him the drainage was in perfect order; after that we made our preparations for sitting up all night.

"First, we borrowed two policemen's dark lanterns from the station nearby, and where the superintendent and I were friendly, and as soon as it was really dusk, the landlord went up to his house for his gun. I had the sword bayonet I have told you about; and when the landlord got back, we sat talking in my study until nearly midnight.

"Then we lit the lanterns and went upstairs. We placed the lanterns, gun and bayonet handy on the table; then I shut and sealed the bedroom doors; afterward we took our seats, and turned off the lights.

"From then until two o'clock, nothing happened; but a little after two, as I found by holding my watch near the faint glow of the closed lanterns, I had a time of extraordinary nervousness; and I bent towards the landlord, and whispered to him that I had a queer feeling something was about to happen, and to be ready with his lantern; at the same time I reached out towards mine. In the very instant I made this movement, the darkness which filled the passage seemed to become suddenly of a dull violet colour; not, as if a light had been shone; but as if the natural blackness of the night had changed colour. And then, coming through this violet night, through this violet-coloured gloom, came a little naked Child, running. In an extraordinary way, the Child seemed not to be distinct from the surrounding gloom; but almost as if it were a concentration of that extraordinary atmosphere; as if that gloomy colour which had changed the night, came from the Child. It seems impossible to make clear to you; but try to understand it.

"The Child went past me, running, with the natural movement of the legs of a chubby human child, but in an absolute and inconceivable silence. It was a very small Child, and must have passed under the table; but I saw the Child through the table, as if it had been only a slightly darker shadow than the coloured gloom. In the same instant, I saw that a fluctuating glimmer of violet light outlined the metal of the gun-barrels and the blade of the sword bayonet, making them seem like faint shapes of glimmering light, floating unsupported where the tabletop should have shown solid.

"Now, curiously, as I saw these things, I was subconsciously aware that I heard the anxious breathing of the landlord, quite clear and laboured, close to my elbow, where he waited nervously with his hands on the lantern. I realised in that moment that he saw nothing; but waited in the darkness, for my warning to come true.

"Even as I took heed of these minor things, I saw the Child jump to one side, and hide behind some half-seen object that was certainly nothing belonging to the passage. I stared, intently, with a most extraordinary thrill of expectant wonder, with fright making goose flesh of my back. And even as I stared, I solved for myself the less important problem of what the two black clouds were that hung over a part of the table. I think it very curious and interesting, the double working of the mind, often so much more apparent during times of stress. The two clouds came from two faintly shining shapes, which I knew must be the metal of the lanterns; and the things that looked black to the sight with which I was then seeing, could be nothing else but what to normal human sight is known as light. This phenomenon I have always remembered. I have twice seen a somewhat similar thing; in the Dark Light Case and in that trouble of Maetheson's, which you know about.

"Even as I understood this matter of the lights, I was looking to my left, to understand why the Child was hiding. And suddenly, I heard the landlord shout out: 'The Woman!' But I saw nothing. I had a disagreeable sense that something repugnant was near to me, and I was aware in the same moment that the landlord was gripping my arm in a hard, frightened grip. Then I was looking back to where the Child had hidden. I saw the Child peeping out from behind its hiding place, seeming to be looking up the passage; but whether in fear I could not tell. Then it came out, and ran headlong away, through the place where should have been the wall of my mother's bedroom; but the Sense with which I was seeing these things, showed me the wall only as a vague, upright shadow, unsubstantial. And immediately the child was lost to me, in the dull violet gloom. At the same time, I felt the landlord press back against me, as if something had passed close to him; and he called out again, a hoarse sort of cry: 'The Woman! The Woman!' and turned the shade clumsily from off his lantern. But I had seen no Woman; and the passage showed empty, as he shone the beam of his light jerkily to and fro; but chiefly in the direction of the doorway of my mother's room.

"He was still clutching my arm, and had risen to his feet; and now, mechanically and almost slowly, I picked up my lantern and turned on the light. I shone it, a little dazedly, at the seals upon the doors; but none were broken; then I sent the light to and fro, up and down the passage; but there was nothing; and I turned to the landlord, who was saying something in a rather incoherent fashion. As my light passed over his face, I noted, in a dull sort of way, that he was drenched with sweat.

"Then my wits became more handleable, and I began to catch the drift of his words: 'Did you see her? Did you see her?' he was saying, over and over again; and then I found myself telling him, in quite a level voice, that I had not seen any Woman. He became more coherent then, and I found that he had seen a Woman come from the end of the passage, and go past us; but he could not describe her, except that she kept stopping and looking about her, and had even peered at the wall, close beside him, as if looking for something. But what seemed to trouble him most, was that she had not seemed to see him at all. He repeated this so often, that in the end I told him, in an absurd sort of way, that he ought to be very glad she had not. 'What did it all mean?' was the question; somehow I was not so frightened, as utterly bewildered. I had seen less then, than since; but what I had seen, had made me feel adrift from my anchorage of Reason.

"What did it mean? He had seen a Woman, searching for something. *I* had not seen this Woman. *I* had seen a Child, running away, and hiding from Something or Someone. *He* had not seen the Child, or the other things – only the Woman. And *I* had not seen her. What did it all mean?

"I had said nothing to the landlord about the Child. I had been too bewildered, and I realised that it would be futile to attempt an explanation. He was already stupid with the thing he had seen; and not the kind of man to understand. All this went through my mind as we stood there, shining the lanterns to and fro. All the time, intermingled with a streak of practical reasoning, I was questioning myself, what did it all mean? What was the Woman searching for; what was the Child running from?

"Suddenly, as I stood there, bewildered and nervous, making random answers to the landlord, a door below was violently slammed, and directly I caught the horrible reek of which I have told you.

"'There!' I said to the landlord, and caught his arm, in my turn. 'The Smell! Do *you* smell it?'

"He looked at me so stupidly that in a sort of nervous anger, I shook him.

"'Yes,' he said, in a queer voice, trying to shine the light from his shaking lantern at the stair head.

"'Come on!' I said, and picked up my bayonet; and he came, carrying his gun awkwardly. I think he came, more because he was afraid to be left alone, than because he had any pluck left, poor beggar. I never sneer at that kind of funk, at least very seldom; for when it takes hold of you, it makes rags of your courage.

"I led the way downstairs, shining my light into the lower passage, and afterward at the doors to see whether they were shut; for I had closed and latched them, placing a corner of a mat against each door, so I should know which had been opened.

"I saw at once that none of the doors had been opened; then I threw the beam of my light down alongside the stairway, in order to see the mat I had placed against the door at the top of the cellar stairs. I got a horrid thrill; for the mat was flat! I paused a couple of seconds, shining my light to and fro in the passage, and holding fast to my courage, I went down the stairs.

"As I came to the bottom step, I saw patches of wet all up and down the passage. I shone my lantern on them. It was the imprint of a wet foot on the oilcloth of the passage; not an ordinary footprint, but a queer, soft, flabby, spreading imprint, that gave me a feeling of extraordinary horror.

"Backward and forward I flashed the light over the impossible marks and saw them everywhere. Suddenly I noticed that they led to each of the closed doors. I felt something touch my back, and glanced 'round swiftly, to find the landlord had come close to me, almost pressing against me, in his fear.

"'It's all right,' I said, but in a rather breathless whisper, meaning to put a little courage into him; for I could feel that he was shaking through all his body. Even then as I tried to get him steadied enough to be of some use, his gun went off with a tremendous bang. He jumped, and yelled with sheer terror; and I swore because of the shock.

"'Give it to me, for God's sake!' I said, and slipped the gun from his hand; and in the same instant there was a sound of running steps up the garden path, and immediately the flash of a bull's-eye lantern upon the fan light over the front door. Then the door was tried, and directly afterward there came a thunderous knocking, which told me a policeman had heard the shot.

"I went to the door, and opened it. Fortunately the constable knew me, and when I had beckoned him in, I was able to explain matters in a very short time. While doing this, Inspector Johnstone came up the path, having missed the officer, and seeing lights and the open door. I told him as briefly as possible what had occurred, and did not mention the Child or the Woman; for it would have seemed too fantastic for him to notice. I showed him the queer, wet footprints and how they went towards the closed doors. I explained quickly about the mats, and how that the one against the cellar door was flat, which showed the door had been opened.

"The inspector nodded, and told the constable to guard the door at the top of the cellar stairs. He then asked the hall lamp to be lit, after which he took the policeman's lantern, and led the way into the front room. He paused with the door wide open, and threw the light all 'round; then he jumped into the room, and looked behind the door; there was no one there; but all over the polished oak floor, between the scattered rugs, went the marks of those horrible spreading footprints; and the room permeated with the horrible odour.

"The inspector searched the room carefully, and then went into the middle room, using the same precautions. There was nothing in the middle room, or in the kitchen or pantry; but everywhere went the wet footmarks through all the rooms, showing plainly wherever there were woodwork or oilcloth; and always there was the smell.

"The inspector ceased from his search of the rooms, and spent a minute in trying whether the mats would really fall flat when the doors were open, or merely ruckle up in a way as to appear they had been untouched; but in each case, the mats fell flat, and remained so.

"'Extraordinary!' I heard Johnstone mutter to himself. And then he went towards the cellar door. He had inquired at first whether there were windows to the cellar, and when he learned there was no way out, except by the door, he had left this part of the search to the last.

"As Johnstone came up to the door, the policeman made a motion of salute, and said something in a low voice; and something in the tone made me flick my light across him. I saw then that the man was very white, and he looked strange and bewildered.

"'What?' said Johnstone impatiently. 'Speak up!'

"'A woman come along 'ere, sir, and went through this 'ere door,' said the constable, clearly, but with a curious monotonous intonation that is sometimes heard from an unintelligent man.

"'Speak up!' shouted the inspector.

"'A woman come along and went through this 'ere door,' repeated the man, monotonously.

"The inspector caught the man by the shoulder, and deliberately sniffed his breath.

"'No!' he said. And then sarcastically: 'I hope you held the door open politely for the lady.'

"'The door weren't opened, sir,' said the man, simply.

"'Are you mad—' began Johnstone.

"'No,' broke in the landlord's voice from the back. Speaking steadily enough. 'I saw the Woman upstairs.' It was evident that he had got back his control again.

"'I'm afraid, Inspector Johnstone,' I said, 'that there's more in this than you think. I certainly saw some very extraordinary things upstairs.'

"The inspector seemed about to say something; but instead, he turned again to the door, and flashed his light down and 'round about the mat. I saw then that the strange, horrible footmarks came straight up to the cellar door; and the last print showed *under* the door; yet the policeman said the door had not been opened.

"And suddenly, without any intention, or realisation of what I was saying, I asked the landlord:

"'What were the feet like?'

"I received no answer; for the inspector was ordering the constable to open the cellar door, and the man was not obeying. Johnstone repeated the order, and at last, in a queer automatic way, the man obeyed, and pushed the door open. The loathsome smell beat up at us, in a great wave of horror, and the inspector came backward a step.

"'My God!' he said, and went forward again, and shone his light down the steps; but there was nothing visible, only that on each step showed the unnatural footprints.

"The inspector brought the beam of the light vividly on the top step; and there, clear in the light, there was something small, moving. The inspector bent to look, and the policeman and I with him. I don't want to disgust you; but the thing we looked at was a maggot. The policeman backed suddenly out of the doorway:

"'The churchyard,' he said, '…at the back of the 'ouse.'

"'Silence!' said Johnstone, with a queer break in the word, and I knew that at last he was frightened. He put his lantern into the doorway, and shone it from step to step, following the footprints down into the darkness; then he stepped back from the open doorway, and we all gave back with him. He looked 'round, and I had a feeling that he was looking for a weapon of some kind.

"'Your gun,' I said to the landlord, and he brought it from the front hall, and passed it over to the inspector, who took it and ejected the empty shell from the right barrel. He held out his hand for a live cartridge, which the landlord brought from his pocket. He loaded the gun and snapped the breech. He turned to the constable:

"'Come on,' he said, and moved towards the cellar doorway.

"'I ain't comin', sir,' said the policeman, very white in the face.

"With a sudden blaze of passion, the inspector took the man by the scruff and hove him bodily down into the darkness, and he went downward, screaming. The inspector followed him instantly, with his lantern and the gun; and I after the inspector, with the bayonet ready. Behind me, I heard the landlord.

"At the bottom of the stairs, the inspector was helping the policeman to his feet, where he stood swaying a moment, in a bewildered fashion; then the inspector went into the front cellar, and his man followed him in stupid fashion; but evidently no longer with any thought of running away from the horror.

"We all crowded into the front cellar, flashing our lights to and fro. Inspector Johnstone was examining the floor, and I saw that the footmarks went all 'round the cellar, into all the corners, and across the floor. I thought suddenly of the Child that was running away from Something. Do you see the thing that I was seeing vaguely?

"We went out of the cellar in a body, for there was nothing to be found. In the next cellar, the footprints went everywhere in that queer erratic fashion, as of someone searching for something, or following some blind scent.

"In the third cellar the prints ended at the shallow well that had been the old water supply of the house. The well was full to the brim, and the water so clear that the pebbly bottom was plainly to be seen, as we shone the lights into the water. The search came to an abrupt end, and we stood about the well, looking at one another, in an absolute, horrible silence.

"Johnstone made another examination of the footprints; then he shone his light again into the clear shallow water, searching each inch of the plainly seen bottom; but there was nothing there. The cellar was full of the dreadful smell; and everyone stood silent, except for the constant turning of the lamps to and fro around the cellar.

"The inspector looked up from his search of the well, and nodded quietly across at me, with his sudden acknowledgment that our belief was now his belief, the smell in the cellar seemed to grow more dreadful, and to be, as it were, a menace – the material expression that some monstrous thing was there with us, invisible.

"'I think—' began the inspector, and shone his light towards the stairway; and at this the constable's restraint went utterly, and he ran for the stairs, making a queer sound in his throat.

"The landlord followed, at a quick walk, and then the inspector and I. He waited a single instant for me, and we went up together, treading on the same steps, and with our lights held backward. At the top, I slammed and locked the stair door, and wiped my forehead, and my hands were shaking.

"The inspector asked me to give his man a glass of whisky, and then he sent him on his beat. He stayed a short while with the landlord and me, and it was arranged that he would join us again the following night and watch the Well with us from midnight until daylight. Then he left us, just as the dawn was coming in. The landlord and I locked up the house, and went over to his place for a sleep.

"In the afternoon, the landlord and I returned to the house, to make arrangements for the night. He was very quiet, and I felt he was to be relied on, now that he had been 'salted', as it were, with his fright of the previous night.

"We opened all the doors and windows, and blew the house through very thoroughly; and in the meanwhile, we lit the lamps in the house, and took them into the cellars, where we set them all about, so as to have light everywhere. Then we carried down three chairs and a table, and set them in the cellar where the well was sunk. After that, we stretched thin piano wire across the cellar, about nine inches from the floor, at such a height that it should catch anything moving about in the dark.

"When this was done, I went through the house with the landlord, and sealed every window and door in the place, excepting only the front door and the door at the top of the cellar stairs.

"Meanwhile, a local wire-smith was making something to my order; and when the landlord and I had finished tea at his house, we went down to see how the smith was getting on. We found the thing complete. It looked rather like a huge parrot's cage, without any bottom, of very heavy gauge wire, and stood about seven feet high and was four feet in diameter. Fortunately, I remembered to have it made longitudinally in two halves, or else we should never have got it through the doorways and down the cellar stairs.

"I told the wire-smith to bring the cage up to the house so he could fit the two halves rigidly together. As we returned, I called in at an ironmonger's, where I bought some thin hemp rope and an iron rack pulley, like those used in Lancashire for hauling up the ceiling clothes racks, which you will find in every cottage. I bought also a couple of pitchforks.

"'We shan't want to touch it,' I said to the landlord; and he nodded, rather white all at once.

"As soon as the cage arrived and had been fitted together in the cellar, I sent away the smith; and the landlord and I suspended it over the well, into which it fitted easily. After a lot of trouble, we managed to hang it so perfectly central from the rope over the iron pulley, that when hoisted to the ceiling and dropped, it went every time plunk into the well, like a candle-extinguisher. When we had it finally arranged, I hoisted it up once more, to the ready position, and made the rope fast to a heavy wooden pillar, which stood in the middle of the cellar.

"By ten o'clock, I had everything arranged, with the two pitchforks and the two police lanterns; also some whisky and sandwiches. Underneath the table I had several buckets full of disinfectant.

"A little after eleven o'clock, there was a knock at the front door, and when I went, I found Inspector Johnstone had arrived, and brought with him one of his plainclothes men. You will understand how pleased I was to see there would be this addition to our watch; for he looked a tough, nerveless man, brainy and collected; and one I should have picked to help us with the horrible job I felt pretty sure we should have to do that night.

"When the inspector and the detective had entered, I shut and locked the front door; then, while the inspector held the light, I sealed the door carefully, with tape and wax. At the head of the cellar stairs, I shut and locked that door also, and sealed it in the same way.

"As we entered the cellar, I warned Johnstone and his man to be careful not to fall over the wires; and then, as I saw his surprise at my arrangements, I began to explain my ideas and intentions, to all of which he listened with strong approval. I was pleased to see also that the detective was nodding his head, as I talked, in a way that showed he appreciated all my precautions.

"As he put his lantern down, the inspector picked up one of the pitchforks, and balanced it in his hand; he looked at me, and nodded.

"'The best thing,' he said. 'I only wish you'd got two more.'

"Then we all took our seats, the detective getting a washing stool from the corner of the cellar. From then, until a quarter to twelve, we talked quietly, whilst we made a light supper of whisky and sandwiches; after which, we cleared everything off the table, excepting the lanterns and the pitchforks. One of the latter, I handed to the inspector; the other I took myself, and then, having set my chair so as to be handy to the rope which lowered the cage into the well, I went 'round the cellar and put out every lamp.

"I groped my way to my chair, and arranged the pitchfork and the dark lantern ready to my hand; after which I suggested that everyone should keep an absolute silence throughout the watch. I asked, also, that no lantern should be turned on, until I gave the word.

"I put my watch on the table, where a faint glow from my lantern made me able to see the time. For an hour nothing happened, and everyone kept an absolute silence, except for an occasional uneasy movement.

"About half-past one, however, I was conscious again of the same extraordinary and peculiar nervousness, which I had felt on the previous night. I put my hand out quickly, and eased the hitched rope from around the pillar. The inspector seemed aware of the movement; for I saw the faint light from his lantern, move a little, as if he had suddenly taken hold of it, in readiness.

"A minute later, I noticed there was a change in the colour of the night in the cellar, and it grew slowly violet tinted upon my eyes. I glanced to and fro, quickly, in the new darkness, and even as I looked, I was conscious that the violet colour deepened. In the direction of the well, but seeming to be at a great distance, there was, as it were, a nucleus to the change; and the nucleus came swiftly towards us, appearing to come from a great space, almost in a single moment. It came near, and I saw again that it was a little naked Child, running, and seeming to be of the violet night in which it ran.

"The Child came with a natural running movement, exactly as I described it before; but in a silence so peculiarly intense, that it was as if it brought the silence with it. About half-way between the well and the table, the Child turned swiftly, and looked back at something invisible to me; and suddenly it went down into a crouching attitude, and seemed to be hiding behind something that showed vaguely; but there was nothing there, except the bare floor of the cellar; nothing, I mean, of our world.

"I could hear the breathing of the three other men, with a wonderful distinctness; and also the tick of my watch upon the table seemed to sound as loud and as slow as the tick of an old grandfather's clock. Someway I knew that none of the others saw what I was seeing.

"Abruptly, the landlord, who was next to me, let out his breath with a little hissing sound; I knew then that something was visible to him. There came a creak from the table, and I had a feeling that the inspector was leaning forward, looking at something that I could not see. The landlord reached out his hand through the darkness, and fumbled a moment to catch my arm:

"'The Woman!' he whispered, close to my ear. 'Over by the well.'

"I stared hard in that direction; but saw nothing, except that the violet colour of the cellar seemed a little duller just there.

"I looked back quickly to the vague place where the Child was hiding. I saw it was peering back from its hiding place. Suddenly it rose and ran straight for the middle of the table, which showed only as vague shadow half-way between my eyes and the unseen floor. As the Child ran under the table, the steel prongs of my pitchfork glimmered with a violet, fluctuating light. A little way off, there showed high up in the gloom, the vaguely shining outline of the other fork, so I knew the inspector had it raised in his hand, ready. There was no doubt but that he saw something. On the table, the metal of the five lanterns shone with the same strange glow; and about each lantern there was a little cloud of absolute blackness, where the phenomenon that is light to our natural eyes, came through the fittings; and in this complete darkness, the metal of each lantern showed plain, as might a cat's-eye in a nest of black cotton wool.

"Just beyond the table, the Child paused again, and stood, seeming to oscillate a little upon its feet, which gave the impression that it was lighter and vaguer than a thistle-down; and yet, in the same moment, another part of me seemed to know that it was to me, as something that might be beyond thick, invisible glass, and subject to conditions and forces that I was unable to comprehend.

"The Child was looking back again, and my gaze went the same way. I stared across the cellar, and saw the cage hanging clear in the violet light, every wire and tie outlined with its glimmering; above it there was a little space of gloom, and then the dull shining of the iron pulley which I had screwed into the ceiling.

"I stared in a bewildered way 'round the cellar; there were thin lines of vague fire crossing the floor in all directions; and suddenly I remembered the piano wire that the landlord and I had stretched. But there was nothing else to be seen, except that near the table there were indistinct glimmerings of light, and at the far end the outline of a dull glowing revolver, evidently in the detective's pocket. I remember a sort of subconscious satisfaction, as I settled the point in a queer automatic fashion. On the table, near to me, there was a little shapeless collection of the light; and this I knew, after an instant's consideration, to be the steel portions of my watch.

"I had looked several times at the Child, and 'round at the cellar, whilst I was decided these trifles; and had found it still in that attitude of hiding from something. But now, suddenly, it ran clear away into the distance, and was nothing more than a slightly deeper coloured nucleus far away in the strange coloured atmosphere.

"The landlord gave out a queer little cry, and twisted over against me, as if to avoid something. From the inspector there came a sharp breathing sound, as if he had been suddenly drenched with cold water. Then suddenly the violet colour went out of the night, and I was conscious of the nearness of something monstrous and repugnant.

"There was a tense silence, and the blackness of the cellar seemed absolute, with only the faint glow about each of the lanterns on the table. Then, in the darkness and the silence, there came a faint tinkle of water from the well, as if something were rising noiselessly out of it, and the water running back with a gentle tinkling. In the same instant, there came to me a sudden waft of the awful smell.

"I gave a sharp cry of warning to the inspector, and loosed the rope. There came instantly the sharp splash of the cage entering the water; and then, with a stiff, frightened movement, I opened the shutter of my lantern, and shone the light at the cage, shouting to the others to do the same.

"As my light struck the cage, I saw that about two feet of it projected from the top of the well, and there was something protruding up out of the water, into the cage. I stared, with a feeling that I recognised the thing; and then, as the other lanterns were opened, I saw that it was a leg of mutton. The thing was held by a brawny fist and arm, that rose out of the water. I stood utterly bewildered, watching to see what was coming. In a moment there rose into view a great bearded face, that I felt for one quick instant was the face of a drowned man, long dead. Then the face opened at the mouth part, and spluttered and coughed. Another big hand came into view, and wiped the water from the eyes, which blinked rapidly, and then fixed themselves into a stare at the lights.

"From the detective there came a sudden shout:

"'Captain Tobias!' he shouted, and the inspector echoed him; and instantly burst into loud roars of laughter.

"The inspector and the detective ran across the cellar to the cage; and I followed, still bewildered. The man in the cage was holding the leg of mutton as far away from him as possible, and holding his nose.

"'Lift thig dam trap, quig!' he shouted in a stifled voice; but the inspector and the detective simply doubled before him, and tried to hold their noses, whilst they laughed, and the light from their lanterns went dancing all over the place.

"'Quig! Quig!' said the man in the cage, still holding his nose, and trying to speak plainly.

"Then Johnstone and the detective stopped laughing, and lifted the cage. The man in the well threw the leg across the cellar, and turned swiftly to go down into the well; but the officers were too quick for him, and had him out in a twinkling. Whilst they held him, dripping upon the floor, the inspector jerked his thumb in the direction of the offending leg, and the landlord, having harpooned it with one of the pitchforks, ran with it upstairs and so into the open air.

"Meanwhile, I had given the man from the well a stiff tot of whisky; for which he thanked me with a cheerful nod, and having emptied the glass at a draught, held his hand for the bottle, which he finished, as if it had been so much water.

"As you will remember, it was a Captain Tobias who had been the previous tenant; and this was the very man, who had appeared from the well. In the course of the talk that followed, I learned the reason for Captain Tobias leaving the house; he had been wanted by the police for smuggling. He had undergone imprisonment; and had been released only a couple of weeks earlier.

"He had returned to find new tenants in his old home. He had entered the house through the well, the walls of which were not continued to the bottom (this I will deal with later); and gone up by a little stairway in the cellar wall, which opened at the top through a panel beside my mother's bedroom. This panel was opened, by revolving the left doorpost of the bedroom door, with the result that the bedroom door always became unlatched, in the process of opening the panel.

"The captain complained, without any bitterness, that the panel had warped, and that each time he opened it, it made a cracking noise. This had been evidently what I mistook for raps. He would not give his reason for entering the house; but it was pretty obvious that he had hidden something, which he wanted to get. However, as he found it impossible to get into the house without the risk of being caught, he decided to try to drive us out, relying on the bad reputation of the house, and his own artistic efforts as a ghost. I must say he succeeded. He intended then to rent the house again, as before; and would then, of course have plenty of time to get whatever he had hidden. The house suited him admirably;

for there was a passage – as he showed me afterward – connecting the dummy well with the crypt of the church beyond the garden wall; and these, in turn, were connected with certain caves in the cliffs, which went down to the beach beyond the church.

"In the course of his talk, Captain Tobias offered to take the house off my hands; and as this suited me perfectly, for I was about stalled with it, and the plan also suited the landlord, it was decided that no steps should be taken against him; and that the whole business should be hushed up.

"I asked the captain whether there was really anything queer about the house; whether he had ever seen anything. He said yes, that he had twice seen a Woman going about the house. We all looked at one another, when the captain said that. He told us she never bothered him, and that he had only seen her twice, and on each occasion it had followed a narrow escape from the Revenue people.

"Captain Tobias was an observant man; he had seen how I had placed the mats against the doors; and after entering the rooms, and walking all about them, so as to leave the foot-marks of an old pair of wet woollen slippers everywhere, he had deliberately put the mats back as he found them.

"The maggot which had dropped from his disgusting leg of mutton had been an accident, and beyond even his horrible planning. He was hugely delighted to learn how it had affected us.

"The mouldy smell I had noticed was from the little closed stairway, when the captain opened the panel. The door slamming was also another of his contributions.

"I come now to the end of the captain's ghost play; and to the difficulty of trying to explain the other peculiar things. In the first place, it was obvious there was something genuinely strange in the house; which made itself manifest as a Woman. Many different people had seen this Woman, under differing circumstances, so it is impossible to put the thing down to fancy; at the same time it must seem extraordinary that I should have lived two years in the house, and seen nothing; whilst the policeman saw the Woman, before he had been there twenty minutes; the landlord, the detective, and the inspector all saw her.

"I can only surmise that *fear* was in every case the key, as I might say, which opened the senses to the presence of the Woman. The policeman was a highly-strung man, and when he became frightened, was able to see the Woman. The same reasoning applies all 'round. *I* saw nothing, until I became really frightened; then I saw, not the Woman; but a Child, running away from Something or Someone. However, I will touch on that later. In short, until a very strong degree of fear was present, no one was affected by the Force which made Itself evident, as a Woman. My theory explains why some tenants were never aware of anything strange in the house, whilst others left immediately. The more sensitive they were, the less would be the degree of fear necessary to make them aware of the Force present in the house.

"The peculiar shining of all the metal objects in the cellar, had been visible only to me. The cause, naturally I do not know; neither do I know why I, alone, was able to see the shining."

"The Child," I asked. "Can you explain that part at all? Why *you* didn't see the Woman, and why *they* didn't see the Child. Was it merely the same Force, appearing differently to different people?"

"No," said Carnacki, "I can't explain that. But I am quite sure that the Woman and the Child were not only two complete and different entities; but even they were each not in quite the same planes of existence.

"To give you a root idea, however, it is held in the Sigsand MS. that a child 'stillborn' is 'Snatyched back bye thee Haggs'. This is crude; but may yet contain an elemental truth. Yet, before I make this clearer, let me tell you a thought that has often been made. It may be that physical birth is but a secondary process; and that prior to the possibility, the Mother Spirit searches for, until it finds, the small Element – the primal Ego or child's soul. It may be that a certain waywardness would cause such to strive to evade capture by the Mother Spirit. It may have been such a thing as this, that I saw. I have always tried to think so; but it is impossible to ignore the sense of repulsion that I felt when the unseen Woman went past me. This repulsion carries forward the idea suggested in the Sigsand MS., that a stillborn child is thus, because its ego or spirit has been snatched back by the 'Hags'. In other words, by certain of the Monstrosities of the Outer Circle. The thought is inconceivably terrible, and probably the more so because it is so fragmentary. It leaves us with the conception of a child's soul adrift half-way between two lives, and running through Eternity from Something incredible and inconceivable (because not understood) to our senses.

"The thing is beyond further discussion; for it is futile to attempt to discuss a thing, to any purpose, of which one has a knowledge so fragmentary as this. There is one thought, which is often mine. Perhaps there is a Mother Spirit—"

"And the well?" said Arkwright. "How did the captain get in from the other side?"

"As I said before," answered Carnacki. "The side walls of the well did not reach to the bottom; so that you had only to dip down into the water, and come up again on the other side of the wall, under the cellar floor, and so climb into the passage. Of course, the water was the same height on both sides of the walls. Don't ask me who made the well entrance or the little stairway; for I don't know. The house was very old, as I have told you; and that sort of thing was useful in the old days."

"And the Child," I said, coming back to the thing which chiefly interested me. "You would say that the birth must have occurred in that house; and in this way, one might suppose that the house to have become *en rapport*, if I can use the word in that way, with the Forces that produced the tragedy?"

"Yes," replied Carnacki. "This is, supposing we take the suggestion of the Sigsand MS., to account for the phenomenon."

"There may be other houses—" I began.

"There are," said Carnacki; and stood up.

"Out you go," he said, genially, using the recognised formula. And in five minutes we were on the Embankment, going thoughtfully to our various homes.

If you enjoyed this, you might also like...
The House Among the Laurels, see page 25
The Sea Horses, see page 184

The Thing Invisible

CARNACKI HAD JUST RETURNED to Cheyne Walk, Chelsea. I was aware of this interesting fact by reason of the curt and quaintly worded postcard which I was rereading, and by which I was requested to present myself at his house not later than seven o'clock on that evening. Mr. Carnacki had, as I and the others of his strictly limited circle of friends knew, been away in Kent for the past three weeks; but beyond that, we had no knowledge. Carnacki was genially secretive and curt, and spoke only when he was ready to speak. When this stage arrived, I and his three other friends – Jessop, Arkright, and Taylor – would receive a card or a wire, asking us to call. Not one of us ever willingly missed, for after a thoroughly sensible little dinner Carnacki would snuggle down into his big armchair, light his pipe, and wait whilst we arranged ourselves comfortably in our accustomed seats and nooks. Then he would begin to talk.

Upon this particular night I was the first to arrive and found Carnacki sitting, quietly smoking over a paper. He stood up, shook me firmly by the hand, pointed to a chair, and sat down again, never having uttered a word.

For my part, I said nothing either. I knew the man too well to bother him with questions or the weather, and so took a seat and a cigarette. Presently the three others turned up and after that we spent a comfortable and busy hour at dinner.

Dinner over, Carnacki snugged himself down into his great chair, as I have said was his habit, filled his pipe and puffed for awhile, his gaze directed thoughtfully at the fire. The rest of us, if I may so express it, made ourselves cosy, each after his own particular manner. A minute or so later Carnacki began to speak, ignoring any preliminary remarks, and going straight to the subject of the story we knew he had to tell:

"I have just come back from Sir Alfred Jarnock's place at Burtontree, in South Kent," he began, without removing his gaze from the fire. "Most extraordinary things have been happening down there lately and Mr. George Jarnock, the eldest son, wired to ask me to run over and see whether I could help to clear matters up a bit. I went.

"When I got there, I found that they have an old Chapel attached to the castle which has had quite a distinguished reputation for being what is popularly termed 'haunted'. They have been rather proud of this, as I managed to discover, until quite lately when something very disagreeable occurred, which served to remind them that family ghosts are not always content, as I might say, to remain purely ornamental.

"It sounds almost laughable, I know, to hear of a long-respected supernatural phenomenon growing unexpectedly dangerous; and in this case, the tale of the haunting was considered as little more than an old myth, except after nightfall, when possibly it became more plausible seeming.

"But however this may be, there is no doubt at all but that what I might term the Haunting Essence which lived in the place, had become suddenly dangerous – deadly dangerous too, the old butler being nearly stabbed to death one night in the Chapel, with a peculiar old dagger.

"It is, in fact, this dagger which is popularly supposed to 'haunt' the Chapel. At least, there has been always a story handed down in the family that this dagger would attack any enemy who should dare to venture into the Chapel, after nightfall. But, of course, this had been taken with just about the same amount of seriousness that people take most ghost tales, and that is not usually of a worryingly *real* nature. I mean that most people never quite know how much or how little they believe of matters ab-human or ab-normal, and generally they never have an opportunity to learn. And, indeed, as you are all aware, I am as big a sceptic concerning the truth of ghost tales as any man you are likely to meet; only I am what I might term an unprejudiced sceptic. I am not given to either believing or disbelieving things 'on principle', as I have found many idiots prone to be, and what is more, some of them not ashamed to boast of the insane fact. I view all reported 'hauntings' as unproven until I have examined into them, and I am bound to admit that ninety-nine cases in a hundred turn out to be sheer bosh and fancy. But the hundredth! Well, if it were not for the hundredth, I should have few stories to tell you – eh?

"Of course, after the attack on the butler, it became evident that there was at least 'something' in the old story concerning the dagger, and I found everyone in a half belief that the queer old weapon did really strike the butler, either by the aid of some inherent force, which I found them peculiarly unable to explain, or else in the hand of some invisible thing or monster of the Outer World!

"From considerable experience, I knew that it was much more likely that the butler had been 'knifed' by some vicious and quite material human!

"Naturally, the first thing to do, was to test this probability of human agency, and I set to work to make a pretty drastic examination of the people who knew most about the tragedy.

"The result of this examination, both pleased and surprised me, for it left me with very good reasons for belief that I had come upon one of those extraordinary rare 'true manifestations' of the extrusion of a Force from the Outside. In more popular phraseology – a genuine case of haunting.

"These are the facts: On the previous Sunday evening but one, Sir Alfred Jarnock's household had attended family service, as usual, in the Chapel. You see, the Rector goes over to officiate twice each Sunday, after concluding his duties at the public Church about three miles away.

"At the end of the service in the Chapel, Sir Alfred Jarnock, his son Mr. George Jarnock, and the Rector had stood for a couple of minutes, talking, whilst old Bellett the butler went 'round, putting out the candles.

"Suddenly, the Rector remembered that he had left his small prayer book on the Communion table in the morning; he turned, and asked the butler to get it for him before he blew out the chancel candles.

"Now I have particularly called your attention to this because it is important in that it provides witnesses in a most fortunate manner at an extraordinary moment. You see, the Rector's turning to speak to Bellett had naturally caused both Sir Alfred Jarnock and his son to glance in the direction of the butler, and it was at this identical instant and whilst all three were looking at him, that the old butler was stabbed – there, full in the candlelight, before their eyes.

"I took the opportunity to call early upon the Rector, after I had questioned Mr. George Jarnock, who replied to my queries in place of Sir Alfred Jarnock, for the older man was in a nervous and shaken condition as a result of the happening, and his son wished him to avoid dwelling upon the scene as much as possible.

"The Rector's version was clear and vivid, and he had evidently received the astonishment of his life. He pictured to me the whole affair – Bellett, up at the chancel gate, going for the prayer book, and absolutely alone; and then the *blow*, out of the Void, he described it; and the *force* prodigious – the old man being driven headlong into the body of the Chapel. Like the kick of a great horse, the Rector said, his benevolent old eyes bright and intense with the effort he had actually witnessed, in defiance of all that he had hitherto believed.

"When I left him, he went back to the writing which he had put aside when I appeared. I feel sure that he was developing the first unorthodox sermon that he had ever evolved. He was a dear old chap, and I should certainly like to have heard it.

"The last man I visited was the butler. He was, of course, in a frightfully weak and shaken condition, but he could tell me nothing that did not point to there being a Power abroad in the Chapel. He told the same tale, in every minute particle, that I had learned from the others. He had been just going up to put out the altar candles and fetch the Rector's book, when something struck him an enormous blow high up on the left breast and he was driven headlong into the aisle.

"Examination had shown that he had been stabbed by the dagger – of which I will tell you more in a moment – that hung always above the altar. The weapon had entered, fortunately some inches above the heart, just under the collarbone, which had been broken by the stupendous force of the blow, the dagger itself being driven clean through the body, and out through the scapula behind.

"The poor old fellow could not talk much, and I soon left him; but what he had told me was sufficient to make it unmistakable that no living person had been within yards of him when he was attacked; and, as I knew, this fact was verified by three capable and responsible witnesses, independent of Bellett himself.

"The thing now was to search the Chapel, which is small and extremely old. It is very massively built, and entered through only one door, which leads out of the castle itself, and the key of which is kept by Sir Alfred Jarnock, the butler having no duplicate.

"The shape of the Chapel is oblong, and the altar is railed off after the usual fashion. There are two tombs in the body of the place; but none in the chancel, which is bare, except for the tall candlesticks, and the chancel rail, beyond which is the undraped altar of solid marble, upon which stand four small candlesticks, two at each end.

"Above the altar hangs the 'waeful dagger', as I had learned it was named. I fancy the term has been taken from an old vellum, which describes the dagger and its supposed abnormal properties. I took the dagger down, and examined it minutely and with method. The blade is ten inches long, two inches broad at the base, and tapering to a rounded but sharp point, rather peculiar. It is double-edged.

"The metal sheath is curious for having a crosspiece, which, taken with the fact that the sheath itself is continued three parts up the hilt of the dagger (in a most inconvenient fashion), gives it the appearance of a cross. That this is not unintentional is shown by an engraving of the Christ crucified upon one side, whilst upon the other, in Latin, is the inscription: 'Vengeance is Mine, I will Repay.' A quaint and rather terrible conjunction of ideas. Upon the blade of the dagger is graven in old English capitals: *I WATCH. I STRIKE.* On the butt of the hilt there is carved deeply a Pentacle.

"This is a pretty accurate description of the peculiar old weapon that has had the curious and uncomfortable reputation of being able (either of its own accord or in the hand of something invisible) to strike murderously any enemy of the Jarnock family who may chance to enter the Chapel after nightfall. I may tell you here and now, that before I left, I had very good reason to put certain doubts behind me; for I tested the deadliness of the thing myself.

"As you know, however, at this point of my investigation, I was still at that stage where I considered the existence of a supernatural Force unproven. In the meanwhile, I treated the Chapel drastically, sounding and scrutinising the walls and floor, dealing with them almost foot by foot, and particularly examining the two tombs.

"At the end of this search, I had in a ladder, and made a close survey of the groined roof. I passed three days in this fashion, and by the evening of the third day I had proved to my entire satisfaction that there is no place in the whole of that Chapel where any living being could have hidden, and also that the only way of ingress and egress to and from the Chapel is through the doorway which leads into the castle, the door of which was always kept locked, and the key kept by Sir Alfred Jarnock himself, as I have told you. I mean, of course, that this doorway is the only entrance practicable to material people.

"Yes, as you will see, even had I discovered some other opening, secret or otherwise, it would not have helped at all to explain the mystery of the incredible attack, in a normal fashion. For the butler, as you know, was struck in full sight of the Rector, Sir Jarnock and his son. And old Bellett himself knew that no living person had touched him…. 'Out of the Void,' the Rector had described the inhumanly brutal attack. 'Out of the Void!' A strange feeling it gives one – eh?

"And this is the thing that I had been called in to bottom!

"After considerable thought, I decided on a plan of action. I proposed to Sir Alfred Jarnock that I should spend a night in the Chapel, and keep a constant watch upon the dagger. But to this, the old knight – a little, wizened, nervous man – would not listen for a moment. He, at least, I felt assured had no doubt of the reality of some dangerous supernatural Force a roam at night in the Chapel. He informed me that it had been his habit every evening to lock the Chapel door, so that no one might foolishly or heedlessly run the risk of any peril that it might hold at night, and that he could not allow me to attempt such a thing after what had happened to the butler.

"I could see that Sir Alfred Jarnock was very much in earnest, and would evidently have held himself to blame had he allowed me to make the experiment and any harm come to me; so I said nothing in argument; and presently, pleading the fatigue of his years and health, he said goodnight, and left me; having given me the impression of being a polite but rather superstitious, old gentleman.

"That night, however, whilst I was undressing, I saw how I might achieve the thing I wished, and be able to enter the Chapel after dark, without making Sir Alfred Jarnock nervous. On the morrow, when I borrowed the key, I would take an impression, and have a duplicate made. Then, with my private key, I could do just what I liked.

"In the morning I carried out my idea. I borrowed the key, as I wanted to take a photograph of the chancel by daylight. When I had done this I locked up the Chapel and handed the key to Sir Alfred Jarnock, having first taken an impression in soap. I had brought out the exposed plate – in its slide – with me; but the camera I had left exactly as it was, as I wanted to take a second photograph of the chancel that night, from the same position.

"I took the dark slide into Burtontree, also the cake of soap with the impress. The soap I left with the local ironmonger, who was something of a locksmith and promised to let me have my duplicate, finished, if I would call in two hours. This I did, having in the meanwhile found out a photographer where I developed the plate, and left it to dry, telling him I would call next day. At the end of the two hours I went for my key and found it ready, much to my satisfaction. Then I returned to the castle.

"After dinner that evening, I played billiards with young Jarnock for a couple of hours. Then I had a cup of coffee and went off to my room, telling him I was feeling awfully tired. He nodded and told me he felt the same way. I was glad, for I wanted the house to settle as soon as possible.

"I locked the door of my room, then from under the bed – where I had hidden them earlier in the evening – I drew out several fine pieces of plate armour, which I had removed from the armoury. There was also a shirt of chain mail, with a sort of quilted hood of mail to go over the head.

"I buckled on the plate armour, and found it extraordinarily uncomfortable, and over all I drew on the chain mail. I know nothing about armour, but from what I have learned since, I must have put on parts of two suits. Anyway, I felt beastly, clamped and clumsy and unable to move my arms and legs naturally. But I knew that the thing I was thinking of doing called for some sort of protection for my body. Over the armour I pulled on my dressing gown and shoved my revolver into one of the side pockets – and my repeating flash-light into the other. My dark lantern I carried in my hand.

"As soon as I was ready I went out into the passage and listened. I had been some considerable time making my preparations and I found that now the big hall and staircase were in darkness and all the house seemed quiet. I stepped back and closed and locked my door. Then, very slowly and silently I went downstairs to the hall and turned into the passage that led to the Chapel.

"I reached the door and tried my key. It fitted perfectly and a moment later I was in the Chapel, with the door locked behind me, and all about me the utter dree silence of the place, with just the faint showings of the outlines of the stained, leaded windows, making the darkness and lonesomeness almost the more apparent.

"Now it would be silly to say I did not feel queer. I felt very queer indeed. You just try, any of you, to imagine yourself standing there in the dark silence and remembering not only the legend that was attached to the place, but what had really happened to the old butler only a little while gone, I can tell you, as I stood there, I could believe that something invisible was coming towards me in the air of the Chapel. Yet, I had got to go through with the business, and I just took hold of my little bit of courage and set to work.

"First of all I switched on my light, then I began a careful tour of the place; examining every corner and nook. I found nothing unusual. At the chancel gate I held up my lamp and flashed the light at the dagger. It hung there, right enough, above the altar, but I remember thinking of the word 'demure', as I looked at it. However, I pushed the thought away, for what I was doing needed no addition of uncomfortable thoughts.

"I completed the tour of the place, with a constantly growing awareness of its utter chill and unkind desolation – an atmosphere of cold dismalness seemed to be everywhere, and the quiet was abominable.

"At the conclusion of my search I walked across to where I had left my camera focused upon the chancel. From the satchel that I had put beneath the tripod I took out a dark slide and inserted it in the camera, drawing the shutter. After that I uncapped the lens, pulled out my flashlight apparatus, and pressed the trigger. There was an intense, brilliant flash, that made the whole of the interior of the Chapel jump into sight, and disappear as quickly. Then, in the light from my lantern, I inserted the shutter into the slide, and reversed the slide, so as to have a fresh plate ready to expose at any time.

"After I had done this I shut off my lantern and sat down in one of the pews near to my camera. I cannot say what I expected to happen, but I had an extraordinary feeling, almost a conviction, that something peculiar or horrible would soon occur. It was, you know, as if I knew.

"An hour passed, of absolute silence. The time I knew by the far-off, faint chime of a clock that had been erected over the stables. I was beastly cold, for the whole place is without any kind of heating pipes or furnace, as I had noticed during my search, so that the temperature was sufficiently uncomfortable to suit my frame of mind. I felt like a kind of human periwinkle encased in boilerplate and frozen with cold and funk. And, you know, somehow the dark about me seemed to press coldly against my face. I cannot say whether any of you have ever had the feeling, but if you have, you will know just how disgustingly unnerving it is. And then, all at once, I had a horrible sense that something was moving in the place. It was not that I could hear anything but I had a kind of intuitive knowledge that something had stirred in the darkness. Can you imagine how I felt?

"Suddenly my courage went. I put up my mailed arms over my face. I wanted to protect it. I had got a sudden sickening feeling that something was hovering over me in the dark. Talk about fright! I could have shouted if I had not been afraid of the noise… And then, abruptly, I heard something. Away up the aisle, there sounded a dull clang of metal, as it might be the tread of a mailed heel upon the stone of the aisle. I sat immovable. I was fighting with all my strength to get back my courage. I could not take my arms down from over my face, but I knew that I was getting hold of the gritty part of me again. And suddenly I made a mighty effort and lowered my arms. I held my face up in the darkness. And, I tell you, I respect myself for the act, because I thought truly at that moment that I was going to die. But I think, just then, by the slow revulsion of feeling which had assisted my effort, I was less sick, in that instant, at the thought of having to die, than at the knowledge of the utter weak cowardice that had so unexpectedly shaken me all to bits, for a time.

"Do I make myself clear? You understand, I feel sure, that the sense of respect, which I spoke of, is not really unhealthy egotism; because, you see, I am not blind to the state of mind which helped me. I mean that if I had uncovered my face by a sheer effort of will, unhelped by any revulsion of feeling, I should have done a thing much more worthy of mention. But, even as it was, there were elements in the act, worthy of respect. You follow me, don't you?

"And, you know, nothing touched me, after all! So that, in a little while, I had got back a bit to my normal, and felt steady enough to go through with the business without any more funking.

"I daresay a couple of minutes passed, and then, away up near the chancel, there came again that clang, as though an armoured foot stepped cautiously. By Jove! But it made me stiffen. And suddenly the thought came that the sound I heard might be the rattle of the dagger above the altar. It was not a particularly sensible notion, for the sound was far too heavy and resonant for such a cause. Yet, as can be easily understood, my reason was bound to submit somewhat to my fancy at such a time. I remember now, that the idea of that insensate thing becoming animate, and attacking me, did not occur to me with any sense of possibility or reality. I thought rather, in a vague way, of some invisible monster of outer space fumbling at the dagger. I remembered the old Rector's description of the attack on the butler…. *of the void*. And he had described the stupendous force of the blow as being 'like the kick of a great horse'. You can see how uncomfortably my thoughts were running.

"I felt 'round swiftly and cautiously for my lantern. I found it close to me, on the pew seat, and with a sudden, jerky movement, I switched on the light. I flashed it up the aisle, to and fro across the chancel, but I could see nothing to frighten me. I turned quickly, and sent the jet of light darting across and across the rear end of the Chapel; then on each side of me, before and behind, up at the roof and down at the marble floor, but nowhere was there any visible thing to put me in fear, not a thing that need have set my flesh thrilling; just the quiet Chapel, cold, and eternally silent. You know the feeling.

"I had been standing, whilst I sent the light about the Chapel, but now I pulled out my revolver, and then, with a tremendous effort of will, switched off the light, and sat down again in the darkness, to continue my constant watch.

"It seemed to me that quite half an hour, or even more, must have passed, after this, during which no sound had broken the intense stillness. I had grown less nervously tense, for the flashing of the light 'round the place had made me feel less out of all bounds of the normal – it had given me something of that unreasoned sense of safety that a nervous child obtains at night, by covering its head up with the bedclothes. This just about illustrates the completely human illogicalness of the workings of my feelings; for, as you know, whatever Creature, Thing, or Being it was that had made that extraordinary and horrible attack on the old butler, it had certainly not been visible.

"And so you must picture me sitting there in the dark; clumsy with armour, and with my revolver in one hand, and nursing my lantern, ready, with the other. And then it was, after this little time of partial relief from intense nervousness, that there came a fresh strain on me; for somewhere in the utter quiet of the Chapel, I thought I heard something. I listened, tense and rigid, my heart booming just a little in my ears for a moment; then I thought I heard it again. I felt sure that something had moved at the top of the aisle. I strained in the darkness, to hark; and my eyes showed me blackness within blackness, wherever I glanced, so that I took no heed of what they told me; for even if I looked at the dim loom of the stained window at the top of the chancel, my sight gave me the shapes of vague shadows passing noiseless and ghostly across, constantly. There was a time of almost peculiar silence, horrible to me, as I felt just then. And suddenly I seemed to hear a sound again, nearer to me, and repeated, infinitely stealthy. It was as if a vast, soft tread were coming slowly down the aisle.

"Can you imagine how I felt? I do not think you can. I did not move, any more than the stone effigies on the two tombs; but sat there, *stiffened*. I fancied now, that I heard the tread all about the Chapel. And then, you know, I was just as sure in a moment that I could not hear it – that I had never heard it.

"Some particularly long minutes passed, about this time; but I think my nerves must have quieted a bit; for I remember being sufficiently aware of my feelings, to realise that the muscles of my shoulders *ached*, with the way that they must have been contracted, as I sat there, hunching myself, rigid. Mind you, I was still in a disgusting funk; but what I might call the 'imminent sense of danger' seemed to have eased from around me; at any rate, I felt, in some curious fashion, that there was a respite – a temporary cessation of malignity from about me. It is impossible to word my feelings more clearly to you, for I cannot see them more clearly than this, myself.

"Yet, you must not picture me as sitting there, free from strain; for the nerve tension was so great that my heart action was a little out of normal control, the blood beat making a dull booming at times in my ears, with the result that I had the sensation that I could not hear acutely. This is a simply beastly feeling, especially under such circumstances.

"I was sitting like this, listening, as I might say with body and soul, when suddenly I got that hideous conviction again that something was moving in the air of the place. The feeling seemed to stiffen me, as I sat, and my head appeared to tighten, as if all the scalp had grown *tense*. This was so real, that I suffered an actual pain, most peculiar and at the same time intense; the whole head pained. I had a fierce desire to cover my face again with my mailed arms, but I fought it off. If I had given way then to that, I should simply have bunked straight out of the place. I sat and sweated coldly (that's the bald truth), with the 'creep' busy at my spine....

"And then, abruptly, once more I thought I heard the sound of that huge, soft tread on the aisle, and this time closer to me. There was an awful little silence, during which I had the feeling that something enormous was bending over towards me, from the aisle.... And then, through the booming of the blood in my ears, there came a slight sound from the place where my camera stood – a disagreeable sort of slithering sound, and then a sharp tap. I had the lantern ready in my left hand, and now I snapped it on, desperately, and shone it straight above me, for I had a conviction that there was something there. But I saw nothing. Immediately I flashed the light at the camera, and along the aisle, but again there was nothing visible. I wheeled 'round, shooting the beam of light in a great circle about the place; to and fro I shone it, jerking it here and there, but it showed me nothing.

"I had stood up the instant that I had seen that there was nothing in sight over me, and now I determined to visit the chancel, and see whether the dagger had been touched. I stepped out of the pew into the aisle, and here I came to an abrupt pause, for an almost invincible, sick repugnance was fighting me back from the upper part of the Chapel. A constant, queer prickling went up and down my spine, and a dull ache took me in the small of the back, as I fought with myself to conquer this sudden new feeling of terror and horror. I tell you, that no one who has not been through these kinds of experiences, has any idea of the sheer, actual physical pain attendant upon, and resulting from, the intense nerve strain that ghostly fright sets up in the human system. I stood there feeling positively ill. But I got myself in hand, as it were, in about half a minute, and then I went, walking, I expect, as jerky as a mechanical tin man, and switching the light from side to side, before and behind, and over my head continually. And the hand that held my revolver sweated so much, that the thing fairly slipped in my fist. Does not sound very heroic, does it?

"I passed through the short chancel, and reached the step that led up to the small gate in the chancel rail. I threw the beam from my lantern upon the dagger. Yes, I thought, it's all right. Abruptly, it seemed to me that there was something wanting, and I leaned forward over the chancel gate to peer, holding the light high. My suspicion was hideously correct. *The dagger had gone.* Only the cross-shaped sheath hung there above the altar.

"In a sudden, frightened flash of imagination, I pictured the thing adrift in the Chapel, moving here and there, as though of its own volition; for whatever Force wielded it, was certainly beyond visibility. I turned my head stiffly over to the left, glancing frightenedly behind me, and flashing the light to help my eyes. In the same instant I was struck a tremendous blow over the left breast, and hurled backward from the chancel rail, into the aisle, my armour clanging loudly in the horrible silence. I landed on my back, and slithered along on the polished marble. My shoulder struck the corner of a pew front, and brought me up, half stunned. I scrambled to my feet, horribly sick and shaken; but the fear that was on me, making little of that at the moment. I was minus both revolver and lantern, and utterly bewildered as to just where I was standing. I bowed my head, and made a scrambling run in the complete darkness and dashed into a pew. I jumped back, staggering, got my bearings a little, and raced down the centre of the aisle, putting my mailed arms over my face. I plunged into my camera, hurling it among the pews. I crashed into the font, and reeled back. Then I was at the exit. I fumbled madly in my dressing gown pocket for the key. I found it and scraped at the door, feverishly, for the keyhole. I found the keyhole, turned the key, burst the door open, and was into the passage. I slammed the door and leant hard against it, gasping, whilst I felt crazily again for the keyhole, this time to lock the door upon what was in the Chapel. I succeeded, and began to feel my way stupidly along the wall of the corridor. Presently I had come to the big hall, and so in a little to my room.

"In my room, I sat for a while, until I had steadied down something to the normal. After a time I commenced to strip off the armour. I saw then that both the chain mail and the plate armour had been pierced over the breast. And, suddenly, it came home to me that the Thing had struck for my heart.

"Stripping rapidly, I found that the skin of the breast over the heart had just been cut sufficiently to allow a little blood to stain my shirt, nothing more. Only, the whole breast was badly bruised and intensely painful. You can imagine what would have happened if I had not worn the armour. In any case, it is a marvel that I was not knocked senseless.

"I did not go to bed at all that night, but sat upon the edge, thinking, and waiting for the dawn; for I had to remove my litter before Sir Alfred Jarnock should enter, if I were to hide from him the fact that I had managed a duplicate key.

"So soon as the pale light of the morning had strengthened sufficiently to show me the various details of my room, I made my way quietly down to the Chapel. Very silently, and with tense nerves, I opened the door. The chill light of the dawn made distinct the whole place – everything seeming instinct with a ghostly, unearthly quiet. Can you get the feeling? I waited several minutes at the door, allowing the morning to grow, and likewise my courage, I suppose. Presently the rising sun threw an odd beam right in through the big, East window, making coloured sunshine all the length of the Chapel. And then, with a tremendous effort, I forced myself to enter.

"I went up the aisle to where I had overthrown my camera in the darkness. The legs of the tripod were sticking up from the interior of a pew, and I expected to find the machine smashed to pieces; yet, beyond that the ground glass was broken, there was no real damage done.

"I replaced the camera in the position from which I had taken the previous photography; but the slide containing the plate I had exposed by flashlight I removed and put into one of my side pockets, regretting that I had not taken a second flash picture at the instant when I heard those strange sounds up in the chancel.

"Having tidied my photographic apparatus, I went to the chancel to recover my lantern and revolver, which had both – as you know – been knocked from my hands when I was stabbed. I found the lantern lying, hopelessly bent, with smashed lens, just under the pulpit. My revolver I must have held until my shoulder struck the pew, for it was lying there in the aisle, just about where I believe I cannoned into the pew corner. It was quite undamaged.

"Having secured these two articles, I walked up to the chancel rail to see whether the dagger had returned, or been returned, to its sheath above the altar. Before, however, I reached the chancel rail, I had a slight shock; for there on the floor of the chancel, about a yard away from where I had been struck, lay the dagger, quiet and demure upon the polished marble pavement. I wonder whether you will, any of you, understand the nervousness that took me at the sight of the thing. With a sudden, unreasoned action, I jumped forward and put my foot on it, to hold it there. Can you understand? Do you?

And, you know, I could not stoop down and pick it up with my hands for quite a minute, I should think. Afterward, when I had done so, however, and handled it a little, this feeling passed away and my Reason (and also, I expect, the daylight) made me feel that I had been a little bit of an ass. Quite natural, though, I assure you! Yet it was a new kind of fear to me. I'm taking no notice of the cheap joke about the ass! I am talking about the curiousness of learning in that moment a new shade or quality of fear that had hitherto been outside of my knowledge or imagination. Does it interest you?

"I examined the dagger, minutely, turning it over and over in my hands and never – as I suddenly discovered – holding it loosely. It was as if I were subconsciously surprised that it lay quiet in my hands. Yet even this feeling passed, largely, after a short while. The curious weapon showed no signs of the blow, except that the dull colour – of the blade was slightly brighter on the rounded point that had cut through the armour.

"Presently, when I had made an end of staring at the dagger, I went up the chancel step and in through the little gate. Then, kneeling upon the altar, I replaced the dagger in its sheath, and came outside of the rail again, closing the gate after me and feeling awarely uncomfortable because the horrible old weapon was back again in its accustomed place. I suppose, without analysing my feelings very deeply, I had an unreasoned and only half-conscious belief that there was a greater probability of danger when the dagger hung in its five century resting place than when it was out of it! Yet, somehow I don't think this is a very good explanation, when I remember the *demure* look the thing seemed to have when I saw it lying on the floor of the chancel. Only I know this, that when I had replaced the dagger I had quite a touch of nerves and I stopped only to pick up my lantern from where I had placed it whilst I examined the weapon, after which I went down the quiet aisle at a pretty quick walk, and so got out of the place.

"That the nerve tension had been considerable, I realised, when I had locked the door behind me. I felt no inclination now to think of old Sir Alfred as a hypochondriac because he had taken such hyperseeming precautions regarding the Chapel. I had a sudden wonder as to whether he might not have some knowledge of a long prior tragedy in which the dagger had been concerned.

"I returned to my room, washed, shaved and dressed, after which I read awhile. Then I went downstairs and got the acting butler to give me some sandwiches and a cup of coffee.

"Half an hour later I was heading for Burtontree, as hard as I could walk; for a sudden idea had come to me, which I was anxious to test. I reached the town a little before eight thirty, and found the local photographer with his shutters still up. I did not wait, but knocked until he appeared with his coat off, evidently in the act of dealing with his breakfast. In a few words I made clear that I wanted the use of his dark room immediately, and this he at once placed at my disposal.

"I had brought with me the slide which contained the plate that I had used with the flashlight, and as soon as I was ready I set to work to develop. Yet, it was not the plate which I had exposed, that I first put into the solution, but the second plate, which had been ready in the camera during all the time of my waiting in the darkness. You see, the lens had been uncapped all that while, so that the whole chancel had been, as it were, under observation.

"You all know something of my experiments in 'Lightless Photography', that is, appreciating light. It was X-ray work that started me in that direction. Yet, you must understand, though I was attempting to develop this 'unexposed' plate, I had no definite idea of results – nothing more than a vague hope that it might show me something.

"Yet, because of the possibilities, it was with the most intense and absorbing interest that I watched the plate under the action of the developer. Presently I saw a faint smudge of black appear in the upper part, and after that others, indistinct and wavering of outline. I held the negative up to the light. The marks were rather small, and were almost entirely confined to one end of the plate, but as I have said, lacked definiteness. Yet, such as they were, they were sufficient to make me very excited and I shoved the thing quickly back into the solution.

"For some minutes further I watched it, lifting it out once or twice to make a more exact scrutiny, but could not imagine what the markings might represent, until suddenly it occurred to me that in one of two places they certainly had shapes suggestive of a cross hilted dagger. Yet, the shapes were sufficiently indefinite to make me careful not to let myself be overimpressed by the uncomfortable resemblance, though I must confess, the very thought was sufficient to set some odd thrills adrift in me.

"I carried development a little further, then put the negative into the hypo, and commenced work upon the other plate. This came up nicely, and very soon I had a really decent negative that appeared similar in every respect (except for the difference of lighting) to the negative I had taken during the previous day. I fixed the plate, then having washed both it and the 'unexposed' one for a few minutes under the tap, I put them into methylated spirits for fifteen minutes, after which I carried them into the photographer's kitchen and dried them in the oven.

"Whilst the two plates were drying the photographer and I made an enlargement from the negative I had taken by daylight. Then we did the same with the two that I had just developed, washing them as quickly as possible, for I was not troubling about the permanency of the prints, and drying them with spirits.

"When this was done I took them to the window and made a thorough examination, commencing with the one that appeared to show shadowy daggers in several places. Yet, though it was now enlarged, I was still unable to feel convinced that the marks truly represented anything abnormal; and because of this, I put it on one side, determined not to let my imagination play too large a part in constructing weapons out of the indefinite outlines.

"I took up the two other enlargements, both of the chancel, as you will remember, and commenced to compare them. For some minutes I examined them without being able to distinguish any difference in the scene they portrayed, and then abruptly, I saw something in which they varied. In the second enlargement – the one made from the flashlight negative – the dagger was not in its sheath. Yet, I had felt sure it was there but a few minutes before I took the photograph.

"After this discovery I began to compare the two enlargements in a very different manner from my previous scrutiny. I borrowed a pair of callipers from the photographer and with these I carried out a most methodical and exact comparison of the details shown in the two photographs.

"Suddenly I came upon something that set me all tingling with excitement. I threw the callipers down, paid the photographer, and walked out through the shop into the street. The three enlargements I took with me, making them into a roll as I went. At the corner of the street I had the luck to get a cab and was soon back at the castle.

"I hurried up to my room and put the photographs away; then I went down to see whether I could find Sir Alfred Jarnock; but Mr. George Jarnock, who met me, told me that his father was too unwell to rise and would prefer that no one entered the Chapel unless he were about.

"Young Jarnock made a half apologetic excuse for his father; remarking that Sir Alfred Jarnock was perhaps inclined to be a little over careful; but that, considering what had happened, we must agree that the need for his carefulness had been justified. He added, also, that even before the horrible attack on the butler his father had been just as particular, always keeping the key and never allowing the door to be unlocked except when the place was in use for Divine Service, and for an hour each forenoon when the cleaners were in.

"To all this I nodded understandingly; but when, presently, the young man left me I took my duplicate key and made for the door of the Chapel. I went in and locked it behind me, after which I carried out some intensely interesting and rather weird experiments. These proved successful to such an extent that I came out of the place in a perfect fever of excitement. I inquired for Mr. George Jarnock and was told that he was in the morning room.

"'Come along,' I said, when I had found him. 'Please give me a lift. I've something exceedingly strange to show you.'

"He was palpably very much puzzled, but came quickly. As we strode along he asked me a score of questions, to all of which I just shook my head, asking him to wait a little.

"I led the way to the Armoury. Here I suggested that he should take one side of a dummy, dressed in half plate armour, whilst I took the other. He nodded, though obviously vastly bewildered, and together we carried the thing to the Chapel door. When he saw me take out my key and open the way for us he appeared even more astonished, but held himself in, evidently waiting for me to explain. We entered the Chapel and I locked the door behind us, after which we carted the armoured dummy up the aisle to the gate of the chancel rail where we put it down upon its round, wooden stand.

"'Stand back!' I shouted suddenly as young Jarnock made a movement to open the gate. 'My God, man! You mustn't do that!'

"'Do what?' he asked, half-startled and half-irritated by my words and manner.

"'One minute,' I said. 'Just stand to the side a moment, and watch.'

"He stepped to the left whilst I took the dummy in my arms and turned it to face the altar, so that it stood close to the gate. Then, standing well away on the right side, I pressed the back of the thing so that it leant forward a little upon the gate, which flew open. In the same instant, the dummy was struck a tremendous blow that hurled it into the aisle, the armour rattling and clanging upon the polished marble floor.

"'Good God!' shouted young Jarnock, and ran back from the chancel rail, his face very white.

"'Come and look at the thing,' I said, and led the way to where the dummy lay, its armoured upper limbs all splayed adrift in queer contortions. I stooped over it and pointed. There, driven right through the thick steel breastplate, was the 'waeful dagger'.

"'Good God!' said young Jarnock again. 'Good God! It's the dagger! The thing's been stabbed, same as Bellett!'

"'Yes,' I replied, and saw him glance swiftly towards the entrance of the Chapel. But I will do him the justice to say that he never budged an inch.

"'Come and see how it was done,' I said, and led the way back to the chancel rail. From the wall to the left of the altar I took down a long, curiously ornamented, iron instrument, not unlike a short spear. The sharp end of this I inserted in a hole in the left-hand gatepost of the chancel gateway. I lifted hard, and a section of the post, from the floor upward, bent inward towards the altar, as though hinged at the bottom. Down it went, leaving the remaining part of the post standing. As I bent the movable portion lower there came a quick click and a section of the floor slid to one side, showing a long, shallow cavity, sufficient to enclose the post. I put my weight to the lever and hove the post down into the niche. Immediately there was a sharp clang, as some catch snicked in, and held it against the powerful operating spring.

"I went over now to the dummy, and after a few minute's work managed to wrench the dagger loose out of the armour. I brought the old weapon and placed its hilt in a hole near the top of the post where it fitted loosely, the point upward. After that I went again to the lever and gave another strong heave, and the post descended about a foot, to the bottom of the cavity, catching there with another clang. I withdrew the lever and the narrow strip of floor slid back, covering post and dagger, and looking no different from the surrounding surface.

"Then I shut the chancel gate, and we both stood well to one side. I took the spear-like lever, and gave the gate a little push, so that it opened. Instantly there was a loud thud, and something sang through the air, striking the bottom wall of the Chapel. It was the dagger. I showed Jarnock then that the other half of the post had sprung back into place, making the whole post as thick as the one upon the right-hand side of the gate.

"'There!' I said, turning to the young man and tapping the divided post. 'There's the 'invisible' thing that used the dagger, but who the deuce is the person who sets the trap?' I looked at him keenly as I spoke.

"'My father is the only one who has a key,' he said. 'So it's practically impossible for anyone to get in and meddle.'

"I looked at him again, but it was obvious that he had not yet reached out to any conclusion.

"'See here, Mr. Jarnock,' I said, perhaps rather curter than I should have done, considering what I had to say. 'Are you quite sure that Sir Alfred is quite balanced – mentally?'

"He looked at me, half frightenedly and flushing a little. I realised then how badly I put it.

"'I – I don't know,' he replied, after a slight pause and was then silent, except for one or two incoherent half remarks.

"'Tell the truth,' I said. 'Haven't you suspected something, now and again? You needn't be afraid to tell me.'

"'Well,' he answered slowly, 'I'll admit I've thought Father a little – a little strange, perhaps, at times. But I've always tried to think I was mistaken. I've always hoped no one else would see it. You see, I'm very fond of the old guvnor.'

"I nodded.

"'Quite right, too,' I said. 'There's not the least need to make any kind of scandal about this. We must do something, though, but in a quiet way. No fuss, you know. I should go and have a chat with your father, and tell him we've found out about this thing.' I touched the divided post.

Young Jarnock seemed very grateful for my advice and after shaking my hand pretty hard, took my key, and let himself out of the Chapel. He came back in about an hour, looking rather upset. He told me that my conclusions were perfectly correct. It was Sir Alfred Jarnock who had set the trap, both on the night that the butler was nearly killed, and on the past night. Indeed, it seemed that the old gentleman had set it every night for many years. He had learnt of its existence from an old manuscript book in the Castle library. It had been planned and used in an earlier age as a protection for the gold vessels of the ritual, which were, it seemed, kept in a hidden recess at the back of the altar.

"This recess Sir Alfred Jarnock had utilised, secretly, to store his wife's jewelry. She had died some twelve years back, and the young man told me that his father had never seemed quite himself since.

"I mentioned to young Jarnock how puzzled I was that the trap had been set *before* the service, on the night that the butler was struck; for, if I understood him aright, his father had been in the habit of setting the trap late every night and unsetting it each morning before anyone entered the Chapel. He replied that his father, in a fit of temporary forgetfulness (natural enough in his neurotic condition), must have set it too early and hence what had so nearly proved a tragedy.

"That is about all there is to tell. The old man is not (so far as I could learn), really insane in the popularly accepted sense of the word. He is extremely neurotic and has developed into a hypochondriac, the whole condition probably brought about by the shock and sorrow resultant on the death of his wife, leading to years of sad broodings and to overmuch of his own company and thoughts. Indeed, young Jarnock told me that his father would sometimes pray for hours together, alone in the Chapel." Carnacki made an end of speaking and leant forward for a spill.

"But you've never told us just *how* you discovered the secret of the divided post and all that," I said, speaking for the four of us.

"Oh, that!" replied Carnacki, puffing vigorously at his pipe. "I found on comparing the photos, that the one taken in the daytime, showed a thicker left-hand gatepost, than the one taken at night by the flashlight. That put me on to the track. I saw at once that there might be some mechanical dodge at the back of the whole queer business and nothing at all of an abnormal nature. I examined the post and the rest was simple enough, you know.

"By the way," he continued, rising and going to the mantelpiece, "you may be interested to have a look at the so-called 'waeful dagger'. Young Jarnock was kind enough to present it to me, as a little memento of my adventure."

He handed it 'round to us and whilst we examined it, stood silent before the fire, puffing meditatively at his pipe.

"Jarnock and I made the trap so that it won't work," he remarked after a few moments. "I've got the dagger, as you see, and old Bellett's getting about again, so that the whole business can be hushed up, decently. All the same I fancy the Chapel will never lose its reputation as a dangerous place. Should be pretty safe now to keep valuables in."

"There's two things you haven't explained yet," I said. "What do you think caused the two clangey sounds when you were in the Chapel in the dark? And do you believe the soft tready sounds were real, or only a fancy, with your being so worked up and tense?"

"Don't know for certain about the clangs," replied Carnacki.

"I've puzzled quite a bit about them. I can only think that the spring which worked the post must have 'given' a trifle, slipped you know, in the catch. If it did, under such a tension, it would make a bit of a ringing noise. And a little sound goes a long way in the middle of the night when you're thinking of 'ghostesses'. You can understand that – eh?"

"Yes," I agreed. "And the other sounds?"

"Well, the same thing – I mean the extraordinary quietness – may help to explain these a bit. They may have been some usual enough sound that would never have been noticed under ordinary conditions, or they may have been only fancy. It is just impossible to say. They were disgustingly real to me. As for the slithery noise, I am pretty sure that one of the tripod legs of my camera must have slipped a few inches: if it did so, it may easily have jolted the lens cap off the baseboard, which would account for that queer little tap which I heard directly after."

"How do you account for the dagger being in its place above the altar when you first examined it that night?" I asked. "How could it be there, when at that very moment it was set in the trap?"

"That was my mistake," replied Carnacki. "The dagger could not possibly have been in its sheath at the time, though I thought it was. You see, the curious cross-hilted sheath gave the appearance of the complete weapon, as you can understand. The hilt of the dagger protrudes very little above the continued portion of the sheath – a most inconvenient arrangement for drawing quickly!" He nodded sagely at the lot of us and yawned, then glanced at the clock.

"Out you go!" he said, in friendly fashion, using the recognised formula. "I want a sleep."

We rose, shook him by the hand, and went out presently into the night and the quiet of the Embankment, and so to our homes.

If you enjoyed this, you might also like...
The Goddess of Death, see page 286
The Horse of the Invisible, see page 48

The Haunted 'Jarvee'

"SEEN ANYTHING of Carnacki lately?" I asked Arkright when we met in the City.

"No," he replied. "He's probably off on one of his jaunts. We'll be having a card one of these days inviting us to No. 472, Cheyne Walk, and then we'll hear all about it. Queer chap that."

He nodded, and went on his way. It was some months now since we four – Jessop, Arkright, Taylor and myself – had received the usual summons to drop in at No. 472 and hear Carnacki's story of his latest case. What talks they were! Stories of all kinds and true in every word, yet full of weird and extraordinary incidents that held one silent and awed until he had finished.

Strangely enough, the following morning brought me a curtly worded card telling me to be at No. 472 at seven o'clock promptly. I was the first to arrive, Jessop and Taylor soon followed and just before dinner was announced Arkright came in.

Dinner over, Carnacki as usual passed round his smokes, snuggled himself down luxuriously in his favourite armchair and went straight to the story we knew he had invited us to hear.

"I've been on a trip in one of the real old-time sailing ships," he said without any preliminary remarks. "The *Jarvee*, owned by my old friend Captain Thompson. I went on the voyage primarily for my health, but I picked on the old *Jarvee* because Captain Thompson had often told me there was something queer about her. I used to ask him up here whenever he came ashore and try to get him to tell me more about it, you know; but the funny thing was he never could tell me anything definite concerning her queerness. He seemed always to know but when it came to putting his knowledge into words it was as if he found that the reality melted out of it. He would end up usually by saying that you saw things and then he would wave his hands vaguely, but further than that he never seemed able to pass on the knowledge of something strange which he had noticed about the ship, except odd outside details.

"'Can't keep men in her no-how,' he often told me. 'They get frightened and they see things and they feel things. An' I've lost a power o' men out of her. Fallen from aloft, you know. She's getting a bad name.' And then he'd shake his head very solemnly.

"Old Thompson was a brick in every way. When I got aboard I found that he had given me the use of a whole empty cabin opening off my own as my laboratory and workshop. He gave the carpenter orders to fit up the empty cabin with shelves and other conveniences according to my directions and in a couple of days I had all the apparatus, both mechanical and electric with which I had conducted my other ghost-hunts, neatly and safely stowed away, for I took a great deal of gear with me as I intended to interest myself by examining thoroughly into the mystery about which the captain was at once so positive and so vague.

"During the first fortnight out I followed my usual methods of making a thorough and exhaustive search. This I did with the most scrupulous care, but found nothing abnormal of any kind in the whole vessel. She was an old wooden ship and I took care to sound and measure every casement and bulkhead, to examine every exit from the holds and to seal all the hatches. These and many other precautions I took, but at the end of the fortnight I had neither seen anything nor found anything.

"The old barque was just, to all seeming, a healthy, average old-timer jogging along comfortably from one port to another. And save for an indefinable sense of what I could now describe as 'abnormal peace' about the ship I could find nothing to justify the old captain's solemn and frequent assurances that I would see soon enough for myself. This he would say often as we walked the poop together; afterwards stopping to take a long, expectant, half-fearful look at the immensity of the sea around.

"Then on the eighteenth day something truly happened. I had been pacing the poop as usual with old Thompson when suddenly he stopped and looked up at the mizzen royal which had just begun to flap against the mast. He glanced at the wind-vane near him, then ruffled his hat back and stared at the sea.

"'Wind's droppin', mister. There'll be trouble tonight,' he said. 'D'you see yon?' And he pointed away to windward.

"'What?' I asked, staring with a curious little thrill that was due to more than curiosity. 'Where?'

"'Right off the beam,' he said. 'Comin' from under the sun.'

"'I don't see anything,' I explained after a long stare at the wide-spreading silence of the sea that was already glassing into a dead calm surface now that the wind had died.

"'Yon shadow fixin',' said the old man, reaching for his glasses.

"He focussed them and took a long look, then passed them across to me and pointed with his finger. 'Just under the sun,' he repeated. 'Comin' towards us at the rate o' knots.' He was curiously calm and matter-of-fact and yet I felt that a certain excitement had him in the throat; so that I took the glasses eagerly and stared according to his directions.

"After a minute I saw it – a vague shadow upon the still surface of the sea that seemed to move towards us as I stared. For a moment I gazed fascinated, yet ready every moment to swear that I saw nothing and in the same instant to be assured that there was truly something out there upon the water, apparently coming towards the ship.

"'It's only a shadow, captain,' I said at length.

"'Just so, mister,' he replied simply. 'Have a look over the stern to the norrard.' He spoke in the quietest way, as a man speaks who is sure of all his facts and who is facing an experience he has faced before, yet who salts his natural matter-of-factness with a deep and constant excitement.

"At the captain's hint I turned about and directed the glasses to the northward. For a while I searched, sweeping my aided vision to and fro over the greying arc of the sea.

"Then I saw the thing plain in the field of the glass – a vague something, a shadow upon the water and the shadow seemed to be moving towards the ship.

"'That's queer,' I muttered with a funny little stirring at the back of my throat.

"'Now to the west'ard, mister,' said the captain, still speaking in his peculiar level way.

"I looked to the westward and in a minute I picked up the thing – a third shadow that seemed to move across the sea as I watched it.

"'My God, captain,' I exclaimed, 'what does it mean?'

"'That's just what I want to know, mister,' said the captain. 'I've seen 'em before and thought sometimes I must be going mad. Sometimes they're plain an' sometimes they're scarce to be seen, an' sometimes they're like livin' things, an' sometimes they're like nought at all but silly fancies. D' you wonder I couldn't name 'em proper to you?'

"I did not answer for I was staring now expectantly towards the south along the length of the barque. Afar off on the horizon my glasses picked up something dark and vague upon the surface of the sea, a shadow it seemed which grew plainer.

"'My God!' I muttered again. 'This is real. This—' I turned again to the eastward.

"'Comin' in from the four points, ain't they,' said Captain Thompson and he blew his whistle.

"'Take them three r'yals off her,' he told the mate, 'an' tell one of the boys to shove lanterns up on the sherpoles. Get the men down smart before dark,' he concluded as the mate moved off to see the orders carried out.

"'I'm sendin' no men aloft tonight,' he said to me. 'I've lost enough that way.'

"'They may be only shadows, captain, after all,' I said, still looking earnestly at that far-off grey vagueness on the eastward sea. 'Bit of mist or cloud floating low.' Yet though I said this I had no belief that it was so. And as for old Captain Thompson, he never took the trouble to answer, but reached for his glasses which I passed to him.

"'Gettin' thin an' disappearin' as they come near,' he said presently. 'I know, I've seen 'em do that oft an' plenty before. They'll be close round the ship soon but you nor me won't see them, nor no one else, but they'll be there. I wish 'twas mornin'. I do that!'

"He had handed the glasses back to me and I had been staring at each of the oncoming shadows in turn. It was as Captain Thompson had said. As they drew nearer they seemed to spread and thin out and presently to become dissipated into the grey of the gloaming so that I could easily have imagined that I watched merely four little portions of grey cloud, expanding naturally into impalpableness and invisibility.

"'Wish I'd took them t'gallants off her while I was about it,' remarked the old man presently. 'Can't think to send no one off the decks tonight, not unless there's real need.' He slipped away from me and peered at the aneroid in the skylight. 'Glass steady, anyhow,' he muttered as he came away, seeming more satisfied.

"By this time the men had all returned to the decks and the night was down upon us so that I could watch the queer, dissolving shadows which approached the ship.

"Yet as I walked the poop with old Captain Thompson, you can imagine how I grew to feel. Often I found myself looking over my shoulder with quick, jerky glances; for it seemed to me that in the curtains of gloom that hung just beyond the rails there must be a vague, incredible thing looking inboard.

"I questioned the captain in a thousand ways, but could get little out of him beyond what I knew. It was as if he had no power to convey to another the knowledge which he possessed and I could ask no one else, for every other man in the ship was newly signed on, including the mates, which was in itself a significant fact.

"'You'll see for yourself, mister,' was the refrain with which the captain parried my questions, so that it began to seem as if he almost feared to put anything he knew into words. Yet once, when I had jerked round with a nervous feeling that something was at my back he said calmly enough: 'Naught to fear, mister, whilst you're in the light and on the decks.' His attitude was extraordinary in the way in which he accepted the situation. He appeared to have no personal fear.

"The night passed quietly until about eleven o'clock when suddenly and without one atom of warning a furious squall burst on the vessel. There was something monstrous and abnormal in the wind; it was as if some power were using the elements to an infernal purpose. Yet the captain met the situation calmly. The helm was put down and the sails shaken while the three t'gallants were lowered. Then the three upper topsails. Yet still the breeze roared over us, almost drowning the thunder which the sails were making in the night.

"'Split 'em to ribbons!' the captain yelled in my ear above the noise of the wind. 'Can't help it. I ain't sendin' no men aloft tonight unless she seems like to shake the sticks out of her. That's what bothers me.'

"For nearly an hour after that, until eight bells went at midnight, the wind showed no signs of easing but breezed up harder than ever. And all the while the skipper and I walked the poop, he ever and again peering up anxiously through the darkness at the banging and thrashing sails.

"For my part I could do nothing except stare round and round at the extraordinarily dark night in which the ship seemed to be embedded solidly. The very feel and sound of the wind gave me a sort of constant horror, for there seemed to be an unnaturalness rampant in the atmosphere. But how much this was the effect of my over-strung nerves and excited imagination, I cannot say. Certainly, in all my experience I had never come across anything just like what I felt and endured through that peculiar squall.

"At eight bells when the other watch came on deck the captain was forced to send all hands aloft to make the canvas fast, as he had begun to fear that he would actually lose his masts if he delayed longer. This was done and the barque snugged right down.

"Yet, though the work was done successfully, the captain's fears were justified in a sufficiently horrible way, for as the men were beginning to make their way in off the wards there was a loud crying and shouting aloft and immediately afterwards a crash down on the main deck, followed instantly by a second crash.

"'My God! Two of 'em!' shouted the skipper as he snatched a lamp from the forrard binnacle. Then down on to the main deck. It was as he had said. Two of the men had fallen, or – as the thought came to me – been thrown from aloft and were lying silent on the deck. Above us in the darkness I heard a few vague shouts followed by a curious quiet, save for the constant blast of the wind whose whistling and howling in the rigging seemed but to accentuate the complete and frightened silence of the men aloft. Then I was aware that the men were coming down swiftly and presently one after the other came with a quick leap out of the rigging and stood about the two fallen men with odd exclamations and questions which always merged off instantly into new silence.

"And all the time I was conscious of a most extraordinary sense of oppression and frightened distress and fearful expectation, for it seemed to me, standing there near the dead in that unnatural wind that a power of evil filled all the night about the ship and that some fresh horror was imminent.

"The following morning there was a solemn little service, very rough and crude, but undertaken with a nice reverence and the two men who had fallen were tilted off from a hatch-cover and plunged suddenly out of sight. As I watched them vanish in the deep blue of the water an idea came to me and I spent part of the afternoon talking it over with the captain, after which I passed the rest of the time until sunset was upon us in arranging and fitting up a part of my electrical apparatus. Then I went on deck and had a good look round. The evening was beautifully calm and ideal for the experiment which I had in mind, for the wind had died away with a peculiar suddenness after the death of the two men and all that day the sea had been like glass.

"To a certain extent I believed that I comprehended the primary cause of the vague but peculiar manifestations which I had witnessed the previous evening and which Captain Thompson believed implicitly to be intimately connected with the death of the two sailormen.

"I believed the origin of the happenings to lie in a strange but perfectly understandable cause, i.e., in that phenomenon known technically as 'attractive vibrations'. Harzam, in his monograph on 'Induced Hauntings', points out that such are invariably produced by 'induced vibrations', that is, by temporary vibrations set up by some outside cause.

"This is somewhat abstruse to follow out in a story of this kind, but it was on a long consideration of these points that I had resolved to make experiments to see whether I could not produce a counter or 'repellent' vibration, a thing which Harzam had succeeded in producing on three occasions and in which I have had a partial success once, failing only because of the imperfectness of the apparatus I had aboard.

"As I have said, I can scarcely follow the reasoning further in a brief record such as this, neither do I think it would be of interest to you who are interested only in the startling and weird side of my investigations. Yet I have told you sufficient to show you the germ of my reasonings and to enable you to follow intelligently my hopes and expectations in sending out what I hoped would prove 'repellent' vibrations.

"Therefore it was that when the sun had descended to within ten degrees of the visible horizon the captain and I began to watch for the appearance of the shadows. Presently, under the sun, I discovered the same peculiar appearance of a moving greyness which I had seen on the preceding night and almost immediately Captain Thompson told me that he saw the same to the south.

"To the north and east we perceived the same extraordinary thing and I at once set my electric apparatus at work, sending out the strange repelling force to the dim, far shadows of mystery which moved steadily out of the distance towards the vessel.

"Earlier in the evening the captain had snugged the barque right down to her topsails, for as he said, until the calm went he would risk nothing. According to him it was always during calm weather that the extraordinary manifestations occurred. In this case he was certainly justified, for a most tremendous squall struck the ship in the middle watch, taking the fore upper topsail right out of the ropes.

"At the time when it came I was lying down on a locker in the saloon, but I ran up on to the poop as the vessel canted under the enormous force of the wind. Here I found the air pressure tremendous and the noise of the squall stunning. And over it all and through it all I was conscious of something abnormal and threatening that set my nerves uncomfortably acute. The thing was not natural.

"Yet, despite the carrying away of the topsail, not a man was sent aloft.

"'Let 'em all go!' said old Captain Thompson. 'I'd have shortened her down to the bare sticks if I'd done all I wanted!'

"About two a.m. the squall passed with astonishing suddenness and the night showed clear above the vessel. From then onward I paced the poop with the skipper, often pausing at the break to look along the lighted main deck. It was on one of these occasions that I saw something peculiar. It was like a vague flitting of an impossible shadow between me and the whiteness of the well-scrubbed decks. Yet, even as I stared, the thing was gone and I could not say with surety that I had seen anything.

"'Pretty plain to see, mister,' said the captain's voice at my elbow. 'I've only seen that once before an' we lost half of the hands that trip. We'd better be at 'ome, I'm thinkin'. It'll end in scrappin' her, sure.'

"The old man's calmness bewildered me almost as much as the confirmation his remark gave that I had really seen something abnormal floating between me and the deck eight feet below us.

"'Good lord, Captain Thompson,' I exclaimed, 'this is simply infernal!'

"'Just that,' he agreed. 'I said, mister, you'd see if you'd wait. And this ain't the half. You wait till you sees 'em looking like little black clouds all over the sea round the ship and movin' steady with the ship. All the same, I ain't seen 'em aboard but the once. Guess we're in for it.'

"'How do you mean?' I asked. But though I questioned him in every way I could get nothing satisfactory out of him.

"'You'll see, mister. You wait an' see. She's a queer un.' And that was about the extent of his further efforts and methods of enlightening me.

"From then on through the rest of the watch I leaned over the break of the poop, staring down at the maindeck and odd whiles taking quick glances to the rear. The skipper had resumed his steady pacing of the poop, but now and again he would come to a pause beside me and ask calmly enough whether I had seen any more of 'them there'.

"Several times I saw the vagueness of something drifting in the lights of the lanterns and a sort of wavering in the air in this place and that, as if it might be an attenuated something having movement, that was half-seen for a moment and then gone before my brain could record anything definite.

"Towards the end of the watch, however, both the captain and I saw something very extraordinary. He had just come beside me and was leaning over the rail across the break. 'Another of 'em there,' he remarked in his calm way, giving me a gentle nudge and nodding his head towards the port side of the maindeck, a yard or two to our left.

"In the place he had indicated there was a faint, dull shadowy spot seeming suspended about a foot above the deck. This grew more visible and there was movement in it and a constant, oily-seeming whirling from the centre outwards. The thing expanded to several feet across, with the lighted planks of the deck showing vaguely through. The movement from the centre outwards was now becoming very distinct, till the whole strange shape blackened and grew more dense, so that the deck below was hidden.

"Then as I stared with the most intense interest there went a thinning movement over the thing and almost directly it had dissolved so that there was nothing more to be seen than a vague rounded shape of shadow, hovering and convoluting dimly between us and the deck below. This gradually thinned out and vanished and we were both of us left staring down at a piece of the deck where the planking and pitched seams showed plain and distinct in the light from the lamps that were now hung nightly on the sherpoles.

"'Mighty queer that, mister,' said the captain meditatively as he fumbled for his pipe. 'Mighty queer.' Then he lit his pipe and began again his pacing of the poop.

"The calm lasted for a week with the sea like glass and every night without warning there was a repetition of the extraordinary squall, so that the captain had everything made fast at dusk and waited patiently for a trade wind.

"Each evening I experimented further with my attempts to set up 'repellent' vibrations, but without result. I am not sure whether I ought to say that my meddling produced no result; for the calm gradually assumed a more unnatural permanent aspect whilst the sea looked more than ever like a plain of glass, bulged anon with the low oily roll of some deep swell. For the rest, there was by day a silence so profound as to give a sense of unrealness, for never a sea-bird hove in sight whilst the movement of the vessel was so slight as scarce to keep up the constant creak, creak of spars and gear, which is the ordinary accompaniment of a calm.

"The sea appeared to have become an emblem of desolation and freeness, so that it seemed to me at last that there was no more any known world, but just one great ocean going on for ever into the far distances in every direction. At night the strange squalls assumed a far greater violence so that sometimes it seemed as if the very spars would be ripped and twisted out of the vessel, yet fortunately no harm came in that wise.

"As the days passed I became convinced at last that my experiments were producing very distinct results, though the opposite to those which I hoped to produce, for now at each sunset a sort of grey cloud resembling light smoke would appear far away in every quarter almost immediately upon the commencement of the vibrations, with the effect that I desisted from any prolonged attempt and became more tentative in my experiments.

"At last, however, when we had endured this condition of affairs for a week, I had a long talk with old Captain Thompson and he agreed to let me carry out a bold experiment to its conclusion. It was to keep the vibrations going steadily at full power from a little before sunset until the dawn and to take careful notes of the results.

"With this in view, all was made ready. The royal and t'gallant yards were sent down, all the sails stowed and everything about the decks made fast. A sea anchor was rigged out over the bows and a long line of cable veered away. This was to ensure the vessel coming head to wind should one of those strange squalls strike us from any quarter during the night.

"Late in the afternoon the men were sent into the fo'c'sle and told that they might please themselves and turn in or do anything they liked, but that they were not to come on deck during the night whatever happened. To ensure this the port and starboard doors were padlocked. Afterwards I made the first and the eighth signs of the Saaamaaa Ritual opposite each door-post, connecting them with triple lines crossed at every seventh inch. You've dipped deeper into the science of magic than I have, Arkright, and you will know what that means. Following this I ran a wire entirely around the outside of the fo'c'sle and connected it up with my machinery, which I had erected in the sail-locker aft.

"'In any case,' I explained to the captain, 'they run practically no risk other than the general risk which we may expect in the form of a terrific storm-burst. The real danger will be to those who are 'meddling'. The 'path of the vibrations' will make a kind of 'halo' round the apparatus. I shall have to be there to control and I'm willing to risk it, but you'd better get into your cabin and the three mates must do the same.'

"This the old captain refused to do and the three mates begged to be allowed to stay and 'see the fun'. I warned them very seriously that there might be a very disagreeable and unavoidable danger, but they agreed to risk it and I can tell you I was not sorry to have their companionship.

"I set to work then, making them help where I needed help, and so presently I had all my gear in order. Then I led my wires up through the skylight from the cabin and set the vibrator dial and trembler-box level, screwing them solidly down to the poop-deck, in the clear space that lay between the foreside of the skylight and the lid of the sail locker.

"I got the three mates and the captain to take their places close together and I warned them not to move whatever happened. I set to work then, alone, and chalked a temporary pentacle about the whole lot of us, including the apparatus. Afterwards I made haste to get the tubes of my electric pentacle fitted all about us, for it was getting on to dusk. As soon as this was done I switched on the current into the vacuum tubes and immediately the pale sickly glare shone dull all about us, seeming cold and unreal in the last light of the evening.

"Immediately afterwards I set the vibrations beating out into all space and then I took my seat beside the control board. Here I had a few words with the others, warning them again whatever they might hear or see not to leave the pentacle, if they valued their lives. They nodded to this and I knew that they were fully impressed with the possibility of the unknown danger that we were meddling with.

"Then we settled down to watch. We were all in our oilskins, for I expected the experiment to include some very peculiar behaviour on the part of the elements and so we were ready to face the night. One other thing I was careful to do and that was to confiscate all matches so that no one should forgetfully light his pipe, for the light rays are 'paths' to certain of the Forces.

"With a pair of marine glasses I was staring round at the horizon. All around, but miles away in the greying of the evening, there seemed to be a strange, vague darkening of the surface of the sea. This became more distinct and it seemed to me presently that it might be a slight, low-lying mist far away about the ship. I watched it very intently and the captain and the three mates were doing likewise through their glasses.

"'Coming in on us at the rate o' knots, mister,' said the old man in a low voice. 'This is what I call playin' with 'ell. I only hope it'll all come right.' That was all he said and afterwards there was absolute silence from him and the others through the strange hours that followed.

"As the night stole down upon the sea we lost sight of the peculiar incoming circle of mist and there was a period of the most intense and oppressive silence to the five of us, sitting there watchful and quiet within the pale glow of the electric pentacle.

"A while later there came a sort of strange, noiseless lightning. By noiseless I mean that while the flashes appeared to be near at hand and lit up all the vague sea around, yet there was no thunder; neither, so it appeared to me, did there seem to be any reality in the flashes. This is a queer thing to say but it describes my impressions. It was as if I saw a representation of lightning rather than the physical electricity itself. No, of course, I am not pretending to use the word in its technical sense.

"Abruptly a strange quivering went through the vessel from end to end and died away. I looked fore and aft and then glanced at the four men who stared back at me with a sort of dumb and half-frightened wonder, but no one said anything. About five minutes passed with no sound anywhere except the faint buzz of the apparatus and nothing visible anywhere except the noiseless lightning which came down, flash after flash, lighting the sea all around the vessel.

"Then a most extraordinary thing happened. The peculiar quivering passed again through the ship and died away. It was followed immediately by a kind of undulation of the vessel, first fore and aft and then from side to side. I can give you no better illustration of the strangeness of the movement on that glass-like sea than to say that it was just such a movement as might have been given her had an invisible giant hand lifted her and toyed with her, canting her this way and that with a certain curious and rather sickening rhythm of movement. This appeared to last about two minutes, so far as I can guess, and ended with the ship being shaken up and down several times, after which there came again the quivering and then quietness.

"A full hour must have passed during which I observed nothing except that twice the vessel was faintly shaken and the second time this was followed by a slight repetition of the curious undulations. This, however, lasted but a few seconds and afterwards there was only the abnormal and oppressive silence of the night, punctured time after time by these noiseless flashes of lightning. All the time I did my best to study the appearance of the sea and atmosphere around the ship.

"One thing was apparent, that the surrounding wall of vagueness had drawn in more upon the ship, so that the brightest flashes now showed me no more than about a clear quarter of a mile of ocean around us, after which the sight was just lost in trying to penetrate a kind of shadowy distance that yet had no depth in it, but which still lacked any power to arrest the vision at any particular point so that one could not know definitely whether there was anything there or not, but only that one's sight was limited by some phenomenon which hid all the distant sea. Do I make this clear?

"The strange, noiseless lightning increased in vividness and the flashes began to come more frequently. This went on till they were almost continuous, so that all the near sea could be watched with scarce an intermission. Yet the brightness of the flashes seemed to have no power to dull the pale light of the curious detached glows that circled in silent multitudes about us.

"About this time I became aware of a strange sense of breathlessness. Each breath seemed to be drawn with difficulty and presently with a sense of positive distress. The three mates and the captain were breathing with curious little gasps and the faint buzz of the vibrator seemed to come from a great distance away. For the rest there was such a silence as made itself known like a dull, numbing ache upon the brain.

"The minutes passed slowly and then, abruptly, I saw something new. There were grey things floating in the air about the ship which were so vague and attenuated that at first I could not be sure that I saw anything, but in a while there could be no doubt that they were there.

"They began to show plainer in the constant glare of the quiet lightning and growing darker and darker they increased visibly in size. They appeared to be but a few feet above the level of the sea and they began to assume humped shapes.

"For quite half an hour, which seemed indefinitely longer, I watched those strange humps like little hills of blackness floating just above the surface of the water and moving round and round the vessel with a slow, everlasting circling that produced on my eyes the feeling that it was all a dream.

"It was later still that I discovered still another thing. Each of those great vague mounds had begun to oscillate as it circled round about us. I was conscious at the same time that there was communicated to the vessel the beginning of a similar oscillating movement, so very slight at first that I could scarcely be sure she so much as moved.

"The movement of the ship grew with a steady oscillation, the bows lifting first and then the stern, as if she were pivoted amidships. This ceased and she settled down on to a level keel with a series of queer jerks as if her weight were being slowly lowered again to the buoying of the water.

"Suddenly there came a cessation of the extraordinary lightning and we were in an absolute blackness with only the pale sickly glow of the electric pentacle above us and the faint buzz of the apparatus seeming far away in the night. Can you picture it all? The five of us there, tense and watchful and wondering what was going to happen.

"The thing began gently – a little jerk upward of the starboard side of the vessel, then a second jerk, then a third and the whole ship was canted distinctly to port. It continued in a kind of slow rhythmic tilting with curious timed pauses between the jerks and suddenly, you know, I saw that we were in absolute danger, for the vessel was being capsized by some enormous Force in the utter silence and blackness of that night.

""My God, mister, stop it!" came the captain's voice, quick and very hoarse. "She'll be gone in a moment! She'll be gone!"

"He had got on to his knees and was staring round and gripping at the deck. The three mates were also gripping at the deck with their palms to stop them from sliding down the violent slope. In that moment came a final tilting of the side of the vessel and the deck rose up almost like a wall. I snatched at the lever of the vibrator and switched it over.

"Instantly the angle of the deck decreased as the vessel righted several feet with a jerk. The righting movement continued with little rhythmic jerks until the ship was once more on an even keel.

"And even as she righted I was aware of an alteration in the tenseness of the atmosphere and a great noise far off to starboard. It was the roaring of wind. A huge flash of lightning was followed by others and the thunder crashed continually overhead. The noise of the wind to starboard rose to a loud screaming and drove towards us through the night. Then the lightning ceased and the deep roll of the thunder was lost in the nearer sound of the wind which was now within a mile of us and making a most hideous, bellowing scream. The shrill howling came at us out of the dark and covered every other sound. It was as if all the night on that side were a vast cliff, sending down high and monstrous echoes upon us. This is a queer thing to say, I know, but it may help you to get the feeling of the thing; for that just describes exactly how it felt to me at the time – that queer, echoing, empty sense above us in the night, yet all the emptiness filled with sound on high. Do you get it? It was most extraordinary and there was a grand something about it all as if one had come suddenly upon the steeps of some monstrous lost world.

"Then the wind rushed out at us and stunned us with its sound and force and fury. We were smothered and half-stunned. The vessel went over on to her port side merely from pressure of the wind on her naked spars and side. The whole night seemed one yell and the foam roared and snowed over us in countless tonnes. I have never known anything like it. We were all splayed about the poop, holding on to anything we could, while the pentacle was smashed to atoms so that we were in complete darkness. The storm-burst had come down on us.

"Towards morning the storm calmed and by evening we were running before a fine breeze; yet the pumps had to be kept going steadily for we had sprung a pretty bad leak, which proved so serious that we had to take to the boats two days later. However, we were picked up that night so that we had only a short time of it. As for the *Jarvee*, she is now safely at the bottom of the Atlantic, where she had better remain forever."

Carnacki came to an end and tapped out his pipe.

"But you haven't explained," I remonstrated. "What made her like that? What made her different from other ships? Why did those shadows and things come to her? What's your idea?"

"Well," replied Carnacki, "in my opinion she was a focus. That is a technical term which I can best explain by saying that she possessed the 'attractive vibration' that is the power to draw to her any psychic waves in the vicinity, much in the way of a medium. The way in which the 'vibration' is acquired – to use a technical term again – is, of course, purely a matter for supposition. She may have developed it during the years, owing to a suitability of conditions or it may have been in her ('of her' is a better term) from the very day her keel was laid. I mean the direction in which she lay the condition of the atmosphere, the state of the 'electric tensions', the very blows of the hammers and the accidental combining of materials suited to such an end – all might tend to such a thing. And this is only to speak of the known. The vast unknown it is vain to speculate upon in a brief chatter like this.

"I would like to remind you here of that idea of mine that certain forms of so-called 'hauntings' may have their cause in the 'attractive vibrations'. A building or a ship – just as I have indicated – may develop 'vibrations', even as certain materials in combination under the proper conditions will certainly develop an electric current.

"To say more in a talk of this scope is useless. I am more inclined to remind you of the glass which will vibrate to a certain note struck upon a piano and to silence all your worrying questions with that simple little unanswered one: What is electricity? When we've got that clear it will be time to take the next step in a more dogmatic fashion. We are but speculating on the coasts of a strange country of mystery. In this case, I think the next best step for you all will be home and bed."

And with this terse ending, in the most genial way possible, Carnacki ushered us out presently on to the quiet chill of the Embankment, replying heartily to our various goodnights.

If you enjoyed this, you might also like…

The Hog, see page 402
The Derelict, see page 349

Dangers
at Sea

A Tropical Horror

WE ARE a hundred and thirty days out from Melbourne, and for three weeks we have lain in this sweltering calm.

It is midnight, and our watch on deck until four a.m. I go out and sit on the hatch. A minute later, Joky, our youngest 'prentice, joins me for a chatter. Many are the hours we have sat thus and talked in the night watches; though, to be sure, it is Joky who does the talking. I am content to smoke and listen, giving an occasional grunt at seasons to show that I am attentive.

Joky has been silent for some time, his head bent in meditation. Suddenly he looks up, evidently with the intention of making some remark. As he does so, I see his face stiffen with a nameless horror. He crouches back, his eyes staring past me at some unseen fear. Then his mouth opens. He gives forth a strangulated cry and topples backward off the hatch, striking his head against the deck. Fearing I know not what, I turn to look.

Great Heavens! Rising above the bulwarks, seen plainly in the bright moonlight, is a vast slobbering mouth a fathom across. From the huge dripping lips hang great tentacles. As I look the Thing comes further over the rail. It is rising, rising, higher and higher. There are no eyes visible; only that fearful slobbering mouth set on the tremendous trunk-like neck; which, even as I watch, is curling inboard with the stealthy celerity of an enormous eel. Over it comes in vast heaving folds. Will it never end? The ship gives a slow, sullen roll to starboard as she feels the weight. Then the tail, a broad, flat-shaped mass, slips over the teak rail and falls with a loud slump on to the deck.

For a few seconds the hideous creature lies heaped in writhing, slimy coils. Then, with quick, darting movements, the monstrous head travels along the deck. Close by the mainmast stand the harness casks, and alongside of these a freshly opened cask of salt beef with the top loosely replaced. The smell of the meat seems to attract the monster, and I can hear it sniffing with a vast indrawing breath. Then those lips open, displaying four huge fangs; there is a quick forward motion of the head, a sudden crashing, crunching sound, and beef and barrel have disappeared. The noise brings one of the ordinary seamen out of the fo'cas'le. Coming into the night, he can see nothing for a moment. Then, as he gets further aft, he sees, and with horrified cries rushes forward. Too late! From the mouth of the Thing there flashes forth a long, broad blade of glistening white, set with fierce teeth. I avert my eyes, but cannot shut out the sickening "Glut! Glut!" that follows.

The man on the 'look-out', attracted by the disturbance, has witnessed the tragedy, and flies for refuge into the fo'cas'le, flinging to the heavy iron door after him.

The carpenter and sailmaker come running out from the half-deck in their drawers. Seeing the awful Thing, they rush aft to the cabin with shouts of fear. The second mate, after one glance over the break of the poop, runs down the companion-way with the helmsman after him. I can hear them barring the scuttle, and abruptly I realise that I am on the main deck alone.

So far I have forgotten my own danger. The past few minutes seem like a portion of an awful dream. Now, however, I comprehend my position and, shaking off the horror that has held me, turn to seek safety. As I do so my eyes fall upon Joky, lying huddled and senseless with fright where he has fallen. I cannot leave him there. Close by stands the empty half-deck – a little steel-built house with iron doors. The lee one is hooked open. Once inside I am safe.

Up to the present the Thing has seemed to be unconscious of my presence. Now, however, the huge barrel-like head sways in my direction; then comes a muffled bellow, and the great tongue flickers in and out as the brute turns and swirls aft to meet me. I know there is not a moment to lose, and, picking up the helpless lad, I make a run for the open door. It is only distant a few yards, but that awful shape is coming down the deck to me in great wreathing coils. I reach the house and tumble in with my burden; then out on deck again to unhook and close the door. Even as I do so something white curls round the end of the house. With a bound I am inside and the door is shut and bolted. Through the thick glass of the ports I see the Thing sweep round the house, in vain search for me.

Joky has not moved yet; so, kneeling down, I loosen his shirt collar and sprinkle some water from the breaker over his face. While I am doing this I hear Morgan shout something; then comes a great shriek of terror, and again that sickening "Glut! Glut!"

Joky stirs uneasily, rubs his eyes, and sits up suddenly.

"Was that Morgan shouting—?" He breaks off with a cry. "Where are we? I have had such awful dreams!"

At this instant there is a sound of running footsteps on the deck and I hear Morgan's voice at the door.

"Tom, open—!"

He stops abruptly and gives an awful cry of despair. Then I hear him rush forward. Through the porthole, I see him spring into the fore rigging and scramble madly aloft. Something steals up after him. It shows white in the moonlight. It wraps itself around his right ankle. Morgan stops dead, plucks out his sheath-knife, and hacks fiercely at the fiendish thing. It lets go, and in a second he is over the top and running for dear life up the t'gallant rigging.

A time of quietness follows, and presently I see that the day is breaking. Not a sound can be heard save the heavy gasping breathing of the Thing. As the sun rises higher the creature stretches itself out along the deck and seems to enjoy the warmth. Still no sound, either from the men forward or the officers aft. I can only suppose that they are afraid of attracting its attention. Yet, a little later, I hear the report of a pistol away aft, and looking out I see the serpent raise its huge head as though listening. As it does so I get a good view of the fore part, and in the daylight see what the night has hidden.

There, right about the mouth, is a pair of little pig-eyes, that seem to twinkle with a diabolical intelligence. It is swaying its head slowly from side to side; then, without warning, it turns quickly and looks right in through the port. I dodge out of sight; but not soon enough. It has seen me, and brings its great mouth up against the glass.

I hold my breath. My God! If it breaks the glass! I cower, horrified. From the direction of the port there comes a loud, harsh, scraping sound. I shiver. Then I remember that there are little iron doors to shut over the ports in bad weather. Without a moment's waste of time I rise to my feet and slam to the door over the port. Then I go round to the others and do the same. We are now in darkness, and I tell Joky in a whisper to light the lamp, which, after some fumbling, he does.

About an hour before midnight I fall asleep. I am awakened suddenly some hours later by a scream of agony and the rattle of a water-dipper. There is a slight scuffling sound; then that soul-revolting "Glut! Glut!"

I guess what has happened. One of the men forrad has slipped out of the fo'cas'le to try and get a little water. Evidently he has trusted to the darkness to hide his movements. Poor beggar! He has paid for his attempt with his life!

After this I cannot sleep, though the rest of the night passes quietly enough. Towards morning I doze a bit, but wake every few minutes with a start. Joky is sleeping peacefully; indeed, he seems worn out with the terrible strain of the past twenty-four hours. About eight a.m. I call him, and we make a light breakfast off the dry ship's biscuit and water. Of the latter happily we have a good supply. Joky seems more himself, and starts to talk a little – possibly somewhat louder than is safe; for, as he chatters on, wondering how it will end, there comes a tremendous blow against the side of the house, making it ring again. After this Joky is very silent. As we sit there I cannot but wonder what all the rest are doing, and how the poor beggars forrad are faring, cooped up without water, as the tragedy of the night has proved.

Towards noon, I hear a loud bang, followed by a terrific bellowing. Then comes a great smashing of woodwork, and the cries of men in pain. Vainly I ask myself what has happened. I begin to reason. By the sound of the report it was evidently something much heavier than a rifle or pistol, and judging from the mad roaring of the Thing, the shot must have done some execution. On thinking it over further, I become convinced that, by some means, those aft have got hold of the small signal cannon we carry, and though I know that some have been hurt, perhaps killed, yet a feeling of exultation seizes me as I listen to the roars of the Thing, and realise that it is badly wounded, perhaps mortally. After a while, however, the bellowing dies away, and only an occasional roar, denoting more of anger than aught else, is heard.

Presently I become aware, by the ship's canting over to starboard, that the creature has gone over to that side, and a great hope springs up within me that possibly it has had enough of us and is going over the rail into the sea. For a time all is silent and my hope grows stronger. I lean across and nudge Joky, who is sleeping with his head on the table. He starts up sharply with a loud cry.

"Hush!" I whisper hoarsely. "I'm not certain, but I do believe it's gone."

Joky's face brightens wonderfully, and he questions me eagerly. We wait another hour or so, with hope ever rising. Our confidence is returning fast. Not a sound can we hear, not even the breathing of the Beast. I get out some biscuits, and Joky, after rummaging in the locker, produces a small piece of pork and a bottle of ship's vinegar. We fall to with a relish. After our long abstinence from food the meal acts on us like wine, and what must Joky do but insist on opening the door, to make sure the Thing has gone. This I will not allow, telling him that at least it will be safer to open the iron port-covers first and have a look out. Joky argues, but I am immovable. He becomes excited. I believe the youngster is lightheaded. Then, as I turn to unscrew one of the after-covers, Joky makes a dash at the door. Before he can undo the bolts I have him, and after a short struggle lead him back to the table. Even as I endeavour to quieten him there comes at the starboard door – the door that Joky has tried to open – a sharp, loud sniff, sniff, followed immediately by a thunderous grunting howl and a foul stench of putrid breath sweeps in under the door. A great trembling takes me, and were it not for the carpenter's tool-chest I should fall. Joky turns very white and is violently sick, after which he is seized by a hopeless fit of sobbing.

Hour after hour passes, and, weary to death, I lie down on the chest upon which I have been sitting, and try to rest.

It must be about half-past two in the morning, after a somewhat longer doze, that I am suddenly awakened by a most tremendous uproar away forrad – men's voices shrieking, cursing, praying; but in spite of the terror expressed, so weak and feeble; while in the midst, and at times broken off short with that hellishly suggestive "Glut! Glut!" is the unearthly bellowing of the Thing. Fear incarnate seizes me, and I can only fall on my knees and pray. Too well I know what is happening.

Joky has slept through it all, and I am thankful.

Presently, under the door there steals a narrow ribbon of light, and I know that the day has broken on the second morning of our imprisonment. I let Joky sleep on. I will let him have peace while he may. Time passes, but I take little notice. The Thing is quiet, probably sleeping. About midday I eat a little biscuit and drink some of the water. Joky still sleeps. It is best so.

A sound breaks the stillness. The ship gives a slight heave, and I know that once more the Thing is awake. Round the deck it moves, causing the ship to roll perceptibly. Once it goes forrad – I fancy to again explore the fo'cas'le. Evidently it finds nothing, for it returns almost immediately. It pauses a moment at the house, then goes on further aft. Up aloft, somewhere in the fore-rigging, there rings out a peal of wild laughter, though sounding very faint and far away. The Horror stops suddenly. I listen intently, but hear nothing save a sharp creaking beyond the after end of the house, as though a strain had come upon the rigging.

A minute later I hear a cry aloft, followed almost instantly by a loud crash on deck that seems to shake the ship. I wait in anxious fear. What is happening? The minutes pass slowly. Then comes another frightened shout. It ceases suddenly. The suspense has become terrible, and I am no longer able to bear it. Very cautiously I open one of the after port-covers, and peep out to see a fearful sight. There, with its tail upon the deck and its vast body curled round the mainmast, is the monster, its head above the topsail yard, and its great claw-armed tentacle waving in the air. It is the first proper sight that I have had of the Thing. Good Heavens! It must weigh a hundred tonnes! Knowing that I shall have time, I open the port itself, then crane my head out and look up. There on the extreme end of the lower topsail yard I see one of the able seamen. Even down here I note the staring horror of his face. At this moment he sees me and gives a weak, hoarse cry for help. I can do nothing for him. As I look the great tongue shoots out and licks him off the yard, much as might a dog a fly off the window-pane.

Higher still, but happily out of reach, are two more of the men. As far as I can judge they are lashed to the mast above the royal yard. The Thing attempts to reach them, but after a futile effort it ceases, and starts to slide down, coil on coil, to the deck. While doing this I notice a great gaping wound on its body some twenty feet above the tail.

I drop my gaze from aloft and look aft. The cabin door is torn from its hinges, and the bulkhead – which, unlike the half-deck, is of teak wood – is partly broken down. With a shudder I realise the cause of those cries after the cannon-shot. Turning I screw my head round and try to see the foremast, but cannot. The sun, I notice, is low, and the night is near. Then I draw in my head and fasten up both port and cover.

How will it end? Oh! how will it end?

After a while Joky wakes up. He is very restless, yet though he has eaten nothing during the day I cannot get him to touch anything.

Night draws on. We are too weary – too dispirited to talk. I lie down, but not to sleep.... Time passes.

* * *

A ventilator rattles violently somewhere on the main deck, and there sounds constantly that slurring, gritty noise. Later I hear a cat's agonised howl, and then again all is quiet. Some time after comes a great splash alongside. Then, for some hours all is silent as the grave. Occasionally I sit up on the chest and listen, yet never a whisper of noise comes to me. There is an absolute silence, even the monotonous creak of the gear has died away entirely, and at last a real hope is springing up within me. That splash, this silence – surely I am justified in hoping. I do not wake Joky this time. I will prove first for myself that all is safe. Still I wait. I will run no unnecessary risks. After a time I creep to the after-port and will listen; but there is no sound. I put up my hand and feel at the screw, then again I hesitate, yet not for long. Noiselessly I begin to unscrew the fastening of the heavy shield. It swings loose on its hinge, and I pull it back and peer out. My heart is beating madly. Everything seems strangely dark outside. Perhaps the moon has gone behind a cloud. Suddenly a beam of moonlight enters through the port, and goes as quickly. I stare out. Something moves. Again the light streams in, and now I seem to be looking into a great cavern, at the bottom of which quivers and curls something palely white.

My heart seems to stand still! It is the Horror! I start back and seize the iron port-flap to slam it to. As I do so, something strikes the glass like a steam ram, shatters it to atoms, and flicks past me into the berth. I scream and spring away. The port is quite filled with it. The lamp shows it dimly. It is curling and twisting here and there. It is as thick as a tree, and covered with a smooth slimy skin. At the end is a great claw, like a lobster's, only a thousand times larger. I cower down into the farthest corner.... It has broken the tool-chest to pieces with one click of those frightful mandibles. Joky has crawled under a bunk. The Thing sweeps round in my direction. I feel a drop of sweat trickle slowly down my face – it tastes salty. Nearer comes that awful death.... Crash! I roll over backwards. It has crushed the water breaker against which I leant, and I am rolling in the water across the floor. The claw drives up, then down, with a quick uncertain movement, striking the deck a dull, heavy blow, a foot from my head. Joky gives a little gasp of horror. Slowly the Thing rises and starts feeling its way round the berth. It plunges into a bunk and pulls out a bolster, nips it in half and drops it, then moves on. It is feeling along the deck. As it does so it comes across a half of the bolster. It seems to toy with it, then picks it up and takes it out through the port....

A wave of putrid air fills the berth. There is a grating sound, and something enters the port again – something white and tapering and set with teeth. Hither and thither it curls, rasping over the bunks, ceiling, and deck, with a noise like that of a great saw at work. Twice it flickers above my head, and I close my eyes. Then off it goes again. It sounds now on the opposite side of the berth and nearer to Joky. Suddenly the harsh, raspy noise becomes muffled, as though the teeth were passing across some soft substance. Joky gives a horrid little scream, that breaks off into a bubbling, whistling sound. I open my eyes. The tip of the vast tongue is curled tightly round something that drips, then is quickly withdrawn, allowing the moonbeams to steal again into the berth. I rise to my feet. Looking round, I note in a mechanical sort of way the wrecked state of the berth – the shattered chests, dismantled bunks, and something else –

"Joky!" I cry, and tingle all over.

There is that awful Thing again at the port. I glance round for a weapon. I will revenge Joky. Ah! there, right under the lamp, where the wreck of the carpenter's chest strews the floor, lies a small hatchet. I spring forward and seize it. It is small, but so keen – so keen! I feel its razor edge lovingly. Then I am back at the port. I stand to one side and raise my weapon. The great tongue is feeling its way to those fearsome remains. It reaches them. As it does so, with a scream of "Joky! Joky!" I strike savagely again and again and again, gasping as I strike; once more, and the monstrous mass falls to the deck, writhing like a hideous eel. A vast, warm flood rushes in through the porthole. There is a sound of breaking steel and an enormous bellowing. A singing comes in my ears and grows louder – louder. Then the berth grows indistinct and suddenly dark.

* * *

Extract from the log of the steamship *Hispaniola*.

> *June 24.—Lat.—N. Long.—W. 11 a.m. – Sighted four-masted barque about four points on the port bow, flying signal of distress. Ran down to her and sent a boat aboard. She proved to be the Glen Doon, homeward bound from Melbourne to London. Found things in a terrible state. Decks covered with blood and slime. Steel deck-house stove in. Broke open door, and discovered youth of about nineteen in last stage of inanition, also part remains of boy about fourteen years of age. There was a great quantity of blood in the place, and a huge curled-up mass of whitish flesh, weighing about half a tonne, one end of which appeared to have been hacked through with a sharp instrument. Found forecastle door open and hanging from one hinge. Doorway bulged, as though something had been forced through. Went inside. Terrible state of affairs, blood everywhere, broken chests, smashed bunks, but no men nor remains. Went aft again and found youth showing signs of recovery. When he came round, gave the name of Thompson. Said they had been attacked by a huge serpent – thought it must have been sea-serpent. He was too weak to say much, but told us there were some men up the mainmast. Sent a hand aloft, who reported them lashed to the royal mast, and quite dead. Went aft to the cabin. Here we found the bulkhead smashed to pieces, and the cabin-door lying on the deck near the after-hatch. Found body of captain down lazarette, but no officers. Noticed amongst the wreckage part of the carriage of a small cannon. Came aboard again.*
>
> *Have sent the second mate with six men to work her into port. Thompson is with us. He has written out his version of the affair. We certainly consider that the state of the ship, as we found her, bears out in every respect his story. (Signed) William Norton (Master). Tom Briggs (1st Mate).*

If you enjoyed this, you might also like...
The Thing in the Weeds, see page 340
The Mystery of the Derelict, see page 138

From the Tideless Sea: Part One

THE CAPTAIN of the schooner leant over the rail, and stared for a moment, intently.

"Pass us them glasses, Jock," he said, reaching a hand behind him.

Jock left the wheel for an instant, and ran into the little companionway. He emerged immediately with a pair of marine-glasses, which he pushed into the waiting hand.

For a little, the Captain inspected the object through the binoculars. Then he lowered them, and polished the object glasses.

"Seems like er water-logged barr'l as sumone's been doin' fancy paintin' on," he remarked after a further stare. "Shove ther 'elm down er bit, Jock, an' we'll 'ave er closer look at it."

Jock obeyed, and soon the schooner bore almost straight for the object which held the Captain's attention. Presently, it was within some fifty feet, and the Captain sung out to the boy in the caboose to pass along the boathook.

Very slowly, the schooner drew nearer, for the wind was no more than breathing gently. At last the cask was within reach, and the Captain grappled at it with the boathook. It bobbed in the calm water, under his ministrations; and, for a moment, the thing seemed likely to elude him. Then he had the hook fast in a bit of rotten-looking rope which was attached to it. He did not attempt to lift it by the rope; but sung out to the boy to get a bowline round it. This was done, and the two of them hove it up on to the deck.

The Captain could see now, that the thing was a small water-breaker, the upper part of which was ornamented with the remains of a painted name.

"H—M—E—B——" spelt out the Captain with difficulty, and scratched his head. "'ave er look at this 'ere, Jock. See wot you makes of it."

Jock bent over from the wheel, expectorated, and then stared at the breaker. For nearly a minute he looked at it in silence.

"I'm thinkin' some of the letterin's washed awa'," he said at last, with considerable deliberation. "I have ma doots if he'll be able to read it.

"Hadn't ye no better knock in the end?" he suggested, after a further period of pondering. "I'm thinkin' ye'll be lang comin' at them contents otherwise."

"It's been in ther water er thunderin' long time," remarked the Captain, turning the bottom side upwards. "Look at them barnacles!"

Then, to the boy:

"Pass erlong ther 'atchet outer ther locker."

Whilst the boy was away, the Captain stood the little barrel on end, and kicked away some of the barnacles from the underside. With them, came away a great shell of pitch. He bent, and inspected it.

"Blest if ther thing ain't been pitched!" he said. "This 'ere's been put afloat er purpose, an' they've been, mighty anxious as ther stuff in it shouldn't be 'armed.

He kicked away another mass of the barnacle-studded pitch. Then, with a sudden impulse, he picked up the whole thing and shook it violently. It gave out a light, dull, thudding sound, as though something soft and small were within. Then the boy came with the hatchet.

"Stan' clear!" said the Captain, and raised the implement. The next instant, he had driven in one end of the barrel. Eagerly, he stooped forward. He dived his hand down and brought out a little bundle stitched up in oilskin.

"I don' spect as it's anythin' of valley," he remarked. "But I guess as there's sumthin' 'ere as 'll be worth tellin' 'bout w'en we gets 'ome."

He slit up the oilskin as he spoke. Underneath, there was another covering of the same material, and under that a third. Then a longish bundle done up in tarred canvas. This was removed, and a black, cylindrical shaped case disclosed to view. It proved to be a tin canister, pitched over. Inside of it, neatly wrapped within a last strip of oilskin, was a roll of papers, which, on opening, the Captain found to be covered with writing. The Captain shook out the various wrappings; but found nothing further. He handed the MS. across to Jock.

"More 'n your line 'n mine, I guess," he remarked. "Jest you read it up, an' I'll listen."

He turned to the boy.

"Fetch thef dinner erlong 'ere. Me an' ther Mate 'll 'ave it comfortable up 'ere, an' you can take ther wheel.... Now then, Jock!"

And, presently, Jock began to read.

The Losing of the Homebird

"THE 'OMEBIRD!" exclaimed the Captain. "Why, she were lost w'en I wer' quite a young feller. Let me see – seventy-three. That were it. Tail end er seventy-three w'en she left 'ome, an' never 'eard of since; not as I knows. Go a'ead with ther yarn, Jock."

"It is Christmas eve. Two years ago today, we became lost to the world. Two years! It seems like twenty since I had my last Christmas in England. Now, I suppose, we are already forgotten – and this ship is but one more among the missing! My God! To think upon our loneliness gives me a choking feeling, a tightness across the chest!

"I am writing this in the saloon of the sailing ship, *Homebird*, and writing with but little hope of human eye ever seeing that which I write; for we are in the heart of the dread Sargasso Sea – the Tideless Sea of the North Atlantic. From the stump of our mizzen mast, one may see, spread out to the far horizon, an interminable waste of weed – a treacherous, silent vastitude of slime and hideousness!

"On our port side, distant some seven or eight miles, there is a great, shapeless, discoloured mass. No one, seeing it for the first time, would suppose it to be the hull of a long lost vessel. It bears but little resemblance to a sea-going craft, because of a strange superstructure which has been built upon it. An examination of the vessel herself, through a telescope, tells one that she is unmistakably ancient. Probably a hundred, possibly two hundred, years. Think of it! Two hundred years in the midst of this desolation! It is an eternity.

"At first we wondered at that extraordinary superstructure. Later, we were to learn its use – and profit by the teaching of hands long withered. It is inordinately strange that we should have come upon this sight for the dead! Yet, thought suggests, that there may be many such, which have lain here through the centuries in this World of Desolation. I had not imagined that the earth contained so much loneliness, as is held within the circle, seen from the stump of our shattered mast. Then comes the thought that I might wander a hundred miles in any direction – and still be lost.

"And that craft yonder, that one break in the monotony, that monument of a few men's misery, serves only to make the solitude the more atrocious; for she is a very effigy of terror, telling of tragedies in the past, and to come!

"And now to get back to the beginnings of it. I joined the *Homebird*, as a passenger, in the early part of November. My health was not quite the thing, and I hoped the voyage would help to set me up. We had a lot of dirty weather for the first couple of weeks out, the wind dead ahead. Then we got a Southerly slant, that carried us down through the forties; but a good deal more to the Westward than we desired. Here we ran right into a tremendous cyclonic storm. All hands were called to shorten sail, and so urgent seemed our need, that the very officers went aloft to help make up the sails, leaving only the Captain (who had taken the wheel) and myself upon the poop. On the maindeck; the cook was busy letting go such ropes as the Mates desired.

"Abruptly, some distance ahead, through the vague sea-mist, but rather on the port bow, I saw loom up a great black wall of cloud.

"'Look, Captain!' I exclaimed; but it had vanished before I had finished speaking. A minute later it came again, and this time the Captain saw it.

"'O, my God!' he cried, and dropped his hands from the wheel. He leapt into the companionway, and seized a speaking trumpet. Then out on deck. He put it to his lips.

"'Come down from aloft! Come down! Come down!' he shouted. And suddenly I lost his voice in a terrific mutter of sound from somewhere to port. It was the voice of the storm – shouting. My God! I had never heard anything like it! It ceased as suddenly as it had begun, and, in the succeeding quietness, I heard the whining of the kicking-tackles through the blocks. Then came a quick clang of brass upon the deck, and I turned quickly. The Captain had thrown down the trumpet, and sprung back to the wheel. I glanced aloft, and saw that many of the men were already in the rigging, and racing down like cats.

"I heard the Captain draw his breath with a quick gasp.

"'Hold on for your lives!' he shouted, in a hoarse, unnatural voice.

"I looked at him. He was staring to windward with a fixed stare of painful intentness, and my gaze followed his. I saw, not four hundred yards distant, an enormous mass of foam and water coming down upon us. In the same instant, I caught the hiss of it, and immediately it was a shriek, so intense and awful, that I cringed impotently with sheer terror.

"The smother of water and foam took the ship a little fore-side of the beam, and the wind was with it. Immediately, the vessel rolled over on to her side, the sea-froth flying over her in tremendous cataracts.

"It seemed as though nothing could save us. Over, over we went, until I was swinging against the deck, almost as against the side of a house; for I had grasped the weather rail at the Captain's warning. As I swung there, I saw a strange thing. Before me was the port quarter boat. Abruptly, the canvas cover was flipped clean off it, as though by a vast, invisible hand.

"The next instant, a flurry of oars, boats' masts and odd gear flittered up into the air, like so many feathers, and blew to leeward and was lost in the roaring chaos of foam. The boat, herself, lifted in her chocks, and suddenly was blown clean down on to the maindeck, where she lay all in a ruin of white-painted timbers.

"A minute of the most intense suspense passed; then, suddenly, the ship righted, and I saw that the three masts had carried away. Yet, so hugely loud was the crying of the storm, that no sound of their breaking had reached me.

"I looked towards the wheel; but no one was there. Then I made out something crumpled up against the lee rail. I struggled across to it, and found that it was the Captain. He was insensible, and queerly limp in his right arm and leg. I looked round. Several of the men were crawling aft along the poop. I beckoned to them, and pointed to the wheel, and then to the Captain. A couple of them came towards me, and one went to the wheel. Then I made out through the spray the form of the Second Mate. He had several more of the men with him, and they had a coil of rope, which they took forrard. I learnt afterwards that they were hastening to get out a sea-anchor, so as to keep the ship's head towards the wind.

"We got the Captain below, and into his bunk. There, I left him in the hands of his daughter and the steward, and returned on deck.

"Presently, the Second Mate came back, and with him the remainder of the men. I found then that only seven had been saved in all. The rest had gone.

"The day passed terribly – the wind getting stronger hourly; though, at its worst, it was nothing like so tremendous as that first burst.

"The night came – a night of terror, with the thunder and hiss of the giant seas in the air above us, and the wind bellowing like some vast Elemental beast.

"Then, just before the dawn, the wind lulled, almost in a moment; the ship rolling and wallowing fearfully, and the water coming aboard – hundreds of tonnes at a time. Immediately afterwards it caught us again; but more on the beam, and bearing the vessel over on to her side, and this only by the pressure of the element upon the stark hull. As we came head to wind again, we righted, and rode, as we had for hours, amid a thousand fantastic hills of phosphorescent flame.

"Again the wind died – coming again after a longer pause, and then, all at once, leaving us. And so, for the space of a terrible half hour, the ship lived through the most awful, windless sea that can be imagined. There was no doubting but that we had driven right into the calm centre of the cyclone – calm only so far as lack of wind, and yet more dangerous a thousand times than the most furious hurricane that ever blew.

"For now we were beset by the stupendous Pyramidal Sea; a sea once witnessed, never forgotten; a sea in which the whole bosom of the ocean is projected towards heaven in monstrous hills of water; not leaping forward, as would be the case if there were wind; but hurling upwards in jets and peaks of living brine, and falling back in a continuous thunder of foam.

"Imagine this, if you can, and then have the clouds break away suddenly overhead, and the moon shine down upon that hellish turmoil, and you will have such a sight as has been given to mortals but seldom, save with death. And this is what we saw, and to my mind there is nothing within the knowledge of man to which I can liken it.

"Yet we lived through it, and through the wind that came later. But two more complete days and nights had passed, before the storm ceased to be a terror to us, and then, only because it had carried us into the seaweed laden waters of the vast Sargasso Sea.

"Here, the great billows first became foamless; and dwindled gradually in size as we drifted further among the floating masses of weed. Yet the wind was still furious, so that the ship drove on steadily, sometimes between banks, and other times over them.

"For a day and a night we drifted thus; and then astern I made out a great bank of weed, vastly greater than any which hitherto we had encountered. Upon this, the wind drove us stern foremost, so that we over-rode it. We had been forced some distance across it, when it occurred to me that our speed was slackening. I guessed presently that the sea-anchor, ahead, had caught in the weed, and was holding. Even as I surmised this, I heard from beyond the bows a faint, droning, twanging sound, blending with the roar of the wind. There came an indistinct report, and the ship lurched backwards through the weed. The hawser, connecting us with the sea-anchor, had parted.

"I saw the Second Mate run forrard with several men. They hauled in upon the hawser, until the broken end was aboard. In the meantime, the ship, having nothing ahead to keep her 'bows on', began to slew broadside towards the wind. I saw the men attach a chain to the end of the broken hawser; then they paid it out again, and the ship's head came back to the gale.

"When the Second Mate came aft, I asked him why this had been done, and he explained that so long as the vessel was end-on, she would travel over the weed. I inquired why he wished her to go over the weed, and he told me that one of the men had made out what appeared to be clear water astern, and that – could we gain it – we might win free.

"Through the whole of that day, we moved rearwards across the great bank; yet, so far from the weed appearing to show signs of thinning, it grew steadily thicker, and, as it became denser, so did our speed slacken, until the ship was barely moving. And so the night found us.

"The following morning discovered to us that we were within a quarter of a mile of a great expanse of clear water – apparently the open sea; but unfortunately the wind had dropped to a moderate breeze, and the vessel was motionless, deep sunk in the weed; great tufts of which rose up on all sides, to within a few feet of the level of our maindeck.

"A man was sent up the stump of the mizzen, to take a look round. From there, he reported that he could see something, that might be weed, across the water; but it was too far distant for him to be in any way certain. Immediately afterwards, he called out that there was something, away on our port beam; but what it was, he could not say, and it was not until a telescope was brought to bear, that we made it out to be the hull of the ancient vessel I have previously mentioned.

"And now, the Second Mate began to cast about for some means by which he could bring the ship to the clear water astern. The first thing which he did, was to bend a sail to a spare yard, and hoist it to the top of the mizzen stump. By this means, he was able to dispense with the cable towing over the bows, which, of course, helped to prevent the ship from moving. In addition, the sail would prove helpful to force the vessel across the weed. Then he routed out a couple of kedges. These, he bent on to the ends of a short piece of cable, and, to the bight of this, the end of a long coil of strong rope.

"After that, he had the starboard quarter boat lowered into the weed, and in it he placed the two kedge anchors. The end of another length of rope, he made fast to the boat's painter. This done, he took four of the men with him, telling them to bring chain-hooks, in addition to the oars – his intention being to force the boat through the weed, until he reached the clear water. There, in the marge of the weed, he would plant the two anchors in the thickest clumps of the growth; after which we were to haul the boat back to the ship, by means of the rope attached to the painter.

"'Then,' as he put it, 'we'll take the kedge-rope to the capstan, and heave her out of this blessed cabbage heap!'

"The weed proved a greater obstacle to the progress of the boat, than, I think, he had anticipated. After half an hour's work, they had gone scarcely more than some two hundred feet from the vessel; yet, so thick was the stuff, that no sign could we see of them, save the movement they made among the weed, as they forced the boat along.

"Another quarter of an hour passed away, during which the three men left upon the poop, paid out the ropes as the boat forged slowly ahead. All at once, I heard my name called. Turning, I saw the Captain's daughter in the companionway, beckoning to me. I walked across to her.

"'My father has sent me up to know, Mr. Philips, how they are getting on?'

"'Very slowly, Miss Knowles,' I replied. 'Very slowly indeed. The weed is so extraordinarily thick.'

"She nodded intelligently, and turned to descend; but I detained her a moment.

"'Your father, how is he?' I asked.

"She drew her breath swiftly.

"'Quite himself,' she said; 'but so dreadfully weak. He—'

"An outcry from one of the men broke across her speech:

"'Lord 'elp us, mates! Wot were that!'

"I turned sharply. The three of them were staring over the taffrail. I ran towards them, and Miss Knowles followed.

"'Hush!' she said, abruptly. 'Listen!'

"I stared astern to where I knew the boat to be. The weed all about it was quaking queerly – the movement extending far beyond the radius of their hooks and oars. Suddenly, I heard the Second Mate's voice:

"'Look out, lads! My God, look out!'

"And close upon this, blending almost with it, came the hoarse scream of a man in sudden agony.

"I saw an oar come up into view, and descend violently, as though someone struck at something with it. Then the Second Mate's voice, shouting:

"'Aboard there! Aboard there! Haul in on the rope! Haul in on the rope—!' It broke off into a sharp cry.

"As we seized hold of the rope, I saw the weed hurled in all directions, and a great crying and choking swept to us over the brown hideousness around.

"'Pull!' I yelled, and we pulled. The rope tautened; but the boat never moved.

"'Tek it ter ther capsting!' gasped one of the men.

"Even as he spoke, the rope slackened. "'It's coming!' cried Miss Knowles. 'Pull! Oh! Pull!'

"She had hold of the rope along with us, and together we hauled, the boat yielding to our strength with surprising ease.

"'There it is!' I shouted, and then I let go of the rope. There was no one in the boat.

"'For the half of a minute, we stared, dumfoundered. Then my gaze wandered astern to the place from which we had plucked it. There was a heaving movement among the great weed masses. I saw something waver up aimlessly against the sky; it was sinuous, and it flickered once or twice from side to side; then sank back among the growth, before I could concentrate my attention upon it.

"I was recalled to myself by a sound of dry sobbing. Miss Knowles was kneeling upon the deck, her hands clasped round one of the iron uprights of the rail. She seemed momentarily all to pieces.

"'Come! Miss Knowles,' I said, gently. 'You must be brave. We cannot let your father know of this in his present state.'

"She allowed me to help her to her feet. I could feel that she was trembling badly. Then, even as I sought for words with which to reassure her, there came a dull thud from the direction of the companionway. We looked round. On the deck, face downward, lying half in and half out of the scuttle, was the Captain. Evidently, he had witnessed everything. Miss Knowles gave out a wild cry, and ran to her father. I beckoned to one of the men to help me, and, together, we carried him back to his bunk. An hour later, he recovered from his swoon. He was quite calm, though very weak, and evidently in considerable pain.

"Through his daughter, he made known to me that he wished me to take the reins of authority in his place. This, after a slight demur, I decided to do; for, as I reassured myself, there were no duties required of me, needing any special knowledge of shipcraft. The vessel was fast; so far as I could see, irrevocably fast. It would be time to talk of freeing her, when the Captain was well enough to take charge once more.

"I returned on deck, and made known to the men the Captain's wishes. Then I chose one to act as a sort of bo'sun over the other two, and to him I gave orders that everything should be put to rights before the night came. I had sufficient sense to leave him to manage matters in his own way; for, whereas my knowledge of what was needful, was fragmentary, his was complete.

"By this time, it was near to sunsetting, and it was with melancholy feelings that I watched the great hull of the sun plunge lower. For awhile, I paced the poop, stopping ever and anon to stare over the dreary waste by which we were surrounded. The more I looked about, the more a sense of lonesomeness and depression and fear assailed me. I had pondered much upon the dread happening of the day, and all my ponderings led to a vital questioning: – What was there among all that quiet weed, which had come upon the crew of the boat, and destroyed them? And I could not make answer, and the weed was silent – dreadly silent!

"The sun had drawn very near to the dim horizon, and I watched it, moodily, as it splashed great clots of red fire across the water that lay stretched into the distance across our stern. Abruptly, as I gazed, its perfect lower edge was marred by an irregular shape. For a moment, I stared, puzzled. Then I fetched a pair of glasses from the holdfast in the companion. A glance through these, and I knew the extent of our fate. That line, blotching the round of the sun, was the conformation of another enormous weed bank.

"I remembered that the man had reported something as showing across the water, when he was sent up to the top of the mizzen stump in the morning; but, what it was, he had been unable to say. The thought flashed into my mind that it had been only *just* visible from aloft in the morning, and now it was in sight from the deck. It occurred to me that the wind might be compacting the weed, and driving the bank which surrounded the ship, down upon a larger portion. Possibly, the clear stretch of water had been but a temporary rift within the heart of the Sargasso Sea. It seemed only too probable.

"Thus it was that I meditated, and so, presently, the night found me. For some hours further, I paced the deck in the darkness, striving to understand the incomprehensible; yet with no better result than to weary myself to death. Then, somewhere about midnight, I went below to sleep.

"The following morning, on going on deck, I found that the stretch of clear water had disappeared entirely, during the night, and now, so far as the eye could reach, there was nothing but a stupendous desolation of weed.

"The wind had dropped completely, and no sound came from all that weed-ridden immensity. We had, in truth, reached the Cemetery of the Ocean!

"The day passed uneventfully enough. It was only when I served out some food to the men, and one of them asked whether they could have a few raisins, that I remembered, with a pang of sudden misery, that it was Christmas day. I gave them the fruit, as they desired, and they spent the morning in the galley, cooking their dinner. Their stolid indifference to the late terrible happenings appalled me somewhat, until I remembered what their lives were, and had been. Poor fellows! One of them ventured aft at dinner time, and offered me a slice of what he called 'plum duff'. He brought it on a plate which he had found in the galley and scoured thoroughly with sand and water. He tendered it shyly enough, and I took it, so graciously as I could, for I would not hurt his feelings; though the very smell of the stuff was an abomination.

"During the afternoon, I brought out the Captain's telescope, and made a thorough examination of the ancient hulk on our port beam. Particularly did I study the extraordinary superstructure around her sides; but could not, as I have said before, conceive of its use.

"The evening, I spent upon the poop, my eyes searching wearily across that vile quietness, and so, in a little, the night came – Christmas night, sacred to a thousand happy memories. I found myself dreaming of the night a year previous, and, for a little while, I forgot what was before me. I was recalled suddenly – terribly. A voice rose out of the dark which hid the maindeck. For the fraction of an instant, it expressed surprise; then pain and terror leapt into it. Abruptly, it seemed to come from above, and then from somewhere *beyond* the ship, and so in a moment there was silence, save for a rush of feet and the bang of a door forrard.

"I leapt down the poop ladder, and ran along the maindeck, towards the fo'cas'le. As I ran, something knocked off my cap. I scarcely noticed it *then*. I reached the fo'cas'le, and caught at the latch of the port door. I lifted it and pushed; but the door was fastened.

"'Inside there!' I cried, and banged upon the panels with my clenched fist.

"A man's voice came, incoherently.

"'Open the door!' I shouted. 'Open the door!'

"'Yes, Sir – I'm com—ming, Sir,' said one of them, jerkily.

"I heard footsteps stumble across the planking. Then a hand fumbled at the fastening, and the door flew open under my weight.

"The man who had opened to me, started back. He held a flaring slush-lamp above his head, and, as I entered, he thrust it forward. His hand was trembling visibly, and, behind him, I made out the face of one of his mates, the brow and dirty, clean-shaven upper lip drenched with sweat. The man who held the lamp, opened his mouth, and gabbered at me; but, for a moment, no sound came.

"'Wot— wot were it? Wot we-ere it?' he brought out at last, with a gasp.

"The man behind, came to his side, and gesticulated.

"'What was what?' I asked sharply, and looking from one to the other. 'Where's the other man? What was that screaming?'

"The second man drew the palm of his hand across his brow; then flirted his fingers deckwards.

"'We don't know, Sir! We don't know! It were Jessop! Somethin's took 'im just as we was comin' forrid! We— we— He-he-*Hark!*'

"His head came forward with a jerk as he spoke, and then, for a space, no one stirred. A minute passed, and I was about to speak, when, suddenly, from somewhere out upon the deserted maindeck, there came a queer, subdued noise, as though something moved stealthily hither and thither. The man with the lamp caught me by the sleeve, and then, with an abrupt movement, slammed the door and fastened it.

"'That's *it*, Sir!' he exclaimed, with a note of terror and conviction in his voice.

"I bade him be silent, while I listened; but no sound came to us through the door, and so I turned to the men and told them to let me have all they knew.

"It was little enough. They had been sitting in the galley, yarning, until, feeling tired, they had decided to go forrard and turn-in. They extinguished the light, and came out upon the deck, closing the door behind them. Then, just as they turned to go forrard, Jessop gave out a yell. The next instant they heard him screaming in the air above their heads, and, realising that some terrible thing was upon them, they took forthwith to their heels, and ran for the security of the fo'cas'le.

"Then I had come.

"As the men made an end of telling me, I thought I heard something outside, and held up my hand for silence. I caught the sound again. Someone was calling my name. It was Miss Knowles. Likely enough she was calling me to supper – and she had no knowledge of the dread thing which had happened. I sprang to the door. She might be coming along the maindeck in search of me. And there was Something out there, of which I had no conception – something unseen, but deadly tangible!

"'Stop, Sir!' shouted the men, together; but I had the door open.

"'Mr. Philips!' came the girl's voice at no great distance. 'Mr. Philips!'

"'Coming, Miss Knowles!' I shouted, and snatched the lamp from the man's hand.

"The next instant, I was running aft, holding the lamp high, and glancing fearfully from side to side. I reached the place where the mainmast had been, and spied the girl coming towards me.

"'Go back!' I shouted. 'Go back!'

"She turned at my shout, and ran for the poop ladder. I came up with her, and followed close at her heels. On the poop, she turned and faced me.

"'What is it, Mr. Philips?'

"I hesitated. Then:

"'I don't know!' I said.

"'My father heard something,' she began. 'He sent me. He—'

"I put up my hand. It seemed to me that I had caught again the sound of something stirring on the maindeck.

"'Quick!' I said sharply. 'Down into the cabin!.' And she, being a sensible girl, turned and ran down without waste of time. I followed, closing and fastening the companion-doors behind me.

"In the saloon, we had a whispered talk, and I told her everything. She bore up bravely, and said nothing; though her eyes were very wide, and her face pale. Then the Captain's voice came to us from the adjoining cabin.

"'Is Mr. Philips there, Mary?'

"'Yes, father.'

"'Bring him in.'

"I went in.

"'What was it, Mr. Philips?' he asked, collectedly.

"I hesitated; for I was willing to spare him the ill news; but he looked at me with calm eyes for a moment, and I knew that it was useless attempting to deceive him.

"'Something has happened, Mr. Philips,' he said, quietly. 'You need not be afraid to tell me.'

"At that, I told him so much as I knew, he listening, and nodding his comprehension of the story.

"'It must be something big,' he remarked, when I had made an end. 'And yet you saw nothing when you came aft?'

"'No,' I replied.

"'It is something in the weed,' he went on. 'You will have to keep off the deck at night.'

"After a little further talk, in which he displayed a calmness that amazed me, I left him, and went presently to my berth.

"The following day, I took the two men, and, together, we made a thorough search through the ship; but found nothing. It was evident to me that the Captain was right. There was some dread Thing hidden within the weed. I went to the side and looked down. The two men followed me. Suddenly, one of them pointed.

"'Look, Sir!' he exclaimed. 'Right below you, Sir! Two eyes like blessed great saucers! Look!'

"I stared; but could see nothing. The man left my side, and ran into the galley. In a moment, he was back with a great lump of coal.

"'Just there, Sir,' he said, and hove it down into the weed immediately beneath where we stood.

"Too late, I saw the thing at which he aimed – two immense eyes, some little distance below the surface of the weed. I knew instantly to what they belonged; for I had seen large specimens of the octopus some years previously, during a cruise in Australasian waters.

"'Look out, man!' I shouted, and caught him by the arm. 'It's an octopus! Jump back!' I sprang down on to the deck. In the same instant, huge masses of weed were hurled in all directions, and half a dozen immense tentacles whirled up into the air. One lapped itself about his neck. I caught his leg; but he was torn from my grasp, and I tumbled backwards on to the deck. I heard a scream from the other man as I scrambled to my feet. I looked to where he had been; but of him there was no sign. Regardless of the danger, in my great agitation, I leapt upon the rail, and gazed down with frightened eyes. Yet, neither of him nor his mate, nor the monster, could I perceive a vestige.

"How long I stood there staring down bewilderedly, I cannot say; certainly some minutes. I was so bemazed that I seemed incapable of movement. Then, all at once, I became aware that a light quiver ran across the weed, and the next instant, something stole up out of the depths with a deadly celerity. Well it was for me that I had seen it in time, else should I have shared the fate of those two – and the others. As it was, I saved myself only by leaping backwards on to the deck. For a moment, I saw the feeler wave above the rail with a certain apparent aimlessness; then it sank out of sight, and I was alone.

"An hour passed before I could summon a sufficiency of courage to break the news of this last tragedy to the Captain and his daughter, and when I had made an end, I returned to the solitude of the poop; there to brood upon the hopelessness of our position.

"As I paced up and down, I caught myself glancing continuously at the nearer weed tufts. The happenings of the past two days had shattered my nerves, and I feared every moment to see some slender death-grapple searching over the rail for me. Yet, the poop, being very much higher out of the weed than the maindeck, was comparatively safe; though only comparatively.

"Presently, as I meandered up and down, my gaze fell upon the hulk of the ancient ship, and, in a flash, the reason for that great superstructure was borne upon me. It was intended as a protection against the dread creatures which inhabited the weed. The thought came to me that I would attempt some similar means of protection; for the feeling that, at any moment, I might be caught and lifted out into that slimy wilderness, was not to be borne. In addition, the work would serve to occupy my mind, and help me to bear up against the intolerable sense of loneliness which assailed me.

"I resolved that I would lose no time, and so, after some thought as to the manner in which I should proceed, I routed out some coils of rope and several sails. Then I went down on to the maindeck and brought up an armful of capstan bars. These I lashed vertically to the rail all round the poop. Then I knotted the rope to each, stretching it tightly between them, and over this framework stretched the sails, sewing the stout canvas to the rope, by means of twine and some great needles which I found in the Mate's room.

"It is not to be supposed that this piece of work was accomplished immediately. Indeed, it was only after three days of hard labour that I got the poop completed. Then I commenced work upon the maindeck. This was a tremendous undertaking, and a whole fortnight passed before I had the entire length of it enclosed; for I had to be continually on the watch against the hidden enemy. Once, I was very nearly surprised, and saved myself only by a quick leap. Thereafter, for the rest of that day, I did no more work; being too greatly shaken in spirit. Yet, on the following morning, I recommenced, and from thence, until the end, I was not molested.

"Once the work was roughly completed, I felt at ease to begin and perfect it. This I did, by tarring the whole of the sails with Stockholm tar; thereby making them stiff, and capable of resisting the weather. After that, I added many fresh uprights, and much strengthening ropework, and finally doubled the sailcloth with additional sails, liberally smeared with the tar.

"In this manner, the whole of January passed away, and a part of February. Then, it would be on the last day of the month, the Captain sent for me, and told me, without any preliminary talk, that he was dying. I looked at him; but said nothing; for I had known long that it was so. In return, he stared back with a strange intentness, as though he would read my inmost thoughts, and this for the space of perhaps two minutes.

"'Mr. Philips,' he said at last, 'I may be dead by this time tomorrow. Has it ever occurred to you that my daughter will be alone with you?'

"'Yes, Captain Knowles,' I replied, quietly, and waited.

"For a few seconds, he remained silent; though, from the changing expressions of his face, I knew that he was pondering how best to bring forward the thing which it was in his mind to say.

"'You are a gentleman—' he began, at last.

"'I will marry her,' I said, ending the sentence for him.

"A slight flush of surprise crept into his face.

"'You – you have thought seriously about it?'

"'I have thought very seriously,' I explained.

"'Ah!' he said, as one who comprehends. And then, for a little, he lay there quietly. It was plain to me that memories of past days were with him. Presently, he came out of his dreams, and spoke, evidently referring to my marriage with his daughter.

"'It is the only thing,' he said, in a level voice.

"I bowed, and after that, he was silent again for a space. In a little, however, he turned once more to me:

"'Do you – do you love her?'

"His tone was keenly wistful, and a sense of trouble lurked in his eyes.

"'She will be my wife,' I said, simply; and he nodded.

"'God has dealt strangely with us,' he murmured presently, as though to himself.

"Abruptly, he bade me tell her to come in.

"And then he married us.

"Three days later, he was dead, and we were alone.

"For a while, my wife was a sad woman; but gradually time eased her of the bitterness of her grief.

"Then, some eight months after our marriage, a new interest stole into her life. She whispered it to me, and we, who had borne our loneliness uncomplainingly, had now this new thing to which to look forward. It became a bond between us, and bore promise of some companionship as we grew old. Old! At the idea of age, a sudden flash of thought darted like lightning across the sky of my mind: – *FOOD!* Hitherto, I had thought of myself, almost as of one already dead, and had cared naught for anything beyond the immediate troubles which each day forced upon me. The loneliness of the vast Weed World had become an assurance of doom to me, which had clouded and dulled my faculties, so that I had grown apathetic. Yet, immediately, as it seemed, at the shy whispering of my wife, was all this changed.

"That very hour, I began a systematic search through the ship. Among the cargo, which was of a 'general' nature, I discovered large quantities of preserved and tinned provisions, all of which I put carefully on one side. I continued my examination until I had ransacked the whole vessel. The business took me near upon six months to complete, and when it was finished, I seized paper, and made calculations, which led me to the conclusion that we had sufficient food in the ship to preserve life in three people for some fifteen to seventeen years. I could not come nearer to it than this; for I had no means of computing the quantity the child would need year by year. Yet it is sufficient to show me that seventeen years *must* be the limit. Seventeen years! And then—

"Concerning water, I am not troubled; for I have rigged a great sailcloth tun-dish, with a canvas pipe into the tanks; and from every rain, I draw a supply, which has never run short.

"The child was born nearly five months ago. She is a fine little girl, and her mother seems perfectly happy. I believe I could be quietly happy with them, were it not that I have ever in mind the end of those seventeen years. True! we may be dead long before then; but, if not, our little girl will be in her teens – and it is a hungry age.

"If one of us died – but no! Much may happen in seventeen years. I will wait.

"My method of sending this clear of the weed is likely to succeed. I have constructed a small fire-balloon, and this missive, safely enclosed in a little barrel, will be attached. The wind will carry it swiftly hence.

"Should this ever reach civilised beings, will they see that it is forwarded to:—"

(Here followed an address, which, for some reason, had been roughly obliterated. Then came the signature of the writer)

"Arthur Samuel Philips."

* * *

The captain of the schooner looked over at Jock, as the man made an end of his reading.

"Seventeen years pervisions," he muttered thoughtfully. "An' this 'ere were written sumthin' like twenty-nine years ago!" He nodded his head several times. "Poor creatures!" he exclaimed. "It'd be er long while, Jock – a long while!"

If you enjoyed this, you might also like...

From the Tideless Sea: Part Two, see page 124
The Boats of the 'Glen Carrig', see page 204

From the Tideless Sea: Part Two
Further News of the Homebird

IN THE AUGUST OF 1902, Captain Bateman, of the schooner *Agnes*, picked up a small barrel, upon which was painted a half obliterated word; which, finally, he succeeded in deciphering as 'Homebird', the name of a full-rigged ship, which left London in the November of 1873, and from thenceforth was heard of no more by any man.

Captain Bateman opened the barrel, and discovered a packet of Manuscript, wrapped in oilskin. This, on examination, proved to be an account of the losing of the *Homebird* amid the desolate wastes of the Sargasso Sea. The papers were written by one Arthur Samuel Philips, a passenger in the ship; and, from them, Captain Bateman was enabled to gather that the ship, mastless, lay in the very heart of the dreaded Sargasso; and that all of the crew had been lost – some in the storm which drove them thither, and some in attempts to free the ship from the weed, which locked them in on all sides.

Only Mr. Philips and the Captain's daughter had been left alive, and they two, the dying Captain had married. To them had been born a daughter, and the papers ended with a brief but touching allusion to their fear that, eventually, they must run short of food.

There is need to say but little more. The account was copied into most of the papers of the day, and caused widespread comment. There was even some talk of fitting out a rescue expedition; but this fell through, owing chiefly to lack of knowledge of the whereabouts of the ship in all the vastness of the immense Sargasso Sea. And so, gradually, the matter has slipped into the background of the Public's memory.

Now, however, interest will be once more excited in the lonesome fate of this lost trio; for a second barrel, identical, it would seem, with that found by Captain Bateman, has been picked up by a Mr. Bolton, of Baltimore, master of a small brig, engaged in the South American coast-trade. In this barrel was enclosed a further message from Mr. Philips – the fifth that he has sent abroad to the world; but the second, third and fourth, up to this time, have not been discovered.

This 'fifth message' contains a vital and striking account of their lives during the year 1879, and stands unique as a document informed with human lonesomeness and longing. I have seen it, and read it through, with the most intense and painful interest. The writing, though faint, is very legible; and the whole manuscript bears the impress of the same hand and mind that wrote the piteous account of the losing of the *Homebird*, of which I have already made mention, and with which, no doubt, many are well acquainted.

In closing this little explanatory note, I am stimulated to wonder whether, somewhere, at some time, those three missing messages ever shall be found. And then there may be others. What stories of human, strenuous fighting with Fate may they not contain.

We can but wait and wonder. Nothing more may we ever learn; for what is this one little tragedy among the uncounted millions that the silence of the sea holds so remorselessly. And yet, again, news may come to us out of the Unknown – out of the lonesome silences of the dread Sargasso Sea – the loneliest and the most inaccessible place of all the lonesome and inaccessible places of this earth.

And so I say, let us wait.

W.H.H.

The Fifth Message

"THIS IS THE FIFTH MESSAGE that I have sent abroad over the loathsome surface of this vast Weed-World, praying that it may come to the open sea, ere the lifting power of my fire-balloon be gone, and yet, if it come there – the which I could now doubt – how shall I be the better for it! Yet write I must, or go mad, and so I choose to write, though feeling as I write that no living creature, save it be the giant octopi that live in the weed about me, will ever see the thing I write.

"My first message I sent out on Christmas Eve, 1875, and since then, each eve of the birth of Christ has seen a message go skywards upon the winds, towards the open sea. It is as though this approaching time, of festivity and the meeting of parted loved ones, overwhelms me, and drives away the half apathetic peace that has been mine through spaces of these years of lonesomeness; so that I seclude myself from my wife and the little one, and with ink, pen, and paper, try to ease my heart of the pent emotions that seem at times to threaten to burst it.

"It is now six completed years since the Weed-World claimed us from the World of the Living – six years away from our brothers and sisters of the human and living world – It has been six years of living in a grave! And there are all the years ahead! Oh! My God! My God! I dare not think upon them! I must control myself—

"And then there is the little one, she is nearly four and a half now, and growing wonderfully, out among these wilds. Four and a half years, and the little woman has never seen a human face besides ours – think of it! And yet, if she lives four and forty years, she will never see another.... Four and forty years! It is foolishness to trouble about such a space of time; for the future, for us, ends in ten years – eleven at the utmost. Our food will last no longer than that.... My wife does not know; for it seems to me a wicked thing to add unnecessarily to her punishment. She does but know that we must waste no ounce of food-stuff, and for the rest she imagines that the most of the cargo is of an edible nature. Perhaps, I have nurtured this belief. If anything happened to me, the food would last a few extra years; but my wife would have to imagine it an accident, else would each bite she took sicken her.

"I have thought often and long upon this matter, yet I fear to leave them; for who knows but that their very lives might at any time depend upon my strength, more pitifully, perhaps, than upon the food which they must come at last to lack. No, I must not bring upon them, and myself, a *near* and *certain* calamity, to defer one that, though it seems to have but little less certainty, is yet at a further distance.

"Until lately, nothing has happened to us in the past four years, if I except the adventures that attended my mad attempt to cut a way through the surrounding weed to freedom, and from which it pleased God that I and those with me should be preserved.[1] Yet, in the latter part of this year, an adventure, much touched with grimness, came to us most unexpectedly, in a fashion quite unthought of – an adventure that has brought into our lives a fresh and more active peril; for now I have learned that the weed holds other terrors besides that of the giant octopi.

"Indeed, I have grown to believe this world of desolation capable of holding *any* horror, as well it might. Think of it – an interminable stretch of dank, brown loneliness in all directions, to the distant horizon; a place where monsters of the deep and the weed have undisputed reign; where never an enemy may fall upon them; but from which they may strike with sudden deadliness! No human can ever bring an engine of destruction to bear upon them, and the humans whose fate it is to have sight of them, do so only from the decks of lonesome derelicts, whence they stare lonely with fear, and without ability to harm.

"I cannot describe it, nor can any hope ever to imagine it! When the wind falls, a vast silence holds us girt, from horizon to horizon, yet it is a silence through which one seems to feel the pulse of hidden things all about us, watching and waiting – waiting and watching; waiting but for the chance to reach forth a huge and sudden death-grapple…. It is no use! I cannot bring it home to any; nor shall I be better able to convey the frightening sound of the wind, sweeping across these vast, quaking plains – the shrill whispering of the weed-fronds, under the stirring of the winds. To hear it from beyond our canvas screen, is like listening to the uncounted dead of the mighty Sargasso wailing their own requiems. Or again, my fancy, diseased with much loneliness and brooding, likens it to the advancing rustle of armies of the great monsters that are always about us – waiting.

"And so to the coming of this new terror:

"It was in the latter end of October that we first had knowledge of it – a tapping in the night time against the side of the vessel, below the water-line; a noise that came distinct, yet with a ghostly strangeness in the quietness of the night. It was on a Monday night when first I heard it. I was down in the lazarette, overhauling our stores, and suddenly I heard it – tap-tap-tap – against the outside of the vessel upon the starboard side, and below the water line. I stood for awhile listening; but could not discover what it was that should come a-tapping against our side, away out here in this lonesome world of weed and slime. And then, as I stood there listening, the tapping ceased, and so I waited, wondering, and with a hateful sense of fear, weakening my manhood, and taking the courage out of my heart….

"Abruptly, it recommenced; but now upon the opposite side of the vessel, and as it continued, I fell into a little sweat; for it seemed to me that some foul thing out in the night was tapping for admittance. Tap-tap-tap – it went, and continued, and there I stood listening, and so gripped about with frightened thoughts, that I seemed without power to stir myself; for the spell of the Weed-World, and the fear bred of its hidden terrors and the weight and dreeness of its loneliness have entered into my marrow, so that I could, then and now, believe in the likelihood of matters which, ashore and in the midst of my fellows, I might laugh at in contempt. It is the dire lonesomeness of this strange world into which I have entered, that serves so to take the heart out of a man.

"And so, as I have said, I stood there listening, and full of frightened, but undefined, thoughts; and all the while the tapping continued, sometimes with a regular insistence, and anon with a quick spasmodic tap, tap, tap-a-tap, as though some Thing, having Intelligence, signalled to me.

"Presently, however, I shook off something of the foolish fright that had taken me, and moved over to the place from which the tapping seemed to sound. Coming near to it, I bent my head down, close to the side of the vessel, and listened. Thus, I heard the noises with greater plainness, and could distinguish easily, now, that something knocked with a hard object upon the outside of the ship, as though someone had been striking her iron side with a small hammer.

"Then, even as I listened, came a thunderous blow close to my ear, so loud and astonishing, that I leaped sideways in sheer fright. Directly afterwards there came a second heavy blow, and then a third, as though someone had struck the ship's side with a heavy sledge-hammer, and after that, a space of silence, in which I heard my wife's voice at the trap of the lazarette, calling down to me to know what had happened to cause so great a noise.

"'Hush, My Dear!' I whispered; for it seemed to me that the thing outside might hear her; though this could not have been possible, and I do but mention it as showing how the noises had set me off my natural balance.

"At my whispered command, my wife turned her about and came down the ladder into the semi-darkness of the place.

"'What is it, Arthur?' she asked, coming across to me, and slipping her hand between my arm and side.

"As though in reply to her query, there came against the outside of the ship, a fourth tremendous blow, filling the whole of the lazarette with a dull thunder.

"My wife gave out a frightened cry, and sprang away from me; but the next instant, she was back, and gripping hard at my arm.

"'What is it, Arthur? What is it?' she asked me; her voice, though no more than a frightened whisper, easily heard in the succeeding silence.

"'I don't know, Mary,' I replied, trying to speak in a level tone. 'It's—'

"'There's something again,' she interrupted, as the minor tapping noises recommenced.

"For about a minute, we stood silent, listening to those eerie taps. Then my wife turned to me:

"'Is it anything dangerous, Arthur – tell me? I promise you I shall be brave.'

"'I can't possibly say, Mary,' I answered. 'I can't say; but I'm going up on deck to listen…. Perhaps,' I paused a moment to think; but a fifth tremendous blow against the ship's side, drove whatever I was going to say, clean from me, and I could do no more than stand there, frightened and bewildered, listening for further sounds. After a short pause, there came a sixth blow. Then my wife caught me by the arm, and commenced to drag me towards the ladder.

"'Come up out of this dark place, Arthur,' she said. 'I shall be ill if we stay here any longer. Perhaps the – the thing outside can hear us, and it may stop if we go upstairs.'

"By this, my wife was all of a shake, and I but little better, so that I was glad to follow her up the ladder. At the top, we paused for a while to listen, bending down over the open hatchway. A space of, maybe, some five minutes passed away in silence; then there commenced again the tapping noises, the sounds coming clearly up to us where we crouched. Presently, they ceased once more, and after that, though we listened for a further space of some ten minutes, they were not repeated. Neither were there any more of the great bangs.

"In a little, I led my wife away from the hatch, to a seat in the saloon; for the hatch is situated under the saloon table. After that, I returned to the opening, and replaced the cover. Then I went into our cabin – the one which had been the Captain's, her father – and brought from there a revolver, of which we have several. This, I loaded with care, and afterwards placed in my side pocket.

"Having done this, I fetched from the pantry, where I have made it my use to keep such things at hand, a bull's-eye lantern, the same having been used on dark nights when clearing up the ropes from the decks. This, I lit, and afterwards turned the dark-slide to cover the light. Next, I slipped off my boots; and then, as an afterthought, I reached down one of the long-handled American axes from the rack about the mizzenmast – these being keen and very formidable weapons.

"After that, I had to calm my wife and assure her that I would run no unnecessary risks, if, indeed, there were any risks to run; though, as may be imagined, I could not say what new peril might not be upon us. And then, picking up the lantern, I made my way silently on stockinged feet, up the companionway. I had reached the top, and was just stepping out on to the deck, when something caught my arm. I turned swiftly, and perceived that my wife had followed me up the steps, and from the shaking of her hand upon my arm, I gathered that she was very much agitated.

"'Oh, My Dear, My Dear, don't go! don't go!' she whispered, eagerly. 'Wait until it is daylight. Stay below tonight. You don't know what may be about in this horrible place.'

"I put the lantern and the axe upon the deck beside the companion; then bent towards the opening, and took her into my arms, soothing her, and stroking her hair; yet with ever an alert glance to and fro along the indistinct decks. Presently, she was more like her usual self, and listened to my reasoning, that she would do better to stay below, and so, in a little, left me, having made me promise afresh that I would be very wary of danger.

"When she had gone, I picked up the lantern and the axe, and made my way cautiously to the side of the vessel. Here, I paused and listened very carefully, being just above that spot upon the port side where I had heard the greater part of the tapping, and all of the heavy bangs; yet, though I listened, as I have said, with much attention, there was no repetition of the sounds.

"Presently, I rose and made my way forrard to the break of the poop. Here, bending over the rail which ran across, I listened, peering along the dim maindecks; but could neither see nor hear anything; not that, indeed, I had any reason for expecting to see or hear ought unusual *aboard* of the vessel; for all of the noises had come from over the side, and, more than that, from beneath the water-line. Yet in the state of mind in which I was, I had less use for reason than fancy; for that strange thudding and tapping, out here in the midst of this world of loneliness, had set me vaguely imagining unknowable terrors, stealing upon me from every shadow that lay upon the dimly-seen decks.

"Then, as still I listened, hesitating to go down on to the maindeck, yet too dissatisfied with the result of my peerings, to cease from my search, I heard, faint yet clear in the stillness of the night, the tapping noises recommence.

"I took my weight from off the rail, and listened; but I could no longer hear them, and at that, I leant forward again over the rail, and peered down on to the maindeck. Immediately, the sounds came once more to me, and I knew now, that they were borne to me by the medium of the rail, which conducted them to me through the iron stanchions by which it is fixed to the vessel.

"At that, I turned and went aft along the poop deck, moving very warily and with quietness. I stopped over the place where first I had heard the louder noises, and stooped, putting my ear against the rail. Here, the sounds came to me with great distinctness.

"For a little, I listened; then stood up, and slid away that part of the tarred canvas-screen which covers the port opening through which we dump our refuse; they being made here for convenience, one upon each side of the vessel. This, I did very silently; then, leaning forward through the opening, I peered down into the dimness of the weed. Even as I did so, I heard plainly below me a heavy thud, muffled and dull by reason of the intervening water, against the iron side of the ship. It seemed to me that there was some disturbance amid the dark, shadowy masses of the weed. Then I had opened the dark-slide of my lantern, and sent a clear beam of light down into the blackness. For a brief instant, I thought I perceived a multitude of things moving. Yet, beyond that they were oval in shape, and showed white through the weed fronds, I had no clear conception of anything; for with the flash of the light, they vanished, and there lay beneath me only the dark, brown masses of the weed – demurely quiet.

"But an impression they did leave upon my over excited imagination – an impression that might have been due to morbidity, bred of too much loneliness; but nevertheless it seemed to me that I had seen momentarily a multitude of dead white faces, upturned towards me among the meshes of the weed.

"For a little, I leant there, staring down at the circle of illumined weed; yet with my thoughts in such a turmoil of frightened doubts and conjectures, that my physical eyes did but poor work, compared with the orb that looks inward. And through all the chaos of my mind there rose up weird and creepy memories – ghouls, the un-dead. There seemed nothing improbable, in that moment, in associating the terms with the fears that were besetting me. For no man may dare to say what terrors this world holds, until he has become lost to his brother men, amid the unspeakable desolation of the vast and slimy weed-plains of the Sargasso Sea.

"And then, as I leaned there, so foolishly exposing myself to those dangers which I had learnt did truly exist, my eyes caught and subconsciously noted the strange and subtle undulation which always foretells the approach of one of the giant octopi. Instantly, I leapt back, and whipped the tarred canvas-cover across the opening, and so stood alone there in the night, glancing frightenedly before and behind me, the beam from my lamp casting wavering splashes of light to and fro about the decks. And all the time, I was listening – listening; for it seemed to me that some Terror was brooding in the night, that might come upon us at any moment and in some unimagined form.

"Then, across the silence, stole a whisper, and I turned swiftly towards the companionway. My wife was there, and she reached out her arms to me, begging me to come below into safety. As the light from my lantern flashed upon her, I saw that she had a revolver in her right hand, and at that, I asked her what she had it for; whereupon she informed me that she had been watching over me, through the whole of the time that I had been on deck, save for the little while that it had taken her to get and load the weapon.

"At that, as may be imagined, I went and embraced her very heartily, kissing her for the love that had prompted her actions; and then, after that, we spoke a little together in low tones – she asking that I should come down and fasten up the companion-doors, and I demurring, telling her that I felt too unsettled to sleep; but would rather keep watch about the poop for a while longer.

"Then, even as we discussed the matter, I motioned to her for quietness. In the succeeding silence, she heard it, as well as I, a slow – tap! tap! tap! coming steadily along the dark maindecks. I felt a swift vile fear, and my wife's hold upon me became very tense, despite that she trembled a little. I released her grip from my arm, and made to go towards the break of the poop; but she was after me instantly, praying me at least to stay where I was, if I would not go below.

"Upon that, I bade her very sternly to release me, and go down into the cabin; though all the while I loved her for her very solicitude. But she disobeyed me, asserting very stoutly, though in a whisper, that if I went into danger, she would go with me; and at that

I hesitated; but decided, after a moment, to go no further than the break of the poop, and not to venture on to the maindeck.

"I went very silently to the break, and my wife followed me. From the rail across the break, I shone the light of the lantern; but could neither see nor hear anything; for the tapping noise had ceased. Then it recommenced, seeming to have come near to the port side of the stump of the mainmast. I turned the lantern towards it, and, for one brief instant, it seemed to me that I saw something pale, just beyond the brightness of my light. At that, I raised my pistol and fired, and my wife did the same, though without any telling on my part. The noise of the double explosion went very loud and hollow sounding along the decks, and after the echoes had died away, we both of us thought we heard the tapping going away forrard again.

"After that, we stayed awhile, listening and watching; but all was quiet, and, presently, I consented to go below and bar up the companion, as my wife desired; for, indeed, there was much sense in her plea of the futility of my staying up upon the decks.

"The night passed quietly enough, and on the following morning, I made a very careful inspection of the vessel, examining the decks, the weed outside of the ship, and the sides of her. After that, I removed the hatches, and went down into the holds; but could nowhere find anything of an unusual nature.

"That night, just as we were making an end of our supper, we heard three tremendous blows given against the starboard side of the ship, whereat, I sprang to my feet, seized and lit the dark-lantern, which I had kept handy, and ran quickly and silently up on to the deck. My pistol, I had already in my pocket, and as I had soft slippers upon my feet, I needed not to pause to remove my footgear. In the companionway, I had left the axe, and this I seized as I went up the steps.

"Reaching the deck, I moved over quietly to the side, and slid back the canvas door; then I leant out and opened the slide of the lantern, letting its light play upon the weed in the direction from which the bangs had seemed to proceed; but nowhere could I perceive anything out of the ordinary, the weed seeming undisturbed. And so, after a little, I drew in my head, and slid-to the door in the canvas screen; for it was but wanton folly to stand long exposed to any of the giant octopi that might chance to be prowling near, beneath the curtain of the weed.

"From then, until midnight, I stayed upon the poop, talking much in a quiet voice to my wife, who had followed me up into the companion. At times, we could hear the knocking, sometimes against one side of the ship, and again upon the other. And, between the louder knocks, and accompanying them, would sound the minor tap, tap, tap-a-tap, that I had first heard.

"About midnight, feeling that I could do nothing, and no harm appearing to result to us from the unseen things that seemed to be encircling us my wife and I made our way below to rest, securely barring the companion-doors behind us.

"It would be, I should imagine, about two o'clock in the morning, that I was aroused from a somewhat troubled sleep, by the agonised screaming of our great boar, away forrard. I leant up upon my elbow, and listened, and so grew speedily wide awake. I sat up, and slid from my bunk to the floor. My wife, as I could tell from her breathing, was sleeping peacefully, so that I was able to draw on a few clothes without disturbing her.

"Then, having lit the dark-lantern, and turned the slide over the light, I took the axe in my other hand, and hastened towards the door that gives out of the forrard end of the saloon, on to the maindeck, beneath the shelter of the break of the poop. This door, I had locked before turning-in, and now, very noiselessly, I unlocked it, and turned the handle, opening the door with much caution. I peered out along the dim stretch of the maindeck; but could see nothing; then I turned on the slide of the lamp, and let the light play along the decks; but still nothing unusual was revealed to me.

"Away forrard, the shrieking of the pig had been succeeded by an absolute silence, and there was nowhere any noise, if I except an occasional odd tap-a-tap, which seemed to come from the side of the ship. And so, taking hold of my courage, I stepped out on to the maindeck, and proceeded slowly forrard, throwing the beam of light to and fro continuously, as I walked.

"Abruptly, I heard away in the bows of the ship a sudden multitudinous tapping and scraping and slithering; and so loud and near did it sound, that I was brought up all of a round-turn, as the saying is. For, perhaps, a whole minute, I stood there hesitating, and playing the light all about me, not knowing but that some hateful thing might leap upon me from out of the shadows.

"And then, suddenly, I remembered that I had left the door open behind me, that led into the saloon, so that, were there any deadly thing about the decks, it might chance to get in upon my wife and child as they slept. At the thought, I turned and ran swiftly aft again, and in through the door to my cabin. Here, I made sure that all was right with the two sleepers, and after that, I returned to the deck, shutting the door, and locking it behind me.

"And now, feeling very lonesome out there upon the dark decks, and cut off in a way from a retreat, I had need of all my manhood to aid me forrard to learn the wherefore of the pig's crying, and the cause of that manifold tapping. Yet go I did, and have some right to be proud of the act; for the dreeness and lonesomeness and the cold fear of the Weed-World, squeeze the pluck out of one in a very woeful manner.

"As I approached the empty fo'cas'le, I moved with all wariness, swinging the light to and fro, and holding my axe very handily, and the heart within my breast like a shape of water, so in fear was I. Yet, I came at last to the pigsty, and so discovered a dreadful sight. The pig, a huge boar of twenty-score pounds, had been dragged out on to the deck, and lay before the sty with all his belly ripped up, and stone dead. The iron bars of the sty – great bars they are too – had been torn apart, as though they had been so many straws; and, for the rest, there was a deal of blood both within the sty and upon the decks.

"Yet, I did not stay then to see more; for, all of a sudden, the realisation was borne upon me that this was the work of some monstrous thing, which even at that moment might be stealing upon me; and, with the thought, an overwhelming fear leapt upon me, overbearing my courage; so that I turned and ran for the shelter of the saloon, and never stopped until the stout door was locked between me and that which had wrought such destruction upon the pig. And as I stood there, quivering a little with very fright, I kept questioning dumbly as to what manner of wild-beast thing it was that could burst asunder iron bars, and rip the life out of a great boar, as though it were of no more account than a kitten. And then more vital questions: – How did it get aboard, and where had it hidden? And again: – *What was it?* And so in this fashion for a good while, until I had grown something more calmed.

"But through all the remainder of that night, I slept not so much as a wink.

"Then in the morning when my wife awoke, I told her of the happenings of the night; whereat she turned very white, and fell to reproaching me for going out at all on to the deck, declaring that I had run needlessly into danger, and that, at least, I should not have left her alone, sleeping in ignorance of what was towards. And after that, she fell into a fit of crying, so that I had some to-do comforting her. Yet, when she had come back to calmness, she was all for accompanying me about the decks, to see by daylight what had indeed befallen in the night-time. And from this decision, I could not turn her; though I assured her I should have told her nothing, had it not been that I wished to warn her from going to and fro between the saloon and the galley, until I had made a thorough search about the decks. Yet, as I have remarked, I could not turn her from her purpose of accompanying me, and so was forced to let her come, though against my desire.

"We made our way on deck through the door that opens under the break of the poop, my wife carrying her loaded revolver half-clumsily in both hands, whilst I had mine held in my left, and the long-handled axe in my right – holding it very readily.

"On stepping out on to the deck, we closed the door behind us, locking it and removing the key; for we had in mind our sleeping child. Then we went slowly forrard along the decks, glancing about warily. As we came fore-side of the pigsty, and my wife saw that which lay beyond it, she let out a little exclamation of horror, shuddering at the sight of the mutilated pig, as, indeed, well she might.

"For my part, I said nothing; but glanced with much apprehension about us; feeling a fresh access of fright; for it was very plain to me that the boar had been molested since I had seen it – the head having been torn, with awful might, from the body; and there were, besides, other new and ferocious wounds, one of which had come nigh to severing the poor brute's body in half. All of which was so much additional evidence of the formidable character of the monster, or Monstrosity, that had attacked the animal.

"I did not delay by the pig, nor attempt to touch it; but beckoned my wife to follow me up on to the fo'cas'le head. Here, I removed the canvas cover from the small skylight which lights the fo'cas'le beneath; and, after that, I lifted off the heavy top, letting a flood of light down into the gloomy place. Then I leant down into the opening, and peered about; but could discover no signs of any lurking thing, and so returned to the maindeck, and made an entrance into the fo'cas'le through the starboard doorway. And now I made a more minute search; but discovered nothing, beyond the mournful array of sea-chests that had belonged to our dead crew.

"My search concluded, I hastened out from the doleful place, into the daylight, and after that made fast the door again, and saw to it that the one upon the port side was also securely locked. Then I went up again on to the fo'cas'le head, and replaced the skylight-top and the canvas cover, battening the whole down very thoroughly.

"And in this wise, and with an incredible care, did I make my search through the ship, fastening up each place behind me, so that I should be certain that no Thing was playing some dread game of hide and seek with me.

"Yet I found *nothing*, and had it not been for the grim evidence of the dead and mutilated boar, I had been like to have thought nothing more dreadful than an over vivid Imagination had roamed the decks in the darkness of the past night.

"That I had reason to feel puzzled, may be the better understood, when I explain that I had examined the whole of the great, tarred-canvas screen, which I have built about the ship as a protection against the sudden tentacles of any of the roaming giant octopi, without discovering any torn place such as must have been made if any conceivable monster had climbed aboard out of the weed. Also, it must be borne in mind that the ship stands many feet out of the weed, presenting only her smooth iron sides to anything that desires to climb aboard.

"And yet there was the dead pig, lying brutally torn before its empty sty! An undeniable proof that, to go out upon the decks after dark, was to run the risk of meeting a horrible and mysterious death!

"Through all that day, I pondered over this new fear that had come upon us, and particularly upon the monstrous and unearthly power that had torn apart the stout iron bars of the sty, and so ferociously wrenched off the head of the boar. The result of my pondering was that I removed our sleeping belongings that evening from the cabin to the iron half-deck – a little, four-bunked house, standing fore-side of the stump of the main mast, and built entirely of iron, even to the single door, which opens out of the after end.

"Along with our sleeping matters, I carried forrard to our new lodgings, a lamp, and oil, also the dark-lantern, a couple of the axes, two rifles, and all of the revolvers, as well as a good supply of ammunition. Then I bade my wife forage out sufficient provisions to last us for a week, if need be, and whilst she was so busied, I cleaned out and filled the water breaker which belonged to the half-deck.

"At half-past six, I sent my wife forrard to the little iron house, with the baby, and then I locked up the saloon and all of the cabin doors, finally locking after me the heavy, teak door that opened out under the break of the poop.

"Then I went forrard to my wife and child, and shut and bolted the iron door of the half-deck for the night. After that, I went round and saw to it that all of the iron storm-doors, that shut over the eight ports of the house, were in good working order, and so we sat down, as it were, to await the night.

"By eight o'clock, the dusk was upon us, and before half-past, the night hid the decks from my sight. Then I shut down all the iron port-flaps, and screwed them up securely, and after that, I lit the lamp.

"And so a space of waiting ensued, during which I whispered reassuringly to my wife, from time to time, as she looked across at me from her seat beside the sleeping child, with frightened eyes, and a very white face; for somehow there had come upon us within the last hour, a sense of chilly fright, that went straight to one's heart, robbing one vilely of pluck.

"A little later, a sudden sound broke the impressive silence – a sudden dull thud against the side of the ship; and, after that, there came a succession of heavy blows, seeming to be struck all at once upon every side of the vessel; after which there was quietness for maybe a quarter of an hour.

"Then, suddenly, I heard, away forrard, a tap, tap, tap, and then a loud rattling, slurring noise, and a loud crash. After that, I heard many other sounds, and always that tap, tap, tap, repeated a hundred times, as though an army of wooden-legged men were busied all about the decks at the fore end of the ship.

"Presently, there came to me the sound of something coming down the deck, tap, tap, tap, it came. It drew near to the house, paused for nigh a minute; then continued away aft towards the saloon: – tap, tap, tap. I shivered a little, and then, fell half consciously to thanking God that I had been given wisdom to bring my wife and child forrard to the security of the iron deck-house.

"About a minute later, I heard the sound of a heavy blow struck somewhere away aft; and after that a second, and then a third, and seeming by the sounds to have been against iron – the iron of the bulkshead that runs across the break of the poop. There came the noise of a fourth blow, and it blended into the crash of broken woodwork. And therewith, I had a little tense quivering inside me; for the little one and my wife might have been sleeping aft there at that very moment, had it not been for the Providential thought which had sent us forrard to the half-deck.

"With the crash of the broken door, away aft, there came, from forrard of us, a great tumult of noises; and, directly, it sounded as though a multitude of wooden-legged men were coming down the decks from forrard. Tap, tap, tap; tap-a-tap, the noises came, and drew abreast of where we sat in the house, crouched and holding our breaths, for fear that we should make some noise to attract *that* which was without. The sounds passed us, and went tapping away aft, and I let out a little breath of sheer easement. Then, as a sudden thought came to me, I rose and turned down the lamp, fearing that some ray from it might be seen from beneath the door. And so, for the space of an hour, we sat wordless, listening to the sounds which came from away aft, the thud of heavy blows, the occasional crash of wood, and, presently, the tap, tap, tap, again, coming forrard towards us.

"The sounds came to a stop, opposite the starboard side of the house, and, for a full minute, there was quietness. Then suddenly, 'Boom!' a tremendous blow had been struck against the side of the house. My wife gave out a little gasping cry, and there came a second blow; and, at that, the child awoke and began to wail, and my wife was put to it, with trying to soothe her into immediate silence.

"A third blow was struck, filling the little house with a dull thunder of sound, and then I heard the tap, tap, tap, move round to the after end of the house. There came a pause, and then a great blow right upon the door. I grasped the rifle, which I had leant against my chair, and stood up; for I did not know but that the thing might be upon us in a moment, so prodigious was the force of the blows it struck. Once again it struck the door, and after that went tap, tap, tap, round to the port side of the house, and there struck the house again; but now I had more ease of mind; for it was its direct attack upon the door, that had put such horrid dread into my heart.

"After the blows upon the port side of the house, there came a long spell of silence, as though the thing outside were listening; but, by the mercy of God, my wife had been able to soothe the child, so that no sound from us, told of our presence.

"Then, at last, there came again the sounds: – tap, tap, tap, as the voiceless thing moved away forrard. Presently, I heard the noises cease aft; and, after that, there came a multitudinous tap-a-tapping, coming along the decks. It passed the house without so much as a pause, and receded away forrard.

"For a space of over two hours, there was an absolute silence; so that I judged that we were now no longer in danger of being molested. An hour later, I whispered to my wife; but, getting no reply, knew that she had fallen into a doze, and so I sat on, listening tensely; yet making no sort of noise that might attract attention.

"Presently, by the thin line of light from beneath the door, I saw that the day was breaking; and, at that, I rose stiffly, and commenced to unscrew the iron port-covers. I unscrewed the forrard ones first, and looked out into the wan dawn; but could discover nothing unusual about so much of the decks as I could see from there.

"After that, I went round and opened each, as I came to it, in its turn; but it was not until I had uncovered the port which gave me a view of the port side of the after maindeck, that I discovered anything extraordinary. Then I saw, at first dimly, but more clearly as the day brightened, that the door, leading from beneath the break of the poop into the saloon, had been broken to flinders, some of which lay scattered upon the deck, and some of which still hung from the bent hinges; whilst more, no doubt, were strewed in the passage beyond my sight.

"Turning from the port, I glanced towards my wife, and saw that she lay half in and half out of the baby's bunk, sleeping with her head beside the child's, both upon one pillow. At the sight, a great wave of holy thankfulness took me, that we had been so wonderfully spared from the terrible and mysterious danger that had stalked the decks in the darkness of the preceding night. Feeling thus, I stole across the floor of the house, and kissed them both very gently, being full of tenderness, yet not minded to waken them. And, after that, I lay down in one of the bunks, and slept until the sun was high in the heaven.

"When I awoke, my wife was about and had tended to the child and prepared our breakfast, so that I had naught to do but tumble out and set to, the which I did with a certain keenness of appetite, induced, I doubt not, by the stress of the night. Whilst we ate, we discussed the peril through which we had just passed; but without coming any the nearer to a solution of the weird mystery of the Terror.

"Breakfast over, we took a long and final survey of the decks, from the various ports, and then prepared to sally out. This we did with instinctive caution and quietness, both of us armed as on the previous day. The door of the half-deck we closed and locked behind us, thereby ensuring that the child was open to no danger whilst we were in other parts of the ship.

"After a quick look about us, we proceeded aft towards the shattered door beneath the break of the poop. At the doorway, we stopped, not so much with the intent to examine the broken door, as because of an instinctive and natural hesitation to go forward into the saloon, which but a few hours previous had been visited by some incredible monster or monsters. Finally, we decided to go up upon the poop and peer down through the skylight. This we did, lifting the sides of the dome for that purpose; yet though we peered long and earnestly, we could perceive no signs of any lurking thing. But broken woodwork there appeared to be in plenty, to judge by the scattered pieces.

"After that, I unlocked the companion, and pushed back the big, over-arching slide. Then, silently, we stole down the steps and into the saloon. Here, being now able to see the big cabin through all its length, we discovered a most extraordinary scene; the whole place appeared to be wrecked from end to end; the six cabins that line each side had their bulksheading driven into shards and slivers of broken wood in places. Here, a door would be standing untouched, whilst the bulkshead beside it was in a mass of flinders – There a door would be driven completely from its hinges, whilst the surrounding woodwork was untouched. And so it was, wherever we looked.

"My wife made to go towards our cabin; but I pulled her back, and went forward myself. Here the desolation was almost as great. My wife's bunk-board had been ripped out, whilst the supporting side-batten of mine had been plucked forth, so that all the bottom-boards of the bunk had descended to the floor in a cascade.

"But it was neither of these things that touched us so sharply, as the fact that the child's little swing cot had been wrenched from its standards, and flung in a tangled mass of white-painted iron-work across the cabin. At the sight of that, I glanced across at my wife, and she at me, her face grown very white. Then down she slid to her knees, and fell to crying and thanking God together, so that I found myself beside her in a moment, with a very humble and thankful heart.

"Presently, when we were more controlled, we left the cabin, and finished our search. The pantry, we discovered to be entirely untouched, which, somehow, I do not think was then a matter of great surprise to me; for I had ever a feeling that the things which had broken a way into our sleeping cabin, had been looking for us.

"In a little while, we left the wrecked saloon and cabins, and made our way forrard to the pigsty; for I was anxious to see whether the carcass of the pig had been touched. As we came round the corner of the sty, I uttered a great cry; for there, lying upon the deck, on its back, was a gigantic crab, so vast in size that I had not conceived so huge a monster existed. Brown it was in colour, save for the belly part, which was of a light yellow.

"One of its pincer-claws, or mandibles, had been torn off in the fight in which it must have been slain (for it was all disembowelled). And this one claw weighed so heavy that I had some to-do to lift it from the deck; and by this you may have some idea of the size and formidableness of the creature itself.

"Around the great crab, lay half a dozen smaller ones, no more than from seven or eight to twenty inches across, and all white in colour, save for an occasional mottling of brown. These had all been killed by a single nip of an enormous mandible, which had in every case smashed them almost into two halves. Of the carcass of the great boar, not a fragment remained.

"And so was the mystery solved; and, with the solution, departed the superstitious terror which had suffocated me through those three nights, since the tapping had commenced. We had been attacked by a wandering shoal of giant crabs, which, it is quite possible, roam across the weed from place to place, devouring aught that comes in their path.

"Whether they had ever boarded a ship before, and so, perhaps, developed a monstrous lust for human flesh, or whether their attack had been prompted by curiosity, I cannot possibly say. It may be that, at first, they mistook the hull of the vessel for the body of some dead marine monster, and hence their blows upon her sides, by which, possibly, they were endeavouring to pierce through our somewhat unusually tough hide!

"Or, again, it may be that they have some power of scent, by means of which they were able to smell our presence aboard the ship; but this (as they made no general attack upon us in the deck-house) I feel disinclined to regard as probable. And yet – I do not know. Why their attack upon the saloon, and our sleeping-cabin? As I say, I cannot tell, and so must leave it there.

"The way in which they came aboard, I discovered that same day; for, having learned what manner of creature it was that had attacked us, I made a more intelligent survey of the sides of the ship; but it was not until I came to the extreme bows, that I saw how they had managed. Here, I found that some of the gear of the broken bowsprit and jibboom, trailed down on to the weed, and as I had not extended the canvas-screen across the heel of the bowsprit, the monsters had been able to climb up the gear, and thence aboard, without the least obstruction being opposed to their progress.

"This state of affairs, I very speedily remedied; for, with a few strokes of my axe, I cut through the gear, allowing it to drop down among the weed; and after that, I built a temporary breastwork of wood across the gap, between the two ends of the screen; later on making it more permanent.

"Since that time, we have been no more molested by the giant crabs; though for several nights afterwards, we heard them knocking strangely against our sides. Maybe, they are attracted by such refuse as we are forced to dump overboard, and this would explain their first tappings being aft, opposite to the lazarette; for it is from the openings in this part of the canvas-screen that we cast our rubbish.

"Yet, it is weeks now since we heard aught of them, so that I have reason to believe that they have betaken themselves elsewhere, maybe to attack some other lonely humans, living out their short span of life aboard some lone derelict, lost even to memory in the depth of this vast sea of weed and deadly creatures.

"I shall send this message forth on its journey, as I have sent the other four, within a well-pitched barrel, attached to a small fire balloon. The shell of the severed claw of the monster crab, I shall enclose,[2] as evidence of the terrors that beset us in this dreadful place. Should this message, and the claw, ever fall into human hands, let them, contemplating this vast mandible, try to imagine the size of the other crab or crabs that could destroy so formidable a creature as the one to which this claw belonged.

"What other terrors does this hideous world hold for us?

"I had thought of inclosing, along with the claw, the shell of one of the white smaller crabs. It must have been some of these moving in the weed that night, that set my disordered fancy to imagining of ghouls and the Un-Dead. But, on thinking it over, I shall not; for to do so would be to illustrate nothing that needs illustration, and it would but increase needlessly the weight which the balloon will have to lift.

"And so I grow wearied of writing. The night is drawing near, and I have little more to tell. I am writing this in the saloon, and, though I have mended and carpentered so well as I am able, nothing I can do will hide the traces of that night when the vast crabs raided through these cabins, searching for – *what?*

"There is nothing more to say. In health, I am well, and so is my wife and the little one, but…

"I must have myself under control, and be patient. We are beyond all help, and must bear that which is before us, with such bravery as we are able. And with this, I end; for my last word shall not be one of complaint.

"Arthur Samuel Philips."

"Christmas Eve, 1879."

Footnotes for From the Tideless Sea: Part Two

1. This is evidently a reference to something which Mr. Philips has set in an earlier message – one of the three lost messages. – *W.H.H.*
2. Captain Bolton makes no mention of the claw, in the covering letter which he has enclosed with the MS. – *W.H.H.*

If you enjoyed this, you might also like…

The Haunted 'Jarvee', see page 93
The Finding of the Graiken, see page 170

The Mystery of the Derelict

ALL THE NIGHT had the four-masted ship, *Tarawak*, lain motionless in the drift of the Gulf Stream; for she had run into a 'calm patch' – into a stark calm which had lasted now for two days and nights.

On every side, had it been light, might have been seen dense masses of floating gulf-weed, studding the ocean even to the distant horizon. In places, so large were the weed-masses that they formed long, low banks, that by daylight, might have been mistaken for low-lying land.

Upon the lee side of the poop, Duthie, one of the 'prentices, leaned with his elbows upon the rail, and stared out across the hidden sea, to where in the Eastern horizon showed the first pink and lemon streamers of the dawn – faint, delicate streaks and washes of colour.

A period of time passed, and the surface of the leeward sea began to show – a great expanse of grey, touched with odd, wavering belts of silver. And everywhere the black specks and islets of the weed.

Presently, the red dome of the sun protruded itself into sight above the dark rim of the horizon; and, abruptly, the watching Duthie saw something – a great, shapeless bulk that lay some miles away to starboard, and showed black and distinct against the gloomy red mass of the rising sun.

"Something in sight to looard, Sir," he informed the Mate, who was leaning, smoking, over the rail that ran across the break of the poop. "I can't just make out what it is."

The Mate rose from his easy position, stretched himself, yawned, and came across to the boy.

"Whereabouts, Toby?" he asked, wearily, and yawning again.

"There, Sir," said Duthie – alias Toby – "broad away on the beam, and right in the track of the sun. It looks something like a big houseboat, or a hay-stack."

The Mate stared in the direction indicated, and saw the thing which puzzled the boy, and immediately the tiredness went out of his eyes and face.

"Pass me the glasses off the skylight, Toby," he commanded, and the youth obeyed.

After the Mate had examined the strange object through his binoculars for, maybe, a minute, he passed them to Toby, telling him to take a 'squint', and say what he made of it.

"Looks like an old powder-hulk, Sir," exclaimed the lad, after awhile, and to this description the Mate nodded agreement.

Later, when the sun had risen somewhat, they were able to study the derelict with more exactness. She appeared to be a vessel of an exceedingly old type, mastless, and upon the hull of which had been built a roof-like superstructure; the use of which they could not determine. She was lying just within the borders of one of the weed-banks, and all her side was splotched with a greenish growth.

It was her position, within the borders of the weed, that suggested to the puzzled Mate, how so strange and unseaworthy looking a craft had come so far abroad into the greatness of the ocean. For, suddenly, it occurred to him that she was neither more nor less than a derelict from the vast Sargasso Sea – a vessel that had, possibly, been lost to the world, scores and scores of years gone, perhaps hundreds. The suggestion touched the Mate's thoughts with solemnity, and he fell to examining the ancient hulk with an even greater interest, and pondering on all the lonesome and awful years that must have passed over her, as she had lain desolate and forgotten in that grim cemetery of the ocean.

Through all that day, the derelict was an object of the most intense interest to those aboard the *Tarawak*, every glass in the ship being brought into use to examine her. Yet, though within no more than some six or seven miles of her, the Captain refused to listen to the Mate's suggestions that they should put a boat into the water, and pay the stranger a visit; for he was a cautious man, and the glass warned him that a sudden change might be expected in the weather; so that he would have no one leave the ship on any unnecessary business. But, for all that he had caution, curiosity was by no means lacking in him, and his telescope, at intervals, was turned on the ancient hulk through all the day.

Then, it would be about six bells in the second dog watch, a sail was sighted astern, coming up steadily but slowly. By eight bells they were able to make out that a small barque was bringing the wind with her; her yards squared, and every stitch set. Yet the night had advanced apace, and it was nigh to eleven o'clock before the wind reached those aboard the *Tarawak*. When at last it arrived, there was a slight rustling and quaking of canvas, and odd creaks here and there in the darkness amid the gear, as each portion of the running and standing rigging took up the strain.

Beneath the bows, and alongside, there came gentle rippling noises, as the vessel gathered way; and so, for the better part of the next hour, they slid through the water at something less than a couple of knots in the sixty minutes.

To starboard of them, they could see the red light of the little barque, which had brought up the wind with her, and was now forging slowly ahead, being better able evidently than the big, heavy *Tarawak* to take advantage of so slight a breeze.

About a quarter to twelve, just after the relieving watch had been roused, lights were observed to be moving to and fro upon the small barque, and by midnight it was palpable that, through some cause or other, she was dropping astern.

When the Mate arrived on deck to relieve the Second, the latter officer informed him of the possibility that something unusual had occurred aboard the barque, telling of the lights about her decks,[1] and how that, in the last quarter of an hour, she had begun to drop astern.

On hearing the Second Mate's account, the First sent one of the 'prentices for his night-glasses, and, when they were brought, studied the other vessel intently, that is, so well as he was able through the darkness; for, even through the night-glasses, she showed only as a vague shape, surmounted by the three dim towers of her masts and sails.

Suddenly, the Mate gave out a sharp exclamation; for, beyond the barque, there was something else shown dimly in the field of vision. He studied it with great intentness, ignoring for the instant, the Second's queries as to what it was that had caused him to exclaim.

All at once, he said, with a little note of excitement in his voice:

"The derelict! The barque's run into the weed around that old hooker!"

The Second Mate gave a mutter of surprised assent, and slapped the rail.

"That's it!" he said. "That's why we're passing her. And that explains the lights. If they're not fast in the weed, they've probably run slap into the blessed derelict!"

"One thing," said the Mate, lowering his glasses, and beginning to fumble for his pipe, "she won't have had enough way on her to do much damage."

The Second Mate, who was still peering through his binoculars, murmured an absent agreement, and continued to peer. The Mate, for his part, filled and lit his pipe, remarking meanwhile to the unhearing Second, that the light breeze was dropping.

Abruptly, the Second Mate called his superior's attention, and in the same instant, so it seemed, the failing wind died entirely away, the sails settling down into runkles, with little rustles and flutters of sagging canvas.

"What's up?" asked the Mate, and raised his glasses.

"There's something queer going on over yonder," said the Second. "Look at the lights moving about, and— Did you see *that*?"

The last portion of his remark came out swiftly, with a sharp accentuation of the last word.

"What?" asked the Mate, staring hard.

"They're shooting," replied the Second. "Look! There again!"

"Rubbish!" said the Mate, a mixture of unbelief and doubt in his voice.

With the falling of the wind, there had come a great silence upon the sea. And, abruptly, from far across the water, sounded the distant, dullish thud of a gun, followed almost instantly by several minute, but sharply defined, reports, like the cracking of a whip out in the darkness.

"Jove!" cried the Mate, "I believe you're right." He paused and stared. "There!" he said. "I saw the flashes then. They're firing from the poop, I believe.... I must call the Old Man."

He turned and ran hastily down into the saloon, knocked on the door of the Captain's cabin, and entered. He turned up the lamp, and, shaking his superior into wakefulness, told him of the thing he believed to be happening aboard the barque:

"It's mutiny, Sir; they're shooting from the poop. We ought to do something—" The Mate said many things, breathlessly; for he was a young man; but the Captain stopped him, with a quietly lifted hand.

"I'll be up with you in a minute, Mr. Johnson," he said, and the Mate took the hint, and ran up on deck.

Before the minute had passed, the Skipper was on the poop, and staring through his night-glasses at the barque and the derelict. Yet now, aboard of the barque, the lights had vanished, and there showed no more the flashes of discharging weapons – only there remained the dull, steady red glow of the port sidelight; and, behind it, the night-glasses showed the shadowy outline of the vessel.

The Captain put questions to the Mates, asking for further details.

"It all stopped while the Mate was calling you, Sir," explained the Second. "We could hear the shots quite plainly."

"They seemed to be using a gun as well as their revolvers," interjected the Mate, without ceasing to stare into the darkness.

For awhile the three of them continued to discuss the matter, whilst down on the maindeck the two watches clustered along the starboard rail, and a low hum of talk rose, fore and aft.

Presently, the Captain and the Mates came to a decision. If there had been a mutiny, it had been brought to its conclusion, whatever that conclusion might be, and no interference from those aboard the *Tarawak*, at that period, would be likely to do good.

They were utterly in the dark – in more ways than one – and, for all they knew, there might not even have been any mutiny. If there had been a mutiny, and the mutineers had won, then they had done their worst; whilst if the officers had won well and good. They had managed to do so without help. Of course, if the *Tarawak* had been a man-of-war with a large crew, capable of mastering any situation, it would have been a simple matter to send a powerful, armed boat's crew to inquire; but as she was merely a merchant vessel, under-manned, as is the modern fashion, they must go warily. They would wait for the morning, and signal. In a couple of hours it would be light. Then they would be guided by circumstances.

The Mate walked to the break of the poop, and sang out to the men:

"Now then, my lads, you'd better turn in, the watch below, and have a sleep; we may be wanting you by five bells."

There was a muttered chorus of "i, i, Sir," and some of the men began to go forrard to the fo'cas'le; but others of the watch below remained, their curiosity overmastering their desire for sleep.

On the poop, the three officers leaned over the starboard rail, chatting in a desultory fashion, as they waited for the dawn. At some little distance hovered Duthie, who, as eldest 'prentice just out of his time, had been given the post of acting Third Mate.

Presently, the sky to starboard began to lighten with the solemn coming of the dawn. The light grew and strengthened, and the eyes of those in the *Tarawak* scanned with growing intentness that portion of the horizon where showed the red and dwindling glow of the barque's sidelight.

Then, it was in that moment when all the world is full of the silence of the dawn, something passed over the quiet sea, coming out of the East – a very faint, long-drawn-out, screaming, piping noise. It might almost have been the cry of a little wind wandering out of the dawn across the sea – a ghostly, piping skirl, so attenuated and elusive was it; but there was in it a weird, almost threatening note, that told the three on the poop it was no wind that made so dree and inhuman a sound.

The noise ceased, dying out in an indefinite, mosquito-like shrilling, far and vague and minutely shrill. And so came the silence again.

"I heard that, last night, when they were shooting," said the Second Mate, speaking very slowly, and looking first at the Skipper and then at the Mate. "It was when you were below, calling the Captain," he added.

"Ssh!" said the Mate, and held up a warning hand; but though they listened, there came no further sound; and so they fell to disjointed questionings, and guessed their answers, as puzzled men will. And ever and anon, they examined the barque through their glasses; but without discovering anything of note, save that, when the light grew stronger, they perceived that her jibboom had struck through the superstructure of the derelict, tearing a considerable gap therein.

Presently, when the day had sufficiently advanced, the Mate sung out to the Third, to take a couple of the 'prentices, and pass up the signal flags and the code book. This was done, and a 'hoist' made; but those in the barque took not the slightest heed; so that finally the Captain bade them make up the flags and return them to the locker.

After that, he went down to consult the glass, and when he reappeared, he and the Mates had a short discussion, after which, orders were given to hoist out the starboard life-boat. This, in the course of half an hour, they managed; and, after that, six of the men and two of the 'prentices were ordered into her.

Then half a dozen rifles were passed down, with ammunition, and the same number of cutlasses. These were all apportioned among the men, much to the disgust of the two apprentices, who were aggrieved that they should be passed over; but their feelings altered when the Mate descended into the boat, and handed them each a loaded revolver, warning them, however, to play no 'monkey tricks' with the weapons.

Just as the boat was about to push off, Duthie, the eldest 'prentice, came scrambling down the side ladder, and jumped for the after thwart. He landed, and sat down, laying the rifle which he had brought, in the stern; and, after that, the boat put off for the barque.

There were now ten in the boat, and all well armed, so that the Mate had a certain feeling of comfort that he would be able to meet any situation that was likely to arise.

After nearly an hour's hard pulling, the heavy boat had been brought within some two hundred yards of the barque, and the Mate sung out to the men to lie on their oars for a minute. Then he stood up and shouted to the people on the barque; but though he repeated his cry of "Ship ahoy!" several times, there came no reply.

He sat down, and motioned to the men to give way again, and so brought the boat nearer the barque by another hundred yards. Here, he hailed again; but still receiving no reply, he stooped for his binoculars, and peered for awhile through them at the two vessels – the ancient derelict, and the modern sailing-vessel.

The latter had driven clean in over the weed, her stern being perhaps some two score yards from the edge of the bank. Her jibboom, as I have already mentioned, had pierced the green-blotched superstructure of the derelict, so that her cutwater had come very close to the grass-grown side of the hulk.

That the derelict was indeed a very ancient vessel, it was now easy to see; for at this distance the Mate could distinguish which was hull, and which superstructure. Her stern rose up to a height considerably above her bows, and possessed galleries, coming round the counter. In the window frames some of the glass still remained; but others were securely shuttered, and some missing, frames and all, leaving dark holes in the stern. And everywhere grew the dank, green growth, giving to the beholder a queer sense of repulsion. Indeed, there was that about the whole of the ancient craft, that repelled in a curious way – something elusive – a remoteness from humanity, that was vaguely abominable.

The Mate put down his binoculars, and drew his revolver, and, at the action, each one in the boat gave an instinctive glance to his own weapon. Then he sung out to them to give-way, and steered straight for the weed. The boat struck it, with something of a sog; and, after that, they advanced slowly, yard by yard, only with considerable labour.

They reached the counter of the barque, and the Mate held out his hand for an oar. This, he leaned up against the side of the vessel, and a moment later was swarming quickly up it. He grasped the rail, and swung himself aboard; then, after a swift glance fore and aft, gripped the blade of the oar, to steady it, and bade the rest follow as quickly as possible, which they did, the last man bringing up the painter with him, and making it fast to a cleat.

Then commenced a rapid search through the ship. In several places about the maindeck they found broken lamps, and aft on the poop, a shot-gun, three revolvers, and several capstan-bars lying about the poop-deck. But though they pried into every possible corner, lifting the hatches, and examining the lazarette, not a human creature was to be found – the barque was absolutely deserted.

After the first rapid search, the Mate called his men together; for there was an uncomfortable sense of danger in the air, and he felt that it would be better not to straggle. Then, he led the way forrard, and went up on to the t'gallant fo'cas'le head. Here, finding the port sidelight still burning, he bent over the screen, as it were mechanically, lifted the lamp, opened it, and blew out the flame; then replaced the affair on its socket.

After that, he climbed into the bows, and out along the jibboom, beckoning to the others to follow, which they did, no man saying a word, and all holding their weapons handily; for each felt the oppressiveness of the Incomprehensible about them.

The Mate reached the hole in the great superstructure, and passed inside, the rest following. Here they found themselves in what looked something like a great, gloomy barracks, the floor of which was the deck of the ancient craft. The superstructure, as seen from the inside, was a very wonderful piece of work, being beautifully shored and fixed; so that at one time it must have possessed immense strength; though now it was all rotted, and showed many a gape and rip. In one place, near the centre, or midships part, was a sort of platform, high up, which the Mate conjectured might have been used as a 'look-out'; though the reason for the prodigious superstructure itself, he could not imagine.

Having searched the decks of this craft, he was preparing to go below, when, suddenly, Duthie caught him by the sleeve, and whispered to him, tensely, to listen. He did so, and heard the thing that had attracted the attention of the youth – it was a low, continuous shrill whining that was rising from out of the dark hull beneath their feet, and, abruptly, the Mate was aware that there was an intensely disagreeable animal-like smell in the air. He had noticed it, in a subconscious fashion, when entering through the broken superstructure; but now, suddenly, he was *aware* of it.

Then, as he stood there hesitating, the whining noise rose all at once into a piping, screaming squeal, that filled all the space in which they were inclosed, with an awful, inhuman and threatening clamour. The Mate turned and shouted at the top of his voice to the rest, to retreat to the barque, and he, himself, after a further quick nervous glance round, hurried towards the place where the end of the barque's jibboom protruded in across the decks.

He waited, with strained impatience, glancing ever behind him, until all were off the derelict, and then sprang swiftly on to the spar that was their bridge to the other vessel. Even as he did so, the squealing died away into a tiny shrilling, twittering sound, that made him glance back; for the suddenness of the quiet was as effective as though it had been a loud noise. What he saw, seemed to him in that first instant so incredible and monstrous, that he was almost too shaken to cry out. Then he raised his voice in a shout of warning to the men, and a frenzy of haste shook him in every fibre, as he scrambled back to the barque, shouting ever to the men to get into the boat. For in that backward glance, he had seen the whole decks of the derelict a-move with living things – giant rats, thousands and tens of thousands of them; and so in a flash had come to an understanding of the disappearance of the crew of the barque.

He had reached the fo'cas'le head now, and was running for the steps, and behind him, making all the long slanting length of the jibboom black, were the rats, racing after him. He made one leap to the maindeck, and ran. Behind, sounded a queer, multitudinous pattering noise, swiftly surging upon him. He reached the poop steps, and as he sprang up them, felt a savage bite in his left calf. He was on the poop deck now, and running with a stagger. A score of great rats leapt around him, and half a dozen hung grimly to his back, whilst the one that had gripped his calf, flogged madly from side to side as he raced on. He reached the rail, gripped it, and vaulted clean over and down into the weed.

The rest were already in the boat, and strong hands and arms hove him aboard, whilst the others of the crew sweated in getting their little craft round from the ship. The rats still clung to the Mate; but a few blows with a cutlass eased him of his murderous burden. Above them, making the rails and half-round of the poop black and alive, raced thousands of rats.

The boat was now about an oar's length from the barque, and, suddenly, Duthie screamed out that *they* were coming. In the same instant, nearly a hundred of the largest rats launched themselves at the boat. Most fell short, into the weed; but over a score reached the boat, and sprang savagely at the men, and there was a minute's hard slashing and smiting, before the brutes were destroyed.

Once more the men resumed their task of urging their way through the weed, and so in a minute or two, had come to within some fathoms of the edge, working desperately. Then a fresh terror broke upon them. Those rats which had missed their leap, were now all about the boat, and leaping in from the weed, running up the oars, and scrambling in over the sides, and, as each one got inboard, straight for one of the crew it went; so that they were all bitten and be-bled in a score of places.

There ensued a short but desperate fight, and then, when the last of the beasts had been hacked to death, the men lay once more to the task of heaving the boat clear of the weed.

A minute passed, and they had come almost to the edge, when Duthie cried out, to look; and at that, all turned to stare at the barque, and perceived the thing that had caused the 'prentice to cry out; for the rats were leaping down into the weed in black multitudes, making the great weed-fronds quiver, as they hurled themselves in the direction of the boat. In an incredibly short space of time, all the weed between the boat and the barque, was alive with the little monsters, coming at breakneck speed.

The Mate let out a shout, and, snatching an oar from one of the men, leapt into the stern of the boat, and commenced to thrash the weed with it, whilst the rest laboured infernally to pluck the boat forth into the open sea. Yet, despite their mad efforts, and the death-dealing blows of the Mate's great fourteen-foot oar, the black, living mass were all about the boat, and scrambling aboard in scores, before she was free of the weed. As the boat shot into the clear water, the Mate gave out a great curse, and, dropping his oar, began to pluck the brutes from his body with his bare hands, casting them into the sea. Yet, fast almost as he freed himself, others sprang upon him, so that in another minute he was like to have been pulled down, for the boat was alive and swarming with the pests, but that some of the men got to work with their cutlasses, and literally slashed the brutes to pieces, sometimes killing several with a single blow. And thus, in a while, the boat was freed once more; though it was a sorely wounded and frightened lot of men that manned her.

The Mate himself took an oar, as did all those who were able. And so they rowed slowly and painfully away from that hateful derelict, whose crew of monsters even then made the weed all of a-heave with hideous life.

From the *Tarawak* came urgent signals for them to haste; by which the Mate knew that the storm, which the Captain had feared, must be coming down upon the ship, and so he spurred each one to greater endeavour, until, at last, they were under the shadow of their own vessel, with very thankful hearts, and bodies, bleeding, tired and faint.

Slowly and painfully, the boat's crew scrambled up the side-ladder, and the boat was hoisted aboard; but they had no time then to tell their tale; for the storm was upon them.

It came half an hour later, sweeping down in a cloud of white fury from the Eastward, and blotting out all vestiges of the mysterious derelict and the little barque which had proved her victim. And after that, for a weary day and night, they battled with the storm. When it passed, nothing was to be seen, either of the two vessels or of the weed which had studded the sea before the storm; for they had been blown many a score of leagues to the Westward of the spot, and so had no further chance – nor, I ween, inclination – to investigate further the mystery of that strange old derelict of a past time, and her habitants of rats.

Yet, many a time, and in many fo'cas'les has this story been told; and many a conjecture has been passed as to how came that ancient craft abroad there in the ocean. Some have suggested – as indeed I have made bold to put forth as fact – that she must have drifted out of the lonesome Sargasso Sea. And, in truth, I cannot but think this the most reasonable supposition. Yet, of the rats that evidently dwelt in her, I have no reasonable explanation to offer. Whether they were true ship's rats, or a species that is to be found in the weed-haunted plains and islets of the Sargasso Sea, I cannot say. It may be that they are the descendants of rats that lived in ships long centuries lost in the Weed Sea, and which have learned to live among the weed, forming new characteristics, and developing fresh powers and instincts. Yet, I cannot say; for I speak entirely without authority, and do but tell this story as it is told in the fo'cas'le of many an old-time sailing ship – that dark, brine-tainted place where the young men learn somewhat of the mysteries of the all mysterious sea.

Footnotes for The Mystery of the Derelict
1. Unshaded lights are never allowed about the decks at night, as they are likely to blind the vision of the officer of the watch. – W.H.H.

If you enjoyed this, you might also like...
The Thing in the Weeds, see page 340
The Stone Ship, see page 365

Through the Vortex of a Cyclone

IT WAS IN THE MIDDLE of November that the four-masted barque, *Golconda*, came down from Crockett and anchored off Telegraph Hill, San Francisco. She was loaded with grain, and was homeward bound round Cape Horn. Five days later she was towed out through the Golden Gates, and cast loose off the Heads, and so set sail upon the voyage that was to come so near to being her last.

For a fortnight we had baffling winds; but after that time, got a good slant that carried us down to within a couple of degrees of the Line. Here it left us, and over a week passed before we managed to tack and drift our way into the Southern Hemisphere.

About five degrees South of the Line, we met with a fair wind that helped us Southward another ten or twelve degrees, and there, early one morning, it dropped us, ending with a short, but violent, thunder storm, in which, so frequent were the lightning flashes, that I managed to secure a picture of one, whilst in the act of snapshotting the sea and clouds upon our port side.

During the day, the wind, as I have remarked, left us entirely, and we lay becalmed under a blazing hot sun. We hauled up the lower sails to prevent them from chafing as the vessel rolled lazily on the scarce perceptible swells, and busied ourselves, as is customary on such occasions, with much swabbing and cleaning of paint-work.

As the day proceeded, so did the heat seem to increase; the atmosphere lost its clear look, and a low haze seemed to lie about the ship at a great distance. At times, the air seemed to have about it a queer, unbreathable quality; so that one caught oneself breathing with a sense of distress.

And, hour by hour, as the day moved steadily onward, the sense of oppression grew ever more acute.

Then, it was, I should think, about three-thirty in the afternoon, I became conscious of the fact that a strange, unnatural, dull, brick-red glare was in the sky. Very subtle it was, and I could not say that it came from any particular place; but rather it seemed to shine *in* the atmosphere. As I stood looking at it, the Mate came up beside me. After about half a minute, he gave out a sudden exclamation:

"Hark!" he said. "Did you hear that?"

"No, Mr. Jackson," I replied. "What was it like?"

"Listen!" was all his reply, and I obeyed; and so perhaps for a couple of minutes we stood there in silence.

"There! – There it is again!" he exclaimed, suddenly; and in the same instant I heard it… a sound like low, strange growling far away in the North-East. It lasted for about fifteen seconds, and then died away in a low, hollow, moaning noise, that sounded indescribably dree.

After that, for a space longer, we stood listening; and so, at last, it came again…a far, faint, wild-beast growling, away over the North-Eastern horizon. As it died away, with that strange hollow note, the Mate touched my arm:

"Go and call the Old Man," he said, meaning the Captain. "And while you're down, have a look at the barometer."

In both of these matters I obeyed him, and in a few moments the Captain was on deck, standing beside the Mate – listening.

"How's the glass?" asked the Mate, as I came up.

"Steady," I answered, and at that, he nodded his head, and resumed his expectant attitude. Yet, though we stood silent, maybe for the better part of half an hour, there came no further repetition of that weird, far-off growling, and so, as the glass was steady, no serious notice was taken of the matter.

That evening, we experienced a sunset of quite indescribable gorgeousness, which had, to me, an unnatural glow about it, especially in the way in which it lit up the surface of the sea, which was, at this time, stirred by a slight evening breeze. Evidently, the Mate was of the opinion that it foreboded something in the way of ill weather; for he gave orders for the watch on deck to take the three royals off her.

By the time the men had got down from aloft, the sun had set, and the evening was fading into dusk; yet, despite that, all the sky to the North-East was full of the most vivid red and orange; this being, it will be remembered, the direction from which we had heard earlier that sullen growling.

It was somewhat later, I remember, that I heard the Mate remark to the Captain that we were in for bad weather, and that it was his belief a Cyclone was coming down upon us; but this, the Captain – who was quite a young fellow – poo-poohed; telling him that he pinned *his* faith to the barometer, which was perfectly steady. Yet, I could see that the Mate was by no means so sure; but forebore to press further his opinion against his superior's.

Presently, as the night came down upon the world, the orange tints went out of the sky, and only a sombre, threatening red was left, with a strangely bright rift of white light running horizontally across it, about twenty degrees above the North-*Eastern* horizon.

This lasted for nigh on to half an hour, and so did it impress the crew with a sense of something impending, that many of them crouched, staring over the port rail, until long after it had faded into the general greyness.

That night, I recollect, it was my watch on deck from midnight until four in the morning. When the boy came down to wake me, he told me that it had been lightning during the past watch. Even as he spoke, a bright, bluish glare lit up the port-hole; but there was no succeeding thunder.

I sprang hastily from my bunk, and dressed; then, seizing my camera, ran out on deck. I opened the shutter, and the next instant – flash! a great stream of electricity sprang out of the zenith.

Directly afterwards, the Mate called to me from the break of the poop to know whether I had managed to secure *that* one. I replied, Yes, I thought I had, and he told me to come up on to the poop, beside him, and have a further try from there; for he, the Captain and the Second Mate were much interested in my photographic hobby, and did all in their power to aid me in the securing of successful snaps.

That the Mate was uneasy, I very soon perceived; for, presently, a little while after he had relieved the Second Mate, he ceased his pacing of the poop deck, and came and leant over the rail, alongside of me.

"I wish to goodness the Old Man would have her shortened right down to lower topsails," he said, a moment later, in a low voice. "There's some rotten, dirty weather knocking around. I can smell it." And he raised his head, and sniffed at the air.

"Why not shorten her down, on your own?" I asked him.

"Can't!" he replied. "The Old Man's left orders not to touch anything; but to call him if any change occurs. He goes *too* d—n much by the barometer, to suit me, and won't budge a rope's end, because it's steady."

All this time, the lightning had been playing at frequent intervals across the sky; but now there came several gigantic flashes, seeming extraordinarily near to the vessel, pouring down out of a great rift in the clouds – veritable torrents of electric fluid. I switched open the shutter of my camera, and pointed the lens upward; and the following instant, I secured a magnificent photograph of a great flash, which, bursting down from the same rift, divided to the East and West in a sort of vast electric arch.

For perhaps a minute afterwards, we waited, thinking that such a flash *must* be followed by thunder; but none came. Instead, from the darkness to the North-East, there sounded a faint, far-drawn-out wailing noise, that seemed to echo queerly across the quiet sea. And after that, silence.

The Mate stood upright, and faced round at me.

"Do you know," he said, "only once before in my life have I heard anything like that, and that was before the Cyclone in which the *Lancing*, and the *Eurasian* were lost, in the Indian Ocean."

"Do you think then there's *really* any danger of a Cyclone now?" I asked him, with something of a little thrill of excitement.

"I think—" he began, and then stopped, and swore suddenly. "Look!" he said, in a loud voice. "Look! 'Stalk' lightning, as I'm a living man!" And he pointed to the North-East. "Photograph that, while you've got the chance; you'll never have another as long as you live!"

I looked in the direction which he indicated, and there, sure enough, were great, pale, flickering streaks and tongues of flame *rising apparently out of the sea*. They remained steady for some ten or fifteen seconds, and in that time I was able to take a snap of them.

This photograph, as I discovered when I came to develop the negative, has not, I regret to say, taken regard of a strange, indefinable dull-red glare that lit up the horizon at the same time; but, as it is, it remains to me a treasured record of a form of electrical phenomenon but seldom seen, even by those whose good, or ill, fortune has allowed them to come face to face with a Cyclonic Storm. Before leaving this incident, I would once more impress upon the reader that this strange lightning was *not* descending from the atmosphere; but *rising from the sea*.

It was after I had secured this last snap, that the Mate declared it to be his conviction that a great Cyclonic Storm was coming down upon us from the North-East, and, with that – for about the twentieth time that watch – he went below to consult the barometer.

He came back in about ten minutes, to say that it was still steady; but that he had called the Old Man, and told him about the upward 'Stalk' lightning; yet the Captain, upon hearing from him that the glass was still steady, had refused to be alarmed, but had promised to come up and take a look round. This, in a while, he did; but, as Fate would have it, there was no further display of the 'Stalk' lightning, and, as the other kind had now become no more than an occasional dull glare behind the clouds to the North-East, he retired once more, leaving orders to be called if there were any change either in the glass or the weather.

With the sunrise there came a change, a low, slow-moving scud driving down from the North-East, and drifting across the face of the newly-risen sun, which was shining with a queer, unnatural glare. Indeed, so stormy and be-burred looked the sun, that I could have applied to it with truth the line:

"And the red Sun all bearded with the Storm,"

to describe its threatening aspect.

The glass also showed a change at last, rising a little for a short while, and then dropping about a tenth, and, at that, the Mate hurried down to inform the Skipper, who was speedily up on deck.

He had the fore and mizzen t'gallants taken off her; but nothing more; for he declared that he wasn't going to throw away a fine fair wind for any Old Woman's fancies.

Presently, the wind began to freshen; but the orange-red burr about the sun remained, and also it seemed to me that the tint of the water had a 'bad weather' look about it. I mentioned this to the Mate, and he nodded agreement; but said nothing in so many words, for the Captain was standing near.

By eight bells (four a.m.) the wind had freshened so much that we were lying over to it, with a big cant of the decks, and making a good twelve knots, under nothing higher than the main t'gallant.

We were relieved by the other watch, and went below for a short sleep. At eight o'clock, when again I came on deck, I found that the sea had begun to rise somewhat; but that otherwise the weather was much as it had been when I left the decks; save that the sun was hidden by a heavy squall to windward, which was coming down upon us.

Some fifteen minutes later, it struck the ship, making the foam fly, and carrying away the main topsail sheet. Immediately upon this, the heavy iron ring in the clew of the sail began to thrash and beat about, as the sail flapped in the wind, striking great blows against the steel yard; but the clewline was manned, and some of the men went aloft to repair the damage, after which the sail was once more sheeted home, and we continued to carry on.

About this time, the Mate sent me down into the saloon to take another look at the glass, and I found that it had fallen a further tenth. When I reported this to him, he had the main t'gallant taken in; but hung on to the mainsail, waiting for eight bells, when the whole crowd would be on deck to give a hand.

By that time, we had begun to ship water, and most of us were speedily very thoroughly soused; yet, we got the sail off her, and she rode the easier for the relief.

A little after one o'clock in the afternoon, I went out on deck to have a final 'squint' at the weather, before turning-in for a short sleep, and found that the wind had freshened considerably, the seas striking the counter of the vessel at times, and flying to a considerable height in foam.

At four o'clock, when once more I appeared on deck, I discovered the spray flying over us with a good deal of freedom, and the solid water coming aboard occasionally in odd tonnes.

Yet, so far there was, *to a sailorman*, nothing worthy of note, in the severity of the weather. It was merely blowing a moderately heavy gale, before which, under our six topsails and foresail, we were making a good twelve knots an hour to the Southward. Indeed, it seemed to me, at this time, that the Captain was right in his belief that we were not in for any very dirty weather, and I said as much to the Mate; whereat he laughed somewhat bitterly.

"Don't you make any sort of mistake!" he said, and pointed to leeward, where continual flashes of lightning darted down from a dark bank of cloud. "We're already within the borders of the Cyclone. We are travelling, so I take it, about a knot slower an hour to the South than the bodily forward movement of the Storm; so that you may reckon it's overtaking us at the rate of something like a mile an hour. Later on, I expect, it'll get a move on it, and then a torpedo boat wouldn't catch it! This bit of a breeze that we're having now" – and he gestured to windward with his elbow – "is only fluff – nothing more than the outer fringe of the advancing Cyclone! Keep your eye lifting to the North-East, and keep your ears open. Wait until you hear the thing yelling at you as loud as a million mad tigers!"

He came to a pause, and knocked the ashes out of his pipe; then he slid the empty 'weapon' into the side pocket of his long oilskin coat. And all the time, I could see that he was ruminating.

"Mark my words," he said, at last, and speaking with great deliberation. "Within twelve hours it'll be upon us!"

He shook his head at me. Then he added:

"Within twelve hours, my boy, you and I and every other soul in this blessed packet may be down there in the cold!" And the brute pointed downward into the sea, and grinned cheerfully at me.

It was our watch that night from eight to twelve; but, except that the wind freshened a trifle, hourly, nothing of note occurred during our watch. The wind was just blowing a good fresh gale, and giving us all we wanted, to keep the ship doing her best under topsails and foresail.

At midnight, I went below for a sleep. When I was called at four o'clock, I found a very different state of affairs. The day had broken, and showed the sea in a very confused state, with a tendency to run up into heaps, and there was a good deal less wind; but what struck me as most remarkable, and brought home with uncomfortable force the Mate's warning of the previous day, was the colour of the sky, which seemed to be everywhere one great glare of gloomy, orange-coloured light, streaked here and there with red. So intense was this glare that the seas, as they rose clumsily into heaps, caught and reflected the light in an extraordinary manner, shining and glittering gloomily, like vast moving mounds of liquid flame. The whole presenting an effect of astounding and uncanny grandeur.

I made my way up on to the poop, carrying my camera. There, I met the Mate.

"You'll not want that pretty little box of yours," he remarked, and tapped my camera. "I guess you'll find a coffin more useful."

"Then it's coming?" I said.

"Look!" was all his reply, and he pointed into the North-East.

I saw in an instant what it was at which he pointed. It was a great black wall of cloud that seemed to cover about seven points of the horizon, extending almost from North to East, and reaching upward some fifteen degrees towards the zenith. The intense, solid blackness of this cloud was astonishing, and threatening to the beholder, seeming, indeed, to be more like a line of great black cliffs standing out of the sea, than a mass of thick vapour.

I glanced aloft, and saw that the other watch were securing the mizzen upper topsail. At the same moment, the Captain appeared on deck, and walked over to the Mate.

"Glass has dropped another tenth, Mr. Jackson," he remarked, and glanced to windward. "I think we'd better have the fore and main upper topsails off her."

Scarcely had he given the order, before the Mate was down on the maindeck, shouting: – "Fore and main topsail hal'yards! Lower away! Man clewlines and spillinglines!" So eager was he to have the sail off her.

By the time that the upper topsails were furled, I noted that the red glare had gone out of the greater part of the sky to windward, and a stiffish looking squall was bearing down upon us. Away more to the North, I saw that the black rampart of cloud had disappeared, and, in place thereof, it seemed to me that the clouds in that quarter were assuming a hard, tufted appearance, and changing their shapes with surprising rapidity.

The sea also at this time was remarkable, acting uneasily, and hurling up queer little mounds of foam, which the passing squall caught and spread.

All these points, the Mate noted; for I heard him urging the Captain to take in the foresail and mizzen lower topsail. Yet, this, the Skipper seemed unwilling to do; but finally agreed to have the mizzen topsail off her. Whilst the men were up at this, the wind dropped abruptly in the tail of the squall, the vessel rolling heavily, and taking water and spray with every roll.

Now, I want the Reader to try and understand exactly how matters were at this particular and crucial moment. The wind had dropped entirely, and, with the dropping of the wind, a thousand different sounds broke harshly upon the ear, sounding almost unnatural in their distinctness, and impressing the ear with a sense of discomfort. With each roll of the ship, there came a chorus of creaks and groans from the swaying masts and gear, and the sails slatted with a damp, disagreeable sound. Beyond the ship, there was the constant, harsh murmur of the seas, occasionally changing to a low roar, as one broke near us. One other sound there was that punctuated all these, and that was the loud, slapping blows of the seas, as they hove themselves clumsily against the ship; and, for the rest, there was a strange sense of silence.

Then, as sudden as the report of a heavy gun, a great bellowing came out of the North and East, and died away into a series of monstrous grumbles of sound. It was not thunder. *It was the Voice of the approaching Cyclone.*

In the same instant, the Mate nudged my shoulder, and pointed, and I saw, with an enormous feeling of surprise, that a large waterspout had formed about four hundred yards astern, and was coming towards us. All about the base of it, the sea was foaming in a strange manner, and the whole thing seemed to have a curious luminous quality.

Thinking about it now, I cannot say that I perceived it to be in rotation; but nevertheless, I had the impression that it was revolving swiftly. Its general onward motion seemed to be about as fast as would be attained by a well-manned gig.

I remember, in the first moments of astonishment, as I watched it, hearing the Mate shout something to the Skipper about the foresail, then I realised suddenly that the spout was coming straight for the ship. I ran hastily to the taffrail, raised my camera, and snapped it, and then, as it seemed to tower right up above me, gigantic, I ran backwards in sudden fright. In the same instant, there came a blinding flash of lightning, almost in my face, followed instantaneously by a tremendous roar of thunder, and I saw that the thing had burst within about fifty yards of the ship. The sea, immediately beneath where it had been, leapt up in a great hummock of solid water, and foam, as though something as great as a house had been cast into the ocean. Then, rushing towards us, it struck the stern of the vessel, flying as high as our topsail yards in spray, and knocking me backwards on to the deck.

As I stood up, and wiped the water hurriedly from my camera, I heard the Mate shout out to know if I were hurt, and then, in the same moment, and before I could reply, he cried out:

"It's coming! Up hellum! Up hellum! Look out everybody! Hold on for your lives!"

Directly afterwards, a shrill, yelling noise seemed to fill the whole sky with a deafening, piercing sound. I glanced hastily over the port quarter. *In that direction the whole surface of the ocean seemed to be torn up into the air in monstrous clouds of spray.* The yelling sound passed into a vast scream, and the next instant the Cyclone was upon us.

Immediately, the air was so full of flying spray that I could not see a yard before me, and the wind slapped me back against the teak companion, pinning me there for a few moments, helpless. The ship heeled over to a terrible angle, so that, for some seconds, I thought we were going to capsize. Then, with a sudden lurch, she hove herself upright, and I became able to see about me a little, by switching the water from my face, and shielding my eyes. Near to me, the helmsman – a little Dago – was clinging to the wheel, looking like nothing so much as a drowned monkey, and palpably frightened to such an extent that he could hardly stand upright.

From him, I looked round at so much of the vessel as I could see, and up at the spars, and so, presently, I discovered how it was that she had righted. The mizzen topmast was gone just below the heel of the t'gallantmast, and the fore topmast a little above the cap. The main topmast alone stood. It was the losing of these spars which had eased her, and allowed her to right so suddenly. Marvellously enough, the foresail – a small, new, No. 1 canvas stormsail – had stood the strain, and was now bellying out, with a high foot, the sheets evidently having surged under the wind pressure. What was more extraordinary, was that the fore and main lower topsails were standing,[1] and this, despite the fact that the bare upper spars on both the fore and mizzen masts, had been carried away.

And now, the first awful burst of the Cyclone having passed with the righting of the vessel, the three sails stood, though tested to their utmost, and the ship, under the tremendous urging force of the Storm, was tearing forward at a high speed through the seas.

I glanced down now at myself and camera. Both were soaked; yet, as I discovered later, the latter would still take photographs. I struggled forward to the break of the poop, and stared down on to the maindeck. The seas were breaking aboard every moment, and the spray flying over us continually in huge white clouds. And in my ears was the incessant, wild, roaring-scream of the monster Whirl-Storm.

Then I saw the Mate. He was up against the lee rail, chopping at something with a hatchet. At times the water left him visible to his knees; anon he was completely submerged; but ever there was the whirl of his weapon amid the chaos of water, as he hacked and cut at the gear that held the mizzen t'gallant mast crashing against the side.

I saw him glance round once, and he beckoned with the hatchet to a couple of his watch who were fighting their way aft along the streaming decks. He did not attempt to shout, for no shout could have been heard in the incredible roaring of the wind. Indeed, so vastly loud was the noise made by this element, that I had not heard even the topmasts carry away; though the sound of a large spar breaking will make as great a noise as the report of a big gun. The next instant, I had thrust my camera into one of the hencoops upon the poop, and turned to struggle aft to the companionway; for I knew it was no use going to the Mate's aid without axes.

Presently, I was at the companion, and had the fastenings undone; then I opened the door, and sprang in on to the stairs. I slammed-to the door, bolted it, and made my way below, and so, in a minute, had possessed myself of a couple of axes. With these, I returned to the poop, fastening the companion doors carefully behind me, and, in a little, was up to my neck in water on the maindeck, helping to clear away the wreckage. The second axe, I had pushed into the hands of one of the men.

Presently, we had the gear cleared away.

Then we scrambled away forrard along the decks, through the boiling swirls of water and foam that swept the vessel, as the seas thundered aboard; and so we came to the assistance of the Second Mate, who was desperately busied, along with some of his watch, in clearing away the broken fore-topmast and yards that were held by their gear, thundering against the side of the ship.

Yet, it must not be supposed that we were to manage this piece of work, without coming to some harm; for, just as we made an end of it, an enormous sea swept aboard, and dashed one of the men against the spare topmast that was lashed along, inside the bulwarks, below the pin-rail. When we managed to pull the poor senseless fellow out from underneath the spar, where the sea had jammed him, we found that his left arm and collar-bone were broken. We took him forrard to the fo'cas'le, and there, with rough surgery, made him so comfortable as we could; after which we left him, but half conscious, in his bunk.

After that, several wet, weary hours were spent in rigging rough preventer-stays. Then the rest of us, men as well as officers, made our way aft to the poop; there to wait, desperately ready to cope with any emergency where our poor, futile human strength might aid to our salvation.

With great difficulty, the Carpenter had managed to sound the well, and, to our delight, had found that we were not making any water; so that the blows of the broken spars had done us no vital harm.

By midday, the following seas had risen to a truly formidable height, and two hands were working half naked at the wheel; for any carelessness in steering would, most certainly, have had horrible consequences.

In the course of the afternoon, the Mate and I went down into the saloon to get something to eat, and here, out of the deafening roar of the wind, I managed to get a short chat with my senior officer.

Talking about the waterspout which had so immediately preceded the first rush of the Cyclone, I made mention of its luminous appearance; to which he replied that it was due probably to a vast electric action going on between the clouds and the sea.

After that, I asked him why the Captain did not heave to, and ride the Storm out, instead of running before it, and risking being pooped, or broaching to.

To this, the Mate made reply that we were right in the line of translation; in other words, that we were directly in the track of the vortex, or centre, of the Cyclone, and that the Skipper was doing his best to edge the ship to leeward, before the centre, with the awful Pyramidal Sea, should overtake us.

"If we can't manage to get out of the way," he concluded, grimly, "you'll probably have a chance to photograph something that you'll never have time to develop!"

I asked him how he knew that the ship was directly in the track of the vortex, and he replied that the facts that the wind was not hauling, but getting steadily worse, with the barometer constantly falling, were sure signs.

And soon after that we returned to the deck.

As I have said, at midday, the seas were truly formidable; but by four p.m. they were so much worse that it was impossible to pass fore or aft along the decks, the water breaking aboard, as much as a hundred tonnes at a time, and sweeping all before it.

All this time, the roaring and *howling* of the Cyclone was so incredibly loud, that no word spoken, or shouted, out on deck – even though right into one's ear – could be heard distinctly, so that the utmost we could do to convey ideas to one another, was to make signs. And so, because of this, and to get for a little out of the painful and exhausting pressure of the wind, each of the officers would, in turn (sometimes singly and sometimes two at once), go down to the saloon, for a short rest and smoke.

It was in one of those brief 'smoke-ohs' that the Mate told me the vortex of the Cyclone was probably within about eighty or a hundred miles of us, and coming down on us at something like twenty or thirty knots an hour, which – as this speed enormously exceeded ours – made it probable that it would be upon us before midnight.

"Is there no chance of getting out of the way?" I asked. "Couldn't we haul her up a trifle, and cut across the track a bit quicker than we are doing?"

"No," replied the Mate, and shook his head, thoughtfully. "The seas would make a clean breach over us, if we tried that. It's a case of 'run till you're blind, and pray till you bust'!" he concluded with a certain despondent brutalness.

I nodded assent; for I knew that it was true. And after that we were silent. A few minutes later, we went up on deck. There we found that, the wind had increased, and blown the foresail bodily away; yet, despite the greater weight of the wind, there had come a rift in the clouds, through which the sun was shining with a queer brightness.

I glanced at the Mate, and smiled; for it seemed to me a good omen; but he shook his head, as one who should say: "It is no good omen; but a sign of something worse coming."

That he was right in refusing to be assured, I had speedy proof; for within ten minutes the sun had vanished, and the clouds seemed to be right down upon our mastheads – great bellying webs of black vapour, that seemed almost to mingle with the flying clouds of foam and spray. The wind appeared to gain strength minute by minute, rising into an abominable scream, so piercing at times as to seem to pain the ear drums.

In this wise an hour passed, the ship racing onward under her two topsails, seeming to have lost no speed with the losing of the foresail; though it is possible that she was more under water forrard than she had been.

Then, about five-thirty p.m., I heard a louder roar in the air above us, so deep and tremendous that it seemed to daze and stun one; and, in the same instant, the two topsails were blown out of the bolt-ropes, and one of the hencoops was lifted bodily off the poop, and hurled into the air, descending with an *inaudible* crash on to the maindeck. Luckily, it was not the one into which I had thrust my camera.

With the losing of the topsails, we might be very truly described as running under bare poles; for now we had not a single stitch of sail set anywhere. Yet, so furious was the increasing wind, so tremendous the weight of it, that the vessel, though urged forward only by the pressure of the element upon her naked spars and hull, managed to keep ahead of the monstrous following seas, which now were grown to truly awesome proportions.

The next hour or two, I remember only as a time that spread out monotonously. A time miserable and dazing, and dominated always by the deafening, roaring scream of the Storm. A time of wetness and dismalness, in which I knew, more than saw, that the ship wallowed on and on through the interminable seas. And so, hour by hour, the wind increased as the Vortex of the Cyclone – the 'Death-Patch' – drew nearer and ever nearer.

Night came on early, or, if not night, a darkness that was fully its equivalent. And now I was able to see how tremendous was the electric action that was going on all about us. There seemed to be no lightning flashes; but, instead, there came at times across the darkness, queer luminous shudders of light. I am not acquainted with any word that better describes this extraordinary electrical phenomenon, than 'shudders' of light – broad, dull shudders of light, that came in undefined belts across the black, thunderous canopy of clouds, which seemed so low that our main-truck must have 'puddled' them with every roll of the ship.

A further sign of electric action was to be seen in the 'corpse candles', which ornamented every yard-arm. Not only were they upon the yard-arms; but occasionally several at a time would glide up and down one or more of the fore and aft stays, at whiles swinging off to one side or the other, as the ship rolled. The sight having in it a distinct touch of weirdness.

It was an hour or so later, I believe a little after nine p.m., that I witnessed the most striking manifestation of electrical action that I have ever seen; this being neither more nor less than a display of Aurora Borealis lightning – a sight dree and almost frightening, with the sense of unearthliness and mystery that it brings.

I want you to be very clear that I am *not* talking about the Northern Lights – which, indeed, could never be seen at that distance to the Southward; but of an extraordinary electrical phenomenon which occurred when the vortex of the Cyclone was within some twenty or thirty miles of the ship. It occurred suddenly. First, a ripple of 'Stalk' lightning showed right away over the oncoming seas to the Northward; then, abruptly, a red glare shone out in the sky, and, immediately afterwards, vast streamers of greenish flame appeared above the red glare. These lasted, perhaps, half a minute, expanding and contracting over the sky with a curious quivering motion. The whole forming a truly awe-inspiring spectacle.

And then, slowly, the whole thing faded, and only the blackness of the night remained, slit in all directions by the phosphorescent crests of the seas.

I don't know whether I can convey to you any vivid impression of our case and chances at this time. It is so difficult – unless one had been through a similar experience – even to comprehend fully the incredible loudness of the wind. Imagine a noise as loud as the loudest thunder you have ever heard; then imagine this noise to last hour after hour, without intermission, and to have in it a hideously threatening hoarse note, and, blending with this, a constant yelling scream that rises at times to such a pitch that the very ear drums seem to experience pain, and then, perhaps, you will be able to comprehend merely the amount of *sound* that has to be endured during the passage of one of these Storms. And then, the *force* of the wind! Have you ever faced a wind so powerful that it splayed your lips apart, whether you would or not, laying your teeth bare to view? This is only a little thing; but it may help you to conceive something of the strength of a wind that will play such antics with one's mouth. The sensation it gives is extremely disagreeable – a sense of foolish impotence, is how I can best describe it.

Another thing; I learned that, with my face to the wind, I could not breathe. This is a statement baldly put; but it should help me somewhat in my endeavour to bring home to you the force of the wind, as exemplified in the minor details of my experience.

To give some idea of the wind's power, as shown in a larger way, one of the lifeboats on the after skids was up-ended against the mizzen mast, and there crushed flat by the wind, as though a monstrous invisible hand had pinched it. Does this help you a little to gain an idea of wind-force never met with in a thousand ordinary lives?

Apart from the wind, it must be borne in mind that the gigantic seas pitch the ship about in a most abominable manner. Indeed, I have seen the stern of a ship hove up to such a height that I could see the seas ahead over the fore topsail yards, and when I explain that these will be something like seventy to eighty feet above the deck, you may be able to imagine what manner of Sea is to be met with in a great Cyclonic Storm.

Regarding this matter of the size and ferocity of the seas, I possess a photograph that was taken about ten o'clock at night. This was photographed by the aid of flashlight, an operation in which the Captain assisted me. We filled an old, percussion pistol with flashlight powder, with an air-cone of paper down the centre. Then, when I was ready, I opened the shutter of the camera, and pointed it over the stern into the darkness. The Captain fired the pistol, and, in the instantaneous great blaze of light that followed, I saw what manner of sea it was that pursued us. To say it was a mountain, is to be futile. *It was like a moving cliff.*

As I snapped-to the shutter of my camera, the question flashed into my brain: "Are we going to live it out, after all?" And, suddenly, it came home to me that I was a little man in a little ship, in the midst of a very great sea.

And then fresh knowledge came to me; I knew, abruptly, that it would not be a difficult thing to be very much afraid. The knowledge was new, and took me more in the stomach than the heart. Afraid! I had been in so many storms that I had forgotten they might be things to fear. Hitherto, my sensation at the thought of bad weather had been chiefly a feeling of annoyed repugnance, due to many memories of dismal wet nights, in wetter oilskins; with everything about the vessel reeking with damp and cheerless discomfort. But *fear* – No! A sailor has no more normal fear of bad weather, than a steeple-jack fears height. It is, as you might say, his vocation. And now this hateful sense of insecurity!

I turned from the taffrail, and hurried below to wipe the lens and cover of my camera; for the whole air was full of driving spray, that soaked everything, and hurt the face intolerably; being driven with such force by the storm.

Whilst I was drying my camera, the Mate came down for a minute's breathing space.

"Still at it?" he said.

"Yes," I replied, and I noticed, half-consciously, that he made no effort to light his pipe, as he stood with his arm crooked over an empty, brass candle bracket.

"You'll never develop them," he remarked.

"Of course I shall!" I replied, half-irritably; but with a horrid little sense of chilliness at his words, which came so unaptly upon my mind, so lately perturbed by uncomfortable thoughts.

"You'll see," he replied, with a sort of brutal terseness. "We shan't be above water by midnight!"

"You *can't* tell," I said. "What's the use of meeting trouble! Vessels have lived through worse than this?"

"Have they?" he said, very quietly. "Not many vessels have lived through worse than what's to come. I suppose you realise we expect to meet the Centre in less than an hour?"

"Well," I replied, "anyway, I shall go on taking photos. I guess if we come through all right, I shall have something to show people ashore."

He laughed, a queer, little, bitter laugh.

"You may as well do that as anything else," he said. "We can't do anything to help ourselves. If we're not pooped before the Centre reaches us, *IT*'ll finish us in quick time!"

Then that cheerful officer of mine turned slowly, and made his way on deck, leaving me, as may be imagined, particularly exhilarated by his assurances. Presently, I followed, and, having barred the companionway behind me, struggled forward to the break of the poop, clutching blindly at any holdfast in the darkness.

And so, for a space, we waited in the Storm – the wind bellowing fiendishly, and our maindecks one chaos of broken water, swirling and roaring to and fro in the darkness.

It was a little later that some one plucked me hard by the sleeve, and, turning, I made out with difficulty that it was the Captain, trying to attract my attention. I caught his wrist, to show that I comprehended what he desired, and, at that, he dropped on his hands and knees, and crawled aft along the streaming poop deck, I following, my camera held between my teeth by the handle.

He reached the companionway, and unbarred the starboard door; then crawled through, and I followed after him. I fastened the door, and made my way, in his wake, to the saloon. Here he turned to me. He was a curiously devil-may-care sort of man, and I found that he had brought me down to explain that the Vortex would be upon us very soon, and that I should have the chance of a life-time to get a snap of the much talked of Pyramidal Sea. And, in short, that he wished me to have everything prepared, and the pistol ready loaded with flashlight powder; for, as he remarked:

"*If* we get through, it'll be a rare curiosity to show some of those unbelieving devils ashore."

In a little, we had everything ready, and then we made our way once more up on deck; the Captain placing the pistol in the pocket of his silk oilskin coat.

There, together, under the after weather-cloth, we waited. The Second Mate, I could not see; but occasionally I caught a vague sight of the First Mate, standing near the after binnacle,[2] and obviously watching the steering. Apart from the puny halo that emanated from the binnacle, all else was blind darkness, save for the phosphorescent lights of the overhanging crests of the seas.

And above us and around us, filling all the sky with sound, was the incessant mad yowling of the Cyclone; the noise so vast, and the volume and mass of the wind so enormous that I am impressed now, looking back, with a sense of having been in a semi-stunned condition through those last minutes.

I am conscious now that a vague time passed. A time of noise and wetness and lethargy and immense tiredness. Abruptly, a tremendous flash of lightning burst through the clouds. It was followed, almost directly, by another, which seemed to rive the sky apart. Then, so quickly that the succeeding thunder-clap was *audible* to our wind-deafened ears, the wind ceased, and, in the comparative, but hideously unnatural, silence, I caught the Captain's voice shouting:

"The Vortex – quick!"

Even as I pointed my camera over the rail, and opened the shutter, my brain was working with a preternatural avidity, drinking in a thousand uncanny sounds and echoes that seemed to come upon me from every quarter, brutally distinct against the background of the Cyclone's distant howling. There were the harsh, bursting, frightening, intermittent noises of the seas, making tremendous, slopping crashes of sound; and, mingling with these, the shrill, hissing scream of the foam;[3] the dismal sounds, that suggested dankness, of water swirling over our decks; and oddly, the faintly-heard creaking of the gear and shattered spars; and then – *Flash*, in the same instant in which I had taken in these varied impressions, the Captain had fired the pistol, and I saw the Pyramidal Sea…. A sight never to be forgotten. A sight rather for the Dead than the Living. A sea such as I could never have imagined. Boiling and bursting upward in monstrous hillocks of water and foam as big as houses. I heard, without knowing I heard, the Captain's expression of amazement. Then a thunderous roar was in my ears. One of those vast, flying hills of water had struck the ship, and, for some moments, I had a sickening feeling that she was sinking beneath me. The water cleared, and I found myself clinging to the iron weather-cloth staunchion; the weather-cloth itself had gone. I wiped my eyes, and coughed dizzily for a little; then I stared round for the Captain. I could see something dimly up against the rail; something that moved and stood upright. I sung out to know whether it was the Captain, and whether he was all right? To which he replied, heartily enough, but with a gasp, that he was all right so far.

From him, I glanced across to the wheel. There was no light in the binnacle, and, later, I found that it had been washed away, and with it one of the helmsmen. The other man also was gone; but we discovered him, nigh an hour later, jammed half through the rail that ran round the poop. To leeward, I heard the Mate singing out to know whether we were safe; to which both the Captain and I shouted a reply, so as to assure him. It was then I became aware that my camera had been washed out of my hands. I found it eventually among a tangle of ropes and gear to leeward.

Again and again the great hills of water struck the vessel, seeming to rise up on every side at once – towering, live pyramids of brine, in the darkness, hurling upward with a harsh unceasing roaring.

From her taffrail to her knight-heads, the ship was swept, fore and aft, so that no living thing could have existed for a moment down upon the maindeck, which was practically submerged. Indeed, the whole vessel seemed at times to be lost beneath the chaos of water that thundered down and over her in clouds and cataracts of brine and foam, so that each moment seemed like to be our last.

Occasionally, I would hear the hoarse voice of the Captain or the Mate, calling through the gloom to one another, or to the figures of the clinging men. And then again would come the thunder of water, as the seas burst over us. And all this in an almost impenetrable darkness, save when some unnatural glare of lightning sundered the clouds, and lit up the thirty-mile cauldron that had engulfed us.

And, anon, all this while, round about, seeming to come from every point of the horizon, sounded a vast, but distant, bellowing and screaming noise, that I caught sometimes above the harsh, slopping roarings of the bursting water-hills all about us. The sound appeared now to be growing louder upon our port beam. It was the Storm circling far round us.

Some time later, there sounded an intense roar in the air above the ship, and then came a far-off shrieking, that grew rapidly into a mighty whistling-scream, and a minute afterwards a most tremendous gust of wind struck the ship on her port side, hurling her over on to her starboard broadside. For many minutes she lay there, her decks under water almost up to the coamings of the hatches.[4] Then she righted, sullenly and slowly, freeing herself from, maybe, half a thousand tonnes of water.

Again there came a short period of windlessness, and then once more the yelling of an approaching gust. It struck us; but now the vessel had paid off before the wind, and she was not again forced over on to her side.

From now onward, we drove forward over vast seas, with the Cyclone bellowing and wailing over us in one unbroken roar…. *The Vortex had passed*, and, could we but last out a few more hours, then might we hope to win through.

With the return of the wind, the Mate and one of the men had taken the wheel; but, despite the most careful steering, we were pooped several times;[5] for the seas were hideously broken and confused, we being still in the wake of the Vortex, and the wind not having had time as yet to smash the Pyramidal Sea into the more regular storm waves, which, though huge in size, give a vessel a chance to rise to them.

It was later that some of us, headed by the Mate – who had relinquished his place at the wheel to one of the men – ventured down on to the maindeck with axes and knives, to clear away the wreckage of some of the spars which we had lost in the Vortex. Many a grim risk was run in that hour; but we cleared the wreck, and after that, scrambled back, dripping, to the poop, where the Steward, looking woefully white and scared, served out rum to us from a wooden deck-bucket.

It was decided now that we should bring her head to the seas, so as to make better weather of it. To reduce the risk as much as possible, we had already put out two fresh oil-bags, which we had prepared, and which, indeed, we ought to have done earlier; for though they were being constantly washed aboard again, we had begun at once to take less water.

Now, we took a hawser from the bows, outside of everything, and right away aft to the poop, where we bent on our sea-anchor, which was like an enormous log-bag, or drogue, made of triple canvas.

We bent on our two oil-bags to the sea-anchor, and then dropped the whole business over the side. When the vessel took the pull of it, we put down our helm, and came up into the wind, very quick, and without taking any great water. And a risk it was; but a deal less than some we had come through already.

Slowly, with an undreamt of slowness, the remainder of the night passed, minute by minute, and at last the day broke in a weary dawn; the sky full of a stormy, sickly light. On every side tumbled an interminable chaos of seas. And the vessel herself—! A wreck, she appeared. The mizzenmast had gone, some dozen feet above the deck; the main topmast had gone, and so had the jigger-topmast. I struggled forrard to the break of the poop, and glanced along the decks. The boats had gone. All the iron scupper-doors were either bent, or had disappeared. On the starboard side, opposite to the stump of the mizzenmast, was a great ragged gap in the steel bulwarks, where the mast must have struck, when it carried away. In several other places, the t'gallant rail was smashed or bent, where it had been struck by falling spars. The side of the teak deck-house had been stove, and the water was roaring in and out with each roll of the ship. The sheep-pen had vanished, and so – as I discovered later – had the pigsty.

Further forrard, my glance went, and I saw that the sea had breached the bulkshead, across the after end of the fo'cas'le, and, with each biggish sea that we shipped, a torrent of water drove in, and then flowed out, sometimes bearing with it an odd board, or perhaps a man's boot, or some article of wearing apparel. In two places on the maindeck, I saw men's sea-chests, washing to and fro in the water that streamed over the deck. And, suddenly, there came into my mind a memory of the poor fellow who had broken his arm when we were cutting loose the wreck of the fore-topmast.

Already, the strength of the Cyclone was spent, so far, at least, as we were concerned; and I was thinking of making a try for the fo'cas'le, when, close beside me, I heard the Mate's voice. I turned, with a little start. He had evidently noticed the breach in the bulkshead; for he told me to watch a chance, and see if we could get forrard.

This, we did; though not without a further thorough sousing; as we were still shipping water by the score of tonnes. Moreover, the risk was considerably greater than might be conceived; for the doorless scupper-ports offered uncomfortable facilities for gurgling out into the ocean, along with a tonne or two of brine from the decks.

We reached the fo'cas'le, and pulled open the lee door. We stepped inside. It was like stepping into a dank, gloomy cavern. Water was dripping from every beam and staunchion. We struggled across the slippery deck, to where we had left the sick man in his bunk. In the dim light, we saw that man and bunk, everything, had vanished; only the bare steel sides of the vessel remained. Every bunk and fitting in the place had been swept away, and all of the men's sea-chests. Nothing remained, save, it might be, an odd soaked rag of clothing, or a sodden bunk-board.

The Mate and I looked at one another, in silence.

"Poor devil!" he said. He repeated his expression of pity, staring at the place where had been the bunk. Then, grave of face, he turned to go out on deck. As he did so, a heavier sea than usual broke aboard; flooded roaring along the decks, and swept in through the broken bulkshead and the lee doorway. It swirled round the sides, caught us, and threw us down in a heap; then swept out through the breach and the doorway, carrying the Mate with it. He managed to grasp the lintel of the doorway, else, I do believe, he would have gone out through one of the open scupper traps. A doubly hard fate, after having come safely through the Cyclone.

Outside of the fo'cas'le, I saw that the ladders leading up to the fo'cas'le head had both gone; but I managed to scramble up. Here, I found that both anchors had been washed away, and the rails all round; only the bare staunchions remaining.

Beyond the bows, the jibboom had gone, and all the gear was draggled inboard over the fo'cas'le head, or trailing in the sea.

We made our way aft, and reported; then the roll was called, and we found that no one else was missing, besides the two I have already mentioned, and the man we found jammed half through the poop rails, who was now under the Steward's care.

From that time on, the sea went down steadily, until, presently, it ceased to threaten us, and we proceeded to get the ship cleared up a bit; after which, one watch turned-in on the floor of the saloon, and the other was told to 'stand easy'.

Hour by hour, through that day and the next, the sea went down, until it was difficult to believe that we had so lately despaired for our lives. And so the second evening came, calm and restful, the wind no more than a light summer's breeze, and the sea calming steadily.

About seven bells that second night, a big steamer crossed our stern, and slowed down to ask us if we were in need of help; for, even by moonlight, it was easy to see our dismantled condition. This offer, however, the Captain refused; and with many good wishes, the big vessel swung off into the moon-wake, and so, presently, we were left alone in the quiet night; safe at last, and rich in a completed experience.

Footnotes for Through the Vortex of a Cyclone

1. I suggest the existence of smaller air vortices within the Cyclone. By air vortices, I mean vorticular air whorls – as it might be the upper portions of uncompleted waterspouts. How else explain the naked mizzen and fore topmasts and t'gallant masts being twisted off (as later appeared to have been the case), and yet the great spread of the lower topsails and the foresail not suffering? I am convinced that the unequal force of the first wind-burst is only thus to be explained.
2. It occurs to me here, as showing in another way the unusual wind-strength, to mention that, having tried in vain every usual method of keeping the wind from blowing out the binnacle lamps; such as stuffing all the crevices with rags, and making temporary shields for the chimneys, the Skipper had at last resorted to a tiny electric watch light, which he fixed in the binnacle, and which now enabled me to get an odd vague glimpse of the Mate, as he hovered near the compass.
3. A description absolute and without exaggeration. Who that has ever heard the weird, crisp screaming of the foam, in some momentary lull in a great storm, when a big sea has reared itself within a few fathoms of one, can ever forget it?
4. The Second Mate, who was holding to the rail across the break of the poop, gave me this information later; he being in a position to see the maindecks at the time.

5. Possibly, our being pooped at this time, was due chiefly to the fact that our speed through the water had diminished, owing to our having lost more of our spars whilst in the Vortex, and some of the gear still towing. And a Mercy our sides were not stove a thousand times!

If you enjoyed this, you might also like...
The Shamraken Homeward-Bounder, see page 162
The Real Thing: 'S.O.S.', see page 198

The Shamraken
Homeward-Bounder

Chapter I

THE OLD *SHAMRAKEN*, sailing-ship, had been many days upon the waters. She was old
– older than her masters, and that was saying a good deal. She seemed in no hurry, as she
lifted her bulging, old, wooden sides through the seas. What need for hurry! She would
arrive some time, in some fashion, as had been her habit heretofore.

Two matters were especially noticeable among her crew – who were also her masters;
the first the agedness of each and everyone; the second the *family* sense which appeared
to bind them, so that the ship seemed manned by a crew, all of whom were related one to
the other; yet it was not so.

A strange company were they, each man bearded, aged and grizzled; yet there was
nothing of the inhumanity of old age about them, save it might be in their freedom from
grumbling, and the calm content which comes only to those in whom the more violent
passions have died.

Had anything to be done, there was nothing of the growling, inseparable from the
average run of sailor men. They went aloft to the 'job' – whatever it might be – with
the wise submission which is brought only by age and experience. Their work was
gone through with a certain slow pertinacity – a sort of tired steadfastness, born of the
knowledge that such work *had* to be done. Moreover, their hands possessed the ripe
skill which comes only from exceeding practice, and which went far to make amends
for the feebleness of age. Above all, their movements, slow as they might be, were
remorseless in their lack of faltering. They had so often performed the same kind of
work, that they had arrived, by the selection of utility, at the shortest and most simple
methods of doing it.

They had, as I have said, been many days upon the water, though I am not sure that
any man in her knew to a nicety the number of those days. Though Skipper Abe Tombes
– addressed usually as Skipper Abe – may have had some notion; for he might be seen at
times gravely adjusting a prodigious quadrant, which suggests that he kept some sort of
record of time and place.

Of the crew of the *Shamraken*, some half dozen were seated, working placidly at such
matters of seamanship as were necessary. Besides these, there were others about the
decks. A couple who paced the lee side of the main deck, smoking, and exchanging an
occasional word. One who sat by the side of a worker, and made odd remarks between
draws at his pipe. Another, out upon the jibboom, who fished, with a line, hook and white
rag, for bonito. This last was Nuzzie, the ship's boy. He was grey-bearded, and his years
numbered five and fifty. A boy of fifteen he had been, when he joined the *Shamraken*, and
'boy' he was still, though forty years had passed into eternity, since the day of his 'signing

on'; for the men of the *Shamraken* lived in the past, and thought of him only as the 'boy' of that past.

It was Nuzzie's watch below – his time for sleeping. This might have been said also of the other three men who talked and smoked; but for themselves they had scarce a thought of sleep. Healthy age sleeps little, and they were in health, though so ancient.

Presently, one of those who walked the lee side of the main deck, chancing to cast a glance forrard, observed Nuzzie still to be out upon the jibboom, jerking his line so as to delude some foolish bonito into the belief that the white rag was a flying-fish.

The smoker nudged his companion.

"Time thet b'y 'ad 'is sleep."

"i, i, mate," returned the other, withdrawing his pipe, and giving a steadfast look at the figure seated out upon the jibboom.

For the half of a minute they stood there, very effigies of Age's implacable determination to rule rash Youth. Their pipes were held in their hands, and the smoke rose up in little eddies from the smouldering contents of the bowls.

"Thar's no tamin' of thet b'y!" said the first man, looking very stern and determined. Then he remembered his pipe, and took a draw.

"B'ys is tur'ble queer critters," remarked the second man, and remembered his pipe in turn.

"Fishin' w'en 'e orter be sleepin'," snorted the first man.

"B'ys needs a tur'ble lot er sleep," said the second man. "I 'member w'en I wor a b'y. I reckon it's ther growin'."

And all the time poor Nuzzie fished on.

"Guess I'll jest step up an' tell 'im ter come in outer thet," exclaimed the first man, and commenced to walk towards the steps leading up on to the fo'cas'le head.

"B'y!" he shouted, as soon as his head was above the level of the fo'cas'le deck. "B'y!"

Nuzzie looked round, at the second call.

"Eh?" he sung out.

"Yew come in outer thet," shouted the older man, in the somewhat shrill tone which age had brought to his voice. "Reckon we'll be 'avin' yer sleepin' at the wheel ter night."

"i," joined in the second man, who had followed his companion up on to the fo'cas'le head. "Come in, b'y, an' get ter yer bunk."

"Right," called Nuzzie, and commenced to coil up his line. It was evident that he had no thought of disobeying. He came in off the spar, and went past them without a word, on the way to turn in.

They, on their part, went down slowly off the fo'cas'le head, and resumed their walk fore and aft along the lee side of the main deck.

Chapter II

"I RECKON, ZEPH," said the man who sat upon the hatch and smoked, "I reckon as Skipper Abe's 'bout right. We've made a trifle o' dollars outer the old 'ooker, an' we don't get no younger."

"Ay, thet's so, right 'nuff," returned the man who sat beside him, working at the stropping of a block.

"An' it's 'bout time's we got inter the use o' bein' ashore," went on the first man, who was named Job.

Zeph gripped the block between his knees, and fumbled in his hip pocket for a plug. He bit off a chew and replaced the plug.

"Seems cur'ous this is ther last trip, w'en yer comes ter think uv it," he remarked, chewing steadily, his chin resting on his hand.

Job took two or three deep draws at his pipe before he spoke.

"Reckon it had ter come sumtime," he said, at length. "I've a purty leetle place in me mind w'er' I'm goin' ter tie up. 'Ave yer thought erbout it, Zeph?"

The man who held the block between his knees, shook his head, and stared away moodily over the sea.

"Dunno, Job, as I know what I'll do w'en ther old 'ooker's sold," he muttered. "Sence M'ria went, I don't seem nohow ter care 'bout bein' 'shore."

"I never 'ad no wife," said Job, pressing down the burning tobacco in the bowl of his pipe. "I reckon seafarin' men don't ought ter have no truck with wives."

"Thet's right 'nuff, Job, fer yew. Each man ter 'is taste. I wer' tur'ble fond uv M'ria—" he broke off short, and continued to stare out over the sea.

"I've allus thought I'd like ter settle down on er farm o' me own. I guess the dollars I've arned 'll do the trick," said Job.

Zeph made no reply, and, for a time, they sat there, neither speaking.

Presently, from the door of the fo'cas'le, on the starboard side, two figures emerged. They were also of the 'watch below'. If anything, they seemed older than the rest of those about the decks; their beards, white, save for the stain of tobacco juice, came nearly to their waists. For the rest, they had been big vigorous men; but were now sorely bent by the burden of their years. They came aft, walking slowly. As they came opposite to the main hatch, Job looked up and spoke –

"Say, Nehemiah, thar's Zeph here's been thinkin' 'bout M'ria, an' I ain't bin able ter peek 'im up nohow."

The smaller of the two newcomers shook his head slowly.

"We hev oor trubbles," he said. "We hev oor trubbles. I hed mine w'en I lost my datter's gell. I wor powerful took wi' thet gell, she wor that winsome; but it wor like ter be – it wor like ter be, an' Zeph's hed his trubble sence then."

"M'ria wer' a good wife ter me, she wer'," said Zeph, speaking slowly. "An' now th' old 'ooker's goin', I'm feared as I'll find it mighty lonesome ashore yon," and he waved his hand, as though suggesting vaguely that the shore lay anywhere beyond the starboard rail.

"Ay," remarked the second of the newcomers. "It's er weary thing tu me as th' old packet's goin'. Six and sixty year hev I sailed in her. Six and sixty year!" He nodded his head, mournfully, and struck a match with shaky hands.

"It's like ter be," said the smaller man. "It's like ter be."

And, with that, he and his companion moved over to the spar that lay along under the starboard bulwarks, and there seated themselves, to smoke and meditate.

Chapter III

SKIPPER ABE, and Josh Matthews, the First Mate, were standing together beside the rail which ran across the break of the poop. Like the rest of the men of the *Shamraken*, their age had come upon them, and the frost of eternity had touched their beards and hair.

Skipper Abe was speaking:

"It's harder 'n I'd thought," he said, and looked away from the Mate, staring hard along the worn, white-scoured decks.

"Dunno w'at I'll du, Abe, w'en she's gone," returned the old Mate. "She's been a 'ome fer us these sixty years an' more." He knocked out the old tobacco from his pipe, as he spoke, and began to cut a bowl-full of fresh.

"It's them durned freights!" exclaimed the Skipper. "We're jest losin' dollars every trip. It's them steam packets as hes knocked us out."

He sighed wearily, and bit tenderly at his plug.

"She's been a mighty comfortable ship," muttered Josh, in soliloquy. "An' sence thet b'y o' mine went, I sumhow thinks less o' goin' ashore 'n I used ter. I ain't no folk left on all thar 'arth."

He came to an end, and began with his old trembling fingers to fill his pipe.

Skipper Abe said nothing. He appeared to be occupied with his own thoughts. He was leaning over the rail across the break of the poop, and chewing steadily. Presently, he straightened himself up and walked over to leeward. He expectorated, after which he stood there for a few moments, taking a short look round – the result of half a century of habit. Abruptly, he sung out to the Mate…

"Wat d'yer make outer it?" he queried, after they had stood awhile, peering.

"Dunno, Abe, less'n it's some sort o' mist, riz up by ther 'eat."

Skipper Abe shook his head; but having nothing better to suggest, held his peace for awhile.

Presently, Josh spoke again:

"Mighty cur'us, Abe. These are strange parts."

Skipper Abe nodded his assent, and continued to stare at that which had come into sight upon the lee bow. To them, as they looked, it seemed that a vast wall of rose-coloured mist was rising towards the zenith. It showed nearly ahead, and at first had seemed no more than a bright cloud upon the horizon; but already had reached a great way into the air, and the upper edge had taken on wondrous flame-tints.

"It's powerful nice-lookin'," said Josh. "I've allus 'eard as things was diff'rent out 'n these parts."

Presently, as the *Shamraken* drew near to the mist, it appeared to those aboard that it filled all the sky ahead of them, being spread out now far on either bow. And so in a while they entered into it, and, at once, the aspect of all things was changed… The mist, in great rosy wreaths, floated all about them, seeming to soften and beautify every rope and spar, so that the old ship had become, as it were, a fairy craft in an unknown world.

"Never seen nothin' like it, Abe – nothin'!" said Josh. "Ey! but it's fine! It's fine! Like 's ef we'd run inter ther sunset."

"I'm mazed, just mazed!" exclaimed Skipper Abe, "but I'm 'gree'ble as it's purty, mighty purty."

For a further while, the two old fellows stood without speech, just gazing and gazing. With their entering into the mist, they had come into a greater quietness than had been theirs out upon the open sea. It was as though the mist muffled and toned down the creak, creak, of the spars and gear; and the big, foamless seas that rolled past them, seemed to have lost something of their harsh whispering roar of greeting.

"Sort o' unarthly, Abe," said Josh, later, and speaking but little above a whisper. "Like as ef yew was in church."

"Ay," replied Skipper Abe. "It don't seem nat'rel."

"Shouldn't think as 'eaven was all thet diff'rent," whispered Josh. And Skipper Abe said nothing in contradiction.

Chapter IV

SOMETIME LATER, the wind began to fail, and it was decided that, when eight bells was struck, all hands should set the main t'gallant. Presently, Nuzzie having been called (for he was the only one aboard who had turned in) eight bells went, and all hands put aside their pipes, and prepared to tail on to the ha'lyards; yet no one of them made to go up to loose the sail. That was the b'y's job, and Nuzzie was a little late in coming out on deck. When, in a minute, he appeared, Skipper Abe spoke sternly to him.

"Up now, b'y, an' loose thet sail. D'y think to let er grown man dew suchlike work! Shame on yew!"

And Nuzzie, the grey-bearded 'b'y' of five and fifty years, went aloft humbly, as he was bidden.

Five minutes later, he sung out that all was ready for hoisting, and the string of ancient Ones took a strain on the ha'lyards. Then Nehemiah, being the chaunty man, struck up in his shrill quaver:

"Thar wor an ole farmer in Yorkshire did dwell."

And the shrill piping of the ancient throats took up the refrain:

"Wi' me ay, ay, blow thar lan' down."

Nehemiah caught up the story:

"'e 'ad 'n ole wife, 'n 'e wished 'er in 'ell."

"Give us some time ter blow thar lan' down," came the quavering chorus of old voices.

"O, thar divvel come to 'im one day at thar plough," continued old Nehemiah; and the crowd of ancients followed up with the refrain: "Wi' me ay, ay, blow thar lan' down."

"I've comed fer th' ole woman, I mun 'ave 'er now," sang Nehemiah. And again the refrain: "Give us some time ter blow thar lan' down," shrilled out.

And so on to the last couple of stanzas. And all about them, as they chaunteyed, was that extraordinary, rose-tinted mist; which, above, blent into a marvellous radiance of flame-colour, as though, just a little higher than their mastheads, the sky was one red ocean of silent fire.

"Thar wor three leetle divvels chained up ter thar wall," sang Nehemiah, shrilly.

"Wi' me ay, ay, blow thar lan' down," came the piping chorus.

"She tuk off 'er clog, 'n she walloped 'em all," chaunted old Nehemiah, and again followed the wheezy, age-old refrain.

"These three leetle divvels fer marcy did bawl," quavered Nehemiah, cocking one eye upward to see whether the yard was nearly mast-headed.

"Wi' me ay, ay, blow thar lan' down," came the chorus.

"Chuck out this ole hag, or she'll mur—"

"Belay," sung out Josh, cutting across the old sea song, with the sharp command. The chaunty had ceased with the first note of the Mate's voice, and a couple of minutes later, the ropes were coiled up, and the old fellows back to their occupations.

It is true that eight bells had gone, and that the watch was supposed to be changed; and changed it was, so far as the wheel and look-out were concerned; but otherwise little enough difference did it make to those sleep-proof ancients. The only change visible in the men about the deck, was that those who had previously only smoked, now smoked and worked; while those who had hitherto worked and smoked, now only smoked. Thus matters went on in all amity; while the old *Shamraken* passed onward like a rose-tinted shadow through the shining mist, and only the great, silent, lazy seas that came at her, out from the enshrouding redness, seemed aware that she was anything more than the shadow she appeared.

Presently, Zeph sung out to Nuzzie to get their tea from the galley, and so, in a little, the watch below were making their evening meal. They ate it as they sat upon the hatch or spar, as the chance might be; and, as they ate, they talked with their mates, of the watch on deck, upon the matter of the shining mist into which they had plunged. It was obvious, from their talk, that the extraordinary phenomenon had impressed them vastly, and all the superstition in them seemed to have been waked to fuller life. Zeph, indeed, made no bones of declaring his belief that they were nigh to something more than earthly. He said that he had a feeling that 'M'ria' was somewhere near to him.

"Meanin' ter say as we've come purty near ter 'eaven?" said Nehemiah, who was busy thrumming a paunch mat, for chafing gear.

"Dunno," replied Zeph; "but" – making a gesture towards the hidden sky – "yew'll 'low as it's mighty wonderful, 'n I guess ef 'tis 'eaven, thar's some uv us as is growin' powerful wearied uv 'arth. I guess I'm feelin' peeky fer a sight uv M'ria."

Nehemiah nodded his head slowly, and the nod seemed to run round the group of white-haired ancients.

"Reckon my datter's gell 'll be thar," he said, after a space of pondering. "Be s'prisin' ef she 'n M'ria 'd made et up ter know one anuther."

"M'ria wer' great on makin' friends," remarked Zeph, meditatively, "an gells wus awful friendly wi' 'er. Seemed as she hed er power thet way."

"I never 'ad no wife," said Job, at this point, somewhat irrelevantly. It was a fact of which he was proud, and he made a frequent boast of it.

"Thet's naught ter cocker thysel on, lad," exclaimed one of the white-beards, who, until this time, had been silent. "Thou'lt find less folk in heaven t' greet thee."

"Thet's trewth, sure 'nuff, Jock," assented Nehemiah, and fixed a stern look on Job; whereat Job retired into silence.

Presently, at three bells, Josh came along and told them to put away their work for the day.

Chapter V

THE SECOND DOG WATCH came, and Nehemiah and the rest of his side, made their tea out upon the main hatch, along with their mates. When this was finished, as though by common agreement, they went every one and sat themselves upon the pin-rail running along under the t'gallant bulwarks; there, with their elbows upon the rail, they faced outward to gaze their full at the mystery of colour which had wrapped them about. From time to time, a pipe would be removed, and some slowly evolved thought given an utterance.

Eight bells came and went; but, save for the changing of the wheel and look-out, none moved from his place.

Nine o'clock, and the night came down upon the sea; but to those within the mist, the only result was a deepening of the rose colour into an intense red, which seemed to shine with a light of its own creating. Above them, the unseen sky seemed to be one vast blaze of silent, blood-tinted flame.

"Piller uv cloud by day, 'n er piller uv fire by night," muttered Zeph to Nehemiah, who crouched near.

"I reckon's them's Bible words," said Nehemiah.

"Dunno," replied Zeph; "but them's thar very words as I heerd passon Myles a sayin' w'en thar timber wor afire down our way. 'Twer' mostly smoke 'n daylight; but et tamed ter 'n etarnal fire w'en thar night comed."

At four bells, the wheel and look-out were relieved, and a little later, Josh and Skipper Abe came down on to the main deck.

"Tur'ble queer," said Skipper Abe, with an affectation of indifference.

"Aye, 'tes, sure," said Nehemiah.

And after that, the two old men sat among the others, and watched.

At five bells, half-past ten, there was a murmur from those who sat nearest to the bows, and a cry from the man on the look-out. At that, the attention of all was turned to a point nearly right ahead. At this particular spot, the mist seemed to be glowing with a curious, unearthly red brilliance; and, a minute later, there burst upon their vision a vast arch, formed of blazing red clouds.

At the sight, each and every one cried out their amazement, and immediately began to run towards the fo'cas'le head. Here they congregated in a clump, the Skipper and the Mate among them. The arch appeared now to extend its arc far beyond either bow, so that the ship was heading to pass right beneath it.

"Tis 'eaven fer sure," murmured Josh to himself; but Zeph heard him.

"Reckon's them's ther Gates uv Glory thet M'ria wus allus talkin' 'bout," he replied.

"Guess I'll see thet b'y er mine in er little," muttered Josh, and he craned forward, his eyes very bright and eager.

All about the ship was a great quietness. The wind was no more now than a light steady breath upon the port quarter; but from right ahead, as though issuing from the mouth of the radiant arch, the long-backed, foamless seas rolled up, black and oily.

Suddenly, amid the silence, there came a low musical note, rising and falling like the moan of a distant aeolian harp. The sound appeared to come from the direction of the arch, and the surrounding mist seemed to catch it up and send it sobbing and sobbing in low echoes away into the redness far beyond sight.

"They'm singin'," cried Zeph. "M'ria wer' allus tur'ble fond uv singin'. Hark ter—"

"Sh!" interrupted Josh. "Thet's my b'y!" His shrill old voice had risen almost to a scream.

"It's wunnerful – wunnerful; just mazin'!" exclaimed Skipper Abe.

Zeph had gone a little forrard of the crowd. He was shading his eyes with his hands, and staring intently, his expression denoting the most intense excitement.

"B'lieve I see 'er. B'lieve I see 'er," he was muttering to himself, over and over again.

Behind him, two of the old men were steadying Nehemiah, who felt, as he put it, "a bit mazy at thar thought o' seein' thet gell."

Away aft, Nuzzie, the 'b'y' was at the wheel. He had heard the moaning; but, being no more than a boy, it must be supposed that he knew nothing of the *nearness* of the next world, which was so evident to the men, his masters.

A matter of some minutes passed, and Job, who had in mind that farm upon which he had set his heart, ventured to suggest that heaven was less near than his mates supposed; but no one seemed to hear him, and he subsided into silence.

It was the better part of an hour later, and near to midnight, when a murmur among the watchers announced that a fresh matter had come to sight. They were yet a great way off from the arch; but still the thing showed clearly – a prodigious umbel, of a deep, burning red; but the crest of it was black, save for the very apex which shone with an angry red glitter.

"Thar Throne uv God!" cried out Zeph, in a loud voice, and went down upon his knees. The rest of the old men followed his example, and even old Nehemiah made a great effort to get to that position.

"Simly we'm a'most 'n 'eaven," he muttered huskily.

Skipper Abe got to his feet, with an abrupt movement. He had never heard of that extraordinary electrical phenomenon, seen once perhaps in a hundred years – the 'Fiery Tempest' which precedes certain great Cyclonic Storms; but his experienced eye had suddenly discovered that the red-shining umbel was truly a low, whirling water-hill, reflecting the red light. He had no theoretical knowledge to tell him that the thing was produced by an enormous air-vortice; but he had often seen a waterspout form. Yet, he was still undecided. It was all so beyond him; though, certainly, that monstrous gyrating hill of water, sending out a reflected glitter of burning red, appealed to him as having no place in his ideas of Heaven. And then, even as he hesitated, came the first, wild-beast bellow of the coming Cyclone. As the sound smote upon their ears, the old men looked at one another with bewildered, frightened eyes.

"Reck'n thet's God speakin'," whispered Zeph. "Guess we're on'y mis'rable sinners."

The next instant, the breath of the Cyclone was in their throats, and the *Shamraken*, homeward-bounder, passed in through the everlasting portals.

If you enjoyed this, you might also like...
Out of the Storm, see page 337
Through the Vortex of a Cyclone, see page 146

The Finding of the Graiken

Chapter I

WHEN A YEAR had passed, and still there was no news of the full-rigged ship *Graiken*, even the most sanguine of my old chum's friends had ceased to hope perchance, somewhere, she might be above water.

Yet Ned Barlow, in his inmost thoughts, I knew, still hugged to himself the hope that she would win home. Poor, dear old fellow, how my heart did go out towards him in his sorrow!

For it was in the *Graiken* that his sweetheart had sailed on that dull January day some twelve months previously.

The voyage had been taken for the sake of her health; yet since then – save for a distant signal recorded at the Azores – there had been from all the mystery of ocean no voice; the ship and they within her had vanished utterly.

And still Barlow hoped. He said nothing actually, but at times his deeper thoughts would float up and show through the sea of his usual talk, and thus I would know in an indirect way of the thing that his heart was thinking.

Nor was time a healer.

It was later that my present good fortune came to me. My uncle died, and I – hitherto poor – was now a rich man. In a breath, it seemed, I had become possessor of houses, lands, and money; also – in my eyes almost more important – a fine fore-and-aft-rigged yacht of some two hundred tonnes register.

It seemed scarcely believable that the thing was mine, and I was all in a scutter to run away down to Falmouth and get to sea.

In old times, when my uncle had been more than usually gracious, he had invited me to accompany him for a trip round the coast or elsewhere, as the fit might take him; yet never, even in my most hopeful moments, had it occurred to me that ever she might be mine.

And now I was hurrying my preparations for a good long sea trip – for to me the sea is, and always has been, a comrade.

Still, with all the prospects before me, I was by no means completely satisfied, for I wanted Ned Barlow with me, and yet was afraid to ask him.

I had the feeling that, in view of his overwhelming loss, he must positively hate the sea; and yet I could not be happy at the thought of leaving him, and going alone.

He had not been well lately, and a sea voyage would be the very thing for him, if only it were not going to freshen painful memories.

Eventually I decided to suggest it, and this I did a couple of days before the date I had fixed for sailing.

"Ned," I said, "you need a change."

"Yes," he assented wearily.

"Come with me, old chap," I went on, growing bolder. "I'm taking a trip in the yacht. It would be splendid to have—"

To my dismay, he jumped to his feet and came towards me excitedly.

"I've upset him now," was my thought. "I *am* a fool!"

"Go to sea!" he said. "My God! I'd give—" He broke off short, and stood suppressed opposite to me, his face all of a quiver with suppressed emotion. He was silent a few seconds, getting himself in hand; then he proceeded more quietly: "Where to?"

"Anywhere," I replied, watching him keenly, for I was greatly puzzled by his manner. "I'm not quite clear yet. Somewhere south of here – the West Indies, I have thought. It's all so new, you know – just fancy being able to go just where we like. I can hardly realise it yet."

I stopped; for he had turned from me and was staring out of the window.

"You'll come, Ned?" I cried, fearful that he was going to refuse me.

He took a pace away, and came back.

"I'll come," he said, and there was a look of strange excitement in his eyes that set me off on a tack of vague wonder; but I said nothing, just told him how he had pleased me.

Chapter II

WE HAD BEEN AT SEA a couple of weeks, and were alone upon the Atlantic – at least, so much of it as presented itself to our view.

I was leaning over the taffrail, staring down into the boil of the wake; yet I noticed nothing, for I was wrapped in a tissue of somewhat uncomfortable thought. It was about Ned Barlow.

He had been queer, decidedly queer, since leaving port. His whole attitude mentally had been that of a man under the influence of an all-pervading excitement. I had said that he was in need of a change, and had trusted that the splendid tonic of the sea breeze would serve to put him soon to rights mentally and physically; yet here was the poor old chap acting in a manner calculated to cause me anxiety as to his balance.

Scarcely a word had been spoken since leaving the Channel. When I ventured to speak to him, often he would take not the least notice, other times he would answer only by a brief word; but talk – never.

In addition, his whole time was spent on deck among the men, and with some of them he seemed to converse both long and earnestly; yet to me, his chum and true friend, not a word.

Another thing came to me as a surprise – Barlow betrayed the greatest interest in the position of the vessel, and the courses set, all in such a manner as left me no room to doubt but that his knowledge of navigation was considerable.

Once I ventured to express my astonishment at this knowledge, and ask a question or two as to the way in which he had gathered it, but had been treated with such an absurdly stony silence that since then I had not spoken to him.

With all this it may be easily conceived that my thoughts, as I stared down into the wake, were troublesome.

Suddenly I heard a voice at my elbow:

"I should like to have a word with you, sir." I turned sharply. It was my skipper, and something in his face told me that all was not as it should be.

"Well, Jenkins, fire away."

He looked round, as if afraid of being overheard; then came closer to me.

"Someone's been messing with the compasses, sir," he said in a low voice.

"What?" I asked sharply.

"They've been meddled with, sir. The magnets have been shifted, and by someone who's a good idea of what he's doing."

"What on earth do you mean?" I inquired. "Why should anyone mess about with them? What good would it do them? You must be mistaken."

"No, sir, I'm not. They've been touched within the last forty-eight hours, and by someone that understands what he's doing."

I stared at him. The man was so certain. I felt bewildered.

"But why should they?"

"That's more than I can say, sir; but it's a serious matter, and I want to know what I'm to do. It looks to me as though there were something funny going on. I'd give a month's pay to know just who it was, for certain."

"Well," I said, "if they have been touched, it can only be by one of the officers. You say the chap who has done it must understand what he is doing."

He shook his head. "No sir—" he began, and then stopped abruptly. His gaze met mine. I think the same thought must have come to us simultaneously. I gave a little gasp of amazement.

He wagged his head at me. "I've had my suspicions for a bit, sir," he went on; "but seeing that he's – he's—" He was fairly struck for the moment.

I took my weight off the rail and stood upright.

"To whom are you referring?" I asked curtly.

"Why, sir, to him – Mr. Ned—"

He would have gone on, but I cut him short.

"That will do, Jenkins!" I cried. "Mr. Ned Barlow is my friend. You are forgetting yourself a little. You will accuse me of tampering with the compasses next!"

I turned away, leaving little Captain Jenkins speechless. I had spoken with an almost vehement over-loyalty, to quiet my own suspicions.

All the same, I was horribly bewildered, not knowing what to think or do or say, so that, eventually, I did just nothing.

Chapter III

IT WAS EARLY one morning, about a week later, that I opened my eyes abruptly. I was lying on my back in my bunk, and the daylight was beginning to creep wanly in through the ports.

I had a vague consciousness that all was not as it should be, and feeling thus, I made to grasp the edge of my bunk, and situp, but failed, owing to the fact that my wrists were securely fastened by a pair of heavy steel handcuffs.

Utterly confounded, I let my head fall back upon the pillow; and then, in the midst of my bewilderment, there sounded the sharp report of a pistol-shot somewhere on the decks over my head. There came a second, and the sound of voices and footsteps, and then a long spell of silence.

Into my mind had rushed the single word – mutiny! My temples throbbed a little, but I struggled to keep calm and think, and then, all adrift, I fell to searching round for a reason. Who was it? and why?

Perhaps an hour passed, during which I asked myself ten thousand vain questions. All at once I heard a key inserted in the door. So I had been locked in! It turned, and the steward walked into the cabin. He did not look at me, but went to the arm-rack and began to remove the various weapons.

"What the devil is the meaning of all this, Jones?" I roared, getting up a bit on one elbow. "What's happening.?"

But the fool answered not a word – just went to and fro carrying out the weapons from my cabin into the next, so that at last I ceased from questioning him, and lay silent, promising myself future vengeance.

When he had removed the arms, the steward began to go through my table drawers, emptying them, so it appeared to me, of everything that could be used as a weapon or tool.

Having completed his task, he vanished, locking the door after him.

Some time passed, and at last, about seven bells, he reappeared, this time bringing a tray with my breakfast. Placing it upon the table, he came across to me and proceeded to unlock the cuffs from off my wrists. Then for the first time he spoke.

"Mr. Barlow desires me to say, sir, that you have the liberty of your cabin so long as you will agree not to cause any bother. Should you wish for anything, I am under his orders to supply you." He retreated hastily towards the door.

On my part, I was almost speechless with astonishment and rage.

"One minute, Jones!" I shouted, just as he was in the act of leaving the cabin. "Kindly explain what you mean. You said Mr. Barlow. Is it to him that I owe all this?" And I waved my hand towards the irons which the man still held.

"It is by his orders," replied he, and turned once more to leave the cabin.

"I don't understand!" I said, bewildered. "Mr. Barlow is my friend, and this is my yacht! By what right do you dare to take your orders from him? Let me out!"

As I shouted the last command, I leapt from my bunk, and made a dash for the door, but the steward, so far from attempting to bar it, flung it open and stepped quickly through, thus allowing me to see that a couple of the sailors were stationed in the alleyway.

"Get on deck at once!" I said angrily. "What are you doing down here?"

"Sorry sir," said one of the men. "We'd take it kindly if you'd make no trouble. But we ain't lettin' you out, sir. Don't make no bloomin' error."

I hesitated, then went to the table and sat down. I would, at least, do my best to preserve my dignity.

After an inquiry as to whether he could do anything further, the steward left me to breakfast and my thoughts. As may be imagined, the latter were by no means pleasant.

Here was I prisoner in my own yacht, and by the hand of the very man I had loved and befriended through many years. Oh, it was too incredible and mad!

For a while, leaving the table, I paced the deck of my room; then, growing calmer, I sat down again and attempted to make some sort of a meal.

As I breakfasted, my chief thought was as to *why* my one-time chum was treating me thus; and after that I fell to puzzling *how* he had managed to get the yacht into his own hands.

Many things came back to me – his familiarity with the men, his treatment of me – which I had put down to a temporary want of balance – the fooling with the compasses; for I was certain now that he had been the doer of that piece of mischief. But *why?* That was the great point.

As I turned the matter over in my brain, an incident that had occurred some six days back came to me. It had been on the very day after the captain's report to me of the tampering with the compasses.

Barlow had, for the first time, relinquished his brooding and silence, and had started to talk to me, but in such a wild strain that he had made me feel vaguely uncomfortable about his sanity for he told me some yarn of an idea which he had got into his head. And then, in an overbearing way, he demanded that the navigation of the yacht should be put into his hands.

He had been very incoherent, and was plainly in a state of considerable mental excitement. He had rambled on about some derelict, and then had talked in an extraordinary fashion of a vast world of seaweed.

Once or twice in his bewilderingly disconnected speech he had mentioned the name of his sweetheart, and now it was the memory of her name that gave me the first inkling of what might possibly prove a solution of the whole affair.

I wished now that I had encouraged his incoherent ramble of speech, instead of heading him off; but I had done so because I could not bear to have him talk as he had.

Yet, with the little I remembered, I began to shape out a theory. It seemed to me that he might be nursing some idea that had formed – goodness knows how or when – that his sweetheart (still alive) was aboard some derelict in the midst of an enormous 'world', he had termed it, of seaweed.

He might have grown more explicit had I not attempted to reason with him, and so lost the rest.

Yet, remembering back, it seemed to me that he must undoubtedly have meant the enormous Sargasso Sea – that great seaweed-laden ocean, vast almost as Continental Europe, and the final resting-place of the Atlantic's wreckage.

Surely, if he proposed any attempt to search through that, then there could be no doubt but that he was temporarily unbalanced. And yet I could do nothing. I was a prisoner and helpless.

Chapter IV

EIGHT DAYS of variable but strongish winds passed, and still I was a prisoner in my cabin. From the ports that opened out astern and on each side – for my cabin runs right across the whole width of the stern – I was able to command a good view of the surrounding ocean, which now had commenced to be laden with great floating patches of Gulf weed – many of them hundreds and hundreds of yards in length.

And still we held on, apparently towards the nucleus of the Sargasso Sea. This I was able to assume by means of a chart which I found in one of the lockers, and the course I had been able to gather from the 'tell-tale' compass let into the cabin ceiling.

And so another and another day went by, and now we were among weed so thick that at times the vessel found difficulty in forcing her way through, while the surface of the sea had assumed a curious oily appearance, though the wind was still quite strong.

It was later in the day that we encountered a bank of weed so prodigious that we had to up helm and run round it, and after that the same experience was many times repeated; and so the night found us.

The following morning found me at the ports, eagerly peering out across the water. From one of those on the starboard side I could discern at a considerable distance a huge bank of weed that seemed to be unending, and to run parallel with our broadside. It appeared to rise in places a couple of feet above the level of the surrounding sea.

For a long while I stared, then went across to the port side. Here I found that a similar bank stretched away on our port beam. It was as though we were sailing up an immense river, the low banks of which were formed of seaweed instead of land.

And so that day passed hour by hour, the weed-banks growing more definite and seeming to be nearer. Towards evening something came into sight – a far, dim hulk, the masts gone, the whole hull covered with growth, an unwholesome green, blotched with brown in the light from the dying sun.

I saw this lonesome craft from a port on the starboard side, and the sight roused a multitude of questions and thoughts.

Evidently we had penetrated into the unknown central portion of the enormous Sargasso, the Great Eddy of the Atlantic, and this was some lonely derelict, lost ages ago perhaps to the outside world.

Just at the going down of the sun, I saw another; she was nearer, and still possessed two of her masts. which stuck up bare and desolate into the darkening sky. She could not have been more than a quarter of a mile in from the edge of the weed. As we passed her I craned out my head through the port to stare at her. As I stared the dusk grew out of the abyss of the air, and she faded presently from sight into the surrounding loneliness.

Through all that night I sat at the port and watched, listening and peering; for the tremendous mystery of that inhuman weed-world was upon me.

In the air there rose no sound; even the wind was scarcely more than a low hum aloft among the sails and gear, and under me the oily water gave no rippling noise. All was silence, supreme and unearthly.

About midnight the moon rose away on our starboard beam, and from then until the dawn I stared out upon a ghostly world of noiseless weed, fantastic, silent, and unbelievable, under the moonlight.

On four separate occasions my gaze lit on black hulks that rose above the surrounding weeds – the hulks of long-lost vessels. And once, just when the strangeness of dawn was in the sky, a faint, long-drawn wailing seemed to come floating to me across the immeasurable waste of weed.

It startled my strung nerves, and I assured myself that it was the cry of some lone sea bird. Yet, my imagination reached out for some stranger explanation.

The eastward sky began to flush with the dawn, and the morning light grew subtly over the breadth of the enormous ocean of weed until it seemed to me to reach away unbroken on each beam into the grey horizons. Only astern of us, like a broad road of oil, ran the strange river-like gulf up which we had sailed.

Now I noticed that the banks of weed were nearer, very much nearer, and a disagreeable thought came to me. This vast rift that had allowed us to penetrate into the very nucleus of the Sargasso Sea – suppose it should close!

It would mean inevitably that there would be one more among the missing- another unanswered mystery of the inscrutable ocean. I resisted the thought, and came back more directly into the present.

Evidently the wind was still dropping, for we were moving slowly, as a glance at the ever-nearing weed-banks told me. The hours passed on, and my breakfast, when the steward brought it, I took to one of the ports, and there ate; for I would lose nothing of the strange surroundings into which we were so steadily plunging.

And so the morning passed.

Chapter V

IT WAS ABOUT an hour after dinner that I observed the open channel between the weedbanks to be narrowing almost minute by minute with uncomfortable speed. I could do nothing except watch and surmise.

At times I felt convinced that the immense masses of weed were closing in upon us, but I fought off the thought with the more hopeful one that we were surely approaching some narrowing outlet of the gulf that yawned so far across the seaweed.

By the time the afternoon was half-through, the weed-banks had approached so close that occasional out-jutting masses scraped the yacht's sides in passing. It was now with the stuff below my face, within a few feet of my eyes, that I discovered the immense amount of life that stirred among all the hideous waste.

Innumerable crabs crawled among the seaweed, and once, indistinctly, something stirred among the depths of a large outlying tuft of weed. What it was I could not tell, though afterwards I had an idea; but all I saw was something dark and glistening. We were past it before I could see more.

The steward was in the act of bringing in my tea, when from above there came a noise of shouting, and almost immediately a slight jolt. The man put down the tray he was carrying, and glanced at me, with startled expression.

"What is it, Jones?" I questioned.

"I don't know sir. I expect it's the weed," he replied.

I ran to the port, craned out my head, and looked forward. Our bow seemed to be embedded in a mass of weeds, and as I watched it came further aft.

Within the next five minutes we had driven through it into a circle of sea that was free from the weed. Across this we seemed to drift, rather than sail, so slow was our speed.

Upon its opposite margin we brought up the vessel swinging broadside on to the weed, being secured thus with a couple of kedges cast from the bows and stern, though of this I was not aware until later. As we swung, and at last I was able from my port to see ahead, I saw a thing that amazed me.

There, not three hundred feet distant across the quaking weed, a vessel lay embedded. She had been a three-master; but of these only the mizzen was standing. For perhaps a minute I stared, scarcely breathing in my exceeding interest.

All around above her bulwarks to the height of apparently some ten feet, ran a sort of fencing formed, so far as I could make out, from canvas, rope, and spars. Even as I wondered at the use of such a thing, I heard my chum's voice overhead. He was hailing her:

"*Graiken*, ahoy!" he shouted. "*Graiken*, ahoy!"

At that I fairly jumped. *Graiken*! What could he mean! I stared out of the port. The blaze of the sinking sun flashed redly upon her stern, and showed the lettering of her name and port; yet the distance was too great for me to read.

I ran across to my table to see if there were a pair of binoculars in the drawers. I found one in the first I opened; then I ran back to the port, racking them out as I went. I reached it, and clapped them to my eyes. Yes; I saw it plainly, her name *Graiken* and her port London.

From her name my gaze moved to that strange fencing about her. There was a movement in the aft part. As I watched a portion of it slid to one side, and a man's head and shoulders appeared.

I nearly yelled with the excitement of that moment. I could scarcely believe the thing I saw. The man waved an arm, and a vague hail reached us across the weed, then he disappeared.

A moment later a score of people crowded the opening, and among them I made out distinctly the face and figure of a girl.

"He was right, after all!" I heard myself saying out loud in a voice that was toneless through very amazement.

In a minute, I was at the door, beating it with my fists. "Let me out, Ned! Let me out!" I shouted.

I felt that I could forgive him all the indignity that I had suffered. Nay, more; in a queer way way I had a feeling that it was I who needed to ask him for forgiveness. All my bitterness had gone, and I wanted only to be out and give a hand in the rescue.

Yet though I shouted, no one came, so that at last I returned quickly to the port, to see what further developments there were.

Across the weed I now saw that one man had his hands up to his mouth shouting. His voice reached me only as a faint, hoarse cry; the distance was too great for anyone aboard the yacht to distinguish its import.

From the derelict my attention was drawn abruptly to a scene alongside. A plank was thrown down on to the weed, and the next moment I saw my chum swing himself down the side and leap upon it.

I had opened my mouth to call out to him that I would forgive all were I but freed to lend a hand in this unbelievable rescue.

But even as the words formed they died, for though the weed appeared so dense, it was evidently incapable of bearing any considerable weight, and the plank, with Barlow upon it, sank down into the weed almost to his waist.

He turned and grabbed at the rope with both hands, and in the same moment he gave a loud cry of sheer terror, and commenced to scramble up the yacht's side.

As his feet drew clear of the weed I gave a short cry. Something was curled about his left ankle – something oily, supple and tapered. As I stared another rose up out from the weed and swayed through the air, made a grab at his leg, missed and appeared to wave aimlessly. Others came towards him as he struggled upwards.

Then I saw hands reach down from above and seize Barlow beneath the arms. They lifted him by main force, and with a mass of weed that enfolded something leathery, from which numbers of curling arms writhed.

A hand slashed down with a sheath-knife, and the next instant the hideous thing had fallen back among the weed.

For a couple of seconds longer I remained, my head twisted upwards; then faces appeared once more over our rail, and I saw the men extending arms and fingers, pointing. From above me there rose a hoarse chorus of fear and wonder, and I turned my head swiftly to glance down and across that treacherous extraordinary weedworld.

The whole of the hitherto silent surface was all of a move in one stupendous undulation – as though life had come to all that desolation.

The undulatory movement continued, and abruptly, in a hundred places, the seaweed was tossed up into sudden billowy hillocks. From these burst mighty arms, and in an instant the evening air was full of them, hundreds and hundreds, coming towards the yacht.

"Devil-fishes!" shouted a man's voice from the deck. "Octopuses! My Lord!"

Then I caught my chum shouting.

"Cut the mooring ropes!" he yelled.

This must have been done almost on the instant, for immediately there showed between us and the nearest weed a broadening gap of scummy water.

"Haul away, lads!" I heard Barlow shouting; and the same instant I caught the splash, splash of something in the water on our port side. I rushed across and looked out. I found that a rope had been carried across to the opposite seaweed, and that the men were now warping us rapidly from those invading horrors.

I raced back to the starboard port, and, lo! as though by magic, there stretched between us and the *Graiken* only the silent stretch of demure weed and some fifty feet of water. It seemed inconceivable that it was a covering to so much terror.

And then speedily the night was upon us, hiding all; but from the decks above there commenced a sound of hammering that continued long throughout the night – long after I, weary with my previous night's vigil, had passed into a fitful slumber, broken anon by that hammering above.

Chapter VI

"YOUR BREAKFAST, SIR," came respectfully enough in the steward's voice; and I woke with a start. Overhead, there still sounded that persistent hammering, and I turned to the steward for an explanation.

"I don't exactly know, sir," was his reply. "It's something the carpenter's doing to one of the lifeboats." And then he left me.

I ate my breakfast standing at the port, staring at the distant *Graiken*. The weed was perfectly quiet, and we were lying about the centre of the little lake.

As I watched the derelict, it seemed to me that I saw a movement about her side, and I reached for the glasses. Adjusting them, I made out that there were several of the cuttlefish attached to her in different parts, their arms spread out almost starwise across the lower portions of her hull.

Occasionally a feeler would detached itself and wave aimlessly. This it was that had drawn my attention. The sight of these creatures, in conjunction with that extraordinary scene the previous evening, enabled me to guess the use of the great screen running about the *Graiken*. It had obviously been erected as a protection against the vile inhabitants of that strange weedworld.

From that my thoughts passed to the problem of reaching and rescuing the crew of the derelict. I could by no means conceive how this was to be effected.

As I stood pondering, whilst I ate, I caught the voices of men chaunteying on deck. For a while this continued; then came Barlow's voice shouting orders, and almost immediately a splash in the water on the starboard side.

I poked my head out through the port, and stared. They had got one of the lifeboats into the water. To the gunnel of the boat they had added a superstructure ending in a roof, the whole somewhat resembling a gigantic dog-kennel.

From under the two sharp ends of the boat rose a couple of planks at an angle or thirty degrees. These appeared to be firmly bolted to the boat and the superstructure. I guessed that their purpose was to enable the boat to over-ride the seaweed, instead of ploughing into it and getting fast.

In the stern of the boat was fixed a strong ringbolt, into which was spliced the end of a coil of one-inch manila rope. Along the sides of the boat, and high above the gunnel, the superstructure was pierced with holes for oars. In one side of the roof was placed a trapdoor. The idea struck me as wonderfully ingenious, and a very probable solution of the difficulty of rescuing the crew of the *Graiken*.

A few minutes later one of the men threw over a rope on to the roof of the boat. He opened the trap, and lowered himself into the interior. I noticed that he was armed with one of the yacht's cutlasses and a revolver.

It was evident that my chum fully appreciated the difficulties that were to be overcome. In a few seconds the man was followed by four others of the crew, similarly armed; and then Barlow.

Seeing him, I craned my head as far as possible, and sang out to him.

"Ned! Ned, old man!" I shouted. "Let me come along with you!"

He appeared never to have heard me. I noticed his face, just before he shut down the trap above him. The expression was fixed and peculiar. It had the uncomfortable remoteness of a sleep-walker.

"Confound it!" I muttered, and after that I said nothing; for it hurt my dignity to supplicate before the men.

From the interior of the boat I heard Barlow's voice, muffled. Immediately four oars were passed out through the holes in the sides, while from slots in the front and rear of the superstructure were thrust a couple of oars with wooden chocks nailed to the blades.

These, I guessed, were intended to assist in steering the boat, that in the bow being primarily for pressing down the weed before the boat, so as to allow her to surmount it the more easily.

Another muffled order came from the interior of the queer-looking craft, and immediately the four oars dipped, and the boat shot towards the weed, the rope trailing out astern as it was paid out from the deck above me.

The board-assisted bow of the lifeboat took the weed with a sort of squashy surge, rose up, and the whole craft appeared to leap from the water down in among the quaking mass.

I saw now the reason why the oar-holes had been placed so high. For of the boat itself nothing could be seen, only the upper portion of the superstructure wallowing amid the weed. Had the holes been lower, there would have been no handling the oars.

I settled myself to watch. There was the probability of a prodigious spectacle, and as I could not help, I would, at least, use my eyes.

Five minutes passed, during which nothing happened, and the boat made slow progress towards the derelict. She had accomplished perhaps some twenty or thirty yards, when suddenly from the *Graiken* there reached my ears a hoarse shout.

My glance leapt from the boat to the derelict. I saw that the people aboard had the sliding part of the screen to one side, and were waving their arms frantically, as though motioning the boat back.

Amongst them I could see the girlish figure that had attracted my attention the previous evening. For a moment I stared, then my gaze travelled back to the boat. All was quiet.

The boat had now covered a quarter of the distance, and I began to persuade myself that she would get across without being attacked.

Then, as I gazed anxiously, from a point in the weed a little ahead of the boat there came a sudden quaking ripple that shivered through the weed in a sort of queer tremor. The next instant, like a shot from a gun, a huge mass drove up clear through the tangled weed, hurling it in all directions, and almost capsizing the boat.

The creature had driven up rear foremost. It fell back with a mighty splash, and in the same moment its monstrous arms were reached out to the boat. They grasped it, enfolding themselves about it horribly. It was apparently attempting to drag the boat under.

From the boat came a regular volley of revolver shots. Yet, though the brute writhed, it did not relinquish its hold. The shots closed, and I saw the dull flash of cutlass blades. The men were attempting to hack at the thing through the oar holes, but evidently with little effect.

All at once the enormous creature seemed to make an effort to overturn the boat. I saw the half-submerged boat go over to one side, until it seemed to me that nothing could right it, and at the sight I went mad with excitement to help them.

I pulled my head in from the port, and glanced round the cabin. I wanted to break down the door, but there was nothing with which to do this.

Then my sight fell on my bunkboard, which fitted into a sliding groove. It was made of teak wood, and very solid and heavy. I lifted it out, and charged the door with the end of it.

The panels split from top to bottom, for I am a heavy man. Again I struck, and drove the two portions of the door apart. I hove down the bunk-board, and rushed through.

There was no one on guard; evidently they had gone on deck to view the rescue. The gunroom door was to my right, and I had the key in my pocket.

In an instant, I had it open, and was lifting down from its rack a heavy elephant gun. Seizing a box of cartridges, I tore off the lid, and emptied the lot into my pocket; then I leapt up the companionway on the deck.

The steward was standing near. He turned at my step; his face was white and he took a couple of paces towards me doubtfully.

"They're – they're—" he began; but I never let him finish.

"Get out of my way!" I roared, and swept him to one side. I ran forward.

"Haul in on that rope!" I shouted. "Tail on to it! Are you going to stand there like a lot of owls and see them drown!"

The men only wanted a leader to show them what to do, and, without showing any thought of insubordination, they tacked on to the rope that was fastened to the stern of the boat, and hauled her back across the weed – cuttle-fish and all.

The strain on the rope had thrown her on an even keel again, so that she took the water safely, though that foul thing was straddled all across her.

"Vast hauling!" I shouted. "Get the doc's cleavers, some of you – anything that'll cut!"

"This is the sort, sir!" cried the bo'sun; from somewhere he had got hold of a formidable doublebladed whale lance.

The boat, still under the impetus given by our pull, struck the side of the yacht immediately beneath where I was waiting with the gun. Astern of it towed the body of the monster, its two eyes – monstrous orbs of the Profound – staring out vilely from behind its arms.

I leant my elbows on the rail, and aimed full at the right eye. As I pulled on the trigger one of the great arms detached itself from the boat, and swirled up towards me. There was a thunderous bang as the heavy charge drove its way through that vast eye, and at the same instant something swept over my head.

There came a cry from behind: "Lookout, sir!" A flame of steel before my eyes, and a truncated something fell upon my shoulder, and thence to the deck.

Down below, the water was being churned to a froth, and three more arms sprang into the air, and then down among us.

One grasped the bo'sun, lifting him like a child. Two cleavers gleamed, and he fell to the deck from a height of some twelve feet, along with the severed portion of the limb.

I had my weapons reloaded again by now, and ran forward along the deck somewhat, to be clear of the flying arms that flailed on the rails and deck.

I fired again into the hulk of the brute, and then again. At the second shot, the murderous din of the creature ceased, and, with an ineffectual flicker of its remaining tentacles, it sank out of sight beneath the water.

A minute later we had the hatch in the roof of the superstructure open, and the men out, my chum coming last. They had been mightily shaken, but otherwise were none the worse.

As Barlow came over the gangway, I stepped up to him and gripped his shoulder. I was strangely muddled in my feelings. I felt that I had no sure position aboard my own yacht. Yet all I said was:

"Thank God, you're safe, old man!" And I meant it from my heart.

He looked at me in a doubtful, puzzled sort of manner, and passed his hand across his forehead.

"Yes," he replied; but his voice was strangely toneless, save that some puzzledness seemed to have crept into it. For a couple of moments he stared at me in an unseeing way, and once more I was struck by the immobile, tensed-up expression of his features.

Immediately afterwards he turned away – having shown neither friendliness nor enmity – and commenced to clamber back over the side into the boat.

"Come up, Ned!" I cried. "It's no good. You'll never manage it that way. Look!" and I stretched out my arm, pointing. Instead of looking, he passed his hand once more across his forehead, with that gesture of puzzled doubt. Then, to my relief, he caught at the rope ladder, and commenced to make his way slowly up the side.

Reaching the deck, he stood for nearly a minute without saying a word, his back turned to the derelict. Then, still wordless, he walked slowly across to the opposite side, and leant his elbows upon the rail, as though looking back along the way the yacht had come.

For my part, I said nothing, dividing my attention between him and the men, with occasional glances at the quaking weed and the – apparently – hopelessly surrounded *Graiken*.

The men were quiet, occasionally turning towards Barlow, as though for some further order. Of me they appeared to take little notice. In this wise, perhaps a quarter of an hour went by; then abruptly Barlow stood upright, waving his arms and shouting:

"It comes! It comes!" He turned towards us, and his face seemed transfigured, his eyes gleaming almost maniacally.

I ran across the deck to his side, and looked away to port, and now I saw what it was that had excited him. The weed-barrier through which we had come on our inward journey was divided, a slowly broadening river of oil water showing clean across it.

Even as I watched it grew broader, the immense masses of weed being moved by some unseen impulsion.

I was still staring, amazed, when a sudden cry went up from some of the men to starboard. Turning quickly, I saw that the yawning movement was being continued to the mass of weed that lay between us and the *Graiken*.

Slowly, the weed was divided, surely as though an invisible wedge were being driven through it. The gulf of weed-clear water reached the derelict, and passed beyond. And now there was no longer anything to stop our rescue of the crew of the derelict.

Chapter VII

IT WAS BARLOW'S VOICE that gave the order for the mooring ropes to be cast off, and then, as the light wind was right against us, a boat was out ahead, and the yacht was towed towards the ship, whilst a dozen of the men stood ready with their rifles on the fo'c's'le head.

As we drew nearer, I began to distinguish the features of the crew, the men strangely grizzled and old looking. And among them, white-faced with emotion, was my chum's lost sweetheart. I never expect to know a more extraordinary moment.

I looked at Barlow; he was staring at the white-faced girl with an extraordinary fixidity of expression that was scarcely the look of a sane man.

The next minute we were alongside, crushing to a pulp between our steel sides one of those remaining monsters of the deep that had continued to cling steadfastly to the *Graiken*.

Yet of that I was scarcely aware, for I had turned again to look at Ned Barlow. He was swaying slowly to his feet, and just as the two vessels closed he reached up both hands to his head, and fell like a log.

Brandy was brought, and later Barlow carried to his cabin; yet we had won clear of that hideous weed-world before he recovered consciousness.

During his illness I learned from his sweetheart how, on a terrible night a long year previously, the *Graiken* had been caught in a tremendous storm and dismasted, and how, helpless and driven by the gale, they at last found themselves surrounded by the great banks of floating weed, and finally held fast in the remorseless grip of the dread Sargasso.

She told me of their attempts to free the ship from the weed, and of the attacks of the cuttlefish. And later of various other matters; for all of which I have no room in this story.

In return I told her of our voyage, and her lover's strange behaviour. How he had wanted to undertake the navigation of the yacht, and had talked of a great world of weed. How I had – believing him unhinged – refused to listen to him.

How he had taken matters into his own hands, without which she would most certainly have ended her days surrounded by the quaking weed and those great beasts of the deep waters.

She listened with an ever-growing seriousness, so that I had, time and again, to assure her that I bore my old chum no ill, but rather held myself to be in the wrong. At which she shook her head, but seemed mightily relieved.

It was during Barlow's recovery that I made the astonishing discovery that he remembered no detail of his imprisoning of me.

I am convinced now that for days and weeks he must have lived in a sort of dream in a hyper state, in which I can only imagine that he had possibly been sensitive to more subtle understandings than normal bodily and mental health allows.

One other thing there is in closing. I found that the captain and the two mates had been confined to their cabins by Barlow. The captain was suffering from a pistol-shot in the arm, due to his having attempted to resist Barlow's assumption of authority.

When I released him he vowed vengeance. Yet Ned Barlow being my chum, I found means to slake both the captain's and the two mates' thirst for vengeance, and the slaking thereof is – well, another story.

If you enjoyed this, you might also like...
From the Tideless Sea: Part Two, see page 124
The Derelict, see page 349

The Sea Horses

"An' we's under the sea, b'ys,
Where the Wild Horses go,
Horses wiv tails
As big as ole whales
All jiggin' around in a row,
An' when you ses Whoa!
Them divvils does go!"

Chapter I

"HOW WAS IT you catched my one, granfer?" asked Nebby, as he had asked the same question any time during the past week, whenever his burly, blue-guernseyed grandfather crooned out the old Ballade of the Sea-Horses, which, however, he never carried past the portion given above.

"Like as he was a bit weak, Nebby b'y; an' I gev him a smart clip wiv the axe, 'fore he could bolt off," explained his grandfather, lying with inimitable gravity and relish.

Nebby dismounted from his curious-looking go-horse, by the simple method of dragging it forward from between his legs. He examined its peculiar, unicorn-like head, and at last put his finger on a bruised indentation in the black paint that covered the nose.

"'S that where you welted him, granfer?" he asked, seriously.

"Aye," said his granfer Zacchy, taking the strangely-shaped go-horse, and examining the contused paint. "Aye, I shore hit 'm a tumble welt."

"Are he dead, granfer?" asked the boy.

"Well," said the burly old man, feeling the go-horse all over with an enormous finger and thumb, "betwixt an' between, like." He opened the cleverly hinged mouth, and looked at the bone teeth with which he had fitted it, and then squinted earnestly, with one eye, down the red-painted throat. "Aye," he repeated, "betwixt an' between, Nebby. Don't you never let 'm go to water, b'y; for he'd maybe come alive ag'in, an' ye'd lose 'm sure."

Perhaps old Diver-Zacchy, as he was called in the little sea-village, was thinking that water would prove unhealthy to the glue, with which he had fixed-on the big bonito's tail, at what he termed the starn-end of the curious looking beast. He had cut the whole thing out of a nice, four-foot by ten-inch piece of soft, knot-less yellow pine; and, to the rear, he had attached, thwart-ship, the afore-mentioned bonito's tail; for the thing was no ordinary horse, as you may think; but a *gen-u-ine* (as Zacchy described it) Sea-Horse, which he had brought up from the sea bottom for his small grandson, whilst following his occupation as diver.

The animal had taken him many a long hour to carve, and had been made during his spell-ohs, between dives, aboard the diving-barge. The creature itself was a combined production of his own extremely fertile fancy, plus his small grandson's Faith. For Zacchy had manufactured unending and peculiar stories of what he saw daily at the bottom of the sea, and during many a winter's evening, Nebby had 'cut boats' around the big stove, whilst the old man smoked and yarned the impossible yarns that were so marvellously real and possible to the boy. And of all the tales that the old diver told in his whimsical fashion, there was none that so stirred Nebby's feelings as the one about the Sea-Horses.

At first it had been but a scrappy and a fragmentary yarn, suggested as like as not, by the old ballade which Zacchy so often hummed, half-unconsciously. But Nebby's constant questionings had provided so many suggestions for fresh additions, that at last it took nearly the whole of a long evening for the Tale of the Sea-Horses to be told properly, from where the first Horse was seen by Zacchy, eatin' sea-grass as nat'rel as ye like, to where Zacchy had seen li'l Martha Tullet's b'y ridin' one like a reel cow-puncher; and from that tremendous effort of imagination, the Horse Yarn had speedily grown to include every child that wended the Long Road out of the village.

"Shall I go ridin' them Sea-Horses, Granfer, when I dies?" Nebby had asked, earnestly.

"Aye," Granfer Zacchy had replied, absently, puffing at his corn-cob. "Aye, like's not, Nebby. Like as not."

"Mebbe I'll die middlin' soon, Granfer?" Nebby had suggested, longingly. "There's plenty li'l boys dies 'fore they gets growed up."

"Husht! b'y! Husht!" Granfer had said, wakening suddenly to what the child was saying.

Later, when Nebby had many times betrayed his exceeding high requirement of death, that he might ride the Sea-Horses all round his Granfer at work on the sea-bottom, old Zacchy had suddenly evolved a less drastic solution of the difficulty.

"I'll ketch ye one, Nebby, sure," he said, "an' ye kin ride it round the kitchen."

The suggestion pleased Nebby enormously, and practically nullified his impatience regarding the date of his death, which was to give him the freedom of the sea and all the Sea-Horses therein.

For a long month, old Zacchy was met each evening by a small and earnest boy, desirous of learning whether he had "catched one" that day, or not. Meanwhile, Zacchy had been dealing honestly with that four-foot by ten-inch piece of yellow pine, already described. He had carved out his notion of what might be supposed to constitute a veritable Sea-Horse, aided in his invention by Nebby's illuminating questions as to whether Sea-Horses had tails like a real horse or like real fishes; did they wear horse-shoes; did they bite?

These were three points upon which Nebby's curiosity was definite; and the results were definite enough in the finished work; for Granfer supplied the peculiar creature with "reel" bone teeth and a workable jaw; two squat, but prodigious legs, near what he termed the "bows"; whilst to the "starn" he affixed the bonito-tail which has already had mention, setting it the way Dame Nature sets it on the bonito, that is, "thwart-ships", so that its two flukes touched the ground when the go-horse was in position, and thus steadied it admirably with this hint taken direct from the workmanship of the Great Carpenter.

There came a day when the horse was finished and the last coat of paint had dried smooth and hard. That evening, when Nebby came running to meet Zacchy, he was aware of his Grandfather's voice in the dusk, shouting: – "Whoa, Mare! Whoa, Mare!" followed immediately by the cracking of a whip.

Nebby shrilled out a call, and raced on, mad with excitement, towards the noise. He knew instantly that at last Granfer had managed to catch one of the wily Sea-Horses. Presumably the creature was somewhat intractable; for when Nebby arrived, he found the burly form of Granfer straining back tremendously upon stout reins, which Nebby saw vaguely in the dusk were attached to a squat, black monster:

"Whoa, Mare!" roared Granfer, and lashed the air furiously with his whip. Nebby shrieked delight, and ran round and round, whilst Granfer struggled with the animal.

"Hi! Hi! Hi!" shouted Nebby, dancing from foot to foot. "Ye've catched 'm, Granfer! Ye've catched 'm, Granfer!"

"Aye," said Granfer, whose struggles with the creature must have been prodigious; for he appeared to pant. "She'll go quiet now, b'y. Take a holt!" And he handed the reins and the whip over to the excited, but half-fearful Nebby. "Put y'r hand on 'er, Neb," said old Zacchy. "That'll quiet 'er."

Nebby did so, a little nervously, and drew away in a moment.

"She's all wet 's wet!" he cried out.

"Aye," said Granfer, striving to hide the delight in his voice. "She'm straight up from the water, b'y."

This was quite true; it was the final artistic effort of Granfer's imagination; he had dipped the horse overside, just before leaving the diving barge. He took his towel from his pocket, and wiped the horse down, hissing as he did so.

"Now, b'y," he said, "welt 'er good, an' make her take ye home."

Nebby straddled the go-horse, made an ineffectual effort to crack the whip, shouted: – "Gee-up! Gee-up!" And was off – two small, lean bare legs twinkling away into the darkness at a tremendous rate, accompanied by shrill and recurrent "Gee-ups!"

Granfer Zacchy stood in the dusk, laughing happily, and pulled out his pipe. He filled it slowly, and as he applied the light, he heard the galloping of the horse, returning. Nebby dashed up, and circled his Granfer in splendid fashion, singing in a rather breathless voice:

'An' we's under the sea, b'ys.
Where the Wild Horses go,
Horses wiv tails
As big as ole whales
All jiggin' around in a row,
An' when you ses Whoa!
Them debbils does go!"

And away he went again at the gallop.

This had happened a week earlier; and now we have Nebby questioning Granfer Zacchy as to whether the Sea-Horse is really alive or dead.

"Should think they has Sea-Horses 'n heaven, Granfer?" said Nebby, thoughtfully, as he once more straddled the go-horse.

"Sure," said Granfer Zacchy.

"Is Martha Tullet's li'l b'y gone to heaven?" asked Nebby.

"Sure," said Granfer again, as he sucked at his pipe.

Nebby was silent a good while, thinking. It was obvious that he confused heaven with the Domain of the Sea-Horses; for had not Granfer himself seen Martha Tullet's li'l b'y riding one of the Sea-Horses. Nebby had told Mrs. Tullet about it; but she had only thrown her apron over her head, and cried, until at last Nebby had stolen away, feeling rather dumpy.

"Has you ever seed any angels wiv wings on the Sea-Horses, Granfer?" Nebby asked, presently; determined to have further information with which to assure his ideas.

"Aye," said Granfer Zacchy. "Shoals of 'em. Shoals of 'em, b'y."

Nebby was greatly pleased.

"Could they ride some, Granfer?" he questioned.

"Sure," said old Zacchy, reaching for his pouch.

"As good 's me?" asked Nebby, anxiously.

"Middlin' near. Middlin' near, b'y," said Granfer Zacchy. "Why, Neb," he continued, waking up with a sudden relish to the full possibilities of the question, "thar's some of them lady ayngels as c'ud do back-somersaults an' never take a throw, b'y."

It is to be feared that Granfer Zacchy's conception of a lady angel had been formed during odd visits to the circus. But Nebby was duly impressed, and bumped his head badly the same day, trying to achieve the rudiments of a back-somersault.

Chapter II

SOME EVENINGS LATER, Nebby came running to meet old Zacchy, with an eager question:

"Has you seed Jane Melly's li'l gel ridin' the Horses, Granfer?" he asked, earnestly.

"Aye," said Granfer. Then, realising suddenly what the question portended:

"What's wrong wiv Mrs. Melly's wee gel?" he queried.

"Dead," said Nebby, calmly. "Mrs. Kay ses it's the fever come to the village again, Granfer."

Nebby's voice was cheerful; for the fever had visited the village some months before, and Granfer Zacchy had taken Nebby to live on the barge, away from danger of infection. Nebby had enjoyed it all enormously, and had often prayed God since to send another fever, with its attendant possibilities of life again aboard the diving-barge.

"Shall we live in the barge, Granfer?" he asked, as he swung along with the old man.

"Maybe! Maybe!" said old Zacchy, absently, in a somewhat troubled voice.

Granfer left Nebby in the kitchen, and went on up the village to make inquiries; the result was that he packed Nebby's clothes and toys into a well-washed sugar-bag, and the next day took the boy down to the barge, to live. But whereas Granfer walked, carrying the sack of gear, Nebby rode all the way, most of it at an amazing gallop. He even rode daringly down the narrow, railless gang-plank. It is true that Granfer Zacchy took care to keep close behind, in as unobtrusive a fashion as possible; but of this, or the need of such watchfulness, Nebby was most satisfactorily ignorant. He was welcomed in the heartiest fashion by Ned, the pump-man, and Binny, who attended to the air-pipe and life-line when Granfer Zacchy was down below.

Chapter III

LIFE ABOARD the diving-barge was a very happy time for Nebby. It was a happy time also for Granfer Zacchy and his two men; for the child, playing constantly in their midst, brought back to them an adumbration of their youth. There was only one point upon which there arose any trouble, and that was Nebby's forgetfulness, in riding across the air-tube, when he was exercising his Sea-Horse.

Ned, the pump-man, had spoken very emphatically to Nebby on this point, and Nebby had promised to remember; but, as usual, soon forgot. They had taken the barge outside the bar, and anchored her over the buoy that marked Granfer's submarine operations. The day was gloriously fine, and so long as the weather remained fixed, they meant to keep the barge out there, merely sending the little punt ashore for provisions.

To Nebby, it was all just splendid! When he was not riding his Sea-Horse, he was talking to the men, or waiting at the gangway eagerly for Granfer's great copper head-piece to come up out of the water, as the air-tube and life-line were slowly drawn aboard. Or else his shrill young voice was sure to be heard, as he leant over the rail and peered into the depths below, singing:

> *'An' we's under the sea, b'ys.*
> *Where the Wild Horses go,*
> *Horses wiv tails*
> *As big as ole whales*
> *All jiggin' around in a row.*
> *An' when you ses Whoa!*
> *Them debbils does go!"*

Possibly, he considered it as some kind of charm with which to call the Sea-Horses up to view.

Each time the boat went ashore, it brought sad news, that first this and then that one had gone the Long Road; but it was chiefly the children that interested Nebby. Each time that his Granfer came up out of the depths, Nebby would dance round him impatiently, until the big helmet was unscrewed; then would come his inevitable, eager question: Had Granfer seen Carry Andrew's li'l gel; or had Granfer seen Marty's li'l b'y riding the Sea-Horses? And so on.

"Sure," Granfer would reply; though, several times, it was his first intimation that the child mentioned had died; the news having reached the barge through some passing boat, whilst he was on the sea-bottom.

Chapter IV

"LOOK YOU, NEBBY!" shouted Ned, the pump-man, angrily. "I'll shore break that horse of yours up for kindlin' next time you goes steppin' on the air-pipe."

It was all too true; Nebby had forgotten, and done it again; but whereas, generally, he took Ned's remonstrances in good part, and promised better things, he stood now, looking with angry defiance at the man. The suggestion that his Sea-Horse was made of wood, bred in him a tempest of bitterness. Never for one moment to himself had he allowed so horrible a thought to enter his own head; not even when, in a desperate charge, he had knocked a chip off the nose of the Sea-Horse, and betrayed the merciless wood below. He had simply refused to look particularly at the place; his fresh, child's imagination allowing him presently to grow assured again that all was well; that he truly rode a "gen-u-ine" Sea-Horse. In his earnestness of determined make-believe, he had even avoided showing Granfer Zacchy the place, and asking him to mend it, much as he wanted it mended. Granfer always mended his toys for him; but *this* could not be mended. It was a *real* Sea-Horse; not a toy. Nebby resolutely averted his thoughts from the possibility of any other Belief; though it is likely that such mental processes were more subconscious than conscious.

And now, Ned had said the deadly thing, practically in so many naked words. Nebby trembled with anger and a furious mortification of his pride of Sea-Horse-Ownership. He looked round swiftly for the surest way to avenge the brutish insult, and saw the air-pipe; the thing around which the bother had been made. Yes, that would make Ned angry! Nebby turned his strange steed, and charged straight away back at the pipe. There, with an angry and malicious deliberateness, he halted, and made the big front hoofs of his extraordinary monster, stamp upon the air-pipe.

"You young devil!" roared Ned, scarcely able to believe the thing he saw. "You young devil!"

Nebby continued to stamp the big hoofs upon the pipe, glaring with fierce, defiant, blue eyes at Ned. Whereupon, Ned's patience arose and departed, and Ned himself arrived bodily in haste and with considerable vigour. He gave one kick, and the Sea-Horse went flying across the deck, and crashed into the low bulwarks. Nebby screamed; but it was far more a scream of tremendous anger, than of fear.

"I'll heave the blamed thing over the side!" said Ned, and ran to complete his dreadful sacrilege. The following instant, something clasped his right leg, and small, distinctly sharp teeth bit his bare shin, below the up-rolled trousers. Ned yelled, and sat rapidly and luridly upon the deck, in a fashion calculated to shock his system, in every sense of the word.

Nebby had loosed from him, the instant his bite had taken effect; and now he was nursing and examining the black monster of his dreams and waking moments. He knelt there, near the bulwarks, looking with burning eyes of anger and enormous distress at the effects of Ned's great kick; for Ned wore his bluchers on his bare feet. Ned himself still endured a sitting conjunction with the deck; he had not yet finished expressing himself; not that Nebby was in the least interested... anger and distress had built a wall of fierce indifference about his heart. He desired chiefly Ned's death.

If Ned, himself, had been less noisy, he would have heard Binny even earlier than he did; for that sane man had jumped to the air-pump, luckily for Granfer Zacchy, and was now, as he worked, emptying his soul of most of its contents upon the derelict Ned. As it was, Ned's memory and ears did duty together, and he remembered that he had committed the last crime in the Pumpman's Calendar... he had left the pump, whilst his diver was still below water. Powder ignited in quite a considerable quantity beneath him, could scarcely have moved Ned more speedily. He gave out one yell, and leaped for the pump; at the same instant he discovered that Binny was there, and his gasp of relief was as vehement as prayer. He remembered his leg, and concluded his journey to the pump, with a limp. Here, with one hand he pumped, whilst with the other, he investigated Nebby's teeth-marks. He found that the skin was barely broken; but it was his temper that most needed mending; and, of course, it had been very naughty of Nebby to attempt such a familiarity.

* * *

Binny was drawing in the life-line and air-pipe; for Granfer Zacchy was ascending the long rope-ladder, that led up from the sea-bottom, to learn what had caused the unprecedented interruption of his air-supply.

It was a very angry Granfer who, presently, having heard a fair representation of the facts, applied a wet but horny hand to Nebby's anatomy, in a vigorous and decided manner. Yet Nebby neither cried nor spoke; he merely clung on tightly to the Sea-Horse; and Granfer whacked on. At last Granfer grew surprised at the continued absence of remonstrance on Nebby's part, and turned that young man the other end about, to discover the wherefore of so determined a silence.

Nebby's face was very white, and tears seemed perilously near; yet even the nearness of these, did not in any way detract from the expression of unutterable defiance that looked out at Granfer and all the world, from his face. Granfer regarded him for a few moments with earnest attention and doubt, and decided to cease whipping that atom of blue-eyed stubbornness. He looked at the Sea-Horse that Nebby clutched so tightly, in his silence, and perceived the way to make Nebby climb down... Nebby must go and beg Ned's pardon for trying to eat him (Granfer smothered a chuckle), or else the Sea-Horse would be taken away.

Nebby's face, however, showed no change, unless it was that the blue eyes shone with a fiercer defiance, which dried out of them that suspicion of tears. Granfer pondered over him, and had a fresh idea. He would take the Sea-Horse back again to the bottom of the sea; and it would then come alive once more and swim away, and Nebby would never see it again, if Nebby did not go at once to Ned and beg Ned's pardon, that very minute. Granfer was prodigiously stern.

There came, perhaps, the tiniest flash of fright into the blue eyes; but it was blurred with unbelief; and, anyway, it had no power at that stage of Nebby's temper to budge him from his throne of enormous anger. He decided, with that fierce courage of the burner of boats, that if Granfer did truly do such a dreadful thing, he (Nebby) would "kneel down proper" and pray God to kill Ned. An added relish of vengeance came to his child's mind.... He would kneel down in front of Ned; he would pray to God "out loud". Ned should thus learn beforehand that he was doomed.

In that moment of inspired Intention, Nebby became trebly fixed into his Aura of Implacable Anger. He voiced his added grimness of heart in the most tremendous words possible:

"It's wood!" said Nebby, glaring at Granfer, in a kind of fierce, sick, horrible triumph. "It carn't come back alive again!"

Then he burst into tears, at this dreadful act of disillusionment, and wrenching himself free from Granfer's gently-detaining hand, he dashed away aft, and down the scuttle into the cuddy, where for an hour he hid himself under a bunk, and refused, in dreary silence, any suggestion of dinner.

After dinner, however, he emerged, tear-stained but unbroken. He had brought the Sea-Horse below with him; and now, as the three men watched him, unobtrusively, from their seats around the little cuddy-table, it was plain to them that Nebby had some definite object in view, which he was attempting to mask under an attitude of superb but ineffectual casualness.

"B'y," said Granfer Zacchy, in a very stern voice, "come you an' beg Ned's pard'n, or I'll shore take th' Sea-Horse down wiv me, an' you'll never see 'm no more, an' I'll never ketch ye another, Nebby."

Nebby's reply was an attempted dash for the scuttle-ladder; but Granfer reached out a long arm, that might have been described as possessing the radius of the small cuddy. As a result, Nebby was put with his face in a corner, whilst Granfer Zacchy laid the Sea-Horse across his knees, and stroked it meditatively, as he smoked a restful after-dinner pipe.

Presently, he knocked out his pipe, and, reaching round, brought Nebby to stand at his knee.

"Nebby, b'y," he said, in his grave, kindly fashion, "go you an' beg Ned's pard'n, an' ye shall hev this right back to play wiv."

But Nebby had not been given time yet to ease himself clear of the cloud of his indignation; and even as he stood there by Granfer, he could see the great bruise in the paint, where Ned's blucher had taken effect; and the broken fluke of the tail, that had been smashed when the poor Sea-Horse brought up so violently against the low bulwarks of the barge.

"Ned's a wicked pig man!" said Nebby, with a fresh intensity of anger against the pump-hand.

"Hush, b'y!" said Granfer, with real sternness. "Ye've had fair chance to come round, an' ye've not took it, an' now I'll read ye a lesson as ye'll shore mind!"

He stood up, and put the Sea-Horse under his arm; then, with one hand on Nebby's shoulder, he went to the ladder, and so in a minute they were all on the deck of the barge. Presently, Granfer was once more transformed from a genial and burly giant, into an indiarubber-covered and dome-ended monster. Then, with a slowness and solemnity befitting so terrible an execution of justice, Granfer made a fathom, or so, of spunyard fast about the Sea-Horse's neck, whilst Nebby looked on, white-faced.

When this was accomplished, Granfer stood up and marched with ponderous steps to the side, the Sea-Horse under his arm. He began to go slowly down the wooden rungs of the rope-ladder, and presently there were only his shoulders and copper-headpiece visible. Nebby stared down in an anguish; he could see the Sea-Horse vaguely. It seemed to waggle in the crook of Granfer's arm. It was surely about to swim away. Then Granfer's shoulders, and finally his great copper head disappeared from sight, and there was soon only the slight working of the ladder, and the paying out of the air-pipe and life-line, to tell that any one was down there in all that greyness of the water-dusk; for Granfer had often explained to Nebby that it was always "evenin' at th' sea-bottom".

Nebby sobbed once or twice, in a dry, horrid way, in his throat; then, for quite half an hour, he lay flat on his stomach in the gangway, silent and watchful, staring down into the water. Several times he felt *quite* sure he saw something swimming with a queer, waggling movement, a little under the water; and presently he started to sing in a low voice:

> "An' we's under the sea, b'ys,
> Where the Wild Horses go,
> Horses wiv tails
> As big as ole whales
> All jiggin' around in a row,
> An' when you ses Whoa!
> Them debbils does go!"

But it seemed to have no power to charm the Sea-Horse up to the surface; and he fell silent, after singing it through, maybe a dozen times. He was waiting for Granfer. He had a vague hope, which grew, that Granfer had meant to tie it up with the spunyard, so that it could not swim away; and perhaps Granfer would bring it up with him when he came. Nebby felt that he would really beg Ned's pardon, if only Granfer brought the Sea-Horse up with him again.

A little later, there came the signal that Granfer was about to ascend, and Nebby literally trembled with excitement, as the life-line and air-pipe came in slowly, hand over hand. He saw the big dome of the helmet come vaguely into view, with the line of the air-pipe leading down at the usual "funny" angle, right into the top of the dome (it was an old type of helmet). Then the helmet broke the water, and Nebby could not see anything, because the "rimples" on the water stopped him seeing. Granfer's big shoulders came into view, and then sufficient of him for Nebby to see that the Sea-Horse was truly not with him. Nebby whitened. Granfer had *really* let the Sea-Horse go. As a matter of fact, Granfer Zacchy had tethered the Sea-Horse to some tough marine weed-rootlets at the sea-bottom, so as to prevent it floating traitorously to the surface; but to Nebby it was plain only that the Sea-Horse had truly "come alive" and swum away.

Granfer stepped on to the deck, and Binny eased off the great helmet, whilst Ned ceased his last, slow revolution of the pump-handle.

It was at this moment that Nebby faced round on Ned, with a white, set, little face, in which his blue eyes literally burned. Ned was surely doomed in that instant! And then, even in the Moment of his Intention, Nebby heard Granfer say to Binny:

"Aye, I moored it wiv the spunyarn safe enough."

Nebby's anger lost its deadliness abruptly, under the sudden sweet chemistry of hope. He oscillated an instant between a new, vague thought, and his swiftly-lessening requirement of vengeance. The new, vague thought became less vague, and he swayed the more towards it; and so, in a moment, had rid himself of his Dignity, and run across to Granfer Zacchy:

"Has it comed alive, Granfer?" he asked, breathlessly, with the infinite eagerness and expectancy of a child.

"Aye!" said Granfer Zacchy, with apparent sternness. "Ye've sure lost it now, b'y. 'Tis swimmin' an' swimmin' roun' an' roun' all the time."

Nebby's eyes shone with sudden splendour, as the New Idea took now a most definite form in his young brain.

Granfer, looking at him with eyes of tremendous sternness, was quite non-plussed at the harmless effect of his expectedly annihilative news concerning the final and obvious lostness of the Sea-Horse. Yet, Nebby said never a word to give Granfer an inkling of the stupendous plan that was settling fast in his daring child's-mind. He opened his mouth once or twice upon a further question; then relapsed into the safety of silence again, as though instinctively realising that he might ask something that would make Granfer suspicious.

Presently, Nebby had stolen away once more to the gangway, and there, lying on his stomach, he began again to look down into the sea. His anger now was almost entirely submerged in the great, glorious New Idea, that filled him with such tremendous exaltation that he could scarcely lie quiet, or cease from singing aloud at the top of his voice.

A few moments earlier, he had meant to "kneel down proper" and pray God "out loud" for Ned to be killed quickly and painfully; but now all was changed. Though, in an indifferent sort of way, in his healthily-savage child's-mind, he did not *forgive* Ned.... Ned's sin had, of course, been unforgivable, presumably "for ever and ever and ever" – Certainly until tomorrow! Meanwhile, Nebby never so much as thought of him, except it might be as one whose bewilderment should presently be the last lustre of the glory of his (Nebby's) proposed achievement. Not that Nebby thought it all out like this into separate ideas; but it was all there in that young and surging head... in what I might term a Chaos of Determination, buoying up (as it might be a lonesome craft) one clear, vigorous Idea.

Granfer Zacchy went down twice more before evening, and each time that he returned, Nebby questioned him earnestly as to the doings of the Sea-Horse; and each time, Granfer told the same tale (in accents of would-be sternness) that the Sea-Horse was "jest swimmin' roun' an' roun'; an' maybe ye wish now ye'd begged Ned's pardon, when ye was bid!"

But, in his heart, Granfer decided that the Sea-Horse might be safely re-caught on the morrow.

Chapter V

THAT NIGHT, when the three men were asleep in the little cuddy, Nebby's small figure slipped noiselessly out of the bunk that lay below Granfer Zacchy's. He flitted silently to the ladder, and stole up into the warm night, his shirt (a quaint cut-down of Granfer's) softly flicking his lean, bare legs, as he moved through the darkness, along the barge's decks.

Nebby came to a stop where Granfer's diving-suit was hung up carefully on the "frame"; but this was not what Nebby wanted. He stooped to the bottom of the "frame", and pulled up the small hatch of a square locker, where reposed the big, domed, copper helmet, glimmering dully in the vague starlight.

Nebby reached into the locker, and lugged the helmet out bodily, hauling with both hands upon the air-pipe. He carried it across clumsily to the gangway, the air-pipe unreeling off the winch, with each step that he took.

He found the helmet too clumsy and rotund to lift easily on to his own curly head, and so, after an attempt or two, evolved the method of turning the helmet upon its side, and then kneeling down and thrusting his head into it; after which, with a prodigious effort, he rose victoriously to his knees, and began to fumble himself backwards over the edge of the gangway, on to the wooden rungs of Granfer's rope-ladder, which had not been hauled up. He managed a firm foot-hold with his left foot, and then with his right; and so began to descend, slowly and painfully, the great helmet rocking clumsily on his small shoulders.

His right foot touched the water at the fourth rung, and he paused, bringing the other foot down beside the first. The water was pleasantly warm, and Nebby hesitated only a very little while, ere he ventured the next step. Then he stopped again, and tried to look down into the water. The action swayed the big helmet backwards, so that – inside of it – Nebby's delightfully impudent little nose received a bang that made his determined blue eyes water. He loosed his left hand from the ladder, holding on with his right, and tried to push the clumsy helmet forward again into place.

He was, as you will understand, up to his knees in the water, and the rung, on which he perched, was slippery with that peculiar slipperiness, that wood and water together know so well how to breed. One of Nebby's bare feet slipped, and immediately the other. The great helmet gave a prodigious wobble, and completed the danger; for the sudden strain wrenched his grip from the rope between the rungs. There was a muffled little cry inside the helmet, and Nebby swung a small, desperate hand through the darkness towards the ladder; but it was too late; he was falling. There was a splash; not a very big splash for so big a boy's-heart and courage; and no one heard it, or the little bubbling squeak that came out of the depths of the big copper helmet. And then, in a moment, there was only the vaguely disturbed surface of the water, and the air-pipe was running out smoothly and swiftly off the drum.

Chapter VI

IT WAS in the strange, early-morning light, when the lemon and gold-of-light of dawn was in the grey East, that Granfer discovered the thing which had happened. With the wakefulness that is so often an asset of healthy age, he had turned-out in the early hours, to fill his pipe, and had discovered that Nebby's bunk was empty.

He went swiftly up the small ladder. On the deck, the out-trailed air-pipe whispered its tale in silence, and Granfer rushed to it, shouting in a dreadful voice for Binny and Ned, who came bounding up, sleepily, in their heavy flannel drawers.

They hauled in the air-pipe, swiftly but carefully; but when the great dome of the helmet came up to them, there was no Nebby; only, tangled from the thread of one of the old-fashioned thumb-screws, they found several golden, curly strands of Nebby's hair.

Granfer, his great muscular hands trembling, began to get into his rubber suit, the two men helping him, wordless. Within a hundred and fifty seconds, he was dwindling away down under the quiet sea that spread, all grey and lemon-hued and utterly calm, in the dawn. Ned was turning the pump-handle, and wiping his eyes undisguisedly from time to time with the back of one hairy, disengaged hand. Binny, who was of a sterner type, though no less warm-hearted, was grimly silent, giving his whole attention to the air-pipe and the life-line; his hand delicate upon the line, awaiting the signal. He could tell from the feel and the coming-up and going-out of the pipe and the line, that Granfer Zacchy was casting round and round, in ever largening circles upon the sea-bottom.

All that day, Granfer quartered the sea-bottom; staying down so long each time, that at last Binny and Ned were forced to remonstrate. But the old man turned on them, and snarled in a kind of speechless anger and agony that forced them to be silent and let him go his own gait.

For three days, Granfer continued his search, the sea remaining calm; but found nothing. On the fourth day, Granfer Zacchy was forced to take the barge in over the bar; for the wind breezed up hard out of the North, and blew for a dreary and savage fortnight, each day of which found Granfer, with Binny and Ned, searching the shore for the "giving up" of the sea. But the sea had one of its secret moods, and gave up nothing.

At the end of the fortnight of heavy weather, it fell calm, and they took the barge out again, to start once more their daily work. There was little use now in searching further for the boy. The barge was moored again over the old spot, and Granfer descended; and the first thing he saw in the grey half-light of the water, was the Sea-Horse, still moored securely by the length of spunyarn to the rootlets of heavy weed at the sea-bottom.

The sight of the creature, gave old Zacchy a dreadful feeling; it was, at once, so familiar of Nebby, as to give him the sensation and unreasoning impression that the "b'y" must be surely close at hand; and yet, at the same time, the grotesque, inanimate creature was the visible incarnation of the Dire Cause of the unspeakable loneliness and desolation that now possessed his old heart so utterly. He glared at it, through the thick glass of his helmet, and half raised his axe to strike at it. Then, with a sudden revulsion, he reached out, and pulled the silent go-horse to him, and hugged it madly, as if, indeed, it were the boy himself.

Presently, old Granfer Zacchy grew calmer, and turned to his work; yet a hundred times, he would find himself staring round in the watery twilight towards it – staring eagerly and unreasoningly, and actually listening, inside his helmet, for sounds that the eternal silence of the sea might never bring through its dumb waters, that are Barriers of Silence about the lonesome diver in the strange underworld of the waters. And then, realising freshly that there was no longer One who might make the so-craved-for sounds, Granfer would turn again, grey-souled and lonely, to his work. Yet, in a while, he would be staring and listening once more.

In the course of days, old Zacchy grew calmer and more resigned; yet he kept the motionless Sea-Horse tethered, in the quiet twilight of the water, to the weed-rootlets at the sea-bottom. And more and more, he grew to staring round at it; and less and less did it seem a futile or an unreasonable thing to do.

In weeks, the habit grew to such an extent, that he had ceased to be aware of it. He prolonged his hours under water, out of all reason, so far as his health was concerned; and turned queerly "dour" when Ned and Binny remonstrated with him, warning him not to stay down so long, or he would certainly have to pay the usual penalty.

Only once did Granfer say a word in explanation, and then it was obviously an unintentional remark, jerked out of him by the intensity of his feelings:

"Like as I feel 'm nigh me, w'en I'm below," he had muttered, in a half coherent fashion. And the two men understood; for it was just what they had vaguely supposed. They had no reply to make; and the matter dropped.

Generally now, on descending each morning, Granfer would stop near the Sea-Horse, and "look it over". Once, he discovered that the bonito-tail had come unglued; but this he remedied neatly, by lashing it firmly into position with a length of roping-twine. Sometimes, he would pat the head of the horse, with one great hand, and mutter a quite unconscious: "Whoa, mare!" as it bobbed silently under his touch. Occasionally, as he swayed heavily past it, in his clumsy dress, the slight swirl of the water in his "wake" would make the Horse slue round uncannily towards him; and thereafter, it would swing and oscillate for a brief time, slowly back into quietness; the while that Granfer would stand and watch it, unconsciously straining his ears, in that place of no-sound.

Two months passed in this way, and Granfer was vaguely aware that his health was failing; but the knowledge brought no fear to him; only the beginnings of an indefinite contentment – a feeling that maybe he would be "soon seein' Nebby". Yet the thought was never definitely conscious; nor ever, of course, in any form, phrased. Yet it had its effect, in the vague contentment which I have hinted at, which brought a new sense of ease round Granfer's heart; so that, one day, as he worked, he found himself crooning unconsciously the old Ballade of the Sea Horses.

He stopped on the instant, all an ache with memory; then turned and peered towards the Sea-Horse, which loomed, a vague shadow, silent in the still water. It had seemed to him, in that moment, that he had heard a subtle echo of his crooned song, in the quiet deeps around him. Yet, he saw nothing, and presently assured himself that he heard nothing; and so came round again upon his work.

A number of times in the early part of that day, old Granfer caught himself crooning the old Ballade, and each time he shut his lips fiercely on the sound, because of the ache of memory that the old song bred in him; but, presently, all was forgotten in an intense listening; for, abruptly, old Zacchy was sure that he heard the song, coming from somewhere out of the eternal twilight of the waters. He slued himself round, trembling, and stared towards the Sea-Horse; but there was nothing new to be seen, neither was he any more sure that he had ever heard anything.

Several times this happened, and on each occasion Granfer would heave himself round ponderously in the water, and listen with an intensity that had in it, presently, something of desperateness.

In the late afternoon of that day, Granfer again heard something; but refused now to credit his hearing, and continued grimly at work. And then, suddenly, there was no longer any room for doubt… a shrill, sweet child's voice was singing, somewhere among the grey twilights far to his back. He heard it with astounding clearness, helmet and surrounding water notwithstanding. It was a sound, indeed, that he would have heard through all the Mountains of Eternity. He stared round, shaking violently.

The sound appeared to come from the greyness that dwelt away beyond a little wood of submarine growths, that trailed up their roots, so hushed and noiseless, out of a nearby vale in the sea-bottom.

As Granfer stared, everything about him darkened into a wonderful and rather dreadful Blackness. This passed, and he was able to see again; but somehow, as it might be said, newly. The shrill, sweet, childish singing had ceased; but there was something beside the Sea-Horse... a little, agile figure, that caused the Sea-Horse to bob and bound at its moorings. And, suddenly, the little figure was astride the Sea-Horse, and the Horse was free, and two twinkling legs urged it across the sea-bottom towards Granfer.

Granfer thought that he stood up, and ran to meet the boy; but Nebby dodged him, the Sea-Horse curvetting magnificently; and immediately Nebby began to gallop round and round Granfer, singing:

"An' we's under the sea, b'ys,
Where the Wild Horses go,
Horses wiv tails
As big as ole whales
All jiggin' around in a row,
An' when you ses Whoa!
Them debbils does go!"

The voice of the blue-eyed mite was ineffably gleeful; and, abruptly, tremendous youth invaded Granfer, and a glee beyond all understanding.

Chapter VII

ON THE DECK of the barge, Ned and Binny were in great doubt and trouble. The weather had been growing heavy and threatening, during all the late afternoon; and now it was culminating in a tremendous, black squall, which was coming swiftly down upon them.

Time after time, Binny had attempted to signal Granfer Zacchy to come up; but Granfer had taken a turn with his life-line round a hump of rock that protruded out of the sea-bottom; so that Binny was powerless to do aught; for there was no second set of diving gear aboard.

All that the two men could do, was to wait, in deep anxiety, keeping the pump going steadily, and standing-by for the signal that was never to come; for by that time, old Granfer Zacchy was sitting very quiet and huddled against the rock, round which he had hitched his line to prevent Binny from signalling him, as Binny had become prone to do, when Granfer stayed below, out of all reason and wisdom.

And all the time, Ned kept the un-needed pump going, and far down in the grey depth, the air came out in a continual series of bubbles, around the big copper helmet. But Granfer was breathing an air of celestial sweetness, all unwotting and un-needing of the air that Ned laboured faithfully to send to him.

The squall came down in a fierce haze of rain and foam, and the ungainly old craft swung round, jibbing heavily at her kedge-rope, which gave out a little twanging sound, that was lost in the roar of the wind. The unheard twanging of the rope, ended suddenly in a dull thud, as it parted; and the bluff old barge fell off, broadside on to the weight of the squall. She drifted with astonishing rapidity, and the life-line and the air-pipe flew out, with a buzz of the unwinding drums, and parted, with two differently toned reports, that were plain in an instant's lull in the roaring of the squall.

Binny had run forrard to the bows, to try to get over another kedge; but now he came racing aft again, shouting. Ned still pumped on mechanically, with a look of dull, stunned horror in his eyes; the pump driving a useless jet of air through the broken remnant of the air-pipe. Already, the barge was a quarter of a mile to leeward of the diving-ground, and the men could do no more than hoist the foresail, and try to head her in safely over the bar, which was now right under their lee.

Down in the sea, old Granfer Zacchy had altered his position; the jerk upon the air-pipe had done that. But Granfer was well enough content; not only for the moment; but for Eternity; for as Nebby rode so gleefully round and round him, there had come a change in all things; there were strange and subtile lights in all the grey twilights of the deep, that seemed to lead away and away into stupendous and infinitely beautiful distances.

"Is you listenin', Granfer?" Old Zacchy heard Nebby say; and discovered suddenly that Nebby was insisting that he should race him across the strangely glorified twilights, that bounded them now eternally.

"Sure, b'y," said Granfer Zacchy, undismayed; and Nebby wheeled his charger.

"Gee-Up!" shouted Nebby, excitedly, and his small legs began to twinkle ahead in magnificent fashion; with Granfer running a cheerful and deliberate second.

And so passed Granfer Zacchy and Nebby into the Land where little boys may ride Sea-Horses for ever, and where Parting becomes one of the Lost Sorrows.

And Nebby led the way at a splendid gallop; maybe, for all that I have any right to know, to the very Throne of the Almighty, singing, shrill and sweet:

> *"An' we's under the sea, b'ys,*
> *Where the Wild Horses go,*
> *Horses wiv tails*
> *As big as ole whales*
> *All jiggin' around in a row,*
> *An' when you ses Whoa!*
> *Them debbils does go!"*

And overhead (was it *only* a dozen fathoms!) there rushed the white-maned horses of the sea, mad with the glory of the storm, and tossing ruthless from crest to crest, a wooden go-horse, from which trailed a length of broken spunyarn.

If you enjoyed this, you might also like...
The Shamraken Homeward-Bounder, see page 162
The Horse of the Invisible, see page 48

The Real Thing: 'S.O.S.'

"BIG LINER ON FIRE in 55.43 N. and 32.19 W.," shouts the Captain, diving into his chart-room. "Here we are! Give me the parallels!" The First Officer and the Captain figure busily for a minute.

"North, 15 West," says the Master; and "North, 15 West," assents the First Officer, flinging down his pencil. "A hundred and seventeen miles, dead in the wind!"

"Come on!" says the Captain; and the two of them dash out of the chart-room into the roaring black night, and up on to the bridge.

"North, 15 West!" the Master shouts in the face of the burly helmsman. "Over with her, smart!"

"North, 15 West, Sir," shouts back the big quartermaster, and whirls the spokes to starboard, with the steering-gear engine roaring.

The great vessel swings round against the night, with enormous scends, smiting the faces of the great seas with her seventy-feet-high bows.

Crash! A roar of water aboard, as a hundred phosphorescent tonnes of sea-water hurls inboard out of the darkness, and rushes aft along the lower decks, boiling and surging over the hatchways, capstans, deck-fittings, and round the corners of the deck-houses.

The ship has hit the fifty-mile-an-hour gale full in the face, and the engine telegraph stands at full speed. The Master has word with that King of the Underworld, the Chief Engineer; and the Chief goes below himself to take charge, just as the Master has taken charge on deck.

There is fresh news from the Operator's Room. The vessel somewhere out in the night and the grim storm is the 8.8. *Vanderfeld*, with sixty first-class passengers and seven hundred steerage and she is alight forrard. The fire has got a strong hold, and they have already lost three boats, smashed to pieces as they tried to launch them, and every man, woman, and child in the boats crushed to death or drowned.

"Damn these old-fashioned davits!" says the Master, as he reads the wireless operator's notes. "They won't lift a boat out clear of the ship's side, if she's rolling a bit. The boats in a ship are just ornaments, if you've not got proper machinery for launching them. We've got the new derricks, and we can lower a boat, so she strikes the water, forty feet clear of the side, instead of bashing to pieces, like a sixty-foot pendulum, against our side!"

He shouts a question over his shoulder, standing there by the binnacle:

"What's she doing, Mister Andrews?"

"Twenty and three-quarter knots, Sir," says the Second Officer, who has been in charge. "But the Chief's raising her revolutions every minute… She's nearly on to the twenty-one now."

"And even if we lick that we'll be over five hours reaching her," mutters the Master to himself.

Meanwhile the wireless is beating a message of hope across a hundred miles of night and storm and wild waters.

"Coming! The R.M.S. *Cornucopia* is proceeding at full speed in your direction. Keep us informed how you are...."

Then follows a brief unofficial statement, a heart-to-heart word between the young men operators of the two ships, across the hundred-mile gulf of black seas:

"Buck up, old man. We'll do it yet! We're simply piling into the storm, like a giddy cliff. She's doing close on twenty-one, they've just told me, against this breeze; and the Chief's down in the stokeholds himself with a fourteen-inch wrench and a double watch of stokers! Keep all your peckers up. I'll let you know if we speed-up any more!"

The Operator has been brief and literal, and has rather under-stated the facts. The Leviathan is now hurling all her fifty-thousand-ton length through the great seas at something approaching a twenty-two knot stride; and the speed is rising.

Down in the engine-room and stokeholds, the Chief, minus his overalls, is a coatless demi-god, with life in one hand and a fourteen-inch wrench in the other; not that this wrench is in any way necessary, for the half-naked men stream willing sweat in a silence broken only by the rasp of the big shovels and the clang of the furnace-doors, and the Chief's voice.

The Chief is young again; young and a King tonight, and the rough days of his youth have surged back over him. He has picked up the wrench unconsciously, and he walks about, twirling it in his fist; and the stokers work the better for the homely sight of it, and the sharp tang of his words, that miss no man of them all.

And the great ship feels the effect. Her giant tread has broken into an everlasting thunder, as her shoulders hurl the seas to port and starboard, in shattered hills of water, that surge to right and left in half-mile drifts of phosphorescent foam, under the roll of her Gargantuan flanks.

* * *

The first hour has passed, and there have been two fresh messages from that vessel, flaming far off, lost and alone, out in the wild roar of the waters. There has been an explosion forrard in the burning ship, and the fire has come aft as far as the main bunkers. There has been a panic attempt to lower two more of the boats, and each has been smashed to flinders of wood against the side of the burning ship, as she rolled. Every soul in them has been killed or drowned, and the Operator in the burning ship asks a personal question that has the first touch of real despair in it; and there ensues another little heart-to-heart talk between the two young men:

"Honest now, do you think you can do it?"

"Sure," says the Operator in the *Cornucopia*. "We're doing what we've never done at sea before in heavy weather. We're touching within a knot of our 'trials' speed – we're doing twenty-four and a half knots; and we're doing it against *this*! Honour bright, old man! I'll not deceive you at a time like this. I never saw anything like what we're doing. All the engineers are in the engine-room, and all the officers are on the boat-deck, overhauling the boats and gear. We've got those new forty-foot boat derricks, and we can shove a boat into the water with 'em, with the ship rolling half under. The Old Man's on the bridge; and I guess you're just going to be saved all right... You ought to hear us! I tell you, man, she's just welting the seas to a pulp, and skating along to you on the top of them."

The Operator is right. The great ship seems alive tonight, along all her shapely eight hundred feet of marvellous, honest, beautiful steel. Her enormous bows take the seas as on a horn, and hurl them roaring into screaming drifts of foam. She is singing a song, fore and aft, and the thunder of her grey steel flanks is stupendous, as she spurns the mutilated seas and the gale and the bleak intolerable miles into her wake.

* * *

The second and third hours pass, and part of the fourth, in an intermittent thunder of speed. And the speed has been further increased; for now the Leviathan is laying the miles astern, twenty-nine in each hour; her sides drunken with black water and spume – a dripping, league-conquering, fifty-thousand-ton shape of steel and steam and brains, going like some stupendous Angel of Help across the black Desolation of the night.

* * *

Incredibly far away, down on the black horizons of the night, there shows a faint red glow. There is shouting along the bridge.
"There she is!" goes the word fore and aft. "There she is!"
Meanwhile the wireless messages pulse across the darkness: The fire is burning with terrible fury. The fore-part of the *Vanderfield's* iron skin is actually glowing red-hot in places. Despair is seizing everyone. Will the coming *Cornucopia* never, never come?
The young Operators talk, using informal words:
"Look out to the South of you, for our searchlight," replies the man in the wireless-room of the Cornucopia. "The Old Man's going to play it against the clouds, to let you see we're coming. Tell 'em all to look out for it. It'll cheer them up. We're walking along through the smother like an express. Man! Man! we're doing our 'trials' speed, twenty-five and a half knots, *against this*. Do you realise it – *against this*! Look along to the South. Now!"

* * *

There is a hissing on the fore-bridge, quite unheard in the roar of the storm; and then there shoots out across the miles of night and broken seas the white fan-blaze of the searchlight. It beats like an enormous baton against the black canopy of the monstrous storm-clouds, beating to the huge, thundering melody of the roar and onward hurl of the fifty-thousand-ton rescuer, tossing the billows to right and left, as she strides through the miles.
And what a sight it is, in the glare of the great light, as it descends and shows the huge seas! A great cliff of black water rears up, and leaps forward at the ship's bows. There is a thunderous impact, and the ship has smitten the great sea in twain, and tossed it boiling and roaring on to her iron flanks; and is treading it into the welter of foam that surrounds her on every side – a raging testimony, of foam and shattered seas, to the might of her mile-devouring stride.
Another, and another, and another black, moving cliff rises up out of the water-valleys, which she strides across; and each is broken and tossed mutilated from her shapely, mighty, unafraid shoulders.

* * *

A message is coming, very weak and faint, through the receiver:

"We've picked up your searchlight, old man. It's comforted us mightily; but we can't last much longer. The dynamo's stopped. I'm running on my batteries...." It dwindles off into silence, broken by fragments of a message, too weakly projected to be decipherable.

* * *

"Look at her!" the officers shout to one another on the bridge; for the yell of the wind and the ship-thunder is too great for ordinary speech to be heard. They are staring through their glasses. Under a black canopy of bellied storm-clouds, shot with a dull red glowing, there is tossed up on the backs of far-away seas, a far-off ship, seeming incredibly minute, because of the distance; and from her fore-part spouts a swaying tower of flame.

"We'll never do it in time!" says the young Sixth Officer into the ear of the Fifth.

* * *

The burning ship is now less than three miles away, and the black backs of the great seas are splashed with huge, ever shifting reflections.

Through the glasses it is possible now to see the details of the tremendous hold the fire has got on the ship; and, away aft, the huddled masses of the six hundred odd remaining passengers.

As they watch, one of the funnels disappears with an unheard crash, and a great spout of flame and sparks shoot up.

"It'll go through her bottom!" shouts the Second Officer; but they know this does not happen, for she still floats.

* * *

Suddenly comes the thrilling cry of "Out derricks!" and there is a racing of feet and shouted orders. Then the great derricks swing out from the ship's side, a boat's length above the boat-deck. They are hinged, and supported down almost to the draught line of the ship. They reach out forty feet clear of the ship's side.

The Leviathan is bursting through the final miles of wild seas; and then the telegraph bell rings, and she slows down, not more than ten or twelve hundred yards to wind'ard of the burning hull, which rises and falls, a stupendous spectacle on the waste of black seas.

The fifty-thousand-ton racer has performed her noble work, and now the work lies with the boats and the men.

* * *

The searchlight flashes down on to the near water, and the boats shoot out in the 'travellers', then are dropped clear of the mighty flanks of the Mother Ship.

The Leviathan lies to windward of them, to break the force of the seas, and oil bags are put out.

The people in the burning ship greet the ship with mad cheers. The women are hove bodily into the seas, on the ends of lines. They float in their cork jackets. Men take children in their arms, and jump, similarly equipped. And all are easily picked up by the boats, in the blaze of the rescuer's searchlights that brood on leagues of ocean, strangely subdued by the floods of oil which the big ship is pumping on to the seas. Everywhere lies the strange sheen of oil, here in a sudden valley of brine, unseen, or there on the shoulder of some monstrous wave, suddenly eased of its deadliness; or again, the same fluorescence swirls over some half-league of eddy-flattened ocean, resting between efforts – tossing minor oil-soothed ridges into the tremendous lights.

Then the Leviathan steams to leeward of the burning ship, and picks up her boats. She takes the rescued passengers aboard, and returns to windward; then drops the boats again, and repeats the previous operations, until every man, woman, and child is saved.

As the last boat swings up at the end of the great derricks aboard the *Cornucopia* there is a final volcano of flame from the burning ship, lighting up the black belly of the sky into billowing clouds of redness. There falls the eternal blackness of the night... The *Vanderfield* has gone.

The Leviathan swings round through the night, with her six hundred saved; and begins to sing again in her deep heart, laying the miles and the storm astern once more, in a deep low thunder.

If you enjoyed this, you might also like...
Through the Vortex of a Cyclone, see page 146
Out of the Storm, see page 337

The Boats of the 'Glen Carrig'

The Boats of the 'Glen Carrig'

Being an account of their Adventures in the Strange places of the Earth, after the foundering of the good ship Glen Carrig through striking upon a hidden rock in the unknown seas to the Southward. As told by John Winterstraw, Gent., to his son James Winterstraw, in the year 1757, and by him committed very properly and legibly to manuscript.

Madre Mia

*People may say thou art no longer young
And yet, to me, thy youth was yesterday,
A yesterday that seems
Still mingled with my dreams.
Ah! how the years have o'er thee flung
Their soft mantilla, grey.*

*And e'en to them thou art not over old;
How could'st thou be! Thy hair
Hast scarcely lost its deep old glorious dark:
Thy face is scarcely lined. No mark
Destroys its calm serenity. Like gold
Of evening light, when winds scarce stir,
The soul-light of thy face is pure as prayer.*

Chapter I
The Land of Lonesomeness

NOW WE HAD BEEN five days in the boats, and in all this time made no discovering of land. Then upon the morning of the sixth day came there a cry from the bo'sun, who had the command of the lifeboat, that there was something which might be land afar upon our larboard bow; but it was very low lying, and none could tell whether it was land or but a morning cloud. Yet, because there was the beginning of hope within our hearts, we pulled wearily towards it, and thus, in about an hour, discovered it to be indeed the coast of some flat country.

Then, it might be a little after the hour of midday, we had come so close to it that we could distinguish with ease what manner of land lay beyond the shore, and thus we found it to be of an abominable flatness, desolate beyond all that I could have imagined. Here and there it appeared to be covered with clumps of queer vegetation; though whether they were small trees or great bushes, I had no means of telling; but this I know, that they were like unto nothing which ever I had set eyes upon before.

So much as this I gathered as we pulled slowly along the coast, seeking an opening whereby we could pass inward to the land; but a weary time passed or ere we came upon that which we sought. Yet, in the end, we found it – a slimy-banked creek, which proved to be the estuary of a great river, though we spoke of it always as a creek. Into this we entered, and proceeded at no great pace upwards along its winding course; and as we made forward, we scanned the low banks upon each side, perchance there might be some spot where we could make to land; but we found none – the banks being composed of a vile mud which gave us no encouragement to venture rashly upon them.

Now, having taken the boat something over a mile up the great creek, we came upon the first of that vegetation which I had chanced to notice from the sea, and here, being within some score yards of it, we were the better able to study it. Thus I found that it was indeed composed largely of a sort of tree, very low and stunted, and having what might be described as an unwholesome look about it. The branches of this tree, I perceived to be the cause of my inability to recognise it from a bush, until I had come close upon it; for they grew thin and smooth through all their length, and hung towards the earth; being weighted thereto by a single, large cabbage-like plant which seemed to sprout from the extreme tip of each.

Presently, having passed beyond this clump of the vegetation, and the banks of the river remaining very low, I stood me upon a thwart, by which means I was enabled to scan the surrounding country. This I discovered, so far as my sight could penetrate, to be pierced in all directions with innumerable creeks and pools, some of these latter being very great of extent; and, as I have before made mention, everywhere the country was low set – as it might be a great plain of mud; so that it gave me a sense of dreariness to look out upon it. It may be, all unconsciously, that my spirit was put in awe by the extreme silence of all the country around; for in all that waste I could see no living thing, neither bird nor vegetable, save it be the stunted trees, which, indeed, grew in clumps here and there over all the land, so much as I could see.

This silence, when I grew fully aware of it was the more uncanny; for my memory told me that never before had I come upon a country which contained so much quietness. Nothing moved across my vision – not even a lone bird soared up against the dull sky; and, for my hearing, not so much as the cry of a sea-bird came to me – no! nor the croak of a frog, nor the plash of a fish. It was as though we had come upon the Country of Silence, which some have called the Land of Lonesomeness.

Now three hours had passed whilst we ceased not to labour at the oars, and we could no more see the sea; yet no place fit for our feet had come to view, for everywhere the mud, grey and black, surrounded us – encompassing us veritably by a slimy wilderness. And so we were fain to pull on, in the hope that we might come ultimately to firm ground.

Then, a little before sundown, we halted upon our oars, and made a scant meal from a portion of our remaining provisions; and as we ate, I could see the sun sinking away over the wastes, and I had some slight diversion in watching the grotesque shadows which it cast from the trees into the water upon our larboard side; for we had come to a pause opposite a clump of the vegetation. It was at this time, as I remember, that it was borne in upon me afresh how very silent was the land; and that this was not due to my imagination, I remarked that the men both in our own and in the bo'sun's boat, seemed uneasy because of it; for none spoke save in undertones, as though they had fear of breaking it.

And it was at this time, when I was awed by so much solitude, that there came the first telling of life in all that wilderness. I heard it first in the far distance, away inland – a curious, low, sobbing note it was, and the rise and the fall of it was like to the sobbing of a lonesome wind through a great forest. Yet was there no wind. Then, in a moment, it had died, and the silence of the land was awesome by reason of the contrast. And I looked about me at the men, both in the boat in which I was and that which the bo'sun commanded; and not one was there but held himself in a posture of listening. In this wise a minute of quietness passed, and then one of the men gave out a laugh, born of the nervousness which had taken him.

The bo'sun muttered to him to hush, and, in the same moment, there came again the plaint of that wild sobbing. And abruptly it sounded away on our right, and immediately was caught up, as it were, and echoed back from some place beyond us afar up the creek. At that, I got me upon a thwart, intending to take another look over the country about us; but the banks of the creek had become higher; moreover the vegetation acted as a screen, even had my stature and elevation enabled me to overlook the banks.

And so, after a little while, the crying died away, and there was another silence. Then, as we sat each one harking for what might next befall, George, the youngest 'prentice boy, who had his seat beside me, plucked me by the sleeve, inquiring in a troubled voice whether I had any knowledge of that which the crying might portend; but I shook my head, telling him that I had no knowing beyond his own; though, for his comfort, I said that it might be the wind. Yet, at that, he shook his head; for indeed, it was plain that it could not be by such agency, for there was a stark calm.

Now, I had scarce made an end of my remark, when again the sad crying was upon us. It appeared to come from far up the creek, and from far down the creek, and from inland and the land between us and the sea. It filled the evening air with its doleful wailing, and I remarked that there was in it a curious sobbing, most human in its despairful crying. And so awesome was the thing that no man of us spoke; for it seemed that we harked to the weeping of lost souls. And then, as we waited fearfully, the sun sank below the edge of the world, and the dusk was upon us.

And now a more extraordinary thing happened; for, as the night fell with swift gloom, the strange wailing and crying was hushed, and another sound stole out upon the land – a far, sullen growling. At the first, like the crying, it came from far inland; but was caught up speedily on all sides of us, and presently the dark was full of it. And it increased in volume, and strange trumpetings fled across it. Then, though with slowness, it fell away to a low, continuous growling, and in it there was that which I can only describe as an insistent, hungry snarl. Aye! no other word of which I have knowledge so well describes it as that – a note of *hunger*, most awesome to the ear. And this, more than all the rest of those incredible voicings, brought terror into my heart.

Now as I sat listening, George gripped me suddenly by the arm, declaring in a shrill whisper that something had come among the clump of trees upon the left-hand bank. Of the truth of this, I had immediately a proof; for I caught the sound of a continuous rustling among them, and then a nearer note of growling, as though a wild beast purred at my elbow. Immediately upon this, I caught the bo'sun's voice, calling in a low tone to Josh, the eldest 'prentice, who had the charge of our boat, to come alongside of him; for he would have the boats together. Then got we out the oars and laid the boats together in the midst of the creek; and so we watched through the night, being full of fear, so that we kept our speech low; that is, so low as would carry our thoughts one to the other through the noise of the growling.

And so the hours passed, and naught happened more than I have told, save that once, a little after midnight, the trees opposite to us seemed to be stirred again, as though some creature, or creatures, lurked among them; and there came, a little after that, a sound as of something stirring the water up against the bank; but it ceased in a while and the silence fell once more.

Thus, after a weariful time, away Eastwards the sky began to tell of the coming of the day; and, as the light grew and strengthened, so did that insatiable growling pass hence with the dark and the shadows. And so at last came the day, and once more there was borne to us the sad wailing that had preceded the night. For a certain while it lasted, rising and falling most mournfully over the vastness of the surrounding wastes, until the sun was risen some degrees above the horizon; after which it began to fail, dying away in lingering echoes, most solemn to our ears. And so it passed, and there came again the silence that had been with us in all the daylight hours.

Now, it being day, the bo'sun bade us make such sparse breakfast as our provender allowed; after which, having first scanned the banks to discern if any fearful thing were visible, we took again to our oars, and proceeded on our upward journey; for we hoped presently to come upon a country where life had not become extinct, and where we could put foot to honest earth. Yet, as I have made mention earlier, the vegetation, where it grew, did flourish most luxuriantly; so that I am scarce correct when I speak of life as being extinct in that land. For, indeed, now I think of it, I can remember that the very mud from which it sprang seemed veritably to have a fat, sluggish life of its own, so rich and viscid was it.

Presently it was midday; yet was there but little change in the nature of the surrounding wastes; though it may be that the vegetation was something thicker, and more continuous along the banks. But the banks were still of the same thick, clinging mud; so that nowhere could we effect a landing; though, had we, the rest of the country beyond the banks seemed no better.

And all the while, as we pulled, we glanced continuously from bank to bank; and those who worked not at the oars were fain to rest a hand by their sheath-knives; for the happenings of the past night were continually in our minds, and we were in great fear; so that we had turned back to the sea but that we had come so nigh to the end of our provisions.

Chapter II
The Ship in the Creek

THEN, IT WAS NIGH on to evening, we came upon a creek opening into the greater one through the bank upon our left. We had been like to pass it – as, indeed, we had passed many throughout the day – but that the bo'sun, whose boat had the lead, cried out that there was some craft lying-up, a little beyond the first bend. And, indeed, so it seemed; for one of the masts of her – all jagged, where it had carried away – stuck up plain to our view.

Now, having grown sick with so much lonesomeness, and being in fear of the approaching night, we gave out something near to a cheer, which, however, the bo'sun silenced, having no knowledge of those who might occupy the stranger. And so, in silence, the bo'sun turned his craft towards the creek, whereat we followed, taking heed to keep quietness, and working the oars warily. So, in a little, we came to the shoulder of the bend, and had plain sight of the vessel some little way beyond us. From the distance she had no appearance of being inhabited; so that after some small hesitation, we pulled towards her, though still being at pains to keep silence.

The strange vessel lay against that bank of the creek which was upon our right, and over above her was a thick clump of the stunted trees. For the rest, she appeared to be firmly imbedded in the heavy mud, and there was a certain look of age about her which carried to me a doleful suggestion that we should find naught aboard of her fit for an honest stomach.

We had come to a distance of maybe some ten fathoms from her starboard bow – for she lay with her head down towards the mouth of the little creek – when the bo'sun bade his men to back water, the which Josh did regarding our own boat. Then, being ready to fly if we had been in danger, the bo'sun hailed the stranger; but got no reply, save that some echo of his shout seemed to come back at us. And so he sung out again to her, chance there might be some below decks who had not caught his first hail; but, for the second time, no answer came to us, save the low echo – naught, but that the silent trees took on a little quivering, as though his voice had shaken them.

At that, being confident now within our minds, we laid alongside, and, in a minute had shinned up the oars and so gained her decks. Here, save that the glass of the skylight of the main cabin had been broken, and some portion of the framework shattered, there was no extraordinary litter; so that it appeared to us as though she had been no great while abandoned.

So soon as the bo'sun had made his way up from the boat, he turned aft towards the scuttle, the rest of us following. We found the leaf of the scuttle pulled forward to within an inch of closing, and so much effort did it require of us to push it back, that we had immediate evidence of a considerable time since any had gone down that way.

However, it was no great while before we were below, and here we found the main cabin to be empty, save for the bare furnishings. From it there opened off two state-rooms at the forrard end, and the captain's cabin in the after part, and in all of these we found matters of clothing and sundries such as proved that the vessel had been deserted apparently in haste. In further proof of this we found, in a drawer in the captain's room, a considerable quantity of loose gold, the which it was not to be supposed would have been left by the free-will of the owner.

Of the staterooms, the one upon the starboard side gave evidence that it had been occupied by a woman – no doubt a passenger. The other, in which there were two bunks, had been shared, so far as we could have any certainty, by a couple of young men; and this we gathered by observation of various garments which were scattered carelessly about.

Yet it must not be supposed that we spent any great time in the cabins; for we were pressed for food, and made haste – under the directing of the bo'sun – to discover if the hulk held victuals whereby we might be kept alive.

To this end, we removed the hatch which led down to the lazarette, and, lighting two lamps which we had with us in the boats, went down to make a search. And so, in a little while, we came upon two casks which the bo'sun broke open with a hatchet. These casks were sound and tight, and in them was ship's biscuit, very good and fit for food. At this, as may be imagined, we felt eased in our minds, knowing that there was no immediate fear of starvation. Following this, we found a barrel of molasses; a cask of rum; some cases of dried fruit – these were mouldy and scarce fit to be eaten; a cask of salt beef, another of pork; a small barrel of vinegar; a case of brandy; two barrels of flour – one of which proved to be damp-struck; and a bunch of tallow dips.

In a little while we had all these things up in the big cabin, so that we might come at them the better to make choice of that which was fit for our stomachs, and that which was otherwise. Meantime, whilst the bo'sun overhauled these matters, Josh called a couple of the men, and went on deck to bring up the gear from the boats, for it had been decided that we should pass the night aboard the hulk.

When this was accomplished, Josh took a walk forward to the fo'cas'le; but found nothing beyond two seamen's chests; a sea-bag, and some odd gear. There were, indeed, no more than ten bunks in the place; for she was but a small brig, and had no call for a great crowd. Yet Josh was more than a little puzzled to know what had come to the odd chests; for it was not to be supposed that there had been no more than two – and a sea-bag – among ten men. But to this, at that time, he had no answer, and so, being sharp for supper, made a return to the deck, and thence to the main cabin.

Now while he had been gone, the bo'sun had set the men to clearing out the main cabin; after which, he had served out two biscuits apiece all round, and a tot of rum. To Josh, when he appeared, he gave the same, and, in a little, we called a sort of council; being sufficiently stayed by the food to talk.

Yet, before we came to speech, we made shift to light our pipes; for the bo'sun had discovered a case of tobacco in the captain's cabin, and after this we came to the consideration of our position.

We had provender, so the bo'sun calculated, to last us for the better part of two months, and this without any great stint; but we had yet to prove if the brig held water in her casks, for that in the creek was brackish, even so far as we had penetrated from the sea; else we had not been in need. To the charge of this, the bo'sun set Josh, along with two of the men. Another, he told to take charge of the galley, so long as we were in the hulk. But for that night, he said we had no need to do aught; for we had sufficient of water in the boats' breakers to last us till the morrow. And so, in a little, the dusk began to fill the cabin; but we talked on, being greatly content with our present ease and the good tobacco which we enjoyed.

In a little while, one of the men cried out suddenly to us to be silent, and, in that minute, all heard it – a far, drawn-out wailing; the same which had come to us in the evening of the first day. At that we looked at one another through the smoke and the growing dark, and, even as we looked, it became plainer heard, until, in a while, it was all about us – aye! it seemed to come floating down through the broken framework of the skylight as though some weariful, unseen thing stood and cried upon the decks above our heads.

Now through all that crying, none moved; none, that is, save Josh and the bo'sun, and they went up into the scuttle to see whether anything was in sight; but they found nothing, and so came down to us; for there was no wisdom in exposing ourselves, unarmed as we were, save for our sheath-knives.

And so, in a little, the night crept down upon the world, and still we sat within the dark cabin, none speaking, and knowing of the rest only by the glows of their pipes.

All at once there came a low, muttered growl, stealing across the land; and immediately the crying was quenched in its sullen thunder. It died away, and there was a full minute of silence; then, once more it came, and it was nearer and more plain to the ear. I took my pipe from my mouth; for I had come again upon the great fear and uneasiness which the happenings of the first night had bred in me, and the taste of the smoke brought me no more pleasure. The muttered growl swept over our heads and died away into the distance, and there was a sudden silence.

Then, in that quietness, came the bo'sun's voice. He was bidding us haste everyone into the captain's cabin. As we moved to obey him, he ran to draw over the lid of the scuttle; and Josh went with him, and, together, they had it across; though with difficulty. When we had come into the captain's cabin, we closed and barred the door, piling two great sea chests up against it; and so we felt near safe; for we knew that no thing, man nor beast, could come at us there. Yet, as may be supposed, we felt not altogether secure; for there was that in the growling which now filled the darkness, that seemed demoniac, and we knew not what horrid Powers were abroad.

And so through the night the growling continued, seeming to be mighty near unto us – aye! almost over our heads, and of a loudness far surpassing all that had come to us on the previous night; so that I thanked the Almighty that we had come into shelter in the midst of so much fear.

Chapter III
The Thing That Made Search

NOW AT TIMES, I fell upon sleep, as did most of the others; but, for the most part, I lay half sleeping and half waking – being unable to attain to true sleep by reason of the everlasting growling above us in the night, and the fear which it bred in me. Thus, it chanced that just after midnight, I caught a sound in the main cabin beyond the door, and immediately I was fully waked. I sat me up and listened, and so became aware that something was fumbling about the deck of the main cabin. At that, I got to my feet and made my way to where the bo'sun lay, meaning to waken him, if he slept; but he caught me by the ankle, as I stooped to shake him, and whispered to me to keep silence; for he too had been aware of that strange noise of something fumbling beyond in the big cabin.

In a little, we crept both of us so close to the door as the chests would allow, and there we crouched, listening; but could not tell what manner of thing it might be which produced so strange a noise. For it was neither shuffling, nor treading of any kind, nor yet was it the whirr of a bat's wings, the which had first occurred to me, knowing how vampires are said to inhabit the nights in dismal places. Nor yet was it the slurr of a snake; but rather it seemed to us to be as though a great wet cloth were being rubbed everywhere across the floor and bulkheads. We were the better able to be certain of the truth of this likeness, when, suddenly, it passed across the further side of the door behind which we listened: at which, you may be sure, we drew backwards both of us in fright; though the door, and the chests, stood between us and that which rubbed against it.

Presently, the sound ceased, and, listen as we might, we could no longer distinguish it. Yet, until the morning, we dozed no more; being troubled in mind as to what manner of thing it was which had made search in the big cabin.

Then in time the day came, and the growling ceased. For a mournful while the sad crying filled our ears, and then at last the eternal silence that fills the day hours of that dismal land fell upon us.

So, being at last in quietness, we slept, being greatly aweakried. About seven in the morning, the bo'sun waked me, and I found that they had opened the door into the big cabin; but though the bo'sun and I made careful search, we could nowhere come upon anything to tell us aught concerning the thing which had put us so in fright. Yet, I know not if I am right in saying that we came upon nothing; for, in several places, the bulkheads had a *chafed* look; but whether this had been there before that night, we had no means of telling.

Of that which we had heard, the bo'sun bade me make no mention, for he would not have the men put more in fear than need be. This I conceived to be wisdom, and so held my peace. Yet I was much troubled in my mind to know what manner of thing it was which we had need to fear, and more – I desired greatly to know whether we should be free of it in the daylight hours; for there was always with me, as I went hither and thither, the thought that *it* – for that is how I designated it in my mind – might come upon us to our destruction.

Now after breakfast, at which we had each a portion of salt pork, besides rum and biscuit (for by now the fire in the caboose had been set going), we turned-to at various matters, under the directing of the bo'sun. Josh and two of the men made examination of the water casks, and the rest of us lifted the main hatch-covers, to make inspection of her cargo; but lo! we found nothing, save some three feet of water in her hold.

By this time, Josh had drawn some water off from the casks; but it was most unsuitable for drinking, being vile of smell and taste. Yet the bo'sun bade him draw some into buckets, so that the air might haply purify it; but though this was done, and the water allowed to stand through the morning, it was but little better.

At this, as might be imagined, we were exercised in our minds as to the manner in which we should come upon suitable water; for by now we were beginning to be in need of it. Yet though one said one thing, and another said another, no one had wit enough to call to mind any method by which our need should be satisfied. Then, when we had made an end of dining, the bo'sun sent Josh, with four of the men, up stream, perchance after a mile or two the water should prove of sufficient freshness to meet our purpose. Yet they returned a little before sundown having no water; for everywhere it was salt.

Now the bo'sun, foreseeing that it might be impossible to come upon water, had set the man whom he had ordained to be our cook, to boiling the creek water in three great kettles. This he had ordered to be done soon after the boat left; and over the spout of each, he had hung a great pot of iron, filled with cold water from the hold – this being cooler than that from the creek – so that the steam from each kettle impinged upon the cold surface of the iron pots, and being by this means condensed, was caught in three buckets placed beneath them upon the floor of the caboose. In this way, enough water was collected to supply us for the evening and the following morning; yet it was but a slow method, and we had sore need of a speedier, were we to leave the hulk so soon as I, for one, desired.

We made our supper before sunset, so as to be free of the crying which we had reason to expect. After that, the bo'sun shut the scuttle, and we went every one of us into the captain's cabin, after which we barred the door, as on the previous night; and well was it for us that we acted with this prudence.

By the time that we had come into the captain's cabin, and secured the door, it was upon sunsetting, and as the dusk came on, so did the melancholy wailing pass over the land; yet, being by now somewhat inured to so much strangeness, we lit our pipes, and smoked; though I observed that none talked; for the crying without was not to be forgotten.

Now, as I have said, we kept silence; but this was only for a time, and our reason for breaking it was a discovery made by George, the younger apprentice. This lad, being no smoker, was fain to do something to while away the time, and with this intent, he had raked out the contents of a small box, which had lain upon the deck at the side of the forrard bulkhead.

The box had appeared filled with odd small lumber of which a part was a dozen or so grey paper wrappers, such as are used, I believe, for carrying samples of corn; though I have seen them put to other purposes, as, indeed, was now the case. At first George had tossed these aside; but it growing darker the bo'sun lit one of the candles which we had found in the lazarette. Thus, George, who was proceeding to tidy back the rubbish which was cumbering the place, discovered something which caused him to cry out to us his astonishment.

Now, upon hearing George call out, the bo'sun bade him keep silence, thinking it was but a piece of boyish restlessness; but George drew the candle to him, and bade us to listen; for the wrappers were covered with fine handwriting after the fashion of a woman's.

Even as George told us of that which he had found we became aware that the night was upon us; for suddenly the crying ceased, and in place thereof there came out of the far distance the low thunder of the night-growling, that had tormented us through the past two nights. For a space, we ceased to smoke, and sat – listening; for it was a very fearsome sound. In a very little while it seemed to surround the ship, as on the previous nights; but at length, using ourselves to it, we resumed our smoking, and bade George to read out to us from the writing upon the paper wrappers.

Then George, though shaking somewhat in his voice, began to decipher that which was upon the wrappers, and a strange and awesome story it was, and bearing much upon our own concerns:

"Now, when they discovered the spring among the trees that crown the bank, there was much rejoicing; for we had come to have much need of water. And some, being in fear of the ship (declaring, because of all our misfortune and the strange disappearances of their messmates and the brother of my lover, that she was haunted by a devil), declared their intention of taking their gear up to the spring, and there making a camp. This they conceived and carried out in the space of one afternoon; though our Captain, a good and true man, begged of them, as they valued life, to stay within the shelter of their living-place. Yet, as I have remarked, they would none of them hark to his counselling, and, because the Mate and the bo'sun were gone he had no means of compelling them to wisdom—"

At this point, George ceased to read, and began to rustle among the wrappers, as though in search for the continuation of the story.

Presently he cried out that he could not find it, and dismay was upon his face.

But the bo'sun told him to read on from such sheets as were left; for, as he observed, we had no knowledge if more existed; and we were fain to know further of that spring, which, from the story, appeared to be over the bank near to the vessel.

George, being thus adjured, picked up the topmost sheet; for they were, as I heard him explain to the bo'sun, all oddly numbered, and having but little reference one to the other. Yet we were mightily keen to know even so much as such odd scraps might tell unto us. Whereupon, George read from the next wrapper, which ran thus:

"Now, suddenly, I heard the Captain cry out that there was something in the main cabin, and immediately my lover's voice calling to me to lock my door, and on no condition to open it. Then the door of the Captain's cabin slammed, and there came a silence, and the silence was broken by a *sound*. Now, this was the first time that I had heard the Thing make search through the big cabin; but, afterwards, my lover told me it had happened aforetime, and they had told me naught, fearing to frighten me needlessly; though now I understood why my lover had bidden me never to leave my stateroom door unbolted in the nighttime. I remember also, wondering if the noise of breaking glass that had waked me somewhat from my dreams a night or two previously, had been the work of this indescribable Thing; for on the morning following that night, the glass in the skylight had been smashed. Thus it was that my thoughts wandered out to trifles, while yet my soul seemed ready to leap out from my bosom with fright.

"I had, by reason of usage, come to ability to sleep despite of the fearsome growling; for I had conceived its cause to be the mutter of spirits in the night, and had not allowed myself to be unnecessarily frightened with doleful thoughts; for my lover had assured me of our safety, and that we should yet come to our home. And now, beyond my door, I could hear that fearsome sound of the Thing searching—"

George came to a sudden pause; for the bo'sun had risen and put a great hand upon his shoulder. The lad made to speak; but the bo'sun beckoned to him to say no word, and at that we, who had grown to nervousness through the happenings in the story, began every one to listen. Thus we heard a sound which had escaped us in the noise of the growling without the vessel, and the interest of the reading.

For a space we kept very silent, no man doing more than let the breath go in and out of his body, and so each one of us knew that something moved without, in the big cabin. In a little, something touched upon our door, and it was, as I have mentioned earlier, as though a great swab rubbed and scrubbed at the woodwork. At this, the men nearest unto the door came backwards in a surge, being put in sudden fear by reason of the Thing being so near; but the bo'sun held up a hand, bidding them, in a low voice, to make no unneedful noise. Yet, as though the sounds of their moving had been heard, the door was shaken with such violence that we waited, everyone, expecting to see it torn from its hinges; but it stood, and we hasted to brace it by means of the bunk boards, which we placed between it and the two great chests, and upon these we set a third chest, so that the door was quite hid.

Now, I have no remembrance whether I have put down that when we came first to the ship, we had found the stern window upon the larboard side to be shattered; but so it was, and the bo'sun had closed it by means of a teak-wood cover which was made to go over it in stormy weather, with stout battens across, which were set tight with wedges. This he had done upon the first night, having fear that some evil thing might come upon us through the opening, and very prudent was this same action of his, as shall be seen. Then George cried out that something was at the cover of the larboard window, and we stood back, growing ever more fearful because that some evil creature was so eager to come at us. But the bo'sun, who was a very courageous man, and calm withal, walked over to the closed window, and saw to it that the battens were secure; for he had knowledge sufficient to be sure, if this were so, that no creature with strength less than that of a whale could break it down, and in such case its bulk would assure us from being molested.

Then, even as he made sure of the fastenings, there came a cry of fear from some of the men; for there had come at the glass of the unbroken window, a reddish mass, which plunged up against it, sucking upon it, as it were. Then Josh, who was nearest to the table, caught up the candle, and held it towards the Thing; thus I saw that it had the appearance of a many-flapped thing shaped as it might be, out of raw beef – *but it was alive.*

At this, we stared, everyone being too bemused with terror to do aught to protect ourselves, even had we been possessed of weapons. And as we remained thus, an instant, like silly sheep awaiting the butcher, I heard the framework creak and crack, and there ran splits all across the glass. In another moment, the whole thing would have been torn away, and the cabin undefended, but that the bo'sun, with a great curse at us for our landlubberly lack of use, seized the other cover, and clapped it over the window. At that, there was more help than could be made to avail, and the battens and wedges were in place in a trice. That this was no sooner accomplished than need be, we had immediate proof; for there came a rending of wood and a splintering of glass, and after that a strange yowling out in the dark, and the yowling rose above and drowned the continuous growling that filled the night. In a little, it died away, and in the brief silence that seemed to ensue, we heard a slobby fumbling at the teak cover; but it was well secured, and we had no immediate cause for fear.

Chapter IV
The Two Faces

OF THE REMAINDER of that night, I have but a confused memory. At times we heard the door shaken behind the great chests; but no harm came to it. And, odd whiles, there was a soft thudding and rubbing upon the decks over our heads, and once, as I recollect, the Thing made a final try at the teak covers across the windows; but the day came at last, and found me sleeping. Indeed, we had slept beyond the noon, but that the bo'sun, mindful of our needs, waked us, and we removed the chests. Yet, for perhaps the space of a minute, none durst open the door, until the bo'sun bid us stand to one side. We faced about at him then, and saw that he held a great cutlass in his right hand.

He called to us that there were four more of the weapons, and made a backward motion with his left hand towards an open locker. At that, as might be supposed, we made some haste to the place to which he pointed, and found that, among some other gear, there were three more weapons such as he held; but the fourth was a straight cut-and-thrust, and this I had the good fortune to secure.

Being now armed, we ran to join the bo'sun; for by this he had the door open, and was scanning the main cabin. I would remark here how a good weapon doth seem to put heart into a man; for I, who but a few, short hours since had feared for my life, was now right full of lustiness and fight; which, mayhap, was no matter for regret.

From the main cabin, the bo'sun led up on to the deck, and I remember some surprise at finding the lid of the scuttle even as we had left it the previous night; but then I recollected that the skylight was broken, and there was access to the big cabin that way. Yet, I questioned within myself as to what manner of thing it could be which ignored the convenience of the scuttle, and descended by way of the broken skylight.

We made a search of the decks and fo'cas'le, but found nothing, and, after that, the bo'sun stationed two of us on guard, whilst the rest went about such duties as were needful. In a little, we came to breakfast, and, after that, we prepared to test the story upon the sample wrappers and see perchance whether there was indeed a spring of fresh water among the trees.

Now between the vessel and the trees, lay a slope of the thick mud, against which the vessel rested. To have scrambled up this bank had been next to impossible, by reason of its fat richness; for, indeed, it looked fit to crawl; but that Josh called out to the bo'sun that he had come upon a ladder, lashed across the fo'cas'le head. This was brought, also several hatch covers. The latter were placed first upon the mud, and the ladder laid upon them; by which means we were enabled to pass up to the top of the bank without contact with the mud.

Here, we entered at once among the trees; for they grew right up to the edge; but we had no trouble in making a way; for they were nowhere close together; but standing, rather, each one in a little open space by itself.

We had gone a little way among the trees, when, suddenly, one who was with us cried out that he could see something away on our right, and we clutched everyone his weapon the more determinedly, and went towards it. Yet it proved to be but a seaman's chest, and a space further off, we discovered another. And so, after a little walking, we found the camp;

but there was small semblance of a camp about it; for the sail of which the tent had been formed, was all torn and stained, and lay muddy upon the ground. Yet the spring was all we had wished, clear and sweet, and so we knew we might dream of deliverance.

Now, upon our discovery of the spring, it might be thought that we should set up a shout to those upon the vessel; but this was not so; for there was something in the air of the place which cast a gloom upon our spirits, and we had no disinclination to return unto the vessel.

Upon coming to the brig, the bo'sun called to four of the men to go down into the boats, and pass up the breakers: also, he collected all the buckets belonging to the brig, and forthwith each of us was set to our work. Some, those with the weapons, entered into the wood, and gave down the water to those stationed upon the bank, and these, in turn, passed it to those in the vessel. To the man in the galley, the bo'sun gave command to fill a boiler with some of the most select pieces of the pork and beef from the casks and get them cooked so soon as might be, and so we were kept at it; for it had been determined – now that we had come upon water – that we should stay not an hour longer in that monster-ridden craft, and we were all agog to get the boats revictualled, and put back to the sea, from which we had too gladly escaped.

So we worked through all that remainder of the morning, and right on into the afternoon; for we were in mortal fear of the coming dark. Towards four o'clock, the bo'sun sent the man, who had been set to do our cooking, up to us with slices of salt meat upon biscuits, and we ate as we worked, washing our throats with water from the spring, and so, before the evening, we had filled our breakers, and near every vessel which was convenient for us to take in the boats. More, some of us snatched the chance to wash our bodies; for we were sore with brine, having dipped in the sea to keep down thirst as much as might be.

Now, though it had not taken us so great a while to make a finish of our water-carrying if matters had been more convenient; yet because of the softness of the ground under our feet, and the care with which we had to pick our steps, and some little distance between us and the brig, it had grown later than we desired, before we had made an end. Therefore, when the bo'sun sent word that we should come aboard, and bring our gear, we made all haste. Thus, as it chanced, I found that I had left my sword beside the spring, having placed it there to have two hands for the carrying of one of the breakers. At my remarking my loss, George, who stood near, cried out that he would run for it, and was gone in a moment, being greatly curious to see the spring.

Now, at this moment, the bo'sun came up, and called for George; but I informed him that he had run to the spring to bring me my sword. At this, the bo'sun stamped his foot, and swore a great oath, declaring that he had kept the lad by him all the day; having a wish to keep him from any danger which the wood might hold, and knowing the lad's desire to adventure there. At this, a matter which I should have known, I reproached myself for so gross a piece of stupidity, and hastened after the bo'sun, who had disappeared over the top of the bank. I saw his back as he passed into the wood, and ran until I was up with him; for, suddenly, as it were, I found that a sense of chilly dampness had come among the trees; though a while before the place had been full of the warmth of the sun. This, I put to the account of evening, which was drawing on apace; and also, it must be borne in mind, that there were but the two of us.

We came to the spring; but George was not to be seen, and I saw no sign of my sword. At this, the bo'sun raised his voice, and cried out the lad's name. Once he called, and again; then at the second shout we heard the boy's shrill halloo, from some distance ahead among the trees. At that, we ran towards the sound, plunging heavily across the ground, which was everywhere covered with a thick scum, that clogged the feet in walking. As we ran, we hallooed, and so came upon the boy, and I saw that he had my sword.

The bo'sun ran towards him, and caught him by the arm, speaking with anger, and commanding him to return with us immediately to the vessel.

But the lad, for reply, pointed with my sword, and we saw that he pointed at what appeared to be a bird against the trunk of one of the trees. This, as I moved closer, I perceived to be a part of the tree, and no bird; but it had a very wondrous likeness to a bird; so much so that I went up to it, to see if my eyes had deceived me. Yet it seemed no more than a freak of nature, though most wondrous in its fidelity; being but an excrescence upon the trunk. With a sudden thought that it would make me a curio, I reached up to see whether I could break it away from the tree; but it was above my reach, so that I had to leave it. Yet, one thing I discovered; for, in stretching towards the protuberance, I had placed a hand upon the tree, and its trunk was soft as pulp under my fingers, much after the fashion of a mushroom.

As we turned to go, the bo'sun inquired of George his reason for going beyond the spring, and George told him that he had seemed to hear someone calling to him among the trees, and there had been so much pain in the voice that he had run towards it; but been unable to discover the owner. Immediately afterwards he had seen the curious, bird-like excrescence upon a tree nearby. Then we had called, and of the rest we had knowledge.

We had come nigh to the spring on our return journey, when a sudden low whine seemed to run among the trees. I glanced towards the sky, and realised that the evening was upon us. I was about to remark upon this to the bo'sun, when, abruptly, he came to a stand, and bent forward to stare into the shadows to our right. At that, George and I turned ourselves about to perceive what matter it was which had attracted the attention of the bo'sun; thus we made out a tree some twenty yards away, which had all its branches wrapped about its trunk, much as the lash of a whip is wound about its stock. Now this seemed to us a very strange sight, and we made all of us towards it, to learn the reason of so extraordinary a happening.

Yet, when we had come close upon it, we had no means of arriving at a knowledge of that which it portended; but walked each of us around the tree, and were more astonished, after our circumnavigation of the great vegetable than before.

Now, suddenly, and in the distance, I caught the far wailing that came before the night, and abruptly, as it seemed to me, the tree wailed at us. At that I was vastly astonished and frightened; yet, though I retreated, I could not withdraw my gaze from the tree; but scanned it the more intently; and, suddenly, I saw a brown, human face peering at us from between the wrapped branches. At this, I stood very still, being seized with that fear which renders one shortly incapable of movement. Then, before I had possession of myself, I saw that it was of a part with the trunk of the tree; for I could not tell where it ended and the tree began.

Then I caught the bo'sun by the arm, and pointed; for whether it was a part of the tree or not, it was a work of the devil; but the bo'sun, on seeing it, ran straightway so close to the tree that he might have touched it with his hand, and I found myself beside him. Now, George, who was on the bo'sun's other side, whispered that there was another face, not unlike to a woman's, and, indeed, so soon as I perceived it, I saw that the tree had a second excrescence, most strangely after the face of a woman. Then the bo'sun cried out with an oath, at the strangeness of the thing, and I felt the arm, which I held, shake somewhat, as it might be with a deep emotion. Then, far away, I heard again the sound of the wailing and, immediately, from among the trees about us, there came answering wails and a great sighing. And before I had time to be more than aware of these things, the tree wailed again at us. And at that, the bo'sun cried out suddenly that he knew; though of what it was that he knew I had at that time no knowledge. And, immediately, he began with his cutlass to strike at the tree before us, and to cry upon God to blast it; and lo! at his smiting a very fearsome thing happened, for the tree did bleed like any live creature. Thereafter, a great yowling came from it, and it began to writhe. And, suddenly, I became aware that all about us the trees were a-quiver.

Then George cried out, and ran round upon my side of the bo'sun, and I saw that one of the great cabbage-like things pursued him upon its stem, even as an evil serpent; and very dreadful it was, for it had become blood red in colour; but I smote it with the sword, which I had taken from the lad, and it fell to the ground.

Now from the brig I heard them hallooing, and the trees had become like live things, and there was a vast growling in the air, and hideous trumpetings. Then I caught the bo'sun again by the arm, and shouted to him that we must run for our lives; and this we did, smiting with our swords as we ran; for there came things at us, out from the growing dusk.

Thus we made the brig, and, the boats being ready, I scrambled after the bo'sun into his, and we put straightway into the creek, all of us, pulling with so much haste as our loads would allow. As we went I looked back at the brig, and it seemed to me that a multitude of things hung over the bank above her, and there seemed a flicker of things moving hither and thither aboard of her. And then we were in the great creek up which we had come, and so, in a little, it was night.

All that night we rowed, keeping very strictly to the centre of the big creek, and all about us bellowed the vast growling, being more fearsome than ever I had heard it, until it seemed to me that we had waked all that land of terror to a knowledge of our presence. But, when the morning came, so good a speed had we made, what with our fear, and the current being with us, that we were nigh upon the open sea; whereat each one of us raised a shout, feeling like freed prisoners.

And so, full of thankfulness to the Almighty, we rowed outward to the sea.

Chapter V
The Great Storm

NOW, AS I HAVE SAID, we came at last in safety to the open sea, and so for a time had some degree of peace; though it was long ere we threw off all of the terror which the Land of Lonesomeness had cast over our hearts.

And one more matter there is regarding that land, which my memory recalls. It will be remembered that George found certain wrappers upon which there was writing. Now, in the haste of our leaving, he had given no thought to take them with him; yet a portion of one he found within the side pocket of his jacket, and it ran somewhat thus:

"But I hear my lover's voice wailing in the night, and I go to find him; for my loneliness is not to be borne. May God have mercy upon me!"

And that was all.

For a day and a night we stood out from the land towards the North, having a steady breeze to which we set our lug sails, and so made very good way, the sea being quiet, though with a slow, lumbering swell from the Southward.

It was on the morning of the second day of our escape that we met with the beginnings of our adventure into the Silent Sea, the which I am about to make as clear as I am able.

The night had been quiet, and the breeze steady until near on to the dawn, when the wind slacked away to nothing, and we lay there waiting, perchance the sun should bring the breeze with it. And this it did; but no such wind as we did desire; for when the morning came upon us, we discovered all that part of the sky to be full of a fiery redness, which presently spread away down to the South, so that an entire quarter of the heavens was, as it seemed to us, a mighty arc of blood-coloured fire.

Now, at the sight of these omens, the bo'sun gave orders to prepare the boats for the storm which we had reason to expect, looking for it in the South, for it was from that direction that the swell came rolling upon us. With this intent, we roused out so much heavy canvas as the boats contained, for we had gotten a bolt and a half from the hulk in the creek; also the boat covers which we could lash down to the brass studs under the gunnels of the boats. Then, in each boat, we mounted the whaleback – which had been stowed along the tops of the thwarts – also its supports, lashing the same to the thwarts below the knees. Then we laid two lengths of the stout canvas the full length of the boat over the whaleback, overlapping and nailing them to the same, so that they sloped away down over the gunnels upon each side as though they had formed a roof to us. Here, whilst some stretched the canvas, nailing its lower edges to the gunnels, others were employed in lashing together the oars and the mast, and to this bundle they secured a considerable length of new three-and-a-half-inch hemp rope, which we had brought away from the hulk along with the canvas. This rope was then passed over the bows and in through the painter ring, and thence to the forrard thwarts, where it was made fast, and we gave attention to parcel it with odd strips of canvas against danger of chafe. And the same was done in both of the boats, for we could not put our trust in the painters, besides which they had not sufficient length to secure safe and easy riding.

Now by this time we had the canvas nailed down to the gunnels around our boat, after which we spread the boat-cover over it, lacing it down to the brass studs beneath the gunnel. And so we had all the boat covered in, save a place in the stern where a man might stand to wield the steering oar, for the boats were double bowed. And in each boat we made the same preparation, lashing all movable articles, and preparing to meet so great a storm as might well fill the heart with terror; for the sky cried out to us that it would be no light wind, and further, the great swell from the South grew more huge with every hour that passed; though as yet it was without virulence, being slow and oily and black against the redness of the sky.

Presently we were ready, and had cast over the bundle of oars and the mast, which was to serve as our sea anchor, and so we lay waiting. It was at this time that the bo'sun called over to Josh certain advice with regard to that which lay before us. And after that the two of them sculled the boats a little apart; for there might be a danger of their being dashed together by the first violence of the storm.

And so came a time of waiting, with Josh and the bo'sun each of them at the steering oars, and the rest of us stowed away under the coverings. From where I crouched near the bo'sun, I had sight of Josh away upon our port side: he was standing up black as a shape of night against the mighty redness, when the boat came to the foamless crowns of the swells, and then gone from sight in the hollows between.

Now midday had come and gone, and we had made shift to eat so good a meal as our appetites would allow; for we had no knowledge how long it might be ere we should have chance of another, if, indeed, we had ever need to think more of such. And then, in the middle part of the afternoon, we heard the first cryings of the storm – a far-distant moaning, rising and falling most solemnly.

Presently, all the Southern part of the horizon so high up, maybe, as some seven to ten degrees, was blotted out by a great black wall of cloud, over which the red glare came down upon the great swells as though from the light of some vast and unseen fire. It was about this time, I observed that the sun had the appearance of a great full moon, being pale and clearly defined, and seeming to have no warmth nor brilliancy; and this, as may be imagined, seemed most strange to us, the more so because of the redness in the South and East.

And all this while the swells increased most prodigiously; though without making broken water: yet they informed us that we had done well to take so much precaution; for surely they were raised by a very great storm. A little before evening, the moaning came again, and then a space of silence; after which there rose a very sudden bellowing, as of wild beasts, and then once more the silence.

About this time, the bo'sun making no objection, I raised my head above the cover until I was in a standing position; for, until now, I had taken no more than occasional peeps; and I was very glad of the chance to stretch my limbs; for I had grown mightily cramped. Having stirred the sluggishness of my blood, I sat me down again; but in such position that I could see every part of the horizon without difficulty. Ahead of us, that is to the South, I saw now that the great wall of cloud had risen some further degrees, and there was something less of the redness; though, indeed, what there was left of it was sufficiently terrifying; for it appeared to crest the black cloud like red foam, seeming, it might be, as though a mighty sea made ready to break over the world.

Towards the West, the sun was sinking behind a curious red-tinted haze, which gave it the appearance of a dull red disc. To the North, seeming very high in the sky, were some flecks of cloud lying motionless, and of a very pretty rose colour. And here I may remark that all the sea to the North of us appeared as a very ocean of dull red fire; though, as might be expected, the swells, coming up from the South, against the light were so many exceeding great hills of blackness.

It was just after I had made these observations that we heard again the distant roaring of the storm, and I know not how to convey the exceeding terror of that sound. It was as though some mighty beast growled far down towards the South; and it seemed to make very clear to me that we were but two small craft in a very lonesome place. Then, even while the roaring lasted, I saw a sudden light flare up, as it were from the edge of the Southern horizon. It had somewhat the appearance of lightning; yet vanished not immediately, as is the wont of lightning; and more, it had not been my experience to witness such spring up from out of the sea, but, rather, down from the heavens. Yet I have little doubt but that it was a form of lightning; for it came many times after this, so that I had chance to observe it minutely. And frequently, as I watched, the storm would shout at us in a most fearsome manner.

Then, when the sun was low upon the horizon, there came to our ears a very shrill, screaming noise, most penetrating and distressing, and, immediately afterwards the bo'sun shouted out something in a hoarse voice, and commenced to sway furiously upon the steering oar. I saw his stare fixed upon a point a little on our larboard bow, and perceived that in that direction the sea was all blown up into vast clouds of dust-like froth, and I knew that the storm was upon us. Immediately afterwards a cold blast struck us; but we suffered no harm, for the bo'sun had gotten the boat bows-on by this. The wind passed us, and there was an instant of calm. And now all the air above us was full of a continuous roaring, so very loud and intense that I was like to be deafened. To windward, I perceived an enormous wall of spray bearing down upon us, and I heard again the shrill screaming, pierce through the roaring. Then, the bo'sun whipped in his oar under the cover, and, reaching forward, drew the canvas aft, so that it covered the entire boat, and he held it down against the gunnel upon the starboard side, shouting in my ear to do likewise upon the larboard. Now had it not been for this forethought on the part of the bo'sun we had been all dead men; and this may be the better believed when I explain that we felt the water falling upon the stout canvas overhead, tonnes and tonnes, though so beaten to froth as to lack solidity to sink or crush us. I have said 'felt'; for I would make it so clear as may be, here once and for all, that so intense was the roaring and screaming of the elements, there could no sound have penetrated to us, no! not the pealing of mighty thunders. And so for the space of maybe a full minute the boat quivered and shook most vilely, so that she seemed like to have been shaken in pieces, and from a dozen places between the gunnel and the covering canvas, the water spurted in upon us. And here one other thing I would make mention of: During that minute, the boat had ceased to rise and fall upon the great swell, and whether this was because the sea was flattened by the first rush of the wind, or that the excess of the storm held her steady, I am unable to tell; and can put down only that which we felt.

Now, in a little, the first fury of the blast being spent, the boat began to sway from side to side, as though the wind blew now upon the one beam, and now upon the other; and several times we were stricken heavily with the blows of solid water. But presently this ceased, and we returned once again to the rise and fall of the swell, only that now we received a cruel jerk every time that the boat came upon the top of a sea. And so a while passed.

Towards midnight, as I should judge, there came some mighty flames of lightning, so bright that they lit up the boat through the double covering of canvas; yet no man of us heard aught of the thunder; for the roaring of the storm made all else a silence.

And so to the dawn, after which, finding that we were still, by the mercy of God, possessed of our lives, we made shift to eat and drink; after which we slept.

Now, being extremely wearied by the stress of the past night, I slumbered through many hours of the storm, waking at some time between noon and evening. Overhead, as I lay looking upwards, the canvas showed of a dull leadenish colour, blackened completely at whiles by the dash of spray and water. And so, presently, having eaten again, and feeling that all things lay in the hands of the Almighty, I came once more upon sleep.

Twice through the following night was I wakened by the boat being hurled upon her beam-ends by the blows of the seas; but she righted easily, and took scarce any water, the canvas proving a very roof of safety. And so the morning came again.

Being now rested, I crawled after to where the bo'sun lay, and, the noise of the storm lulling odd instants, shouted in his ear to know whether the wind was easing at whiles. To this he nodded, whereat I felt a most joyful sense of hope pulse through me, and ate such food as could be gotten, with a very good relish.

In the afternoon, the sun broke out suddenly, lighting up the boat most gloomily through the wet canvas; yet a very welcome light it was, and bred in us a hope that the storm was near to breaking. In a little, the sun disappeared; but, presently, it coming again, the bo'sun beckoned to me to assist him, and we removed such temporary nails as we had used to fasten down the after part of the canvas, and pushed back the covering a space sufficient to allow our heads to go through into the daylight. On looking out, I discovered the air to be full of spray, beaten as fine as dust, and then, before I could note aught else, a little gout of water took me in the face with such force as to deprive me of breath; so that I had to descend beneath the canvas for a little while.

So soon as I was recovered, I thrust forth my head again, and now I had some sight of the terrors around us. As each huge sea came towards us, the boat shot up to meet it, right up to its very crest, and there, for the space of some instants, we would seem to be swamped in a very ocean of foam, boiling up on each side of the boat to the height of many feet. Then, the sea passing from under us, we would go swooping dizzily down the great, black, froth-splotched back of the wave, until the oncoming sea caught us up most mightily. Odd whiles, the crest of a sea would hurl forward before we had reached the top, and though the boat shot upward like a veritable feather, yet the water would swirl right over us, and we would have to draw in our heads most suddenly; in such cases the wind flapping the cover down so soon as our hands were removed. And, apart from the way in which the boat met the seas, there was a very sense of terror in the air; the continuous roaring and howling of the storm; the *screaming* of the foam, as the frothy summits of the briny mountains hurled past us, and the wind that tore the breath out of our weak human throats, are things scarce to be conceived.

Presently, we drew in our heads, the sun having vanished again, and nailed down the canvas once more, and so prepared for the night.

From here on until the morning, I have very little knowledge of any happenings; for I slept much of the time, and, for the rest, there was little to know, cooped up beneath the cover. Nothing save the interminable, thundering swoop of the boat downwards, and then the halt and upward hurl, and the occasional plunges and surges to larboard or starboard, occasioned, I can only suppose, by the indiscriminate might of the seas.

I would make mention here, how that I had little thought all this while for the peril of the other boat, and, indeed, I was so very full of our own that it is no matter at which to wonder. However, as it proved, and as this is a most suitable place in which to tell it, the boat that held Josh and the rest of the crew came through the storm with safety; though it was not until many years afterwards that I had the good fortune to hear from Josh himself how that, after the storm, they were picked up by a homeward-bound vessel, and landed in the Port of London.

And now, to our own happenings.

Chapter VI
The Weed-Choked Sea

IT WAS SOME LITTLE WHILE before midday that we grew conscious that the sea had become very much less violent; and this despite the wind roaring with scarce abated noise. And, presently, everything about the boat, saving the wind, having grown indubitably calmer, and no great water breaking over the canvas, the bo'sun beckoned me again to assist him lift the after part of the cover. This we did, and put forth our heads to inquire the reason of the unexpected quietness of the sea; not knowing but that we had come suddenly under the lee of some unknown land. Yet, for a space, we could see nothing, beyond the surrounding billows; for the sea was still very furious, though no matter to cause us concern, after that through which we had come.

Presently, however, the bo'sun, raising himself, saw something, and, bending cried in my ear that there was a low bank which broke the force of the sea; but he was full of wonder to know how that we had passed it without shipwreck. And whilst he was still pondering the matter I raised myself, and took a look on all sides of us, and so I discovered that there lay another great bank upon our larboard side, and this I pointed out to him. Immediately afterwards, we came upon a great mass of seaweed swung up on the crest of a sea, and, presently, another. And so we drifted on, and the seas grew less with astonishing rapidity, so that, in a little, we stripped off the cover so far as the midship thwart; for the rest of the men were sorely in need of the fresh air, after so long a time below the canvas covering.

It was after we had eaten, that one of them made out that there was another low bank astern upon which we were drifting. At that, the bo'sun stood up and made an examination of it, being much exercised in his mind to know how we might come clear of it with safety. Presently, however, we had come so near to it that we discovered it to be composed of seaweed, and so we let the boat drive upon it, making no doubt but that the other banks, which we had seen, were of a similar nature.

In a little, we had driven in among the weed; yet, though our speed was greatly slowed, we made some progress, and so in time came out upon the other side, and now we found the sea to be near quiet, so that we hauled in our sea anchor – which had collected a great mass of weed about it – and removed the whaleback and canvas coverings, after which we stepped the mast, and set a tiny storm-foresail upon the boat; for we wished to have her under control, and could set no more than this, because of the violence of the breeze.

Thus we drove on before the wind, the bo'sun steering, and avoiding all such banks as showed ahead, and ever the sea grew calmer. Then, when it was near on to evening, we discovered a huge stretch of the weed that seemed to block all the sea ahead, and, at that, we hauled down the foresail, and took to our oars, and began to pull, broadside on to it, towards the West. Yet so strong was the breeze, that we were being driven down rapidly upon it. And then, just before sunset, we opened out the end of it, and drew in our oars, very thankful to set the little foresail, and run off again before the wind.

And so, presently, the night came down upon us, and the bo'sun made us take turn and turn about to keep a look-out; for the boat was going some knots through the water, and we were among strange seas; but *he* took no sleep all that night, keeping always to the steering oar.

I have memory, during my time of watching, of passing odd floating masses, which I make no doubt were weed, and once we drove right atop of one; but drew clear without much trouble. And all the while, through the dark to starboard, I could make out the dim outline of that enormous weed extent lying low upon the sea, and seeming without end. And so, presently, my time to watch being at an end, I returned to my slumber, and when next I waked it was morning.

Now the morning discovered to me that there was no end to the weed upon our starboard side; for it stretched away into the distance ahead of us so far as we could see; while all about us the sea was full of floating masses of the stuff. And then, suddenly, one of the men cried out that there was a vessel in among the weed. At that, as may be imagined, we were very greatly excited, and stood upon the thwarts that we might get better view of her. Thus I saw her a great way in from the edge of the weed, and I noted that her foremast was gone near to the deck, and she had no main topmast; though, strangely enough, her mizzen stood unharmed. And beyond this, I could make out but little, because of the distance; though the sun, which was upon our larboard side, gave me some sight of her hull, but not much, because of the weed in which she was deeply embedded; yet it seemed to me that her sides were very weather-worn, and in one place some glistening brown object, which may have been a fungus, caught the rays of the sun, sending off a wet sheen.

There we stood, all of us, upon the thwarts, staring and exchanging opinions, and were like to have overset the boat; but that the bo'sun ordered us down. And after this we made our breakfast, and had much discussion regarding the stranger, as we ate.

Later, towards midday, we were able to set our mizzen; for the storm had greatly modified, and so, presently, we hauled away to the West, to escape a great bank of the weed which ran out from the main body. Upon rounding this, we let the boat off again, and set the main lug, and thus made very good speed before the wind. Yet though we ran all that afternoon parallel with the weed to starboard, we came not to its end. And three separate times we saw the hulks of rotting vessels, some of them having the appearance of a previous age, so ancient did they seem.

Now, towards evening, the wind dropped to a very little breeze, so that we made but slow way, and thus we had better chance to study the weed. And now we saw that it was full of crabs; though for the most part so very minute as to escape the casual glance; yet they were not all small, for in a while I discovered a swaying among the weed, a little way in from the edge, and immediately I saw the mandible of a very great crab stir amid the weed. At that, hoping to obtain it for food, I pointed it out to the bo'sun, suggesting that we should try and capture it. And so, there being by now scarce any wind, he bade us get out a couple of the oars, and back the boat up to the weed. This we did, after which he made fast a piece of salt meat to a bit of spun yarn, and bent this on to the boat hook. Then he made a running bowline, and slipped the loop on to the shaft of the boat hook, after which he held out the boat hook, after the fashion of a fishing rod, over the place where I had seen the crab. Almost immediately, there swept up an enormous claw, and grasped the meat, and at that, the bo'sun cried out to me to take an oar and slide the bowline along the boat-hook, so that it should fall over the claw, and this I did, and immediately some of us hauled upon the line, taughtening it about the great claw. Then the bo'sun sung out to us to haul the crab aboard, that we had it most securely; yet on the instant we had reason to wish that we had been less successful; for the creature, feeling the tug of our pull upon it, tossed the weed in all directions, and thus we had full sight of it, and discovered it to be so great a crab as is scarce conceivable – a very monster. And further, it was apparent to us that the brute had no fear of us, nor intention to escape; but rather made to come at us; whereat the bo'sun, perceiving our danger, cut the line, and bade us put weight upon the oars, and so in a moment we were in safety, and very determined to have no more meddlings with such creatures.

Presently, the night came upon us, and, the wind remaining low, there was everywhere about us a great stillness, most solemn after the continuous roaring of the storm which had beset us in the previous days. Yet now and again a little wind would rise and blow across the sea, and where it met the weed, there would come a low, damp rustling, so that I could hear the passage of it for no little time after the calm had come once more all about us.

Now it is a strange thing that I, who had slept amid the noise of the past days, should find sleeplessness amid so much calm; yet so it was, and presently I took the steering oar, proposing that the rest should sleep, and to this the bo'sun agreed, first warning me, however, most particularly to have care that I kept the boat off the weed (for we had still a little way on us), and, further, to call him should anything unforeseen occur. And after that, almost immediately he fell asleep, as indeed did the most of the men.

From the time that I relieved the bo'sun, until midnight, I sat upon the gunnel of the boat, with the steering oar under my arm, and watched and listened, most full of a sense of the strangeness of the seas into which we had come. It is true that I had heard tell of seas choked up with weed – seas that were full of stagnation, having no tides; but I had not thought to come upon such an one in my wanderings; having, indeed, set down such tales as being bred of imagination, and without reality in fact.

Then, a little before the dawn, and when the sea was yet full of darkness, I was greatly startled to hear a prodigious splash amid the weed, mayhaps at a distance of some hundred yards from the boat. Then, as I stood full of alertness, and knowing not what the next moment might bring forth, there came to me across the immense waste of weed, a long, mournful cry, and then again the silence. Yet, though I kept very quiet, there came no further sound, and I was about to re-seat myself, when, afar off in that strange wilderness, there flashed out a sudden flame of fire.

Now upon seeing fire in the midst of so much lonesomeness, I was as one amazed, and could do naught but stare. Then, my judgement returning to me, I stooped and waked the bo'sun; for it seemed to me that this was a matter for his attention. He, after staring at it awhile, declared that he could see the shape of a vessel's hull beyond the flame; but, immediately, he was in doubt, as, indeed, I had been all the while. And then, even as we peered, the light vanished, and though we waited for the space of some minutes; watching steadfastly, there came no further sight of that strange illumination.

From now until the dawn, the bo'sun remained awake with me, and we talked much upon that which we had seen; yet could come to no satisfactory conclusion; for it seemed impossible to us that a place of so much desolation could contain any living being. And then, just as the dawn was upon us, there loomed up a fresh wonder – the hull of a great vessel maybe a couple or three score fathoms in from the edge of the weed. Now the wind was still very light, being no more than an occasional breath, so that we went past her at a drift, thus the dawn had strengthened sufficiently to give to us a clear sight of the stranger, before we had gone more than a little past her. And now I perceived that she lay full broadside on to us, and that her three masts were gone close down to the deck. Her side was streaked in places with rust, and in others a green scum overspread her; but it was no more than a glance that I gave at any of those matters; for I had spied something which drew all my attention – great leathery arms splayed all across her side, some of them crooked inboard over the rail, and then, low down, seen just above the weed, the huge, brown, glistening bulk of so great a monster as ever I had conceived. The bo'sun saw it in the same instant and cried out in a hoarse whisper that it was a mighty devilfish, and then, even as he spoke, two of the arms flickered up into the cold light of the dawn, as though the creature had been asleep, and we had waked it. At that, the bo'sun seized an oar, and I did likewise, and, so swiftly as we dared, for fear of making any unneedful noise, we pulled the boat to a safer distance. From there and until the vessel had become indistinct by reason of the space we put between us, we watched that great creature clutched to the old hull, as it might be a limpet to a rock.

Presently, when it was broad day, some of the men began to rouse up, and in a little we broke our fast, which was not displeasing to me, who had spent the night watching. And so through the day we sailed with a very light wind upon our larboard quarter. And all the while we kept the great waste of weed upon our starboard side, and apart from the mainland of the weed, as it were, there were scattered about an uncountable number of weed islets and banks, and there were thin patches of it that appeared scarce above the water, and through these later we let the boat sail; for they had not sufficient density to impede our progress more than a little.

And then, when the day was far spent, we came in sight of another wreck amid the weeds. She lay in from the edge perhaps so much as the half of a mile, and she had all three of her lower masts in, and her lower yards squared. But what took our eyes more than aught else was a great superstructure which had been built upward from her rails, almost half-way to her main tops, and this, as we were able to perceive, was supported by ropes let down from the yards; but of what material the superstructure was composed, I have no knowledge; for it was so over-grown with some form of green stuff – as was so much of the hull as showed above the weed – as to defy our guesses. And because of this growth, it was borne upon us that the ship must have been lost to the world a very great age ago. At this suggestion, I grew full of solemn thought; for it seemed to me that we had come upon the cemetery of the oceans.

Now, in a little while after we had passed this ancient craft, the night came down upon us, and we prepared for sleep, and because the boat was making some little way through the water, the bo'sun gave out that each of us should stand our turn at the steering-oar, and that he was to be called should any fresh matter transpire. And so we settled down for the night, and owing to my previous sleeplessness, I was full weary, so that I knew nothing until the one whom I was to relieve shook me into wakefulness. So soon as I was fully waked, I perceived that a low moon hung above the horizon, and shed a very ghostly light across the great weed world to starboard. For the rest, the night was exceeding quiet, so that no sound came to me in all that ocean, save the rippling of the water upon our bends as the boat forged slowly along. And so I settled down to pass the time ere I should be allowed to sleep; but first I asked the man whom I had relieved, how long a time had passed since moon-rise; to which he replied that it was no more than the half of an hour, and after that I questioned whether he had seen aught strange amid the weed during his time at the oar; but he had seen nothing, except that once he had fancied a light had shown in the midst of the waste; yet it could have been naught save a humour of the imagination; though apart from this, he had heard a strange crying a little after midnight, and twice there had been great splashes among the weed. And after that he fell asleep, being impatient at my questioning.

Now it so chanced that my watch had come just before the dawn; for which I was full of thankfulness, being in that frame of mind when the dark breeds strange and unwholesome fancies. Yet, though I was so near to the dawn, I was not to escape free of the eerie influence of that place; for, as I sat, running my gaze to and fro over its grey immensity, it came to me that there were strange movements among the weed, and I seemed to see vaguely, as one may see things in dreams, dim white faces peer out at me here and there; yet my common sense assured me that I was but deceived by the uncertain light and the sleep in my eyes; yet for all that, it put my nerves on the quiver.

A little later, there came to my ears the noise of a very great splash amid the weed; but though I stared with intentness, I could nowhere discern aught as likely to be the cause thereof. And then, suddenly, between me and the moon, there drove up from out of that great waste a vast bulk, flinging huge masses of weed in all directions. It seemed to be no more than a hundred fathoms distant, and, against the moon, I saw the outline of it most clearly – a mighty devilfish. Then it had fallen back once more with a prodigious splash, and so the quiet fell again, finding me sore afraid, and no little bewildered that so monstrous a creature could leap with such agility. And then (in my fright I had let the boat come near to the edge of the weed) there came a subtle stir opposite to our starboard bow, and something slid down into the water. I swayed upon the oar to turn the boat's head outward, and with the same movement leant forward and sideways to peer, bringing my face near to the boat's rail. In the same instant, I found myself looking down into a white demoniac face, human save that the mouth and nose had greatly the appearance of a beak. The thing was gripping at the side of the boat with two flickering hands – gripping the bare, smooth outer surface, in a way that woke in my mind a sudden memory of the great devilfish which had clung to the side of the wreck we had passed in the previous dawn. I saw the face come up towards me, and one misshapen hand fluttered almost to my throat, and there came a sudden, hateful reek in my nostrils – foul and abominable. Then, I came into possession of my faculties, and drew back with great haste and a wild cry of fear. And then I had the steering-oar by the middle, and was smiting downward with the loom over the side of the boat; but the thing was gone from my sight. I remember shouting out to the bo'sun and to the men to awake, and then the bo'sun had me by the shoulder, was calling in my ear to know what dire thing had come about. At that, I cried out that I did not know, and, presently, being somewhat calmer, I told them of the thing that I had seen; but even as I told of it, there seemed to be no truth in it, so that they were all at a loss to know whether I had fallen asleep, or that I had indeed seen a devil.

And presently the dawn was upon us.

Chapter VII
The Island in the Weed

IT WAS AS WE WERE all discussing the matter of the devil face that had peered up at me out of the water, that Job, the ordinary seaman, discovered the island in the light of the growing dawn, and, seeing it, sprang to his feet, with so loud a cry that we were like for the moment to have thought he had seen a second demon. Yet when we made discovery of that which he had already perceived, we checked our blame at his sudden shout; for the sight of land, after so much desolation, made us very warm in our hearts.

Now at first the island seemed but a very small matter; for we did not know at that time that we viewed it from its end; yet despite this, we took to our oars and rowed with all haste towards it, and so, coming nearer, were able to see that it had a greater size than we had imagined. Presently, having cleared the end of it, and keeping to that side which was further from the great mass of the weed-continent, we opened out a bay that curved inward to a sandy beach, most seductive to our tired eyes. Here, for the space of a minute, we paused to survey the prospect, and I saw that the island was of a very strange shape, having a great hump of black rock at either end, and dipping down into a steep valley between them. In this valley there seemed to be a deal of a strange vegetation that had the appearance of mighty toadstools; and down nearer the beach there was a thick grove of a kind of very tall reed, and these we discovered afterwards to be exceeding tough and light, having something of the qualities of the bamboo.

Regarding the beach, it might have been most reasonably supposed that it would be very thick with the driftweed; but this was not so, at least, not at that time; though a projecting horn of the black rock which ran out into the sea from the upper end of the island, was thick with it.

And now, the bo'sun having assured himself that there was no appearance of any danger, we bent to our oars, and presently had the boat aground upon the beach, and here, finding it convenient, we made our breakfast. During this meal, the bo'sun discussed with us the most proper thing to do, and it was decided to push the boat off from the shore, leaving Job in her, whilst the remainder of us made some exploration of the island.

And so, having made an end of eating, we proceeded as we had determined, leaving Job in the boat, ready to scull ashore for us if we were pursued by any savage creature, while the rest of us made our way towards the nearer hump, from which, as it stood some hundred feet above the sea, we hoped to get a very good idea of the remainder of the island. First, however, the bo'sun handed out to us the two cutlasses and the cut-and-thrust (the other two cutlasses being in Josh's boat), and, taking one himself, he passed me the cut-and-thrust, and gave the other cutlass to the biggest of the men. Then he bade the others keep their sheath knives handy, and was proceeding to lead the way, when one of them called out to us to wait a moment, and, with that, ran quickly to the clump of reeds. Here, he took one with both his hands and bent upon it; but it would not break, so that he had to notch it about with his knife, and thus, in a little, he had it clear. After this, he cut off the upper part, which was too thin and lissome for his purpose, and then thrust the handle of his knife into the end of the portion which he had retained, and in this wise he had a most serviceable lance or spear. For the reeds were very strong, and hollow after the fashion of bamboo, and when he had bound some yarn about the end into which he had thrust his knife, so as to prevent it splitting, it was a fit enough weapon for any man.

Now the bo'sun, perceiving the happiness of the fellow's idea, bade the rest make to themselves similar weapons, and whilst they were busy thus, he commended the man very warmly. And so, in a little, being now most comfortably armed, we made inland towards the nearer black hill, in very good spirits. Presently, we were come to the rock which formed the hill, and found that it came up out of the sand with great abruptness, so that we could not climb it on the seaward side. At that, the bo'sun led us round a space towards that side where lay the valley, and here there was under-foot neither sand nor rock; but ground of strange and spongy texture, and then suddenly, rounding a jutting spur of the rock, we came upon the first of the vegetation – an incredible mushroom; nay, I should say toadstool; for it had no healthy look about it, and gave out a heavy, mouldy odour. And now we perceived that the valley was filled with them, all, that is, save a great circular patch where nothing appeared to be growing; though we were not yet at a sufficient height to ascertain the reason of this.

Presently, we came to a place where the rock was split by a great fissure running up to the top, and showing many ledges and convenient shelves upon which we might obtain hold and footing. And so we set-to about climbing, helping one another so far as we had ability, until, in about the space of some ten minutes, we reached the top, and from thence had a very fine view. We perceived now that there was a beach upon that side of the island which was opposed to the weed; though, unlike that upon which we had landed, it was greatly choked with weed which had drifted ashore. After that, I gave notice to see what space of water lay between the island and the edge of the great weed-continent, and guessed it to be no more than maybe some ninety yards, at which I fell to wishing that it had been greater, for I was grown much in awe of the weed and the strange things which I conceived it to contain.

Abruptly, the bo'sun clapped me upon the shoulder, and pointed to some object that lay out in the weed at a distance of not much less than the half of a mile from where we stood. Now, at first, I could not conceive what manner of thing it was at which I stared, until the bo'sun, remarking my bewilderment, informed me that it was a vessel all covered in, no doubt as a protection against the devil-fish and other strange creatures in the weed. And now I began to trace the hull of her amid all that hideous growth; but of her masts, I could discern nothing; and I doubted not but that they had been carried away by some storm ere she was caught by the weed; and then the thought came to me of the end of those who had built up that protection against the horrors which the weed-world held hidden amid its slime.

Presently, I turned my gaze once more upon the island, which was very plain to see from where we stood. I conceived, now that I could see so much of it, that its length would be near to half a mile, though its breadth was something under four hundred yards; thus it was very long in proportion to its width. In the middle part it had less breadth than at the ends, being perhaps three hundred yards at its narrowest, and a hundred yards wider at its broadest.

Upon both sides of the island, as I have made already a mention, there was a beach, though this extended no great distance along the shore, the remainder being composed of the black rock of which the hills were formed. And now, having a closer regard to the beach upon the weed-side of the island, I discovered amid the wrack that had been cast ashore, a portion of the lower mast and topmast of some great ship, with rigging attached; but the yards were all gone. This find, I pointed out to the bo'sun, remarking that it might prove of use for firing; but he smiled at me, telling me that the dried weed would make a very abundant fire, and this without going to the labour of cutting the mast into suitable logs.

And now, he, in turn, called my attention to the place where the huge fungi had come to a stop in their growing, and I saw that in the centre of the valley there was a great circular opening in the earth, like to the mouth of a prodigious pit, and it appeared to be filled to within a few feet of the mouth with water, over which spread a brown and horrid scum. Now, as may be supposed, I stared with some intentness at this; for it had the look of having been made with labour, being very symmetrical, yet I could not conceive but that I was deluded by the distance, and that it would have a rougher appearance when viewed from a nearer standpoint.

From contemplating this, I looked down upon the little bay in which our boat floated. Job was sitting in the stern, sculling gently with the steering oar and watching us. At that, I waved my hand to him in friendly fashion, and he waved back, and then, even as I looked, I saw something in the water under the boat – something dark coloured that was all of a-move. The boat appeared to be floating over it as over a mass of sunk weed, and then I saw that, whatever it was, it was rising to the surface. At this a sudden horror came over me, and I clutched the bo'sun by the arm, and pointed, crying out that there was something under the boat. Now the bo'sun, so soon as he saw the thing, ran forward to the brow of the hill and, placing his hands to his mouth after the fashion of a trumpet, sang out to the boy to bring the boat to the shore and make fast the painter to a large piece of rock. At the bo'sun's hail, the lad called out "I, I," and, standing up, gave a sweep with his oar that brought the boat's head round towards the beach. Fortunately for him he was no more than some thirty yards from the shore at this time, else he had never come to it in this life; for the next moment the moving brown mass beneath the boat shot out a great tentacle and the oar was torn out of Job's hands with such power as to throw him right over on to the starboard gunnel of the boat. The oar itself was drawn down out of sight, and for the minute the boat was left untouched. Now the bo'sun cried out to the boy to take another oar, and get ashore while still he had chance, and at that we all called out various things, one advising one thing, and another recommending some other; yet our advice was vain, for the boy moved not, at which some cried out that he was stunned. I looked now to where the brown thing had been, for the boat had moved a few fathoms from the spot, having got some way upon her before the oar was snatched, and thus I discovered that the monster had disappeared, having, I conceived, sunk again into the depths from which it had risen; yet it might re-appear at any moment, and in that case the boy would be taken before our eyes.

At this juncture, the bo'sun called to us to follow him, and led the way to the great fissure up which we had climbed, and so, in a minute, we were, each of us, scrambling down with what haste we could make towards the valley. And all the while as I dropped from ledge to ledge, I was full of torment to know whether the monster had returned.

The bo'sun was the first man to reach the bottom of the cleft, and he set off immediately round the base of the rock to the beach, the rest of us following him as we made safe our footing in the valley. I was the third man down; but, being light and fleet of foot, I passed the second man and caught up with the bo'sun just as he came upon the sand. Here, I found that the boat was within some five fathoms of the beach, and I could see Job still lying insensible; but of the monster there was no sign.

And so matters were, the boat nearly a dozen yards from the shore, and Job lying insensible in her; with, somewhere near under her keel (for all that we knew) a great monster, and we helpless upon the beach.

Now I could not imagine how to save the lad, and indeed I fear he had been left to destruction – for I had deemed it madness to try to reach the boat by swimming – but for the extraordinary bravery of the bo'sun, who, without hesitating, dashed into the water and swam boldly out to the boat, which, by the grace of God, he reached without mishap, and climbed in over the bows. Immediately, he took the painter and hove it to us, bidding us tail on to it and bring the boat to shore without delay, and by this method of gaining the beach he showed wisdom; for in this wise he escaped attracting the attention of the monster by unneedful stirring of the water, as he would surely have done had he made use of an oar.

Yet, despite his care, we had not finished with the creature; for, just as the boat grounded, I saw the lost steering oar shoot up half its length out of the sea, and immediately there was a mighty splather in the water astern, and the next instant the air seemed full of huge, whirling arms. At that, the bo'sun gave one look behind, and, seeing the thing upon him, snatched the boy into his arms, and sprang over the bows on to the sand. Now, at sight of the devil-fish, we had all made for the back of the beach at a run, none troubling even to retain the painter, and because of this, we were like to have lost the boat; for the great cuttlefish had its arms all splayed about it, seeming to have a mind to drag it down into the deep water from whence it had risen, and it had possibly succeeded, but that the bo'sun brought us all to our senses; for, having laid Job out of harm's way, he was the first to seize the painter, which lay trailed upon the sand, and, at that, we got back our courage and ran to assist him.

Now there happened to be convenient a great spike of rock, the same, indeed, to which the bo'sun had bidden Job tie the boat, and to this we ran the painter, taking a couple of turns about it and two half-hitches, and now, unless the rope carried away, we had no reason to fear the loss of the boat; though there seemed to us to be a danger of the creature's crushing it. Because of this, and because of a feeling of natural anger against the thing, the bo'sun took up from the sand one of the spears which had been cast down when we hauled the boat ashore. With this, he went down so far as seemed safe, and prodded the creature in one of its tentacles – the weapon entering easily, at which I was surprised, for I had understood that these monsters were near to invulnerable in all parts save their eyes. At receiving this stab, the great fish appeared to feel no hurt for it showed no signs of pain, and, at that, the bo'sun was further emboldened to go nearer, so that he might deliver a more deadly wound; yet scarce had he taken two steps before the hideous thing was upon him, and, but for an agility wonderful in so great a man, he had been destroyed. Yet, spite of so narrow an escape from death, he was not the less determined to wound or destroy the creature, and, to this end, he dispatched some of us to the grove of reeds to get half a dozen of the strongest, and when we returned with these, he bade two of the men lash their spears securely to them, and by this means they had now spears of a length of between thirty and forty feet. With these, it was possible to attack the devilfish without coming within reach of its tentacles. And now being ready, he took one of the spears, telling the biggest of the men to take the other. Then he directed him to aim for the right eye of the huge fish whilst he would attack the left.

Now since the creature had so nearly captured the bo'sun, it had ceased to tug at the boat, and lay silent, with its tentacles spread all about it, and its great eyes appearing just over the stern, so that it presented an appearance of watching our movements; though I doubt if it saw us with any clearness; for it must have been dazed with the brightness of the sunshine.

And now the bo'sun gave the signal to attack, at which he and the man ran down upon the creature with their lances, as it were in rest. The bo'sun's spear took the monster truly in its left eye; but the one wielded by the man was too bendable, and sagged so much that it struck the stern-post of the boat, the knife blade snapping off short. Yet it mattered not; for the wound inflicted by the bo'sun's weapon was so frightful, that the giant cuttlefish released the boat, and slid back into deep water, churning it into foam, and gouting blood.

For some minutes we waited to make sure that the monster had indeed gone, and after that, we hastened to the boat, and drew her up so far as we were able; after which we unloaded the heaviest of her contents, and so were able to get her right clear of the water.

And for an hour afterwards the sea all about the little beach was stained black, and in places red.

Chapter VIII
The Noises in the Valley

NOW, SO SOON as we had gotten the boat into safety, the which we did with a most feverish haste, the bo'sun gave his attention to Job; for the boy had not yet recovered from the blow which the loom of the oar had dealt him beneath the chin when the monster snatched at it. For awhile, his attentions produced no effect; but presently, having bathed the lad's face with water from the sea, and rubbed rum into his chest over the heart, the youth began to show signs of life, and soon opened his eyes, whereupon the bo'sun gave him a stiff jorum of the rum, after which he asked him how he seemed in himself. To this Job replied in a weak voice that he was dizzy and his head and neck ached badly, on hearing which, the bo'sun bade him keep lying until he had come more to himself. And so we left him in quietness under a little shade of canvas and reeds; for the air was warm and the sand dry, and he was not like to come to any harm there.

At a little distance, under the directing of the bo'sun, we made to prepare dinner, for we were now very hungry, it seeming a great while since we had broken our fast. To this end, the bo'sun sent two of the men across the island to gather some of the dry seaweed; for we intended to cook some of the salt meat, this being the first cooked meal since ending the meat which we had boiled before leaving the ship in the creek.

In the meanwhile, and until the return of the men with the fuel, the bo'sun kept us busied in various ways. Two he sent to cut a bundle of the reeds, and another couple to bring the meat and the iron boiler, the latter being one that we had taken from the old brig.

Presently, the men returned with the dried seaweed, and very curious stuff it seemed, some of it being in chunks near as thick as a man's body; but exceeding brittle by reason of its dryness. And so in a little, we had a very good fire going, which we fed with the seaweed and pieces of the reeds, though we found the latter to be but indifferent fuel, having too much sap, and being troublesome to break into convenient size.

Now when the fire had grown red and hot, the bo'sun half filled the boiler with sea water, in which he placed the meat; and the pan, having a stout lid, he did not scruple to place it in the very heart of the fire, so that soon we had the contents boiling merrily.

Having gotten the dinner under way, the bo'sun set about preparing our camp for the night, which we did by making a rough framework with the reeds, over which we spread the boat's sails and the cover, pegging the canvas down with tough splinters of the reed. When this was completed, we set-to and carried there all our stores, after which the bo'sun took us over to the other side of the island to gather fuel for the night, which we did, each man bearing a great double armful.

Now by the time that we had brought over, each of us, two loads of the fuel, we found the meat to be cooked, and so, without more to-do, set ourselves down and made a very good meal off it and some biscuits, after which we had each of us a sound tot of the rum. Having made an end of eating and drinking, the bo'sun went over to where Job lay, to inquire how he felt, and found him lying very quiet, though his breathing had a heavy touch about it. However, we could conceive of nothing by which he might be bettered, and so left him, being more hopeful that Nature would bring him to health than any skill of which we were possessed.

By this time it was late afternoon, so that the bo'sun declared we might please ourselves until sunset, deeming that we had earned a very good right to rest; but that from sunset till the dawn we should, he told us, have each of us to take turn and turn about to watch; for though we were no longer upon the water, none might say whether we were out of danger or not, as witness the happening of the morning; though, certainly, he apprehended no danger from the devil-fish so long as we kept well away from the water's edge.

And so from now until dark most of the men slept; but the bo'sun spent much of that time in overhauling the boat, to see how it might chance to have suffered during the storm, and also whether the struggles of the devil-fish had strained it in any way. And, indeed, it was speedily evident that the boat would need some attention; for the plank in her bottom next but one to the keel, upon the starboard side, had been burst inwards; this having been done, it would seem, by some rock in the beach hidden just beneath the water's edge, the devil-fish having, no doubt, ground the boat down upon it. Happily, the damage was not great; though it would most certainly have to be carefully repaired before the boat would be again seaworthy. For the rest, there seemed to be no other part needing attention.

Now I had not felt any call to sleep, and so had followed the bo'sun to the boat, giving him a hand to remove the bottom-boards, and finally to slue her bottom a little upwards, so that he might examine the leak more closely. When he had made an end with the boat, he went over to the stores, and looked closely into their condition, and also to see how they were lasting. And, after that, he sounded all the water-breakers; having done which, he remarked that it would be well for us if we could discover any fresh water upon the island.

By this time it was getting on towards evening, and the bo'sun went across to look at Job, finding him much as he had been when we visited him after dinner. At that, the bo'sun asked me to bring across one of the longer of the bottom-boards, which I did, and we made use of it as a stretcher to carry the lad into the tent. And afterwards, we carried all the loose woodwork of the boat into the tent, emptying the lockers of their contents, which included some oakum, a small boat's hatchet, a coil of one-and-a-half-inch hemp line, a good saw, an empty colza-oil tin, a bag of copper nails, some bolts and washers, two fishing-lines, three spare tholes, a three-pronged grain without the shaft, two balls of spun yarn, three hanks of roping-twine, a piece of canvas with four roping-needles stuck in it, the boat's lamp, a spare plug, and a roll of light duck for making boat's sails.

And so, presently, the dark came down upon the island, at which the bo'sun waked the men, and bade them throw more fuel on to the fire, which had burned down to a mound of glowing embers much shrouded in ash. After that, one of them part filled the boiler with fresh water, and soon we were occupied most pleasantly upon a supper of cold, boiled salt-meat, hard biscuits, and rum mixed with hot water. During supper, the bo'sun made clear to the men regarding the watches, arranging how they should follow, so that I found I was set down to take my turn from midnight until one of the clock. Then, he explained to them about the burst plank in the bottom of the boat, and how that it would have to be put right before we could hope to leave the island, and that after that night we should have to go most strictly with the victuals; for there seemed to be nothing upon the island, that we had up till then discovered, fit to satisfy our bellies. More than this, if we could find no fresh water, he should have to distil some to make up for that which we had drunk, and this must be done before leaving the island.

Now by the time that the bo'sun had made an end of explaining these matters, we had ceased from eating, and soon after this we made each one of us a comfortable place in the sand within the tent, and lay down to sleep. For a while, I found myself very wakeful, which may have been because of the warmth of the night, and, indeed, at last I got up and went out of the tent, conceiving that I might the better find sleep in the open air. And so it proved; for, having lain down at the side of the tent, a little way from the fire, I fell soon into a deep slumber, which at first was dreamless. Presently, however, I came upon a very strange and unsettling dream; for I dreamed that I had been left alone on the island, and was sitting very desolate upon the edge of the brown-scummed pit. Then I was aware suddenly that it was very dark and very silent, and I began to shiver; for it seemed to me that something which repulsed my whole being had come quietly behind me. At that I tried mightily to turn and look into the shadows among the great fungi that stood all about me; but I had no power to turn. And the thing was coming nearer, though never a sound came to me, and I gave out a scream, or tried to; but my voice made no stir in the rounding quiet; and then something wet and cold touched my face, and slithered down and covered my mouth, and paused there for a vile, breathless moment. It passed onward and fell to my throat – and stayed there...

Someone stumbled and felt over my feet, and at that, I was suddenly awake. It was the man on watch making a walk round the back of the tent, and he had not known of my presence till he fell over my boots. He was somewhat shaken and startled, as might be supposed; but steadied himself on learning that it was no wild creature crouched there in the shadow; and all the time, as I answered his inquiries, I was full of a strange, horrid feeling that something had left me at the moment of my awakening. There was a slight, hateful odour in my nostrils that was not altogether unfamiliar, and then, suddenly, I was aware that my face was damp and that there was a curious sense of tingling at my throat. I put up my hand and felt my face, and the hand when I brought it away was slippery with slime, and at that, I put up my other hand, and touched my throat, and there it was the same, only, in addition, there was a slight swelled place a little to one side of the wind-pipe, the sort of place that the bite of a mosquito will make; but I had no thought to blame any mosquito.

Now the stumbling of the man over me, my awakening, and the discovery that my face and throat were be-slimed, were but the happenings of some few, short instants; and then I was upon my feet, and following him round to the fire; for I had a sense of chilliness and a great desire not to be alone. Now, having come to the fire, I took some of the water that had been left in the boiler, and washed my face and neck, after which I felt more my own man. Then I asked the man to look at my throat, so that he might give me some idea of what manner of place the swelling seemed, and he, lighting a piece of the dry seaweed to act as a torch, made examination of my neck; but could see little, save a number of small ring-like marks, red inwardly, and white at the edges, and one of them was bleeding slightly. After that, I asked him whether he had seen anything moving round the tent; but he had seen nothing during all the time that he had been on watch; though it was true that he had heard odd noises; but nothing very near at hand. Of the places on my throat he seemed to think but little, suggesting that I had been bitten by some sort of sand-fly; but at that, I shook my head, and told him of my dream, and after that, he was as anxious to keep near me as I to him. And so the night passed onward, until my turn came to watch.

For a little while, the man whom I had relieved sat beside me; having, I conceived, the kindly intent of keeping me company; but so soon as I perceived this, I entreated him to go and get his sleep, assuring him that I had no longer any feelings of fear – such as had been mine upon awakening and discovering the state of my face and throat – and, upon this, he consented to leave me, and so, in a little, I sat alone beside the fire.

For a certain space, I kept very quiet, listening; but no sound came to me out of the surrounding darkness, and so, as though it were a fresh thing, it was borne in upon me how that we were in a very abominable place of lonesomeness and desolation. And I grew very solemn.

Thus as I sat, the fire, which had not been replenished for a while, dwindled steadily until it gave but a dullish glow around. And then, in the direction of the valley, I heard suddenly the sound of a dull thud, the noise coming to me through the stillness with a very startling clearness. At that, I perceived that I was not doing my duty to the rest, nor to myself, by sitting and allowing the fire to cease from flaming; and immediately reproaching myself, I seized and cast a mass of the dry weed upon the fire, so that a great blaze shot up into the night, and afterwards I glanced quickly to right and to left, holding my cut-and-thrust very readily, and most thankful to the Almighty that I had brought no harm to any by reason of my carelessness, which I incline me to believe was that strange inertia which is bred by fear. And then, even as I looked about me, there came to me across the silence of the beach a fresh noise, a continual soft slithering to and fro in the bottom of the valley, as though a multitude of creatures moved stealthily. At this, I threw yet more fuel upon the fire, and after that I fixed my gaze in the direction of the valley: thus in the following instant it seemed to me that I saw a certain thing, as it might be a shadow, move on the outer borders of the firelight. Now the man who had kept watch before me had left his spear stuck upright in the sand convenient to my grasp, and, seeing something moving, I seized the weapon and hurled it with all my strength in its direction; but there came no answering cry to tell that I had struck anything living, and immediately afterwards there fell once more a great silence upon the island, being broken only by a far splash out upon the weed.

It may be conceived with truth that the above happenings had put a very considerable strain upon my nerves, so that I looked to and fro continually, with ever and anon a quick glance behind me; for it seemed to me that I might expect some demoniac creature to rush upon me at any moment. Yet, for the space of many minutes, there came to me neither any sight nor sound of living creature; so that I knew not what to think, being near to doubting if I had heard aught beyond the common.

And then, even as I made halt upon the threshold of doubt, I was assured that I had not been mistaken; for, abruptly, I was aware that all the valley was full of a rustling, scampering sort of noise, through which there came to me occasional soft thuds, and anon the former slithering sounds. And at that, thinking a host of evil things to be upon us, I cried out to the bo'sun and the men to awake.

Immediately upon my shout, the bo'sun rushed out from the tent, the men following, and everyone with his weapon, save the man who had left his spear in the sand, and that lay now somewhere beyond the light of the fire. Then the bo'sun shouted, to know what thing had caused me to cry out; but I replied nothing, only held up my hand for quietness, yet when this was granted, the noises in the valley had ceased; so that the bo'sun turned to me, being in need of some explanation; but I begged him to hark a little longer, which he did, and, the sounds re-commencing almost immediately, he heard sufficient to know that I had not waked them all without due cause. And then, as we stood each one of us staring into the darkness where lay the valley, I seemed to see again some shadowy thing upon the boundary of the firelight; and, in the same instant, one of the men cried out and cast his spear into the darkness. But the bo'sun turned upon him with a very great anger; for in throwing his weapon, the man had left himself without, and thus brought danger to the whole; yet, as will be remembered, I had done likewise but a little since.

Presently, there coming again a quietness within the valley, and none knowing what might be toward, the bo'sun caught up a mass of the dry weed, and, lighting it at the fire, ran with it towards that portion of the beach which lay between us and the valley. Here he cast it upon the sand, singing out to some of the men to bring more of the weed, so that we might have a fire there, and thus be able to see if anything made to come at us out of the deepness of the hollow.

Presently, we had a very good fire, and by the light of this the two spears were discovered, both of them stuck in the sand, and no more than a yard one from the other, which seemed to me a very strange thing.

Now, for a while after the lighting of the second fire, there came no further sounds from the direction of the valley; nothing indeed to break the quietness of the island, save the occasional lonely splashes that sounded from time to time out in the vastness of the weed-continent. Then, about an hour after I had waked the bo'sun, one of the men who had been tending the fires came up to him to say that we had come to the end of our supply of weed-fuel. At that, the bo'sun looked very blank, the which did the rest of us, as well we might; yet there was no help for it, until one of the men bethought him of the remainder of the bundle of reeds which we had cut, and which, burning but poorly, we had discarded for the weed. This was discovered at the back of the tent, and with it we fed the fire that burned between us and the valley; but the other we suffered to die out, for the reeds were not sufficient to support even the one until the dawn.

At last, and whilst it was still dark, we came to the end of our fuel, and as the fire died down, so did the noises in the valley recommence. And there we stood in the growing dark, each one keeping a very ready weapon, and a more ready glance. And at times the island would be mightily quiet, and then again the sounds of things crawling in the valley. Yet, I think the silences tried us the more.

And so at last came the dawn.

Chapter IX
What Happened in the Dusk

NOW WITH THE COMING of the dawn, a lasting silence stole across the island and into the valley, and, conceiving that we had nothing more to fear, the bo'sun bade us get some rest, whilst he kept watch. And so I got at last a very substantial little spell of sleep, which made me fit enough for the day's work.

Presently, after some hours had passed, the bo'sun roused us to go with him to the further side of the island to gather fuel, and soon we were back with each a load, so that in a little we had the fire going right merrily.

Now for breakfast, we had a hash of broken biscuit, salt meat and some shell-fish which the bo'sun had picked up from the beach at the foot of the further hill; the whole being right liberally flavoured with some of the vinegar, which the bo'sun said would help keep down any scurvy that might be threatening us. And at the end of the meal he served out to us each a little of the molasses, which we mixed with hot water, and drank.

The meal being ended, he went into the tent to take a look at Job, the which he had done already in the early morning; for the condition of the lad preyed somewhat upon him; he being, for all his size and top-roughness, a man of surprisingly tender heart. Yet the boy remained much as on the previous evening, so that we knew not what to do with him to bring him into better health. One thing we tried, knowing that no food had passed his lips since the previous morning, and that was to get some little quantity of hot water, rum and molasses down his throat; for it seemed to us he might die from very lack of food; but though we worked with him for more than the half of an hour, we could not get him to come-to sufficiently to take anything, and without that we had fear of suffocating him. And so, presently, we had perforce to leave him within the tent, and go about our business; for there was very much to be done.

Yet, before we did aught else, the bo'sun led us all into the valley, being determined to make a very thorough exploration of it, perchance there might be any lurking beast or devil-thing waiting to rush out and destroy us as we worked, and more, he would make search that he might discover what manner of creatures had disturbed our night.

Now in the early morning, when we had gone for the fuel, we had kept to the upper skirt of the valley where the rock of the nearer hill came down into the spongy ground, but now we struck right down into the middle part of the vale, making a way amid the mighty fungi to the pit-like opening that filled the bottom of the valley. Now though the ground was very soft, there was in it so much of springiness that it left no trace of our steps after we had gone on a little way, none, that is, save that in odd places, a wet patch followed upon our treading. Then, when we got ourselves near to the pit, the ground became softer, so that our feet sank into it, and left very real impressions; and here we found tracks most curious and bewildering; for amid the slush that edged the pit – which I would mention here had less the look of a pit now that I had come near to it – were multitudes of markings which I can liken to nothing so much as the tracks of mighty slugs amid the mud, only that they were not altogether like to that of slugs; for there were other markings such as might have been made by bunches of eels cast down and picked up continually, at least, this is what they suggested to me, and I do but put it down as such.

Apart from the markings which I have mentioned, there was everywhere a deal of slime, and this we traced all over the valley among the great toadstool plants; but, beyond that which I have already remarked, we found nothing. Nay, but I was near to forgetting, we found a quantity of this thin slime upon those fungi which filled the end of the little valley nearest to our encampment, and here also we discovered many of them fresh broken or uprooted, and there was the same mark of the beast upon them all, and now I remember the dull thuds that I had heard in the night, and made little doubt but that the creatures had climbed the great toadstools so that they might spy us out; and it may be that many climbed upon one, so that their weight broke the fungi, or uprooted them. At least, so the thought came to me.

And so we made an end of our search, and after that, the bo'sun set each one of us to work. But first he had us all back to the beach to give a hand to turn over the boat, so that he might get to the damaged part. Now, having the bottom of the boat full to his view, he made discovery that there was other damage beside that of the burst plank; for the bottom plank of all had come away from the keel, which seemed to us a very serious matter; though it did not show when the boat was upon her bilges. Yet the bo'sun assured us that he had no doubts but that she could be made seaworthy, though it would take a greater while than hitherto he had thought needful.

Having concluded his examination of the boat, the bo'sun sent one of the men to bring the bottom-boards out of the tent; for he needed some planking for the repair of the damage. Yet when the boards had been brought, he needed still something which they could not supply, and this was a length of very sound wood of some three inches in breadth each way, which he intended to bolt against the starboard side of the keel, after he had gotten the planking replaced so far as was possible. He had hopes that by means of this device he would be able to nail the bottom plank to this, and then caulk it with oakum, so making the boat almost so sound as ever.

Now hearing him express his need for such a piece of timber, we were all adrift to know from whence such a thing could be gotten, until there came suddenly to me a memory of the mast and topmast upon the other side of the island, and at once I made mention of them. At that, the bo'sun nodded, saying that we might get the timber out of it, though it would be a work requiring some considerable labour, in that we had only a hand-saw and a small hatchet. Then he sent us across to be getting it clear of the weed, promising to follow when he had made an end of trying to get the two displaced planks back into position.

Having reached the spars, we set-to with a very good will to shift away the weed and wrack that was piled over them, and very much entangled with the rigging. Presently we had laid them bare, and so we discovered them to be in remarkably sound condition, the lower-mast especially being a fine piece of timber. All the lower and topmast standing rigging was still attached, though in places the lower rigging was stranded so far as half-way up the shrouds; yet there remained much that was good and all of it quite free from rot, and of the very finest quality of white hemp, such as is to be seen only in the best found vessels.

About the time that we had finished clearing the weed, the bo'sun came over to us, bringing with him the saw and the hatchet. Under his directions, we cut the lanyards of the topmast rigging, and after that sawed through the topmast just above the cap. Now this was a very tough piece of work, and employed us a great part of the morning, even though we took turn and turn at the saw, and when it was done we were mightily glad that the bo'sun bade one of the men go over with some weed and make up the fire for dinner, after which he was to put on a piece of the salt meat to boil.

In the meanwhile, the bo'sun had started to cut through the topmast, about fifteen feet beyond the first cut, for that was the length of the batten he required; yet so wearisome was the work, that we had not gotten more than half through with it before the man whom the bo'sun had sent, returned to say that the dinner was ready. When this was dispatched, and we had rested a little over our pipes, the bo'sun rose and led us back; for he was determined to get through with the topmast before dark.

Presently, relieving each other frequently, we completed the second cut, and after that the bo'sun set us to saw a block about twelve inches deep from the remaining portion of the topmast. From this, when we had cut it, he proceeded to hew wedges with the hatchet. Then he notched the end of the fifteen-foot log, and into the notch he drove the wedges, and so, towards evening, as much, maybe, by good luck as good management, he had divided the log into two halves – the split running very fairly down the centre.

Now, perceiving how that it drew near to sundown, he bade the men haste and gather weed and carry it across to our camp; but one he sent along the shore to make a search for shell-fish among the weed; yet he himself ceased not to work at the divided log, and kept me with him as helper. Thus, within the next hour, we had a length, maybe some four inches in diameter, split off the whole length of one of the halves, and with this he was very well content; though it seemed but a very little result for so much labour.

By this time the dusk was upon us, and the men, having made an end of weed carrying, were returned to us, and stood about, waiting for the bo'sun to go into camp. At this moment, the man the bo'sun had sent to gather shellfish, returned, and he had a great crab upon his spear, which he had spitted through the belly. This creature could not have been less than a foot across the back, and had a very formidable appearance; yet it proved to be a most tasty matter for our supper, when it had been placed for a while in boiling water.

Now so soon as this man was returned, we made at once for the camp, carrying with us the piece of timber which we had hewn from the topmast. By this time it was quite dusk, and very strange amid the great fungi as we struck across the upper edge of the valley to the opposite beach. Particularly, I noticed that the hateful, mouldy odour of these monstrous vegetables was more offensive than I had found it to be in the daytime; though this may be because I used my nose the more, in that I could not use my eyes to any great extent.

We had gotten halfway across the top of the valley, and the gloom was deepening steadily, when there stole to me upon the calmness of the evening air, a faint smell; something quite different from that of the surrounding fungi. A moment later I got a great whiff of it, and was near sickened with the abomination of it; but the memory of that foul thing which had come to the side of the boat in the dawn-gloom, before we discovered the island, roused me to a terror beyond that of the sickness of my stomach; for, suddenly, I knew what manner of thing it was that had beslimed my face and throat upon the previous night, and left its hideous stench lingering in my nostrils. And with the knowledge, I cried out to the bo'sun to make haste, for there were demons with us in the valley. And at that, some of the men made to run; but he bade them, in a very grim voice, stay where they were, and keep well together, else would they be attacked and overcome, straggled all among the fungi in the dark. And this, being, I doubt not, as much in fear of the rounding dark as of the bo'sun, they did, and so we came safely out of the valley; though there seemed to follow us a little lower down the slope an uncanny slithering.

Now so soon as we reached the camp, the bo'sun ordered four fires to be lit – one on each side of the tent, and this we did, lighting them at the embers of our old fire, which we had most foolishly allowed to die down. When the fires had been got going, we put on the boiler, and treated the great crab as I have already mentioned, and so fell-to upon a very hearty supper; but, as we ate, each man had his weapon stuck in the sand beside him; for we had knowledge that the valley held some devilish thing, or maybe many; though the knowing did not spoil our appetites.

And so, presently, we came to an end of eating, whereat each man pulled out his pipe, intending to smoke; but the bo'sun told one of the men to get him upon his feet and keep watch, else might we be in danger of surprise, with every man lolling upon the sand; and this seemed to me very good sense; for it was easy to see that the men, too readily, deemed themselves secure, by reason of the brightness of the fires about them.

Now, whilst the men were taking their ease within the circle of the fires, the bo'sun lit one of the dips which we had out of the ship in the creek, and went in to see how Job was, after the day's rest. At that, I rose up, reproaching myself for having forgotten the poor lad, and followed the bo'sun into the tent. Yet, I had but reached the opening, when he gave out a loud cry, and held the candle low down to the sand. At that, I saw the reason for his agitation, for, in the place where we had left Job, there was nothing. I stepped into the tent, and, in the same instant, there came to my nostrils the faint odour of the horrible stench which had come to me in the valley, and before then from the thing that came to the side of the boat. And, suddenly, I knew that Job had fallen prey of those foul things, and, knowing this, I called out to the bo'sun that *they* had taken the boy, and then my eyes caught the smear of slime upon the sand, and I had proof that I was not mistaken.

Now, so soon as the bo'sun knew all that was in my mind; though indeed it did but corroborate that which had come to his own, he came swiftly out from the tent, bidding the men to stand back; for they had come all about the entrance, being very much discomposed at that which the bo'sun had discovered. Then the bo'sun took from a bundle of the reeds, which they had cut at the time when he had bidden them gather fuel, several of the thickest, and to one of these he bound a great mass of the dry weed; whereupon the men, divining his intention, did likewise with the others, and so we had each of us the wherewithal for a mighty torch.

So soon as we had completed our preparations, we took each man his weapon and, plunging our torches into the fires, set off along the track which had been made by the devil-things and the body of poor Job; for now that we had suspicion that harm had come to him, the marks in the sand, and the slime, were very plain to be seen, so that it was a wonder that we had not discovered them earlier.

Now the bo'sun led the way, and, finding the marks led direct to the valley, he broke into a run, holding his torch well above his head. At that, each of us did likewise; for we had a great desire to be together, and further than this, I think with truth I may say, we were all fierce to avenge Job, so that we had less of fear in our hearts than otherwise had been the case.

In less than the half of a minute we had reached the end of the valley; but here, the ground being of a nature not happy in the revealing of tracks, we were at fault to know in which direction to continue. At that, the bo'sun set up a loud shout to Job, perchance he might be yet alive; but there came no answer to us, save a low and uncomfortable echo.

Then the bo'sun, desiring to waste no more time, ran straight down towards the centre of the valley, and we followed, and kept our eyes very open about us. We had gotten perhaps halfway, when one of the men shouted that he saw something ahead; but the bo'sun had seen it earlier; for he was running straight down upon it, holding his torch high and swinging his great cutlass. Then, instead of smiting, he fell upon his knees beside it, and the following instant we were up with him, and in that same moment it seemed to me that I saw a number of white shapes melt swiftly into the shadows further ahead: but I had no thought for these when I perceived that by which the bo'sun knelt; for it was the stark body of Job, and no inch of it but was covered with the little ringed marks that I had discovered upon my throat, and from every place there ran a trickle of blood, so that he was a most horrid and fearsome sight.

At the sight of Job so mangled and be-bled, there came over us the sudden quiet of a mortal terror, and in that space of silence, the bo'sun placed his hand over the poor lad's heart; but there was no movement, though the body was still warm. Immediately upon that, he rose to his feet, a look of vast wrath upon his great face. He plucked his torch from the ground, into which he had plunged the haft, and stared round into the silence of the valley; but there was no living thing in sight, nothing save the giant fungi and the strange shadows cast by our great torches, and the loneliness.

At this moment, one of the men's torches, having burnt near out, fell all to pieces, so that he held nothing but the charred support, and immediately two more came to a like end. Upon this, we became afraid that they would not last us back to the camp, and we looked to the bo'sun to know his wish; but the man was very silent, and peering everywhere into the shadows. Then a fourth torch fell to the ground in a shower of embers, and I turned to look. In the same instant there came a great flare of light behind me, accompanied by the dull thud of a dry matter set suddenly alight. I glanced swiftly back to the bo'sun, and he was staring up at one of the giant toadstools which was in flames all along its nearer edge, and burning with an incredible fury, sending out spirits of flame, and anon giving out sharp reports, and at each report, a fine powder was belched in thin streams; which, getting into our throats and nostrils, set us sneezing and coughing most lamentably; so that I am convinced, had any enemy come upon us at that moment, we had been undone by reason of our uncouth helplessness.

Now whether it had come to the bo'sun to set alight this first of the fungi, I know not; for it may be that his torch coming by chance against it, set it afire. However it chanced, the bo'sun took it as a veritable hint from Providence, and was already setting his torch to one a little further off, whilst the rest of us were near to choking with our coughings and sneezings. Yet, that we were so suddenly overcome by the potency of the powder, I doubt if a full minute passed before we were each one busied after the manner of the bo'sun; and those whose torches had burned out, knocked flaming pieces from the burning fungus, and with these impaled upon their torch-sticks, did so much execution as any.

And thus it happened that within five minutes of this discovery of Job's body, the whole of that hideous valley sent up to heaven the reek of its burning; whilst we, filled with murderous desires, ran hither and thither with our weapons, seeking to destroy the vile creatures that had brought the poor lad to so unholy a death. Yet nowhere could we discover any brute or creature upon which to ease our vengeance, and so, presently, the valley becoming impassable by reason of the heat, the flying sparks and the abundance of the acrid dust, we made back to the body of the boy, and bore him thence to the shore.

And during all that night no man of us slept, and the burning of the fungi sent up a mighty pillar of flame out of the valley, as out of the mouth of a monstrous pit and when the morning came it still burned. Then when it was daylight, some of us slept, being greatly aweariied; but some kept watch.

And when we waked there was a great wind and rain upon the island.

Chapter X
The Light in the Weed

NOW THE WIND was very violent from the sea, and threatened to blow down our tent, the which, indeed, it achieved at last as we made an end of a cheerless breakfast. Yet, the bo'sun bade us not trouble to put it up again; but spread it out with the edges raised upon props made from the reeds, so that we might catch some of the rainwater; for it was become imperative that we should renew our supply before putting out again to sea. And whilst some of us were busied about this, he took the others and set up a small tent made of the spare canvas, and under this he sheltered all of our matters like to be harmed by the rain.

In a little, the rain continuing very violent, we had near a breaker-full of water collected in the canvas, and were about to run it off into one of the breakers, when the bo'sun cried out to us to hold, and first taste the water before we mixed it with that which we had already. At that, we put down our hands and scooped up some of the water to taste, and thus we discovered it to be brackish and quite undrinkable, at which I was amazed, until the bo'sun reminded us that the canvas had been saturated for many days with salt water, so that it would take a great quantity of fresh before all the salt was washed out. Then he told us to lay it flat upon the beach, and scour it well on both sides with the sand, which we did, and afterwards let the rain rinse it well, whereupon the next water that we caught we found to be near fresh; though not sufficiently so for our purpose. Yet when we had rinsed it once more, it became clear of the salt, so that we were able to keep all that we caught further.

And then, something before noon, the rain ceased to fall, though coming again at odd times in short squalls; yet the wind died not, but blew steadily, and continued so from that quarter during the remainder of the time that we were upon the island.

Upon the ceasing of the rain, the bo'sun called us all together, that we might make a decent burial of the unfortunate lad, whose remains had lain during the night upon one of the bottom-boards of the boat. After a little discussion, it was decided to bury him in the beach; for the only part where there was soft earth was in the valley, and none of us had a stomach for that place. Moreover, the sand was soft and easy to dig, and as we had no proper tools, this was a great consideration. Presently, using the bottom-boards and the oars and the hatchet, we had a place large and deep enough to hold the boy, and into this we placed him. We made no prayer over him; but stood about the grave for a little space, in silence. Then, the bo'sun signed to us to fill in the sand; and, therewith, we covered up the poor lad, and left him to his sleep.

And, presently, we made our dinner, after which the bo'sun served out to each one of us a very sound tot of the rum; for he was minded to bring us back again to a cheerful state of mind.

After we had sat awhile, smoking, the bo'sun divided us into two parties to make a search through the island among the rocks, perchance we should find water, collected from the rain, among the hollows and crevasses; for though we had gotten some, through our device with the sail, yet we had by no means caught sufficient for our needs. He was especially anxious for haste, in that the sun had come out again; for he was feared that such small pools as we should find would be speedily dried up by its heat.

Now the bo'sun headed one party, and set the big seaman over the other, bidding all to keep their weapons very handy. Then he set out to the rocks about the base of the nearer hill, sending the others to the farther and greater one, and in each party we carried an empty breaker slung from a couple of the stout reeds, so that we might put all such driblets as we should find, straight away into it, before they had time to vanish into the hot air; and for the purpose of bailing up the water, we had brought with us our tin pannikins, and one of the boat's bailers.

In a while, and after much scrambling amid the rocks, we came upon a little pool of water that was remarkably sweet and fresh, and from this we removed near three gallons before it became dry; and after that we came across, maybe, five or six others; but not one of them near so big as the first; yet we were not displeased; for we had near three parts filled the breaker, and so we made back to the camp, having some wonder as to the luck of the other party.

When we came near the camp, we found the others returned before us, and seeming in a very high content with themselves; so that we had no need to call to them as to whether they had filled their breaker. When they saw us, they set out to us at a run to tell us that they had come upon a great basin of fresh water in a deep hollow a third of the distance up the side of the far hill, and at this the bo'sun bade us put down our breaker and make all of us to the hill, so that he might examine for himself whether their news was so good as it seemed.

Presently, being guided by the other party, we passed around to the back of the far hill, and discovered it to go upward to the top at an easy slope, with many ledges and broken places, so that it was scarce more difficult than a stair to climb. And so, having climbed perhaps ninety or a hundred feet, we came suddenly upon the place which held the water, and found that they had not made too much of their discovery; for the pool was near twenty feet long by twelve broad, and so clear as though it had come from a fountain; yet it had considerable depth, as we discovered by thrusting a spear shaft down into it.

Now the bo'sun, having seen for himself how good a supply of water there was for our needs, seemed very much relieved in his mind, and declared that within three days at the most we might leave the island, at which we felt none of us any regret. Indeed, had the boat escaped harm, we had been able to leave that same day; but this could not be; for there was much to be done before we had her seaworthy again.

Having waited until the bo'sun had made complete his examination, we turned to descend, thinking that this would be the bo'sun's intention; but he called to us to stay, and, looking back, we saw that he made to finish the ascent of the hill. At that, we hastened to follow him; though we had no notion of his reason for going higher. Presently, we were come to the top, and here we found a very spacious place, nicely level save that in one or two parts it was crossed by deepish cracks, maybe half a foot to a foot wide, and perhaps three to six fathoms long; but, apart from these and some great boulders, it was, as I have mentioned, a spacious place; moreover it was bone dry and pleasantly firm under one's feet, after so long upon the sand.

I think, even this early, I had some notion of the bo'sun's design; for I went to the edge that overlooked the valley, and peered down, and, finding it nigh a sheer precipice, found myself nodding my head, as though it were in accordance with some part formed wish. Presently, looking about me, I discovered the bo'sun to be surveying that part which looked over towards the weed, and I made across to join him. Here, again, I saw that the hill fell away very sheer, and after that we went across to the seaward edge, and there it was near as abrupt as on the weed side.

Then, having by this time thought a little upon the matter, I put it straight to the bo'sun that here would make indeed a very secure camping place, with nothing to come at us upon our sides or back; and our front, where was the slope, could be watched with ease. And this I put to him with great warmth; for I was mortally in dread of the coming night.

Now when I had made an end of speaking, the bo'sun disclosed to me that this was, as I had suspicion, his intent, and immediately he called to the men that we should haste down, and ship our camp to the top of the hill. At that, the men expressed their approbation, and we made haste every one of us to the camp, and began straightway to move our gear to the hilltop.

In the meanwhile, the bo'sun, taking me to assist him, set-to again upon the boat, being intent to get his batten nicely shaped and fit to the side of the keel, so that it would bed well to the keel, but more particularly to the plank which had sprung outward from its place. And at this he laboured the greater part of that afternoon, using the little hatchet to shape the wood, which he did with surprising skill; yet when the evening was come, he had not brought it to his liking. But it must not be thought that he did naught but work at the boat; for he had the men to direct, and once he had to make his way to the top of the hill to fix the place for the tent. And after the tent was up, he set them to carry the dry weed to the new camp, and at this he kept them until near dusk; for he had vowed never again to be without a sufficiency of fuel. But two of the men he sent to collect shell-fish – putting two of them to the task, because he would not have one alone upon the island, not knowing but that there might be danger, even though it were bright day; and a most happy ruling it proved; for, a little past the middle of the afternoon, we heard them shouting at the other end of the valley, and, not knowing but that they were in need of assistance, we ran with all haste to discover the reason of their calling, passing along the right-hand side of the blackened and sodden vale. Upon reaching the further beach, we saw a most incredible sight; for the two men were running towards us through the thick masses of the weed, while, no more than four or five fathoms behind, they were pursued by an enormous crab. Now I had thought the crab we had tried to capture before coming to the island, a prodigy unsurpassed; but this creature was more than treble its size, seeming as though a prodigious table were a-chase of them, and moreover, spite of its monstrous bulk, it made better way over the weed than I should have conceived to be possible – running almost sideways, and with one enormous claw raised near a dozen feet into the air.

Now whether, omitting accidents, the men would have made good their escape to the firmer ground of the valley, where they could have attained to a greater speed, I do not know; but suddenly one of them tripped over a loop of the weed, and the next instant lay helpless upon his face. He had been dead the following moment, but for the pluck of his companion, who faced round manfully upon the monster, and ran at it with his twenty-foot spear. It seemed to me that the spear took it about a foot below the overhanging armour of the great back shell, and I could see that it penetrated some distance into the creature, the man having, by the aid of Providence, stricken it in a vulnerable part. Upon receiving this thrust, the mighty crab ceased at once its pursuit, and clipped at the haft of the spear with its great mandible, snapping the weapon more easily than I had done the same thing to a straw. By the time we had raced up to the men, the one who had stumbled was again upon his feet, and turning to assist his comrade; but the bo'sun snatched his spear from him, and leapt forward himself; for the crab was making now at the other man. Now the bo'sun did not attempt to thrust the spear into the monster; but instead he made two swift blows at the great protruding eyes, and in a moment the creature had curled itself up, helpless, save that the huge claw waved about aimlessly. At that, the bo'sun drew us off, though the man who had attacked the crab desired to make an end of it, averring that we should get some very good eating out of it; but to this the bo'sun would not listen, telling him that it was yet capable of very deadly mischief, did any but come within reach of its prodigious mandible.

And after this, he bade them look no more for shellfish; but take out the two fishing-lines which we had, and see if they could catch aught from some safe ledge on the further side of the hill upon which we had made our camp. Then he returned to his mending of the boat.

It was a little before the evening came down upon the island, that the bo'sun ceased work; and, after that, he called to the men, who, having made an end of their fuel carrying, were standing near, to place the full breakers – which we had not thought needful to carry to the new camp on account of their weight – under the upturned boat, some holding up the gunnel whilst the others pushed them under. Then the bo'sun laid the unfinished batten along with them, and we lowered the boat again over all, trusting to its weight to prevent any creature from meddling with aught.

After that, we made at once to the camp, being wearifully tired, and with a hearty anticipation of supper. Upon reaching the hilltop, the men whom the bo'sun had sent with the lines, came to show him a very fine fish, something like to a huge king-fish, which they had caught a few minutes earlier. This, the bo'sun, after examining, did not hesitate to pronounce fit for food; whereupon they set-to and opened and cleaned it. Now, as I have said, it was not unlike a great king-fish, and like it, had a mouth full of very formidable teeth; the use of which I understood the better when I saw the contents of its stomach, which seemed to consist of nothing but the coiled tentacles of squid or cuttlefish, with which, as I have shown, the weed-continent swarmed. When these were upset upon the rock, I was confounded to perceive the length and thickness of some of them; and could only conceive that this particular fish must be a very desperate enemy to them, and able successfully to attack monsters of a bulk infinitely greater than its own.

After this, and whilst the supper was preparing, the bo'sun called to some of the men to put up a piece of the spare canvas upon a couple of the reeds, so as to make a screen against the wind, which up there was so fresh that it came near at times to scattering the fire abroad. This they found not difficult; for a little on the windward side of the fire there ran one of the cracks of which I have made previous mention, and into this they jammed the supports, and so in a very little time had the fire screened.

Presently, the supper was ready, and I found the fish to be very fair eating; though somewhat coarse; but this was no great matter for concern with so empty a stomach as I contained. And here I would remark, that we made our fishing save our provisions through all our stay on the island. Then, after we had come to an end of our eating, we lay down to a most comfortable smoke; for we had no fear of attack, at that height, and with precipices upon all sides save that which lay in front. Yet, so soon as we had rested and smoked a while, the bo'sun set the watches; for he would run no risk through carelessness.

By this time the night was drawing on apace; yet it was not so dark but that one could perceive matters at a very reasonable distance. Presently, being in a mood that tended to thoughtfulness, and feeling a desire to be alone for a little, I strolled away from the fire to the leeward edge of the hilltop. Here, I paced up and down awhile, smoking and meditating. Anon, I would stare out across the immensity of the vast continent of weed and slime that stretched its incredible desolation out beyond the darkening horizon, and there would come the thought to me of the terror of men whose vessels had been entangled among its strange growths, and so my thoughts came to the lone derelict that lay out there in the dusk, and I fell to wondering what had been the end of her people, and at that I grew yet more solemn in my heart. For it seemed to me that they must have died at last by starvation, and if not by that, then by the act of some one of the devil-creatures which inhabited that lonely weed-world. And then, even as I fell upon this thought, the bo'sun clapped me upon the shoulder, and told me in a very hearty way to come to the light of the fire, and banish all melancholy thoughts; for he had a very penetrating discernment, and had followed me quietly from the camping place, having had reason once or twice before to chide me for gloomy meditations. And for this, and many other matters, I had grown to like the man, the which I could almost believe at times, was his regarding of me; but his words were too few for me to gather his feelings; though I had hope that they were as I surmised.

And so I came back to the fire, and presently, it not being my time to watch until after midnight, I turned into the tent for a spell of sleep, having first arranged a comfortable spread of some of the softer portions of the dry weed to make me a bed.

Now I was very full of sleep, so that I slept heavily, and in this wise heard not the man on watch call the bo'sun; yet the rousing of the others waked me, and so I came to myself and found the tent empty, at which I ran very hurriedly to the doorway, and so discovered that there was a clear moon in the sky, the which, by reason of the cloudiness that had prevailed, we had been without for the past two nights. Moreover, the sultriness had gone, the wind having blown it away with the clouds; yet though, maybe, I appreciated this, it was but in a half-conscious manner; for I was put about to discover the whereabouts of the men, and the reason of their leaving the tent. With this purpose, I stepped out from the entrance, and the following instant discovered them all in a clump beside the leeward edge of the hilltop. At that, I held my tongue; for I knew not but that silence might be their desire; but I ran hastily over to them, and inquired of the bo'sun what manner of thing it was which called them from their sleep, and he, for answer, pointed out into the greatness of the weed-continent.

At that, I stared out over the breadth of the weed, showing very ghostly in the moonlight; but, for the moment, I saw not the thing to which he purposed to draw my attention. Then, suddenly, it fell within the circle of my gaze – a little light out in the lonesomeness. For the space of some moments, I stared with bewildered eyes; then it came to me with abruptness that the light shone from the lone derelict lying out in the weed, the same that upon that very evening, I had looked with sorrow and awe, because of the end of those who had been in her – and now, behold, a light burning, seemingly within one of her after cabins; though the moon was scarce powerful enough to enable the outline of the hulk to be seen clear of the rounding wilderness.

And from this time, until the day, we had no more sleep; but made up the fire, and sat round it, full of excitement and wonder, and getting up continually to discover if the light still burned. This it ceased to do about an hour after I had first seen it; but it was the more proof that some of our kind were no more than the half of a mile from our camp.

And at last the day came.

Chapter XI
The Signals from the Ship

NOW SO SOON as it was clearly light, we went all of us to the leeward brow of the hill to stare upon the derelict, which now we had cause to believe no derelict, but an inhabited vessel. Yet though we watched her for upwards of two hours, we could discover no sign of any living creature, the which, indeed, had we been in cooler minds, we had not thought strange, seeing that she was all so shut in by the great superstructure; but we were hot to see a fellow creature, after so much lonesomeness and terror in strange lands and seas, and so could not by any means contain ourselves in patience until those aboard the hulk should choose to discover themselves to us.

And so, at last, being wearied with watching, we made it up together to shout when the bo'sun should give us the signal, by this means making a good volume of sound which we conceived the wind might carry down to the vessel. Yet though we raised many shouts, making as it seemed to us a very great noise, there came no response from the ship, and at last we were fain to cease from our calling, and ponder some other way of bringing ourselves to the notice of those within the hulk.

For a while we talked, some proposing one thing, and some another; but none of them seeming like to achieve our purpose. And after that we fell to marvelling that the fire which we had lit in the valley had not awakened them to the fact that some of their fellow creatures were upon the island; for, had it, we could not suppose but that they would have kept a perpetual watch upon the island until such time as they should have been able to attract our notice. Nay! more than this, it was scarce credible that they should not have made an answering fire, or set some of their bunting above the superstructure, so that our gaze should be arrested upon the instant we chanced to glance towards the hulk. But so far from this, there appeared even a purpose to shun our attention; for that light which we had viewed in the past night was more in the way of an accident, than of the nature of a purposeful exhibition.

And so, presently, we went to breakfast, eating heartily; our night of wakefulness having given us mighty appetites; but, for all that, we were so engrossed by the mystery of the lonesome craft, that I doubt if any of us knew what manner of food it was with which we filled our bellies. For first one view of the matter would be raised, and when this had been combated, another would be broached, and in this wise it came up finally that some of the men were falling in doubt whether the ship was inhabited by anything human, saying rather that it might be held by some demoniac creature of the great weed-continent. At this proposition, there came among us a very uncomfortable silence; for not only did it chill the warmth of our hopes; but seemed like to provide us with a fresh terror, who were already acquainted with too much. Then the bo'sun spoke, laughing with a hearty contempt at our sudden fears, and pointed out that it was just as like that they aboard the ship had been put in fear by the great blaze from the valley, as that they should take it for a sign that fellow creatures and friends were at hand. For, as he put it to us, who of us could say what fell brutes and demons the weed-continent did hold, and if we had reason to know that there were very dread things among the weed, how much the more must they, who had, for all that we knew, been many years beset around by such. And so, as he went on to make clear, we might suppose that they were very well aware there had come some creatures to the island; yet, maybe, they desired not to make themselves known until they had been given sight of them, and because of this, we must wait until they chose to discover themselves to us.

Now when the bo'sun had made an end, we felt each one of us greatly cheered; for his discourse seemed very reasonable. Yet still there were many matters that troubled our company; for, as one put it, was it not mightily strange that we had not had previous sight of their light, or, in the day, of the smoke from their galley fire? But to this the bo'sun replied that our camp hitherto had lain in a place where we had not sight, even of the great world of weed, leaving alone any view of the derelict. And more, that at such times as we had crossed to the opposite beach, we had been occupied too sincerely to have much thought to watch the hulk, which, indeed, from that position showed only her great superstructure. Further, that, until the preceding day, we had but once climbed to any height; and that from our present camp the derelict could not be viewed, and to do so, we had to go near to the leeward edge of the hill-top.

And so, breakfast being ended, we went all of us to see if there were yet any signs of life in the hulk; but when an hour had gone, we were no wiser. Therefore, it being folly to waste further time, the bo'sun left one man to watch from the brow of the hill, charging him very strictly to keep in such position that he could be seen by any aboard the silent craft, and so took the rest down to assist him in the repairing of the boat. And from thence on, during the day, he gave the men a turn each at watching, telling them to wave to him should there come any sign from the hulk. Yet, excepting the watch, he kept every man so busy as might be, some bringing weed to keep up a fire which he had lit near the boat; one to help him turn and hold the batten upon which he laboured; and two he sent across to the wreck of the mast, to detach one of the futtock shrouds, which (as is most rare) were made of iron rods. This, when they brought it, he bade me heat in the fire, and afterwards beat out straight at one end, and when this was done, he set me to burn holes with it through the keel of the boat, at such places as he had marked, these being for the bolts with which he had determined to fasten on the batten.

In the meanwhile, he continued to shape the batten until it was a very good and true fit according to his liking. And all the while he cried out to this man and to that one to do this or that; and so I perceived that, apart from the necessity of getting the boat into a seaworthy condition, he was desirous to keep the men busied; for they were become so excited at the thought of fellow creatures almost within hail, that he could not hope to keep them sufficiently in hand without some matter upon which to employ them.

Now, it must not be supposed that the bo'sun had no share of our excitement; for I noticed that he gave ever and anon a glance to the crown of the far hill, perchance the watchman had some news for us. Yet the morning went by, and no signal came to tell us that the people in the ship had design to show themselves to the man upon watch, and so we came to dinner. At this meal, as might be supposed, we had a second discussion upon the strangeness of the behaviour of those aboard the hulk; yet none could give any more reasonable explanation than the bo'sun had given in the morning, and so we left it at that.

Presently, when we had smoked and rested very comfortably, for the bo'sun was no tyrant, we rose at his bidding to descend once more to the beach. But at this moment, one of the men having run to the edge of the hill to take a short look at the hulk, cried out that a part of the great superstructure over the quarter had been removed, or pushed back, and that there was a figure there, seeming, so far as his unaided sight could tell, to be looking through a spy-glass at the island. Now it would be difficult to tell of all our excitement at this news, and we ran eagerly to see for ourselves if it could be as he informed us. And so it was; for we could see the person very clearly; though remote and small because of the distance. That he had seen us, we discovered in a moment; for he began suddenly to wave something, which I judged to be the spy-glass, in a very wild manner, seeming also to be jumping up and down. Yet, I doubt not but that we were as much excited; for suddenly I discovered myself to be shouting with the rest in a most insane fashion, and moreover I was waving my hands and running to and fro upon the brow of the hill. Then, I observed that the figure on the hulk had disappeared; but it was for no more than a moment, and then it was back and there were near a dozen with it, and it seemed to me that some of them were females; but the distance was over great for surety. Now these, all of them, seeing us upon the brow of the hill, where we must have shown up plain against the sky, began at once to wave in a very frantic way, and we, replying in like manner, shouted ourselves hoarse with vain greetings. But soon we grew wearied of the unsatisfactoriness of this method of showing our excitement, and one took a piece of the square canvas, and let it stream out into the wind, waving it to them, and another took a second piece and did likewise, while a third man rolled up a short bit into a cone and made use of it as a speaking trumpet; though I doubt if his voice carried any the further because of it. For my part, I had seized one of the long bamboo-like reeds which were lying about near the fire, and with this I was making a very brave show. And so it may be seen how very great and genuine was our exaltation upon our discovery of these poor people shut off from the world within that lonesome craft.

Then, suddenly, it seemed to come to us to realise that *they* were among the weed, and *we* upon the hilltop, and that we had no means of bridging that which lay between. And at this we faced one another to discuss what we should do to effect the rescue of those within the hulk. Yet it was little that we could even suggest; for though one spoke of how he had seen a rope cast by means of a mortar to a ship that lay off shore, yet this helped us not, for we had no mortar; but here the same man cried out that they in the ship might have such a thing, so that they would be able to shoot the rope to us, and at this we thought more upon his saying; for if they had such a weapon, then might our difficulties be solved. Yet we were greatly at a loss to know how we should discover whether they were possessed of one, and further to explain our design to them. But here the bo'sun came to our help, and bade one man go quickly and char some of the reeds in the fire, and whilst this was doing he spread out upon the rock one of the spare lengths of canvas; then he sung out to the man to bring him one of the pieces of charred reed, and with this he wrote our question upon the canvas, calling for fresh charcoal as he required it. Then, having made an end of writing, he bade two of the men take hold of the canvas by the ends and expose it to the view of those in the ship, and in this manner we got them to understand our desires. For, presently, some of them went away, and came back after a little, and held up for us to see, a very great square of white, and upon it a great "NO," and at this were we again at our wits' ends to know how it would be possible to rescue those within the ship; for, suddenly, our whole desire to leave the island, was changed into a determination to rescue the people in the hulk, and, indeed, had our intentions not been such we had been veritable curs; though I am happy to tell that we had no thought at this juncture but for those who were now looking to us to restore them once more to the world to which they had been so long strangers.

Now, as I have said, we were again at our wits' ends to know how to come at those within the hulk, and there we stood all of us, talking together, perchance we should hit upon some plan, and anon we would turn and wave to those who watched us so anxiously. Yet, a while passed, and we had come no nearer to a method of rescue. Then a thought came to me (waked perchance by the mention of shooting the rope over to the hulk by means of a mortar) how that I had read once in a book, of a fair maid whose lover effected her escape from a castle by a similar artifice, only that in his case he made use of a bow in place of a mortar, and a cord instead of a rope, his sweetheart hauling up the rope by means of the cord.

Now it seemed to me a possible thing to substitute a bow for the mortar, if only we could find the material with which to make such a weapon, and with this in view, I took up one of the lengths of the bamboo-like reed, and tried the spring of it, which I found to be very good; for this curious growth, of which I have spoken hitherto as a reed, had no resemblance to that plant, beyond its appearance; it being extraordinarily tough and woody, and having considerably more nature than a bamboo. Now, having tried the spring of it, I went over to the tent and cut a piece of sampsonline which I found among the gear, and with this and the reed I contrived a rough bow. Then I looked about until I came upon a very young and slender reed which had been cut with the rest, and from this I fashioned some sort of an arrow, feathering it with a piece of one of the broad, stiff leaves, which grew upon the plant, and after that I went forth to the crowd about the leeward edge of the hill. Now when they saw me thus armed, they seemed to think that I intended a jest, and some of them laughed, conceiving that it was a very odd action on my part; but when I explained that which was in my mind, they ceased from laughter, and shook their heads, making that I did but waste time; for, as they said, nothing save gunpowder could cover so great a distance. And after that they turned again to the bo'sun with whom some of them seemed to be in argument. And so for a little space I held my peace, and listened; thus I discovered that certain of the men advocated the taking of the boat – so soon as it was sufficiently repaired – and making a passage through the weed to the ship, which they proposed to do by cutting a narrow canal. But the bo'sun shook his head, and reminded them of the great devil-fish and crabs, and the worse things which the weed concealed, saying that those in the ship would have done it long since had it been possible, and at that the men were silenced, being robbed of their unreasoning ardour by his warnings.

Now just at this point there happened a thing which proved the wisdom of that which the bo'sun contended; for, suddenly, one of the men cried out to us to look, and at that we turned quickly, and saw that there was a great commotion among those who were in the open place in the superstructure; for they were running this way and that, and some were pushing to the slide which filled the opening. And then, immediately, we saw the reason for their agitation and haste; for there was a stir in the weed near to the stem of the ship, and the next instant, monstrous tentacles were reached up to the place where had been the opening; but the door was shut, and those aboard the hulk in safety. At this manifestation, the men about me who had proposed to make use of the boat, and the others also, cried out their horror of the vast creature, and, I am convinced, had the rescue depended upon their use of the boat, then had those in the hulk been forever doomed.

Now, conceiving that this was a good point at which to renew my importunities, I began once again to explain the probabilities of my plan succeeding, addressing myself more particularly to the bo'sun. I told how that I had read that the ancients made mighty weapons, some of which could throw a great stone so heavy as two men, over a distance surpassing a quarter of a mile; moreover, that they compassed huge catapults which threw a lance, or great arrow, even further. On this, he expressed much surprise, never having heard of the like; but doubted greatly that we should be able to construct such a weapon. Yet, I told him that I was prepared; for I had the plan of one clearly in my mind, and further I pointed out to him that we had the wind in our favour, and that we were a great height up, which would allow the arrow to travel the farther before it came so low as the weed.

Then I stepped to the edge of the hill, and, bidding him watch, fitted my arrow to the string, and, having bent the bow, loosed it, whereupon, being aided by the wind and the height on which I stood, the arrow plunged into the weed at a distance of near two hundred yards from where we stood, that being about a quarter of the distance on the road to the derelict. At that, the bo'sun was won over to my idea; though, as he remarked, the arrow had fallen nearer had it been drawing a length of yarn after it, and to this I assented; but pointed out that my bow and arrow was but a rough affair, and, more, that I was no archer; yet I promised him, with the bow that I should make, to cast a shaft clean over the hulk, did he but give me his assistance, and bid the men to help.

Now, as I have come to regard it in the light of greater knowledge, my promise was exceeding rash; but I had faith in my conception, and was very eager to put it to the test; the which, after much discussion at supper, it was decided I should be allowed to do.

Chapter XII
The Making of the Great Bow

THE FOURTH NIGHT upon the island was the first to pass without incident. It is true that a light showed from the hulk out in the weed; but now that we had made some acquaintance with her inmates, it was no longer a cause for excitement, so much as contemplation. As for the valley where the vile things had made an end of Job, it was very silent and desolate under the moonlight; for I made a point to go and view it during my time on watch; yet, for all that it lay empty, it was very eerie, and a place to conjure up uncomfortable thoughts, so that I spent no great time pondering it.

This was the second night on which we had been free from the terror of the devil-things, and it seemed to me that the great fire had put them in fear of us and driven them away; but of the truth or error of this idea, I was to learn later.

Now it must be admitted that, apart from a short look into the valley, and occasional starings at the light out in the weed, I gave little attention to aught but my plans for the great bow, and to such use did I put my time, that when I was relieved, I had each particular and detail worked out, so that I knew very well just what to set the men doing so soon as we should make a start in the morning.

Presently, when the morning had come, and we had made an end of breakfast, we turned-to upon the great bow, the bo'sun directing the men under my supervision. Now, the first matter to which I bent attention, was the raising, to the top of the hill, of the remaining half of that portion of the topmast which the bo'sun had split in twain to procure the batten for the boat. To this end, we went down, all of us, to the beach where lay the wreckage, and, getting about the portion which I intended to use, carried it to the foot of the hill; then we sent a man to the top to let down the rope by which we had moored the boat to the sea anchor, and when we had bent this on securely to the piece of timber, we returned to the hill-top, and tailed on to the rope, and so, presently, after much weariful pulling, had it up.

The next thing I desired was that the split face of the timber should be rubbed straight, and this the bo'sun understood to do, and whilst he was about it, I went with some of the men to the grove of reeds, and here, with great care, I made a selection of some of the finest, these being for the bow, and after that I cut some which were very clean and straight, intending them for the great arrows. With these we returned once more to the camp, and there I set-to and trimmed them of their leaves, keeping these latter, for I had a use for them. Then I took a dozen reeds and cut them each to a length of twenty-five feet, and afterwards notched them for the strings. In the meanwhile, I had sent two men down to the wreckage of the masts to cut away a couple of the hempen shrouds and bring them to the camp, and they, appearing about this time, I set to work to unlay the shrouds, so that they might get out the fine white yarns which lay beneath the outer covering of tar and blacking. These, when they had come at them, we found to be very good and sound, and this being so, I bid them make three-yarn sennit; meaning it for the strings of the bows. Now, it will be observed that I have said bows, and this I will explain. It had been my original intention to make one great bow, lashing a dozen of the reeds together for the purpose; but this, upon pondering it, I conceived to be but a poor plan; for there would be much life and power lost in the rendering of each piece through the lashings, when the bow was released. To obviate this, and further, to compass the bending of the bow, the which had, at first, been a source of puzzlement to me as to how it was to be accomplished, I had determined to make twelve separate bows, and these I intended to fasten at the end of the stock one above the other, so that they were all in one plane vertically, and because of this conception, I should be able to bend the bows one at a time, and slip each string over the catch-notch, and afterwards frap the twelve strings together in the middle part so that they would be but one string to the butt of the arrow. All this, I explained to the bo'sun, who, indeed, had been exercised in his own mind as to how we should be able to bend such a bow as I intended to make, and he was mightily pleased with my method of evading this difficulty, and also one other, which, else, had been greater than the bending, and that was the *stringing* of the bow, which would have proved a very awkward work.

Presently, the bo'sun called out to me that he had got the surface of the stock sufficiently smooth and nice; and at that I went over to him; for now I wished him to burn a slight groove down the centre, running from end to end, and this I desired to be done very exactly; for upon it depended much of the true flight of the arrow. Then I went back to my own work; for I had not yet finished notching the bows. Presently, when I had made an end of this, I called for a length of the sennit, and, with the aid of another man, contrived to string one of the bows. This, when I had finished, I found to be very springy, and so stiff to bend that I had all that I could manage to do so, and at this I felt very satisfied.

Presently, it occurred to me that I should do well to set some of the men to work upon the line which the arrow was to carry; for I had determined that this should be made also from the white hemp yarns, and, for the sake of lightness, I conceived that one thickness of yarn would be sufficient; but so that it might compass enough of strength, I bid them split the yarns and lay the two halves up together, and in this manner they made me a very light and sound line; though it must not be supposed that it was finished at once; for I needed over half a mile of it, and thus it was later finished than the bow itself.

Having now gotten all things in train, I set me down to work upon one of the arrows; for I was anxious to see what sort of a fist I should make of them, knowing how much would depend upon the balance and truth of the missile. In the end, I made a very fair one, feathering it with its own leaves, and truing and smoothing it with my knife; after which I inserted a small bolt in the forrard end, to act as a head, and, as I conceived, give it balance; though whether I was right in this latter, I am unable to say. Yet, before I had finished my arrow, the bo'sun had made the groove, and called me over to him, that I might admire it, the which I did; for it was done with a wonderful neatness.

Now I have been so busy with my description of how we made the great bow, that I have omitted to tell of the flight of time, and how we had eaten our dinner this long while since, and how that the people in the hulk had waved to us, and we had returned their signals, and then written upon a length of the canvas the one word, "WAIT." And, besides all this, some had gathered our fuel for the coming night.

And so, presently, the evening came upon us; but we ceased not to work; for the bo'sun bade the men to light a second great fire, beside our former one, and by the light of this we worked another long spell; though it seemed short enough, by reason of the interest of the work. Yet, at last, the bo'sun bade us to stop and make supper, which we did, and after that, he set the watches, and the rest of us turned in; for we were very weary.

In spite of my previous weariness, when the man whom I relieved called me to take my watch, I felt very fresh and wide awake, and spent a great part of the time, as on the preceding night, in studying over my plans for completing the great bow, and it was then that I decided finally in what manner I would secure the bows athwart the end of the stock; for until then I had been in some little doubt, being divided between several methods. Now, however, I concluded to make twelve grooves across the sawn end of the stock, and fit the middles of the bows into these, one above the other, as I have already mentioned; and then to lash them at each side to bolts driven into the sides of the stock. And with this idea I was very well pleased; for it promised to make them secure, and this without any great amount of work.

Now, though I spent much of my watch in thinking over the details of my prodigious weapon, yet it must not be supposed that I neglected to perform my duty as watchman; for I walked continually about the top of the hill, keeping my cut-and-thrust ready for any sudden emergency. Yet my time passed off quietly enough; though it is true that I witnessed one thing which brought me a short spell of disquiet thought. It was in this wise: – I had come to that part of the hill-top which overhung the valley, and it came to me, abruptly, to go near to the edge and look over. Thus, the moon being very bright, and the desolation of the valley reasonably clear to the eye, it appeared to me, as I looked that I saw a movement among certain of the fungi which had not burnt, but stood up shrivelled and blackened in the valley. Yet by no means could I be sure that it was not a sudden fancy, born of the eeriness of that desolate looking vale; the more so as I was like to be deceived because of the uncertainty which the light of the moon gives. Yet, to prove my doubts, I went back until I had found a piece of rock easy to throw, and this, taking a short run, I cast into the valley, aiming at the spot where it had seemed to me that there had been a movement. Immediately upon this, I caught a glimpse of some moving thing, and then, more to my right, something else stirred, and at this, I looked towards it; but could discover nothing. Then, looking back at the clump at which I had aimed my missile, I saw that the slime covered pool, which lay near, was all a-quiver, or so it seemed. Yet the next instant I was just as full of doubt; for, even as I watched it, I perceived that it was quite still. And after that, for some time, I kept a very strict gaze into the valley; yet could nowhere discover aught to prove my suspicions, and, at last, I ceased from watching it; for I feared to grow fanciful, and so wandered to that part of the hill which overlooked the weed.

Presently, when I had been relieved, I returned to sleep, and so till the morning. Then, when we had made each of us a hasty breakfast – for all were grown mightily keen to see the great bow completed – we set-to upon it, each at our appointed task. Thus, the bo'sun and I made it our work to make the twelve grooves athwart the flat end of the stock, into which I proposed to fit and lash the bows, and this we accomplished by means of the iron futtock-shroud, which we heated in its middle part, and then, each taking an end (protecting our hands with canvas), we went one on each side and applied the iron until at length we had the grooves burnt out very nicely and accurately. This work occupied us all the morning; for the grooves had to be deeply burnt; and in the meantime the men had completed near enough sennit for the stringing of the bows; yet those who were at work on the line which the arrow was to carry, had scarce made more than half, so that I called off one man from the sennit to turn-to, and give them a hand with the making of the line.

When dinner was ended, the bo'sun and I set-to about fitting the bows into their places, which we did, and lashed them to twenty-four bolts, twelve a side, driven into the timber of the stock, about twelve inches in from the end. After this, we bent and strung the bows, taking very great care to have each bent exactly as the one below it; for we started at the bottom. And so, before sunset, we had that part of our work ended.

Now, because the two fires which we had lit on the previous night had exhausted our fuel, the bo'sun deemed it prudent to cease work, and go down all of us to bring up a fresh supply of the dry seaweed and some bundles of the reeds. This we did, making an end of our journeyings just as the dusk came over the island. Then, having made a second fire, as on the preceding night, we had first our supper, and after that another spell of work, all the men turning to upon the line which the arrow was to carry, whilst the bo'sun and I set-to, each of us, upon the making of a fresh arrow; for I had realised that we should have to make one or two flights before we could hope to find our range and make true our aim.

Later, maybe about nine of the night, the bo'sun bade us all to put away our work, and then he set the watches, after which the rest of us went into the tent to sleep; for the strength of the wind made the shelter a very pleasant thing.

That night, when it came my turn to watch, I minded me to take a look into the valley; but though I watched at intervals through the half of an hour, I saw nothing to lead me to imagine that I had indeed seen aught on the previous night, and so I felt more confident in my mind that we should be troubled no further by the devil-things which had destroyed poor Job. Yet I must record one thing which I saw during my watch; though this was from the edge of the hilltop which overlooked the weed-continent, and was not in the valley, but in the stretch of clear water which lay between the island and the weed. As I saw it, it seemed to me that a number of great fish were swimming across from the island, diagonally towards the great continent of weed: they were swimming in one wake, and keeping a very regular line; but not breaking the water after the manner of porpoises or black fish. Yet, though I have mentioned this, it must not be supposed that I saw any very strange thing in such a sight, and indeed, I thought nothing more of it than to wonder what sort of fish they might be; for, as I saw them indistinctly in the moonlight, they made a queer appearance, seeming each of them to be possessed of two tails, and further, I could have thought I perceived a flicker as of tentacles just beneath the surface; but of this I was by no means sure.

Upon the following morning, having hurried our breakfast, each of us set-to again upon our tasks; for we were in hopes to have the great bow at work before dinner. Soon, the bo'sun had finished his arrow, and mine was completed very shortly after, so that there lacked nothing now to the completion of our work, save the finishing of the line, and the getting of the bow into position. This latter, assisted by the men, we proceeded now to effect, making a level bed of rocks near the edge of the hill which overlooked the weed. Upon this we placed the great bow, and then, having sent the men back to their work at the line, we proceeded to the aiming of the huge weapon. Now, when we had gotten the instrument pointed, as we conceived, straight over the hulk, the which we accomplished by squinting along the groove which the bo'sun had burnt down the centre of the stock, we turned-to upon the arranging of the notch and trigger, the notch being to hold the strings when the weapon was set, and the trigger – a board bolted on loosely at the side just below the notch – to push them upwards out of this place when we desired to discharge the bow.

This part of the work took up no great portion of our time, and soon we had all ready for our first flight. Then we commenced to set the bows, bending the bottom one first, and then those above in turn, until all were set; and, after that, we laid the arrow very carefully in the groove. Then I took two pieces of spun yarn and frapped the strings together at each end of the notch, and by this means I was assured that all the strings would act in unison when striking the butt of the arrow. And so we had all things ready for the discharge; whereupon, I placed my foot upon the trigger, and, bidding the bo'sun watch carefully the flight of the arrow, pushed downwards. The next instant, with a mighty twang, and a quiver that made the great stock stir on its bed of rocks, the bow sprang to its lesser tension, hurling the arrow outwards and upwards in a vast arc. Now, it may be conceived with what mortal interest we watched its flight, and so in a minute discovered that we had aimed too much to the right, for the arrow struck the weed ahead of the hulk – but *beyond* it. At that, I was filled near to bursting with pride and joy, and the men who had come forward to witness the trial, shouted to acclaim my success, whilst the bo'sun clapped me twice upon the shoulder to signify his regard, and shouted as loud as any.

And now it seemed to me that we had but to get the true aim, and the rescue of those in the hulk would be but a matter of another day or two; for, having once gotten a line to the hulk, we should haul across a thin rope by its means, and with this a thicker one; after which we should set this up so taut as possible, and then bring the people in the hulk to the island by means of a seat and block which we should haul to and fro along the supporting line.

Now, having realised that the bow would indeed carry so far as the wreck, we made haste to try our second arrow, and at the same time we bade the men go back to their work upon the line; for we should have need of it in a very little while. Presently, having pointed the bow more to the left, I took the frappings off the strings, so that we could bend the bows singly, and after that we set the great weapon again. Then, seeing that the arrow was straight in the groove, I replaced the frappings, and immediately discharged it. This time, to my very great pleasure and pride, the arrow went with a wonderful straightness towards the ship, and, clearing the superstructure, passed out of our sight as it fell behind it. At this, I was all impatience to try to get the line to the hulk before we made our dinner; but the men had not yet laid-up sufficient; there being then only four hundred and fifty fathoms (which the bo'sun measured off by stretching it along his arms and across his chest). This being so, we went to dinner, and made very great haste through it; and, after that, every one of us worked at the line, and so in about an hour we had sufficient; for I had estimated that it would not be wise to make the attempt with a less length than five hundred fathoms.

Having now completed a sufficiency of the line, the bo'sun set one of the men to flake it down very carefully upon the rock beside the bow, whilst he himself tested it at all such parts as he thought in any way doubtful, and so, presently, all was ready. Then I bent it on to the arrow, and, having set the bow whilst the men were flaking down the line, I was prepared immediately to discharge the weapon.

Now, all the morning, a man upon the hulk had observed us through a spy-glass, from a position that brought his head just above the edge of the superstructure, and, being aware of our intentions – having watched the previous flights – he understood the bo'sun, when he beckoned to him, that we had made ready for a third shot, and so, with an answering wave of his spy-glass, he disappeared from our sight. At that, having first turned to see that all were clear of the line, I pressed down the trigger, my heart beating very fast and thick, and so in a moment the arrow was sped. But now, doubtless because of the weight of the line, it made nowhere near so good a flight as on the previous occasion, the arrow striking the weed some two hundred yards short of the hulk, and at this, I could near have wept with vexation and disappointment.

Immediately upon the failure of my shot, the bo'sun called to the men to haul in the line very carefully, so that it should not be parted through the arrow catching in the weed; then he came over to me, and proposed that we should set-to at once to make a heavier arrow, suggesting that it had been lack of weight in the missile which had caused it to fall short. At that, I felt once more hopeful, and turned-to at once to prepare a new arrow; the bo'sun doing likewise; though in his case he intended to make a lighter one than that which had failed; for, as he put it, though the heavier one fell short, yet might the lighter succeed, and if neither, then we could only suppose that the bow lacked power to carry the line, and in that case, we should have to try some other method.

Now, in about two hours, I had made my arrow, the bo'sun having finished his a little earlier, and so (the men having hauled in all the line and flaked it down ready) we prepared to make another attempt to cast it over the hulk. Yet, a second time we failed, and by so much that it seemed hopeless to think of success; but, for all that it appeared useless, the bo'sun insisted on making a last try with the light arrow, and, presently, when we had gotten the line ready again, we loosed upon the wreck; but in this case so lamentable was our failure, that I cried out to the bo'sun to set the useless thing upon the fire and burn it; for I was sorely irked by its failure, and could scarce abide to speak civilly of it.

Now the bo'sun, perceiving how I felt, sung out that we would cease troubling about the hulk for the present, and go down all of us to gather reeds and weed for the fire; for it was drawing nigh to evening. And this we did, though all in a disconsolate condition of mind; for we had seemed so near to success, and now it appeared to be further than ever from us. And so, in a while, having brought up a sufficiency of fuel, the bo'sun sent two of the men down to one of the ledges which overhung the sea, and bade them see whether they could not secure a fish for our supper. Then, taking our places about the fire, we fell-to upon a discussion as to how we should come at the people in the hulk.

Now, for a while there came no suggestion worthy of notice, until at last there occurred to me a notable idea, and I called out suddenly that we should make a small fire balloon, and float off the line to them by such means. At that, the men about the fire were silent a moment; for the idea was new to them, and moreover they needed to comprehend just what I meant. Then, when they had come fully at it, the one who had proposed that they should make spears of their knives, cried out to know why a kite would not do, and at that I was confounded, in that so simple an expedient had not occurred to any before; for, surely, it would be but a little matter to float a line to them by means of a kite, and, further, such a thing would take no great making.

And so, after a space of talk, it was decided that upon the morrow we should build some sort of kite, and with it fly a line over the hulk, the which should be a task of no great difficulty with so good a breeze as we had continually with us.

And, presently, having made our supper off a very fine fish, which the two fishermen had caught whilst we talked, the bo'sun set the watches, and the rest turned-in.

Chapter XIII
The Weed Men

NOW, ON THAT NIGHT, when I came to my watch, I discovered that there was no moon, and, save for such light as the fire threw, the hill-top was in darkness; yet this was no great matter to trouble me; for we had been unmolested since the burning of the fungi in the valley, and thus I had lost much of the haunting fear which had beset me upon the death of Job. Yet, though I was not so much afraid as I had been, I took all precautions that suggested themselves to me, and built up the fire to a goodly height, after which I took my cut-and-thrust, and made the round of the camping place. At the edges of the cliffs which protected us on three sides, I made some pause, staring down into the darkness, and listening; though this latter was of but small use because of the strength of the wind which roared continually in my ears. Yet though I neither saw nor heard anything, I was presently possessed of a strange uneasiness, which made me return twice or thrice to the edge of the cliffs; but always without seeing or hearing anything to justify my superstitions. And so, presently, being determined to give way to no fancifulness, I avoided the boundary of cliffs, and kept more to that part which commanded the slope, up and down which we made our journeys to and from the island below.

Then, it would be near halfway through my time of watching, there came to me out of the immensity of weed that lay to leeward, a far distant sound that grew upon my ear, rising and rising into a fearsome screaming and shrieking, and then dying away into the distance in queer sobs, and so at last to a note below that of the wind's. At this, as might be supposed, I was somewhat shaken in myself to hear so dread a noise coming out of all that desolation, and then, suddenly, the thought came to me that the screaming was from the ship to leeward of us, and I ran immediately to the edge of the cliff overlooking the weed, and stared into the darkness; but now I perceived, by a light which burned in the hulk, that the screaming had come from some place a great distance to the right of her, and more, as my sense assured me, it could by no means have been possible for those in her to have sent their voices to me against such a breeze as blew at that time.

And so, for a space, I stood nervously pondering, and peering away into the blackness of the night; thus, in a little, I perceived a dull glow upon the horizon, and, presently, there rose into view the upper edge of the moon, and a very welcome sight it was to me; for I had been upon the point of calling the bo'sun to inform him regarding the sound which I had heard; but I had hesitated, being afraid to seem foolish if nothing should befall. Then, even as I stood watching the moon rise into view, there came again to me the beginning of that screaming, somewhat like to the sound of a woman sobbing with a giant's voice, and it grew and strengthened until it pierced through the roar of the wind with an amazing clearness, and then slowly, and seeming to echo and echo, it sank away into the distance, and there was again in my ears no sound beyond that of the wind.

At this, having looked fixedly in the direction from which the sound had proceeded, I ran straightway to the tent and roused the bo'sun; for I had no knowledge of what the noise might portend, and this second cry had shaken from me all my bashfulness. Now the bo'sun was upon his feet almost before I had made an end of shaking him, and catching up his great cutlass which he kept always by his side, he followed me swiftly out on to the hill-top. Here, I explained to him that I had heard a very fearsome sound which had appeared to proceed out of the vastness of the weed-continent, and that, upon a repetition of the noise, I had decided to call him; for I knew not but that it might signal to us of some coming danger. At that, the bo'sun commended me; though chiding me in that I had hesitated to call him at the first occurrence of the crying, and then, following me to the edge of the leeward cliff, he stood there with me, waiting and listening, perchance there might come again a recurrence of the noise.

For perhaps something over an hour we stood there very silent and listening; but there came to us no sound beyond the continuous noise of the wind, and so, by that time, having grown somewhat impatient of waiting, and the moon being well risen, the bo'sun beckoned to me to make the round of the camp with him. Now, just as I turned away, chancing to look downward at the clear water directly below, I was amazed to see that an innumerable multitude of great fish, like unto those which I had seen on the previous night, were swimming from the weed-continent towards the island. At that, I stepped nearer the edge; for they came so directly towards the island that I expected to see them close inshore; yet I could not perceive one; for they seemed all of them to vanish at a point some thirty yards distant from the beach, and at that, being amazed both by the numbers of the fish and their strangeness, and the way in which they came on continually, yet never reached the shore, I called to the bo'sun to come and see; for he had gone on a few paces. Upon hearing my call, he came running back; whereat I pointed into the sea below. At that, he stooped forward and peered very intently, and I with him; yet neither one of us could discover the meaning of so curious an exhibition, and so for a while we watched, the bo'sun being quite so much interested as I.

Presently, however, he turned away, saying that we did foolishly to stand here peering at every curious sight, when we should be looking to the welfare of the camp, and so we began to go the round of the hill-top. Now, whilst we had been watching and listening, we had suffered the fire to die down to a most unwise lowness, and consequently, though the moon was rising, there was by no means the same brightness that should have made the camp light. On perceiving this, I went forward to throw some fuel on to the fire, and then, even as I moved, it seemed to me that I saw something stir in the shadow of the tent. And at that, I ran towards the place, uttering a shout, and waving my cut-and-thrust; yet I found nothing, and so, feeling somewhat foolish, I turned to make up the fire, as had been my intention, and whilst I was thus busied, the bo'sun came running over to me to know what I had seen, and in the same instant there ran three of the men out of the tent, all of them waked by my sudden cry. But I had naught to tell them, save that my fancy had played me a trick, and had shown me something where my eyes could find nothing, and at that, two of the men went back to resume their sleep; but the third, the big fellow to whom the bo'sun had given the other cutlass, came with us, bringing his weapon; and, though he kept silent, it seemed to me that he had gathered something of our uneasiness; and for my part I was not sorry to have his company.

Presently, we came to that portion of the hill which overhung the valley, and I went to the edge of the cliff, intending to peer over; for the valley had a very unholy fascination for me. Yet, no sooner had I glanced down than I started, and ran back to the bo'sun and plucked him by the sleeve, and at that, perceiving my agitation, he came with me in silence to see what matter had caused me so much quiet excitement. Now, when he looked over, he also was astounded, and drew back instantly; then, using great caution, he bent forward once more, and stared down, and, at that, the big seaman came up behind, walking upon his toes, and stooped to see what manner of thing we had discovered. Thus we each of us stared down upon a most unearthly sight; for the valley all beneath us was a-swarm with moving creatures, white and unwholesome in the moonlight, and their movements were somewhat like the movements of monstrous slugs, though the things themselves had no resemblance to such in their contours; but minded me of naked humans, very fleshy and crawling upon their stomachs; yet their movements lacked not a surprising rapidity. And now, looking a little over the bo'sun's shoulder, I discovered that these hideous things were coming up out from the pit-like pool in the bottom of the valley, and, suddenly, I was minded of the multitudes of strange fish which we had seen swimming towards the island; but which had all disappeared before reaching the shore, and I had no doubt but that they entered the pit through some natural passage known to them beneath the water. And now I was made to understand my thought of the previous night, that I had seen the flicker of tentacles; for these things below us had each two short and stumpy arms; but the ends appeared divided into hateful and wriggling masses of small tentacles, which slid hither and thither as the creatures moved about the bottom of the valley, and at their hinder ends, where they should have grown feet, there seemed other flickering bunches; but it must not be supposed that we saw these things clearly.

Now it is scarcely possible to convey the extraordinary disgust which the sight of these human slugs bred in me; nor, could I, do I think I would; for were I successful, then would others be like to retch even as I did, the spasm coming on without premonition, and born of very horror. And then, suddenly, even as I stared, sick with loathing and apprehension, there came into view, not a fathom below my feet, a face like to the face which had peered up into my own on that night, as we drifted beside the weed-continent. At that, I could have screamed, had I been in less terror; for the great eyes, so big as crown pieces, the bill like to an inverted parrot's, and the slug-like undulating of its white and slimy body, bred in me the dumbness of one mortally stricken. And, even as I stayed there, my helpless body bent and rigid, the bo'sun spat a mighty curse into my ear, and, leaning forward, smote at the thing with his cutlass; for in the instant that I had seen it, it had advanced upward by so much as a yard. Now, at this action of the bo'sun's, I came suddenly into possession of myself, and thrust downward with so much vigour that I was like to have followed the brute's carcass; for I overbalanced, and danced giddily for a moment upon the edge of eternity; and then the bo'sun had me by the waistband, and I was back in safety; but in that instant through which I had struggled for my balance, I had discovered that the face of the cliff was near hid with the number of the things which were making up to us, and I turned to the bo'sun, crying out to him that there were thousands of them swarming up to us. Yet, he was gone already from me, running towards the fire, and shouting to the men in the tent to haste to our help for their very lives, and then he came racing back with a great armful of the weed, and after him came the big seaman, carrying a burning tuft from the camp fire, and so in a few moments we had a blaze, and the men were bringing more weed; for we had a very good stock upon the hill-top; for which the Almighty be thanked.

Now, scarce had we lit one fire, when the bo'sun cried out to the big seaman to make another, further along the edge of the cliff, and, in the same instant, I shouted, and ran over to that part of the hill which lay towards the open sea; for I had seen a number of moving things about the edge of the seaward cliff. Now here there was a deal of shadow; for there were scattered certain large masses of rock about this part of the hill, and these held off both the light of the moon, and that from the fires. Here, I came abruptly upon three great shapes moving with stealthiness towards the camp, and, behind these, I saw dimly that there were others. Then, with a loud cry for help, I made at the three, and, as I charged, they rose up on end at me, and I found that they overtopped me, and their vile tentacles were reached out at me. Then I was smiting, and gasping, sick with a sudden stench, the stench of the creatures which I had come already to know. And then something clutched at me, something slimy and vile, and great mandibles champed in my face; but I stabbed upward, and the thing fell from me, leaving me dazed and sick, and smiting weakly. Then there came a rush of feet behind, and a sudden blaze, and the bo'sun crying out encouragement, and, directly, he and the big seaman thrust themselves in front of me, hurling from them great masses of burning weed, which they had borne, each of them, up a long reed. And immediately the things were gone, slithering hastily down over the cliff edge.

And so, presently, I was more my own man, and made to wipe from my throat the slime left by the clutch of the monster: and afterwards I ran from fire to fire with weed, feeding them, and so a space passed, during which we had safety; for by that time we had fires all about the top of the hill, and the monsters were in mortal dread of fire, else had we been dead, all of us, that night.

Now, a while before the dawn, we discovered, for the second time since we had been upon the island, that our fuel could not last us the night at the rate at which we were compelled to burn it, and so the bo'sun told the men to let out every second fire, and thus we staved off for a while the time when we should have to face a spell of darkness, and the things which, at present, the fires held off from us. And so at last, we came to the end of the weed and the reeds, and the bo'sun called out to us to watch the cliff edges very carefully, and smite on the instant that any thing showed; but that, should he call, all were to gather by the central fire for a last stand. And, after that, he blasted the moon which had passed behind a great bank of cloud. And thus matters were, and the gloom deepened as the fires sank lower and lower. Then I heard a man curse, on that part of the hill which lay towards the weed-continent, his cry coming up to me against the wind, and the bo'sun shouted to us to all have a care, and directly afterwards I smote at something that rose silently above the edge of the cliff opposite to where I watched.

Perhaps a minute passed, and then there came shouts from all parts of the hilltop, and I knew that the weed men were upon us, and in the same instant there came two above the edge near me, rising with a ghostly quietness, yet moving lithely. Now the first, I pierced somewhere in the throat, and it fell backward; but the second, though I thrust it through, caught my blade with a bunch of its tentacles, and was like to have snatched it from me; but that I kicked it in the face, and at that, being, I believe, more astonished than hurt, it loosed my sword, and immediately fell away out of sight. Now this had taken, in all, no more than some ten seconds; yet already I perceived so many as four others coming into view a little to my right, and at that it seemed to me that our deaths must be very near, for I knew not how we were to cope with the creatures, coming as they were so boldly and with such rapidity. Yet, I hesitated not, but ran at them, and now I thrust not; but cut at their faces, and found this to be very effectual; for in this wise disposed I of three in as many strokes; but the fourth had come right over the cliff edge, and rose up at me upon its hinder parts, as had done those others when the bo'sun had succoured me. At that, I gave way, having a very lively dread; but, hearing all about me the cries of conflict, and knowing that I could expect no help, I made at the brute: then as it stooped and reached out one of its bunches of tentacles, I sprang back, and slashed at them, and immediately I followed this up by a thrust in the stomach, and at that it collapsed into a writhing white ball, that rolled this way and that, and so, in its agony, coming to the edge of the cliff, it fell over, and I was left, sick and near helpless with the hateful stench of the brutes.

Now by this time all the fires about the edges of the hill were sunken into dull glowing mounds of embers; though that which burnt near to the entrance of the tent was still of a good brightness; yet this helped us but little, for we fought too far beyond the immediate circle of its beams to have benefit of it. And still the moon, at which now I threw a despairing glance, was no more than a ghostly shape behind the great bank of cloud which was passing over it. Then, even as I looked upward, glancing as it might be over my left shoulder, I saw, with a sudden horror, that something had come anigh me, and upon the instant, I caught the reek of the thing, and leapt fearfully to one side, turning as I sprang. Thus was I saved in the very moment of my destruction; for the creature's tentacles smeared the back of my neck as I leapt, and then I had smitten, once and again, and conquered.

Immediately after this, I discovered something to be crossing the dark space that lay between the dull mound of the nearest fire, and that which lay further along the hill-top, and so, wasting no moment of time, I ran towards the thing, and cut it twice across the head before ever it could get upon its hind parts, in which position I had learned greatly to dread them. Yet, no sooner had I slain this one, than there came a rush of maybe a dozen upon me; these having climbed silently over the cliff edge in the meanwhile. At this, I dodged, and ran madly towards the glowing mound of the nearest fire, the brutes following me almost so quick as I could run; but I came to the fire the first, and then, a sudden thought coming to me, I thrust the point of my cut-and-thrust among the embers and switched a great shower of them at the creatures, and at that I had a momentary clear vision of many white, hideous faces stretched out towards me, and brown, champing mandibles which had the upper beak shutting into the lower; and the clumped, wriggling tentacles were all a-flutter. Then the gloom came again; but immediately, I switched another and yet another shower of the burning embers towards them, and so, directly, I saw them give back, and then they were gone. At this, all about the edges of the hilltop, I saw the fires being scattered in like manner; for others had adopted this device to help them in their sore straits.

For a little after this, I had a short breathing space, the brutes seeming to have taken fright; yet I was full of trembling, and I glanced hither and thither, not knowing when some one or more of them would come upon me. And ever I glanced towards the moon, and prayed the Almighty that the clouds would pass quickly, else should we be all dead men; and then, as I prayed, there rose a sudden very terrible scream from one of the men, and in the same moment there came something over the edge of the cliff fronting me; but I cleft it or ever it could rise higher, and in my ears there echoed still the sudden scream which had come from that part of the hill which lay to the left of me: yet I dared not to leave my station; for to have done so would have been to have risked all, and so I stayed, tortured by the strain of ignorance, and my own terror.

Again, I had a little spell in which I was free from molestation; nothing coming into sight so far as I could see to right or left of me; though others were less fortunate, as the curses and sounds of blows told to me, and then, abruptly, there came another cry of pain, and I looked up again to the moon, and prayed aloud that it might come out to show some light before we were all destroyed; but it remained hid. Then a sudden thought came into my brain, and I shouted at the top of my voice to the bo'sun to set the great cross-bow upon the central fire; for thus we should have a big blaze – the wood being very nice and dry. Twice I shouted to him, saying: – "Burn the bow! Burn the bow!" And immediately he replied, shouting to all the men to run to him and carry it to the fire; and this we did and bore it to the centre fire, and then ran back with all speed to our places. Thus in a minute we had some light, and the light grew as the fire took hold of the great log, the wind fanning it to a blaze. And so I faced outwards, looking to see if any vile face showed above the edge before me, or to my right or left. Yet, I saw nothing, save, as it seemed to me, once a fluttering tentacle came up, a little to my right; but nothing else for a space.

Perhaps it was near five minutes later, that there came another attack, and, in this, I came near to losing my life, through my folly in venturing too near to the edge of the cliff; for, suddenly, there shot up out from the darkness below, a clump of tentacles, and caught me about the left ankle, and immediately I was pulled to a sitting posture, so that both my feet were over the edge of the precipice, and it was only by the mercy of God that I had not plunged head foremost into the valley. Yet, as it was, I suffered a mighty peril; for the brute that had my foot, put a vast strain upon it, trying to pull me down; but I resisted, using my hands and seat to sustain me, and so, discovering that it could not compass my end in this wise, it slacked somewhat of the stress, and bit at my boot, shearing through the hard leather, and nigh destroying my small toe; but now, being no longer compelled to use both hands to retain my position, I slashed down with great fury, being maddened by the pain and the mortal fear which the creature had put upon me; yet I was not immediately free of the brute; for it caught my sword blade; but I snatched it away before it could take a proper hold, mayhaps cutting its feelers somewhat thereby; though of this I cannot be sure, for they seemed not to grip around a thing, but to *suck* to it; then, in a moment, by a lucky blow, I maimed it, so that it loosed me, and I was able to get back into some condition of security.

And from this onwards, we were free from molestation; though we had no knowledge but that the quietness of the weed men did but portend a fresh attack, and so, at last, it came to the dawn; and in all this time the moon came not to our help, being quite hid by the clouds which now covered the whole arc of the sky, making the dawn of a very desolate aspect.

And so soon as there was a sufficiency of light, we examined the valley; but there were nowhere any of the weed men, no! Nor even any of their dead for it seemed that they had carried off all such and their wounded, and so we had no opportunity to make an examination of the monsters by daylight. Yet, though we could not come upon their dead, all about the edges of the cliffs was blood and slime, and from the latter there came ever the hideous stench which marked the brutes; but from this we suffered little, the wind carrying it far away to leeward, and filling our lungs with sweet and wholesome air.

Presently, seeing that the danger was past, the bo'sun called us to the centre fire, on which burnt still the remnants of the great bow, and here we discovered for the first time that one of the men was gone from us. At that, we made search about the hilltop, and afterwards in the valley and about the island; but found him not.

Chapter XIV
In Communication

NOW OF THE SEARCH which we made through the valley for the body of Tompkins, that being the name of the lost man, I have some doleful memories. But first, before we left the camp, the bo'sun gave us all a very sound tot of the rum, and also a biscuit apiece, and thereafter we hasted down, each man holding his weapon readily. Presently, when we were come to the beach which ended the valley upon the seaward side, the bo'sun led us along to the bottom of the hill, where the precipices came down into the softer stuff which covered the valley, and here we made a careful search, perchance he had fallen over, and lay dead or wounded near to our hands. But it was not so, and after that, we went down to the mouth of the great pit, and here we discovered the mud all about it to be covered with multitudes of tracks, and in addition to these and the slime, we found many traces of blood; but nowhere any signs of Tompkins. And so, having searched all the valley, we came out upon the weed which strewed the shore nearer to the great weed-continent; but discovered nothing until we had made up towards the foot of the hill, where it came down sheer into the sea. Here, I climbed on to a ledge – the same from which the men had caught their fish – thinking that, if Tompkins had fallen from above, he might lie in the water at the foot of the cliff, which was here, maybe, some ten to twenty feet deep; but, for a little space, I saw nothing. Then, suddenly, I discovered that there was something white, down in the sea away to my left, and, at that, I climbed farther out along the ledge.

In this wise I perceived that the thing which had attracted my notice was the dead body of one of the weed men. I could see it but dimly, catching odd glimpses of it as the surface of the water smoothed at whiles. It appeared to me to be lying curled up, and somewhat upon its right side, and in proof that it was dead, I saw a mighty wound that had come near to shearing away the head; and so, after a further glance, I came in, and told what I had seen. At that, being convinced by this time that Tompkins was indeed done to death, we ceased our search; but first, before we left the spot, the bo'sun climbed out to get a sight of the dead weed man and after him the rest of the men, for they were greatly curious to see clearly what manner of creature it was that had attacked us in the night. Presently, having seen so much of the brute as the water would allow, they came in again to the beach, and afterwards were returned to the opposite side of the island, and so, being there, we crossed over to the boat, to see whether it had been harmed; but found it to be untouched. Yet, that the creatures had been all about it, we could perceive by the marks of slime upon the sand, and also by the strange trail which they had left in the soft surface. Then one of the men called out that there had been something at Job's grave, which, as will be remembered, had been made in the sand some little distance from the place of our first camp. At that, we looked all of us, and it was easy to see that it had been disturbed, and so we ran hastily to it, knowing not what to fear; thus we found it to be empty; for the monsters had digged down to the poor lad's body, and of it we could discover no sign. Upon this, we came to a greater horror of the weed men than ever; for we knew them now to be foul ghouls who could not let even the dead body rest in the grave.

Now after this, the bo'sun led us all back to the hill-top, and there he looked to our hurts; for one man had lost two fingers in the night's fray; another had been bitten savagely in the left arm; whilst a third had all the skin of his face raised in wheals where one of the brutes had fixed its tentacles. And all of these had received but scant attention, because of the stress of the fight, and, after that, through the discovery that Tompkins was missing. Now, however, the bo'sun set-to upon them, washing and binding them up, and for dressings he made use of some of the oakum which we had with us, binding this on with strips torn from the roll of spare duck, which had been in the locker of the boat.

For my part, seizing this chance to make some examination of my wounded toe, the which, indeed, was causing me to limp, I found that I had endured less harm than seemed to me; for the bone of the toe was untouched, though showing bare; yet when it was cleansed, I had not overmuch pain with it; though I could not suffer to have the boot on, and so bound some canvas about my foot, until such time as it should be healed.

Presently, when our wounds were all attended to, the which had taken time, for there was none of us altogether untouched, the bo'sun bade the man whose fingers were damaged, to lie down in the tent, and the same order he gave also to him that was bitten in the arm. Then, the rest of us he directed to go down with him and carry up fuel; for that the night had shown him how our very lives depended upon a sufficiency of this; and so all that morning we brought fuel to the hill-top, both weed and reeds, resting not until midday, when he gave us a further tot of the rum, and after that set one of the men upon the dinner. Then he bade the man, Jessop by name, who had proposed to fly a kite over the vessel in the weed, to say whether he had any craft in the making of such a matter. At that, the fellow laughed, and told the bo'sun that he would make him a kite that would fly very steadily and strongly, and this without the aid of a tail. And so the bo'sun bade him set-to without delay, for that we should do well to deliver the people in the hulk, and afterwards make all haste from the island, which was no better than a nesting place of ghouls.

Now hearing the man say that his kite would fly without a tail, I was mightily curious to see what manner of thing he would make; for I had never seen the like, nor heard that such was possible. Yet he spoke of no more than he could accomplish; for he took two of the reeds and cut them to a length of about six feet; then he bound them together in the middle so that they formed a Saint Andrew's cross, and after that he made two more such crosses, and when these were completed, he took four reeds maybe a dozen feet long, and bade us stand them upright in the shape of a square, so that they formed the four corners, and after that he took one of the crosses, and laid it in the square so that its four ends touched the four uprights, and in this position he lashed it. Then he took the second cross and lashed it midway between the top and bottom of the uprights, and after that he lashed the third at the top, so that the three of them acted as spreaders to keep the four longer reeds in their places as though they were for the uprights of a little square tower. Now, when he had gotten so far as that, the bo'sun called out to us to make our dinners, and this we did, and afterwards had a short time in which to smoke, and whilst we were thus at our ease the sun came out, the which it had not done all the day, and at that we felt vastly brighter; for the day had been very gloomy with clouds until that time, and what with the loss of Tompkins, and our own fears and hurts, we had been exceeding doleful, but now, as I have said, we became more cheerful, and went very alertly to the finishing of the kite.

At this point it came suddenly to the bo'sun that we had made no provision of cord for the flying of the kite, and he called out to the man to know what strength the kite would require, at which Jessop answered him that maybe ten-yarn sennit would do, and this being so, the bo'sun led three of us down to the wrecked mast upon the further beach, and from this we stripped all that was left of the shrouds, and carried them to the top of the hill, and so, presently, having unlaid them, we set-to upon the sennit, using ten yarns; but plaiting two as one, by which means we progressed with more speed than if we had taken them singly.

Now, as we worked, I glanced occasionally towards Jessop, and saw that he stitched a band of the light duck around each end of the framework which he had made, and these bands I judged to be about four feet wide, in this wise leaving an open space between the two, so that now the thing looked something like to a Punchinello show, only that the opening was in the wrong place, and there was too much of it. After that he bent on a bridle to two of the uprights, making this of a piece of good hemp rope which he found in the tent, and then he called out to the bo'sun that the kite was finished. At that, the bo'sun went over to examine it, the which did all of us; for none of us had seen the like of such a thing, and, if I misdoubt not, few of us had much faith that it would fly; for it seemed so big and unwieldy. Now, I think that Jessop gathered something of our thoughts; for, calling to one of us to hold the kite, lest it should blow away, he went into the tent, and brought out the remainder of the hemp line, the same from which he had cut the bridle. This, he bent on to it, and, giving the end into our hands, bade us go back with it until all the slack was taken up, he, in the meanwhile, steadying the kite. Then, when we had gone back to the extent of the line, he shouted to us to take a very particular hold upon it, and then, stooping, caught the kite by the bottom, and threw it into the air, whereupon, to our amazement, having swooped somewhat to one side, it steadied and mounted upwards into the sky like a very bird.

Now at this, as I have made mention, we were astonished, for it appeared like a miracle to us to see so cumbrous a thing fly with so much grace and persistence, and further, we were mightily surprised at the manner in which it pulled upon the rope, tugging with such heartiness that we were like to have loosed it in our first astonishment, had it not been for the warning which Jessop called to us.

And now, being well assured of the properness of the kite, the bo'sun bade us to draw it in, the which we did only with difficulty, because of its bigness and the strength of the breeze. And when we had it back again upon the hilltop, Jessop moored it very securely to a great piece of rock, and, after that, having received our approbation, he turned-to with us upon the making of the sennit.

Presently, the evening drawing near, the bo'sun set us to the building of fires about the hill-top, and after that, having waved our goodnights to the people in the hulk, we made our suppers, and lay down to smoke, after which, we turned-to again at our plaiting of the sennit, the which we were in very great haste to have done. And so, later, the dark having come down upon the island, the bo'sun bade us take burning weed from the centre fire, and set light to the heaps of weed that we had stacked round the edges of the hill for that purpose, and so in a few minutes the whole of the hill-top was very light and cheerful, and afterwards, having put two of the men to keep watch and attend to the fires, he sent the rest of us back to our sennit making, keeping us at it until maybe about ten of the clock, after which he arranged that two men at a time should be on watch throughout the night, and then he bade the rest of us turn-in, so soon as he had looked to our various hurts.

Now, when it came to my turn to watch, I discovered that I had been chosen to accompany the big seaman, at which I was by no means displeased; for he was a most excellent fellow, and moreover a very lusty man to have near, should anything come upon one unawares. Yet, we were happy in that the night passed off without trouble of any sort, and so at last came the morning.

So soon as we had made our breakfast, the bo'sun took us all down to the carrying of fuel; for he saw very clearly that upon a good supply of this depended our immunity from attack. And so for the half of the morning we worked at the gathering of weed and reeds for our fires. Then, when we had obtained a sufficiency for the coming night, he set us all to work again upon the sennit, and so until dinner, after which we turned-to once more upon our plaiting. Yet it was plain that it would take several days to make a sufficient line for our purpose, and because of this, the bo'sun cast about in his mind for some way in which he could quicken its production. Presently, as a result of some little thought, he brought out from the tent the long piece of hemp rope with which we had moored the boat to the sea anchor, and proceeded to unlay it, until he had all three strands separate. Then he bent the three together, and so had a very rough line of maybe some hundred and eighty fathoms in length, yet, though so rough, he judged it strong enough, and thus we had this much the less sennit to make.

Now, presently, we made our dinner, and after that for the rest of the day we kept very steadily to our plaiting, and so, with the previous day's work, had near two hundred fathoms completed by the time that the bo'sun called us to cease and come to supper.

Thus it will be seen that counting all, including the piece of hemp line from which the bridle had been made, we may be said to have had at this time about four hundred fathoms towards the length which we needed for our purpose, this having been reckoned at five hundred fathoms.

After supper, having lit all the fires, we continued to work at the plaiting, and so, until the bo'sun set the watches, after which we settled down for the night, first, however, letting the bo'sun see to our hurts. Now this night, like to the previous, brought us no trouble; and when the day came, we had first our breakfast, and then set-to upon our collecting of fuel, after which we spent the rest of the day at the sennit, having manufactured a sufficiency by the evening, the which the bo'sun celebrated by a very rousing tot of the rum. Then, having made our supper, we lit the fires, and had a very comfortable evening, after which, as on the preceding nights, having let the bo'sun attend our wounds, we settled for the night, and on this occasion the bo'sun let the man who had lost his fingers, and the one who had been bitten so badly in the arm, take their first turn at the watching since the night of the attack.

Now when the morning came we were all of us very eager to come to the flying of the kite; for it seemed possible to us that we might effect the rescue of the people in the hulk before the evening. And, at the thought of this, we experienced a very pleasurable sense of excitement; yet, before the bo'sun would let us touch the kite, he insisted that we should gather our usual supply of fuel, the which order, though full of wisdom, irked us exceedingly, because of our eagerness to set about the rescue. But at last this was accomplished, and we made to get the line ready, testing the knots, and seeing that it was all clear for running. Yet, before setting the kite off, the bo'sun took us down to the further beach to bring up the foot of the royal and t'gallant mast, which remained fast to the topmast, and when we had this upon the hill-top, he set its ends upon two rocks, after which he piled a heap of great pieces around them, leaving the middle part clear. Round this he passed the kite line a couple or three times, and then gave the end to Jessop to bend on to the bridle of the kite, and so he had all ready for paying out to the wreck.

And now, having nothing to do, we gathered round to watch, and, immediately, the bo'sun giving the signal, Jessop cast the kite into the air, and, the wind catching it, lifted it strongly and well, so that the bo'sun could scarce pay out fast enough. Now, before the kite had been let go, Jessop had bent to the forward end of it a great length of the spun yarn, so that those in the wreck could catch it as it trailed over them, and, being eager to witness whether they would secure it without trouble, we ran all of us to the edge of the hill to watch. Thus, within five minutes from the time of the loosing of the kite, we saw the people in the ship wave to us to cease veering, and immediately afterwards the kite came swiftly downwards, by which we knew that they had the tripping-line, and were hauling upon it, and at that we gave out a great cheer, and afterwards we sat about and smoked, waiting until they had read our instructions, which we had written upon the covering of the kite.

Presently, maybe the half of an hour afterwards, they signalled to us to haul upon our line, which we proceeded to do without delay, and so, after a great space, we had hauled in all of our rough line, and come upon the end of theirs, which proved to be a fine piece of three-inch hemp, new and very good; yet we could not conceive that this would stand the stress necessary to lift so great a length clear of the weed, as would be needful, or ever we could hope to bring the people of the ship over it in safety. And so we waited some little while, and, presently, they signalled again to us to haul, which we did, and found that they had bent on a much greater rope to the bight of the three-inch hemp, having merely intended the latter for a hauling-line by which to get the heavier rope across the weed to the island. Thus, after a weariful time of pulling, we got the end of the bigger rope up to the hill-top, and discovered it to be an extraordinarily sound rope of some four inches diameter, and smoothly laid of fine yarns round and very true and well spun, and with this we had every reason to be satisfied.

Now to the end of the big rope they had tied a letter, in a bag of oilskin, and in it they said some very warm and grateful things to us, after which they set out a short code of signals by which we should be able to understand one another on certain general matters, and at the end they asked if they should send us any provision ashore; for, as they explained, it would take some little while to get the rope set taut enough for our purpose, and the carrier fixed and in working order. Now, upon reading this letter, we called out to the bo'sun that he should ask them if they would send us some soft bread; the which he added thereto a request for lint and bandages and ointment for our hurts. And this he bade me write upon one of the great leaves from off the reeds, and at the end he told me to ask if they desired us to send them any fresh water. And all of this, I wrote with a sharpened splinter of reed, cutting the words into the surface of the leaf. Then, when I had made an end of writing, I gave the leaf to the bo'sun, and he enclosed it in the oilskin bag, after which he gave the signal for those in the hulk to haul on the smaller line, and this they did.

Presently, they signed to us to pull in again, the which we did, and so, when we had hauled in a great length of their line, we came to the little oilskin bag, in which we found lint and bandages and ointment, and a further letter, which set out that they were baking bread, and would send us some so soon as it was out from the oven.

Now, in addition to the matters for the healing of our wounds, and the letter, they had included a bundle of paper in loose sheets, some quills and an inkhorn, and at the end of their epistle, they begged very earnestly of us to send them some news of the outer world; for they had been shut up in that strange continent of weed for something over seven years. They told us then that there were twelve of them in the hulk, three of them being women, one of whom had been the captain's wife; but he had died soon after the vessel became entangled in the weed, and along with him more than half of the ship's company, having been attacked by giant devil-fish, as they were attempting to free the vessel from the weed, and afterwards they who were left had built the superstructure as a protection against the devil-fish, and the *devil-men*, as they termed them; for, until it had been built, there had been no safety about the decks, neither day nor night.

To our question as to whether they were in need of water, the people in the ship replied that they had a sufficiency, and, further, that they were very well supplied with provisions; for the ship had sailed from London with a general cargo, among which there was a vast quantity of food in various shapes and forms. At this news we were greatly pleased, seeing that we need have no more anxiety regarding a lack of victuals, and so in the letter which I went into the tent to write, I put down that we were in no great plentitude of provisions, at which hint I guessed they would add somewhat to the bread when it should be ready. And after that I wrote down such chief events as my memory recalled as having occurred in the course of the past seven years, and then, a short account of our own adventures, up to that time, telling them of the attack which we had suffered from the weed men, and asking such questions as my curiosity and wonder prompted.

Now whilst I had been writing, sitting in the mouth of the tent, I had observed, from time to time, how that the bo'sun was busied with the men in passing the end of the big rope round a mighty boulder, which lay about ten fathoms in from the edge of the cliff which overlooked the hulk. This he did, parcelling the rope where the rock was in any way sharp, so as to protect it from being cut; for which purpose he made use of some of the canvas. And by the time that I had the letter completed, the rope was made very secure to the great piece of rock, and, further, they had put a large piece of chafing gear under that part of the rope where it took the edge of the cliff.

Now having, as I have said, completed the letter, I went out with it to the bo'sun; but, before placing it in the oilskin bag he bade me add a note at the bottom, to say that the big rope was all fast, and that they could heave on it so soon as it pleased them, and after that we dispatched the letter by means of the small line, the men in the hulk hauling it off to them so soon as they perceived our signals.

By this, it had come well on to the latter part of the afternoon, and the bo'sun called us to make some sort of a meal, leaving one man to watch the hulk, perchance they should signal to us. For we had missed our dinner in the excitement of the day's work, and were come now to feel the lack of it. Then, in the midst of it, the man upon the lookout cried out that they were signalling to us from the ship, and, at that, we ran all of us to see what they desired, and so, by the code which we had arranged between us, we found that they waited for us to haul upon the small line. This did we, and made out presently that we were hauling something across the weed, of a very fair bulk, at which we warmed to our work, guessing that it was the bread which they had promised us, and so it proved, and done up with great neatness in a long roll of tarpaulin, which had been wrapped around both the loaves and the rope, and lashed very securely at the ends, thus producing a taper shape convenient for passing over the weed without catching. Now, when we came to open this parcel, we discovered that my hint had taken very sound effect; for there were in the parcel, besides the loaves, a boiled ham, a Dutch cheese, two bottles of port well padded from breakage, and four pounds of tobacco in plugs. And at this coming of good things, we stood all of us upon the edge of the hill, and waved our thanks to those in the ship, they waving back in all good will, and after that we went back to our meal, at which we sampled the new victuals with very lusty appetites.

There was in the parcel, one other matter, a letter, most neatly indited, as had been the former epistles, in a feminine handwriting, so that I guessed they had one of the women to be their scribe. This epistle answered some of my queries, and, in particular, I remember that it informed me as to the probable cause of the strange crying which preceded the attack by the weed men, saying that on each occasion when they in the ship had suffered their attacks, there had been always this same crying, being evidently a summoning call or signal to the attack, though how given, the writer had not discovered; for the weed devils – this being how they in the ship spoke always of them – made never a sound when attacking, not even when wounded to the death, and, indeed, I may say here, that we never learnt the way in which that lonesome sobbing was produced, nor, indeed, did they, or we, discover more than the merest tithe of the mysteries which that great continent of weed holds in its silence.

Another matter to which I had referred was the consistent blowing of the wind from one quarter, and this the writer told me happened for as much as six months in the year, keeping up a very steady strength. A further thing there was which gave me much interest; it was that the ship had not been always where we had discovered her; for at one time they had been so far within the weed, that they could scarce discern the open sea upon the far horizon; but that at times the weed opened in great gulfs that went yawning through the continent for scores of miles, and in this way the shape and coasts of the weed were being constantly altered; these happenings being for the most part at the change of the wind.

And much more there was that they told us then and afterwards, how that they dried weed for their fuel, and how the rains, which fell with great heaviness at certain periods, supplied them with fresh water; though, at times, running short, they had learnt to distil sufficient for their needs until the next rains.

Now, near to the end of the epistle, there came some news of their present actions, and thus we learnt that they in the ship were busy at staying the stump of the mizzen-mast, this being the one to which they proposed to attach the big rope, taking it through a great iron-bound snatch-block, secured to the head of the stump, and then down to the mizzen-capstan, by which, and a strong tackle, they would be able to heave the line so taut as was needful.

Now, having finished our meal, the bo'sun took out the lint, bandages and ointment, which they had sent us from the hulk, and proceeded to dress our hurts, beginning with him who had lost his fingers, which, happily, were making a very healthy heal. And afterwards we went all of us to the edge of the cliff, and sent back the look-out to fill such crevices in his stomach as remained yet empty; for we had passed him already some sound hunks of the bread and ham and cheese, to eat whilst he kept watch, and so he had suffered no great harm.

It may have been near an hour after this, that the bo'sun pointed out to me that they in the ship had commenced to heave upon the great rope, and so I perceived, and stood watching it; for I knew that the bo'sun had some anxiety as to whether it would take-up sufficiently clear of the weed to allow those in the ship to be hauled along it, free from molestation by the great devil-fish.

Presently, as the evening began to draw on, the bo'sun bade us go and build our fires about the hilltop, and this we did, after which we returned to learn how the rope was lifting, and now we perceived that it had come clear of the weed, at which we felt mightily rejoiced, and waved encouragement, chance there might be any who watched us from the hulk. Yet, though the rope was up clear of the weed, the bight of it had to rise to a much greater height, or ever it would do for the purpose for which we intended it, and already it suffered a vast strain, as I discovered by placing my hand upon it; for, even to lift the slack of so great a length of line meant the stress of some tonnes. And later I saw that the bo'sun was growing anxious; for he went over to the rock around which he had made fast the rope, and examined the knots, and those places where he had parcelled it, and after that he walked to the place where it went over the edge of the cliff, and here he made a further scrutiny; but came back presently, seeming not dissatisfied.

Then, in a while, the darkness came down upon us, and we lighted our fires and prepared for the night, having the watches arranged as on the preceding nights.

Chapter XV
Aboard the Hulk

NOW WHEN IT CAME to my watch, the which I took in company with the big seaman, the moon had not yet risen, and all the island was vastly dark, save the hill-top, from which the fires blazed in a score of places, and very busy they kept us, supplying them with fuel. Then, when maybe the half of our watch had passed, the big seaman, who had been to feed the fires upon the weed side of the hill-top, came across to me, and bade me come and put my hand upon the lesser rope; for that he thought they in the ship were anxious to haul it in so that they might send some message across to us. At his words, I asked him very anxiously whether he had perceived them waving a light, the which we had arranged to be our method of signalling in the night, in the event of such being needful; but, to this, he said that he had seen naught; and, by now, having come near the edge of the cliff, I could see for myself, and so perceived that there was none signalling to us from the hulk. Yet, to please the fellow, I put my hand upon the line, which we had made fast in the evening to a large piece of rock, and so, immediately, I discovered that something was pulling upon it, hauling and then slackening, so that it occurred to me that the people in the vessel might be indeed wishful to send us some message, and at that, to make sure, I ran to the nearest fire, and, lighting a tuft of weed, waved it thrice; but there came not any answering signal from those in the ship, and at that I went back to feel at the rope, to assure myself that it had not been the pluck of the wind upon it; but I found that it was something very different from the wind, something that plucked with all the sharpness of a hooked fish, only that it had been a mighty great fish to have given such tugs, and so I knew that some vile thing out in the darkness of the weed was fast to the rope, and at this there came the fear that it might break it, and then a second thought that something might be climbing up to us along the rope, and so I bade the big seaman stand ready with his great cutlass, whilst I ran and waked the bo'sun. And this I did, and explained to him how that something meddled with the lesser rope, so that he came immediately to see for himself how this might be, and when he had put his hand upon it, he bade me go and call the rest of the men, and let them stand round by the fires; for that there was something abroad in the night, and we might be in danger of attack; but he and the big seaman stayed by the end of the rope, watching, so far as the darkness would allow, and ever and anon feeling the tension upon it.

Then, suddenly, it came to the bo'sun to look to the second line, and he ran, cursing himself for his thoughtlessness; but because of its greater weight and tension, he could not discover for certain whether anything meddled with it or not; yet he stayed by it, arguing that if aught touched the smaller rope then might something do likewise with the greater, only that the small line lay along the weed, whilst the greater one had been some feet above it when the darkness had fallen over us, and so might be free from any prowling creatures.

And thus, maybe, an hour passed, and we kept watch and tended the fires, going from one to another, and, presently, coming to that one which was nearest to the bo'sun, I went over to him, intending to pass a few minutes in talk; but as I drew nigh to him, I chanced to place my hand upon the big rope, and at that I exclaimed in surprise; for it had become much slacker than when last I had felt it in the evening, and I asked the bo'sun whether he had noticed it, whereat he felt the rope, and was almost more amazed than I had been; for when last he had touched it, it had been taut, and humming in the wind. Now, upon this discovery, he was in much fear that something had bitten through it, and called to the men to come all of them and pull upon the rope, so that he might discover whether it was indeed parted; but when they came and hauled upon it, they were unable to gather in any of it, whereat we felt all of us mightily relieved in our minds; though still unable to come at the cause of its sudden slackness.

And so, a while later, there rose the moon, and we were able to examine the island and the water between it and the weed-continent, to see whether there was anything stirring; yet neither in the valley, nor on the faces of the cliffs, nor in the open water could we perceive aught living, and as for anything among the weed, it was small use trying to discover it among all that shaggy blackness. And now, being assured that nothing was coming at us, and that, so far as our eyes could pierce, there climbed nothing upon the ropes, the bo'sun bade us get turned-in, all except those whose time it was to watch. Yet, before I went into the tent, I made a careful examination of the big rope, the which did also the bo'sun, but could perceive no cause for its slackness; though this was quite apparent in the moonlight, the rope going down with greater abruptness than it had done in the evening. And so we could but conceive that they in the hulk had slacked it for some reason; and after that we went to the tent and a further spell of sleep.

In the early morning we were waked by one of the watchmen, coming into the tent to call the bo'sun; for it appeared that the hulk had moved in the night, so that its stern was now pointed somewhat towards the island. At this news, we ran all of us from the tent to the edge of the hill, and found it to be indeed as the man had said, and now I understood the reason of that sudden slackening of the rope; for, after withstanding the stress upon it for some hours, the vessel had at last yielded, and slewed its stern towards us, moving also to some extent bodily in our direction.

And now we discovered that a man in the look-out place in the top of the structure was waving a welcome to us, at which we waved back, and then the bo'sun bade me haste and write a note to know whether it seemed to them likely that they might be able to heave the ship clear of the weed, and this I did, greatly excited within myself at this new thought, as, indeed, was the bo'sun himself and the rest of the men. For could they do this, then how easily solved were every problem of coming to our own country. But it seemed too good a thing to have come true, and yet I could but hope. And so, when my letter was completed, we put it up in the little oilskin bag, and signalled to those in the ship to haul in upon the line. Yet, when they went to haul, there came a mighty splather amid the weed, and they seemed unable to gather in any of the slack, and then, after a certain pause, I saw the man in the look-out point something, and immediately afterwards there belched out in front of him a little puff of smoke, and, presently, I caught the report of a musket, so that I knew that he was firing at something in the weed. He fired again, and yet once more, and after that they were able to haul in upon the line, and so I perceived that his fire had proved effectual; yet we had no knowledge of the thing at which he had discharged his weapon.

Now, presently, they signalled to us to draw back the line, the which we could do only with great difficulty, and then the man in the top of the super-structure signed to us to vast hauling, which we did, whereupon he began to fire again into the weed; though with what effect we could not perceive. Then, in a while he signalled to us to haul again, and now the rope came more easily; yet still with much labour, and a commotion in the weed over which it lay and, in places, sank. And so, at last, as it cleared the weed because of the lift of the cliff, we saw that a great crab had clutched it, and that we hauled it towards us; for the creature had too much obstinacy to let go.

Perceiving this, and fearing that the great claws of the crab might divide the rope, the bo'sun caught up one of the men's lances, and ran to the cliff edge, calling to us to pull in gently, and put no more strain upon the line than need be. And so, hauling with great steadiness, we brought the monster near to the edge of the hill, and there, at a wave from the bo'sun, stayed our pulling. Then he raised the spear, and smote at the creature's eyes, as he had done on a previous occasion, and immediately it loosed its hold, and fell with a mighty splash into the water at the foot of the cliff. Then the bo'sun bade us haul in the rest of the rope, until we should come to the packet, and, in the meantime, he examined the line to see whether it had suffered harm through the mandibles of the crab; yet, beyond a little chafe, it was quite sound.

And so we came to the letter, which I opened and read, finding it to be written in the same feminine hand which had indited the others. From it we gathered that the ship had burst through a very thick mass of the weed which had compacted itself about her, and that the second mate, who was the only officer remaining to them, thought there might be good chance to heave the vessel out; though it would have to be done with great slowness, so as to allow the weed to part gradually, otherwise the ship would but act as a gigantic rake to gather up weed before it, and so form its own barrier to clear water. And after this there were kind wishes and hopes that we had spent a good night, the which I took to be prompted by the feminine heart of the writer, and after that I fell to wondering whether it was the captain's wife who acted as scribe. Then I was waked from my pondering, by one of the men crying out that they in the ship had commenced to heave again upon the big rope, and, for a time, I stood and watched it rise slowly, as it came to tautness.

I had stood there awhile, watching the rope, when, suddenly, there came a commotion amid the weed, about two-thirds of the way to the ship, and now I saw that the rope had freed itself from the weed, and clutching it, were, maybe, a score of giant crabs. At this sight, some of the men cried out their astonishment, and then we saw that there had come a number of men into the look-out place in the top of the superstructure, and, immediately, they opened a very brisk fire upon the creatures, and so, by ones and twos they fell back into the weed, and after that, the men in the hulk resumed their heaving, and so, in a while, had the rope some feet clear of the surface.

Now, having tautened the rope so much as they thought proper, they left it to have its due effect upon the ship, and proceeded to attach a great block to it; then they signalled to us to slack away on the little rope until they had the middle part of it, and this they hitched around the neck of the block, and to the eye in the strop of the block they attached a bo'sun's chair, and so they had ready a carrier, and by this means we were able to haul stuff to and from the hulk without having to drag it across the surface of the weed; being, indeed, the fashion in which we had intended to haul ashore the people in the ship. But now we had the bigger project of salvaging the ship herself, and, further, the big rope, which acted as support for the carrier, was not yet of a sufficient height above the weed-continent for it to be safe to attempt to bring any ashore by such means; and now that we had hopes of saving the ship, we did not intend to risk parting the big rope, by trying to attain such a degree of tautness as would have been necessary at this time to have raised its bight to the desired height.

Now, presently, the bo'sun called out to one of the men to make breakfast, and when it was ready we came to it, leaving the man with the wounded arm to keep watch; then when we had made an end, he sent him, that had lost his fingers, to keep a look-out whilst the other came to the fire and ate his breakfast. And in the meanwhile, the bo'sun took us down to collect weed and reeds for the night, and so we spent the greater part of the morning, and when we had made an end of this, we returned to the top of the hill, to discover how matters were going forward; thus we found, from the one at the look-out, that they, in the hulk, had been obliged to heave twice upon the big rope to keep it off the weed, and by this we knew that the ship was indeed making a slow sternway towards the island – slipping steadily through the weed, and as we looked at her, it seemed almost that we could perceive that she was nearer; but this was no more than imagination; for, at most, she could not have moved more than some odd fathoms. Yet it cheered us greatly, so that we waved our congratulations to the man who stood in the lookout in the superstructure, and he waved back.

Later, we made dinner, and afterwards had a very comfortable smoke, and then the bo'sun attended to our various hurts. And so through the afternoon we sat about upon the crest of the hill overlooking the hulk, and thrice had they in the ship to heave upon the big rope, and by evening they had made near thirty fathoms towards the island, the which they told us in reply to a query which the bo'sun desired me to send them, several messages having passed between us in the course of the afternoon, so that we had the carrier upon our side. Further than this, they explained that they would tend the rope during the night, so that the strain would be kept up, and, more, this would keep the ropes off the weed.

And so, the night coming down upon us, the bo'sun bade us light the fires about the top of the hill, the same having been laid earlier in the day, and thus, our supper having been dispatched, we prepared for the night. And all through it there burned lights aboard the hulk, the which proved very companionable to us in our times of watching; and so, at last came the morning, the darkness having passed without event. And now, to our huge pleasure, we discovered that the ship had made great progress in the night; being now so much nearer that none could suppose it a matter of imagination; for she must have moved nigh sixty fathoms nearer to the island, so that now we seemed able almost to recognise the face of the man in the look-out; and many things about the hulk we saw with greater clearness, so that we scanned her with a fresh interest. Then the man in the look-out waved a morning greeting to us, the which we returned very heartily, and, even as we did so, there came a second figure beside the man, and waved some white matter, perchance a handkerchief, which is like enough, seeing that it was a woman, and at that, we took off our head coverings, all of us, and shook them at her, and after this we went to our breakfast; having finished which, the bo'sun dressed our hurts, and then, setting the man, who had lost his fingers, to watch, he took the rest of us, excepting him that was bitten in the arm, down to collect fuel, and so the time passed until near dinner.

When we returned to the hill-top, the man upon the look-out told us that they in the ship had heaved not less than four separate times upon the big rope, the which, indeed, they were doing at that present minute; and it was very plain to see that the ship had come nearer even during the short space of the morning. Now, when they had made an end of tautening the rope, I perceived that it was, at last, well clear of the weed through all its length, being at its lowest part nigh twenty feet above the surface, and, at that, a sudden thought came to me which sent me hastily to the bo'sun; for it had occurred to me that there existed no reason why we should not pay a visit to those aboard the hulk. But when I put the matter to him, he shook his head, and, for awhile, stood out against my desire; but, presently, having examined the rope, and considering that I was the lightest of any in the island, he consented, and at that I ran to the carrier which had been hauled across to our side, and got me into the chair. Now, the men, so soon as they perceived my intention, applauded me very heartily, desiring to follow; but the bo'sun bade them be silent, and, after that, he lashed me into the chair, with his own hands, and then signalled to those in the ship to haul upon the small rope; he, in the meanwhile, checking my descent towards the weeds, by means of our end of the hauling-line.

And so, presently, I had come to the lowest part, where the bight of the rope dipped downward in a bow towards the weed, and rose again to the mizzenmast of the hulk. Here I looked downward with somewhat fearful eyes; for my weight on the rope made it sag somewhat lower than seemed to me comfortable, and I had a very lively recollection of some of the horrors which that quiet surface hid. Yet I was not long in this place; for they in the ship, perceiving how the rope let me nearer to the weed than was safe, pulled very heartily upon the hauling-line, and so I came quickly to the hulk.

Now, as I drew nigh to the ship, the men crowded upon a little platform which they had built in the superstructure somewhat below the broken head of the mizzen, and here they received me with loud cheers and very open arms, and were so eager to get me out of the bo'sun's chair, that they cut the lashings, being too impatient to cast them loose. Then they led me down to the deck, and here, before I had knowledge of aught else, a very buxom woman took me into her arms, kissing me right heartily, at which I was greatly taken aback; but the men about me did naught but laugh, and so, in a minute, she loosed me, and there I stood, not knowing whether to feel like a fool or a hero; but inclining rather to the latter. Then, at this minute, there came a second woman, who bowed to me in a manner most formal, so that we might have been met in some fashionable gathering, rather than in a cast-away hulk in the lonesomeness and terror of that weed-choked sea; and at her coming all the mirth of the men died out of them, and they became very sober, whilst the buxom woman went backward for a piece, and seemed somewhat abashed. Now, at all this, I was greatly puzzled, and looked from one to another to learn what it might mean; but in the same moment the woman bowed again, and said something in a low voice touching the weather, and after that she raised her glance to my face, so that I saw her eyes, and they were so strange and full of melancholy, that I knew on the instant why she spoke and acted in so unmeaning a way; for the poor creature was out of her mind, and when I learnt afterwards that she was the captain's wife, and had seen him die in the arms of a mighty devil-fish, I grew to understand how she had come to such a pass.

Now for a minute after I had discovered the woman's madness, I was so taken aback as to be unable to answer her remark; but for this there appeared no necessity; for she turned away and went aft towards the saloon stairway, which stood open, and here she was met by a maid very bonny and fair, who led her tenderly down from my sight. Yet, in a minute, this same maid appeared, and ran along the decks to me, and caught my two hands, and shook them, and looked up at me with such roguish, playful eyes, that she warmed my heart, which had been strangely chilled by the greeting of the poor mad woman. And she said many hearty things regarding my courage, to which I knew in my heart I had no claim; but I let her run on, and so, presently, coming more to possession of herself, she discovered that she was still holding my hands, the which, indeed, I had been conscious of the while with a very great pleasure; but at her discovery she dropped them with haste, and stood back from me a space, and so there came a little coolness into her talk: yet this lasted not long; for we were both of us young, and, I think, even thus early we attracted one the other; though, apart from this, there was so much that we desired each to learn, that we could not but talk freely, asking question for question, and giving answer for answer. And thus a time passed, in which the men left us alone, and went presently to the capstan, about which they had taken the big rope, and at this they toiled awhile; for already the ship had moved sufficiently to let the line fall slack.

Presently, the maid, whom I had learnt was niece to the captain's wife, and named Mary Madison, proposed to take me the round of the ship, to which proposal I agreed very willingly; but first I stopped to examine the mizzen stump, and the manner in which the people of the ship had stayed it, the which they had done very cunningly, and I noted how that they had removed some of the superstructure from about the head of the mast, so as to allow passage for the rope, without putting a strain upon the superstructure itself. Then when I had made an end upon the poop, she led me down on to the main-deck, and here I was very greatly impressed by the prodigious size of the structure which they had built about the hulk, and the skill with which it had been carried out, the supports crossing from side to side and to the decks in a manner calculated to give great solidity to that which they upheld. Yet, I was very greatly puzzled to know where they had gotten a sufficiency of timber to make so large a matter; but upon this point she satisfied me by explaining that they had taken up the 'tween decks, and used all such bulkheads as they could spare, and, further, that there had been a good deal among the dunnage which had proved usable.

And so we came at last to the galley, and here I discovered the buxom woman to be installed as cook, and there were in with her a couple of fine children, one of whom I guessed to be a boy of maybe some five years, and the second a girl, scarce able to do more than toddle. At this I turned and asked Mistress Madison whether these were her cousins; but in the next moment I remembered that they could not be; for, as I knew, the captain had been dead some seven years; yet it was the woman in the galley who answered my question; for she turned and, with something of a red face, informed me that they were hers, at which I felt some surprise; but supposed that she had taken passage in the ship with her husband; yet in this I was not correct; for she proceeded to explain that, thinking they were cut off from the world for the rest of this life, and falling very fond of the carpenter, they had made it up together to make a sort of marriage, and had gotten the second mate to read the service over them. She told me then, how that she had taken passage with her mistress, the captain's wife, to help her with her niece, who had been but a child when the ship sailed; for she had been very attached to them both, and they to her. And so she came to an end of her story, expressing a hope that she had done no wrong by her marriage, as none had been intended. And to this I made answer, assuring her that no decent-minded man could think the worse of her; but that I, for my part, thought rather the better, seeing that I liked the pluck which she had shown. At that she cast down the soup ladle, which she had in her fist, and came towards me, wiping her hands; but I gave back, for I shamed to be hugged again, and before Mistress Mary Madison, and at that she came to a stop and laughed very heartily; but, all the same, called down a very warm blessing upon my head; for which I had no cause to feel the worse. And so I passed on with the captain's niece.

Presently, having made the round of the hulk, we came aft again to the poop, and discovered that they were heaving once more upon the big rope, the which was very heartening, proving, as it did, that the ship was still a-move. And so, a little later, the girl left me, having to attend to her aunt. Now whilst she was gone, the men came all about me, desiring news of the world beyond the weed-continent, and so for the next hour I was kept very busy, answering their questions. Then the second mate called out to them to take another heave upon the rope, and at that they turned to the capstan, and I with them, and so we hove it taut again, after which they got about me once more, questioning; for so much seemed to have happened in the seven years in which they had been imprisoned. And then, after a while, I turned-to and questioned them on such points as I had neglected to ask Mistress Madison, and they discovered to me their terror and sickness of the weed-continent, its desolation and horror, and the dread which had beset them at the thought that they should all of them come to their ends without sight of their homes and countrymen.

Now, about this time, I became conscious that I had grown very empty; for I had come off to the hulk before we had made our dinner, and had been in such interest since, that the thought of food had escaped me; for I had seen none eating in the hulk, they, without doubt, having dined earlier than my coming. But now, being made aware of my state by the grumbling of my stomach, I inquired whether there was any food to be had at such a time, and, at that, one of the men ran to tell the woman in the galley that I had missed my dinner, at which she made much ado, and set-to and prepared me a very good meal, which she carried aft and set out for me in the saloon, and after that she sent me down to it.

Presently, when I had come near to being comfortable, there chanced a lightsome step upon the floor behind me, and, turning, I discovered that Mistress Madison was surveying me with a roguish and somewhat amused air. At that, I got hastily to my feet; but she bade me sit down, and therewith she took a seat opposite, and so bantered me with a gentle playfulness that was not displeasing to me, and at which I played so good a second as I had ability. Later, I fell to questioning her, and, among other matters, discovered that it was she who acted as scribe for the people in the hulk, at which I told her that I had done likewise for those on the island. After that, our talk became somewhat personal, and I learnt that she was near on to nineteen years of age, whereat I told her that I had passed my twenty-third. And so we chatted on, until, presently, it occurred to me that I had better be preparing to return to the island, and I rose to my feet with this intention; yet feeling that I had been very much happier to have stayed, the which I thought, for a moment, had not been displeasing to her, and this I imagined, noting somewhat in her eyes when I made mention that I must be gone. Yet it may be that I flattered myself.

Now when I came out on deck, they were busied again in heaving taut the rope, and, until they had made an end, Mistress Madison and I filled the time with such chatter as is wholesome between a man and maid who have not long met, yet find one another pleasing company. Then, when at last the rope was taut, I went up to the mizzen staging, and climbed into the chair, after which some of the men lashed me in very securely. Yet when they gave the signal to haul me to the island, there came for awhile no response, and then signs that we could not understand; but no movement to haul me across the weed. At that, they unlashed me from the chair, bidding me get out, whilst they sent a message to discover what might be wrong. And this they did, and, presently, there came back word that the big rope had stranded upon the edge of the cliff, and that they must slacken it somewhat at once, the which they did, with many expressions of dismay. And so, maybe an hour passed, during which we watched the men working at the rope, just where it came down over the edge of the hill, and Mistress Madison stood with us and watched; for it was very terrible, this sudden thought of failure (though it were but temporary) when they were so near to success. Yet, at last there came a signal from the island for us to loose the hauling-line, the which we did, allowing them to haul across the carrier, and so, in a little while, they signalled back to us to pull in, which, having done, we found a letter in the bag lashed to the carrier, in which the bo'sun made it plain that he had strengthened the rope, and placed fresh chafing gear about it, so that he thought it would be so safe as ever to heave upon; but to put it to a less strain. Yet he refused to allow me to venture across upon it, saying that I must stay in the ship until we were clear of the weed; for if the rope had stranded in one place, then had it been so cruelly tested that there might be some other points at which it was ready to give. And this final note of the bo'sun's made us all very serious; for, indeed, it seemed possible that it was as he suggested; yet they reassured themselves by pointing out that, like enough, it had been the chafe upon the cliff edge which had frayed the strand, so that it had been weakened before it parted; but I, remembering the chafing gear which the bo'sun had put about it in the first instance, felt not so sure; yet I would not add to their anxieties.

And so it came about that I was compelled to spend the night in the hulk; but, as I followed Mistress Madison into the big saloon, I felt no regret, and had near forgotten already my anxiety regarding the rope.

And out on deck there sounded most cheerily the clack of the capstan.

Chapter XVI
Freed

NOW, WHEN MISTRESS MADISON had seated herself, she invited me to do likewise, after which we fell into talk, first touching upon the matter of the stranding of the rope, about which I hastened to assure her, and later to other things, and so, as is natural enough with a man and maid, to ourselves, and here we were very content to let it remain.

Presently, the second mate came in with a note from the bo'sun, which he laid upon the table for the girl to read, the which she beckoned me to do also, and so I discovered that it was a suggestion, written very rudely and ill-spelt, that they should send us a quantity of reeds from the island, with which we might be able to ease the weed somewhat from around the stern of the hulk, thus aiding her progress. And to this the second mate desired the girl to write a reply, saying that we should be very happy for the reeds, and would endeavour to act upon his hint, and this Mistress Madison did, after which she passed the letter to me, perchance I desired to send any message. Yet I had naught that I wished to say, and so handed it back, with a word of thanks, and, at once, she gave it to the second mate, who went, forthwith, and dispatched it.

Later, the stout woman from the galley came aft to set out the table, which occupied the centre of the saloon, and whilst she was at this, she asked for information on many things, being very free and unaffected in her speech, and seeming with less of deference to my companion, than a certain motherliness; for it was very plain that she loved Mistress Madison, and in this my heart did not blame her. Further, it was plain to me that the girl had a very warm affection for her old nurse, which was but natural, seeing that the old woman had cared for her through all the past years, besides being companion to her, and a good and cheerful one, as I could guess.

Now awhile I passed in answering the buxom woman's questions, and odd times such occasional ones as were slipped in by Mistress Madison; and then, suddenly there came the clatter of men's feet overhead, and, later, the thud of something being cast down upon the deck, and so we knew that the reeds had come. At that, Mistress Madison cried out that we should go and watch the men try them upon the weed; for that if they proved of use in easing that which lay in our path, then should we come the more speedily to the clear water, and this without the need of putting so great a strain upon the hawser, as had been the case hitherto.

When we came to the poop, we found the men removing a portion of the superstructure over the stern, and after that they took some of the stronger reeds, and proceeded to work at the weed that stretched away in a line with our taffrail. Yet that they anticipated danger, I perceived; for there stood by them two of the men and the second mate, all armed with muskets, and these three kept a very strict watch upon the weed, knowing, through much experience of its terrors, how that there might be a need for their weapons at any moment. And so a while passed, and it was plain that the men's work upon the weed was having effect; for the rope grew slack visibly, and those at the capstan had all that they could do, taking fleet and fleet with the tackle, to keep it anywhere near to tautness, and so, perceiving that they were kept so hard at it, I ran to give a hand, the which did Mistress Madison, pushing upon the capstan-bars right merrily and with heartiness. And thus a while passed, and the evening began to come down upon the lonesomeness of the weed-continent. Then there appeared the buxom woman, and bade us come to our suppers, and her manner of addressing the two of us was the manner of one who might have mothered us; but Mistress Madison cried out to her to wait, that we had found work to do, and at that the big woman laughed, and came towards us threateningly, as though intending to remove us hence by force.

And now, at this moment, there came a sudden interruption which checked our merriment; for, abruptly, there sounded the report of a musket in the stern, and then came shouts, and the noise of the two other weapons, seeming like thunder, being pent by the over-arching superstructure. And, directly, the men about the taffrail gave back, running here and there, and so I saw that great arms had come all about the opening which they had made in the superstructure, and two of these flickered in-board, searching hither and thither; but the stout woman took a man near to her, and thrust him out of danger, and after that, she caught Mistress Madison up in her big arms, and ran down on to the main-deck with her, and all this before I had come to a full knowledge of our danger. But now I perceived that I should do well to get further back from the stern, the which I did with haste, and, coming to a safe position, I stood and stared at the huge creature, its great arms, vague in the growing dusk, writhing about in vain search for a victim. Then returned the second mate, having been for more weapons, and now I observed that he armed all the men, and had brought up a spare musket for my use, and so we commenced, all of us, to fire at the monster, whereat it began to lash about most furiously, and so, after some minutes, it slipped away from the opening and slid down into the weed. Upon that several of the men rushed to replace those parts of the superstructure which had been removed, and I with them; yet there were sufficient for the job, so that I had no need to do aught; thus, before they had made up the opening, I had been given chance to look out upon the weed, and so discovered that all the surface which lay between our stern and the island, was moving in vast ripples, as though mighty fish were swimming beneath it, and then, just before the men put back the last of the great panels, I saw the weed all tossed up like to a vast pot a-boil, and then a vague glimpse of thousands of monstrous arms that filled the air, and came towards the ship.

And then the men had the panel back in its place, and were hasting to drive the supporting struts into their positions. And when this was done, we stood awhile and listened; but there came no sound above that of the wail of the wind across the extent of the weed-continent. And at that, I turned to the men, asking how it was that I could hear no sounds of the creatures attacking us, and so they took me up into the look-out place, and from there I stared down at the weed; but it was without movement, save for the stirring of the wind, and there was nowhere any sign of the devil-fish. Then, seeing me amazed, they told me how that anything which moved the weed seemed to draw them from all parts; but that they seldom touched the hulk unless there was something visible to them which had movement. Yet, as they went on to explain, there would be hundreds and hundreds of them lying all about the ship, hiding in the weed; but that if we took care not to show ourselves within their reach, they would have gone most of them by the morning. And this the men told me in a very matter-of-fact way; for they had become inured to such happenings.

Presently, I heard Mistress Madison calling to me by name, and so descended out of the growing darkness, to the interior of the superstructure, and here they had lit a number of rude slush-lamps, the oil for which, as I learned later, they obtained from a certain fish which haunted the sea, beneath the weed, in very large schools, and took near any sort of bait with great readiness. And so, when I had climbed down into the light, I found the girl waiting for me to come to supper, for which I discovered myself to be in a mightily agreeable humour.

Presently, having made an end of eating, she leaned back in her seat and commenced once more to bait me in her playful manner, the which appeared to afford her much pleasure, and in which I joined with no less, and so we fell presently to more earnest talk, and in this wise we passed a great space of the evening. Then there came to her a sudden idea, and what must she do but propose that we should climb to the lookout, and to this I agreed with a very happy willingness. And to the lookout we went. Now when we had come there, I perceived her reason for this freak; for away in the night, astern the hulk, there blazed half-way between the heaven and the sea, a mighty glow, and suddenly, as I stared, being dumb with admiration and surprise, I knew that it was the blaze of our fires upon the crown of the bigger hill; for, all the hill being in shadow, and hidden by the darkness, there showed only the glow of the fires, hung, as it were, in the void, and a very striking and beautiful spectacle it was. Then, as I watched, there came, abruptly a figure into view upon the edge of the glow, showing black and minute, and this I knew to be one of the men come to the edge of the hill to take a look at the hulk, or test the strain on the hawser. Now, upon my expressing admiration of the sight to Mistress Madison, she seemed greatly pleased, and told me that she had been up many times in the darkness to view it. And after that we went down again into the interior of the superstructure, and here the men were taking a further heave upon the big rope, before settling the watches for the night, the which they managed, by having one man at a time to keep awake and call the rest whenever the hawser grew slack.

Later Mistress Madison showed me where I was to sleep, and so, having bid one another a very warm good-night, we parted, she going to see that her aunt was comfortable, and I out on to the main-deck to have a chat with the man on watch. In this way, I passed the time until midnight, and in that while we had been forced to call the men thrice to heave upon the hawser, so quickly had the ship begun to make way through the weed. Then, having grown sleepy, I said goodnight, and went to my berth, and so had my first sleep upon a mattress, for some weeks.

Now when the morning was come, I waked, hearing Mistress Madison calling upon me from the other side of my door, and rating me very saucily for a lie-a-bed, and at that I made good speed at dressing, and came quickly into the saloon, where she had ready a breakfast that made me glad I had waked. But first, before she would do aught else, she had me out to the lookout place, running up before me most merrily and singing in the fullness of her glee, and so, when I had come to the top of the superstructure, I perceived that she had very good reason for so much merriment, and the sight which came to my eyes, gladdened me most mightily, yet at the same time filling me with a great amazement; for, behold! in the course of that one night, we had made near unto two hundred fathoms across the weed, being now, with what we had made previously, no more than some thirty fathoms in from the edge of the weed. And there stood Mistress Madison beside me, doing somewhat of a dainty step-dance upon the flooring of the look-out, and singing a quaint old lilt that I had not heard that dozen years, and this little thing, I think, brought back more clearly to me than aught else how that this winsome maid had been lost to the world for so many years, having been scarce of the age of twelve when the ship had been lost in the weed-continent.

Then, as I turned to make some remark, being filled with many feelings, there came a hail, from far above in the air, as it might be, and, looking up, I discovered the man upon the hill to be standing along the edge, and waving to us, and now I perceived how that the hill towered a very great way above us, seeming, as it were, to overhang the hulk though we were yet some seventy fathoms distant from the sheer sweep of its nearer precipice. And so, having waved back our greeting, we made down to breakfast, and, having come to the saloon, set-to upon the good victuals, and did very sound justice thereto.

Presently, having made an end of eating, and hearing the clack of the capstan-pawls, we hurried out on deck, and put our hands upon the bars, intending to join in that last heave which should bring the ship free out of her long captivity, and so for a time we moved round about the capstan, and I glanced at the girl beside me; for she had become very solemn, and indeed it was a strange and solemn time for her; for she, who had dreamed of the world as her childish eyes had seen it, was now, after many hopeless years, to go forth once more to it – to live in it, and to learn how much had been dreams, and how much real; and with all these thoughts I credited her; for they seemed such as would have come to me at such a time, and, presently, I made some blundering effort to show to her that I had understanding of the tumult which possessed her, and at that she smiled up at me with a sudden queer flash of sadness and merriment, and our glances met, and I saw something in hers, which was but newborn, and though I was but a young man, my heart interpreted it for me, and I was all hot suddenly with the pain and sweet delight of this new thing; for I had not dared to think upon that which already my heart had made bold to whisper to me, so that even thus soon I was miserable out of her presence. Then she looked downward at her hands upon the bar; and, in the same instant, there came a loud, abrupt cry from the second mate, to vast heaving, and at that all the men pulled out their bars and cast them upon the deck, and ran, shouting, to the ladder that led to the look-out, and we followed, and so came to the top, and discovered that at last the ship was clear of the weed, and floating in the open water between it and the island.

Now at the discovery that the hulk was free, the men commenced to cheer and shout in a very wild fashion, as, indeed, is no cause for wonder, and we cheered with them. Then, suddenly, in the midst of our shouting, Mistress Madison plucked me by the sleeve and pointed to the end of the island where the foot of the bigger hill jutted out in a great spur, and now I perceived a boat, coming round into view, and in another moment I saw that the bo'sun stood in the stern, steering; thus I knew that he must have finished repairing her whilst I had been on the hulk. By this, the men about us had discovered the nearness of the boat, and commenced shouting afresh, and they ran down, and to the bows of the vessel, and got ready a rope to cast. Now when the boat came near, the men in her scanned us very curiously, but the bo'sun took off his head-gear, with a clumsy grace that well became him; at which Mistress Madison smiled very kindly upon him, and, after that, she told me with great frankness that he pleased her, and, more, that she had never seen so great a man, which was not strange seeing that she had seen but few since she had come to years when men become of interest to a maid.

After saluting us the bo'sun called out to the second mate that he would tow us round to the far side of the island, and to this the officer agreed, being, I surmised, by no means sorry to put some solid matter between himself and the desolation of the great weed-continent; and so, having loosed the hawser, which fell from the hill-top with a prodigious splash, we had the boat head, towing. In this wise we opened out, presently, the end of the hill; but feeling now the force of the breeze, we bent a kedge to the hawser, and, the bo'sun carrying it seawards, we warped ourselves to windward of the island, and here, in forty fathoms, we vast heaving, and rode to the kedge.

Now when this was accomplished they called to our men to come aboard, and this they did, and spent all of that day in talk and eating; for those in the ship could scarce make enough of our fellows. And then, when it had come to night, they replaced that part of the superstructure which they had removed from about the head of the mizzen-stump, and so, all being secure, each one turned-in and had a full night's rest, of the which, indeed, many of them stood in sore need.

The following morning, the second mate had a consultation with the bo'sun, after which he gave the order to commence upon the removal of the great superstructure, and to this each one of us set himself with vigour. Yet it was a work requiring some time, and near five days had passed before we had the ship stripped clear. When this had been accomplished, there came a busy time of routing out various matter of which we should have need in jury rigging her; for they had been so long in disuse, that none remembered where to look for them. At this a day and a half was spent, and after that we set-to about fitting her with such jury-masts as we could manage from our material.

Now, after the ship had been dismasted, all those seven years gone, the crew had been able to save many of her spars, these having remained attached to her, through their inability to cut away all of the gear; and though this had put them in sore peril at the time, of being sent to the bottom with a hole in their side, yet now had they every reason to be thankful; for, by this accident, we had now a foreyard, a topsail-yard, a main t'gallant-yard, and the fore-topmast. They had saved more than these; but had made use of the smaller spars to shore up the superstructure, sawing them into lengths for that purpose. Apart from such spars as they had managed to secure, they had a spare topmast lashed along under the larboard bulwarks, and a spare t'gallant and royal mast lying along the starboard side.

Now, the second mate and the bo'sun set the carpenter to work upon the spare topmast, bidding him make for it some trestle-trees and bolsters, upon which to lay the eyes of the rigging; but they did not trouble him to shape it. Further, they ordered the same to be fitted to the foretopmast and the spare t'gallant and royal mast. And in the meanwhile, the rigging was prepared, and when this was finished, they made ready the shears to hoist the spare topmast, intending this to take the place of the main lower-mast. Then, when the carpenter had carried out their orders, he was set to make three partners with a step cut in each, these being intended to take the heels of the three masts, and when these were completed, they bolted them securely to the decks at the fore part of each one of the stumps of the three lower-masts. And so, having all ready, we hove the mainmast into position, after which we proceeded to rig it. Now, when we had made an end of this, we set-to upon the foremast, using for this the foretopmast which they had saved, and after that we hove the mizzenmast into place, having for this the spare t'gallant and royal mast.

Now the manner in which we secured the masts, before ever we came to the rigging of them, was by lashing them to the stumps of the lower-masts, and after we had lashed them, we drove dunnage and wedges between the masts and the lashings, thus making them very secure. And so, when we had set up the rigging, we had confidence that they would stand all such sail as we should be able to set upon them. Yet, further than this, the bo'sun bade the carpenter make wooden caps of six inch oak, these caps to fit over the *squared* heads of the lower-mast stumps, and having a hole, each of them, to embrace the jury-mast, and by making these caps in two halves, they were able to bolt them on after the masts had been hove into position.

And so, having gotten in our three jury lower-masts, we hoisted up the foreyard to the main, to act as our mainyard, and did likewise with the topsail-yard to the fore, and after that, we sent up the t'gallant-yard to the mizzen. Thus we had her sparred, all but a bowsprit and jibboom; yet this we managed by making a stumpy, spike bowsprit from one of the smaller spars which they had used to shore up the superstructure, and because we feared that it lacked strength to bear the strain of our fore and aft stays, we took down two hawsers from the fore, passing them in through the hawse-holes and setting them up there. And so we had her rigged, and, after that, we bent such sail as our gear abled us to carry, and in this wise had the hulk ready for sea.

Now, the time that it took us to rig the ship, and fit her out, was seven weeks, saving one day. And in all this time we suffered no molestation from any of the strange habitants of the weed-continent; though this may have been because we kept fires of dried weed going all the night about the decks, these fires being lit on big flat pieces of rock which we had gotten from the island. Yet, for all that we had not been troubled, we had more than once discovered strange things in the water swimming near to the vessel; but a flare of weed, hung over the side, on the end of a reed, had sufficed always to scare away such unholy visitants.

And so at last we came to the day on which we were in so good a condition that the bo'sun and the second mate considered the ship to be in a fit state to put to sea – the carpenter having gone over so much of her hull as he could get at and found her everywhere very sound; though her lower parts were hideously overgrown with weed, barnacles and other matters; yet this we could not help, and it was not wise to attempt to scrape her, having consideration to the creatures which we knew to abound in those waters.

Now in those seven weeks, Mistress Madison and I had come very close to one another, so that I had ceased to call her by any name save Mary, unless it were a dearer one than that; though this would be one of my own invention, and would leave my heart too naked did I put it down here.

Of our love one for the other, I think yet, and ponder how that mighty man, the bo'sun, came so quickly to a knowledge of the state of our hearts; for he gave me a very sly hint one day that he had a sound idea of the way in which the wind blew, and yet, though he said it with a half-jest, methought there was something wistful in his voice, as he spoke, and at that I just clapped my hand in his, and he gave it a very huge grip. And after that he ceased from the subject.

Chapter XVII
How We Came to Our Own Country

NOW, WHEN THE DAY CAME ON which we made to leave the nearness of the island, and the waters of that strange sea, there was great lightness of heart among us, and we went very merrily about such tasks as were needful. And so, in a little, we had the kedge tripped, and had cast the ship's head to starboard, and presently, had her braced up upon the larboard tack, the which we managed very well; though our gear worked heavily, as might be expected. And after that we had gotten under way, we went to the lee side to witness the last of that lonesome island, and with us came the men of the ship, and so, for a space, there was a silence among us; for they were very quiet, looking astern and saying naught; but we had sympathy with them, knowing somewhat of those past years.

And now the bo'sun came to the break of the poop, and called down to the men to muster aft, the which they did, and I with them; for I had come to regard them as my very good comrades; and rum was served out to each of them, and to me along with the rest, and it was Mistress Madison herself who dipped it out to us from the wooden bucket; though it was the buxom woman who had brought it up from the lazarette. Now, after the rum, the bo'sun bade the crew to clear up the gear about the decks, and get matters secured, and at that I turned to go with the men, having become so used to work with them; but he called to me to come up to him upon the poop, the which I did, and there he spoke respectfully, remonstrating with me, and reminding me that now there was need no longer for me to toil; for that I was come back to my old position of passenger, such as I had been in the *Glen Carrig*, ere she foundered. But to this talk of his, I made reply that I had as good a right to work my passage home as any other among us; for though I had paid for a passage in the *Glen Carrig*, I had done no such thing regarding the *Seabird* – this being the name of the hulk – and to this, my reply, the bo'sun said little; but I perceived that he liked my spirit, and so from thence until we reached the Port of London, I took my turn and part in all seafaring matters, having become by this quite proficient in the calling. Yet, in one matter, I availed myself of my former position; for I chose to live aft, and by this was abled to see much of my sweetheart, Mistress Madison.

Now after dinner upon the day on which we left the island, the bo'sun and the second mate picked the watches, and thus I found myself chosen to be in the bo'sun's, at which I was mightly pleased. And when the watches had been picked, they had all hands to 'bout ship, the which, to the pleasure of all, she accomplished; for under such gear and with so much growth upon her bottom, they had feared that we should have to veer, and by this we should have lost much distance to leeward, whereas we desired to edge so much to windward as we could, being anxious to put space between us and the weed-continent. And twice more that day we put the ship about, though the second time it was to avoid a great bank of weed that lay floating athwart our bows; for all the sea to windward of the island, so far as we had been able to see from the top of the higher hill, was studded with floating masses of the weed, like unto thousands of islets, and in places like to far-spreading reefs. And, because of these, the sea all about the island remained very quiet and unbroken, so that there was never any surf, no, nor scarce a broken wave upon its shore, and this, for all that the wind had been fresh for many days.

When the evening came, we were again upon the larboard tack, making, perhaps, some four knots in the hour; though, had we been in proper rig, and with a clean bottom, we had been making eight or nine, with so good a breeze and so calm a sea. Yet, so far, our progress had been very reasonable; for the island lay, maybe, some five miles to leeward, and about fifteen astern. And so we prepared for the night. Yet, a little before dark, we discovered that the weed-continent trended out towards us; so that we should pass it, maybe, at a distance of something like half a mile, and, at that, there was talk between the second mate and the bo'sun as to whether it was better to put the ship about, and gain a greater sea-room before attempting to pass this promontory of weed; but at last they decided that we had naught to fear; for we had fair way through the water, and further, it did not seem reasonable to suppose that we should have aught to fear from the habitants of the weed-continent, at so great a distance as the half of a mile. And so we stood on; for, once past the point, there was much likelihood of the weed trending away to the Eastward, and if this were so, we could square-in immediately and get the wind upon our quarter, and so make better way.

Now it was the bo'sun's watch from eight of the evening until midnight, and I, with another man, had the lookout until four bells. Thus it chanced that, coming abreast of the point during our time of watching, we peered very earnestly to leeward; for the night was dark, having no moon until nearer the morning; and we were full of unease in that we had come so near again to the desolation of that strange continent. And then, suddenly, the man with me clutched my shoulder, and pointed into the darkness upon our bow, and thus I discovered that we had come nearer to the weed than the bo'sun and the second mate had intended; they, without doubt, having miscalculated our leeway. At this, I turned and sang out to the bo'sun that we were near to running upon the weed, and, in the same moment, he shouted to the helmsman to luff, and directly afterwards our starboard side was brushing against the great outlying tufts of the point, and so, for a breathless minute, we waited. Yet the ship drew clear, and so into the open water beyond the point; but I had seen something as we scraped against the weed, a sudden glimpse of white, gliding among the growth, and then I saw others, and, in a moment, I was down on the main-deck, and running aft to the bo'sun; yet midway along the deck a horrid shape came above the starboard rail, and I gave out a loud cry of warning. Then I had a capstan-bar from the rack near, and smote with it at the thing, crying all the while for help, and at my blow the thing went from my sight, and the bo'sun was with me, and some of the men.

Now the bo'sun had seen my stroke, and so sprang upon the t'gallant rail, and peered over; but gave back on the instant, shouting to me to run and call the other watch, for that the sea was full of the monsters swimming off to the ship, and at that I was away at a run, and when I had waked the men, I raced aft to the cabin and did likewise with the second mate, and so returned in a minute, bearing the bo'sun's cutlass, my own cut-and-thrust, and the lantern that hung always in the saloon. Now when I had gotten back, I found all things in a mighty scurry – men running about in their shirts and drawers, some in the galley bringing fire from the stove, and others lighting a fire of dry weed to leeward of the galley, and along the starboard rail there was already a fierce fight, the men using capstan-bars, even as I had done. Then I thrust the bo'sun's cutlass into his hand, and at that he gave a great shout, part of joy, and part of approbation, and after that he snatched the lantern from me, and had run to the larboard side of the deck, before I was well aware that he had taken the light; but now I followed him, and happy it was for all of us in the ship that he had thought to go at that moment; for the light of the lantern showed me the vile faces of three of the weed men climbing over the larboard rail; yet the bo'sun had cleft them or ever I could come near; but in a moment I was full busy; for there came nigh a dozen heads above the rail a little aft of where I was, and at that I ran at them, and did good execution; but some had been aboard, if the bo'sun had not come to my help. And now the decks were full of light, several fires having been lit, and the second mate having brought out fresh lanterns; and now the men had gotten their cutlasses, the which were more handy than the capstan-bars; and so the fight went forward, some having come over to our side to help us, and a very wild sight it must have seemed to any onlooker; for all about the decks burned the fires and the lanterns, and along the rails ran the men, smiting at hideous faces that rose in dozens into the wild glare of our fighting lights. And everywhere drifted the stench of the brutes. And up on the poop, the fight was as brisk as elsewhere; and here, having been drawn by a cry for help, I discovered the buxom woman smiting with a gory meat-axe at a vile thing which had gotten a clump of its tentacles upon her dress; but she had dispatched it, or ever my sword could help her, and then, to my astonishment, even at that time of peril, I discovered the captain's wife, wielding a small sword, and the face of her was like to the face of a tiger; for her mouth was drawn, and showed her teeth clenched; but she uttered no word nor cry, and I doubt not but that she had some vague idea that she worked her husband's vengeance.

Then, for a space, I was as busy as any, and afterwards I ran to the buxom woman to demand the whereabouts of Mistress Madison, and she, in a very breathless voice, informed me that she had locked her in her room out of harm's way, and at that I could have embraced the woman; for I had been sorely anxious to know that my sweetheart was safe.

And, presently, the fight diminished, and so, at last, came to an end, the ship having drawn well away from the point, and being now in the open. And after that I ran down to my sweetheart, and opened her door, and thus, for a space, she wept, having her arms about my neck; for she had been in sore terror for me, and for all the ship's company. But, soon, drying her tears, she grew very indignant with her nurse for having locked her into her room, and refused to speak to that good woman for near an hour. Yet I pointed out to her that she could be of very great use in dressing such wounds as had been received, and so she came back to her usual brightness, and brought out bandages, and lint, and ointment, and thread, and was presently very busy.

Now it was later that there rose a fresh commotion in the ship; for it had been discovered that the captain's wife was a-missing. At this, the bo'sun and the second mate instituted a search; but she was nowhere to be found, and, indeed, none in the ship ever saw her again, at which it was presumed that she had been dragged over by some of the weed men, and so come upon her death. And at this, there came a great prostration to my sweetheart so that she would not be comforted for the space of nigh three days, by which time the ship had come clear of those strange seas, having left the incredible desolation of the weed-continent far under our starboard counter.

And so, after a voyage which lasted for nine and seventy days since getting under weigh, we came to the Port of London, having refused all offers of assistance on the way.

Now here, I had to say farewell to my comrades of so many months and perilous adventures; yet, being a man not entirely without means, I took care that each of them should have a certain gift by which to remember me.

And I placed monies in the hands of the buxom woman, so that she could have no reason to stint my sweetheart, and she having – for the comfort of her conscience – taken her good man to the church, set up a little house upon the borders of my estate; but this was not until Mistress Madison had come to take her place at the head of my hall in the County of Essex.

Now one further thing there is of which I must tell. Should any, chancing to trespass upon my estate, come upon a man of very mighty proportions, albeit somewhat bent by age, seated comfortably at the door of his little cottage, then shall they know him for my friend the bo'sun; for to this day do he and I fore-gather, and let our talk drift to the desolate places of this earth, pondering upon that which we have seen

– the weed-continent, where reigns desolation and the terror of its strange habitants. And, after that, we talk softly of the land where God hath made monsters after the fashion of trees. Then, maybe, my children come about me, and so we change to other matters; for the little ones love not terror.

If you enjoyed this, you might also like...
The House on the Borderland, see page 303
From the Tideless Sea: Part One, see page 111

The Weird
and Strange

The Goddess of Death

IT WAS IN THE LATTER END of November when I reached T—worth to find the little town almost in a panic. In answer to my half-jesting inquiry as to whether the French were attempting to land, I was told a harrowing tale of some restless statute that had a habit of running amuck among the worthy townspeople. Nearly a dozen had already fallen victims, the first having been pretty Sally Morgan, the town belle.

These and other matters I learnt. Wherever I went it was the same story. "Good Heavens! What ignorance, what superstition!" This I thought, imagining that they were the dupes of some murderous rogue. Afterwards I was to change my mind. I gathered that the tragedies had all happened in some park near by, where, during the day, this Walking Marble rested innocently enough upon its pedestal.

Though I scouted the story of the walking statue, I was greatly interested in the matter. Already it had come to me to look into it and show these benighted people how mistaken they had been; besides, the thing promised some excitement. As I strolled through the town I laughed, picturing to myself the absurdity of some people believing in a walking marble statue. Pooh! What fools there are! Arriving at my hotel, I was pleased to learn from my landlord that my old friend and schoolmate, William Turner, had been staying there for some time.

That evening while I was at dinner he burst into my room, and was delighted at seeing me.

"I suppose you've heard of the town bogey by now?" he said presently, dropping his voice. "It's a dangerous enough bogey, and we're all puzzled to explain how on earth it has escaped detection so long. Of course," he went on, "this story about the walking statue is all rubbish, though it's surprising what a number of people believe it."

"What do you say to trying our hands at catching it?" I said. "There would be a little excitement, and we should be doing the town a public benefit."

Will smiled. "I'm game if you are, Herton – we could take a stroll in the park tonight, if you like; perhaps we might see something."

"Right," I answered heartily. "What time do you propose going?"

Will pulled out his watch. "It's half-past eight now; shall we say eleven o'clock? It ought to be late enough then."

I assented and invited him to join me at my wine. He did so, and we passed the time away very pleasantly in reminiscences of old times.

"What about weapons?" I asked presently. "I suppose it will be advisable to take something in that line?"

For answer Will unbuttoned his coat, and I saw the gleam of a brace of pistols. I nodded, and, going to my trunk, opened it and showed him a couple of beautiful little pistols I often carried. Having loaded them, I put them in my side pockets. Shortly afterwards, eleven chimed, and getting into our cloaks, we left the house.

It was very cold, and a wintry wind moaned through the night. As we entered the park, we involuntarily kept closer together.

Somehow, my desire for adventure seemed to be ebbing away, and I wanted to get out from the place, and into the lighted streets.

"We'll just have a look at the statue," said Will; "then home and to bed."

A few minutes later we reached a little clearing among the bushes.

"Here we are," Will whispered. "I wish the moon would come out a moment; it would enable us to get a glance at the thing." He peered into the gloom on our right. "I'm hanged," he muttered, "if I can see it at all!"

Glancing to our left, I noticed that the path now led along the edge of a steep slope, at the bottom of which, some considerable distance below us, I caught the gleam of water.

"The park lake," Will explained in answer to a short query on my part. "Beastly deep too!"

He turned away, and we both gazed into the dark gap among the bushes.

A moment afterwards the clouds cleared for an instant, and a ray of light struck down full upon us, lighting up the little circle of bushes and showing the clearing plainly. It was only a momentary gleam, but quite sufficient. There stood a *pedestal great and black*; but *there was no statue upon it*!

Will gave a quick gasp, and for a minute we stood stupidly; then we commenced to retrace our steps hurriedly. Neither of us spoke. As we moved we glanced fearfully from side to side. Nearly half the return journey was accomplished, when, happening to look behind me, I saw in the dim shadows to my left the bushes part, and a huge, white, carven face, crowned with black, suddenly protruded.

I gave a sharp cry and reeled backwards. Will turned. "Oh, mercy upon us!" I heard him shout, and he started to run.

The Thing came out of the shadow. It looked like a giant. I stood rooted; then it came towards me, and I turned and ran. In the hands I had seen something that looked like a twisted cloth. Will was some dozen yards ahead. Behind, silent and vast, ran that awful being.

We neared the park entrance. I looked over my shoulder. It was gaining on us rapidly. Onwards we tore. A hundred yards further lay the gates; and safety in the lighted streets. Would we do it? Only fifty yards to go, and my chest seemed bursting. The distance shortened. The gates were close…. We were through. Down the street we ran; then turned to look. It had vanished.

"Thank Heaven!" I gasped, panting heavily.

A minute later Will said: "What a blue funk we've been in." I said nothing. We were making towards the hotel. I was bewildered and wanted to get by myself to think.

Next morning, while I was sitting dejectedly at breakfast, Will came in. We looked at one another shamefacedly. Will sat down. Presently he spoke:

"What cowards we are!"

I said nothing. It was too true; and the knowledge weighed on me like lead.

"Look here!" and Will spoke sharply and sternly. "We've got to go through with this matter to the end, if only for our own sakes."

I glanced at him eagerly. His determined tone seemed to inspire me with fresh hope and courage.

"What we've got to do first," he continued, "is to give that marble god a proper overhauling, and make sure no one has been playing tricks with us – perhaps it's possible to move it in some way."

I rose from the table, and went to the window. It had snowed heavily the preceding day, and the ground was covered with an even layer of white. As I looked out, a sudden idea came to me, and I turned quickly to Will.

"The snow!" I cried. "It will show the footprints, if there are any."

Will stared, puzzled.

"Round the statue," I explained, "if we go at once."

He grasped my meaning, and stood up. A few minutes later we were striding out briskly for the Park. A sharp walk brought us to the place. As we came in sight, I gave a cry of astonishment. The pedestal was occupied by a figure, identical with the thing that had chased us the night before. There it stood, erect and rigid, its sightless eyes glaring into space.

Will's face wore a look of expectation.

"See," he said, "it's back again. It cannot have managed that by itself, and we shall see by the footprints how many scoundrels there are in the affair."

He moved forward across the snow. I followed. Reaching the pedestal, we made a careful examination of the ground; but to our utter perplexity the snow was undisturbed. Next, we turned our attention to the figure itself, and though Will, who had seen it often before, searched carefully, he could find nothing amiss.

This it must be remembered, was my first sight of it, for – now that my mind was rational – I would not admit, even to myself, that what we had seen in the darkness was anything more than a masquerade, intended to lead people to the belief that it was the dead marble they saw walking.

Seen in the broad daylight, the thing looked what it was, a marble statue, intended to represent some deity. Which, I could not tell; and when I asked Will he shook his head.

In height it might have been eight feet, or perhaps a trifle under. The face was large – as indeed was the whole figure – and in expression cruel to the last degree.

Above his brow was a large, strangely shaped headdress, carved out of some jet-black substance. The body was carved from a single block of milk-white marble, and draped gracefully and plainly in a robe confined at the waist by a narrow black girdle. The arms drooped loosely by the sides, and in the right hand hung a twisted cloth of a similar hue to the girdle. The left was empty and half gripped.

Will had always spoken of the statue as a *god*. Now, however, as my eyes ran over the various details, a doubt formed itself in my mind, and I suggested to Will that he was possibly mistaken as to the intended sex of the image.

For a moment he looked interested; then remarked gloomily that he didn't see it mattered much whether the thing was a man-god or a woman-god. The point was, had it the power to come off its pedestal or not?

I looked at him reproachfully.

"Surely you are not really going to believe that silly superstition?" I expostulated.

He shook his head moodily. "No, but can you or anyone else explain away last night's occurrences in any ordinary manner?"

To this there was no satisfactory reply, so I held my tongue.

"Pity," remarked Will presently, "that we know so little about this god. And the one man who might have enlightened us dead and gone – goodness knows where!"

"Who's that?" I queried.

"Oh, of course. I was forgetting, you don't know! Well, it's the way: For some years an old Indian colonel, called Whigman, lived here. He was a queer old stick, and absolutely refused to have anything to do with anybody. In fact, with the exception of an old Hindoo serving-man, he saw no one. About nine months ago he and his servant were found brutally murdered – strangled, so the doctors said. And now comes the most surprising part of it all.

In his will he had left the whole of his huge estate to the citizens of T—worth to be used as a park."

"Strangled, I think you said?" and I looked at Will questioningly.

He glanced at me a moment absently, then the light of comprehension flashed across his face. He looked startled. "Jove! You don't mean that?"

"I do though, old chap. The murder of these others has in every case been accomplished by strangling – their bodies, so you've told me, have shown that much. Then there are other things that point to my theory being the right one."

"What! You really think that the Colonel met his death at the same hands as—?"

He did not finish.

I nodded assent.

"Well, if you are correct, what about the length of time between them and Sally Morgan's murder – seven months, isn't it – and not a soul hurt all that time, and now—" He threw up his arms with an expressive gesture.

"Heaven knows!" I replied, "I don't."

For some length of time we discussed the matter in all its bearings, but without arriving at any satisfactory conclusion.

On our way back to town Will showed me a tiny piece of white marble which he had surreptitiously chipped from the statue. I examined it closely. Yes, it was marble, and somehow the certainty of that seemed to give us more confidence.

"Marble is marble," Will said, "and it's ridiculous to suppose anything else." I did not attempt to deny this.

During the next few days we paid visits to the park, but without result. The statue remained as we had left it.

A week passed. Then, one morning early, before the dawn, we were roused by a frightful scream, followed by a cry of deepest agony. It ended in a murmuring gurgle, and all was silent.

Without hesitation, we seized pistols, and with lighted candles rushed from our rooms to the great entrance door. This we hurriedly opened. Outside, the night was very quiet. It had been snowing and the ground was covered with a sheet of white.

For a moment we saw nothing. Then we distinguished the form of a woman lying across the steps leading up to the door. Running out, we seized her and carried her into the hall. There we recognised her as one of the waitresses of the hotel. Will turned back her collar and exposed the throat, showing a livid weal round it.

He was very serious, and his voice trembled, though not with fear, as he spoke to me. "We must dress and follow the tracks; there is no time to waste." He smiled gravely. "I don't think *we* shall do the running away this time."

At this moment the landlord appeared. On seeing the girl, and hearing our story, he seemed thunderstruck with fear and amazement, and could do nothing save wring his hands helplessly. Leaving him with the body, we went to our rooms and dressed quickly; then down again into the hall, where we found a crowd of fussy womenfolk around the poor victim.

In the taproom I heard voices, and pushing my way in, discovered several of the serving men discussing the tragedy in excited tones. As they turned at my entrance, I called to them to know who would volunteer to accompany us. At once a strongly built young fellow stepped forward, followed, after a slight hesitation, by two older men. Then, as we had sufficient for our purpose, I told them to get heavy sticks and bring lanterns.

As soon as they were ready we sallied out: Will and I first, the others following and keeping well together. The night was not particularly dark – the snow seemed to lighten it. At the bottom of High Street one of the men gave a short gasp, and pointed ahead.

There, dimly seen, and stealing across the snow with silent strides, was a giant form draped in white. Signing to the men to keep quiet, we ran quickly forward, the snow muffling our footsteps. We neared it rapidly. Suddenly Will stumbled and fell forward on his face, one of his pistols going off with the shock.

Instantly the Thing ahead looked round, and next moment was bounding from us in great leaps. Will was on his feet in a second, and, with a muttered curse at his own clumsiness, joined in the chase again. Through the park gates it went, and we followed hard. As we got nearer, I could plainly see the black headdress, and in the right hand there was a dark something; but what struck me most was the enormous size of the thing; it was certainly quite as tall as the marble goddess.

On we went. We were within a hundred feet of it when it stopped dead and turned towards us, and never shall I forget the fear that chilled me, for there, from head to foot, perfect in every detail, stood the marble goddess. At the movement, we had brought up standing; but now I raised a pistol and fired. That seemed to break the spell, and like one man we leapt forward. As we did so, the thing circled like a flash, and resumed its flight at a speed that bade fair to leave us behind in short time.

Then the thought came to me to head it off. This I did by sending the three men round to the right-hand side of the park lake, while Will and I continued the pursuit. A minute later, the monster disappeared around a bend in the path; but this troubled me little, as I felt convinced that it would blunder right into the arms of the men, and they would turn it back, and then – ah! then this mystery and horror would be solved.

On we ran. A minute, perhaps, passed. All at once I heard a hoarse cry ahead followed by a loud scream, which ceased suddenly. With fear plucking at my heart, I spurted forward, Will close behind. Round the corner we burst, and I saw the two men bending over something on the ground.

"Have you got it?" I shouted excitedly. The men turned quickly, and, seeing me, beckoned hurriedly. A moment later I was with them, and kneeling alongside a silent form. Alas! it was the brave young fellow who had been the first to volunteer. His neck seemed to be broken. Standing up, I turned to the men for an explanation.

"It was this way, sir; Johnson, that's him," nodding to the dead man, "he was smarter on his legs than we be, and he got ahead. Just before we reached him we heard him shout. We was close behind, and I don't think it could ha' been half a minute before we was up and found him."

"Did you see anything—" I hesitated. I felt sick. Then I continued, "anything of *that* – you know what I mean?"

"Yes, sir; leastways, my mate did. He saw it run across to those bushes an'—"

"Come on, Will," I cried, without waiting to hear more; and throwing the light of our lanterns ahead of us, we burst into the shrubberies. Scarcely had we gone a dozen paces when the light struck full upon a towering figure. There was a crash, and my lantern was smashed all to pieces. I was thrown to the ground, and something slid through the bushes. Springing to the edge, we were just in time to catch sight of it running in the direction of the lake. Simultaneously we raised our pistols and fired. As the smoke cleared away, I saw the Thing bound over the railings into the water. A faint splash was borne to our ears, then – silence.

Hurriedly we ran to the spot, but could see nothing.

"Perhaps we hit it," I ventured.

"You forget," laughed Will hysterically, "marble won't float."

"Don't talk rubbish," I answered angrily. Yet I felt that I would have given something to know what it was *really*.

For some minutes we waited; then, as nothing came to view, we moved away towards the gate – the men going on ahead, carrying their dead comrade. Our way led past the little clearing where the statue stood. It was still dark when we reached it.

"Look, Herton, look!" Will's voice rose to a shriek. I turned sharply. I had been lost momentarily in perplexing thought. Now, I saw that we were right opposite the place of the marble statue, and Will was shining the light of the lantern in its direction; but it showed me nothing save the pedestal, bare and smooth.

I glanced at Will. The lantern was shaking visibly in his grasp. Then I looked towards the pedestal again in a dazed manner. I stepped up to it and passed my hand slowly over the top. I felt very queer.

After that, I walked round it once or twice, No use! There was no mistake this time. My eyes showed me nothing, save that vacant place, where, but a few hours previously, had stood the massive marble.

Silently we left the spot. The men had preceded us with their sad burden. Fortunately, in the dim light, they had failed to note the absence of the goddess.

Dawn was breaking as in mournful procession we entered the town. Already the news seemed to have spread, and quite a body of the town people escorted us to the hotel.

During the day a number of men went up to the park, armed with hammers, intending to destroy the statue, but returned later silent and awestruck, declaring that it had disappeared bodily, only the great altar remaining.

I was feeling unwell. The shock thoroughly upset me, and a sense of helplessness assailed me.

About midnight, feeling worn out, I went to bed. It was late on the following morning when I woke with a start. An idea had some to me, and, rising, I dressed quickly and went downstairs. In the bar I found the landlord, and to him I applied for information as to where the library of the late Colonel Whigman had been removed.

He scratched his head a moment reflectively.

"I couldn't rightly say, sir; but I know Mr. Jepson, the town clerk, will be able to, and I daresay he wouldn't mind telling you anything you might want to know."

Having inquired where I was likely to meet this official, I set off, and in a short while found myself chatting to a pleasant, ruddy-faced man of about forty.

"The late colonel's library!" he said genially, "Certainly, come this way, Sir Horton," and he ushered me into a long room, lined with books.

What I wanted was to find if the colonel had left among his library any diary or written record of his life in India. For a couple of hours I searched persistently. Then, just as I was giving up hope, I found it – a little green-backed book, filled with closely-written and crabbed writing.

Opening it, I found staring me in the face, a rough pen-and-ink sketch of – the marble goddess.

The following pages I read eagerly. They told a strange story of how, while engaged in the work of exterminating Thugs, the colonel and his men had found a large idol of white marble, quite unlike any Indian Deity the colonel had ever seen.

After a full description – in which I recognised once more the statue in Bungalow Park – there was some reference to an exciting skirmish with the priests of the temple, in which the colonel had a narrow escape from death at the hands of the high priest, 'who was a most enormous man and mad with fury.'

Finally, having obtained possession, they found among other things that the Deity of the temple was another – and, to Europeans, unknown – form of Kali, the Goddess of Death. The temple itself being a sort of Holy of Holies of Thugdom, where they carried on their brutal and disgusting rites.

After this, the diary went on to say that, loath to destroy the idol, the colonel brought it back with him from Calcutta, having first demolished the temple in which it had been found.

Later, he found occasion to ship it off to England. Shortly after this his life was attempted, and, his time of service being up, he came home.

Here it ended, and yet I was no nearer to the solution than I had been when first I opened the book.

Standing up, I placed it on the table; then, as I reached for my hat, I noticed on the floor a half-sheet of paper, which had evidently fallen from the diary as I read. Stooping, I picked it up. It was soiled, and in parts illegible; but what I saw there filled me with astonishment. Here, at last, in my hands, I held the key to the horrible mystery that surrounded us!

Hastily I crumpled the paper into my pocket, and, opening the door, rushed from the room. Reaching the hotel, I bounded upstairs to where Will sat reading.

"I've found it out! I've found it out!" I gasped. Will sprang from his seat, his eyes blazing with excitement. I seized him by the arm and, without stopping to explain, dragged him hatless into the street.

"Come on," I cried.

As we ran through the streets people looked up wonderingly, and many joined in the race.

At last we reached the open space and the open pedestal. Here I paused a moment to gain breath. Will looked at me curiously. The crowd formed round in a semi-circle, at some little distance.

Then without a word I stepped up to the altar, and, stooping, reached up under it. There was a loud click, and I sprang back sharply. Something rose from the centre of the pedestal with a slow, stately movement. For a second no one spoke; then a great cry of fear came from the crowd: "The image! The image!" and some began to run. There was another click and Kali, the Goddess of Death, stood fully revealed.

Again I stepped up to the altar. The crowd watched me breathlessly and the timid ceased to fly. For a moment I fumbled. Then one side of the pedestal swung back. I held up my hand for silence. Someone procured a lantern, which I lit and lowered through the opening. It went down some ten feet, then rested on the earth beneath. I peered down, and as my eyes became accustomed to the darkness, I made out a square-shaped pit in the ground directly below the pedestal.

Will came to my side and looked over my shoulder.

"We must get a ladder," he said. I nodded, and he sent a man for one. When it came we pushed it through until it rested firmly; then after a final survey, we climbed cautiously down.

I remember feeling surprised at the size of the place. It was as big as a good-sized room. At this moment, as I stood glancing round, Will called to me. His voice denoted great perplexity. Crossing over, I found him staring at a litter of things which strewed the ground: tins, bottles, cans, rubbish, a bucket with some water in it, and, further on, a kind of rude bed.

"Someone's been living here!" and he looked at me blankly. "It wasn't—" he began, then hesitated. "It wasn't that after all," and he indicated with his head.

"No," I replied, "It wasn't *that*."

I assented. Will's face was a study. Then he seemed to grasp the full significance of the fact, and a great look of relief crossed his features.

A moment later I made a discovery. On the left side in the far corner was a low curved entrance, like a small tunnel. On the opposite side was a similar opening. Lowering the lantern, I looked into the right-hand one, but could see nothing. By stooping somewhat we could walk along it, which we did for some distance, until it ended in a heap of stones and earth. Returning to the hollow under the pedestal, we tried the other, and, after a little, noticed that it trended steadily downwards.

"It seems to be going in the direction of the lake," I remarked; "we had better be careful."

A few feet further on the tunnel broadened and heightened considerably, and I saw a faint glimmer, which, on reaching, proved to be water.

"Can't get any further," Will cried. "You were right. We have got down to the level of the lake."

"But what on earth was this tunnel designed for?" I asked, glancing around. "You see it reaches below the surface of the lake."

"Goodness knows," Will answered. "I expect it was one of those secret passages made centuries ago – most likely in Crowell's time. You see, Colonel Whigman's was a very old place, built I can't say how long ago. It belonged once to an old baron. However, there is nothing here; we might as well go."

"Just a second, Will," I said, the recollection of the statue's wild leap into the lake at the moment occurring to me.

I stooped and held the lantern close over the water which blocked our further progress.

As I did so I thought I saw something of an indistinct whiteness floating a few inches beneath the surface. Involuntarily my left hand took a firmer grip of the lantern, and the fingers of my right hand opened out convulsively.

What was it I saw? I could feel myself becoming as icy cold as the water itself. I glanced at Will. He was standing disinterestedly a little behind me. Evidently he had, so far, seen nothing.

Again, I looked, and a horrible sensation of fear and awe crept over me as I seemed to see, staring up at me, the face of Kali, the Goddess of Death.

"See, Will!" I said quickly. "Is it fancy?"

Following the direction of my grimace, he peered down into the gloomy water, then started back with a cry.

"What is it Herton? I seemed to see a face like—"

"Take the lantern, Will." I said, as a sudden inspiration came to me: "I've an idea what it is"; and leaning forward, I plunged my arms in up to the elbows, and grasped something cold and hard. I shuddered, but held on, and pulled, and slowly up from the water rose a vast white face, which came away in my hands. It was a huge mask – an exact facsimile of the features of the statue above us.

Thoroughly shaken, we retreated to the pedestal with our trophy, and from thence up the ladder into the blessed daylight.

Here, to a crowd of eager listeners, we told our story; and so left it.

Little remains to be told.

Workmen were sent down, and from the water they drew forth the dead body of an enormous Hindoo, draped from head to foot in white. In the body were a couple of bullet wounds. Our fire had been true that night, and he had evidently died trying to enter the pedestal through the submerged opening of the passage.

Who he was, or where he came from, no one could explain.

Afterwards, among the colonel's papers, we found a reference to the High Priest which led us to suppose that it was he, who, in vengeance for the sacrilege against his appalling deity, had, to such terrible purpose, impersonated Kali, the Goddess of Death.

If you enjoyed this, you might also like...

The House Among the Laurels, see page 25
The Thing Invisible, see page 78

The Voice in the Night

IT WAS A DARK, starless night. We were becalmed in the Northern Pacific. Our exact position I do not know; for the sun had been hidden during the course of a weary, breathless week, by a thin haze which had seemed to float above us, about the height of our mastheads, at whiles descending and shrouding the surrounding sea.

With there being no wind, we had steadied the tiller, and I was the only man on deck. The crew, consisting of two men and a boy, were sleeping forrard in their den; while Will – my friend, and the master of our little craft – was aft in his bunk on the port side of the little cabin.

Suddenly, from out of the surrounding darkness, there came a hail:

"Schooner, ahoy!"

The cry was so unexpected that I gave no immediate answer, because of my surprise.

It came again – a voice curiously throaty and inhuman, calling from somewhere upon the dark sea away on our port broadside:

"Schooner, ahoy!"

"Hullo!" I sung out, having gathered my wits somewhat. "What are you? What do you want?"

"You need not be afraid," answered the queer voice, having probably noticed some trace of confusion in my tone. "I am only an old man."

The pause sounded oddly; but it was only afterwards that it came back to me with any significance.

"Why don't you come alongside, then?" I queried somewhat snappishly; for I liked not his hinting at my having been a trifle shaken.

"I – I – can't. It wouldn't be safe. I—" The voice broke off, and there was silence.

"What do you mean?" I asked, growing more and more astonished. "Why not safe? Where are you?"

I listened for a moment; but there came no answer. And then, a sudden indefinite suspicion, of I knew not what, coming to me, I stepped swiftly to the binnacle, and took out the lighted lamp. At the same time, I knocked on the deck with my heel to waken Will. Then I was back at the side, throwing the yellow funnel of light out into the silent immensity beyond our rail. As I did so, I heard a slight, muffled cry, and then the sound of a splash as though someone had dipped oars abruptly. Yet I cannot say that I saw anything with certainty; save, it seemed to me, that with the first flash of the light, there had been something upon the waters, where now there was nothing.

"Hullo, there!" I called. "What foolery is this!"

But there came only the indistinct sounds of a boat being pulled away into the night.

Then I heard Will's voice, from the direction of the after scuttle:

"What's up, George?"

"Come here, Will!" I said.

"What is it?" he asked, coming across the deck.

I told him the queer thing which had happened. He put several questions; then, after a moment's silence, he raised his hands to his lips, and hailed:

"Boat, ahoy!"

From a long distance away there came back to us a faint reply, and my companion repeated his call. Presently, after a short period of silence, there grew on our hearing the muffled sound of oars; at which Will hailed again.

This time there was a reply:

"Put away the light."

"I'm damned if I will," I muttered; but Will told me to do as the voice bade, and I shoved it down under the bulwarks.

"Come nearer," he said, and the oar-strokes continued. Then, when apparently some half-dozen fathoms distant, they again ceased.

"Come alongside," exclaimed Will. "There's nothing to be frightened of aboard here!"

"Promise that you will not show the light?"

"What's to do with you," I burst out, "that you're so infernally afraid of the light?"

"Because—" began the voice, and stopped short.

"Because what?" I asked quickly.

Will put his hand on my shoulder.

"Shut up a minute, old man," he said, in a low voice. "Let me tackle him."

He leant more over the rail.

"See here, Mister," he said, "this is a pretty queer business, you coming upon us like this, right out in the middle of the blessed Pacific. How are we to know what sort of a hanky-panky trick you're up to? You say there's only one of you. How are we to know, unless we get a squint at you – eh? What's your objection to the light, anyway?"

As he finished, I heard the noise of the oars again, and then the voice came; but now from a greater distance, and sounding extremely hopeless and pathetic.

"I am sorry – sorry! I would not have troubled you, only I am hungry, and – so is she."

The voice died away, and the sound of the oars, dipping irregularly, was borne to us.

"Stop!" sung out Will. "I don't want to drive you away. Come back! We'll keep the light hidden, if you don't like it."

He turned to me:

"It's a damned queer rig, this; but I think there's nothing to be afraid of?"

There was a question in his tone, and I replied.

"No, I think the poor devil's been wrecked around here, and gone crazy."

The sound of the oars drew nearer.

"Shove that lamp back in the binnacle," said Will; then he leaned over the rail and listened. I replaced the lamp, and came back to his side. The dipping of the oars ceased some dozen yards distant.

"Won't you come alongside now?" asked Will in an even voice. "I have had the lamp put back in the binnacle."

"I – I cannot," replied the voice. "I dare not come nearer. I dare not even pay you for the – the provisions."

"That's all right," said Will, and hesitated. "You're welcome to as much grub as you can take—" Again he hesitated.

"You are very good," exclaimed the voice. "May God, Who understands everything, reward you—" it broke off huskily.

"The – the lady?" said Will abruptly. "Is she—"

"I have left her behind upon the island," came the voice.

"What island?" I cut in.

"I know not its name," returned the voice. "I would to God—!" it began, and checked itself as suddenly.

"Could we not send a boat for her?" asked Will at this point.

"No!" said the voice, with extraordinary emphasis. "My God! No!" There was a moment's pause; then it added, in a tone which seemed a merited reproach:

"It was because of our want I ventured – because her agony tortured me."

"I am a forgetful brute," exclaimed Will. "Just wait a minute, whoever you are, and I will bring you up something at once."

In a couple of minutes he was back again, and his arms were full of various edibles. He paused at the rail.

"Can't you come alongside for them?" he asked.

"No – *I dare not*," replied the voice, and it seemed to me that in its tones I detected a note of stifled craving – as though the owner hushed a mortal desire. It came to me then in a flash, that the poor old creature out there in the darkness, was *suffering* for actual need of that which Will held in his arms; and yet, because of some unintelligible dread, refraining from dashing to the side of our little schooner, and receiving it. And with the lightning-like conviction, there came the knowledge that the Invisible was not mad; but sanely facing some intolerable horror.

"Damn it, Will!" I said, full of many feelings, over which predominated a vast sympathy. "Get a box. We must float off the stuff to him in it."

This we did – propelling it away from the vessel, out into the darkness, by means of a boathook. In a minute, a slight cry from the Invisible came to us, and we knew that he had secured the box.

A little later, he called out a farewell to us, and so heartful a blessing, that I am sure we were the better for it. Then, without more ado, we heard the ply of oars across the darkness.

"Pretty soon off," remarked Will, with perhaps just a little sense of injury.

"Wait," I replied. "I think somehow he'll come back. He must have been badly needing that food."

"And the lady," said Will. For a moment he was silent; then he continued:

"It's the queerest thing ever I've tumbled across, since I've been fishing."

"Yes," I said, and fell to pondering.

And so the time slipped away – an hour, another, and still Will stayed with me; for the queer adventure had knocked all desire for sleep out of him.

The third hour was three parts through, when we heard again the sound of oars across the silent ocean.

"Listen!" said Will, a low note of excitement in his voice.

"He's coming, just as I thought," I muttered.

The dipping of the oars grew nearer, and I noted that the strokes were firmer and longer. The food had been needed.

They came to a stop a little distance off the broadside, and the queer voice came again to us through the darkness:

"Schooner, ahoy!"

"That you?" asked Will.

"Yes," replied the voice. "I left you suddenly; but – but there was great need."

"The lady?" questioned Will.

"The – lady is grateful now on earth. She will be more grateful soon in – in heaven."

Will began to make some reply, in a puzzled voice; but became confused, and broke off short. I said nothing. I was wondering at the curious pauses, and, apart from my wonder, I was full of a great sympathy.

The voice continued:

"We – she and I, have talked, as we shared the result of God's tenderness and yours—"

Will interposed; but without coherence.

"I beg of you not to – to belittle your deed of Christian charity this night," said the voice. "Be sure that it has not escaped His notice."

It stopped, and there was a full minute's silence. Then it came again:

"We have spoken together upon that which – which has befallen us. We had thought to go out, without telling any, of the terror which has come into our – lives. She is with me in believing that tonight's happenings are under a special ruling, and that it is God's wish that we should tell to you all that we have suffered since – since—"

"Yes?" said Will softly.

"Since the sinking of the *Albatross*."

"Ah!" I exclaimed involuntarily. "She left Newcastle for 'Frisco some six months ago, and hasn't been heard of since."

"Yes," answered the voice. "But some few degrees to the North of the line she was caught in a terrible storm, and dismasted. When the day came, it was found that she was leaking badly, and, presently, it falling to a calm, the sailors took to the boats, leaving – leaving a young lady – my fiancée – and myself upon the wreck.

"We were below, gathering together a few of our belongings, when they left. They were entirely callous, through fear, and when we came up upon the deck, we saw them only as small shapes afar off upon the horizon. Yet we did not despair, but set to work and constructed a small raft. Upon this we put such few matters as it would hold including a quantity of water and some ship's biscuit. Then, the vessel being very deep in the water, we got ourselves on to the raft, and pushed off.

"It was later, when I observed that we seemed to be in the way of some tide or current, which bore us from the ship at an angle; so that in the course of three hours, by my watch, her hull became invisible to our sight, her broken masts remaining in view for a somewhat longer period. Then, towards evening, it grew misty, and so through the night. The next day we were still encompassed by the mist, the weather remaining quiet.

"For four days we drifted through this strange haze, until, on the evening of the fourth day, there grew upon our ears the murmur of breakers at a distance. Gradually it became plainer, and, somewhat after midnight, it appeared to sound upon either hand at no very great space. The raft was raised upon a swell several times, and then we were in smooth water, and the noise of the breakers was behind.

"When the morning came, we found that we were in a sort of great lagoon; but of this we noticed little at the time; for close before us, through the enshrouding mist, loomed the hull of a large sailing-vessel. With one accord, we fell upon our knees and thanked God; for we thought that here was an end to our perils. We had much to learn.

"The raft drew near to the ship, and we shouted on them to take us aboard; but none answered. Presently the raft touched against the side of the vessel, and, seeing a rope hanging downwards, I seized it and began to climb. Yet I had much ado to make my way up, because of a kind of grey, lichenous fungus which had seized upon the rope, and which blotched the side of the ship lividly.

"I reached the rail and clambered over it, on to the deck. Here I saw that the decks were covered, in great patches, with grey masses, some of them rising into nodules several feet in height; but at the time I thought less of this matter than of the possibility of there being people aboard the ship. I shouted; but none answered. Then I went to the door below the poop deck. I opened it, and peered in. There was a great smell of staleness, so that I knew in a moment that nothing living was within, and with the knowledge, I shut the door quickly; for I felt suddenly lonely.

"I went back to the side where I had scrambled up. My – my sweetheart was still sitting quietly upon the raft. Seeing me look down she called up to know whether there were any aboard of the ship. I replied that the vessel had the appearance of having been long deserted; but that if she would wait a little I would see whether there was anything in the shape of a ladder by which she could ascend to the deck. Then we would make a search through the vessel together. A little later, on the opposite side of the decks, I found a rope side-ladder. This I carried across, and a minute afterwards she was beside me.

"Together we explored the cabins and apartments in the after part of the ship; but nowhere was there any sign of life. Here and there within the cabins themselves, we came across odd patches of that queer fungus; but this, as my sweetheart said, could be cleansed away.

"In the end, having assured ourselves that the after portion of the vessel was empty, we picked our ways to the bows, between the ugly grey nodules of that strange growth; and here we made a further search which told us that there was indeed none aboard but ourselves.

"This being now beyond any doubt, we returned to the stern of the ship and proceeded to make ourselves as comfortable as possible. Together we cleared out and cleaned two of the cabins: and after that I made examination whether there was anything eatable in the ship. This I soon found was so, and thanked God in my heart for His goodness. In addition to this I discovered the whereabouts of the fresh-water pump, and having fixed it I found the water drinkable, though somewhat unpleasant to the taste.

"For several days we stayed aboard the ship, without attempting to get to the shore. We were busily engaged in making the place habitable. Yet even thus early we became aware that our lot was even less to be desired than might have been imagined; for though, as a first step, we scraped away the odd patches of growth that studded the floors and walls of the cabins and saloon, yet they returned almost to their original size within the space of twenty-four hours, which not only discouraged us, but gave us a feeling of vague unease.

"Still we would not admit ourselves beaten, so set to work afresh, and not only scraped away the fungus, but soaked the places where it had been, with carbolic, a can-full of which I had found in the pantry. Yet, by the end of the week the growth had returned in full strength, and, in addition, it had spread to other places, as though our touching it had allowed germs from it to travel elsewhere.

"On the seventh morning, my sweetheart woke to find a small patch of it growing on her pillow, close to her face. At that, she came to me, so soon as she could get her garments upon her. I was in the galley at the time lighting the fire for breakfast.

"Come here, John," she said, and led me aft. When I saw the thing upon her pillow I shuddered, and then and there we agreed to go right out of the ship and see whether we could not fare to make ourselves more comfortable ashore.

"Hurriedly we gathered together our few belongings, and even among these I found that the fungus had been at work; for one of her shawls had a little lump of it growing near one edge. I threw the whole thing over the side, without saying anything to her.

"The raft was still alongside, but it was too clumsy to guide, and I lowered down a small boat that hung across the stern, and in this we made our way to the shore. Yet, as we drew near to it, I became gradually aware that here the vile fungus, which had driven us from the ship, was growing riot. In places it rose into horrible, fantastic mounds, which seemed almost to quiver, as with a quiet life, when the wind blew across them. Here and there it took on the forms of vast fingers, and in others it just spread out flat and smooth and treacherous. Odd places, it appeared as grotesque stunted trees, seeming extraordinarily kinked and gnarled – the whole quaking vilely at times.

"At first, it seemed to us that there was no single portion of the surrounding shore which was not hidden beneath the masses of the hideous lichen; yet, in this, I found we were mistaken; for somewhat later, coasting along the shore at a little distance, we descried a smooth white patch of what appeared to be fine sand, and there we landed. It was not sand. What it was I do not know. All that I have observed is that upon it the fungus will not grow; while everywhere else, save where the sand-like earth wanders oddly, path-wise, amid the grey desolation of the lichen, there is nothing but that loathsome greyness.

"It is difficult to make you understand how cheered we were to find one place that was absolutely free from the growth, and here we deposited our belongings. Then we went back to the ship for such things as it seemed to us we should need. Among other matters, I managed to bring ashore with me one of the ship's sails, with which I constructed two small tents, which, though exceedingly rough-shaped, served the purpose for which they were intended. In these we lived and stored our various necessities, and thus for a matter of some four weeks all went smoothly and without particular unhappiness. Indeed, I may say with much of happiness – for – for we were together.

"It was on the thumb of her right hand that the growth first showed. It was only a small circular spot, much like a little grey mole. My God! How the fear leapt to my heart when she showed me the place. We cleansed it, between us, washing it with carbolic and water. In the morning of the following day she showed her hand to me again. The grey warty thing had returned. For a little while, we looked at one another in silence. Then, still wordless, we started again to remove it. In the midst of the operation she spoke suddenly.

"'What's that on the side of your face, dear?' Her voice was sharp with anxiety. I put my hand up to feel.

"'There! Under the hair by your ear. A little to the front a bit.' My finger rested upon the place, and then I knew.

"'Let us get your thumb done first,' I said. And she submitted, only because she was afraid to touch me until it was cleansed. I finished washing and disinfecting her thumb, and then she turned to my face. After it was finished we sat together and talked awhile of many things for there had come into our lives sudden, very terrible thoughts. We were, all at once, afraid of something worse than death. We spoke of loading the boat with provisions and water and making our way out on to the sea; yet we were helpless, for many causes, and – and the growth had attacked us already. We decided to stay. God would do with us what was His will. We would wait.

"A month, two months, three months passed and the places grew somewhat, and there had come others. Yet we fought so strenuously with the fear that its headway was but slow, comparatively speaking.

"Occasionally we ventured off to the ship for such stores as we needed. There we found that the fungus grew persistently. One of the nodules on the maindeck became soon as high as my head.

"We had now given up all thought or hope of leaving the island. We had realised that it would be unallowable to go among healthy humans, with the things from which we were suffering.

"With this determination and knowledge in our minds we knew that we should have to husband our food and water; for we did not know, at that time, but that we should possibly live for many years.

"This reminds me that I have told you that I am an old man. Judged by the years this is not so. But – but—"

He broke off; then continued somewhat abruptly:

"As I was saying, we knew that we should have to use care in the matter of food. But we had no idea then how little food there was left of which to take care. It was a week later that I made the discovery that all the other bread tanks – which I had supposed full – were empty, and that (beyond odd tins of vegetables and meat, and some other matters) we had nothing on which to depend, but the bread in the tank which I had already opened.

"After learning this I bestirred myself to do what I could, and set to work at fishing in the lagoon; but with no success. At this I was somewhat inclined to feel desperate until the thought came to me to try outside the lagoon, in the open sea.

"Here, at times, I caught odd fish; but so infrequently that they proved of but little help in keeping us from the hunger which threatened.

It seemed to me that our deaths were likely to come by hunger, and not by the growth of the thing which had seized upon our bodies.

"We were in this state of mind when the fourth month wore out. When I made a very horrible discovery. One morning, a little before midday. I came off from the ship with a portion of the biscuits which were left. In the mouth of her tent I saw my sweetheart sitting, eating something.

"'What is it, my dear?' I called out as I leapt ashore. Yet, on hearing my voice, she seemed confused, and, turning, slyly threw something towards the edge of the little clearing. It fell short, and a vague suspicion having arisen within me, I walked across and picked it up. It was a piece of the grey fungus.

"As I went to her with it in my hand, she turned deadly pale; then rose red.

"I felt strangely dazed and frightened.

"'My dear! My dear!' I said, and could say no more. Yet at words she broke down and cried bitterly. Gradually, as she calmed, I got from her the news that she had tried it the preceding day, and – and liked it. I got her to promise on her knees not to touch it again, however great our hunger. After she had promised she told me that the desire for it had come suddenly, and that, until the moment of desire, she had experienced nothing towards it but the most extreme repulsion.

"Later in the day, feeling strangely restless, and much shaken with the thing which I had discovered, I made my way along one of the twisted paths – formed by the white, sand-like substance – which led among the fungoid growth. I had, once before, ventured along there; but not to any great distance. This time, being involved in perplexing thought, I went much further than hitherto.

"Suddenly I was called to myself by a queer hoarse sound on my left. Turning quickly I saw that there was movement among an extraordinarily shaped mass of fungus, close to my elbow. It was swaying uneasily, as though it possessed life of its own. Abruptly, as I stared, the thought came to me that the thing had a grotesque resemblance to the figure of a distorted human creature. Even as the fancy flashed into my brain, there was a slight, sickening noise of tearing, and I saw that one of the branch-like arms was detaching itself from the surrounding grey masses, and coming towards me. The head of the thing – a shapeless grey ball, inclined in my direction. I stood stupidly, and the vile arm brushed across my face. I gave out a frightened cry, and ran back a few paces. There was a sweetish taste upon my lips where the thing had touched me. I licked them, and was immediately filled with an inhuman desire. I turned and seized a mass of the fungus. Then more and – more. I was insatiable. In the midst of devouring, the remembrance of the morning's discovery swept into my mazed brain. It was sent by God. I dashed the fragment I held to the ground. Then, utterly wretched and feeling a dreadful guiltiness, I made my way back to the little encampment.

"I think she knew, by some marvellous intuition which love must have given, so soon as she set eyes on me. Her quiet sympathy made it easier for me, and I told her of my sudden weakness; yet omitted to mention the extraordinary thing which had gone before. I desired to spare her all unnecessary terror.

"But, for myself, I had added an intolerable knowledge, to breed an incessant terror in my brain; for I doubted not but that I had seen the end of one of those men who had come to the island in the ship in the lagoon; and in that monstrous ending I had seen our own.

"Thereafter we kept from the abominable food, though the desire for it had entered into our blood. Yet our drear punishment was upon us; for, day by day, with monstrous rapidity, the fungoid growth took hold of our poor bodies. Nothing we could do would check it materially, and so – and so – we who had been human, became – well, it matters less each day. Only – only we had been man and maid!

"And day by day the fight is more dreadful, to withstand the hungerlust for the terrible lichen.

"A week ago we ate the last of the biscuit, and since that time I have caught three fish. I was out here fishing tonight when your schooner drifted upon me out of the mist. I hailed you. You know the rest, and may God, out of His great heart, bless you for your goodness to a – a couple of poor outcast souls."

There was the dip of an oar – another. Then the voice came again, and for the last time, sounding through the slight surrounding mist, ghostly and mournful.

"God bless you! Goodbye!"

"Goodbye," we shouted together, hoarsely, our hearts full of many emotions.

I glanced about me. I became aware that the dawn was upon us.

The sun flung a stray beam across the hidden sea; pierced the mist dully, and lit up the receding boat with a gloomy fire. Indistinctly I saw something nodding between the oars. I thought of a sponge – a great, grey nodding sponge – The oars continued to ply. They were grey – as was the boat – and my eyes searched a moment vainly for the conjunction of hand and oar. My gaze flashed back to the – head. It nodded forward as the oars went backward for the stroke. Then the oars were dipped, the boat shot out of the patch of light, and the – the thing went nodding into the mist.

If you enjoyed this, you might also like…
The Derelict, see page 349
The Whistling Room, see page 37

The House on the Borderland
Chapters I-XI

Author's Introduction to the Manuscript

Many are the hours in which I have pondered upon the story that is set forth in the following pages. I trust that my instincts are not awry when they prompt me to leave the account, in simplicity, as it was handed to me.

And the MS. itself – You must picture me, when first it was given into my care, turning it over, curiously, and making a swift, jerky examination. A small book it is; but thick, and all, save the last few pages, filled with a quaint but legible handwriting, and writ very close. I have the queer, faint, pit-water smell of it in my nostrils now as I write, and my fingers have subconscious memories of the soft, 'cloggy' feel of the long-damp pages.

I read, and, in reading, lifted the Curtains of the Impossible that blind the mind, and looked out into the unknown. Amid stiff, abrupt sentences I wandered; and, presently, I had no fault to charge against their abrupt tellings; for, better far than my own ambitious phrasing, is this mutilated story capable of bringing home all that the old Recluse, of the vanished house, had striven to tell.

Of the simple, stiffly given account of weird and extraordinary matters, I will say little. It lies before you. The inner story must be uncovered, personally, by each reader, according to ability and desire. And even should any fail to see, as now I see, the shadowed picture and conception of that to which one may well give the accepted titles of Heaven and Hell; yet can I promise certain thrills, merely taking the story as a story.

WILLIAM HOPE HODGSON December 17, 1907

Chapter I
The Finding of the Manuscript

RIGHT AWAY in the west of Ireland lies a tiny hamlet called Kraighten. It is situated, alone, at the base of a low hill. Far around there spreads a waste of bleak and totally inhospitable country; where, here and there at great intervals, one may come upon the ruins of some long desolate cottage – unthatched and stark. The whole land is bare and unpeopled, the very earth scarcely covering the rock that lies beneath it, and with which the country abounds, in places rising out of the soil in wave-shaped ridges.

Yet, in spite of its desolation, my friend Tonnison and I had elected to spend our vacation there. He had stumbled on the place by mere chance the year previously, during the course of a long walking tour, and discovered the possibilities for the angler in a small and unnamed river that runs past the outskirts of the little village.

I have said that the river is without name; I may add that no map that I have hitherto consulted has shown either village or stream. They seem to have entirely escaped observation: indeed, they might never exist for all that the average guide tells one. Possibly this can be partly accounted for by the fact that the nearest railway station (Ardrahan) is some forty miles distant.

It was early one warm evening when my friend and I arrived in Kraighten. We had reached Ardrahan the previous night, sleeping there in rooms hired at the village post office, and leaving in good time on the following morning, clinging insecurely to one of the typical jaunting cars.

It had taken us all day to accomplish our journey over some of the roughest tracks imaginable, with the result that we were thoroughly tired and somewhat bad tempered. However, the tent had to be erected and our goods stowed away before we could think of food or rest. And so we set to work, with the aid of our driver, and soon had the tent up upon a small patch of ground just outside the little village, and quite near to the river.

Then, having stored all our belongings, we dismissed the driver, as he had to make his way back as speedily as possible, and told him to come across to us at the end of a fortnight. We had brought sufficient provisions to last us for that space of time, and water we could get from the stream. Fuel we did not need, as we had included a small oil-stove among our outfit, and the weather was fine and warm.

It was Tonnison's idea to camp out instead of getting lodgings in one of the cottages. As he put it, there was no joke in sleeping in a room with a numerous family of healthy Irish in one corner and the pigsty in the other, while overhead a ragged colony of roosting fowls distributed their blessings impartially, and the whole place so full of peat smoke that it made a fellow sneeze his head off just to put it inside the doorway.

Tonnison had got the stove lit now and was busy cutting slices of bacon into the frying pan; so I took the kettle and walked down to the river for water. On the way, I had to pass close to a little group of the village people, who eyed me curiously, but not in any unfriendly manner, though none of them ventured a word.

As I returned with my kettle filled, I went up to them and, after a friendly nod, to which they replied in like manner, I asked them casually about the fishing; but, instead of answering, they just shook their heads silently, and stared at me. I repeated the question, addressing more particularly a great, gaunt fellow at my elbow; yet again I received no answer. Then the man turned to a comrade and said something rapidly in a language that I did not understand; and, at once, the whole crowd of them fell to jabbering in what, after a few moments, I guessed to be pure Irish. At the same time they cast many glances in my direction. For a minute, perhaps, they spoke among themselves thus; then the man I had addressed faced 'round at me and said something. By the expression of his face I guessed that he, in turn, was questioning me; but now I had to shake my head, and indicate that I did not comprehend what it was they wanted to know; and so we stood looking at one another, until I heard Tonnison calling to me to hurry up with the kettle. Then, with a smile and a nod, I left them, and all in the little crowd smiled and nodded in return, though their faces still betrayed their puzzlement.

It was evident, I reflected as I went towards the tent, that the inhabitants of these few huts in the wilderness did not know a word of English; and when I told Tonnison, he remarked that he was aware of the fact, and, more, that it was not at all uncommon in that part of the country, where the people often lived and died in their isolated hamlets without ever coming in contact with the outside world.

"I wish we had got the driver to interpret for us before he left," I remarked, as we sat down to our meal. "It seems so strange for the people of this place not even to know what we've come for."

Tonnison grunted an assent, and thereafter was silent for a while.

Later, having satisfied our appetites somewhat, we began to talk, laying our plans for the morrow; then, after a smoke, we closed the flap of the tent, and prepared to turn in.

"I suppose there's no chance of those fellows outside taking anything?" I asked, as we rolled ourselves in our blankets.

Tonnison said that he did not think so, at least while we were about; and, as he went on to explain, we could lock up everything, except the tent, in the big chest that we had brought to hold our provisions. I agreed to this, and soon we were both asleep.

Next morning, early, we rose and went for a swim in the river; after which we dressed and had breakfast. Then we roused out our fishing tackle and overhauled it, by which time, our breakfasts having settled somewhat, we made all secure within the tent and strode off in the direction my friend had explored on his previous visit.

During the day we fished happily, working steadily upstream, and by evening we had one of the prettiest creels of fish that I had seen for a long while. Returning to the village, we made a good feed off our day's spoil, after which, having selected a few of the finer fish for our breakfast, we presented the remainder to the group of villagers who had assembled at a respectful distance to watch our doings. They seemed wonderfully grateful, and heaped mountains of what I presumed to be Irish blessings upon our heads.

Thus we spent several days, having splendid sport, and first-rate appetites to do justice upon our prey. We were pleased to find how friendly the villagers were inclined to be, and that there was no evidence of their having ventured to meddle with our belongings during our absences.

It was on a Tuesday that we arrived in Kraighten, and it would be on the Sunday following that we made a great discovery. Hitherto we had always gone up-stream; on that day, however, we laid aside our rods, and, taking some provisions, set off for a long ramble in the opposite direction. The day was warm, and we trudged along leisurely enough, stopping about midday to eat our lunch upon a great flat rock near the riverbank. Afterward we sat and smoked awhile, resuming our walk only when we were tired of inaction.

For perhaps another hour we wandered onward, chatting quietly and comfortably on this and that matter, and on several occasions stopping while my companion – who is something of an artist – made rough sketches of striking bits of the wild scenery.

And then, without any warning whatsoever, the river we had followed so confidently, came to an abrupt end – vanishing into the earth.

"Good Lord!" I said. "Whoever would have thought of this?"

And I stared in amazement; then I turned to Tonnison. He was looking, with a blank expression upon his face, at the place where the river disappeared.

In a moment he spoke.

"Let us go on a bit; it may reappear again – anyhow, it is worth investigating."

I agreed, and we went forward once more, though rather aimlessly; for we were not at all certain in which direction to prosecute our search. For perhaps a mile we moved onward; then Tonnison, who had been gazing about curiously, stopped and shaded his eyes.

"See!" he said, after a moment. "Isn't that mist or something, over there to the right – away in a line with that great piece of rock?" And he indicated with his hand.

I stared, and, after a minute, seemed to see something, but could not be certain, and said so.

"Anyway," my friend replied, "we'll just go across and have a glance." And he started off in the direction he had suggested, I following. Presently, we came among bushes, and, after a time, out upon the top of a high, boulder-strewn bank, from which we looked down into a wilderness of bushes and trees.

"Seems as though we had come upon an oasis in this desert of stone," muttered Tonnison, as he gazed interestedly. Then he was silent, his eyes fixed; and I looked also; for up from somewhere about the centre of the wooded lowland there rose high into the quiet air a great column of hazelike spray, upon which the sun shone, causing innumerable rainbows.

"How beautiful!" I exclaimed.

"Yes," answered Tonnison, thoughtfully. "There must be a waterfall, or something, over there. Perhaps it's our river come to light again. Let's go and see."

Down the sloping bank we made our way, and entered among the trees and shrubberies. The bushes were matted, and the trees overhung us, so that the place was disagreeably gloomy; though not dark enough to hide from me the fact that many of the trees were fruit trees, and that, here and there, one could trace indistinctly, signs of a long departed cultivation. Thus it came to me that we were making our way through the riot of a great and ancient garden. I said as much to Tonnison, and he agreed that there certainly seemed reasonable grounds for my belief.

What a wild place it was, so dismal and somber! Somehow, as we went forward, a sense of the silent loneliness and desertion of the old garden grew upon me, and I felt shivery. One could imagine things lurking among the tangled bushes; while, in the very air of the place, there seemed something uncanny. I think Tonnison was conscious of this also, though he said nothing.

Suddenly, we came to a halt. Through the trees there had grown upon our ears a distant sound. Tonnison bent forward, listening. I could hear it more plainly now; it was continuous and harsh – a sort of droning roar, seeming to come from far away. I experienced a queer, indescribable, little feeling of nervousness. What sort of place was it into which we had got? I looked at my companion, to see what he thought of the matter; and noted that there was only puzzlement in his face; and then, as I watched his features, an expression of comprehension crept over them, and he nodded his head.

"That's a waterfall," he exclaimed, with conviction. "I know the sound now." And he began to push vigorously through the bushes, in the direction of the noise.

As we went forward, the sound became plainer continually, showing that we were heading straight towards it. Steadily, the roaring grew louder and nearer, until it appeared, as I remarked to Tonnison, almost to come from under our feet – and still we were surrounded by the trees and shrubs.

"Take care!" Tonnison called to me. "Look where you're going." And then, suddenly, we came out from among the trees, on to a great open space, where, not six paces in front of us, yawned the mouth of a tremendous chasm, from the depths of which the noise appeared to rise, along with the continuous, mistlike spray that we had witnessed from the top of the distant bank.

For quite a minute we stood in silence, staring in bewilderment at the sight; then my friend went forward cautiously to the edge of the abyss. I followed, and, together, we looked down through a boil of spray at a monster cataract of frothing water that burst, spouting, from the side of the chasm, nearly a hundred feet below.

"Good Lord!" said Tonnison.

I was silent, and rather awed. The sight was so unexpectedly grand and eerie; though this latter quality came more upon me later.

Presently, I looked up and across to the further side of the chasm. There, I saw something towering up among the spray: it looked like a fragment of a great ruin, and I touched Tonnison on the shoulder. He glanced 'round, with a start, and I pointed towards the thing. His gaze followed my finger, and his eyes lighted up with a sudden flash of excitement, as the object came within his field of view.

"Come along," he shouted above the uproar. "We'll have a look at it. There's something queer about this place; I feel it in my bones." And he started off, 'round the edge of the craterlike abyss. As we neared this new thing, I saw that I had not been mistaken in my first impression. It was undoubtedly a portion of some ruined building; yet now I made out that it was not built upon the edge of the chasm itself, as I had at first supposed; but perched almost at the extreme end of a huge spur of rock that jutted out some fifty or sixty feet over the abyss. In fact, the jagged mass of ruin was literally suspended in midair.

Arriving opposite it, we walked out on to the projecting arm of rock, and I must confess to having felt an intolerable sense of terror as I looked down from that dizzy perch into the unknown depths below us – into the deeps from which there rose ever the thunder of the falling water and the shroud of rising spray.

Reaching the ruin, we clambered 'round it cautiously, and, on the further side, came upon a mass of fallen stones and rubble. The ruin itself seemed to me, as I proceeded now to examine it minutely, to be a portion of the outer wall of some prodigious structure, it was so thick and substantially built; yet what it was doing in such a position I could by no means conjecture. Where was the rest of the house, or castle, or whatever there had been?

I went back to the outer side of the wall, and thence to the edge of the chasm, leaving Tonnison rooting systematically among the heap of stones and rubbish on the outer side. Then I commenced to examine the surface of the ground, near the edge of the abyss, to see whether there were not left other remnants of the building to which the fragment of ruin evidently belonged. But though I scrutinised the earth with the greatest care, I could see no signs of anything to show that there had ever been a building erected on the spot, and I grew more puzzled than ever.

Then, I heard a cry from Tonnison; he was shouting my name, excitedly, and without delay I hurried along the rocky promontory to the ruin. I wondered whether he had hurt himself, and then the thought came, that perhaps he had found something.

I reached the crumbled wall and climbed 'round. There I found Tonnison standing within a small excavation that he had made among the *débris*: he was brushing the dirt from something that looked like a book, much crumpled and dilapidated; and opening his mouth, every second or two, to bellow my name. As soon as he saw that I had come, he handed his prize to me, telling me to put it into my satchel so as to protect it from the damp, while he continued his explorations. This I did, first, however, running the pages through my fingers, and noting that they were closely filled with neat, old-fashioned writing which was quite legible, save in one portion, where many of the pages were almost destroyed, being muddied and crumpled, as though the book had been doubled back at that part. This, I found out from Tonnison, was actually as he had discovered it, and the damage was due, probably, to the fall of masonry upon the opened part. Curiously enough, the book was fairly dry, which I attributed to its having been so securely buried among the ruins.

Having put the volume away safely, I turned-to and gave Tonnison a hand with his self-imposed task of excavating; yet, though we put in over an hour's hard work, turning over the whole of the upheaped stones and rubbish, we came upon nothing more than some fragments of broken wood, that might have been parts of a desk or table; and so we gave up searching, and went back along the rock, once more to the safety of the land.

The next thing we did was to make a complete tour of the tremendous chasm, which we were able to observe was in the form of an almost perfect circle, save for where the ruin-crowned spur of rock jutted out, spoiling its symmetry.

The abyss was, as Tonnison put it, like nothing so much as a gigantic well or pit going sheer down into the bowels of the earth.

For some time longer, we continued to stare about us, and then, noticing that there was a clear space away to the north of the chasm, we bent our steps in that direction.

Here, distant from the mouth of the mighty pit by some hundreds of yards, we came upon a great lake of silent water – silent, that is, save in one place where there was a continuous bubbling and gurgling.

Now, being away from the noise of the spouting cataract, we were able to hear one another speak, without having to shout at the tops of our voices, and I asked Tonnison what he thought of the place – I told him that I didn't like it, and that the sooner we were out of it the better I should be pleased.

He nodded in reply, and glanced at the woods behind furtively. I asked him if he had seen or heard anything. He made no answer; but stood silent, as though listening, and I kept quiet also.

Suddenly, he spoke.

"Hark!" he said, sharply. I looked at him, and then away among the trees and bushes, holding my breath involuntarily. A minute came and went in strained silence; yet I could hear nothing, and I turned to Tonnison to say as much; and then, even as I opened my lips to speak, there came a strange wailing noise out of the wood on our left.... It appeared to float through the trees, and there was a rustle of stirring leaves, and then silence.

All at once, Tonnison spoke, and put his hand on my shoulder. "Let us get out of here," he said, and began to move slowly towards where the surrounding trees and bushes seemed thinnest. As I followed him, it came to me suddenly that the sun was low, and that there was a raw sense of chilliness in the air.

Tonnison said nothing further, but kept on steadily. We were among the trees now, and I glanced around, nervously; but saw nothing, save the quiet branches and trunks and the tangled bushes. Onward we went, and no sound broke the silence, except the occasional snapping of a twig under our feet, as we moved forward. Yet, in spite of the quietness, I had a horrible feeling that we were not alone; and I kept so close to Tonnison that twice I kicked his heels clumsily, though he said nothing. A minute, and then another, and we reached the confines of the wood coming out at last upon the bare rockiness of the countryside. Only then was I able to shake off the haunting dread that had followed me among the trees.

Once, as we moved away, there seemed to come again a distant sound of wailing, and I said to myself that it was the wind – yet the evening was breathless.

Presently, Tonnison began to talk.

"Look you," he said with decision, "I would not spend the night in *that* place for all the wealth that the world holds. There is something unholy – diabolical – about it. It came to me all in a moment, just after you spoke. It seemed to me that the woods were full of vile things – you know!"

"Yes," I answered, and looked back towards the place; but it was hidden from us by a rise in the ground.

"There's the book," I said, and I put my hand into the satchel.

"You've got it safely?" he questioned, with a sudden access of anxiety.

"Yes," I replied.

"Perhaps," he continued, "we shall learn something from it when we get back to the tent. We had better hurry, too; we're a long way off still, and I don't fancy, now, being caught out here in the dark."

It was two hours later when we reached the tent; and, without delay, we set to work to prepare a meal; for we had eaten nothing since our lunch at midday.

Supper over, we cleared the things out of the way, and lit our pipes. Then Tonnison asked me to get the manuscript out of my satchel. This I did, and then, as we could not both read from it at the same time, he suggested that I should read the thing out loud. "And mind," he cautioned, knowing my propensities, "don't go skipping half the book."

Yet, had he but known what it contained, he would have realised how needless such advice was, for once at least. And there seated in the opening of our little tent, I began the strange tale of *The House on the Borderland* (for such was the title of the MS.); this is told in the following pages.

Chapter II
The Plain of Silence

I AM AN old man. I live here in this ancient house, surrounded by huge, unkempt gardens.

The peasantry, who inhabit the wilderness beyond, say that I am mad. That is because I will have nothing to do with them. I live here alone with my old sister, who is also my housekeeper. We keep no servants – I hate them. I have one friend, a dog; yes, I would sooner have old Pepper than the rest of Creation together. He, at least, understands me – and has sense enough to leave me alone when I am in my dark moods.

I have decided to start a kind of diary; it may enable me to record some of the thoughts and feelings that I cannot express to anyone; but, beyond this, I am anxious to make some record of the strange things that I have heard and seen, during many years of loneliness, in this weird old building.

For a couple of centuries, this house has had a reputation, a bad one, and, until I bought it, for more than eighty years no one had lived here; consequently, I got the old place at a ridiculously low figure.

I am not superstitious; but I have ceased to deny that things happen in this old house – things that I cannot explain; and, therefore, I must needs ease my mind, by writing down an account of them, to the best of my ability; though, should this, my diary, ever be read when I am gone, the readers will but shake their heads, and be the more convinced that I was mad.

This house, how ancient it is! Though its age strikes one less, perhaps, than the quaintness of its structure, which is curious and fantastic to the last degree. Little curved towers and pinnacles, with outlines suggestive of leaping flames, predominate; while the body of the building is in the form of a circle.

I have heard that there is an old story, told amongst the country people, to the effect that the devil built the place. However, that is as may be. True or not, I neither know nor care, save as it may have helped to cheapen it, ere I came.

I must have been here some ten years before I saw sufficient to warrant any belief in the stories, current in the neighbourhood, about this house. It is true that I had, on at least a dozen occasions, seen, vaguely, things that puzzled me, and, perhaps, had felt more than I had seen. Then, as the years passed, bringing age upon me, I became often aware of something unseen, yet unmistakably present, in the empty rooms and corridors. Still, it was as I have said many years before I saw any real manifestations of the so-called supernatural.

It was not Halloween. If I were telling a story for amusement's sake, I should probably place it on that night of nights; but this is a true record of my own experiences, and I would not put pen to paper to amuse anyone. No. It was after midnight on the morning of the twenty-first day of January. I was sitting reading, as is often my custom, in my study. Pepper lay, sleeping, near my chair.

Without warning, the flames of the two candles went low, and then shone with a ghastly green effulgence. I looked up, quickly, and as I did so I saw the lights sink into a dull, ruddy tint; so that the room glowed with a strange, heavy, crimson twilight that gave the shadows behind the chairs and tables a double depth of blackness; and wherever the light struck, it was as though luminous blood had been splashed over the room.

Down on the floor, I heard a faint, frightened whimper, and something pressed itself in between my two feet. It was Pepper, cowering under my dressing gown. Pepper, usually as brave as a lion!

It was this movement of the dog's, I think, that gave me the first twinge of *real* fear. I had been considerably startled when the lights burnt first green and then red; but had been momentarily under the impression that the change was due to some influx of noxious gas into the room. Now, however, I saw that it was not so; for the candles burned with a steady flame, and showed no signs of going out, as would have been the case had the change been due to fumes in the atmosphere.

I did not move. I felt distinctly frightened; but could think of nothing better to do than wait. For perhaps a minute, I kept my glance about the room, nervously. Then I noticed that the lights had commenced to sink, very slowly; until presently they showed minute specks of red fire, like the gleamings of rubies in the darkness. Still, I sat watching; while a sort of dreamy indifference seemed to steal over me; banishing altogether the fear that had begun to grip me.

Away in the far end of the huge old-fashioned room, I became conscious of a faint glow. Steadily it grew, filling the room with gleams of quivering green light; then they sank quickly, and changed – even as the candle flames had done – into a deep, somber crimson that strengthened, and lit up the room with a flood of awful glory.

The light came from the end wall, and grew ever brighter until its intolerable glare caused my eyes acute pain, and involuntarily I closed them. It may have been a few seconds before I was able to open them. The first thing I noticed was that the light had decreased, greatly; so that it no longer tried my eyes. Then, as it grew still duller, I was aware, all at once, that, instead of looking at the redness, I was staring through it, and through the wall beyond.

Gradually, as I became more accustomed to the idea, I realised that I was looking out on to a vast plain, lit with the same gloomy twilight that pervaded the room. The immensity of this plain scarcely can be conceived. In no part could I perceive its confines. It seemed to broaden and spread out, so that the eye failed to perceive any limitations. Slowly, the details of the nearer portions began to grow clear; then, in a moment almost, the light died away, and the vision – if vision it were – faded and was gone.

Suddenly, I became conscious that I was no longer in the chair. Instead, I seemed to be hovering above it, and looking down at a dim something, huddled and silent. In a little while, a cold blast struck me, and I was outside in the night, floating, like a bubble, up through the darkness. As I moved, an icy coldness seemed to enfold me, so that I shivered.

After a time, I looked to right and left, and saw the intolerable blackness of the night, pierced by remote gleams of fire. Onward, outward, I drove. Once, I glanced behind, and saw the earth, a small crescent of blue light, receding away to my left. Further off, the sun, a splash of white flame, burned vividly against the dark.

An indefinite period passed. Then, for the last time, I saw the earth – an enduring globule of radiant blue, swimming in an eternity of ether. And there I, a fragile flake of soul dust, flickered silently across the void, from the distant blue, into the expanse of the unknown.

A great while seemed to pass over me, and now I could nowhere see anything. I had passed beyond the fixed stars and plunged into the huge blackness that waits beyond. All this time I had experienced little, save a sense of lightness and cold discomfort. Now however the atrocious darkness seemed to creep into my soul, and I became filled with fear and despair. What was going to become of me? Where was I going? Even as the thoughts were formed, there grew against the impalpable blackness that wrapped me a faint tinge of blood. It seemed extraordinarily remote, and mistlike; yet, at once, the feeling of oppression was lightened, and I no longer despaired.

Slowly, the distant redness became plainer and larger; until, as I drew nearer, it spread out into a great, somber glare – dull and tremendous. Still, I fled onward, and, presently, I had come so close, that it seemed to stretch beneath me, like a great ocean of somber red. I could see little, save that it appeared to spread out interminably in all directions.

In a further space, I found that I was descending upon it; and, soon, I sank into a great sea of sullen, red-hued clouds. Slowly, I emerged from these, and there, below me, I saw the stupendous plain that I had seen from my room in this house that stands upon the borders of the Silences.

Presently, I landed, and stood, surrounded by a great waste of loneliness. The place was lit with a gloomy twilight that gave an impression of indescribable desolation.

Afar to my right, within the sky, there burnt a gigantic ring of dull-red fire, from the outer edge of which were projected huge, writhing flames, darted and jagged. The interior of this ring was black, black as the gloom of the outer night. I comprehended, at once, that it was from this extraordinary sun that the place derived its doleful light.

From that strange source of light, I glanced down again to my surroundings. Everywhere I looked, I saw nothing but the same flat weariness of interminable plain. Nowhere could I descry any signs of life; not even the ruins of some ancient habitation.

Gradually, I found that I was being borne forward, floating across the flat waste. For what seemed an eternity, I moved onward. I was unaware of any great sense of impatience; though some curiosity and a vast wonder were with me continually. Always, I saw around me the breadth of that enormous plain; and, always, I searched for some new thing to break its monotony; but there was no change – only loneliness, silence, and desert.

Presently, in a half-conscious manner, I noticed that there was a faint mistiness, ruddy in hue, lying over its surface. Still, when I looked more intently, I was unable to say that it was really mist; for it appeared to blend with the plain, giving it a peculiar unrealness, and conveying to the senses the idea of unsubstantiality.

Gradually, I began to weary with the sameness of the thing. Yet, it was a great time before I perceived any signs of the place, towards which I was being conveyed.

At first, I saw it, far ahead, like a long hillock on the surface of the Plain. Then, as I drew nearer, I perceived that I had been mistaken; for, instead of a low hill, I made out, now, a chain of great mountains, whose distant peaks towered up into the red gloom, until they were almost lost to sight.

Chapter III
The House in the Arena

AND SO, AFTER A TIME, I came to the mountains. Then, the course of my journey was altered, and I began to move along their bases, until, all at once, I saw that I had come opposite to a vast rift, opening into the mountains. Through this, I was borne, moving at no great speed. On either side of me, huge, scarped walls of rocklike substance rose sheer. Far overhead, I discerned a thin ribbon of red, where the mouth of the chasm opened, among inaccessible peaks. Within, was gloom, deep and somber, and chilly silence. For a while, I went onward steadily, and then, at last, I saw, ahead, a deep, red glow, that told me I was near upon the further opening of the gorge.

A minute came and went, and I was at the exit of the chasm, staring out upon an enormous amphitheatre of mountains. Yet, of the mountains, and the terrible grandeur of the place, I recked nothing; for I was confounded with amazement to behold, at a distance of several miles and occupying the centre of the arena, a stupendous structure built apparently of green jade. Yet, in itself, it was not the discovery of the building that had so astonished me; but the fact, which became every moment more apparent, that in no particular, save in colour and its enormous size, did the lonely structure vary from this house in which I live.

For a while, I continued to stare, fixedly. Even then, I could scarcely believe that I saw aright. In my mind, a question formed, reiterating incessantly: "What does it mean?" "What does it mean?" and I was unable to make answer, even out of the depths of my imagination. I seemed capable only of wonder and fear. For a time longer, I gazed, noting continually some fresh point of resemblance that attracted me. At last, wearied and sorely puzzled, I turned from it, to view the rest of the strange place on to which I had intruded.

Hitherto, I had been so engrossed in my scrutiny of the House, that I had given only a cursory glance 'round. Now, as I looked, I began to realise upon what sort of a place I had come. The arena, for so I have termed it, appeared a perfect circle of about ten to twelve miles in diameter, the House, as I have mentioned before, standing in the centre. The surface of the place, like to that of the Plain, had a peculiar, misty appearance, that was yet not mist.

From a rapid survey, my glance passed quickly upward along the slopes of the circling mountains. How silent they were. I think that this same abominable stillness was more trying to me than anything that I had so far seen or imagined. I was looking up, now, at the great crags, towering so loftily. Up there, the impalpable redness gave a blurred appearance to everything.

And then, as I peered, curiously, a new terror came to me; for away up among the dim peaks to my right, I had descried a vast shape of blackness, giantlike. It grew upon my sight. It had an enormous equine head, with gigantic ears, and seemed to peer steadfastly down into the arena. There was that about the pose that gave me the impression of an eternal watchfulness – of having warded that dismal place, through unknown eternities. Slowly, the monster became plainer to me; and then, suddenly, my gaze sprang from it to something further off and higher among the crags. For a long minute, I gazed, fearfully. I was strangely conscious of something not altogether unfamiliar – as though something stirred in the back of my mind. The thing was black, and had four grotesque arms. The features showed indistinctly, 'round the neck, I made out several light-coloured objects. Slowly, the details came to me, and I realised, coldly, that they were skulls. Further down the body was another circling belt, showing less dark against the black trunk. Then, even as I puzzled to know what the thing was, a memory slid into my mind, and straightway, I knew that I was looking at a monstrous representation of Kali, the Hindu goddess of death.

Other remembrances of my old student days drifted into my thoughts. My glance fell back upon the huge beast-headed Thing. Simultaneously, I recognised it for the ancient Egyptian god Set, or Seth, the Destroyer of Souls. With the knowledge, there came a great sweep of questioning – "Two of the—!" I stopped, and endeavoured to think. Things beyond my imagination peered into my frightened mind. I saw, obscurely. "The old gods of mythology!" I tried to comprehend to what it was all pointing. My gaze dwelt, flickeringly, between the two. "If—"

An idea came swiftly, and I turned, and glanced rapidly upward, searching the gloomy crags, away to my left. Something loomed out under a great peak, a shape of greyness. I wondered I had not seen it earlier, and then remembered I had not yet viewed that portion. I saw it more plainly now. It was, as I have said, grey. It had a tremendous head; but no eyes. That part of its face was blank.

Now, I saw that there were other things up among the mountains. Further off, reclining on a lofty ledge, I made out a livid mass, irregular and ghoulish. It seemed without form, save for an unclean, half-animal face, that looked out, vilely, from somewhere about its middle. And then I saw others – there were hundreds of them. They seemed to grow out of the shadows. Several I recognised almost immediately as mythological deities; others were strange to me, utterly strange, beyond the power of a human mind to conceive.

On each side, I looked, and saw more, continually. The mountains were full of strange things – Beast-gods, and Horrors so atrocious and bestial that possibility and decency deny any further attempt to describe them. And I – I was filled with a terrible sense of overwhelming horror and fear and repugnance; yet, spite of these, I wondered exceedingly. Was there then, after all, something in the old heathen worship, something more than the mere deifying of men, animals, and elements? The thought gripped me – was there?

Later, a question repeated itself. What were they, those Beast-gods, and the others? At first, they had appeared to me just sculptured Monsters placed indiscriminately among the inaccessible peaks and precipices of the surrounding mountains. Now, as I scrutinised them with greater intentness, my mind began to reach out to fresh conclusions. There was something about them, an indescribable sort of silent vitality that suggested, to my broadening consciousness, a state of life-in-death – a something that was by no means life, as we understand it; but rather an inhuman form of existence, that well might be likened to a deathless trance – a condition in which it was possible to imagine their continuing, eternally. "Immortal!" the word rose in my thoughts unbidden; and, straightway, I grew to wondering whether this might be the immortality of the gods.

And then, in the midst of my wondering and musing, something happened. Until then, I had been staying just within the shadow of the exit of the great rift. Now, without volition on my part, I drifted out of the semi-darkness and began to move slowly across the arena – towards the House. At this, I gave up all thoughts of those prodigious Shapes above me – and could only stare, frightenedly, at the tremendous structure towards which I was being conveyed so remorselessly. Yet, though I searched earnestly, I could discover nothing that I had not already seen, and so became gradually calmer.

Presently, I had reached a point more than halfway between the House and the gorge. All around was spread the stark loneliness of the place, and the unbroken silence. Steadily, I neared the great building. Then, all at once, something caught my vision, something that came 'round one of the huge buttresses of the House, and so into full view. It was a gigantic thing, and moved with a curious lope, going almost upright, after the manner of a man. It was quite unclothed, and had a remarkable luminous appearance. Yet it was the face that attracted and frightened me the most. It was the face of a swine.

Silently, intently, I watched this horrible creature, and forgot my fear, momentarily, in my interest in its movements. It was making its way, cumbrously 'round the building, stopping as it came to each window to peer in and shake at the bars, with which – as in this house – they were protected; and whenever it came to a door, it would push at it, fingering the fastening stealthily. Evidently, it was searching for an ingress into the House.

I had come now to within less than a quarter of a mile of the great structure, and still I was compelled forward. Abruptly, the Thing turned and gazed hideously in my direction. It opened its mouth, and, for the first time, the stillness of that abominable place was broken, by a deep, booming note that sent an added thrill of apprehension through me. Then, immediately, I became aware that it was coming towards me, swiftly and silently. In an instant, it had covered half the distance that lay between. And still, I was borne helplessly to meet it. Only a hundred yards, and the brutish ferocity of the giant face numbed me with a feeling of unmitigated horror. I could have screamed, in the supremeness of my fear; and then, in the very moment of my extremity and despair, I became conscious that I was looking down upon the arena, from a rapidly increasing height. I was rising, rising. In an inconceivably short while, I had reached an altitude of many hundred feet. Beneath me, the spot that I had just left, was occupied by the foul Swine-creature. It had gone down on all fours and was snuffing and rooting, like a veritable hog, at the surface of the arena. A moment and it rose to its feet, clutching upward, with an expression of desire upon its face such as I have never seen in this world.

Continually, I mounted higher. A few minutes, it seemed, and I had risen above the great mountains – floating, alone, afar in the redness. At a tremendous distance below, the arena showed, dimly; with the mighty House looking no larger than a tiny spot of green. The Swine-thing was no longer visible.

Presently, I passed over the mountains, out above the huge breadth of the plain. Far away, on its surface, in the direction of the ring-shaped sun, there showed a confused blur. I looked towards it, indifferently. It reminded me, somewhat, of the first glimpse I had caught of the mountain-amphitheatre.

With a sense of weariness, I glanced upward at the immense ring of fire. What a strange thing it was! Then, as I stared, out from the dark centre, there spurted a sudden flare of extraordinary vivid fire. Compared with the size of the black centre, it was as naught; yet, in itself, stupendous. With awakened interest, I watched it carefully, noting its strange boiling and glowing. Then, in a moment, the whole thing grew dim and unreal, and so passed out of sight. Much amazed, I glanced down to the Plain from which I was still rising. Thus, I received a fresh surprise. The Plain – everything had vanished, and only a sea of red mist was spread far below me. Gradually as I stared this grew remote, and died away into a dim far mystery of red against an unfathomable night. A while, and even this had gone, and I was wrapped in an impalpable, lightless gloom.

Chapter IV
The Earth

THUS I WAS, and only the memory that I had lived through the dark, once before, served to sustain my thoughts. A great time passed – ages. And then a single star broke its way through the darkness. It was the first of one of the outlying clusters of this universe. Presently, it was far behind, and all about me shone the splendour of the countless stars. Later, years it seemed, I saw the sun, a clot of flame. Around it, I made out presently several remote specks of light – the planets of the Solar system. And so I saw the earth again, blue and unbelievably minute. It grew larger, and became defined.

A long space of time came and went, and then at last I entered into the shadow of the world – plunging headlong into the dim and holy earth night. Overhead were the old constellations, and there was a crescent moon. Then, as I neared the earth's surface, a dimness swept over me, and I appeared to sink into a black mist.

For a while, I knew nothing. I was unconscious. Gradually, I became aware of a faint, distant whining. It became plainer. A desperate feeling of agony possessed me. I struggled madly for breath, and tried to shout. A moment, and I got my breath more easily. I was conscious that something was licking my hand. Something damp swept across my face. I heard a panting, and then again the whining. It seemed to come to my ears, now, with a sense of familiarity, and I opened my eyes. All was dark; but the feeling of oppression had left me. I was seated, and something was whining piteously, and licking me. I felt strangely confused, and, instinctively, tried to ward off the thing that licked. My head was curiously vacant, and, for the moment, I seemed incapable of action or thought. Then, things came back to me, and I called "Pepper", faintly. I was answered by a joyful bark, and renewed and frantic caresses.

In a little while, I felt stronger, and put out my hand for the matches. I groped about, for a few moments, blindly; then my hands lit upon them, and I struck a light, and looked confusedly around. All about me, I saw the old, familiar things. And there I sat, full of dazed wonders, until the flame of the match burnt my finger, and I dropped it; while a hasty expression of pain and anger, escaped my lips, surprising me with the sound of my own voice.

After a moment, I struck another match, and, stumbling across the room, lit the candles. As I did so, I observed that they had not burned away, but had been put out.

As the flames shot up, I turned, and stared about the study; yet there was nothing unusual to see; and, suddenly, a gust of irritation took me. What had happened? I held my head, with both hands, and tried to remember. Ah! the great, silent Plain, and the ring-shaped sun of red fire. Where were they? Where had I seen them? How long ago? I felt dazed and muddled. Once or twice, I walked up and down the room, unsteadily. My memory seemed dulled, and, already, the thing I had witnessed came back to me with an effort.

I have a remembrance of cursing, peevishly, in my bewilderment. Suddenly, I turned faint and giddy, and had to grasp at the table for support. During a few moments, I held on, weakly; and then managed to totter sideways into a chair. After a little time, I felt somewhat better, and succeeded in reaching the cupboard where, usually, I keep brandy and biscuits. I poured myself out a little of the stimulant, and drank it off. Then, taking a handful of biscuits, I returned to my chair, and began to devour them, ravenously. I was vaguely surprised at my hunger. I felt as though I had eaten nothing for an uncountably long while.

As I ate, my glance roved about the room, taking in its various details, and still searching, though almost unconsciously, for something tangible upon which to take hold, among the invisible mysteries that encompassed me. "Surely," I thought, "there must be something" And, in the same instant, my gaze dwelt upon the face of the clock in the opposite corner. Therewith, I stopped eating, and just stared. For, though its ticking indicated most certainly that it was still going, the hands were pointing to a little *before* the hour of midnight; whereas it was, as well I knew, considerably *after* that time when I had witnessed the first of the strange happenings I have just described.

For perhaps a moment I was astounded and puzzled. Had the hour been the same as when I had last seen the clock, I should have concluded that the hands had stuck in one place, while the internal mechanism went on as usual; but that would, in no way, account for the hands having travelled backward. Then, even as I turned the matter over in my wearied brain, the thought flashed upon me that it was now close upon the morning of the twenty-second, and that I had been unconscious to the visible world through the greater portion of the last twenty-four hours. The thought occupied my attention for a full minute; then I commenced to eat again. I was still very hungry.

During breakfast, next morning, I inquired casually of my sister regarding the date, and found my surmise correct. I had, indeed, been absent – at least in spirit – for nearly a day and a night.

My sister asked me no questions; for it is not by any means the first time that I have kept to my study for a whole day, and sometimes a couple of days at a time, when I have been particularly engrossed in my books or work.

And so the days pass on, and I am still filled with a wonder to know the meaning of all that I saw on that memorable night. Yet, well I know that my curiosity is little likely to be satisfied.

Chapter V
The Thing in the Pit

THIS HOUSE IS, as I have said before, surrounded by a huge estate, and wild and uncultivated gardens.

Away at the back, distant some three hundred yards, is a dark, deep ravine – spoken of as the 'Pit', by the peasantry. At the bottom runs a sluggish stream so overhung by trees as scarcely to be seen from above.

In passing, I must explain that this river has a subterranean origin, emerging suddenly at the East end of the ravine, and disappearing, as abruptly, beneath the cliffs that form its Western extremity.

It was some months after my vision (if vision it were) of the great Plain that my attention was particularly attracted to the Pit.

I happened, one day, to be walking along its Southern edge, when, suddenly, several pieces of rock and shale were dislodged from the face of the cliff immediately beneath me, and fell with a sullen crash through the trees. I heard them splash in the river at the bottom; and then silence. I should not have given this incident more than a passing thought, had not Pepper at once begun to bark savagely; nor would he be silent when I bade him, which is most unusual behavior on his part.

Feeling that there must be someone or something in the Pit, I went back to the house, quickly, for a stick. When I returned, Pepper had ceased his barks and was growling and smelling, uneasily, along the top.

Whistling to him to follow me, I started to descend cautiously. The depth to the bottom of the Pit must be about a hundred and fifty feet, and some time as well as considerable care was expended before we reached the bottom in safety.

Once down, Pepper and I started to explore along the banks of the river. It was very dark there due to the overhanging trees, and I moved warily, keeping my glance about me and my stick ready.

Pepper was quiet now and kept close to me all the time. Thus, we searched right up one side of the river, without hearing or seeing anything. Then, we crossed over – by the simple method of jumping – and commenced to beat our way back through the underbrush.

We had accomplished perhaps half the distance, when I heard again the sound of falling stones on the other side – the side from which we had just come. One large rock came thundering down through the treetops, struck the opposite bank, and bounded into the river, driving a great jet of water right over us. At this, Pepper gave out a deep growl; then stopped, and pricked up his ears. I listened, also.

A second later, a loud, half-human, half-piglike squeal sounded from among the trees, apparently about halfway up the South cliff. It was answered by a similar note from the bottom of the Pit. At this, Pepper gave a short, sharp bark, and, springing across the little river, disappeared into the bushes.

Immediately afterward, I heard his barks increase in depth and number, and in between there sounded a noise of confused jabbering. This ceased, and, in the succeeding silence, there rose a semi-human yell of agony. Almost immediately, Pepper gave a long-drawn howl of pain, and then the shrubs were violently agitated, and he came running out with his tail down, and glancing as he ran over his shoulder. As he reached me, I saw that he was bleeding from what appeared to be a great claw wound in the side that had almost laid bare his ribs.

Seeing Pepper thus mutilated, a furious feeling of anger seized me, and, whirling my staff, I sprang across, and into the bushes from which Pepper had emerged. As I forced my way through, I thought I heard a sound of breathing. Next instant, I had burst into a little clear space, just in time to see something, livid white in colour, disappear among the bushes on the opposite side. With a shout, I ran towards it; but, though I struck and probed among the bushes with my stick, I neither saw nor heard anything further; and so returned to Pepper. There, after bathing his wound in the river, I bound my wetted handkerchief 'round his body; having done which, we retreated up the ravine and into the daylight again.

On reaching the house, my sister inquired what had happened to Pepper, and I told her he had been fighting with a wildcat, of which I had heard there were several about.

I felt it would be better not to tell her how it had really happened; though, to be sure, I scarcely knew myself; but this I did know, that the thing I had seen run into the bushes was no wildcat. It was much too big, and had, so far as I had observed, a skin like a hog's, only of a dead, unhealthy white colour. And then – it had run upright, or nearly so, upon its hind feet, with a motion somewhat resembling that of a human being. This much I had noticed in my brief glimpse, and, truth to tell, I felt a good deal of uneasiness, besides curiosity as I turned the matter over in my mind.

It was in the morning that the above incident had occurred.

Then, it would be after dinner, as I sat reading, that, happening to look up suddenly, I saw something peering in over the window ledge the eyes and ears alone showing.

"A pig, by Jove!" I said, and rose to my feet. Thus, I saw the thing more completely; but it was no pig – God alone knows what it was. It reminded me, vaguely, of the hideous Thing that had haunted the great arena. It had a grotesquely human mouth and jaw; but with no chin of which to speak. The nose was prolonged into a snout; thus it was that with the little eyes and queer ears, gave it such an extraordinarily swinelike appearance. Of forehead there was little, and the whole face was of an unwholesome white colour.

For perhaps a minute, I stood looking at the thing with an ever growing feeling of disgust, and some fear. The mouth kept jabbering, inanely, and once emitted a half-swinish grunt. I think it was the eyes that attracted me the most; they seemed to glow, at times, with a horribly human intelligence, and kept flickering away from my face, over the details of the room, as though my stare disturbed it.

It appeared to be supporting itself by two clawlike hands upon the windowsill. These claws, unlike the face, were of a clayey brown hue, and bore an indistinct resemblance to human hands, in that they had four fingers and a thumb; though these were webbed up to the first joint, much as are a duck's. Nails it had also, but so long and powerful that they were more like the talons of an eagle than aught else.

As I have said, before, I felt some fear; though almost of an impersonal kind. I may explain my feeling better by saying that it was more a sensation of abhorrence; such as one might expect to feel, if brought in contact with something superhumanly foul; something unholy – belonging to some hitherto undreamt of state of existence.

I cannot say that I grasped these various details of the brute at the time. I think they seemed to come back to me, afterward, as though imprinted upon my brain. I imagined more than I saw as I looked at the thing, and the material details grew upon me later.

For perhaps a minute I stared at the creature; then as my nerves steadied a little I shook off the vague alarm that held me, and took a step towards the window. Even as I did so, the thing ducked and vanished. I rushed to the door and looked 'round hurriedly; but only the tangled bushes and shrubs met my gaze.

I ran back into the house, and, getting my gun, sallied out to search through the gardens. As I went, I asked myself whether the thing I had just seen was likely to be the same of which I had caught a glimpse in the morning. I inclined to think it was.

I would have taken Pepper with me; but judged it better to give his wound a chance to heal. Besides, if the creature I had just seen was, as I imagined, his antagonist of the morning, it was not likely that he would be of much use.

I began my search, systematically. I was determined, if it were possible, to find and put an end to that swine-thing. This was, at least, a material Horror!

At first, I searched, cautiously; with the thought of Pepper's wound in my mind; but, as the hours passed, and not a sign of anything living showed in the great, lonely gardens, I became less apprehensive. I felt almost as though I would welcome the sight of it. Anything seemed better than this silence, with the ever-present feeling that the creature might be lurking in every bush I passed. Later, I grew careless of danger, to the extent of plunging right through the bushes, probing with my gun barrel as I went.

At times, I shouted; but only the echoes answered back. I thought thus perhaps to frighten or stir the creature to showing itself; but only succeeded in bringing my sister Mary out, to know what was the matter. I told her that I had seen the wildcat that had wounded Pepper, and that I was trying to hunt it out of the bushes. She seemed only half satisfied, and went back into the house, with an expression of doubt upon her face. I wondered whether she had seen or guessed anything. For the rest of the afternoon, I prosecuted the search anxiously. I felt that I should be unable to sleep, with that bestial thing haunting the shrubberies, and yet, when evening fell, I had seen nothing. Then, as

I turned homeward, I heard a short, unintelligible noise, among the bushes to my right. Instantly, I turned, and, aiming quickly, fired in the direction of the sound. Immediately afterward, I heard something scuttling away among the bushes. It moved rapidly, and in a minute had gone out of hearing. After a few steps I ceased my pursuit, realising how futile it must be in the fast gathering gloom; and so, with a curious feeling of depression, I entered the house.

That night, after my sister had gone to bed, I went 'round to all the windows and doors on the ground floor; and saw to it that they were securely fastened. This precaution was scarcely necessary as regards the windows, as all of those on the lower storey are strongly barred; but with the doors – of which there are five – it was wisely thought, as not one was locked.

Having secured these, I went to my study, yet, somehow, for once, the place jarred upon me; it seemed so huge and echoey. For some time I tried to read; but at last finding it impossible I carried my book down to the kitchen where a large fire was burning, and sat there.

I dare say, I had read for a couple of hours, when, suddenly, I heard a sound that made me lower my book, and listen, intently. It was a noise of something rubbing and fumbling against the back door. Once the door creaked, loudly; as though force were being applied to it. During those few, short moments, I experienced an indescribable feeling of terror, such as I should have believed impossible. My hands shook; a cold sweat broke out on me, and I shivered violently.

Gradually, I calmed. The stealthy movements outside had ceased.

Then for an hour I sat silent and watchful. All at once the feeling of fear took me again. I felt as I imagine an animal must, under the eye of a snake. Yet now I could hear nothing. Still, there was no doubting that some unexplained influence was at work.

Gradually, imperceptibly almost, something stole on my ear – a sound that resolved itself into a faint murmur. Quickly it developed and grew into a muffled but hideous chorus of bestial shrieks. It appeared to rise from the bowels of the earth.

I heard a thud, and realised in a dull, half comprehending way that I had dropped my book. After that, I just sat; and thus the daylight found me, when it crept wanly in through the barred, high windows of the great kitchen.

With the dawning light, the feeling of stupor and fear left me; and I came more into possession of my senses.

Thereupon I picked up my book, and crept to the door to listen. Not a sound broke the chilly silence. For some minutes I stood there; then, very gradually and cautiously, I drew back the bolt and opening the door peeped out.

My caution was unneeded. Nothing was to be seen, save the grey vista of dreary, tangled bushes and trees, extending to the distant plantation.

With a shiver, I closed the door, and made my way, quietly, up to bed.

Chapter VI
The Swine-Things

IT WAS EVENING, a week later. My sister sat in the garden, knitting. I was walking up and down, reading. My gun leant up against the wall of the house; for, since the advent of that strange thing in the gardens, I had deemed it wise to take precautions. Yet, through the whole week, there had been nothing to alarm me, either by sight or sound; so that I was able to look back, calmly, to the incident; though still with a sense of unmitigated wonder and curiosity.

I was, as I have just said, walking up and down, and somewhat engrossed in my book. Suddenly, I heard a crash, away in the direction of the Pit. With a quick movement, I turned and saw a tremendous column of dust rising high into the evening air.

My sister had risen to her feet, with a sharp exclamation of surprise and fright.

Telling her to stay where she was, I snatched up my gun, and ran towards the Pit. As I neared it, I heard a dull, rumbling sound, that grew quickly into a roar, split with deeper crashes, and up from the Pit drove a fresh volume of dust.

The noise ceased, though the dust still rose, tumultuously.

I reached the edge, and looked down; but could see nothing save a boil of dust clouds swirling hither and thither. The air was so full of the small particles, that they blinded and choked me; and, finally, I had to run out from the smother to breathe.

Gradually, the suspended matter sank, and hung in a panoply over the mouth of the Pit.

I could only guess at what had happened.

That there had been a land-slip of some kind, I had little doubt; but the cause was beyond my knowledge; and yet, even then, I had half imaginings; for, already, the thought had come to me, of those falling rocks, and that Thing in the bottom of the Pit; but, in the first minutes of confusion, I failed to reach the natural conclusion, to which the catastrophe pointed.

Slowly, the dust subsided, until, presently, I was able to approach the edge, and look down.

For a while, I peered impotently, trying to see through the reek. At first, it was impossible to make out anything. Then, as I stared, I saw something below, to my left, that moved. I looked intently towards it, and, presently, made out another, and then another – three dim shapes that appeared to be climbing up the side of the Pit. I could see them only indistinctly. Even as I stared and wondered, I heard a rattle of stones, somewhere to my right. I glanced across; but could see nothing. I leant forward, and peered over, and down into the Pit, just beneath where I stood; and saw no further than a hideous, white swine-face, that had risen to within a couple of yards of my feet. Below it, I could make out several others. As the Thing saw me, it gave a sudden, uncouth squeal, which was answered from all parts of the Pit. At that, a gust of horror and fear took me, and, bending down, I discharged my gun right into its face. Straightway, the creature disappeared, with a clatter of loose earth and stones.

There was a momentary silence, to which, probably, I owe my life; for, during it, I heard a quick patter of many feet, and, turning sharply, saw a troop of the creatures coming towards me, at a run. Instantly, I raised my gun and fired at the foremost, who plunged head-long, with a hideous howling. Then, I turned to run. More than halfway from the house to the Pit, I saw my sister – she was coming towards me. I could not see her face, distinctly, as the dusk had fallen; but there was fear in her voice as she called to know why I was shooting.

'Run!' I shouted in reply. 'Run for your life!'

Without more ado, she turned and fled – picking up her skirts with both hands. As I followed, I gave a glance behind. The brutes were running on their hind legs – at times dropping on all fours.

I think it must have been the terror in my voice that spurred Mary to run so; for I feel convinced that she had not, as yet, seen those hell creatures that pursued.

THE HOUSE ON THE BORDERLAND: CHAPTERS I-XI

On we went, my sister leading.

Each moment, the nearing sounds of the footsteps, told me that the brutes were gaining on us, rapidly. Fortunately, I am accustomed to live, in some ways, an active life. As it was, the strain of the race was beginning to tell severely upon me.

Ahead, I could see the back door – luckily it was open. I was some half-dozen yards behind Mary, now, and my breath was sobbing in my throat. Then, something touched my shoulder. I wrenched my head 'round, quickly, and saw one of those monstrous, pallid faces close to mine. One of the creatures, having outrun its companions, had almost overtaken me. Even as I turned, it made a fresh grab. With a sudden effort, I sprang to one side, and, swinging my gun by the barrel, brought it crashing down upon the foul creature's head. The Thing dropped, with an almost human groan.

Even this short delay had been nearly sufficient to bring the rest of the brutes down upon me; so that, without an instant's waste of time, I turned and ran for the door.

Reaching it, I burst into the passage; then, turning quickly, slammed and bolted the door, just as the first of the creatures rushed against it, with a sudden shock.

My sister sat, gasping, in a chair. She seemed in a fainting condition; but I had no time then to spend on her. I had to make sure that all the doors were fastened. Fortunately, they were. The one leading from my study into the gardens was the last to which I went. I had just had time to note that it was secured, when I thought I heard a noise outside. I stood perfectly silent, and listened. Yes! Now I could distinctly hear a sound of whispering, and something slithered over the panels, with a rasping, scratchy noise. Evidently, some of the brutes were feeling with their claw-hands, about the door, to discover whether there were any means of ingress.

That the creatures should so soon have found the door was – to me – a proof of their reasoning capabilities. It assured me that they must not be regarded, by any means, as mere animals. I had felt something of this before, when that first Thing peered in through my window. Then I had applied the term superhuman to it, with an almost instinctive knowledge that the creature was something different from the brute-beast. Something beyond human; yet in no good sense; but rather as something foul and hostile to the *great* and *good* in humanity. In a word, as something intelligent, and yet inhuman. The very thought of the creatures filled me with revulsion.

Now, I bethought me of my sister, and, going to the cupboard, I got out a flask of brandy, and a wine-glass. Taking these, I went down to the kitchen, carrying a lighted candle with me. She was not sitting in the chair, but had fallen out, and was lying upon the floor, face downward.

Very gently, I turned her over, and raised her head somewhat. Then, I poured a little of the brandy between her lips. After a while, she shivered slightly. A little later, she gave several gasps, and opened her eyes. In a dreamy, unrealising way, she looked at me. Then her eyes closed, slowly, and I gave her a little more of the brandy. For, perhaps a minute longer, she lay silent, breathing quickly. All at once, her eyes opened again, and it seemed to me, as I looked, that the pupils were dilated, as though fear had come with returning consciousness. Then, with a movement so unexpected that I started backward, she sat up. Noticing that she seemed giddy, I put out my hand to steady her. At that, she gave a loud scream, and, scrambling to her feet, ran from the room.

For a moment, I stayed there – kneeling and holding the brandy flask. I was utterly puzzled and astonished.

Could she be afraid of me? But no! Why should she? I could only conclude that her nerves were badly shaken, and that she was temporarily unhinged. Upstairs, I heard a door bang, loudly, and I knew that she had taken refuge in her room. I put the flask down on the table. My attention was distracted by a noise in the direction of the back door. I went towards it, and listened. It appeared to be shaken, as though some of the creatures struggled with it, silently; but it was far too strongly constructed and hung to be easily moved.

Out in the gardens rose a continuous sound. It might have been mistaken, by a casual listener, for the grunting and squealing of a herd of pigs. But, as I stood there, it came to me that there was sense and meaning to all those swinish noises. Gradually, I seemed able to trace a semblance in it to human speech – glutinous and sticky, as though each articulation were made with difficulty: yet, nevertheless, I was becoming convinced that it was no mere medley of sounds; but a rapid interchange of ideas.

By this time, it had grown quite dark in the passages, and from these came all the varied cries and groans of which an old house is so full after nightfall. It is, no doubt, because things are then quieter, and one has more leisure to hear. Also, there may be something in the theory that the sudden change of temperature, at sundown, affects the structure of the house, somewhat – causing it to contract and settle, as it were, for the night. However, this is as may be; but, on that night in particular, I would gladly have been quit of so many eerie noises. It seemed to me, that each crack and creak was the coming of one of those Things along the dark corridors; though I knew in my heart that this could not be, for I had seen, myself, that all the doors were secure.

Gradually, however, these sounds grew on my nerves to such an extent that, were it only to punish my cowardice, I felt I must make the 'round of the basement again, and, if anything were there, face it. And then, I would go up to my study, for I knew sleep was out of the question, with the house surrounded by creatures, half beasts, half something else, and entirely unholy.

Taking the kitchen lamp down from its hook, I made my way from cellar to cellar, and room to room; through pantry and coal-hole – along passages, and into the hundred-and-one little blind alleys and hidden nooks that form the basement of the old house. Then, when I knew I had been in every corner and cranny large enough to conceal aught of any size, I made my way to the stairs.

With my foot on the first step, I paused. It seemed to me, I heard a movement, apparently from the buttery, which is to the left of the staircase. It had been one of the first places I searched, and yet, I felt certain my ears had not deceived me. My nerves were strung now, and, with hardly any hesitation, I stepped up to the door, holding the lamp above my head. In a glance, I saw that the place was empty, save for the heavy, stone slabs, supported by brick pillars; and I was about to leave it, convinced that I had been mistaken; when, in turning, my light was flashed back from two bright spots outside the window, and high up. For a few moments, I stood there, staring. Then they moved – revolving slowly, and throwing out alternate scintillations of green and red; at least, so it appeared to me. I knew then that they were eyes.

Slowly, I traced the shadowy outline of one of the Things. It appeared to be holding on to the bars of the window, and its attitude suggested climbing. I went nearer to the window, and held the light higher. There was no need to be afraid of the creature; the bars were strong, and there was little danger of its being able to move them. And then, suddenly, in spite of the knowledge that the brute could not reach to harm me, I had a return of the horrible sensation of fear, that had assailed me on that night, a week previously. It was the same feeling of helpless, shuddering fright. I realised, dimly, that the creature's eyes were looking into mine with a steady, compelling stare. I tried to turn away; but could not. I seemed, now, to see the window through a mist. Then, I thought other eyes came and peered, and yet others; until a whole galaxy of malignant, staring orbs seemed to hold me in thrall.

My head began to swim, and throb violently. Then, I was aware of a feeling of acute physical pain in my left hand. It grew more severe, and forced, literally forced, my attention. With a tremendous effort, I glanced down; and, with that, the spell that had held me was broken. I realised, then, that I had, in my agitation, unconsciously caught hold of the hot lamp-glass, and burnt my hand, badly. I looked up to the window, again. The misty appearance had gone, and, now, I saw that it was crowded with dozens of bestial faces. With a sudden access of rage, I raised the lamp, and hurled it, full at the window. It struck the glass (smashing a pane), and passed between two of the bars, out into the garden, scattering burning oil as it went. I heard several loud cries of pain, and, as my sight became accustomed to the dark, I discovered that the creatures had left the window.

Pulling myself together, I groped for the door, and, having found it, made my way upstairs, stumbling at each step. I felt dazed, as though I had received a blow on the head. At the same time, my hand smarted badly, and I was full of a nervous, dull rage against those Things.

Reaching my study, I lit the candles. As they burnt up, their rays were reflected from the rack of firearms on the sidewall. At the sight, I remembered that I had there a power, which, as I had proved earlier, seemed as fatal to those monsters as to more ordinary animals; and I determined I would take the offensive.

First of all, I bound up my hand; for the pain was fast becoming intolerable. After that, it seemed easier, and I crossed the room, to the rifle stand. There, I selected a heavy rifle – an old and tried weapon; and, having procured ammunition, I made my way up into one of the small towers, with which the house is crowned.

From there, I found that I could see nothing. The gardens presented a dim blur of shadows – a little blacker, perhaps, where the trees stood. That was all, and I knew that it was useless to shoot down into all that darkness. The only thing to be done was to wait for the moon to rise; then, I might be able to do a little execution.

In the meantime, I sat still, and kept my ears open. The gardens were comparatively quiet now, and only an occasional grunt or squeal came up to me. I did not like this silence; it made me wonder on what devilry the creatures were bent. Twice, I left the tower, and took a walk through the house; but everything was silent.

Once, I heard a noise, from the direction of the Pit, as though more earth had fallen. Following this, and lasting for some fifteen minutes, there was a commotion among the denizens of the gardens. This died away, and, after that all was again quiet.

About an hour later, the moon's light showed above the distant horizon. From where I sat, I could see it over the trees; but it was not until it rose clear of them, that I could make out any of the details in the gardens below. Even then, I could see none of the brutes; until, happening to crane forward, I saw several of them lying prone, up against the wall of the house. What they were doing, I could not make out. It was, however, a chance too good to be ignored; and, taking aim, I fired at the one directly beneath. There was a shrill scream, and, as the smoke cleared away, I saw that it had turned on its back, and was writhing, feebly. Then, it was quiet. The others had disappeared.

Immediately after this, I heard a loud squeal, in the direction of the Pit. It was answered, a hundred times, from every part of the garden. This gave me some notion of the number of the creatures, and I began to feel that the whole affair was becoming even more serious than I had imagined.

As I sat there, silent and watchful, the thought came to me – Why was all this? What were these Things? What did it mean? Then my thoughts flew back to that vision (though, even now, I doubt whether it was a vision) of the Plain of Silence. What did that mean? I wondered – And that Thing in the arena? Ugh! Lastly, I thought of the house I had seen in that far-away place. That house, so like this in every detail of external structure, that it might have been modelled from it; or this from that. I had never thought of that—

At this moment, there came another long squeal, from the Pit, followed, a second later, by a couple of shorter ones. At once, the garden was filled with answering cries. I stood up, quickly, and looked over the parapet. In the moonlight, it seemed as though the shrubberies were alive. They tossed hither and thither, as though shaken by a strong, irregular wind; while a continuous rustling, and a noise of scampering feet, rose up to me. Several times, I saw the moonlight gleam on running, white figures among the bushes, and, twice, I fired. The second time, my shot was answered by a short squeal of pain.

A minute later, the gardens lay silent. From the Pit came a deep, hoarse Babel of swine-talk. At times, angry cries smote the air, and they would be answered by multitudinous gruntings. It occurred to me that they were holding some kind of a council, perhaps to discuss the problem of entering the house. Also, I thought that they seemed much enraged, probably by my successful shots.

It occurred to me that now would be a good time to make a final survey of our defences. This, I proceeded to do at once; visiting the whole of the basement again, and examining each of the doors. Luckily, they are all, like the back one, built of solid, iron-studded oak. Then, I went upstairs to the study. I was more anxious about this door. It is, palpably, of a more modern make than the others, and, though a stout piece of work, it has little of their ponderous strength.

I must explain here, that there is a small, raised lawn on this side of the house, upon which this door opens – the windows of the study being barred on this account. All the other entrances – excepting the great gateway which is never opened – are in the lower storey.

Chapter VII
The Attack

I SPENT SOME TIME, puzzling how to strengthen the study door. Finally, I went down to the kitchen, and with some trouble, brought up several heavy pieces of timber. These, I wedged up, slantwise, against it, from the floor, nailing them top and bottom. For half-an-hour, I worked hard, and, at last, got it shored to my mind.

Then, feeling easier, I resumed my coat, which I had laid aside, and proceeded to attend to one or two matters before returning to the tower. It was whilst thus employed, that I heard a fumbling at the door, and the latch was tried. Keeping silence, I waited. Soon, I heard several of the creatures outside. They were grunting to one another, softly. Then, for a minute, there was quietness. Suddenly, there sounded a quick, low grunt, and the door creaked under a tremendous pressure. It would have burst inward; but for the supports I had placed. The strain ceased, as quickly as it had begun, and there was more talk.

Presently, one of the Things squealed, softly, and I heard the sound of others approaching. There was a short confabulation; then again, silence; and I realised that they had called several more to assist. Feeling that now was the supreme moment, I stood ready, with my rifle presented. If the door gave, I would, at least, slay as many as possible.

Again came the low signal; and, once more, the door cracked, under a huge force. For, a minute perhaps, the pressure was kept up; and I waited, nervously; expecting each moment to see the door come down with a crash. But no; the struts held, and the attempt proved abortive. Then followed more of their horrible, grunting talk, and, whilst it lasted, I thought I distinguished the noise of fresh arrivals.

After a long discussion, during which the door was several times shaken, they became quiet once more, and I knew that they were going to make a third attempt to break it down. I was almost in despair. The props had been severely tried in the two previous attacks, and I was sorely afraid that this would prove too much for them.

At that moment, like an inspiration, a thought flashed into my troubled brain. Instantly, for it was no time to hesitate, I ran from the room, and up stair after stair. This time, it was not to one of the towers, that I went; but out on to the flat, leaded roof itself. Once there, I raced across to the parapet, that walls it 'round, and looked down. As I did so, I heard the short, grunted signal, and, even up there, caught the crying of the door under the assault.

There was not a moment to lose, and, leaning over, I aimed, quickly, and fired. The report rang sharply, and, almost blending with it, came the loud splud of the bullet striking its mark. From below, rose a shrill wail; and the door ceased its groaning. Then, as I took my weight from off the parapet, a huge piece of the stone coping slid from under me, and fell with a crash among the disorganised throng beneath. Several horrible shrieks quavered through the night air, and then I heard a sound of scampering feet. Cautiously, I looked over. In the moonlight, I could see the great copingstone, lying right across the threshold of the door. I thought I saw something under it – several things, white; but I could not be sure.

And so a few minutes passed.

As I stared, I saw something come 'round, out of the shadow of the house. It was one of the Things. It went up to the stone, silently, and bent down. I was unable to see what it did. In a minute it stood up. It had something in its talons, which it put to its mouth and tore at....

For the moment, I did not realise. Then, slowly, I comprehended. The Thing was stooping again. It was horrible. I started to load my rifle. When I looked again, the monster was tugging at the stone – moving it to one side. I leant the rifle on the coping, and pulled the trigger. The brute collapsed, on its face, and kicked, slightly.

Simultaneously, almost, with the report, I heard another sound – that of breaking glass. Waiting, only to recharge my weapon, I ran from the roof, and down the first two flights of stairs.

Here, I paused to listen. As I did so, there came another tinkle of falling glass. It appeared to come from the floor below. Excitedly, I sprang down the steps, and, guided by the rattle of the window-sash, reached the door of one of the empty bedrooms, at the back of the house. I thrust it open. The room was but dimly illuminated by the moonlight; most of the light being blotted out by moving figures at the window. Even as

I stood, one crawled through, into the room. Levelling my weapon, I fired point-blank at it – filling the room with a deafening bang. When the smoke cleared, I saw that the room was empty, and the window free. The room was much lighter. The night air blew in, coldly, through the shattered panes. Down below, in the night, I could hear a soft moaning, and a confused murmur of swine-voices.

Stepping to one side of the window, I reloaded, and then stood there, waiting. Presently, I heard a scuffling noise. From where I stood in the shadow, I could see, without being seen.

Nearer came the sounds, and then I saw something come up above the sill, and clutch at the broken window-frame. It caught a piece of the woodwork; and, now, I could make out that it was a hand and arm. A moment later, the face of one of the Swine-creatures rose into view. Then, before I could use my rifle, or do anything, there came a sharp crack – cr-ac-k; and the window-frame gave way under the weight of the Thing. Next instant, a squashing thud, and a loud outcry, told me that it had fallen to the ground. With a savage hope that it had been killed, I went to the window. The moon had gone behind a cloud, so that I could see nothing; though a steady hum of jabbering, just beneath where I stood, indicated that there were several more of the brutes close at hand.

As I stood there, looking down, I marvelled how it had been possible for the creatures to climb so far; for the wall is comparatively smooth, while the distance to the ground must be, at least, eighty feet.

All at once, as I bent, peering, I saw something, indistinctly, that cut the grey shadow of the house-side, with a black line. It passed the window, to the left, at a distance of about two feet. Then, I remembered that it was a gutter-pipe, that had been put there some years ago, to carry off the rainwater. I had forgotten about it. I could see, now, how the creatures had managed to reach the window. Even as the solution came to me, I heard a faint slithering, scratching noise, and knew that another of the brutes was coming. I waited some odd moments; then leant out of the window and felt the pipe. To my delight, I found that it was quite loose, and I managed, using the rifle-barrel as a crowbar, to lever it out from the wall. I worked quickly. Then, taking hold with both bands, I wrenched the whole concern away, and hurled it down – with the Thing still clinging to it – into the garden.

For a few minutes longer, I waited there, listening; but, after the first general outcry, I heard nothing. I knew, now, that there was no more reason to fear an attack from this quarter. I had removed the only means of reaching the window, and, as none of the other windows had any adjacent water pipes, to tempt the climbing powers of the monsters, I began to feel more confident of escaping their clutches.

Leaving the room, I made my way down to the study. I was anxious to see how the door had withstood the test of that last assault. Entering, I lit two of the candles, and then turned to the door. One of the large props had been displaced, and, on that side, the door had been forced inward some six inches.

It was Providential that I had managed to drive the brutes away just when I did! And that copingstone! I wondered, vaguely, how I had managed to dislodge it. I had not noticed it loose, as I took my shot; and then, as I stood up, it had slipped away from beneath me… I felt that I owed the dismissal of the attacking force, more to its timely fall than to my rifle. Then the thought came, that I had better seize this chance to shore up the door, again. It was evident that the creatures had not returned since the fall of the copingstone; but who was to say how long they would keep away?

There and then, I set-to, at repairing the door – working hard and anxiously. First, I went down to the basement, and, rummaging 'round, found several pieces of heavy oak planking. With these, I returned to the study, and, having removed the props, placed the planks up against the door. Then, I nailed the heads of the struts to these, and, driving them well home at the bottoms, nailed them again there.

Thus, I made the door stronger than ever; for now it was solid with the backing of boards, and would, I felt convinced, stand a heavier pressure than hitherto, without giving way.

After that, I lit the lamp which I had brought from the kitchen, and went down to have a look at the lower windows.

Now that I had seen an instance of the strength the creatures possessed, I felt considerable anxiety about the windows on the ground floor – in spite of the fact that they were so strongly barred.

I went first to the buttery, having a vivid remembrance of my late adventure there. The place was chilly, and the wind, soughing in through the broken glass, produced an eerie note. Apart from the general air of dismalness, the place was as I had left it the night before. Going up to the window, I examined the bars, closely; noting, as I did so, their comfortable thickness. Still, as I looked more intently, it seemed to me that the middle bar was bent slightly from the straight; yet it was but trifling, and it might have been so for years. I had never, before, noticed them particularly.

I put my hand through the broken window, and shook the bar. It was as firm as a rock. Perhaps the creatures had tried to 'start' it, and, finding it beyond their power, ceased from the effort. After that, I went 'round to each of the windows, in turn; examining them with careful attention; but nowhere else could I trace anything to show that there had been any tampering. Having finished my survey, I went back to the study, and poured myself out a little brandy. Then to the tower to watch.

Chapter VIII
After the Attack

IT WAS NOW about three a.m., and, presently, the Eastern sky began to pale with the coming of dawn. Gradually, the day came, and, by its light, I scanned the gardens, earnestly; but nowhere could I see any signs of the brutes. I leant over, and glanced down to the foot of the wall, to see whether the body of the Thing I had shot the night before was still there. It was gone. I supposed that others of the monsters had removed it during the night.

Then, I went down on to the roof, and crossed over to the gap from which the coping stone had fallen. Reaching it, I looked over. Yes, there was the stone, as I had seen it last; but there was no appearance of anything beneath it; nor could I see the creatures I had killed, after its fall. Evidently, they also had been taken away. I turned, and went down to my study. There, I sat down, wearily. I was thoroughly tired. It was quite light now; though the sun's rays were not, as yet, perceptibly hot. A clock chimed the hour of four.

I awoke, with a start, and looked 'round, hurriedly. The clock in the corner, indicated that it was three o'clock. It was already afternoon. I must have slept for nearly eleven hours.

With a jerky movement, I sat forward in the chair, and listened. The house was perfectly silent. Slowly, I stood up, and yawned. I felt desperately tired, still, and sat down again; wondering what it was that had waked me.

It must have been the clock striking, I concluded, presently; and was commencing to doze off, when a sudden noise brought me back, once more, to life. It was the sound of a step, as of a person moving cautiously down the corridor, towards my study. In an instant, I was on my feet, and grasping my rifle. Noiselessly, I waited. Had the creatures broken in, whilst I slept? Even as I questioned, the steps reached my door, halted momentarily, and then continued down the passage. Silently, I tiptoed to the doorway, and peeped out. Then, I experienced such a feeling of relief, as must a reprieved criminal – it was my sister. She was going towards the stairs.

I stepped into the hall, and was about to call to her, when it occurred to me that it was very queer she should have crept past my door, in that stealthy manner. I was puzzled, and, for one brief moment, the thought occupied my mind, that it was not she, but some fresh mystery of the house. Then, as I caught a glimpse of her old petticoat, the thought passed as quickly as it had come, and I half laughed. There could be no mistaking that ancient garment. Yet, I wondered what she was doing; and, remembering her condition of mind, on the previous day, I felt that it might be best to follow, quietly – taking care not to alarm her – and see what she was going to do. If she behaved rationally, well and good; if not, I should have to take steps to restrain her. I could run no unnecessary risks, under the danger that threatened us.

Quickly, I reached the head of the stairs, and paused a moment. Then, I heard a sound that sent me leaping down, at a mad rate – it was the rattle of bolts being unshot. That foolish sister of mine was actually unbarring the back door.

Just as her hand was on the last bolt, I reached her. She had not seen me, and, the first thing she knew, I had hold of her arm. She glanced up quickly, like a frightened animal, and screamed aloud.

"Come, Mary!" I said, sternly. "What's the meaning of this nonsense? Do you mean to tell me you don't understand the danger, that you try to throw our two lives away in this fashion!"

To this, she replied nothing; only trembled, violently, gasping and sobbing, as though in the last extremity of fear.

Through some minutes, I reasoned with her; pointing out the need for caution, and asking her to be brave. There was little to be afraid of now, I explained – and, I tried to believe that I spoke the truth – but she must be sensible, and not attempt to leave the house for a few days.

At last, I ceased, in despair. It was no use talking to her; she was, obviously, not quite herself for the time being. Finally, I told her she had better go to her room, if she could not behave rationally.

Still, she took not any notice. So, without more ado, I picked her up in my arms, and carried her there. At first, she screamed, wildly; but had relapsed into silent trembling by the time I reached the stairs.

Arriving at her room, I laid her upon the bed. She lay there quietly enough, neither speaking nor sobbing – just shaking in a very ague of fear. I took a rug from a chair nearby, and spread it over her. I could do nothing more for her, and so, crossed to where Pepper lay in a big basket. My sister had taken charge of him since his wound, to nurse him, for it had proved more severe than I had thought, and I was pleased to note that, in spite of her state of mind, she had looked after the old dog, carefully. Stooping, I spoke to him, and, in reply, he licked my hand, feebly. He was too ill to do more.

Then, going to the bed, I bent over my sister, and asked her how she felt; but she only shook the more, and, much as it pained me, I had to admit that my presence seemed to make her worse.

And so, I left her – locking the door, and pocketing the key. It seemed to be the only course to take.

The rest of the day, I spent between the tower and my study. For food, I brought up a loaf from the pantry, and on this, and some claret, I lived for that day.

What a long, weary day it was. If only I could have gone out into the gardens, as is my wont, I should have been content enough; but to be cooped in this silent house, with no companion, save a mad woman and a sick dog, was enough to prey upon the nerves of the hardiest. And out in the tangled shrubberies that surrounded the house, lurked – for all I could tell – those infernal Swine-creatures waiting their chance. Was ever a man in such straits?

Once, in the afternoon, and again, later, I went to visit my sister. The second time, I found her tending Pepper; but, at my approach, she slid over, unobtrusively, to the far corner, with a gesture that saddened me beyond belief. Poor girl! Her fear cut me intolerably, and I would not intrude on her, unnecessarily. She would be better, I trusted, in a few days; meanwhile, I could do nothing; and I judged it still needful – hard as it seemed – to keep her confined to her room. One thing there was that I took for encouragement: she had eaten some of the food I had taken to her, on my first visit.

And so the day passed.

As the evening drew on, the air grew chilly, and I began to make preparations for passing a second night in the tower – taking up two additional rifles, and a heavy ulster. The rifles I loaded, and laid alongside my other; as I intended to make things warm for any of the creatures who might show, during the night. I had plenty of ammunition, and I thought to give the brutes such a lesson, as should show them the uselessness of attempting to force an entrance.

After that, I made the 'round of the house again; paying particular attention to the props that supported the study door. Then, feeling that I had done all that lay in my power to insure our safety, I returned to the tower; calling in on my sister and Pepper, for a final visit, on the way. Pepper was asleep; but woke, as I entered, and wagged his tail, in recognition. I thought he seemed slightly better. My sister was lying on the bed; though whether asleep or not, I was unable to tell; and thus I left them.

Reaching the tower, I made myself as comfortable as circumstances would permit, and settled down to watch through the night. Gradually, darkness fell, and soon the details of the gardens were merged into shadows. During the first few hours, I sat, alert, listening for any sound that might help to tell me if anything were stirring down below. It was far too dark for my eyes to be of much use.

Slowly, the hours passed; without anything unusual happening. And the moon rose, showing the gardens, apparently empty, and silent. And so, through the night, without disturbance or sound.

Towards morning, I began to grow stiff and cold, with my long vigil; also, I was getting very uneasy, concerning the continued quietness on the part of the creatures. I mistrusted it, and would sooner, far, have had them attack the house, openly. Then, at least, I should have known my danger, and been able to meet it; but to wait like this, through a whole night, picturing all kinds of unknown devilment, was to jeopardise one's sanity. Once or twice, the thought came to me, that, perhaps, they had gone; but, in my heart, I found it impossible to believe that it was so.

Chapter IX
In the Cellars

AT LAST, what with being tired and cold, and the uneasiness that possessed me, I resolved to take a walk through the house; first calling in at the study, for a glass of brandy to warm me. This, I did, and, while there, I examined the door, carefully; but found all as I had left it the night before.

The day was just breaking, as I left the tower; though it was still too dark in the house to be able to see without a light, and I took one of the study candles with me on my 'round. By the time I had finished the ground floor, the daylight was creeping in, wanly, through the barred windows. My search had shown me nothing fresh. Everything appeared to be in order, and I was on the point of extinguishing my candle, when the thought suggested itself to me to have another glance 'round the cellars. I had not, if I remember rightly, been into them since my hasty search on the evening of the attack.

For, perhaps, the half of a minute, I hesitated. I would have been very willing to forego the task – as, indeed, I am inclined to think any man well might – for of all the great, awe-inspiring rooms in this house, the cellars are the hugest and weirdest. Great, gloomy caverns of places, unlit by any ray of daylight. Yet, I would not shirk the work. I felt that to do so would smack of sheer cowardice. Besides, as I reassured myself, the cellars were really the most unlikely places in which to come across anything dangerous; considering that they can be entered only through a heavy oaken door, the key of which I carry always on my person.

It is in the smallest of these places that I keep my wine; a gloomy hole close to the foot of the cellar stairs; and beyond which, I have seldom proceeded. Indeed, save for the rummage 'round, already mentioned, I doubt whether I had ever, before, been right through the cellars.

As I unlocked the great door, at the top of the steps, I paused, nervously, a moment, at the strange, desolate smell that assailed my nostrils. Then, throwing the barrel of my weapon forward, I descended, slowly, into the darkness of the underground regions.

Reaching the bottom of the stairs, I stood for a minute, and listened. All was silent, save for a faint drip, drip of water, falling, drop-by-drop, somewhere to my left. As I stood, I noticed how quietly the candle burnt; never a flicker nor flare, so utterly windless was the place.

Quietly, I moved from cellar to cellar. I had but a very dim memory of their arrangement. The impressions left by my first search were blurred. I had recollections of a succession of great cellars, and of one, greater than the rest, the roof of which was upheld by pillars; beyond that my mind was hazy, and predominated by a sense of cold and darkness and shadows. Now, however, it was different; for, although nervous, I was sufficiently collected to be able to look about me, and note the structure and size of the different vaults I entered.

Of course, with the amount of light given by my candle, it was not possible to examine each place, minutely, but I was enabled to notice, as I went along, that the walls appeared to be built with wonderful precision and finish; while here and there, an occasional, massive pillar shot up to support the vaulted roof.

Thus, I came, at last, to the great cellar that I remembered. It is reached, through a huge, arched entrance, on which I observed strange, fantastic carvings, which threw queer shadows under the light of my candle. As I stood, and examined these, thoughtfully, it occurred to me how strange it was, that I should be so little acquainted with my own house. Yet, this may be easily understood, when one realises the size of this ancient pile, and the fact that only my old sister and I live in it, occupying a few of the rooms, such as our wants decide.

Holding the light high, I passed on into the cellar, and, keeping to the right, paced slowly up, until I reached the further end. I walked quietly, and looked cautiously about, as I went. But, so far as the light showed, I saw nothing unusual.

At the top, I turned to the left, still keeping to the wall, and so continued, until I had traversed the whole of the vast chamber. As I moved along, I noticed that the floor was composed of solid rock, in places covered with a damp mould, in others bare, or almost so, save for a thin coating of light-grey dust.

I had halted at the doorway. Now, however, I turned, and made my way up the centre of the place; passing among the pillars, and glancing to right and left, as I moved. About halfway up the cellar, I stubbed my foot against something that gave out a metallic sound. Stooping quickly, I held the candle, and saw that the object I had kicked was a large, metal ring. Bending lower, I cleared the dust from around it, and, presently, discovered that it was attached to a ponderous trap door, black with age.

Feeling excited, and wondering to where it could lead, I laid my gun on the floor, and, sticking the candle in the trigger guard, took the ring in both hands, and pulled. The trap creaked loudly – the sound echoing, vaguely, through the huge place – and opened, heavily.

Propping the edge on my knee, I reached for the candle, and held it in the opening, moving it to right and left; but could see nothing. I was puzzled and surprised. There were no signs of steps, nor even the appearance of there ever having been any. Nothing; save an empty blackness. I might have been looking down into a bottomless, sideless well. Then, even as I stared, full of perplexity, I seemed to hear, far down, as though from untold depths, a faint whisper of sound. I bent my head, quickly, more into the opening, and listened, intently. It may have been fancy; but I could have sworn to hearing a soft titter, that grew into a hideous, chuckling, faint and distant. Startled, I leapt backward, letting the trap fall, with a hollow clang, that filled the place with echoes. Even then, I seemed to hear that mocking, suggestive laughter; but this, I knew, must be my imagination. The sound I had heard was far too slight to penetrate through the cumbrous trap.

For a full minute, I stood there, quivering – glancing, nervously, behind and before; but the great cellar was silent as a grave, and, gradually, I shook off the frightened sensation. With a calmer mind, I became again curious to know into what that trap opened; but could not, then, summon sufficient courage to make a further investigation. One thing I felt, however, was that the trap ought to be secured. This, I accomplished by placing upon it several large pieces of 'dressed' stone, which I had noticed in my tour along the East wall.

Then, after a final scrutiny of the rest of the place, I retraced my way through the cellars, to the stairs, and so reached the daylight, with an infinite feeling of relief, that the uncomfortable task was accomplished.

Chapter X
The Time of Waiting

THE SUN was now warm, and shining brightly, forming a wondrous contrast to the dark and dismal cellars; and it was with comparatively light feelings that I made my way up to the tower, to survey the gardens. There, I found everything quiet, and, after a few minutes, went down to Mary's room.

Here, having knocked, and received a reply, I unlocked the door. My sister was sitting, quietly, on the bed; as though waiting. She seemed quite herself again, and made no attempt to move away, as I approached; yet, I observed that she scanned my face, anxiously, as though in doubt, and but half assured in her mind that there was nothing to fear from me.

To my questions, as to how she felt, she replied, sanely enough, that she was hungry, and would like to go down to prepare breakfast, if I did not mind. For a minute, I meditated whether it would be safe to let her out. Finally, I told her she might go, on condition that she promised not to attempt to leave the house, or meddle with any of the outer doors. At my mention of the doors, a sudden look of fright crossed her face; but she said nothing, save to give the required promise, and then left the room, silently.

Crossing the floor, I approached Pepper. He had waked as I entered; but, beyond a slight yelp of pleasure, and a soft rapping with his tail, had kept quiet. Now, as I patted him, he made an attempt to stand up, and succeeded, only to fall back on his side, with a little yowl of pain.

I spoke to him, and bade him lie still. I was greatly delighted with his improvement, and also with the natural kindness of my sister's heart, in taking such good care of him, in spite of her condition of mind. After a while, I left him, and went downstairs, to my study.

In a little time, Mary appeared, carrying a tray on which smoked a hot breakfast. As she entered the room, I saw her gaze fasten on the props that supported the study door; her lips tightened, and I thought she paled, slightly; but that was all. Putting the tray down at my elbow, she was leaving the room, quietly, when I called her back. She came, it seemed, a little timidly, as though startled; and I noted that her hand clutched at her apron, nervously.

"Come, Mary," I said. "Cheer up! Things look brighter. I've seen none of the creatures since yesterday morning, early."

She looked at me, in a curiously puzzled manner; as though not comprehending. Then, intelligence swept into her eyes, and fear; but she said nothing, beyond an unintelligible murmur of acquiescence. After that, I kept silence; it was evident that any reference to the Swine-things was more than her shaken nerves could bear.

Breakfast over, I went up to the tower. Here, during the greater part of the day, I maintained a strict watch over the gardens. Once or twice, I went down to the basement, to see how my sister was getting along. Each time, I found her quiet, and curiously submissive. Indeed, on the last occasion, she even ventured to address me, on her own account, with regard to some household matter that needed attention. Though this was done with an almost extraordinary timidity, I hailed it with happiness, as being the first word, voluntarily spoken, since the critical moment, when I had caught her unbarring the back door, to go out among those waiting brutes. I wondered whether she was aware of her attempt, and how near a thing it had been; but refrained from questioning her, thinking it best to let well alone.

That night, I slept in a bed; the first time for two nights. In the morning, I rose early, and took a walk through the house. All was as it should be, and I went up to the tower, to have a look at the gardens. Here, again, I found perfect quietness.

At breakfast, when I met Mary, I was greatly pleased to see that she had sufficiently regained command over herself, to be able to greet me in a perfectly natural manner. She talked sensibly and quietly; only keeping carefully from any mention of the past couple of days. In this, I humored her, to the extent of not attempting to lead the conversation in that direction.

Earlier in the morning, I had been to see Pepper. He was mending, rapidly; and bade fair to be on his legs, in earnest, in another day or two. Before leaving the breakfast table, I made some reference to his improvement. In the short discussion that followed, I was surprised to gather, from my sister's remarks, that she was still under the impression that his wound had been given by the wildcat, of my invention. It made me feel almost ashamed of myself for deceiving her. Yet, the lie had been told to prevent her from being frightened. And then, I had been sure that she must have known the truth, later, when those brutes had attacked the house.

During the day, I kept on the alert; spending much of my time, as on the previous day, in the tower; but not a sign could I see of the Swine-creatures, nor hear any sound. Several times, the thought had come to me, that the Things had, at last, left us; but, up to this time, I had refused to entertain the idea, seriously; now, however, I began to feel that there was reason for hope. It would soon be three days since I had seen any of the Things; but still, I intended to use the utmost caution. For all that I could tell, this protracted silence might be a ruse to tempt me from the house – perhaps right into their arms. The thought of such a contingency, was, alone, sufficient to make me circumspect.

So it was, that the fourth, fifth and sixth days went by, quietly, without my making any attempt to leave the house.

On the sixth day, I had the pleasure of seeing Pepper, once more, upon his feet; and, though still very weak, he managed to keep me company during the whole of that day.

Chapter XI
The Searching of the Gardens

HOW SLOWLY the time went; and never a thing to indicate that any of the brutes still infested the gardens.

It was on the ninth day that, finally, I decided to run the risk, if any there were, and sally out. With this purpose in view, I loaded one of the shotguns, carefully – choosing it, as being more deadly than a rifle, at close quarters; and then, after a final scrutiny of the grounds, from the tower, I called Pepper to follow me, and made my way down to the basement.

At the door, I must confess to hesitating a moment. The thought of what might be awaiting me among the dark shrubberies was by no means calculated to encourage my resolution. It was but a second, though, and then I had drawn the bolts, and was standing on the path outside the door.

Pepper followed, stopping at the doorstep to sniff, suspiciously; and carrying his nose up and down the jambs, as though following a scent. Then, suddenly, he turned, sharply, and started to run here and there, in semicircles and circles, all around the door; finally returning to the threshold. Here, he began again to nose about.

Hitherto, I had stood, watching the dog; yet, all the time, with half my gaze on the wild tangle of gardens, stretching 'round me. Now, I went towards him, and, bending down, examined the surface of the door, where he was smelling. I found that the wood was covered with a network of scratches, crossing and recrossing one another, in inextricable confusion. In addition to this, I noticed that the doorposts, themselves, were gnawed in places. Beyond these, I could find nothing; and so, standing up, I began to make the tour of the house wall.

Pepper, as soon as I walked away, left the door, and ran ahead, still nosing and sniffing as he went along. At times, he stopped to investigate. Here, it would be a bullet-hole in the pathway, or, perhaps, a powder stained wad. Anon, it might be a piece of torn sod, or a disturbed patch of weedy path; but, save for such trifles, he found nothing. I observed him, critically, as he went along, and could discover nothing of uneasiness, in his demeanour, to indicate that he felt the nearness of any of the creatures. By this, I was assured that the gardens were empty, at least for the present, of those hateful Things. Pepper could not be easily deceived, and it was a relief to feel that he would know, and give me timely warning, if there were any danger.

Reaching the place where I had shot that first creature, I stopped, and made a careful scrutiny; but could see nothing. From there, I went on to where the great copingstone had fallen. It lay on its side, apparently just as it had been left when I shot the brute that was moving it. A couple of feet to the right of the nearer end, was a great dent in the ground; showing where it had struck. The other end was still within the indentation – half in, and half out. Going nearer, I looked at the stone, more closely. What a huge piece of masonry it was! And that creature had moved it, single-handed, in its attempt to reach what lay below.

I went 'round to the further end of the stone. Here, I found that it was possible to see under it, for a distance of nearly a couple of feet. Still, I could see nothing of the stricken creatures, and I felt much surprised. I had, as I have before said, guessed that the remains had been removed; yet, I could not conceive that it had been done so thoroughly as not to leave some certain sign, beneath the stone, indicative of their fate. I had seen several of the brutes struck down beneath it, with such force that they must have been literally driven into the earth; and now, not a vestige of them was to be seen – not even a bloodstain.

I felt more puzzled, than ever, as I turned the matter over in my mind; but could think of no plausible explanation; and so, finally, gave it up, as one of the many things that were unexplainable.

From there, I transferred my attention to the study door. I could see, now, even more plainly, the effects of the tremendous strain to which it had been subjected; and I marvelled how, even with the support afforded by the props, it had withstood the attacks, so well. There were no marks of blows – indeed, none had been given – but the door had been literally riven from its hinges, by the application of enormous, silent force. One thing that I observed affected me profoundly – the head of one of the props had been driven right through a panel. This was, of itself, sufficient to show how huge an effort the creatures had made to break down the door, and how nearly they had succeeded.

Leaving, I continued my tour 'round the house, finding little else of interest; save at the back, where I came across the piece of piping I had torn from the wall, lying among the long grass underneath the broken window.

Then, I returned to the house, and, having re-bolted the back door, went up to the tower. Here, I spent the afternoon, reading, and occasionally glancing down into the gardens. I had determined, if the night passed quietly, to go as far as the Pit, on the morrow. Perhaps, I should be able to learn, then, something of what had happened. The day slipped away, and the night came, and went much as the last few nights had gone.

When I rose the morning had broken, fine and clear; and I determined to put my project into action. During breakfast, I considered the matter, carefully; after which I went to the study for my shotgun. In addition, I loaded, and slipped into my pocket, a small, but heavy, pistol. I quite understood that, if there were any danger, it lay in the direction of the Pit and I intended to be prepared.

Leaving the study, I went down to the back door, followed by Pepper. Once outside, I took a quick survey of the surrounding gardens, and then set off towards the Pit. On the way, I kept a sharp outlook, holding my gun, handily. Pepper was running ahead, I noticed, without any apparent hesitation. From this, I augured that there was no imminent danger to be apprehended, and I stepped out more quickly in his wake. He had reached the top of the Pit, now, and was nosing his way along the edge.

A minute later, I was beside him, looking down into the Pit. For a moment, I could scarcely believe that it was the same place, so greatly was it changed. The dark, wooded ravine of a fortnight ago, with a foliage-hidden stream, running sluggishly, at the bottom, existed no longer. Instead, my eyes showed me a ragged chasm, partly filled with a gloomy lake of turbid water. All one side of the ravine was stripped of underwood, showing the bare rock.

A little to my left, the side of the Pit appeared to have collapsed altogether, forming a deep V-shaped cleft in the face of the rocky cliff. This rift ran, from the upper edge of the ravine, nearly down to the water, and penetrated into the Pit side, to a distance of some forty feet. Its opening was, at least, six yards across; and, from this, it seemed to taper into about two. But, what attracted my attention, more than even the stupendous split itself, was a great hole, some distance down the cleft, and right in the angle of the V. It was clearly defined, and not unlike an arched doorway in shape; though, lying as it did in the shadow, I could not see it very distinctly.

The opposite side of the Pit, still retained its verdure; but so torn in places, and everywhere covered with dust and rubbish, that it was hardly distinguishable as such.

My first impression, that there had been a land slip, was, I began to see, not sufficient, of itself, to account for all the changes I witnessed. And the water—? I turned, suddenly; for I had become aware that, somewhere to my right, there was a noise of running water. I could see nothing; but, now that my attention had been caught, I distinguished, easily, that it came from somewhere at the East end of the Pit.

Slowly, I made my way in that direction; the sound growing plainer as I advanced, until in a little, I stood right above it. Even then, I could not perceive the cause, until I knelt down, and thrust my head over the cliff. Here, the noise came up to me, plainly; and I saw, below me, a torrent of clear water, issuing from a small fissure in the Pit side, and rushing down the rocks, into the lake beneath. A little further along the cliff, I saw another, and, beyond that again, two smaller ones. These, then, would help to account for the quantity of water in the Pit; and, if the fall of rock and earth had blocked the outlet of the stream at the bottom, there was little doubt but that it was contributing a very large share.

Yet, I puzzled my head to account for the generally *shaken* appearance of the place – these streamlets, and that huge cleft, further up the ravine! It seemed to me, that more than the landslip was necessary to account for these. I could imagine an earthquake, or a great *explosion*, creating some such condition of affairs as existed; but, of these, there had been neither. Then, I stood up, quickly, remembering that crash, and the cloud of dust that had followed, directly, rushing high into the air. But I shook my head, unbelievingly. No! It must have been the noise of the falling rocks and earth, I had heard; of course, the dust would fly, naturally. Still, in spite of my reasoning, I had an uneasy feeling, that this theory did not satisfy my sense of the probable; and yet, was any other, that I could suggest, likely to be half so plausible? Pepper had been sitting on the grass, while I conducted my examination. Now, as I turned up the North side of the ravine, he rose and followed.

Slowly, and keeping a careful watch in all directions, I made the circuit of the Pit; but found little else, that I had not already seen. From the West end, I could see the four waterfalls, uninterruptedly. They were some considerable distance up from the surface of the lake – about fifty feet, I calculated.

For a little while longer, I loitered about; keeping my eyes and ears open, but still, without seeing or hearing anything suspicious. The whole place was wonderfully quiet; indeed, save for the continuous murmur of the water, at the top end, no sound, of any description, broke the silence.

All this while, Pepper had shown no signs of uneasiness. This seemed, to me, to indicate that, for the time being, at least, there was none of the Swine-creatures in the vicinity. So far as I could see, his attention appeared to have been taken, chiefly, with scratching and sniffing among the grass at the edge of the Pit. At times, he would leave the edge, and run along towards the house, as though following invisible tracks; but, in all cases, returning after a few minutes. I had little doubt but that he was really tracing out the footsteps of the Swine-things; and the very fact that each one seemed to lead him back to the Pit, appeared to me, a proof that the brutes had all returned whence they came.

At noon, I went home, for dinner. During the afternoon, I made a partial search of the gardens, accompanied by Pepper; but, without coming upon anything to indicate the presence of the creatures.

Once, as we made our way through the shrubberies, Pepper rushed in among some bushes, with a fierce yelp. At that, I jumped back, in sudden fright, and threw my gun forward, in readiness; only to laugh, nervously, as Pepper reappeared, chasing an unfortunate cat. Towards evening, I gave up the search, and returned to the house. All at once, as we were passing a great clump of bushes, on our right, Pepper disappeared, and I could hear him sniffing and growling among them, in a suspicious manner. With my gun barrel, I parted the intervening shrubbery, and looked inside. There was nothing to be seen, save that many of the branches were bent down, and broken; as though some animal had made a lair there, at no very previous date. It was probably, I thought, one of the places occupied by some of the Swine-creatures, on the night of the attack.

Next day, I resumed my search through the gardens; but without result. By evening, I had been right through them, and now, I knew, beyond the possibility of doubt, that there were no longer any of the Things concealed about the place. Indeed, I have often thought since, that I was correct in my earlier surmise, that they had left soon after the attack.

**The complete and unabridged text is available
online, from** *flametreepublishing.com/extras*

If you enjoyed this, you might also like...
The Hog, see page 402
The Gateway of the Monster, see page 13

Out of the Storm

"HUSH!" said my friend the scientist, as I walked into his laboratory. I had opened my lips to speak; but stood silent for a few minutes at his request.

He was sitting at his instrument, and the thing was tapping out a message in a curiously irregular fashion – stopping a few seconds, then going on at a furious pace.

It was during a somewhat longer than usual pause that, growing slightly impatient, I ventured to address him.

"Anything important?" I asked.

"For God's sake, shut up!" he answered back in a high, strained voice.

I stared. I am used to pretty abrupt treatment from him at times when he is much engrossed in some particular experiment; but this was going a little too far, and I said so.

He was writing, and, for reply, he pushed several loosely written sheets over to me with the one curt word, "Read!"

With a sense half of anger, half of curiosity, I picked up the first and glanced at it. After a few lines, I was gripped and held securely by a morbid interest. I was reading a message from one in the last extremity. I will give it word for word:

"John, we are sinking! I wonder if you really understand what I feel at the present time – you sitting comfortably in your laboratory, I out here upon the waters, already one among the dead. Yes, we are doomed. There is no such thing as help in our case. We are sinking – steadily, remorselessly. God! I must keep up and be a man! I need not tell you that I am in the operator's room. All the rest are on deck – or dead in the hungry thing which is smashing the ship to pieces.

"I do not know where we are, and there is no one of whom I can ask. The last of the officers was drowned nearly an hour ago, and the vessel is now little more than a sort of breakwater for the giant seas.

"Once, about half an hour ago, I went out on to the deck. My God! The sight was terrible. It is a little after midday: but the sky is the colour of mud – do you understand? – grey mud! Down from it there hang vast lappets of clouds. Not such clouds as I have ever before seen; but monstrous, mildewed-looking hulls. They show solid, save where the frightful wind tears their lower edges into great feelers that swirl savagely above us, like the tentacles of some enormous Horror.

"Such a sight is difficult to describe to the living; though the Dead of the Sea know of it without words of mine. It is such a sight that none is allowed to see and live. It is a picture for the doomed and the dead; one of the sea's hell-orgies – one of the Thing's monstrous gloatings over the living – say the alive-in-death, those upon the brink. I have no right to tell of it to you; to speak of it to one of the living is to initiate innocence into one of the infernal mysteries – to talk of foul things to a child. Yet I care not! I will expose, in all its hideous nakedness, the death-side of the sea. The undoomed living shall know some of the things that death has hitherto so well guarded. Death knows not of this little instrument beneath my hands that connects me still with the quick, else would he haste to quiet me.

"Hark you, John! I have learnt undreamt of things in this little time of waiting. I know now why we are afraid of the dark. I had never imagined such secrets of the sea and the grave (which are one and the same).

"Listen! Ah, but I was forgetting you cannot hear! I can! The Sea is— Hush! the Sea is laughing, as though Hell cackled from the mouth of an ass. It is jeering. I can hear its voice echo like Satanic thunder amid the mud overhead— It is calling to me! Call— I must go— The sea calls!

"Oh! God, art Thou indeed God? Canst Thou sit above and watch calmly that which I have just seen? Nay! Thou art no God! Thou art weak and puny beside this foul Thing which Thou didst create in Thy lusty youth. It is now God – and I am one of its children.

"Are you there, John? Why don't you answer! Listen! I ignore God; for there is a stronger than He. My God is here, beside me, around me, and will be soon above me. You know what that means. It is merciless. The sea is now all the God there is! That is one of the things I have learnt.

"Listen! it, is laughing again. God is it, not He.

"It called, and I went out on to the decks. All was terrible. It is in the waist – everywhere. It has swamped the ship. Only the forecastle, bridge and poop stick up out from the bestial, reeking Thing, like three islands in the midst of shrieking foam. At times gigantic billows assail the ship from both sides. They form momentary arches above the vessel – arches of dull, curved water half a hundred feet towards the hideous sky. Then they descend – roaring. Think of it! You cannot.

"There is an infection of sin in the air: it is the exhalations from the Thing. Those left upon the drenched islets of shattered wood and iron are doing the most horrible things. The Thing is teaching them. Later, I felt the vile informing of its breath; but I have fled back here – to pray for death.

"On the forecastle, I saw a mother and her little son clinging to an iron rail. A great billow heaved up above them – descended in a falling mountain of brine. It passed, and they were still there. The Thing was only toying with them; yet, all the same, it had torn the hands of the child from the rail, and the child was clinging frantically to its Mother's arm. I saw another vast hill hurl up to port and hover above them. Then the Mother stooped and bit like a foul beast at the hands of her wee son. She was afraid that his little additional weight would be more than she could hold. I heard his scream even where I stood – it drove to me upon that wild laughter. It told me again that God is not He, but It. Then the hill thundered down upon those two. It seemed to me that the Thing gave a bellow as it leapt. It roared about them churning and growling; then surged away, and there was only one – the Mother. There appeared to me to be blood as well as water upon her face, especially about her mouth; but the distance was too great, and I cannot be sure. I looked away. Close to me, I saw something further – a beautiful young girl (her soul hideous with the breath of the Thing) struggling with her sweetheart for the shelter of the charthouse side. He threw her off; but she came back at him. I saw her hand come from her head, where still clung the wreckage of some form of headgear. She struck at him. He shouted and fell away to leeward, and she – smiled, showing her teeth. So much for that. I turned elsewhere.

"Out upon the Thing, I saw gleams, horrid and suggestive, below the crests of the waves. I have never seen them until this time. I saw a rough sailorman washed away from the vessel. One of the huge breakers snapped at him! – Those things were teeth. It has teeth. I heard them clash. I heard his yell. It was no more than a mosquito's shrilling amid all that laughter: but it was very terrible. There is worse than death.

"The ship is lurching very queerly with a sort of sickening heave—

"I fancy I have been asleep. No – I remember now. I hit my head when she rolled so strangely.

"My leg is doubled under me. I think it is broken; but it does not matter—

"I have been praying. I – I – What was it? I feel calmer, more resigned, now. I think I have been mad. What was it that I was saying? I cannot remember. It was something about – about – God. I – I believe I blasphemed. May He forgive me! Thou knowest, God, that I was not in my right mind. Thou knowest that I am very weak. Be with me in the coming time! I have sinned: but Thou art all merciful.

"Are you there, John? It is very near the end now. I had so much to say; but it all slips from me. What was it that I said? I take it all back. I was mad, and – and God knows. He is merciful, and I have very little pain now. I feel a bit drowsy.

"I wonder whether you are there, John. Perhaps, after all, no one has heard the things I have said. It is better so. The Living are not meant – and yet, I do not know. If you are there, John, you will – you will tell her how it was; but not – not – Hark! There was such a thunder of water overhead just then. I fancy two vast seas have met in mid-air across the top of the bridge and burst all over the vessel. It must be soon now – and there was such a number of things I had to say! I can hear voices in the wind. They are singing. It is like an enormous dirge – I think I have been dozing again. I pray God humbly that it be soon! You will not – not tell her anything about, about what I may have said, will you, John? I mean those things which I ought not to have said. What was it I did say? My head is growing strangely confused. I wonder whether you really do hear me. I may be talking only to that vast roar outside. Still, it is some comfort to go on, and I will not believe that you do not hear all I say. Hark again! A mountain of brine must have swept clean over the vessel. She has gone right over on to her side… She is back again. It will be very soon now—

"Are you there, John? Are you there? It is coming! The Sea has come for me! It is rushing down through the companionway! It – it is like a vast jet! My God! I am dr-own-ing! I – am – dr—"

If you enjoyed this, you might also like…

Through the Vortex of a Cylcone, see page 146
The Shamraken Homeward-Bounder, see page 162

The Thing in the Weeds

Chapter I

THIS IS AN extraordinary tale. We had come up from the Cape, and owing to the Trades heading us more than usual, we had made some hundreds of miles more westing than I ever did before or since.

I remember the particular night of the happening perfectly. I suppose what occurred stamped it solid into my memory, with a thousand little details that, in the ordinary way, I should never have remembered an hour. And, of course, we talked it over so often among ourselves that this, no doubt, helped to fix it all past any forgetting.

I remember the mate and I had been pacing the weather side of the poop and discussing various old shellbacks' superstitions. I was third mate, and it was between four and five bells in the first watch, i.e. between ten and half-past. Suddenly he stopped in his walk and lifted his head and sniffed several times.

"My word, mister," he said, "there's a rum kind of stink somewhere about. Don't you smell it?"

I sniffed once or twice at the light airs that were coming in on the beam; then I walked to the rail and leaned over, smelling again at the slight breeze. And abruptly I got a whiff of it, faint and sickly, yet vaguely suggestive of something I had once smelt before.

"I can smell something, Mr. Lammart," I said. "I could almost give it name; and yet somehow I can't." I stared away into the dark to windward. "What do you seem to smell?" I asked him.

"I can't smell anything now," he replied, coming over and standing beside me. "It's gone again. No! By Jove! There it is again. My goodness! Phew!"

The smell was all about us now, filling the night air. It had still that indefinable familiarity about it, and yet it was curiously strange, and, more than anything else, it was certainly simply beastly.

The stench grew stronger, and presently the mate asked me to go for'ard and see whether the look-out man noticed anything. When I reached the break of the fo'c's'le head I called up to the man, to know whether he smelled anything.

"Smell anythin', sir?" he sang out. "Jumpin' larks! I sh'u'd think I do. I'm fair p'isoned with it."

I ran up the weather steps and stood beside him. The smell was certainly very plain up there, and after savouring it for a few moments I asked him whether he thought it might be a dead whale. But he was very emphatic that this could not be the case, for, as he said, he had been nearly fifteen years in whaling ships, and knew the smell of a dead whale, "like as you would the smell of bad whiskey, sir," as he put it. "'Tain't no whale yon, but the Lord He knows what 'tis. I'm thinking it's Davy Jones come up for a breather."

I stayed with him some minutes, staring out into the darkness, but could see nothing; for, even had there been something big close to us, I doubt whether I could have seen it, so black a night it was, without a visible star, and with a vague, dull haze breeding an indistinctness all about the ship.

I returned to the mate and reported that the look-out complained of the smell, but that neither he nor I had been able to see anything in the darkness to account for it.

By this time the queer, disgusting odour seemed to be in all the air about us, and the mate told me to go below and shut all the ports, so as to keep the beastly smell out of the cabins and the saloon.

When I returned he suggested that we should shut the companion doors, and after that we commenced to pace the poop again, discussing the extraordinary smell, and stopping from time to time to stare through our night-glasses out into the night about the ship.

"I'll tell you what it smells like, mister," the mate remarked once, "and that's like a mighty old derelict I once went aboard in the North Atlantic. She was a proper old-timer, an' she gave us all the creeps. There was just this funny, dank, rummy sort of century-old bilge-water and dead men an' seaweed. I can't stop thinkin' we're nigh some lonesome old packet out there; an' a good thing we've not much way on us!"

"Do you notice how almighty quiet everything's gone the last half-hour or so?" I said a little later. "It must be the mist thickening down."

"It is the mist," said the mate, going to the rail and staring out. "Good Lord, what's that?" he added.

Something had knocked his hat from his head, and it fell with a sharp rap at my feet. And suddenly, you know, I got a premonition of something horrid.

"Come away from the rail, sir!" I said sharply, and gave one jump and caught him by the shoulders and dragged him back. "Come away from the side!"

"What's up, mister?" he growled at me, an twisted his shoulders free. "What's wrong with you? Was it you knocked off my cap?" He stooped and felt around for it, and as he did so I heard something unmistakably fiddling away at the rail which the mate had just left.

"My God, sir!" I said. "There's something there. Hark!"

The mate stiffened up, listening; then he heard it. It was for all the world as if something was feeling and rubbing the rail there in the darkness, not two fathoms away from us.

"Who's there?" said the mate quickly. Then, as there was no answer: "What the devil's this hanky-panky? Who's playing the goat there?" He made a swift step through the darkness towards he rail, but I caught him by the elbow.

"Don't go, mister!" I said, hardly above a whisper. "It's not one of the men. Let me get a light."

"Quick, then!" he said, and I turned and ran aft to the binnacle and snatched out the lighted lamp. As I did so I heard the mate shout something out of the darkness in a strange voice. There came a sharp, loud, rattling sound, and then a crash, and immediately the mate roaring to me to hasten with the light. His voice changed even whilst he shouted, and gave out somthing that was nearer a scream than anything else. There came two loud, dull blows and an extraordinary gasping sound; and then, as I raced along the poop, there was a tremendous smashing of glass and an immediate silence.

"Mr. Lammart!" I shouted. "Mr. Lammart!" And then I had reached the place where I had left the mate for forty seconds before; but he was not there.

"Mr. Lammart!" I shouted again, holding the light high over my head and turning quickly to look behind me. As I did so my foot glided on some slippery substance, and I went headlong to the deck with a tremendous thud, smashing the lamp and putting out the light.

I was on my feet again in an instant. I groped a moment for the lamp, and as I did so I heard the men singing out from the maindeck and the noise of their feet as they came running aft. I found the broken lamp and realised it was useless; then I jumped for the companion-way, and in half a minute I was back with the big saloon lamp glaring bright in my hands.

I ran for'ard again, shielding the upper edge of the glass chimney from the draught of my running, and the blaze of the big lamp seemed to make the weather side of the poop as bright as day, except for the mist, that gave something of a vagueness to things.

Where I had left the mate there was blood upon the deck, but nowhere any signs of the man himself. I ran to the weather rail and held the lamp to it. There was blood upon it, and the rail itself seemed to have been wrenched by some huge force. I put out my hand and found that I could shake it. Then I leaned out-board and held the lamp at arm's length, staring down over the ship's side.

"Mr. Lammart!" I shouted into the night and the thick mist. "Mr. Lammart! Mr. Lammart!" But my voice seemed to go, lost and muffled and infinitely small, away into the billowy darkness.

I heard the men snuffling and breathing, waiting to leeward of the poop. I whirled round to them, holding the lamp high,

"We heard somethin', sir," said Tarpley, the leading seaman in our watch. "Is anythin' wrong, sir?"

"The mate's gone," I said blankly. "We heard something, and I went for the binnacle lamp. Then he shouted, and I heard a sound of things smashing, and when I got back he'd gone clean." I turned and held the light out again over the unseen sea, and the men crowded round along the rail and stared, bewildered.

"Blood, sir," said Tarpley, pointing. "There's somethin' almighty queer out there." He waved a huge hand into the darkness. "That's what stinks—"

He never finished; for suddenly one of the men cried out something in a frightened voice: "Look out, sir! Look out, sir!"

I saw, in one brief flash of sight, something come in with an infernal flicker of movement; and then, before I could form any notion of what I had seen, the lamp was dashed to pieces across the poop deck. In that instant my perceptions cleared, and I saw the incredible folly of what we were doing; for there we were, standing up against the blank, unknowable night, and out there in the darkness there surely lurked some thing of monstrousness; and we were at its mercy. I seemed to feel it hovering – hovering over us, so that I felt the sickening creep of gooseflesh all over me.

"Stand back from the rail!" I shouted. "Stand back from the rail!" There was a rush of feet as the men obeyed, in sudden apprehension of their danger, and I gave back with them. Even as I did so I felt some invisible thing brush my shoulder, and an indescribable smell was in my nostrils from something that moved over me in the dark.

"Down into the saloon everyone!" I shouted. "Down with you all! Don't wait a moment!"

There was a rush along the dark weather deck, and then the men went helter-skelter down the companion steps into the saloon, falling and cursing over one another in the darkness. I sang out to the man at the wheel to join them, and then I followed.

I came upon the men huddled at the foot of the stairs and filling up the passage, all crowding each other in the darkness. The skipper's voice was filling the saloon, and he was demanding in violent adjectives the cause of so tremendous a noise. From the steward's berth there came also a voice and the splutter of a match, and then the glow of a lamp in the saloon itself.

I pushed my way through the men and found the captain in the saloon in his sleeping gear, looking both drowsy and angry, though perhaps bewilderment topped every other feeling. He held his cabin lamp in his hand, and shone the light over the huddle of men.

I hurried to explain, and told him of the incredible disappearance of the mate, and of my conviction that some extraordinary thing was lurking near the ship out in the mist and the darkness. I mentioned the curious smell, and told how the mate had suggested that we had drifted down near some old-time, sea-rotted derelict. And, you know, even as I put it into awkward words, my imagination began to awaken to horrible discomforts; a thousand dreadful impossibilities of the sea became suddenly possible.

The captain (Jeldy was his name) did not stop to dress, but ran back into his cabin, and came out in a few moments with a couple of revolvers and a handful of cartridges. The second mate had come running out of his cabin at the noise, and had listed intensely to what I had to say; and now he jumped back into his berth and brought out his own lamp and a large Smith and Wesson, which was evidently ready loaded.

Captain Jeldy pushed one of his revolvers into my hands, with some of the cartridges, and we began hastily to load the weapons. Then the captain caught up his lamp and made for the stairway, ordering the men into the saloon out of his way.

"Shall you want them, sir?" I asked.

"No," he said. "It's no use their running any unnecessary risks." He threw a word over his shoulder: "Stay quiet here, men; if I want you I'll give you a shout; then come spry!"

"Aye, aye, sir," said the watch in a chorus; and then I was following the captain up the stairs, with the second mate close behind.

We came up through the companion-way on to the silence of the deserted poop. The mist had thickened up, even during the brief time that I had been below, and there was not a breath of wind. The mist was so dense that it seemed to press in upon us, and the two lamps made a kind of luminous halo in the mist, which seemed to absorb their light in a most peculiar way.

"Where was he?" the captain asked me, almost in a whisper.

"On the port side, sir," I said, "a little foreside the charthouse and about a dozen feet in from the rail. I'll show you the exact place."

We went for'ard along what had been the weather side, going quietly and watchfully, though, indeed, it was little enough that we could see, because of the mist. Once, as I led the way, I thought I heard a vague sound somewhere in the mist, but was all unsure because of the slow creak, creak of the spars and gear as the vessel rolled slightly upon an odd, oily swell. Apart from this slight sound, and the far-up rustle of the canvas slatting gently against the masts, there was no sound of all throughout the ship. I assure you the silence seemed to me to be almost menacing, in the tense, nervous state in which I was.

"Hereabouts is where I left him," I whispered to the captain a few seconds later. "Hold your lamp low, sir. There's blood on the deck."

Captain Jeldy did so, and made a slight sound with his mouth at what he saw. Then, heedless of my hurried warning, he walked across to the rail, holding his lamp high up. I followed him, for I could not let him go alone; and the second mate came too, with his lamp. They leaned over the port rail and held their lamps out into the mist and the unknown darkness beyond the ship's side. I remember how the lamps made just two yellow glares in the mist, ineffectual, yet serving somehow to make extraordinarily plain the vastitude of the night and the *possibilities of the dark*. Perhaps that is a queer way to put it, but it gives you the effect of that moment upon my feelings. And all the time, you know, there was upon me the brutal, frightening expectancy of something reaching in at us from out of that everlasting darkness and mist that held all the sea and the night, so that we were just three mist-shrouded, hidden figures, peering nervously.

The mist was now so thick that we could not even see the surface of the water overside, and fore and aft of us the rail vanished away into the fog and the dark. And then, as we stood here staring, I heard something moving down on the maindeck. I caught Captain Jeldy by the elbow.

"Come away from the rail, sir," I said, hardly above a whisper; and he, with the swift premonition of danger, stepped back and allowed me to urge him well inboard. The second mate followed, and the three of us stood there in the mist, staring round about us and holding our revolvers handily, and the dull waves of the mist beating in slowly upon the lamps in vague wreathings and swirls of fog.

"What was it you heard, mister?" asked the captain after a few moments.

"Ssst!" I muttered. "There it is again. There's something moving down on the maindeck!"

Captain Jeldy heard it himself now, and the three of us stood listening intensely. Yet it was hard to know what to make of the sounds. And then suddenly there was the rattle of a deck ringbolt, and then again, as if something or someone were fumbling and playing with it.

"Down there on the maindeck!" shouted the captain abruptly, his voice seeming hoarse close to my ear, yet immediately smothered by the fog. "Down there on the maindeck! Who's there?"

But there came never an answering sound. And the three of us stood there, looking quickly this way and that, and listening. Abruptly the second mate muttered something:

"The look-out, sir! The look-out!"

Captain Jeldy took the hint on the instant.

"On the look-out there!" he shouted.

And then, far away and muffled-sounding, there came the answering cry of the look-out man from the fo'c'sle head:

"Sir-r-r?" A little voice, long drawn out through unknowable alleys of fog.

"Go below into the fo'c'sle and shut both doors, an' don't stir out till you're told!" sung out Captain Jeldy, his voice going lost into the mist. And then the man's answering "Aye, aye, sir!" coming to us faint and mournful. And directly afterwards the clang of a steel door, hollow-sounding and remote; and immediately the sound of another.

"That puts them safe for the present, anyway," said the second mate. And even as he spoke there came again that indefinite noise down upon the maindeck of something moving with an incredible and unnatural stealthiness.

"On the maindeck there!" shouted Captain Jeldy sternly. "If there is anyone there, answer, or I shall fire!"

The reply was both amazing and terrifying, for suddenly a tremendous blow was stricken upon the deck, and then there came the dull, rolling sound of some enormous weight going hollowly across the maindeck. And then an abominable silence.

"My God!' said Captain Jeldy in a low voice, "what was that?" And he raised his pistol, but I caught him by the wrist. "Don't shoot, sir!" I whispered. "It'll be no good. That – that – whatever it is I – mean it's something enormous, sir. I – I really wouldn't shoot." I found it impossible to put my vague idea into words; but I felt there was a force aboard, down on the maindeck, that it would be futile to attack with so ineffectual a thing as a puny revolver bullet.

And then, as I held Captain Jeldy's wrist, and he hesitated, irresolute, there came a sudden bleating of sheep and the sound of lashings being burst and the cracking of wood; and the next instant a huge crash, followed by crash after crash, and the anguished m-aa-a-a-ing of sheep.

"My God!" said the second mate, "the sheep-pen's being beaten to pieces against the deck. Good God! What sort of thing could do that?"

The tremendous beating ceased, and there was a splashing overside; and after that a silence so profound that it seemed as if the whole atmosphere of the night was full of an unbearable, tense quietness. And then the damp slatting of a sail, far up in the night, that made me start – a lonesome sound to break suddenly through that infernal silence upon my raw nerves.

"Get below, both of you. Smartly now!" muttered Captain Jeldy. "There's something run either aboard us or alongside; and we can't do anything till daylight."

We went below and shut the doors of the companion-way, and there we lay in the wide Atlantic, without wheel or look-out or officer in charge, and something incredible down on the dark maindeck.

Chapter II

FOR SOME HOURS we sat in the captain's cabin talking the matter over whilst the watch slept, sprawled in a dozen attitudes on the floor of the saloon. Captain Jeldy and the second mate still wore their pyjamas, and our loaded revolvers lay handy on the cabin table. And so we watched anxiously through the hours for the dawn to come in.

As the light strengthened we endeavoured to get some view of the sea from the ports, but the mist was so thick about us that it was exactly like looking out into a grey nothingness, that became presently white as the day came.

"Now," said Captain Jeldy, "we're going to look into this."

He went out through the saloon to the companion stairs. At the top he opened the two doors, and the mist rolled in on us, white and impenetrable. For a little while we stood there, the three of us, absolutely silent and listening, with our revolvers handy; but never a sound came to us except the odd, vague slatting of a sail or the slight creaking of the gear as the ship lifted on some slow, invisible swell.

Presently the captain stepped cautiously out on to the deck; he was in his cabin slippers, and therefore made no sound. I was wearing gum-boots, and followed him silently, and the second mate after me in his bare feet. Captain Jeldy went a few paces along the deck, and the mist hid him utterly. "Phew!" I heard him mutter, "the stink's worse than ever!" His voice came odd and vague to me through the wreathing of the mist.

"The sun'll soon eat up all this fog," said the second mate at my elbow, in a voice little above a whisper.

We stepped after the captain, and found him a couple of fathoms away, standing shrouded in the mist in an attitude of tense listening.

"Can't hear a thing!" he whispered. "We'll go for'ard to the break, as quiet as you like. Don't make a sound."

We went forward, like three shadows, and suddenly Captain Jeldy kicked his shin against something and pitched headlong over it, making a tremendous noise. He got up quickly, swearing grimly, and the three of us stood there in silence, waiting lest any infernal thing should come upon us out of all that white invisibility. Once I felt sure I saw something coming towards me, and I raised my revolver, but saw in a moment that there was nothing. The tension of imminent, nervous expectancy eased from us, and Captain Jeldy stooped over the object on the deck.

"The port hencoop's been shifted out here!" he muttered. "It's all stove!"

"That must be what I heard last night when the mate went," I whispered. "There was a loud crash just before he sang out to me to hurry with the lamp."

Captain Jeldy left the smashed hencoop, and the three of us tiptoed silently to the rail across the break of the poop. Here we leaned over and stared down into the blank whiteness of the mist that hid everything.

"Can't see a thing," whispered the second mate; yet as he spoke I could fancy that I heard a slight, indefinite, slurring noise somewhere below us; and I caught them each by an arm to draw them back.

"There's something down there," I muttered. "For goodness' sake come back from the rail."

We gave back a step or two, and then stopped to listen; and even as we did so there came a slight air playing through the mist.

"The breeze is coming," said the second mate. "Look, the mist is clearing already."

He was right. Already the look of white impenetrability had gone, and suddenly we could see the corner of the after-hatch coamings through the thinning fog. Within a minute we could see as far for'ard as the mainmast, and then the stuff blew away from us, clear of the vessel, like a great wall of whiteness, that dissipated as it went.

"*Look!*" we all exclaimed together. The whole of the vessel was now clear to our sight; but it was not at the ship herself that we looked, for, after one quick glance along the empty maindeck, we had seen something beyond the ship's side. All around the vessel there lay a submerged spread of weed, for, maybe, a good quarter of a mile upon every side.

"Weed!" sang out Captain Jeldy in a voice of comprehension. "Weed! Look! By Jove, I guess I know now what got the mate!"

He turned and ran to the port side and looked over. And suddenly he stiffened and beckoned silently over his shoulder to us to come and see. We had followed, and now we stood, one on each side of him, staring.

"Look!" whispered the captain, pointing. "See the great brute! Do you see it? There! Look!"

At first I could see nothing except the submerged spread of the weed, into which we had evidently run after dark. Then, as I stared intently, my gaze began to separate from the surrounding weed a leathery-looking something that was somewhat darker in hue than the weed itself.

"My God!" said Captain Jeldy. "What a monster! What a monster! Just look at the brute! Look at the thing's eyes! That's what got the mate. What a creature out of hell itself!"

I saw it plainly now; three of the massive feelers lay twined in and out among the clumpings of the weed; and then, abruptly, I realised that the two extraordinary round discs, motionless and inscrutable, were the creature's eyes, just below the surface of the water. It appeared to be staring, expressionless, up at the steel side of the vessel. I traced, vaguely, the shapeless monstrosity of what must be termed its head. "My God!" I muttered. "It's an enormous squid of some kind! What an awful brute! What—"

The sharp report of the captain's revolver came at that moment. He had fired at the thing, and instantly there was a most awful commotion alongside. The weed was hove upward, literally in tonnes. An enormous quantity was thrown aboard us by the thrashing of the monster's great feelers. The sea seemed almost to boil, in one great cauldron of weed and water, all about the brute, and the steel side of the ship resounded with the dull, tremendous blows that the creature gave in its struggle. And into all that whirling boil of tentacles, weed, and seawater the three of us emptied our revolvers as fast as we could fire and reload. I remember the feeling of fierce satisfaction I had in thus aiding to avenge the death of the mate.

Suddenly the captain roared out to us to jump back, and we obeyed on the instant. As we did so the weed rose up into a great mound over twenty feet in height, and more than a tonne of it slopped aboard. The next instant three of the monstrous tentacles came in over the side, and the vessel gave a slow, sullen roll to port as the weight came upon her, for the monster had literally hove itself almost free of the sea against our port side, in one vast, leathery shape, all wreathed with weed-fronds, and seeming drenched with blood and curious black liquid.

The feelers that had come inboard thrashed round here and there, and suddenly one of them curled in the most hideous, snake-like fashion around the base of the mainmast. This seemed to attract it, for immediately it curled the two others about the mast, and forthwith wrenched upon it with such hideous violence that the whole towering length of spars, through all their height of a hundred and fifty feet, were shaken visibly, whilst the vessel herself vibrated with the stupendous efforts of the brute.

"It'll have the mast down, sir!" said the second mate, with a gasp. "My God! It'll strain her side open! My—"

"One of those blasting cartridges!" I said to Jeldy almost in a shout, as the inspiration took me. "Blow the brute to pieces!"

"Get one, quick!" said the captain, jerking his thumb towards the companion. "You know where they are."

In thirty seconds I was back with the cartridge. Captain Jeldy took out his knife and cut the fuse dead short; then, with a steady hand, he lit the fuse, and calmly held it, until I backed away, shouting to him to throw it, for I knew it must explode in another couple of seconds.

Captain Jeldy threw the thing like one throws a quoit, so that it fell into the sea just on the outward side of the vast bulk of the monster. So well had he timed it that it burst, with a stunning report, just as it struck the water. The effect upon the squid was amazing. It seemed literally to collapse. The enormous tentacles released themselves from the mast and curled across the deck helplessly, and were drawn inertly over the rail, as the enormous bulk sank away from the ship's side, out of sight, into the weed. The ship rolled slowly to starboard, and then steadied. "Thank God!" I muttered, and looked at the two others. They were pallid and sweating, and I must have been the same.

"Here's the breeze again," said the second mate, a minute later. "We're moving." He turned, without another word, and raced aft to the wheel, whilst the vessel slid over and through the weedfield.

"Look where that brute broke up the sheep-pen!" cried Jeldy, pointing. "And here's the skylight of the sail-locker smashed to bits!"

He walked across to it, and glanced down. And suddenly he let out a tremendous shout of astonishment:

"Here's the mate down here!" he shouted. "He's not overboard at all! He's here!"

He dropped himself down through the skylight on to the sails, and I after him; and, surely, there was the mate, lying all huddled and insensible on a hummock of spare sails.

In his right hand he held a drawn sheath-knife, which he was in the habit of carrying A.B. fashion, whilst his left hand was all caked with dried blood, where he had been badly cut. Afterwards, we concluded he had cut himself in slashing at one of the tentacles of the squid, which had caught him round the left wrist, the tip of the tentacle being still curled tight about his arm, just as it had been when he hacked it through. For the rest, he was not seriously damaged, the creature having obviously flung him violently away through the framework of the skylight, so that he had fallen in a studded condition on to the pile of sails.

We got him on deck, and down into his bunk, where we left the steward to attend to him. When we returned to the poop the vessel had drawn clear of the weed-field, and the captain and I stopped for a few moments to stare astern over the taffrail.

As we stood and looked something wavered up out of the heart of the weed – a long, tapering, sinous thing, that curled and wavered against the dawn-light, and presently sank back again into the demure weed – a veritable spider of the deep, waiting in the great web that Dame Nature had spun for it in the eddy of her tides and currents.

And we sailed away northwards, with strengthening 'trades', and left that patch of monstrousness to the loneliness of the sea.

If you enjoyed this, you might also like...
A Tropical Horror, see page 105
From the Tideless Sea: Part One, see page 111

The Derelict

"IT'S THE MATERIAL," said the old ship's doctor.... "The *Material*, plus the Conditions; and, maybe," he added slowly, "a third factor – yes, a third factor; but there, there...." He broke off his half-meditative sentence, and began to charge his pipe.

"Go on, Doctor," we said, encouragingly, and with more than a little expectancy. We were in the smoke-room of the *Sand-a-lea*, running across the North Atlantic; and the Doctor was a character. He concluded the charging of his pipe, and lit it; then settled himself, and began to express himself more fully:

"The *Material*," he said, with conviction, "is inevitably the medium of expression of the Life-Force – the fulcrum, as it were; lacking which, it is unable to exert itself, or, indeed, to express itself in any form or fashion that would be intelligible or evident to us.

"So potent is the share of the *Material* in the production of that thing which we name Life, and so eager the Life-Force to express itself, that I am convinced it would, if given the right Conditions, make itself manifest even through so hopeless-seeming a medium as a simple block of sawn wood; for I tell you, gentlemen, the Life-Force is both as fiercely urgent and as indiscriminate as Fire – the Destructor; yet which some are now growing to consider the very essence of Life rampant.... There is a quaint seeming paradox there," he concluded, nodding his old grey head.

"Yes, Doctor," I said. "In brief, your argument is that Life is a thing, state, fact, or element, call-it-what-you-like, which requires the *Material* through which to manifest itself, and that given the *Material*, plus the Conditions, the result is Life. In other words, that Life is an evolved product, manifested through Matter and bred of Conditions – eh?"

"As we understand the word," said the old Doctor. "Though, mind you, there *may* be a third factor. But, in my heart, I believe that it is a matter of chemistry; Conditions and a suitable medium; but given the Conditions, the Brute is so almighty that it will seize upon anything through which to manifest itself. It is a Force generated by Conditions; but nevertheless this does not bring us one iota nearer to its *explanation*, any more than to the explanation of Electricity or Fire. They are, all three, of the Outer Forces – Monsters of the Void. Nothing we can do will *create* any one of them; our power is merely to be able, by providing the Conditions, to make each one of them manifest to our physical senses. Am I clear?"

"Yes, Doctor, in a way you are," I said. "But I don't agree with you; though I think I understand you. Electricity and Fire are both what I might call natural things; but Life is an abstract something – a kind of all-permeating Wakefulness. Oh, I can't explain it; who could! But it's spiritual; not just a thing bred out of a Condition, like Fire, as you say, or Electricity. It's a horrible thought of yours. Life's a kind of spiritual mystery...."

"Easy, my boy!" said the old Doctor, laughing gently to himself; "or else I may be asking you to demonstrate the spiritual mystery of life of the limpet, or the crab, shall we say."

He grinned at me, with ineffable perverseness. "Anyway," he continued, "as I suppose you've all guessed, I've a yarn to tell you in support of my impression that Life is no more a mystery or a miracle than Fire or Electricity. But, please to remember, gentlemen, that because we've succeeded in naming and making good use of these two Forces, they're just as much mysteries, fundamentally, as ever. And, anyway, the thing I'm going to tell you, won't explain the mystery of Life; but only give you one of my pegs on which I hang my feeling that Life is, as I have said, a Force made manifest through Conditions (that is to say, natural Chemistry), and that it can take for its purpose and Need, the most incredible and unlikely Matter; for without Matter, it cannot come into existence – it cannot become manifest...."

"I don't agree with you, Doctor," I interrupted. "Your theory would destroy all belief in life after death. It would...."

"Hush, sonny," said the old man, with a quiet little smile of comprehension. "Hark to what I've to say first; and, anyway, what objection have you to material life, after death; and if you object to a material framework, I would still have you remember that I am speaking of Life, as we understand the word in this our life. Now do be a quiet lad, or I'll never be done:

"It was when I was a young man, and that is a good many years ago, gentlemen. I had passed my examinations; but was so run down with overwork, that it was decided that I had better take a trip to sea. I was by no means well off, and very glad, in the end, to secure a nominal post as Doctor in a sailing passenger-clipper, running out to China.

"The name of the ship was the *Bheotpte*, and soon after I had got all my gear aboard, she cast off, and we dropped down the Thames, and next day were well away out in the Channel.

"The Captain's name was Gannington, a very decent man; though quite illiterate. The First Mate, Mr. Berlies, was a quiet, sternish, reserved man, very well-read. The Second Mate, Mr. Selvern, was, perhaps, by birth and upbringing, the most socially cultured of the three; but he lacked the stamina and indomitable pluck of the two others. He was more of a sensitive; and emotionally and even mentally, the most alert man of the three.

"On our way out, we called at Madagascar, where we landed some of our passengers; then we ran Eastward, meaning to call at North West Cape; but about a hundred degrees East, we encountered very dreadful weather, which carried away all our sails and sprung the jibboom and fore t'gallant mast.

"The storm carried us Northward for several hundred miles, and when it dropped us finally, we found ourselves in a very bad state. The ship had been strained, and had taken some three feet of water through her seams; the main topmast had been sprung, in addition to the jibboom and fore t'gallant mast; two of our boats had gone, as also one of the pigsties (with three fine pigs), this latter having been washed overboard but some half hour before the wind began to ease, which it did quickly; though a very ugly sea ran for some hours after.

"The wind left us just before dark, and when morning came, it brought splendid weather; a calm, mildly undulating sea, and a brilliant sun, with no wind. It showed us also that we were not alone; for about two miles away to the Westward, was another vessel, which Mr. Selvern, the Second Mate, pointed out to me.

"'That's a pretty rum looking packet, Doctor,' he said, and handed me his glass. I looked through it, at the other vessel, and saw what he meant; at least, I thought I did.

"'Yes, Mr. Selvern,' I said, 'she's got a pretty old-fashioned look about her.'

"He laughed at me, in his pleasant way.

"'It's easy to see you're not a sailor, Doctor,' he remarked. 'There's a dozen rum things about her. She's a derelict, and has been floating round, by the look of her, for many a score of years. Look at the shape of her counter, and the bows and cutwater. She's as old as the hills, as you might say, and ought to have gone down to Davy Jones a long time ago. Look at the growths on her, and the thickness of her standing rigging; that's all salt encrustations, I fancy, if you notice the white colour. She's been a small barque; but don't you see she's not a yard left aloft. They've all dropped out of the slings; everything rotted away; wonder the standing rigging hasn't gone too. I wish the Old Man would let us take the boat, and have a look at her; she'd be well worth it.'

"There seemed little chance, however, of this; for all hands were turned-to and kept hard at it all day long, repairing the damage to the masts and gear, and this took a long while, as you may think. Part of the time, I gave a hand, heaving on one of the deck-capstans; for the exercise was good for my liver. Old Captain Gannington approved, and I persuaded him to come along and try some of the same medicine, which he did; and we grew very chummy over the job.

"We got talking about the derelict, and he remarked how lucky we were not to have run full tilt on to her, in the darkness; for she lay right away to leeward of us, according to the way that we had been drifting in the storm. He also was of the opinion that she had a strange look about her, and that she was pretty old; but on this latter point, he plainly had far less knowledge than the Second Mate; for he was, as I have said, an illiterate man, and knew nothing of sea-craft, beyond what experience had taught him. He lacked the book-knowledge which the Second Mate had, of vessels previous to his day, which it appeared the derelict was.

"'She's an old 'un, Doctor,' was the extent of his observations in this direction.

"Yet, when I mentioned to him that it would be interesting to go aboard, and give her a bit of an overhaul, he nodded his head, as if the idea had been already in his mind, and accorded with his own inclinations.

"'When the work's over, Doctor,' he said. 'Can't spare the men now, ye know. Got to get all shipshape an' ready as smart as we can. But we'll take my gig, an' go off in the Second Dog Watch. The glass is steady, an' it'll be a bit of gam for us.'

"That evening, after tea, the captain gave orders to clear the gig and get her overboard. The Second Mate was to come with us, and the Skipper gave him word to see that two or three lamps were put into the boat, as it would soon fall dark. A little later, we were pulling across the calmness of the sea, with a crew of six at the oars, and making very good speed of it.

"Now, gentlemen, I have detailed to you with great exactness, all the facts, both big and little, so that you can follow step by step each incident in this extraordinary affair; and I want you now to pay the closest attention.

"I was sitting in the stern-sheets, with the Second Mate, and the Captain, who was steering; and as we drew nearer and nearer to the stranger, I studied her with an ever growing attention, as, indeed, did Captain Gannington and the Second Mate. She was, as you know, to the Westward of us, and the sunset was making a great flame of red light to the back of her, so that she showed a little blurred and indistinct, by reason of the halation of the light, which almost defeated the eye in any attempt to see her rotting spars and standing-rigging, submerged as they were in the fiery glory of the sunset.

"It was because of this effect of the sunset, that we had come quite close, comparatively, to the derelict, before we saw that she was all surrounded by a sort of curious scum, the colour of which was difficult to decide upon, by reason of the red light that was in the atmosphere; but which afterwards we discovered to be brown. This scum spread all about the old vessel for many hundreds of yards, in a huge, irregular patch, a great stretch of which reached out to the Eastward, upon our starboard side, some score, or so, fathoms away.

"'Queer stuff,' said Captain Gannington, leaning to the side, and looking over. 'Something in the cargo 'as gone rotten an' worked out through 'er seams.'

"'Look at her bows and stern,' said the Second Mate; 'just look at the growth on her.'

"There were, as he said, great clumpings of strange looking sea-fungi under the bows and the short counter astern. From the stump of her jib-boom and her cutwater, great beards of rime and marine-growths hung downward into the scum that held her in. Her blank starboard side was presented to us, all a dead, dirtyish white, streaked and mottled vaguely with dull masses of heavier colour.

"'There's a steam or haze rising off her,' said the Second Mate, speaking again; 'you can see it against the light. It keeps coming and going. Look!'

"I saw then what he meant – a faint haze or steam, either suspended above the old vessel, or rising from her; and Captain Gannington saw it also:

"'Spontaneous combustion!' he exclaimed. 'We'll 'ave to watch w'en we lift the 'atches; 'nless it's some poor devil that's got aboard of 'er; but that ain't likely.'

"We were now within a couple of hundred yards of the old derelict, and had entered into the brown scum. As it poured off the lifted oars, I heard one of the men mutter to himself: 'Dam treacle!' and, indeed, it was something like it. As the boat continued to forge nearer and nearer to the old ship, the scum grew thicker and thicker; so that, at last, it perceptibly slowed us.

"'Give way, lads! Put some beef to it!' sung out Captain Gannington; and thereafter there was no sound, except the panting of the men, and the faint, reiterated suck, suck, of the sullen brown scum upon the oars, as the boat was forced ahead. As we went, I was conscious of a peculiar smell in the evening air, and whilst I had no doubt that the puddling of the scum, by the oars, made it rise, I felt that in some way, it was vaguely familiar; yet I could give it no name.

"We were now very close to the old vessel, and presently she was high above us, against the dying light. The Captain called out then to: 'In with the bow oars, and stand-by with the boathook,' which was done.

"'Aboard there! Ahoy! Aboard there! Ahoy!' shouted Captain Gannington; but there came no answer, only the flat sound of his voice going lost into the open sea, each time he sung out.

"'Ahoy! Aboard there! Ahoy!' he shouted, time after time; but there was only the weary silence of the old hulk that answered us; and, somehow as he shouted, the while that I stared up half expectantly at her, a queer little sense of oppression, that amounted almost to nervousness, came upon me. It passed; but I remember how I was suddenly aware that it was growing dark. Darkness comes fairly rapidly in the tropics; though not so quickly as many fiction-writers seem to think; but it was not that the coming dusk had perceptibly deepened in that brief time, of only a few moments, but rather that my nerves had made me suddenly a little hyper-sensitive. I mention my state particularly; for I am not a nervy man, normally; and my abrupt touch of nerves is significant, in the light of what happened.

"'There's no one aboard there!' said Captain Gannington. 'Give way, men!' For the boat's crew had instinctively rested on their oars, as the Captain hailed the old craft. The men gave way again; and then the Second Mate called out excitedly: 'Why, look there,

there's our pigsty! See, it's got *Bheotpte* painted on the end. It's drifted down here, and the scum's caught it. What a blessed wonder!'

"It was, as he had said, our pigsty that had been washed overboard in the storm; and most extraordinary to come across it there.

"'We'll tow it off with us, when we go,' remarked the Captain, and shouted to the crew to get-down to their oars; for they were hardly moving the boat, because the scum was so thick, close in around the old ship, that it literally clogged the boat from going ahead. I remember that it struck me, in a half-conscious sort of way, as curious that the pigsty, containing our three dead pigs, had managed to drift in so far, unaided, whilst we could scarcely manage to *force* the boat in, now that we had come right into the scum. But the thought passed from my mind; for so many things happened within the next few minutes.

"The men managed to bring the boat in alongside, within a couple of feet of the derelict, and the man with the boathook, hooked on.

"''Ave ye got 'old there, forrard?' asked Captain Gannington.

"'Yessir!' said the bow-man; and as he spoke, there came a queer noise of tearing.

"'What's that?' asked the Captain.

"'It's tore, Sir. Tore clean away!' said the man; and his tone showed that he had received something of a shock.

"'Get a hold again, then!' said Captain Gannington, irritably. 'You don't s'pose this packet was built yesterday! Shove the hook into the main chains.' The man did so, gingerly, as you might say; for it seemed to me, in the growing dusk, that he put no strain on to the hook; though, of course, there was no need; you see, the boat could not go very far, of herself, in the stuff in which she was embedded. I remember thinking this, also, as I looked up at the bulging side of the old vessel. Then I heard Captain Gannington's voice:

"'Lord! But she's old! An' what a colour, Doctor! She don't half want paint, do she! Now then, somebody, one of them oars.'

"An oar was passed to him, and he leant it up against the ancient, bulging side; then he paused, and called to the Second Mate to light a couple of the lamps, and stand-by to pass them up; for darkness had settled down now upon the sea.

"The Second Mate lit two of the lamps, and told one of the men to light a third, and keep it handy in the boat; then he stepped across, with a lamp in each hand, to where Captain Gannington stood by the oar against the side of the ship.

"'Now, my lad,' said the Captain, to the man who had pulled stroke, 'up with you, an' we'll pass ye up the lamps.'

"The man jumped to obey; caught the oar, and put his weight upon it, and as he did so, something seemed to give a little.

"'Look!' cried out the Second Mate, and pointed, lamp in hand, 'It's sunk in!'

"This was true. The oar had made quite an indentation into the bulging, somewhat slimy side of the old vessel.

"'Mould, I reckon,' said Captain Gannington, bending towards the derelict to look. Then, to the man:

"'Up you go, my lad, and be smart. Don't stand there waitin'!'

"At that, the man, who had paused a moment as he felt the oar give beneath his weight, began to shin up, and in a few seconds he was aboard, and leant out over the rail for the lamps. These were passed up to him, and the Captain called to him to steady the oar. Then Captain Gannington went, calling to me to follow, and after me the Second Mate.

"As the Captain put his face over the rail, he gave a cry of astonishment:

"'Mould, by gum! Mould. tonnes of it! Good Lord!'

"As I heard him shout that, I scrambled the more eagerly after him, and in a moment or two, I was able to see what he meant – everywhere that the light from the two lamps struck, there was nothing but smooth great masses and surfaces of a dirty white mould.

"I climbed over the rail, with the Second Mate close behind, and stood upon the mould-covered decks. There might have been no planking beneath the mould, for all that our feet could feel. It gave under our tread, with a spongy, puddingy feel. It covered the deck-furniture of the old ship, so that the shape of each article and fitment was often no more than suggested through it.

"Captain Gannington snatched a lamp from the man, and the Second Mate reached for the other. They held the lamps high, and we all stared. It was most extraordinary, and, somehow, most abominable. I can think of no other word, gentlemen, that so much describes the predominant feeling that affected me at the moment.

"'Good Lord!' said Captain Gannington, several times. 'Good Lord!' But neither the Second Mate nor the man said anything, and for my part I just stared, and at the same time began to smell a little at the air; for there was again a vague odour of something half familiar, that somehow brought to me a sense of half-known fright.

"I turned this way and that, staring, as I have said. Here and there, the mould was so heavy as to entirely disguise what lay beneath; converting the deck-fittings into indistinguishable mounds of mould, all dirty-white, and blotched and veined with irregular, dull purplish markings.

"There was a strange thing about the mould, which Captain Gannington drew attention to – it was that our feet did not crush into it and break the surface, as might have been expected; but merely indented it.

"'Never seen nothin' like it before! Never!' said the Captain, after having stooped with his lamp to examine the mould under our feet. He stamped with his heel, and the stuff gave out a dull, puddingy sound. He stooped again, with a quick movement, and stared, holding the lamp close to the deck. 'Blest, if it ain't a reg'lar skin to it!' he said.

"The Second Mate and the man and I all stooped, and looked at it. The Second Mate progged it with his forefinger, and I remember I rapped it several times with my knuckles, listening to the dead sound it gave out, and noticing the close, firm texture of the mould.

"'Dough!' said the Second Mate. 'It's just like blessed dough! Pouf!' He stood up with a quick movement. 'I could fancy it stinks a bit,' he said.

"As he said this, I knew suddenly what the familiar thing was, in the vague odour that hung about us – it was that the smell had something animal-like in it; something of the same smell, only *heavier*, that you will smell in any place that is infested with mice. I began to look about with a sudden very real uneasiness.... There might be vast numbers of hungry rats aboard.... They might prove exceedingly dangerous, if in a starving condition; yet, as you will understand, somehow I hesitated to put forward my idea as a reason for caution; it was too fanciful.

"Captain Gannington had begun to go aft, along the mould-covered maindeck, with the Second Mate; each of them holding his lamp high up, so as to cast a good light about the vessel. I turned quickly and followed them, the man with me keeping close to my heels, and plainly uneasy. As we went, I became aware that there was a feeling of moisture in the air, and I remembered the slight mist, or smoke, above the hulk, which had made Captain Gannington suggest spontaneous combustion, in explanation.

"And always, as we went, there was that vague, animal smell; and, suddenly, I found myself wishing we were well away from the old vessel.

"Abruptly, after a few paces, the Captain stopped and pointed at a row of mould-hidden shapes on either side of the maindeck…. 'Guns,' he said. 'Been a privateer in the old days, I guess; maybe worse! We'll 'ave a look below, Doctor; there may be something worth touchin'. She's older than I thought. Mr. Selvern thinks she's about three hundred year old; but I scarce think it.'

"We continued our way aft, and I remember that I found myself walking as lightly and gingerly as possible; as if I were subconsciously afraid of treading through the rotten, mould-hid decks. I think the others had a touch of the same feeling, from the way that they walked. Occasionally, the soft mould would grip our heels, releasing them with a little, sullen suck.

"The Captain forged somewhat ahead of the Second Mate; and I know that the suggestion he had made himself, that perhaps there might be something below, worth the carrying away, had stimulated his imagination. The Second Mate was, however, beginning to feel somewhat the same way that I did; at least, I have that impression. I think, if it had not been for what I might truly describe as Captain Gannington's sturdy courage, we should all of us have just gone back over the side very soon; for there was most certainly an unwholesome feeling abroad, that made one feel queerly lacking in pluck; and you will soon perceive that this feeling was justified.

"Just as the Captain reached the few, mould-covered steps, leading up on to the short half-poop, I was suddenly aware that the feeling of moisture in the air had grown very much more definite. It was perceptible now, intermittently, as a sort of thin, moist, fog-like vapour, that came and went oddly, and seemed to make the decks a little indistinct to the view, this time and that. Once, an odd puff of it beat up suddenly from somewhere, and caught me in the face, carrying a queer, sickly, heavy odour with it, that somehow frightened me strangely, with a suggestion of a waiting and half-comprehended danger.

"We had followed Captain Gannington up the three, mould-covered steps, and now went slowly aft along the raised after-deck.

"By the mizzenmast, Captain Gannington paused, and held his lantern near to it….

"'My word, Mister,' he said to the Second Mate, 'it's fair thickened up with the mould; why, I'll g'antee it's close on four foot thick.' He shone the light down to where it met the deck. 'Good Lord!' he said, 'look at the sea-lice on it!' I stepped up; and it was as he had said; the sea-lice were thick upon it, some of them huge; not less than the size of large beetles, and all a clear, colourless shade, like water, except where there were little spots of grey in them, evidently their internal organisms.

"'I've never seen the like of them, 'cept on a live cod!' said Captain Gannington, in an extremely puzzled voice. 'My word! But they're whoppers!' Then he passed on; but a few paces farther aft, he stopped again, and held his lamp near to the mould-hidden deck.

"'Lord bless me, Doctor!' he called out, in a low voice. 'Did ye ever see the like of that? Why, it's a foot long, if it's a hinch!'

"I stooped over his shoulder, and saw what he meant; it was a clear, colourless creature, about a foot long, and about eight inches high, with a curved back that was extraordinarily narrow. As we stared, all in a group, it gave a queer little flick, and was gone.

"'Jumped!' said the Captain. 'Well, if that ain't a giant of all the sea-lice that ever I've seen! I guess it's jumped twenty-foot clear.' He straightened his back, and scratched his head a moment, swinging the lantern this way and that with the other hand, and staring about us. 'Wot are *they* doin' aboard 'ere!' he said. 'You'll see 'em (little things) on fat cod, an' suchlike.... I'm blowed, Doctor, if I understand.'

"He held his lamp towards a big mound of the mould, that occupied part of the after portion of the low poop-deck, a little fore-side of where there came a two-foot high 'break' to a kind of second and loftier poop, that ran away aft to the taffrail. The mound was pretty big, several feet across, and more than a yard high. Captain Gannington walked up to it:

"'I reck'n this 's the scuttle,' he remarked, and gave it a heavy kick. The only result was a deep indentation into the huge, whitish hump of mould, as if he had driven his foot into a mass of some doughy substance. Yet, I am not altogether correct in saying that this was the only result; for a certain other thing happened – from a place made by the Captain's foot, there came a little gush of a purplish fluid, accompanied by a peculiar smell, that was, and was not, half-familiar. Some of the mould-like substance had stuck to the toe of the Captain's boot, and from this, likewise, there issued a sweat, as it were, of the same colour.

"'Well!' said Captain Gannington, in surprise; and drew back his foot to make another kick at the hump of mould; but he paused, at an exclamation from the Second Mate:

"'Don't, Sir!' said the Second Mate.

"I glanced at him, and the light from Captain Gannington's lamp showed me that his face had a bewildered, half-frightened look, as if he were suddenly and unexpectedly half-afraid of something, and as if his tongue had given away his sudden fright, without any intention on his part to speak.

"The Captain also turned and stared at him:

"'Why, Mister?' he asked, in a somewhat puzzled voice, through which there sounded just the vaguest hint of annoyance. 'We've got to shift this muck, if we're to get below.'

"I looked at the Second Mate, and it seemed to me that, curiously enough, he was listening less to the Captain, than to some other sound.

"Suddenly, he said in a queer voice: 'Listen, everybody!'

"Yet, we heard nothing, beyond the faint murmur of the men talking together in the boat alongside.

"'I don't hear nothin',' said Captain Gannington, after a short pause. 'Do you, Doctor?'

"'No,' I said.

"'Wot was it you thought you heard?' asked the Captain, turning again to the Second Mate. But the Second Mate shook his head, in a curious, almost irritable way; as if the Captain's question interrupted his listening. Captain Gannington stared a moment at him; then held his lantern up, and glanced about him, almost uneasily. I know I felt a queer sense of strain. But the light showed nothing, beyond the greyish dirty-white of the mould in all directions.

"'Mister Selvern,' said the Captain at last, looking at him, 'don't get fancying things. Get hold of your bloomin' self. Ye know ye heard nothin'?'

"'I'm quite sure I heard something, Sir!' said the Second Mate. 'I seemed to hear—' He broke off sharply, and appeared to listen, with an almost painful intensity.

"'What did it sound like?' I asked.

"'It's all right, Doctor,' said Captain Gannington, laughing gently. 'Ye can give him a tonic when we get back. I'm goin' to shift this stuff.'

"He drew back, and kicked for the second time at the ugly mass, which he took to hide the companionway. The result of his kick was startling; for the whole thing wobbled sloppily, like a mound of unhealthy-looking jelly.

"He drew his foot out of it, quickly, and took a step backward, staring, and holding his lamp towards it:

"'By gum!' he said; and it was plain that he was genuinely startled. 'The blessed thing's gone soft!'

"The man had run back several steps from the suddenly flaccid mound, and looked horribly frightened. Though, of what, I am sure he had not the least idea. The Second Mate stood where he was, and stared. For my part, I know I had a most hideous uneasiness upon me. The Captain continued to hold his light towards the wobbling mound, and stare:

"'It's gone squashy all through!' he said. 'There's no scuttle there. There's no bally woodwork inside that lot! Phoo! What a rum smell!'

"He walked round to the after-side of the strange mound, to see whether there might be some signs of an opening into the hull at the back of the great heap of mould-stuff. And then:

"'Listen!' said the Second Mate, again, in the strangest sort of voice.

"Captain Gannington straightened himself upright, and there succeeded a pause of the most intense quietness, in which there was not even the hum of talk from the men alongside in the boat. We all heard it – a kind of dull, soft Thud! Thud! Thud! Thud! Somewhere in the hull under us; yet so vague that I might have been half doubtful I heard it, only that the others did so, too.

"Captain Gannington turned suddenly to where the man stood:

"'Tell them—' he began. But the fellow cried out something, and pointed. There had come a strange intensity into his somewhat unemotional face; so that the Captain's glance followed his action instantly. I stared, also, as you may think. It was the great mound, at which the man was pointing. I saw what he meant.

"From the two gapes made in the mould-like stuff by Captain Gannington's boot, the purple fluid was jetting out in a queerly regular fashion, almost as if it were being forced out by a pump. My word! But I stared! And even as I stared, a larger jet squirted out, and splashed as far as the man, spattering his boots and trouser-legs.

"The fellow had been pretty nervous before, in a stolid, ignorant sort of way; and his funk had been growing steadily; but, at this, he simply let out a yell, and turned about to run. He paused an instant, as if a sudden fear of the darkness that held the decks, between him and the boat, had taken him. He snatched at the Second Mate's lantern; tore it out of his hand, and plunged heavily away over the vile stretch of mould.

"Mr. Selvern, the Second Mate, said not a word; he was just standing, staring at the strange-smelling twin streams of dull purple, that were jetting out from the wobbling mound. Captain Gannington, however, roared an order to the man to come back; but the man plunged on and on across the mould, his feet seeming to be clogged by the stuff, as if it had grown suddenly soft. He zigzagged, as he ran, the lantern swaying in wild circles, as he wrenched his feet free, with a constant plop, plop; and I could hear his frightened gasps, even from where I stood.

"'Come back with that lamp!' roared the Captain again; but still the man took no notice, and Captain Gannington was silent an instant, his lips working in a queer, inarticulate fashion; as if he were stunned momentarily by the very violence of his anger at the man's insubordination. And in the silence, I heard the sounds again: Thud! Thud! Thud! Thud! Quite distinctly now, beating, it seemed suddenly to me, right down under my feet, but deep.

"I stared down at the mould on which I was standing, with a quick, disgusting sense of the terrible all about me; then I looked at the Captain, and tried to say something, without appearing frightened. I saw that he had turned again to the mould, and all the anger had gone out of his face. He had his lamp out towards the mould, and was listening. There was a further moment of absolute silence; at least, I know that I was not conscious of any sound at all, in all the world, except that extraordinary Thud! Thud! Thud! Thud! Down somewhere in the huge bulk under us.

"The Captain shifted his feet, with a sudden, nervous movement; and as he lifted them, the mould went plop! plop! He looked quickly at me, trying to smile, as if he were not thinking anything very much about it: 'What do you make of it, Doctor?' he said.

"'I think—' I began. But the Second Mate interrupted with a single word; his voice pitched a little high, in a tone that made us both stare instantly at him:

"'Look!' he said, and pointed at the mound. The thing was all of a slow quiver. A strange ripple ran outward from it, along the deck, like you will see a ripple run inshore out of a calm sea. It reached a mound a little fore-side of us, which I had supposed to be the cabin-skylight; and in a moment, the second mound sank nearly level with the surrounding decks, quivering floppily in a most extraordinary fashion. A sudden, quick tremor took the mould, right under the Second Mate, and he gave out a hoarse little cry, and held his arms out on each side of him, to keep his balance. The tremor in the mould spread, and Captain Gannington swayed, and spread his feet, with a sudden curse of fright. The Second Mate jumped across to him, and caught him by the wrist:

"'The boat, Sir!' he said, saying the very thing that I had lacked the pluck to say. 'For God's sake—'

"But he never finished; for a tremendous, hoarse scream cut off his words. They hove themselves round, and looked. I could see without turning. The man who had run from us was standing in the waist of the ship, about a fathom from the starboard bulwarks. He was swaying from side to side, and screaming in a dreadful fashion. He appeared to be trying to lift his feet, and the light from his swaying lantern showed an almost incredible sight. All about him the mould was in active movement. His feet had sunk out of sight. The stuff appeared to be *lapping* at his legs; and abruptly his bare flesh showed. The hideous stuff had rent his trouser-legs away, as if they were paper. He gave out a simply sickening scream, and, with a vast effort, wrenched one leg free. It was partly destroyed. The next instant he pitched face downward, and the stuff heaped itself upon him, as if it were actually alive, with a dreadful savage life. It was simply infernal. The man had gone from sight. Where he had fallen was now a writhing, elongated mound, in constant and horrible increase, as the mould appeared to move towards it in strange ripples from all sides.

"Captain Gannington and the Second Mate were stone silent, in amazed and incredulous horror; but I had begun to reach towards a grotesque and terrific conclusion, both helped and hindered by my professional training.

"From the men in the boat alongside, there was a loud shouting, and I saw two of their faces appear suddenly above the rail. They showed clearly, a moment, in the light from the lamp which the man had snatched from Mr. Selvern; for, strangely enough, this lamp was standing upright and unharmed on the deck, a little way fore-side of that dreadful, elongated, growing mound, that still swayed and writhed with an incredible horror. The lamp rose and fell on the passing ripples of the mould, just – for all the world – as you will see a boat rise and fall on little swells. It is of some interest to me now, psychologically, to remember how that rising and falling lantern brought home to me, more than anything, the incomprehensible, dreadful strangeness of it all.

"The men's faces disappeared, with sudden yells, as if they had slipped, or been suddenly hurt; and there was a fresh uproar of shouting from the boat. The men were calling to us to come away; to come away. In the same instant, I felt my left boot drawn suddenly and forcibly downward, with a horrible, painful gripe. I wrenched it free, with a yell of angry fear. Forrard of us, I saw that the vile surface was all a-move; and abruptly I found myself shouting in a queer frightened voice:

"'The boat, Captain! The boat, Captain!'

"Captain Gannington stared round at me, over his right shoulder, in a peculiar, dull way, that told me he was utterly dazed with bewilderment and the incomprehensibleness of it all. I took a quick, clogged, nervous step towards him, and gripped his arm and shook it fiercely.

"'The boat!' I shouted at him. 'The boat! For God's sake, tell the men to bring the boat aft!'

"Then the mould must have drawn his feet down; for, abruptly, he bellowed fiercely with terror, his momentary apathy giving place to furious energy. His thick-set, vastly muscular body doubled and writhed with his enormous effort, and he struck out madly, dropping the lantern. He tore his feet free, something ripping as he did so. The *reality* and necessity of the situation had come upon him, brutishly real, and he was roaring to the men in the boat: "'Bring the boat aft! Bring 'er aft! Bring 'er aft!'

"The Second Mate and I were shouting the same thing, madly.

"'For God's sake be smart, lads!' roared the Captain, and stooped quickly for his lamp, which still burned. His feet were gripped again, and he hove them out, blaspheming breathlessly, and leaping a yard high with his effort. Then he made a run for the side, wrenching his feet free at each step. In the same instant, the Second Mate cried out something, and grabbed at the Captain:

"'It's got hold of my feet! It's got hold of my feet!' he screamed. His feet had disappeared up to his boot-tops; and Captain Gannington caught him round the waist with his powerful left arm, gave a mighty heave, and the next instant had him free; but both his boot-soles had almost gone.

"For my part, I jumped madly from foot to foot, to avoid the plucking of the mould; and suddenly I made a run for the ship's side. But before I could get there, a queer gape came in the mould, between us and the side, at least a couple of feet wide, and how deep I don't know. It closed up in an instant, and all the mould, where the gape had been, went into a sort of flurry of horrible ripplings, so that I ran back from it; for I did not dare to put my foot upon it. Then the Captain was shouting at me:

"Aft, Doctor! Aft, Doctor! This way, Doctor! Run!' I saw then that he had passed me, and was up on the after, raised portion of the poop. He had the Second Mate thrown like a sack, all loose and quiet, over his left shoulder; for Mr. Selvern had fainted, and his long legs flogged, limp and helpless, against the Captain's massive knees as the Captain ran. I saw, with a queer, unconscious noting of minor details, how the torn soles of the Second Mate's boots flapped and jigged, as the Captain staggered aft.

"'Boat ahoy! Boat ahoy! Boat ahoy!' shouted the Captain; and then I was beside him, shouting also. The men were answering with loud yells of encouragement, and it was plain they were working desperately to force the boat aft, through the thick scum about the ship.

"We reached the ancient, mould-hid taffrail, and slewed about, breathlessly, in the half-darkness, to see what was happening. Captain Gannington had left his lantern by the big mound, when he picked up the Second Mate; and as we stood, gasping, we discovered suddenly that all the mould between us and the light was full of movement. Yet, the part on which we stood, for about six or eight feet forrard of us, was still firm.

"Every couple of seconds, we shouted to the men to hasten, and they kept on calling to us that they would be with us in an instant. And all the time, we watched the deck of that dreadful hulk, feeling, for my part, literally sick with mad suspense, and ready to jump overboard into that filthy scum all about us.

"Down somewhere in the huge bulk of the ship, there was all the time that extraordinary, dull, ponderous Thud! Thud! Thud! Thud! Growing ever louder. I seemed to feel the whole hull of the derelict beginning to quiver and thrill with each dull beat. And to me, with the grotesque and monstrous suspicion of what made that noise, it was, at once, the most dreadful and incredible sound I have ever heard.

"As we waited desperately for the boat, I scanned incessantly so much of the grey-white bulk as the lamp showed. The whole of the decks seemed to be in strange movement. Forrard of the lamp, I could see, indistinctly, the moundings of the mould swaying and nodding hideously, beyond the circle of the brightest rays. Nearer, and full in the glow of the lamp, the mound which should have indicated the skylight, was swelling steadily. There were ugly, purple veinings on it, and as it swelled, it seemed to me that the veinings and mottlings on it, were becoming plainer – rising, as though embossed upon it, like you will see the veins stand out on the body of a powerful, full-blooded horse. It was most extraordinary. The mound that we had supposed to cover the companionway, had sunk flat with the surrounding mould, and I could not see that it jetted out any more of the purplish fluid.

"A quaking movement of the mould began, away forrard of the lamp, and came flurrying away aft towards us; and at the sight of that, I climbed up on to the spongy-feeling taffrail, and yelled afresh for the boat. The men answered with a shout, which told me they were nearer; but the beastly scum was so thick that it was evidently a fight to move the boat at all. Beside me, Captain Gannington was shaking the Second Mate furiously, and the man stirred and began to moan. The Captain shook him again.

"'Wake up! Wake up, Mister!' he shouted.

"The Second Mate staggered out of the Captain's arms, and collapsed suddenly, shrieking: 'My feet! Oh, God! My feet!' The Captain and I lugged him up off the mould, and got him into a sitting position upon the taffrail, where he kept up a continual moaning.

"'Hold 'im, Doctor,' said the Captain, and whilst I did so, he ran forrard a few yards, and peered down over the starboard quarter rail. 'For God's sake, be smart, lads! Be smart! Be smart!' he shouted down to the men; and they answered him, breathless, from close at hand; yet still too far away for the boat to be any use to us on the instant.

"I was holding the moaning, half-unconscious officer, and staring forrard along the poop decks. The flurrying of the mould was coming aft, slowly and noiselessly. And then, suddenly, I saw something closer:

"'Look out, Captain!' I shouted; and even as I shouted, the mould near to him gave a sudden peculiar slobber. I had seen a ripple stealing towards him through the horrible stuff. He gave an enormous, clumsy leap, and landed near to us on the sound part of the mould; but the movement followed him. He turned and faced it, swearing fiercely. All about his feet there came abruptly little gapings, which made horrid sucking noises.

"'Come *back*, Captain!' I yelled. 'Come back, *quick!*'

"As I shouted, a ripple came at his feet – lipping at them; and he stamped insanely at it, and leaped back, his boot torn half off his foot. He swore madly with pain and anger, and jumped swiftly for the taffrail.

"'Come on, Doctor! Over we go!' he called. Then he remembered the filthy scum, and hesitated; roaring out desperately to the men to hurry. I stared down, also.

"'The Second Mate?' I said.

"'I'll take charge, Doctor,' said Captain Gannington, and caught hold of Mr. Selvern. As he spoke, I thought I saw something beneath us, outlined against the scum. I leaned out over the stern, and peered. There was something under the port quarter.

"'There's something down there, Captain!' I called, and pointed in the darkness.

"He stooped far over, and stared.

"'A boat, by gum! A Boat!' he yelled, and began to wriggle swiftly along the taffrail, dragging the Second Mate after him. I followed.

"'A boat it is, sure!' he exclaimed, a few moments later; and, picking up the Second Mate clear of the rail, he hove him down into the boat, where he fell with a crash into the bottom.

"'Over ye go, Doctor!' he yelled at me, and pulled me bodily off the rail, and dropped me after the officer. As he did so, I felt the whole of the ancient, spongy rail give a peculiar, sickening quiver, and begin to wobble. I fell on to the Second Mate, and the Captain came after, almost in the same instant; but fortunately, he landed clear of us, on to the fore thwart, which broke under his weight, with a loud crack and splintering of wood.

"'Thank God!' I heard him mutter. 'Thank God! I guess that was a mighty near thing to goin' to hell.'

"He struck a match, just as I got to my feet, and between us we got the Second Mate straightened out on one of the after thwarts. We shouted to the men in the boat, telling them where we were, and saw the light of their lantern shining round the starboard counter of the derelict. They called back to us, to tell us they were doing their best; and then, whilst we waited, Captain Gannington struck another match, and began to overhaul the boat we had dropped into. She was a modern, two-bowed boat, and on the stern, there was painted *Cyclone Glasgow*. She was in pretty fair condition, and had evidently drifted into the scum and been held by it.

"Captain Gannington struck several matches, and went forrard towards the derelict. Suddenly he called to me, and I jumped over the thwarts to him.

"'Look, Doctor,' he said; and I saw what he meant – a mass of bones, up in the bows of the boat. I stooped over them, and looked. There were the bones of at least three people, all mixed together, in an extraordinary fashion, and quite clean and dry. I had a sudden thought concerning the bones; but I said nothing; for my thought was vague, in some ways, and concerned the grotesque and incredible suggestion that had come to me, as to the cause of that ponderous, dull Thud! Thud! Thud! Thud! That beat on so infernally within the hull, and was plain to hear even now that we had got off the vessel herself. And all the while, you know, I had a sick, horrible, mental-picture of that frightful wriggling mound aboard the hulk.

"As Captain Gannington struck a final match, I saw something that sickened me, and the Captain saw it in the same instant. The match went out, and he fumbled clumsily for another, and struck it. We saw the thing again. We had not been mistaken. A great lip of grey-white was protruding in over the edge of the boat – a great lappet of the mould was coming stealthily towards us; a live mass of *the very hull itself*. And suddenly Captain Gannington yelled out, in so many words, the grotesque and incredible thing I was thinking:

"'She's Alive!'

"I never heard such a sound of *comprehension* and terror in a man's voice. The very horrified assurance of it, made actual to me the thing that, before, had only lurked in my subconscious mind. I knew he was right; I knew that the explanation, my reason and my training, both repelled and reached towards, was the true one. I wonder whether anyone can possibly understand our feelings in that moment. The unmitigable horror of it, and the *incredibleness*.

"As the light of the match burned up fully, I saw that the mass of living matter, coming towards us, was streaked and veined with purple, the veins standing out, enormously distended. The whole thing quivered continuously to each ponderous Thud! Thud! Thud! Thud! Of that gargantuan organ that pulsed within the huge grey-white bulk. The flame of the match reached the Captain's fingers, and there came to me a little sickly whiff of burned flesh; but he seemed unconscious of any pain. Then the flame went out, in a brief sizzle; yet at the last moment, I had seen an extraordinary raw look, become visible upon the end of that monstrous, protruding lappet. It had become dewed with a hideous, purplish sweat. And with the darkness, there came a sudden charnel-like stench.

"I heard the match-box split in Captain Gannington's hands, as he wrenched it open. Then he swore, in a queer frightened voice; for he had come to the end of his matches. He turned clumsily in the darkness, and tumbled over the nearest thwart, in his eagerness to get to the stern of the boat; and I after him; for we knew that thing was coming towards us through the darkness; reaching over that piteous mingled heap of human bones, all jumbled together in the bows. We shouted madly to the men, and for answer saw the bows of the boat emerge dimly into view, round the starboard counter of the derelict.

"'Thank God!' I gasped out; but Captain Gannington yelled to them to show a light. Yet this they could not do; for the lamp had just been stepped on, in their desperate efforts to force the boat round to us.

"'Quick! Quick!' I shouted.

"'For God's sake be smart, men!' roared the Captain; and both of us faced the darkness under the port counter, out of which we knew (but could not see) the thing was coming towards us.

"'An oar! Smart now; pass me an oar!' shouted the Captain; and reached out his hands through the gloom towards the oncoming boat. I saw a figure stand up in the bows, and hold something out to us, across the intervening yards of scum. Captain Gannington swept his hands through the darkness, and encountered it.

"'I've got it. Let go there!' he said, in a quick, tense voice.

"In the same instant, the boat we were in was pressed over suddenly to starboard by some tremendous weight. Then I heard the Captain shout: 'Duck y'r head, Doctor'; and directly afterwards he swung the heavy, fourteen-foot ash oar round his head, and struck into the darkness. There came a sudden squelch, and he struck again, with a savage grunt of fierce energy. At the second blow, the boat righted, with a slow movement, and directly afterwards the other boat bumped gently into ours.

"Captain Gannington dropped the oar, and springing across to the Second Mate, hove him up off the thwart, and pitched him with knee and arms clear in over the bows among the men; then he shouted to me to follow, which I did, and he came after me, bringing the oar with him. We carried the Second Mate aft, and the Captain shouted to the men to back the boat a little; then they got her bows clear of the boat we had just left, and so headed out through the scum for the open sea.

"'Where's Tom 'Arrison?' gasped one of the men, in the midst of his exertions. He happened to be Tom Harrison's particular chum; and Captain Gannington answered him briefly enough:

"'Dead! Pull! Don't talk!'

"Now, difficult as it had been to force the boat through the scum to our rescue, the difficulty to get clear seemed tenfold. After some five minutes pulling, the boat seemed hardly to have moved a fathom, if so much; and a quite dreadful fear took me afresh; which one of the panting men put suddenly into words:

"'It's got us!' he gasped out; 'same as poor Tom!' It was the man who had inquired where Harrison was.

"'Shut y'r mouth an' *pull*!' roared the Captain. And so another few minutes passed. Abruptly, it seemed to me that the dull, ponderous Thud! Thud! Thud! Thud! Came more plainly through the dark, and I stared intently over the stern. I sickened a little; for I could almost swear that the dark mass of the monster was actually *nearer*...that it was coming nearer to us through the darkness. Captain Gannington must have had the same thought; for after a brief look into the darkness, he made one jump to the stroke-oar, and began to double-bank it.

"'Get forrid under the thwarts, Doctor!' he said to me, rather breathlessly. 'Get in the bows, an' see if you can't free the stuff a bit round the bows.'

"I did as he told me, and a minute later I was in the bows of the boat, puddling the scum from side to side with the boathook, and trying to break up the viscid, clinging muck. A heavy, almost animal-like odour rose off it, and all the air seemed full of the deadening smell. I shall never find words to tell anyone the whole horror of it all – the threat that seemed to hang in the very air around us; and, but a little astern, that incredible thing, coming, as I firmly believe, nearer, and the scum holding us like half melted glue.

"The minutes passed in a deadly, eternal fashion, and I kept staring back astern into the darkness; but never ceasing to puddle that filthy scum, striking at it and switching it from side to side, until I sweated.

"Abruptly, Captain Gannington sang out:

"'We're gaining, lads. Pull!' And I felt the boat forge ahead perceptibly, as they gave way, with renewed hope and energy. There was soon no doubt of it; for presently that hideous Thud! Thud! Thud! Thud! Had grown quite dim and vague somewhere astern, and I could no longer see the derelict; for the night had come down tremendously dark, and all the sky was thick overset with heavy clouds. As we drew nearer and nearer to the edge of the scum, the boat moved more and more freely, until suddenly we emerged with a clean, sweet, fresh sound, into the open sea.

"'Thank God!' I said aloud, and drew in the boathook, and made my way aft again to where Captain Gannington now sat once more at the tiller. I saw him looking anxiously up at the sky, and across to where the lights of our vessel burned, and again he would seem to listen intently; so that I found myself listening also.

"'What's that, Captain?' I said sharply; for it seemed to me that I heard a sound far astern, something between a queer whine and a low whistling. 'What's that?'

"'It's wind, Doctor,' he said, in a low voice. 'I wish to God we were aboard.'

"Then, to the men: 'Pull! Put y'r backs into it, or ye'll never put y'r teeth through good bread again!'

"The men obeyed nobly, and we reached the vessel safely, and had the boat safely stowed, before the storm came, which it did in a furious white smother out of the West. I could see it for some minutes beforehand, tearing the sea, in the gloom, into a wall of phosphorescent foam; and as it came nearer, that peculiar whining, piping sound grew louder and louder, until it was like a vast steam whistle, rushing towards us across the sea.

"And when it did come, we got it very heavy indeed; so that the morning showed us nothing but a welter of white seas; and that grim derelict was many a score of miles away in the smother, lost as utterly as our hearts could wish to lose her.

"When I came to examine the Second Mate's feet, I found them in a very extraordinary condition. The soles of them had the appearance of having been partly digested. I know of no other word that so exactly describes their condition; and the agony the man suffered must have been dreadful.

"Now," concluded the Doctor, "that is what I call a case in point. If we could know exactly what that old vessel had originally been loaded with, and the juxtaposition of the various articles of her cargo, plus the heat and time she had endured, plus one or two other only guessable quantities, we should have solved the chemistry of the Life-Force, gentlemen. Not necessarily the *origin*, mind you; but, at least, we should have taken a big step on the way. I've often regretted that gale, you know – in a way, that is, in a way! It was a most amazing discovery; but, at the time, I had nothing but thankfulness to be rid of it. A most amazing chance. I often think of the way the monster woke out of its torpor.... And that scum.... The dead pigs caught in it.... I fancy that was a grim kind of net, gentlemen.... It caught many things.... It..."

The old Doctor sighed and nodded.

"If I could have had her bill of lading," he said, his eyes full of regret. "If— It might have told me something to help. But, anyway...." He began to fill his pipe again.... "I suppose," he ended, looking round at us gravely, "I s'pose we humans are an ungrateful lot of beggars, at the best!...But...but what a chance! What a chance – eh?"

If you enjoyed this, you might also like...
The Mystery of the Derelict, see page 138
The Voice in the Night, see page 295

The Stone Ship

RUM THINGS! – Of course there are rum things happen at sea – As rum as ever there were. I remember when I was in the *Alfred Jessop*, a small barque, whose owner was her skipper, we came across a most extraordinary thing.

We were twenty days out from London, and well down into the tropics. It was before I took my ticket, and I was in the fo'cas'le. The day had passed without a breath of wind, and the night found us with all the lower sails up in the buntlines.

Now, I want you to take good note of what I am going to say:

When it was dark in the second dog watch, there was not a sail in sight; not even the far off smoke of a steamer, and no land nearer than Africa, about a thousand miles to the eastward of us.

It was our watch on deck from eight to twelve, midnight, and my look-out from eight to ten. For the first hour, I walked to and fro across the break of the fo'cas'le head, smoking my pipe and just listening to the quiet... Ever hear the kind of silence you can get away out at sea? You need to be in one of the old-time windjammers, with all the lights dowsed, and the sea as calm and quiet as some queer plain of death. And then you want a pipe and the lonesomeness of the fo'cas'le head, with the caps'n to lean against while you listen and think. And all about you, stretching out into the miles, only and always the enormous silence of the sea, spreading out a thousand miles every way into the everlasting, brooding night. And not a light anywhere, out on all the waste of waters; nor ever a sound, as I have told, except the faint moaning of the masts and gear, as they chafe and whine a little to the occasional invisible roll of the ship.

And suddenly, across all this silence, I heard Jensen's voice from the head of the starboard steps, say:

"Did you hear that, Duprey?"

"What?" I asked, cocking my head up. But as I questioned, I heard what he heard – the constant sound of running water, for all the world like the noise of a brook running down a hill-side. And the queer sound was surely not a hundred fathoms off our port bow!

"By gum!" said Jensen's voice, out of the darkness. "That's damned sort of funny!"

"Shut up!" I whispered, and went across, in my bare feet, to the port rail, where I leaned out into the darkness, and stared towards the curious sound.

The noise of a brook running down a hill-side continued, where there was no brook for a thousand sea-miles in any direction.

"What is it?" said Jensen's voice again, scarcely above a whisper now. From below him on the main-deck, there came several voices questioning: – "Hark!" "Stow the talk!" "...there!" "Listen!" "Lord love us, what is it?" ...And then Jensen muttering to them to be quiet.

There followed a full minute, during which we all heard the brook, where no brook could ever run; and then, out of the night there came a sudden hoarse incredible sound: – oooaze, oooaze, arrrr, arrrr, oooaze – a stupendous sort of croak, deep and somehow abominable, out of the blackness. In the same instant, I found myself sniffing the air. There was a queer rank smell, stealing through the night.

"Forrard there on the look-out!" I heard the mate singing out, away aft. "Forrard there! What the blazes are you doing!"

I heard him come clattering down the port ladder from the poop, and then the sound of his feet at a run along the maindeck. Simultaneously, there was a thudding of bare feet, as the watch below came racing out of the fo'cas'le beneath me.

"Now then! Now then! Now then!" shouted the Mate, as he charged up on to the fo'cas'le head.

"What's up?"

"It's something off the port bow, Sir," I said. "Running water! And then that sort of howl.… Your night-glasses," I suggested.

"Can't see a thing," he growled, as he stared away through the dark. "There's a sort of mist. Phoo! What a devil of a stink!"

"Look!" said someone down on the main-deck. "What's that?"

I saw it in the same instant, and caught the Mate's elbow.

"Look, Sir," I said. "There's a light there, about three points off the bow. It's moving."

The Mate was staring through his night-glasses, and suddenly he thrust them into my hands:

"See if you can make it out," he said, and forthwith put his hands round his mouth, and bellowed into the night: – "Ahoy there! Ahoy there! Ahoy there!" his voice going out lost into the silence and darkness all around. But there came never a comprehensible answer, only all the time the infernal noise of a brook running out there on the sea, a thousand miles from any brook of earth; and away on the port bow, a vague shapeless shining.

I put the glasses to my eyes, and stared. The light was bigger and brighter, seen through the binoculars; but I could make nothing of it, only a dull, elongated shining, that moved vaguely in the darkness, apparently a hundred fathoms or so, away on the sea.

"Ahoy there! Ahoy there!" sung out the Mate again. Then, to the men below: – "Quiet there on the main-deck!"

There followed about a minute of intense stillness, during which we all listened; but there was no sound, except the constant noise of water running steadily.

I was watching the curious shining, and I saw it flick out suddenly at the Mate's shout. Then in a moment I saw three dull lights, one under the other, that flicked in and out intermittently.

"Here, give me the glasses!" said the Mate, and grabbed them from me.

He stared intensely for a moment; then swore, and turned to me:

"What do you make of them?" he asked, abruptly.

"I don't know, Sir," I said. "I'm just puzzled. Perhaps it's electricity, or something of that sort."

"Oh hell!" he replied, and leant far out over the rail, staring, "Lord!" he said, for the second time, "what a stink!"

As he spoke, there came a most extraordinary thing; for there sounded a series of heavy reports out of the darkness, seeming in the silence, almost as loud as the sound of small cannon.

"They're shooting!" shouted a man on the main-deck, suddenly.

The Mate said nothing; only he sniffed violently at the night air. "By Gum!" he muttered, "what is it?"

I put my hand over my nose; for there was a terrible, charnel-like stench filling all the night about us.

"Take my glasses, Duprey," said the Mate, after a few minutes further watching. "Keep an eye over yonder. I'm going to call the Captain."

He pushed his way down the ladder, and hurried aft. About five minutes later, he returned forrard with the Captain and the Second and Third Mates, all in their shirts and trousers.

"Anything fresh, Duprey?" asked the Mate.

"No, Sir," I said, and handed him back his glasses. "The lights have gone again, and I think the mist is thicker. There's still the sound of running water out there."

The Captain and the three Mates stood some time along the port rail of the fo'cas'le head, watching through their night-glasses, and listening. Twice the Mate hailed; but there came no reply.

There was some talk, among the officers; and I gathered that the Captain was thinking of investigating.

"Clear one of the life-boats, Mr. Gelt," he said, at last. "The glass is steady; there'll be no wind for hours yet. Pick out a half a dozen men. Take 'em out of either watch, if they want to come. I'll be back when I've got my coat."

"Away aft with you, Duprey, and some of you others," said the Mate. "Get the cover off the port life-boat, and bail her out."

"'I, 'i, Sir," I answered, and went away aft with the others.

We had the boat into the water within twenty minutes, which is good time for a wind-jammer, where boats are generally used as storage receptacles for odd gear.

I was one of the men told off to the boat, with two others from our watch, and one from the starboard.

The Captain came down the end of the main tops'l halyards into the boat, and the Third after him. The Third took the tiller, and gave orders to cast off.

We pulled out clear of our vessel, and the Skipper told us to lie on our oars for a moment while he took his bearings. He leant forward to listen, and we all did the same. The sound of the running water was quite distinct across the quietness; but it struck me as seeming not so loud as earlier.

I remember now, that I noticed how plain the mist had become – a sort of warm, wet mist; not a bit thick; but just enough to make the night very dark, and to be visible, eddying slowly in a thin vapour round the port side-light, looking like a red cloudiness swirling lazily through the red glow of the big lamp.

There was no other sound at this time, beyond the sound of the running water; and the Captain, after handing something to the Third Mate, gave the order to give-way.

I was rowing stroke, and close to the officers, and so was able to see dimly that the Captain had passed a heavy revolver over to the Third Mate.

"Ho!" I thought to myself, "so the Old Man's a notion there's really something dangerous over there."

I slipped a hand quickly behind me, and felt that my sheath knife was clear.

We pulled easily for about three or four minutes, with the sound of the water growing plainer somewhere ahead in the darkness; and astern of us, a vague red glowing through the night and vapour, showed where our vessel was lying.

We were rowing easily, when suddenly the bow-oar muttered "G'lord!" Immediately afterwards, there was a loud splashing in the water on his side of the boat.

"What's wrong in the bows, there?" asked the Skipper, sharply.

"There's somethin' in the water, Sir, messing round my oar," said the man.

I stopped rowing, and looked round. All the men did the same. There was a further sound of splashing, and the water was driven right over the boat in showers. Then the bow-oar called out: – "There's somethin' got a holt of my oar, Sir!"

I could tell the man was frightened; and I knew suddenly that a curious nervousness had come to me – a vague, uncomfortable dread, such as the memory of an ugly tale will bring, in a lonesome place. I believe every man in the boat had a similar feeling. It seemed to me in that moment, that a definite, muggy sort of silence was all round us, and this in spite of the sound of the splashing, and the strange noise of the running water somewhere ahead of us on the dark sea.

"It's let go the oar, Sir!" said the man.

Abruptly, as he spoke, there came the Captain's voice in a roar: – "Back water all!" he shouted. "Put some beef into it now! Back all! Back all!…Why the devil was no lantern put in the boat! Back now! Back! Back!"

We backed fiercely, with a will; for it was plain that the Old Man had some good reason to get the boat away pretty quickly. He was right, too; though, whether it was guess-work, or some kind of instinct that made him shout out at that moment, I don't know; only I am sure he could not have seen anything in that absolute darkness.

As I was saying, he was right in shouting to us to back; for we had not backed more than half a dozen fathoms, when there was a tremendous splash right ahead of us, as if a house had fallen into the sea; and a regular wave of sea-water came at us out of the darkness, throwing our bows up, and soaking us fore and aft.

"Good Lord!" I heard the Third Mate gasp out. "What the devil's that?"

"Back all! Back! Back!" the Captain sung out again.

After some moments, he had the tiller put over, and told us to pull. We gave way with a will, as you may think, and in a few minutes were alongside our own ship again.

"Now then, men," the Captain said, when we were safe aboard, "I'll not order any of you to come; but after the steward's served out a tot of grog each, those who are willing, can come with me, and we'll have another go at finding out what devil's work is going on over yonder."

He turned to the Mate, who had been asking questions:

"Say, Mister," he said, "it's no sort of thing to let the boat go without a lamp aboard. Send a couple of the lads into the lamp locker, and pass out a couple of the anchor-lights, and that deck bull's-eye, you use at nights for clearing up the ropes."

He whipped round on the Third: – "Tell the steward to buck up with that grog, Mr. Andrews," he said, "and while you're there, pass out the axes from the rack in my cabin."

The grog came along a minute later; and then the Third Mate with three big axes from out the cabin rack.

"Now then, men," said the Skipper, as we took our tots off, "those who are coming with me, had better take an axe each from the Third Mate. They're mightly good weapons in any sort of trouble."

We all stepped forward, and he burst out laughing, slapping his thigh.

"That's the kind of thing I like!" he said. "Mr. Andrews, the axes won't go round. Pass out that old cutlass from the steward's pantry. It's a pretty hefty piece of iron!"

The old cutlass was brought, and the man who was short of an axe, collared it. By this time, two of the 'prentices had filled (at least we supposed they had filled them!) two of the ship's anchor-lights; also they had brought out the bull's-eye lamp we used when clearing up the ropes on a dark night. With the lights and the axes and the cutlass, we felt ready to face anything, and down we went again into the boat, with the Captain and the Third Mate after us.

"Lash one of the lamps to one of the boat-hooks, and rig it over the bows," ordered the Captain.

This was done, and in this way the light lit up the water for a couple of fathoms ahead of the boat; and made us feel less that something could come at us without our knowing. Then the painter was cast off, and we gave way again towards the sound of the running water, out there in the darkness.

I remember now that it struck me that our vessel had drifted a bit; for the sounds seemed farther away. The second anchor-light had been put in the stern of the boat, and the Third Mate kept it between his feet, while he steered. The Captain had the bull's-eye in his hand, and was pricking up the wick with his pocket-knife.

As we pulled, I took a glance or two over my shoulder; but could see nothing, except the lamp making a yellow halo in the mist round the boat's bows, as we forged ahead. Astern of us, on our quarter, I could see the dull red glow of our vessel's port light. That was all, and not a sound in all the sea, as you might say, except the roll of our oars in the rowlocks, and somewhere in the darkness ahead, that curious noise of water running steadily; now sounding, as I have said, fainter and seeming farther away.

"It's got my oar again, Sir!" exclaimed the man at the bow oar, suddenly, and jumped to his feet. He hove his oar up with a great splashing of water, into the air, and immediately something whirled and beat about in the yellow halo of light over the bows of the boat. There was a crash of breaking wood, and the boat-hook was broken. The lamp soused down into the sea, and was lost. Then in the darkness, there was a heavy splash, and a shout from the bow-oar: – "It's gone, Sir. It's loosed off the oar!"

"Vast pulling, all!" sung out the Skipper. Not that the order was necessary; for not a man was pulling. He had jumped up, and whipped a big revolver out of his coat pocket.

He had this in his right hand, and the bull's-eye in his left. He stepped forrard smartly over the oars from thwart to thwart, till he reached the bows, where he shone his light down into the water.

"My word!" he said. "Lord in Heaven! Saw anyone ever the like!"

And I doubt whether any man ever did see what we saw then; for the water was thick and living for yards round the boat with the hugest eels I ever saw before or after.

"Give way, Men," said the Skipper, after a minute. "Yon's no explanation of the almighty queer sounds out yonder we're hearing this night. Give way, lads!"

He stood right up in the bows of the boat, shining his bulls'-eye from side to side, and flashing it down on the water.

"Give way, lads!" he said again. "They don't like the light, that'll keep them from the oars. Give way steady now. Mr. Andrews, keep her dead on for the noise out yonder."

We pulled for some minutes, during which I felt my oar plucked at twice; but a flash of the Captain's lamp seemed sufficient to make the brutes loose hold.

The noise of the water running appeared now quite near sounding. About this time, I had a sense again of an added sort of silence to all the natural quietness of the sea. And I had a return of the curious nervousness that had touched me before. I kept listening intensely, as if I expected to hear some other sound than the noise of the water. It came to me suddenly that I had the kind of feeling one has in the aisle of a large cathedral. There was a sort of echo in the night – an incredibly faint reduplicating of the noise of our oars.

"Hark!" I said, audibly; not realising at first that I was speaking aloud. "There's an echo—"

"That's it!" the Captain cut in, sharply. "I thought I heard something rummy!"

"...I thought I heard something rummy," said a thin ghostly echo, out of the night, "...thought I heard something rummy," "...heard something rummy." The words went muttering and whispering to and fro in the night about us, in a rather a horrible fashion.

"Good Lord!" said the Old Man, in a whisper.

We had all stopped rowing, and were staring about us into the thin mist that filled the night. The Skipper was standing with the bull's-eye lamp held over his head, circling the beam of light round from port to starboard, and back again.

Abruptly, as he did so, it came to me that the mist was thinner. The sound of the running water was very near; but it gave back no echo.

"The water doesn't echo, Sir," I said. "That's damn funny!"

"That's damn funny," came back at me, from the darkness to port and starboard, in a multitudinous muttering, "...Damn funny!....funny... eey!"

"Give way!" said the Old Man, loudly. "I'll bottom this!"

"I'll bottom this...Bottom this...this!" The echo came back in a veritable rolling of unexpected sound. And then we had dipped our oars again, and the night was full of the reiterated rolling echoes of our rowlocks.

Suddenly the echoes ceased, and there was, strangely, the sense of a great space about us, and in the same moment the sound of the water running appeared to be directly before us, but somehow up in the air.

"Vast rowing!" said the Captain, and we lay on our oars, staring round into the darkness ahead. The Old Man swung the beam of his lamp upwards, making circles with it in the night, and abruptly I saw something looming vaguely through the thinner-seeming mist.

"Look, Sir," I called to the Captain. "Quick, Sir, your light right above you! There's something up there!"

The Old Man flashed his lamp upwards, and found the thing I had seen. But it was too indistinct to make anything of, and even as he saw it, the darkness and mist seemed to wrap it about.

"Pull a couple of strokes, all!" said the Captain. "Stow your talk, there in the boat! ... Again! ...That'll do! Vast pulling!"

He was sending the beam of his lamp constantly across that part of the night where we had seen the thing, and suddenly I saw it again.

"There, Sir!" I said. "A little starboard with the light."

He flicked the light swiftly to the right, and immediately we all saw the thing plainly – a strangely-made mast, standing up there out of the mist, and looking like no spar I had ever seen.

It seemed now that the mist must lie pretty low on the sea in places; for the mast stood up out of it plainly for several fathoms; but, lower, it was hidden in the mist, which, I thought, seemed heavier now all round us; but thinner, as I have said, above.

"Ship ahoy!" sung out the Skipper, suddenly. "Ship ahoy, there!" But for some moments there came never a sound back to us except the constant noise of the water running, not a score yards away; and then, it seemed to me that a vague echo beat back at us out of the mist, oddly: - "Ahoy! Ahoy! Ahoy!"

"There's something hailing us, Sir," said the Third Mate.

Now, that 'something' was significant. It showed the sort of feeling that was on us all.

"That's na ship's mast as ever I've seen!" I heard the man next to me mutter. "It's got a unnatcheral look."

"Ahoy there!" shouted the Skipper again, at the top of his voice. "Ahoy there!"

With the suddenness of a clap of thunder there burst out at us a vast, grunting: - oooaze; arrrr; arrrr; oooaze – a volume of sound so great that it seemed to make the loom of the oar in my hand vibrate.

"Good Lord!" said the Captain, and levelled his revolver into the mist; but he did not fire.

I had loosed one hand from my oar, and gripped my axe. I remember thinking that the Skipper's pistol wouldn't be much use against whatever thing made a noise like that.

"It wasn't ahead, Sir," said the Third Mate, abruptly, from where he sat and steered. "I think it came from somewhere over to starboard."

"Damn this mist!" said the Skipper. "Damn it! What a devil of a stink! Pass that other anchor-light forrard."

I reached for the lamp, and handed it to the next man, who passed it on.

"The other boat-hook," said the Skipper; and when he'd got it, he lashed the lamp to the hook end, and then lashed the whole arrangement upright in the bows, so that the lamp was well above his head.

"Now," he said. "Give way gently! And stand by to back-water, if I tell you.... Watch my hand, Mister," he added to the Third Mate. "Steer as I tell you."

We rowed a dozen slow strokes, and with every stroke, I took a look over my shoulder. The Captain was leaning forward under the big lamp, with the bull's-eye in one hand and his revolver in the other. He kept flashing the beam of the lantern up into the night.

"Good Lord!" he said, suddenly. "Vast pulling."

We stopped, and I slewed round on the thwart, and stared.

He was standing up under the glow of the anchor-light, and shining the bull's-eye up at a great mass that loomed dully through the mist. As he flicked the light to and fro over the great bulk, I realised that the boat was within some three or four fathoms of the hull of a vessel.

"Pull another stroke," the Skipper said, in a quiet voice, after a few minutes of silence. "Gently now! Gently! ...Vast pulling!"

I slewed round again on my thwart and stared. I could see part of the thing quite distinctly now, and more of it, as I followed the beam of the Captain's lantern. She was a vessel right enough; but such a vessel as I had never seen. She was extraordinarily high out of the water, and seemed very short, and rose up into a queer mass at one end. But what puzzled me more, I think, than anything else, was the queer look of her sides, down which water was streaming all the time.

"That explains the sound of the water running," I thought to myself; "but what on earth is she built of?"

You will understand a little of my bewildered feelings, when I tell you that as the beam of the Captain's lamp shone on the side of this queer vessel, it showed stone everywhere – as if she were built out of stone. I never felt so dumb-founded in my life.

"She's stone, Cap'n" I said. "Look at her, Sir!"

I realised, as I spoke, a certain horribleness, of the unnatural.... A stone ship, floating out there in the night in the midst of the lonely Atlantic!

"She's stone," I said again, in that absurd way in which one reiterates, when one is bewildered.

"Look at the slime on her!" muttered the man next but one forrard of me. "She's a proper Davy Jones ship. By gum! she stinks like a corpse!"

"Ship ahoy!" roared the Skipper, at the top of his voice. "Ship ahoy! Ship ahoy!"

His shout beat back at us, in a curious, dank, yet metallic, echo, something the way one's voice sounds in an old disused quarry.

"There's no one aboard there, Sir," said the Third Mate. "Shall I put the boat alongside?"

"Yes, shove her up, Mister," said the Old Man. "I'll bottom this business. Pull a couple of strokes, aft there! In bow, and stand by to fend off."

The Third Mate laid the boat alongside, and we unshipped our oars.

Then, I leant forward over the side of the boat, and pressed the flat of my hand upon the stark side of the ship. The water that ran down her side, sprayed out over my hand and wrist in a cataract; but I did not think about being wet, for my hand was pressed solid upon stone.... I pulled my hand back with a queer feeling.

"She's stone, right enough, Sir," I said to the Captain.

"We'll soon see what she is," he said. "Shove your oar up against her side, and shin up. We'll pass the lamp up to you as soon as you're aboard. Shove your axe in the back of your belt. I'll cover you with my gun, till you're aboard."

"'I, 'i, Sir," I said; though I felt a bit funny at the thought of having to be the first aboard that damn rummy craft.

I put my oar upright against her side, and took a spring up from the thwart, and in a moment I was grabbing over my head for her rail, with every rag of me soaked through with the water that was streaming down her, and spraying out over the oar and me.

I got a firm grip of the rail, and hoisted my head high enough to look over; but I could see nothing .... what with the darkness, and the water in my eyes.

I knew it was no time for going slow, if there were danger aboard; so I went in over that rail in one spring, my boots coming down with a horrible, ringing, hollow, stony sound on her decks. I whipped the water out of my eyes and the axe out of my belt, all in the same moment; then I took a good stare fore and aft; but it was too dark to see anything.

"Come along, Duprey!" shouted the Skipper. "Collar the lamp."

I leant out sideways over the rail, and grabbed for the lamp with my left hand, keeping the axe ready in my right, and staring inboard; for I tell you, I was just mortally afraid in that moment of what might be aboard of her.

I felt the lamp-ring with my left hand, and gripped it. Then I switched it aboard, and turned fair and square to see where I'd gotten.

Now, you never saw such a packet as that, not in a hundred years, nor yet two hundred, I should think. She'd got a rum little main-deck, about forty feet long, and then came a step about two feet high, and another bit of a deck, with a little house on it.

That was the after end of her; and more I couldn't see, because the light of my lamp went no farther, except to show me vaguely the big, cocked-up stern of her, going up into the darkness. I never saw a vessel made like her; not even in an old picture of old-time ships.

Forrard of me, was her mast – a big lump of a stick it was too, for her size. And here was another amazing thing, the mast of her looked just solid stone.

"Funny, isn't she, Duprey?" said the Skipper's voice at my back, and I came round on him with a jump.

"Yes," I said. "I'm puzzled. Aren't you, Sir?"

"Well," he said, "I am. If we were like the shellbacks they talk of in books, we'd be crossing ourselves. But, personally, give me a good heavy Colt, or the hefty chunk of steel you're cuddling."

He turned from me, and put his head over the rail.

"Pass up the painter, Jales," he said, to the bow-oar. Then to the Third Mate:

"Bring 'em all up, Mister. If there's going to be anything rummy, we may as well make a picnic party of the lot…. Hitch that painter round the cleet yonder, Duprey," he added to me. "It looks good solid stone! …That's right. Come along."

He swung the thin beam of his lantern fore and aft, and then forrard again.

"Lord!" he said. "Look at that mast. It's stone. Give it a whack with the back of your axe, man; only remember she's apparently a bit of an old-timer! So go gently."

I took my axe short, and tapped the mast, and it rang dull, and solid, like a stone pillar, I struck it again, harder, and a sharp flake of stone flew past my cheek. The Skipper thrust his lantern close up to where I'd struck the mast.

"By George," he said, "she's absolute a stone ship – solid stone, afloat here out of Eternity, in the middle of the wide Atlantic…. Why! She must weigh a thousand tonnes more than she's buoyancy to carry. It's just impossible…. It's—"

He turned his head quickly, at a sound in the darkness along the decks. He flashed his light that way, across the after decks; but we could see nothing

"Get a move on you in the boat!" he said sharply, stepping to the rail and looking down. "For once I'd really prefer a little more of your company…." He came round like a flash. "Duprey, what was that?" he asked in a low voice.

"I certainly heard something, Sir," I said. "I wish the others would hurry. By Jove! Look! What's that—"

"Where?" he said, and sent the beam of his lamp to where I pointed with my axe.

"There's nothing," he said, after circling the light all over the deck. "Don't go imagining things. There's enough solid unnatural fact here, without trying to add to it."

There came the splash and thud of feet behind, as the first of the men came up over the side, and jumped clumsily into the lee scuppers, which had water in them. You see she had a cant to that side, and I supposed the water had collected there.

The rest of the men followed, and then the Third Mate. That made six men of us, all well armed; and I felt a bit more comfortable, as you can think.

"Hold up that lamp of yours, Duprey, and lead the way," said the Skipper. "You're getting the post of honour this trip!"

"'I, 'i, Sir," I said, and stepped forward, holding up the lamp in my left hand, and carrying my axe half way down the haft, in my right.

"We'll try aft, first," said the Captain, and led the way himself, flashing the bull's-eye to and fro. At the raised portion of the deck, he stopped.

"Now," he said, in his queer way, "let's have a look at this…. Tap it with your axe, Duprey…. Ah!" he added, as I hit it with the back of my axe. "That's what we call stone at home, right enough. She's just as rum as anything I've seen while I've been fishing. We'll go on aft and have a peep into the deck-house. Keep your axes handy, men."

We walked slowly up to the curious little house, the deck rising to it with quite a slope. At the foreside of the little deck-house, the Captain pulled up, and shone his bull's-eye down at the deck. I saw that he was looking at what was plainly the stump of the after mast. He stepped closer to it, and kicked it with his foot; and it gave out the same dull, solid note that the foremast had done. It was obviously a chunk of stone.

I held up my lamp so that I could see the upper part of the house more clearly. The fore-part had two square window-spaces in it; but there was no glass in either of them; and the blank darkness within the queer little place, just seemed to stare out at us.

And then I saw something suddenly...a great shaggy head of red hair was rising slowly into sight, through the port window, the one nearest to us.

"My God! What's that, Cap'n?" I called out. But it was gone, even as I spoke.

"What?" he asked, jumping at the way I had sung out.

"At the port window, Sir," I said. "A great red-haired head. It came right up to the window-place; and then it went in a moment."

The Skipper stepped right up to the little dark window, and pushed his lantern through into the blackness. He flashed a light round; then withdrew the lantern.

"Bosh, man!" he said. "That's twice you've got fancying things. Ease up your nerves a bit!"

"I did see it!" I said, almost angrily. "It was like a great red-haired head...."

"Stow it, Duprey!" he said, though not sneeringly. "The house is absolutely empty. Come round to the door, if the Infernal Masons that built her, went in for doors! Then you'll see for yourself. All the same, keep your axes ready, lads. I've a notion there's something pretty queer aboard here."

We went up round the after-end of the little house, and here we saw what appeared to be a door.

The Skipper felt at the queer, odd-shapen handle, and pushed at the door; but it had stuck fast.

"Here, one of you!" he said, stepping back. "Have a whack at this with your axe. Better use the back."

One of the men stepped forward, and stood away to give him room. As his axe struck, the door went to pieces with exactly the same sound that a thin slab of stone would make, when broken.

"Stone!" I heard the Captain mutter, under his breath. "By Gum! What is she?"

I did not wait for the Skipper. He had put me a bit on edge, and I stepped bang in through the open doorway, with the lamp high, and holding my axe short and ready; but there was nothing in the place, save a stone seat running all round, except where the doorway opened on to the deck.

"Find your red-haired monster?" asked the Skipper, at my elbow.

I said nothing. I was suddenly aware that he was all on the jump with some inexplicable fear. I saw his glance going everywhere about him. And then his eye caught mine, and he saw that I realised. He was a man almost callous to fear, that is the fear of danger in what I might call any normal sea-faring shape. And this palpable nerviness affected me tremendously. He was obviously doing his best to throttle it; and trying all he knew to hide it. I had a sudden warmth of understanding for him, and dreaded lest the men should realise his state. Funny that I should be able at that moment to be aware of anything but my own bewildered fear and expectancy of intruding upon something monstrous at any instant. Yet I describe exactly my feelings, as I stood there in the house.

"Shall we try below, Sir?" I said, and turned to where a flight of stone steps led down into an utter blackness, out which rose a strange, dank scent of the sea...an imponderable mixture of brine and darkness.

"The worthy Duprey leads the van!" said the Skipper; but I felt no irritation now. I knew that he must cover his fright, until he had got control again; and I think he felt, somehow, that I was backing him up. I remember now that I went down those stairs into that unknowable and ancient cabin, as much aware in that moment of the Captain's state, as of that extraordinary thing I had just seen at the little window, or of my own half-funk of what we might see any moment.

The Captain was at my shoulder, as I went, and behind him came the Third Mate, and then the men, all in single file; for the stairs were narrow,

I counted seven steps down, and then my foot splashed into water on the eighth. I held the lamp low and stared. I had caught no glimpse of a reflection, and I saw now that this was owing to a curious, dull, greyish scum that lay thinly on the water, seeming to match the colour of the stone which composed the steps and bulkheads.

"Stop!" I said. "I'm in water!"

I let my foot down slowly, and got the next step. Then sounded with my axe, and found the floor at the bottom. I stepped down and stood up to my thighs in water.

"It's all right, Sir," I said, suddenly whispering. I held my lamp up, and glanced quickly about me.

"It's not deep. There's two doors here...."

I whirled my axe up as I spoke; for suddenly, I had realised that one of the doors was open a little. It seemed to move, as I stared, and I could have imagined that a vague undulation ran towards me, across the dull scum-covered water.

"The door's opening!" I said, aloud, with a sudden sick feeling. "Look out!"

I backed from the door, staring; but nothing came. And abruptly, I had control of myself; for I realised that the door was not moving. It had not moved at all. It was simply ajar.

"It's all right, sir," I said. "It's not opening."

I stepped forward again a pace towards the doors, as the Skipper and the Third Mate came down with a jump, splashing water all over me.

The Captain still had the 'nerves' on him, as I think I could feel, even then; but he hid it well.

"Try the door, Mister. I've jumped my damn lamp out!" he growled to the Third Mate; who pushed at the door on my right; but it would not open beyond the nine or ten inches it was fixed ajar.

"There's this one here, Sir," I whispered, and held my lantern up to the closed door that lay on my left.

"Try it," said the Skipper, in an undertone. We did so, but it also was fixed. I whirled my axe suddenly, and struck the door heavily in the centre of the main panel, and the whole thing crashed into flinders of stone, that went with hollow sounding splashes into the darkness beyond.

"Goodness!" said the Skipper, in a startled voice; for my action had been so instant and unexpected. He covered his lapse, in a moment, by the warning:

"Look out for bad air!" But I was already inside with the lamp, and holding my axe handily. There was no bad air; for right across from me, was a split clean through the ship's side, that I could have put my two arms through, just above the level of the scummy water.

The place I had broken into, was a cabin, of a kind; but seemed strange and dank, and too narrow to breathe in; and wherever I turned, I saw stone. The Third Mate and the Skipper gave simultaneous expressions of disgust at the wet dismalness of the place.

"It's all of stone," I said, and brought my axe hard against the front of a sort of squat cabinet, which was built into the after bulkheads. It caved in, with a crash of splintered stone.

"Empty!" I said, and turned instantly away.

The Skipper and the Third Mate, with the men who were now peering in at the door, crowded out; and in that moment, I pushed my axe under my arm, and thrust my hand into the burst stone-chest. Twice I did this, with almost the speed of lightning, and shoved what I had seen into the side-pocket of my coat. Then, I was following the others; and not one of them had noticed a thing. As for me, I was quivering with excitement, so that my knees shook; for I had caught the unmistakable gleam of gems; and had grabbed for them in that one swift instant.

I wonder whether anyone can realise what I felt in that moment. I knew that, if my guess were right, I had snatched the power in that one miraculous moment, that would lift me from the weary life of a common shellback, to the life of ease that had been mine during my early years. I tell you, in that instant, as I staggered almost blindly out of that dark little apartment, I had no thought of any horror that might be held in that incredible vessel, out there afloat on the wide Atlantic.

I was full of one blinding thought, that possibly I was rich! And I wanted to get somewhere by myself as soon as possible, to see whether I was right. Also, if I could, I meant to get back to that strange cabinet of stone, if the chance came; for I knew that the two handfuls I had grabbed, had left a lot behind.

Only, whatever I did, I must let no one guess; for then I should probably lose everything, or have but an infinitesimal share doled out to me of the wealth that I believed to be in those glittering things there in the side-pocket of my coat.

I began immediately to wonder what other treasures there might be aboard; and then, abruptly, I realised that the Captain was speaking to me:

"The light, Duprey, damn you!" he was saying, angrily, in a low tone. "What's the matter with you! Hold it up."

I pulled myself together, and shoved the lamp above my head. One of the men was swinging his axe, to beat in the door that seemed to have stood so eternally ajar; and the rest were standing back, to give him room. Crash! went the axe, and half the door fell inward, in a shower of broken stone, making dismal splashes in the darkness. The man struck again, and the rest of the door fell away, with a sullen slump into the water.

"The lamp," muttered the Captain. But I had hold of myself once more, and I was stepping forward slowly through the thigh-deep water, even before he spoke.

I went a couple of paces in through the black gape of the doorway, and then stopped and held the lamp so as to get a view of the place. As I did so, I remember how the intense silence struck home on me. Every man of us must surely have been holding his breath; and there must have been some heavy quality, either in the water, or in the scum that floated on it, that kept it from rippling against the sides of the bulkheads, with the movements we had made.

At first, as I held the lamp (which was burning badly), I could not get its position right to show me anything, except that I was in a very large cabin for so small a vessel. Then I saw that a table ran along the centre, and the top of it was no more than a few inches above the water. On each side of it, there rose the backs of what were evidently two rows of massive, olden looking chairs. At the far end of the table, there was a huge, immobile, humped something.

I stared at this for several moments; then I took three slow steps forward, and stopped again; for the thing resolved itself, under the light from the lamp, into the figure of an enormous man, seated at the end of the table, his face bowed forward upon his arms. I was amazed, and thrilling abruptly with new fears and vague impossible thoughts. Without moving a step, I held the light nearer at arm's length.... The man was of stone, like everything in that extraordinary ship.

"That foot!" said the Captain's voice, suddenly cracking. "Look at that foot!" His voice sounded amazingly startling and hollow in that silence, and the words seemed to come back sharply at me from the vaguely seen bulkheads.

I whipped my light to starboard, and saw what he meant – a huge human foot was sticking up out of the water, on the right hand of the table. It was enormous. I have never seen so vast a foot. And it also was of stone.

And then, as I stared, I saw that there was a great head above the water, over by the bulkhead.

"I've gone mad!" I said, out loud, as I saw something else, more incredible.

"My God! Look at the hair on the head!" said the Captain.... "It's growing!" he called out once more.

I was looking. On the great head, there was becoming visible a huge mass of red hair, that was surely and unmistakably rising up, as we watched it.

"It's what I saw at the window!" I said. "It's what I saw at the window! I told you I saw it!"

"Come out of that, Duprey," said the Third Mate, quietly.

"Let's get out of here!" muttered one of the men. Two or three of them called out the same thing; and then, in a moment, they began a mad rush up the stairway.

I stood dumb, where I was. The hair rose up in a horrible living fashion on the great head, waving and moving. It rippled down over the forehead, and spread abruptly over the whole gargantuan stone face, hiding the features completely. Suddenly, I swore at the thing madly, and I hove my axe at it. Then I was backing crazily for the door, slumping the scum as high as the deck beams, in my fierce haste. I reached the stairs, and caught at the stone rail, that was modelled like a rope; and so hove myself up out of the water. I reached the deck-house, where I had seen the great head of hair. I jumped through the doorway, out on to the decks, and felt the night air sweet on my face.... Goodness! I ran forward along the decks. There was a Babel of shouting in the waist of the ship, and a thudding of feet running. Some of the men were singing out, to get into the boat; but the Third Mate was shouting that they must wait for me.

"He's coming," called someone. And then I was among them.

"Turn that lamp up, you idiot," said the Captain's voice. "This is just where we want light!"

I glanced down, and realised that my lamp was almost out. I turned it up, and it flared, and began again to dwindle.

"Those damned boys never filled it," I said. "They deserve their necks breaking."

The men were literally tumbling over the side, and the Skipper was hurrying them.

"Down with you into the boat," he said to me. "Give me the lamp. I'll pass it down. Get a move on you!"

The Captain had evidently got his nerve back again. This was more like the man I knew. I handed him the lamp, and went over the side. All the rest had now gone, and the Third Mate was already in the stern, waiting.

As I landed on the thwart, there was a sudden strange noise from aboard the ship – a sound, as if some stone object were trundling down the sloping decks, from aft. In that one moment, I got what you might truly call the 'horrors'. I seemed suddenly able to believe incredible possibilities.

"The stone men!" I shouted. "Jump, Captain! Jump! Jump!" The vessel seemed to roll oddly.

Abruptly, the Captain yelled out something, that not one of us in the boat understood. There followed a succession of tremendous sounds, aboard the ship, and I saw his shadow swing out huge against the thin mist, as he turned suddenly with the lamp. He fired twice with his revolver.

"The hair!" I shouted. "Look at the hair!"

We all saw it – the great head of red hair that we had seen grow visibly on the monstrous stone head, below in the cabin. It rose above the rail, and there was a moment of intense stillness, in which I heard the Captain gasping. The Third Mate fired six times at the thing, and I found myself fixing an oar up against the side of that abominable vessel, to get aboard.

As I did so, there came one appalling crash, that shook the stone ship fore and aft, and she began to cant up, and my oar slipped and fell into the boat. Then the Captain's voice screamed something in a choking fashion above us. The ship lurched forward and paused. Then another crash came, and she rocked over towards us; then away from us again. The movement away from us continued, and the round of the vessel's bottom showed, vaguely. There was a smashing of glass above us, and the dim glow of light aboard vanished. Then the vessel fell clean from us, with a giant splash. A huge wave came at us, out of the night, and half filled the boat.

The boat nearly capsized, then righted and presently steadied.

"Captain!" shouted the Third Mate. "Captain!" But there came never a sound; only presently, out of all the night, a strange murmuring of waters.

"Captain!" he shouted once more; but his voice just went lost and remote into the darkness.

"She's foundered!" I said.

"Out oars," sung out the Third. "Put your backs into it. Don't stop to bail!"

For half an hour we circled the spot slowly. But the strange vessel had indeed foundered and gone down into the mystery of the deep sea, with her mysteries.

Finally we put about, and returned to the *Alfred Jessop*.

Now, I want you to realise that what I am telling you is a plain and simple tale of fact. This is no fairy tale, and I've not done yet; and I think this yarn should prove to you that some mighty strange things do happen at sea, and always will while the world lasts. It's the home of all mysteries; for it's the one place that is really difficult for humans to investigate. Now just listen:

The Mate had kept the bell going, from time to time, and so we came back pretty quickly, having as we came, a strange repetition of the echoey reduplication of our oar-sounds; but we never spoke a word; for not one of us wanted to hear those beastly echoes again, after what we had just gone through. I think we all had a feeling that there was something a bit hellish aboard that night.

We got aboard, and the Third explained to the Mate what had happened; but he would hardly believe the yarn. However, there was nothing to do, but wait for daylight; so we were told to keep about the deck, and keep our eyes and ears open.

One thing the Mate did show he was more impressed by our yarn than he would admit. He had all the ships' lanterns lashed up round the decks, to the sheerpoles; and he never told us to give up either the axes or cutlass.

It was while we were keeping about the decks, that I took the chance to have a look at what I had grabbed. I tell you, what I found made me nearly forget the Skipper, and all the rummy things that had happened. I had twenty-six stones in my pocket and four of them were diamonds, respectively 9, 11, 131/2 and 17 carats in weight, uncut, that is. I know quite something about diamonds. I'm not going to tell you how I learnt what I know; but I would not have taken a thousand pounds for the four, as they lay there, in my hand. There was also a big, dull stone, that looked red inside. I'd have dumped it over the side, I thought so little of it; only, I argued that it must be something, or it would never have been among that lot. Lord! but I little knew what I'd got; not then. Why, the thing was as big as a fair-sized walnut. You may think it funny that I thought of the four diamonds first; but you see, I know diamonds when I see them. They're things I understand; but I never saw a ruby, in the rough, before or since. Good Lord! And to think I'd have thought nothing of heaving it over the side!

You see, a lot of the stones were not anything much; that is, not in the modern market. There were two big topazes, and several onyx and corelians – nothing much. There were five hammered slugs of gold about two ounces each they would be. And then a prize – one winking green devil of an emerald. You're got to know an emerald to look for the 'eye' of it, in the rough; but it is there – the eye of some hidden devil staring up at you. Yes, I'd seen an emerald before, and I knew I held a lot of money in that one stone alone.

And then I remembered what I'd missed, and cursed myself for not grabbing a third time. But that feeling lasted only a moment. I thought of the beastly part that had been the Skipper's share; while there I stood safe under one of the lamps, with a fortune in my hands. And then, abruptly, as you can understand, my mind was filled with the crazy wonder and bewilderment of what had happened. I felt how absurdly ineffectual my imagination was to comprehend anything understandable out of it all, except that the Captain had certainly gone, and I had just as certainly had a piece of impossible luck.

Often, during that time of waiting, I stopped to take a look at the things I had in my pocket; always careful that no one about the decks should come near me, to see what I was looking at.

Suddenly the Mate's voice came sharp along the decks:

"Call the doctor, one of you," he said. "Tell him to get the fire in and the coffee made."

"'I, Sir," said one of the men; and I realised that the dawn was growing vaguely over the sea.

Half an hour later, the 'doctor' shoved his head out of the galley doorway, and sung out that coffee was ready.

The watch below turned out, and had theirs with the watch on deck, all sitting along the spar that lay under the port rail.

As the daylight grew, we kept a constant watch over the side; but even now we could see nothing; for the thin mist still hung low on the sea.

"Hear that?" said one of the men, suddenly. And, indeed, the sound must have been plain for a half a mile round.

"Ooaaze, ooaaze, arr, arrrr, oooaze—"

"By George!" said Tallett, one of the other watch; "that's a beastly sort of thing to hear."

"Look!" I said. "What's that out yonder?"

The mist was thinning under the effect of the rising sun, and tremendous shapes seemed to stand towering half-seen, away to port. A few minutes passed, while we stared. Then, suddenly, we heard the Mate's voice –

"All hands on deck!" he was shouting, along the decks.

I ran aft a few steps.

"Both watches are out, Sir," I called.

"Very good!" said the Mate. "Keep handy all of you. Some of you have got the axes. The rest had better take a caps-n-bar each, and stand-by till I find what this devilment is, out yonder."

"'I, 'i Sir," I said, and turned forrard. But there was no need to pass on the Mate's orders; for the men had heard, and there was a rush for the capstanbars, which are a pretty hefty kind of cudgel, as any sailorman knows. We lined the rail again, and stared away to port.

"Look out, you sea-divvils," shouted Timothy Galt, a huge Irishman, waving his bar excitedly, and peering over the rail into the mist, which was steadily thinning, as the day grew.

Abruptly there was a simultaneous cry – "Rocks!" shouted everyone.

I never saw such a sight. As at last the mist thinned, we could see them. All the sea to port was literally cut about with far-reaching reefs of rock. In places the reefs lay just submerged; but in others they rose into extraordinary and fantastic rock-spires, and arches, and islands of jagged rock.

"Jehosaphat!" I heard the Third Mate shout. "Look at that, Mister! Look at that! Lord! How did we take the boat through that, without stoving her!"

Everthing was so still for the moment, with all the men just staring and amazed, that I could hear every word come along the decks.

"There's sure been a submarine earthquake somewhere," I heard the First Mate. "The bottom of the sea's just riz up here, quiet and gentle, during the night; and God's mercy we aren't now a-top of one of those ornaments out there."

And then, you know, I saw it all. Everything that had looked mad and impossible, began to be natural; though it was, none the less, all amazing and wonderful.

There had been during the night, a slow lifting of the sea-bottom, owing to some action of the Internal Pressures. The rocks had risen so gently that they had made never a sound; and the stone ship had risen with them out of the deep sea. She had evidently lain on one of the submerged reefs, and so had seemed to us to be just afloat in the sea. And she accounted for the water we heard running. She was naturally bung full, as you might say, and took longer to shed the water than she did to rise. She had probably some biggish holes in her bottom. I began to get my 'soundings' a bit, as I might call it in sailor talk. The natural wonders of the sea beat all made-up yarns that ever were!

The Mate sung out to us to man the boat again, and told the Third Mate to take her out to where we lost the Skipper, and have a final look round, in case there might be any chance to find the Old Man's body anywhere about.

"Keep a man in the bows to look out for sunk rocks, Mister," the Mate told the Third, as we pulled off. "Go slow. There'll be no wind yet awhile. See if you can fix up what made those noises, while you're looking round."

We pulled right across about thirty fathoms of clear water, and in a minute we were between two great arches of rock. It was then I realised that the reduplicating of our oar-roll was the echo from these on each side of us. Even in the sunlight, it was queer to hear again that same strange cathedral echoey sound that we had heard in the dark.

We passed under the huge arches, all hung with deep-sea slime. And presently we were heading straight for a gap, where two low reefs swept in to the apex of a huge horseshoe. We pulled for about three minutes, and then the Third gave the word to vast pulling.

"Take the boat-hook, Duprey," he said, "and go forrard, and see we don't hit anything."

"'I, 'i, Sir," I said, and drew in my oar.

"Give way again gently!" said the Third; and the boat moved forward for another thirty or forty yards.

"We're right on to a reef, Sir," I said, presently, as I stared down over the bows. I sounded with the boat-hook. "There's about three feet of water, Sir," I told him.

"Vast pulling," ordered the Third. "I reckon we are right over the rock, where we found that rum packet last night." He leant over the side, and stared down.

"There's a stone cannon on the rock, right under the bows of the boat," I said. Immediately afterwards I shouted –

"There's the hair, Sir! There's the hair! It's on the reef. There's two! There's three! There's one on the cannon!"

"All right! All right, Duprey! Keep cool," said the Third Mate. "I can see them. You've enough intelligence not to be superstitious now the whole thing's explained. They're some kind of big hairy sea-caterpillar. Prod one with your boat-hook."

I did so; a little ashamed of my sudden bewilderment. The thing whipped round like a tiger, at the boat-hook. It lapped itself round and round the boat-hook, while the hind portions of it kept gripped to the rock, and I could no more pull the boat-hook from its grip, than fly; though I pulled till I sweated.

"Take the point of your cutlass to it, Varley," said the Third Mate. "Jab it through."

The bow-oar did so, and the brute loosed the boat-hook, and curled up round a chunk of rock, looking like a great ball of red hair.

I drew the boat-hook up, and examined it.

"Goodness!" I said. "That's what killed the Old Man – one of those things! Look at all those marks in the wood, where it's gripped it with about a hundred legs."

I passed the boat-hook aft to the Third Mate to look at.

"They're about as dangerous as they can be, Sir, I reckon," I told him.

"Makes you think of African centipedes, only these are big and strong enough to kill an elephant, I should think."

"Don't lean all on one side of the boat!" shouted the Third Mate, as the men stared over. "Get back to your places. Give way, there! ...Keep a good look-out for any signs of the ship or the Captain, Duprey."

For nearly an hour, we pulled to and fro over the reef; but we never saw either the stone ship or the Old Man again. The queer craft must have rolled off into the profound depths that lay on each side of the reef.

As I leant over the bows, staring down all that long while at the submerged rocks, I was able to understand almost everything, except the various extraordinary noises.

The cannon made it unmistakably clear that the ship which had been hove up from the sea-bottom, with the rising of the reef, had been originally a normal enough wooden vessel of a time far removed from our own. At the sea-bottom, she had evidently undergone some natural mineralising process, and this explained her stony appearance. The stone men had been evidently humans who had been drowned in her cabin, and their swollen tissues had been subjected to the same natural process, which, however, had also deposited heavy encrustations upon them, so that their size, when compared with the normal, was prodigious.

The mystery of the hair, I had already discovered; but there remained, among other things, the tremendous bangs we had heard. These were, possibly, explained later, while we were making a final examination of the rocks to the westward, prior to returning to our ship. Here we discovered the burst and swollen bodies of several extraordinary deep-sea creatures, of the eel variety. They must have had a girth, in life, of many feet, and one that we measured roughly with an oar, must have been quite forty feet long. They had, apparently, burst on being lifted from the tremendous pressure of the deep sea, into the light air pressure above water, and hence might account for the loud reports we had heard; though, personally, I incline to think these loud bangs were more probably caused by the splitting of the rocks under new stresses.

As for the roaring sounds, I can only conclude that they were caused by a peculiar species of grampus-like fish, of enormous size, which we found dead and hugely distended on one of the rocky masses. This fish must have weighed at least four or five tonnes, and when prodded with a heavy oar, there came from its peculiar snout-shaped mouth, a low, hoarse sound, like a weak imitation of the tremendous sounds we had heard during the past night.

Regarding the apparently carved handrail, like a rope up the side of the cabin stairs, I realise that this had undoubtedly been actual rope at one time.

Recalling the heavy, trundling sounds aboard, just after I climbed down into the boat, I can only suppose that these were made by some stone object, possibly a fossilised gun-carriage, rolling down the decks, as the ship began to slip off the rocks, and bows sank lower in the water.

The varying lights must have been the strongly phosphorescent bodies of some of the deep-sea creatures, moving about on the upheaved reefs. As for the giant splash that occurred in the darkness ahead of the boat, this must have been due to some large portion of heaved-up rock, over-balancing and rolling back into the sea.

No one aboard ever learnt about the jewels. I took care of that! I sold the ruby badly, so I've heard since; but I do not grumble even now. Twenty-three thousand pounds I had for it alone, from a merchant in London. I learned afterwards he made double that on it; but I don't spoil my pleasure by grumbling. I wonder often how the stones and things came where I found them; but she carried guns, as I've told, I think; and there's rum doings happen at sea; yes, by George!

The smell – oh that I guess was due to heaving all that deep-sea slime up for human noses to smell at.

This yarn is, of course, known in nautical circles, and was briefly mentioned in the old *Nautical Mercury* of 1879. The series of volcanic reefs (which disappeared in 1883) were charted under the name of the 'Alfred Jessop Shoals and Reefs'; being named after our Captain who discovered them and lost his life on them.

If you enjoyed this, you might also like…
Demons of the Sea, see page 395
From the Tideless Sea: Part One, see page 111

The Baumoff Explosive

DALLY, WHITLAW AND I were discussing the recent stupendous explosion which had occurred in the vicinity of Berlin. We were marvelling concerning the extraordinary period of darkness that had followed, and which had aroused so much newspaper comment, with theories galore.

The papers had got hold of the fact that the War Authorities had been experimenting with a new explosive, invented by a certain chemist, named Baumoff, and they referred to it constantly as 'The New Baumoff Explosive'.

We were in the Club, and the fourth man at our table was John Stafford, who was professionally a medical man, but privately in the Intelligence Department. Once or twice, as we talked, I had glanced at Stafford, wishing to fire a question at him; for he had been acquainted with Baumoff. But I managed to hold my tongue; for I knew that if I asked out pointblank, Stafford (who's a good sort, but a bit of an ass as regards his almost ponderous code-of-silence) would be just as like as not to say that it was a subject upon which he felt he was not entitled to speak.

Oh, I know the old donkey's way; and when he had once said that, we might just make up our minds never to get another word out of him on the matter as long as we lived. Yet, I was satisfied to notice that he seemed a bit restless, as if he were on the itch to shove in his oar; by which I guessed that the papers we were quoting had got things very badly muddled indeed, in some way or other, at least as regarded his friend Baumoff. Suddenly, he spoke:

"What unmitigated, wicked piffle!" said Stafford, quite warm. "I tell you it is wicked, this associating of Baumoff's name with war inventions and such horrors. He was the most intensely poetical and earnest follower of the Christ that I have ever met; and it is just the brutal Irony of Circumstance that has attempted to use one of the products of his genius for a purpose of Destruction. But you'll find they won't be able to use it, in spite of their having got hold of Baumoff's formula. As an explosive it is not practicable. It is, shall I say, too impartial; there is no way of controlling it.

"I know more about it, perhaps, than any man alive; for I was Baumoff's greatest friend, and when he died, I lost the best comrade a man ever had. I need make no secret about it to you chaps. I was 'on duty' in Berlin, and I was deputed to get in touch with Baumoff. The government had long had an eye on him; he was an Experimental Chemist, you know, and altogether too jolly clever to ignore. But there was no need to worry about him. I got to know him, and we became enormous friends; for I soon found that he would never turn his abilities towards any new war-contrivance; and so, you see, I was able to enjoy my friendship with him, with a comfy conscience – a thing our chaps are not always able to do in their friendships. Oh, I tell you, it's a mean, sneaking, treacherous sort of business, ours; though it's necessary; just as some odd man, or other, has to be a hangsman. There's a number of unclean jobs to be done to keep the Social Machine running!

"I think Baumoff was the most enthusiastic intelligent believer in Christ that it will be ever possible to produce. I learned that he was compiling and evolving a treatise of most extraordinary and convincing proofs in support of the more inexplicable things concerning the life and death of Christ. He was, when I became acquainted with him, concentrating his attention particularly upon endeavouring to show that the Darkness of the Cross, between the sixth and the ninth hours, was a very real thing, possessing a tremendous significance. He intended at one sweep to smash utterly all talk of a timely thunderstorm or any of the other more or less inefficient theories which have been brought forward from time to time to explain the occurrence away as being a thing of no particular significance.

"Baumoff had a pet aversion, an atheistic Professor of Physics, named Hautch, who – using the 'marvellous' element of the life and death of Christ, as a fulcrum from which to attack Baumoff's theories – smashed at him constantly, both in his lectures and in print. Particularly did he pour bitter unbelief upon Baumoff"s upholding that the Darkness of the Cross was anything more than a gloomy hour or two, magnified into blackness by the emotional inaccuracy of the Eastern mind and tongue.

"One evening, some time after our friendship had become very real, I called on Baumoff, and found him in a state of tremendous indignation over some article of the Professor's which attacked him brutally; using his theory of the Significance of the 'Darkness', as a target. Poor Baumoff! It was certainly a marvellously clever attack; the attack of a thoroughly trained, well-balanced Logician. But Baumoff was something more; he was Genius. It is a title few have any rights to; but it was his!

"He talked to me about his theory, telling me that he wanted to show me a small experiment, presently, bearing out his opinions. In his talk, he told me several things that interested me extremely. Having first reminded me of the fundamental fact that light is conveyed to the eye through the means of that indefinable medium, named the Aether. He went a step further, and pointed out to me that, from an aspect which more approached the primary, Light was a vibration of the Aether, of a certain definite number of waves per second, which possessed the power of producing upon our retina the sensation which we term Light.

"To this, I nodded; being, as of course is everyone, acquainted with so well-known a statement. From this, he took a quick, mental stride, and told me that an ineffably vague, but measurable, darkening of the atmosphere (greater or smaller according to the personality-force of the individual) was always evoked in the immediate vicinity of the human, during any period of great emotional stress.

"Step by step, Baumoff showed me how his research had led him to the conclusion that this queer darkening (a million times too subtle to be apparent to the eye) could be produced only through something which had power to disturb or temporally interrupt or break up the Vibration of Light. In other words, there was, at any time of unusual emotional activity, some disturbance of the Aether in the immediate vicinity of the person suffering, which had some effect upon the Vibration of Light, interrupting it, and producing the aforementioned infinitely vague darkening.

"'Yes?' I said, as he paused, and looked at me, as if expecting me to have arrived at a certain definite deduction through his remarks. 'Go on.'

"'Well,' he said, 'don't you see, the subtle darkening around the person suffering, is greater or less, according to the personality of the suffering human. Don't you?'

"'Oh!' I said, with a little gasp of astounded comprehension, 'I see what you mean. You – you mean that if the agony of a person of ordinary personality can produce a faint disturbance of the Aether, with a consequent faint darkening, then the Agony of Christ, possessed of the Enormous Personality of the Christ, would produce a terrific disturbance of the Aether, and therefore, it might chance, of the Vibration of Light, and that this is the true explanation of the Darkness of the Cross; and that the fact of such an extraordinary and apparently unnatural and improbable Darkness having been recorded is not a thing to weaken the Marvel of Christ. But one more unutterably wonderful, infallible proof of His God-like power? Is that it? Is it? Tell me?'

"Baumoff just rocked on his chair with delight, beating one fist into the palm of his other hand, and nodding all the time to my summary. How he loved to be understood; as the Searcher always craves to be understood.

"'And now,' he said, 'I'm going to show you something.'

"He took a tiny, corked test-tube out of his waistcoat pocket, and emptied its contents (which consisted of a single, grey-white grain, about twice the size of an ordinary pin's head) on to his dessert plate. He crushed it gently to powder with the ivory handle of a knife, then damped it gently, with a single minim of what I supposed to be water, and worked it up into a tiny patch of grey-white paste. He then took out his gold tooth-pick, and thrust it into the flame of a small chemist's spirit lamp, which had been lit since dinner as a pipe-lighter. He held the gold tooth-pick in the flame, until the narrow, gold blade glowed whitehot.

"'Now look!' he said, and touched the end of the tooth-pick against the infinitesmal patch upon the dessert plate. There came a swift little violet flash, and suddenly I found that I was staring at Baumoff through a sort of transparent darkness, which faded swiftly into a black opaqueness. I thought at first this must be the complementary effect of the flash upon the retina. But a minute passed, and we were still in that extraordinary darkness.

"'My Gracious! Man! What is it?' I asked, at last.

"His voice explained then, that he had produced, through the medium of chemistry, an exaggerated effect which simulated, to some extent, the disturbance in the Aether produced by waves thrown off by any person during an emotional crisis or agony. The waves, or vibrations, sent out by his experiment produced only a partial simulation of the effect he wished to show me – merely the temporary interruption of the Vibration of Light, with the resulting darkness in which we both now sat.

"'That stuff,' said Baumoff, 'would be a tremendous explosive, under certain conditions.'

I heard him puffing at his pipe, as he spoke, but instead of the glow of the pipe shining out visible and red, there was only a faint glare that wavered and disappeared in the most extraordinary fashion.

"'My Goodness!' I said, 'when's this going away?' And I stared across the room to where the big kerosene lamp showed only as a faintly glimmering patch in the gloom; a vague light that shivered and flashed oddly, as though I saw it through an immense gloomy depth of dark and disturbed water.

"'It's all right,' Baumoff's voice said from out of the darkness. 'It's going now; in five minutes the disturbance will have quieted, and the waves of light will flow off evenly from the lamp in their normal fashion. But, whilst we're waiting, isn't it immense, eh?'

"'Yes,' I said. 'It's wonderful; but it's rather unearthly, you know.'

"'Oh, but I've something much finer to show you,' he said. 'The real thing. Wait another minute. The darkness is going. See! You can see the light from the lamp now quite plainly. It looks as if it were submerged in a boil of waters, doesn't it? That are growing clearer and clearer and quieter and quieter all the time.'

"It was as he said; and we watched the lamp, silently, until all signs of the disturbance of the light-carrying medium had ceased. Then Baumoff faced me once more.

"'Now,' he said. 'You've seen the somewhat casual effects of just crude combustion of that stuff of mine. I'm going to show you the effects of combusting it in the human furnace, that is, in my own body; and then, you'll see one of the great wonders of Christ's death reproduced on a miniature scale.'

"He went across to the mantelpiece, and returned with a small, 120 minim glass and another of the tiny, corked test-tubes, containing a single grey-white grain of his chemical substance. He uncorked the test-tube, and shook the grain of substance into the minim glass, and then, with a glass stirring-rod, crushed it up in the bottom of the glass, adding water, drop by drop as he did so, until there were sixty minims in the glass.

"'Now!' he said, and lifting it, he drank the stuff. 'We will give it thirty-five minutes,' he continued; 'then, as carbonisation proceeds, you will find my pulse will increase, as also the respiration, and presently there will come the darkness again, in the subtlest, strangest fashion; but accompanied now by certain physical and psychic phenomena, which will be owing to the fact that the vibrations it will throw off, will be blent into what I might call the emotional-vibrations, which I shall give off in my distress. These will be enormously intensified, and you will possibly experience an extraordinarily interesting demonstration of the soundness of my more theoretical reasonings. I tested it by myself last week' (He waved a bandaged finger at me), 'and I read a paper to the Club on the results. They are very enthusiastic, and have promised their co-operation in the big demonstration I intend to give on next Good Friday – that's seven weeks off, today.'

"He had ceased smoking; but continued to talk quietly in this fashion for the next thirty-five minutes. The Club to which he had referred was a peculiar association of men, banded together under the presidentship of Baumoff himself, and having for their appellation the title of – so well as I can translate it – 'The Believers And Provers Of Christ'. If I may say so, without any thought of irreverence, they were, many of them, men fanatically crazed to uphold the Christ. You will agree later, I think, that I have not used an incorrect term, in describing the bulk of the members of this extraordinary club, which was, in its way, well worthy of one of the religio-maniacal extrudences which have been forced into temporary being by certain of the more religiously-emotional minded of our cousins across the water.

"Baumoff looked at the clock; then held out his wrist to me. 'Take my pulse,' he said, 'it's rising fast. Interesting data, you know.'

"I nodded, and drew out my watch. I had noticed that his respirations were increasing; and I found his pulse running evenly and strongly at 105. Three minutes later, it had risen to 175, and his respirations to 41. In a further three minutes, I took his pulse again, and found it running at 203, but with the rhythm regular. His respirations were then 49. He had, as I knew, excellent lungs, and his heart was sound. His lungs, I may say, were of exceptional capacity, and there was at this stage no marked dyspnoea. Three minutes later I found the pulse to be 227, and the respiration 54.

"'You've plenty of red corpuscles, Baumoff!' I said. 'But I hope you're not going to overdo things.'

"He nodded at me, and smiled; but said nothing. Three minutes later, when I took the last pulse, it was 233, and the two sides of the heart were sending out unequal quantities of blood, with an irregular rhythm. The respiration had risen to 67 and was becoming shallow and ineffectual, and dyspnoea was becoming very marked. The small amount of arterial blood leaving the left side of the heart betrayed itself in the curious bluish and white tinge of the face.

"'Baumoff!' I said, and began to remonstrate; but he checked me, with a queerly invincible gesture.

"'It's all right!' he said, breathlessly, with a little note of impatience. 'I know what I'm doing all the time. You must remember I took the same degree as you in medicine.'

"It was quite true. I remembered then that he had taken his M.D. in London; and this in addition to half a dozen other degrees in different branches of the sciences in his own country. And then, even as the memory reassured me that he was not acting in ignorance of the possible danger, he called out in a curious, breathless voice:

"'The Darkness! It's beginning. Take note of every single thing. Don't bother about me. I'm all right!'

"I glanced swiftly round the room. It was as he had said. I perceived it now. There appeared to be an extraordinary quality of gloom growing in the atmosphere of the room. A kind of bluish gloom, vague, and scarcely, as yet, affecting the transparency of the atmosphere to light.

"Suddenly, Baumoff did something that rather sickened me. He drew his wrist away from me, and reached out to a small metal box, such as one sterilises a hypodermic in. He opened the box, and took out four rather curious looking drawing-pins, I might call them, only they had spikes of steel fully an inch long, whilst all around the rim of the heads (which were also of steel) there projected downward, parallel with the central spike, a number of shorter spikes, maybe an eighth of an inch long.

"He kicked off his pumps; then stooped and slipped his socks off, and I saw that he was wearing a pair of linen inner-socks.

"'Antiseptic!' he said, glancing at me. 'Got my feet ready before you came. No use running unnecessary risks.' He gasped as he spoke. Then he took one of the curious little steel spikes.

"'I've sterilised them,' he said; and therewith, with deliberation, he pressed it in up to the head into his foot between the second and third branches of the dorsal artery.

"'For God's sake, what are you doing!' I said, half rising from my chair.

"'Sit down!' he said, in a grim sort of voice. 'I can't have any interference. I want you simply to observe; keep note of everything. You ought to thank me for the chance, instead of worrying me, when you know I shall go my own way all the time.'

"As he spoke, he had pressed in the second of the steel spikes up to the hilt in his left instep, taking the same precaution to avoid the arteries. Not a groan had come from him; only his face betrayed the effect of this additional distress.

"'My dear chap!' he said, observing my upsetness. 'Do be sensible. I know exactly what I'm doing. There simply must be distress, and the readiest way to reach that condition is through physical pain.' His speech had become a series of spasmodic words, between gasps, and sweat lay in great clear drops upon his lip and forehead. He slipped off his belt and proceeded to buckle it round both the back of his chair and his waist; as if he expected to need some support from falling.

"'It's wicked!' I said. Baumoff made an attempt to shrug his heaving shoulders, that was, in its way, one of the most piteous things that I have seen, in its sudden laying bare of the agony that the man was making so little of.

"He was now cleaning the palms of his hands with a little sponge, which he dipped from time to time in a cup of solution. I knew what he was going to do, and suddenly he jerked out, with a painful attempt to grin, an explanation of his bandaged finger. He had held his finger in the flame of the spirit lamp, during his previous experiment; but now, as he made clear in gaspingly uttered words, he wished to simulate as far as possible the actual conditions of the great scene that he had so much in mind. He made it so clear to me that we might expect to experience something very extraordinary, that I was conscious of a sense of almost superstitious nervousness.

"'I wish you wouldn't, Baumoff!' I said.

"'Don't – be – silly!' he managed to say. But the two latter words were more groans than words; for between each, he had thrust home right to the heads in the palms of his hands the two remaining steel spikes. He gripped his hands shut, with a sort of spasm of savage determination, and I saw the point of one of the spikes break through the back of his hand, between the extensor tendons of the second and third fingers. A drop of blood beaded the point of the spike. I looked at Baumoff's face; and he looked back steadily at me.

"'No interference,' he managed to ejaculate. 'I've not gone through all this for nothing. I know – what – I'm doing. Look – it's coming. Take note – everything!'

"He relapsed into silence, except for his painful gasping. I realised that I must give way, and I stared round the room, with a peculiar commingling of an almost nervous discomfort and a stirring of very real and sober curiosity.

"'Oh,' said Baumoff, after a moment's silence, 'something's going to happen. I can tell. Oh, wait – till I – I have my – big demonstration. I'll show that brute Hautch."

"I nodded; but I doubt that he saw me; for his eyes had a distinctly in-turned look, the iris was rather relaxed. I glanced away round the room again; there was a distinct occasional breaking up of the light-rays from the lamp, giving a coming-and-going effect.

"The atmosphere of the room was also quite plainly darker – heavy, with an extraordinary sense of gloom. The bluish tint was unmistakably more in evidence; but there was, as yet, none of that opacity which we had experienced before, upon simple combustion, except for the occasional, vague coming-and-going of the lamp-light.

"Baumoff began to speak again, getting his words out between gasps. 'Th' – this dodge of mine gets the – pain into the – the – right place. Right association of – of ideas – emotions – for – best – results. You follow me? Parallelising things – as – much as – possible. Fixing whole attention – on the – the death scene—'

"He gasped painfully for a few moments. 'We demonstrate truth of – of The Darkening; but – but there's psychic effect to be – looked for, through – results of parallelisation of – conditions. May have extraordinary simulation of – the actual thing. Keep note. Keep note.' Then, suddenly, with a clear, spasmodic burst: 'My God, Stafford, keep note of everything. Something's going to happen. Something – wonderful – Promise not – to bother me. I know – what I'm doing.'

"Baumoff ceased speaking, with a gasp, and there was only the labour of his breathing in the quietness of the room. As I stared at him, halting from a dozen things I needed to say, I realised suddenly that I could no longer see him quite plainly; a sort of wavering in the atmosphere, between us, made him seem momentarily unreal. The whole room had darkened perceptibly in the last thirty seconds; and as I stared around, I realised that there was a constant invisible swirl in the fast-deepening, extraordinary blue gloom that seemed now to permeate everything. When I looked at the lamp, alternate flashings of light and blue – darkness followed each other with an amazing swiftness.

"'My God!' I heard Baumoff whispering in the half-darkness, as if to himself, 'how did Christ bear the nails!'

"I stared across at him, with an infinite discomfort, and an irritated pity troubling me; but I knew it was no use to remonstrate now. I saw him vaguely distorted through the wavering tremble of the atmosphere. It was somewhat as if I looked at him through convolutions of heated air; only there were marvellous waves of blue-blackness making gaps in my sight. Once I saw his face clearly, full of an infinite pain, that was somehow, seemingly, more spiritual than physical, and dominating everything was an expression of enormous resolution and concentration, making the livid, sweat-damp, agonised face somehow heroic and splendid.

"And then, drenching the room with waves and splashes of opaqueness, the vibration of his abnormally stimulated agony finally broke up the vibration of Light. My last, swift glance round, showed me, as it seemed, the invisible Aether boiling and eddying in a tremendous fashion; and, abruptly, the flame of the lamp was lost in an extraordinary swirling patch of light, that marked its position for several moments, shimmering and deadening, shimmering and deadening; until, abruptly, I saw neither that glimmering patch of light, nor anything else. I was suddenly lost in a black opaqueness of night, through which came the fierce, painful breathing of Baumoff.

"A full minute passed; but so slowly that, if I had not been counting Baumoff's respirations, I should have said that it was five. Then Baumoff spoke suddenly, in a voice that was, somehow, curiously changed – a certain toneless note in it:

"'My God!' he said, from out of the darkness. 'What must Christ have suffered!'

"It was in the succeeding silence, that I had the first realisation that I was vaguely afraid; but the feeling was too indefinite and unfounded, and I might say subconscious, for me to face it out. Three minutes passed, whilst I counted the almost desperate respirations that came to me through the darkness. Then Baumoff began to speak again, and still in that peculiarly altering voice:

"'By Thy Agony and Bloody Sweat,' he muttered. Twice he repeated this. It was plain indeed that he had fixed his whole attention with tremendous intensity, in his abnormal state, upon the death scene.

"The effect upon me of his intensity was interesting and in some ways extraordinary. As well as I could, I analysed my sensations and emotions and general state of mind, and realised that Baumoff was producing an effect upon me that was almost hypnotic.

"Once, partly because I wished to get my level by the aid of a normal remark, and also because I was suddenly newly anxious by a change in the breathsounds, I asked Baumoff how he was. My voice going with a peculiar and really uncomfortable blankness through that impenetrable blackness of opacity.

"He said: 'Hush! I'm carrying the Cross.' And, do you know, the effect of those simple words, spoken in that new, toneless voice, in that atmosphere of almost unbearable tenseness, was so powerful that, suddenly, with eyes wide open, I saw Baumoff clear and vivid against that unnatural darkness, carrying a Cross. Not, as the picture is usually shown of the Christ, with it crooked over the shoulder; but with the Cross gripped just under the cross-piece in his arms, and the end trailing behind, along rocky ground. I saw even the pattern of the grain of the rough wood, where some of the bark had been ripped away; and under the trailing end there was a tussock of tough wire-grass, that had been uprooted by the lowing end, and dragged and ground along upon the rocks, between the end of the Cross and the rocky ground. I can see the thing now, as I speak. Its vividness was extraordinary; but it had come and gone like a flash, and I was sitting there in the darkness, mechanically counting the respirations; yet unaware that I counted.

"As I sat there, it came to me suddenly – the whole entire marvel of the thing that Baumoff had achieved. I was sitting there in a darkness which was an actual reproduction of the miracle of the Darkness of the Cross. In short, Baumoff had, by producing in himself an abnormal condition, developed an Energy of Emotion that must have almost, in its effects, paralleled the Agony of the Cross. And in so doing, he had shown from an entirely new and wonderful point, the indisputable truth of the stupendous personality and the enormous spiritual force of the Christ. He had evolved and made practical to the average understanding a proof that would make to live again the reality of that wonder of the world – CHRIST. And for all this, I had nothing but admiration of an almost stupefied kind.

"But, at this point, I felt that the experiment should stop. I had a strangely nervous craving for Baumoff to end it right there and then, and not to try to parallel the psychic conditions. I had, even then, by some queer aid of sub-conscious suggestion, a vague reaching-out-towards the danger of 'monstrosity' being induced, instead of any actual knowledge gained.

"'Baumoff!' I said. 'Stop it.'

"But he made no reply, and for some minutes there followed a silence, that was unbroken, save by his gasping breathing. Abruptly, Baumoff said, between his gasps: 'Woman – behold – thy – son.' He muttered this several times, in the same uncomfortably toneless voice in which he had spoken since the darkness became complete.

"'Baumoff.' I said again. 'Baumoff! Stop it.' And as I listened for his answer, I was relieved to think that his breathing was less shallow. The abnormal demand for oxygen was evidently being met, and the extravagant call upon the heart's efficiency was being relaxed.

"'Baumoff!' I said, once more. 'Baumoff! Stop it!'

"And, as I spoke, abruptly, I thought the room was shaken a little.

"Now, I had already as you will have realised, been vaguely conscious of a peculiar and growing nervousness. I think that is the word that best describes it, up to this moment. At this curious little shake that seemed to stir through the utterly dark room, I was suddenly more than nervous. I felt a thrill of actual and literal fear; yet with no sufficient cause of reason to justify me; so that, after sitting very tense for some long minutes, and feeling nothing further, I decided that I needed to take myself in hand, and keep a firmer grip upon my nerves. And then, just as I had arrived at this more comfortable state of mind, the room was shaken again, with the most curious and sickening oscillatory movement, that was beyond all comfort of denial.

"'My God!' I whispered. And then, with a sudden effort of courage, I called· 'Baumoff! For God's sake stop it.'

"You've no idea of the effort it took to speak aloud into that darkness; and when I did speak, the sound of my voice set me afresh on edge. It went so empty and raw across the room; and somehow, the room seemed to be incredibly big. Oh, I wonder whether you realise how beastly I felt, without my having to make any further effort to tell you.

"And Baumoff never answered a word; but I could hear him breathing, a little fuller; though still heaving his thorax painfully, in his need for air. The incredible shaking of the room eased away; and there succeeded a spasm of quiet, in which I felt that it was my duty to get up and step across to Baumoffs chair. But I could not do it. Somehow, I would not have touched Baumoff then for any cause whatever. Yet, even in that moment, as now I know, I was not aware that I was afraid to touch Baumoff.

"And then the oscillations commenced again. I felt the seat of my trousers slide against the seat of my chair, and I thrust out my legs, spreading my feet against the carpet, to keep me from sliding off one way or the other on to the floor. To say I was afraid, was not to describe my state at all. I was terrified. And suddenly, I had comfort, in the most extraordinary fashion; for a single idea literally glazed into my brain, and gave me a reason to which to cling. It was a single line:

"'Aether, the soul of iron and sundry stuffs' which Baumoff had once taken as a text for an extraordinary lecture on vibrations, in the earlier days of our friendship. He had formulated the suggestion that, in embryo, Matter was, from a primary aspect, a localised vibration, traversing a closed orbit. These primary localised vibrations were inconceivably minute. But were capable, under certain conditions, of combining under the action of keynote-vibrations into secondary vibrations of a size and shape to be determined by a multitude of only guessable factors. These would sustain their new form, so long as nothing occurred to disorganise their combination or depreciate or divert their energy – their unity being partially determined by the inertia of the still Aether outside of the closed path which their area of activities covered. And such combination of the primary localised vibrations was neither more nor less than matter. Men and worlds, aye! and universes.

"And then he had said the thing that struck me most. He had said, that if it were possible to produce a vibration of the Aether of a sufficient energy, it would be possible to disorganise or confuse the vibration of matter. That, given a machine capable of creating a vibration of the Aether of a sufficient energy, he would engage to destroy not merely the world, but the whole universe itself, including heaven and hell themselves, if such places existed, and had such existence in a material form.

"I remember how I looked at him, bewildered by the pregnancy and scope of his imagination. And now his lecture had come back to me to help my courage with the sanity of reason. Was it not possible that the Aether disturbance which he had produced, had sufficient energy to cause some disorganisation of the vibration of matter, in the immediate vicinity, and had thus created a miniature quaking of the ground all about the house, and so set the house gently a-shake?

"And then, as this thought came to me, another and a greater, flashed into my mind. 'My God!' I said out loud into the darkness of the room. It explains one more mystery of the Cross, the disturbance of the Aether caused by Christ's Agony, disorganised the vibration of matter in the vicinity of the Cross, and there was then a small local earthquake, which opened the graves, and rent the veil, possibly by disturbing its supports. And, of course, the earthquake was an effect, and not a cause, as belittlers of the Christ have always insisted.

"'Baumoff!' I called. 'Baumoff, you've proved another thing. Baumoff! Baumoff! Answer me. Are you all right?'

"Baumoff answered, sharp and sudden out of the darkness; but not to me:

"'My God!' he said. 'My God!' His voice came out at me, a cry of veritable mental agony. He was suffering, in some hypnotic, induced fashion, something of the very agony of the Christ Himself.

"'Baumoff!' I shouted, and forced myself to my feet. I heard his chair clattering, as he sat there and shook. 'Baumoff!'

An extraordinary quake went across the floor of the room, and I heard a creaking of the woodwork, and something fell and smashed in the darkness. Baumoff's gasps hurt me; but I stood there. I dared not go to him. I knew then that I was afraid of him – of his condition, or something I don't know what. But, oh, I was horribly afraid of him.

"'Bau—' I began, but suddenly I was afraid even to speak to him. And I could not move. Abruptly, he cried out in a tone of incredible anguish:

"'Eloi, Eloi, lama sabachthani!' But the last word changed in his mouth, from his dreadful hypnotic grief and pain, to a scream of simply infernal terror.

"And, suddenly, a horrible mocking voice roared out in the room, from Baumoff's chair: 'Eloi, Eloi, lama sabachthani!'

"Do you understand, the voice was not Baumoff's at all. It was not a voice of despair; but a voice sneering in an incredible, bestial, monstrous fashion. In the succeeding silence, as I stood in an ice of fear, I knew that Baumoff no longer gasped. The room was absolutely silent, the most dreadful and silent place in all this world. Then I bolted; caught my foot, probably in the invisible edge of the hearth-rug, and pitched headlong into a blaze of internal brain-stars. After which, for a very long time, certainly some hours, I knew nothing of any kind.

"I came back into this Present, with a dreadful headache oppressing me, to the exclusion of all else. But the Darkness had dissipated. I rolled over on to my side, and saw Baumoff and forgot even the pain in my head. He was leaning forward towards me: his eyes wide open, but dull. His face was enormously swollen, and there was, somehow, something beastly about him. He was dead, and the belt about him and the chair-back alone prevented him from falling forward on to me. His tongue was thrust out of one corner of his mouth. I shall always remember how he looked. He was leering, like a human-beast, more than a man.

"I edged away from him, across the floor; but I never stopped looking at him, until I had got to the other side of the door, and closed between us. Of course, I got my balance in a bit, and went back to him; but there was nothing I could do.

"Baumoff died of heart-failure, of course, obviously! I should never be so foolish as to suggest to any sane jury that, in his extraordinary, self-hypnotised, defenceless condition, he was 'entered' by some Christ-apeing Monster of the Void. I've too much respect for my own claim to be a common-sensible man, to put forward such an idea with seriousness! Oh, I know I may seem to speak with a jeer; but what can I do but jeer at myself and all the world, when I dare not acknowledge, even secretly to myself, what my own thoughts are. Baumoff did, undoubtedly die of heart-failure; and, for the rest, how much was I hypnotised into believing. Only, there was over by the far wall, where it had been shaken down to the floor from a solidly fastened-up bracket, a little pile of glass that had once formed a piece of beautiful Venetian glassware. You remember that I heard something fall, when the room shook. Surely the room did shake? Oh, I must stop thinking. My head goes round.

"The explosive the papers are talking about. Yes, that's Baumoff's; that makes it all seem true, doesn't it? They had the darkness at Berlin, after the explosion. There is no getting away from that. The Government know only that Baumoff's formulae is capable of producing the largest quantity of gas, in the shortest possible time. That, in short, it is ideally explosive. So it is; but I imagine it will prove an explosive, as I have already said, and as experience has proved, a little too impartial in its action for it to create enthusiasm on either side of a battlefield. Perhaps this is but a mercy, in disguise; certainly a mercy, if Baumoff's theories as to the possibility of disorganising matter, be anywhere near to the truth.

"I have thought sometimes that there might be a more normal explanation of the dreadful thing that happened at the end. Baumoff may have ruptured a blood-vessel in the brain, owing to the enormous arterial pressure that his experiment induced; and the voice I heard and the mockery and the horrible expression and leer may have been nothing more than the immediate outburst and expression of the natural 'obliqueness' of a deranged mind, which so often turns up a side of a man's nature and produces an inversion of character, that is the very complement of his normal state. And certainly, poor Baumoff's normal religious attitude was one of marvellous reverence and loyalty towards the Christ.

"Also, in support of this line of explanation, I have frequently observed that the voice of a person suffering from mental derangement is frequently wonderfully changed, and has in it often a very repellant and inhuman quality. I try to think that this explanation fits the case. But I can never forget that room. Never."

If you enjoyed this, you might also like...

Out of the Storm, see page 337
Demons of the Sea, see page 395

Demons of the Sea

"COME OUT ON DECK and have a look, Darky!" Jepson cried, rushing into the half deck. "The Old Man says there's been a submarine earthquake, and the sea's all bubbling and muddy!"

Obeying the summons of Jepson's excited tone, I followed him out. It was as he had said; the everlasting blue of the ocean was mottled with splotches of a muddy hue, and at times a large bubble would appear, to burst with a loud 'pop'. Aft, the skipper and the three mates could be seen on the poop, peering at the sea through their glasses. As I gazed out over the gently heaving water, far off to windward something was hove up into the evening air. It appeared to be a mass of seaweed, but fell back into the water with a sullen plunge as though it were something more substantial. Immediately after this strange occurrence, the sun set with tropical swiftness, and in the brief afterglow things assumed a strange unreality.

The crew were all below, no one but the mate and the helmsman remaining on the poop. Away forward, on the topgallant forecastle head the dim figure of the man on lookout could be seen, leaning against the forestay. No sound was heard save the occasional jingle of a chain sheet, of the flog of the steering gear as a small swell passed under our counter. Presently the mate's voice broke the silence, and, looking up, I saw that the Old Man had come on deck, and was talking with him. From the few stray words that could be overheard, I knew they were talking of the strange happenings of the day.

Shortly after sunset, the wind, which had been fresh during the day, died down, and with its passing the air grew oppressively hot. Not long after two bells, the mate sung out for me, and ordered me to fill a bucket from overside and bring it to him. When I had carried out his instructions, he placed a thermometer in the bucket.

"Just as I thought," he muttered, removing the instrument and showing it to the skipper; "ninety-nine degrees. Why, the sea's hot enough to make tea with!"

"Hope it doesn't get any hotter," growled the latter; "if it does, we shall all be boiled alive."

At a sign from the mate, I emptied the bucket and replaced it in the rack, after which I resumed my former position by the rail. The Old Man and the mate walked the poop side by side. The air grew hotter as the hours passed and after a long period of silence broken only by the occasional 'pop' of a bursting gas bubble, the moon arose. It shed but a feeble light, however, as a heavy mist had arisen from the sea, and through this, the moonbeams struggled weakly. The mist, we decided, was due to the excessive heat of the sea water; it was a very wet mist, and we were soon soaked to the skin. Slowly the interminable night wore on, and the sun arose, looking dim and ghostly through the mist that rolled and billowed about the ship. From time to time we took the temperature of the sea, although we found but a slight increase therein. No work was done, and a feeling as of something impending pervaded the ship.

The fog horn was kept going constantly, as the lookout peered through the wreathing mists. The captain walked the poop in company with the mates, and once the third mate spoke and pointed out into the clouds of fog. All eyes followed his gesture; we saw what was apparently a black line, which seemed to cut the whiteness of the billows. It reminded us of nothing so much as an enormous cobra standing on its tail. As we looked it vanished. The grouped mates were evidently puzzled; there seemed to be a difference of opinion among them. Presently as they argued, I heard the second mate's voice:

"That's all rot," he said. "I've seen things in fog before, but they've always turned out to be imaginary."

The third shook his head and made some reply I could not overhear, but no further comment was made. Going below that afternoon, I got a short sleep, and on coming on deck at eight bells, I found that the steam still held us; if anything, it seemed to be thicker than ever. Hansard, who had been taking the temperatures during my watch below, informed me that the sea was three degrees hotter, and that the Old Man was getting into a rare old state. At three bells I went forward to have a look over the bows, and a chin with Stevenson, whose lookout it was. On gaining the forecastle head, I went to the side and looked down into the water. Stevenson came over and stood beside me.

"Rum go, this," he grumbled.

He stood by my side for a time in silence; we seemed to be hypnotised by the gleaming surface of the sea. Suddenly out of the depths, right before us, there arose a monstrous black face. It was like a frightful caricature of a human countenance. For a moment we gazed petrified; my blood seemed to suddenly turn to ice water; I was unable to move. With a mighty effort of will, I regained my self-control and, grasping Stevenson's arm, I found I could do no more than croak, my powers of speech seemed gone. "Look!" I gasped. "Look!"

Stevenson continued to stare into the sea, like a man turned to stone. He seemed to stoop further over, as if to examine the thing more closely. "Lord," he exclaimed, "it must be the devil himself!"

As though the sound of his voice had broken a spell, the thing disappeared. My companion looked at me, while I rubbed my eyes, thinking that I had been asleep, and that the awful vision had been a frightful nightmare. One look at my friend, however, disabused me of any such thought. His face wore a puzzled expression.

"Better go aft and tell the Old Man," he faltered.

I nodded and left the forecastle head, making my way aft like one in a trance. The skipper and the mate were standing at the break of the poop, and running up the ladder I told them what we had seen.

"Bosh!" sneered the Old Man. "You've been looking at your own ugly reflection in the water."

Nevertheless, in spite of his ridicule, he questioned me closely. Finally he ordered the mate forward to see if he could see anything. The latter, however, returned in a few moments, to report that nothing unusual could be seen. Four bells were struck, and we were relieved for tea. Coming on deck afterward, I found the men clustered together forward. The sole topic of conversation with them was the thing that Stevenson and I had seen.

"I suppose, Darky, it couldn't have been a reflection by any chance, could it?" one of the older men asked.

"Ask Stevenson," I replied as I made my way aft.

At eight bells, my watch came on deck again, to find that nothing further had developed. But, about an hour before midnight, the mate, thinking to have a smoke, sent me to his room for a box of matches with which to light his pipe. It took me no time to clatter down the brass-treaded ladder, and back to the poop, where I handed him the desired article.

Taking the box, he removed a match and struck it on the heel of his boot. As he did so, far out in the night a muffled screaming arose. Then came a clamour as of hoarse braying, like an ass but considerably deeper, and with a horribly suggestive human note running through it.

"Good God! Did you hear that, Darky?" asked the mate in awed tones.

"Yes, sir," I replied, listening – and scarcely noticing his question – for a repetition of the strange sounds. Suddenly the frightful bellowing broke out afresh. The mate's pipe fell to the deck with a clatter.

"Run for'ard!" he cried. "Quick, now, and see if you can see anything."

With my heart in my mouth, and pulses pounding madly I raced forward. The watch were all up on the forecastle head, clustered around the lookout. Each man was talking and gesticulating wildly. They became silent, and turned questioning glances towards me as I shouldered my way among them.

"Have you seen anything?" I cried.

Before I could receive an answer, a repetition of the horrid sounds broke out again, profaning the night with their horror. They seemed to have definite direction now, in spite of the fog that enveloped us. Undoubtedly, too, they were nearer. Pausing a moment to make sure of their bearing, I hastened aft and reported to the mate. I told him that nothing could be seen, but that the sounds apparently came from right ahead of us. On hearing this he ordered the man at the wheel to let the ship's head come off a couple of points. A moment later a shrill screaming tore its way through the night, followed by the hoarse braying sounds once more.

"It's close on the starboard bow!" exclaimed the mate, as he beckoned the helmsman to let her head come off a little more. Then, singing out for the watch, he ran forward, slacking the lee braces on the way. When he had the yards trimmed to his satisfaction on the new course, he returned to the poop and hung far out over the rail listening intently. Moments passed that seemed like hours, yet the silence remained unbroken. Suddenly the sounds began again, and so close that it seemed as though they must be right aboard of us. At this time I noticed a strange booming note mingled with the brays. And once or twice there came a sound that can only be described as a sort of "gug, gug". Then would come a wheezy whistling, for all the world like an asthmatic person breathing.

All this while the moon shone wanly through the steam, which seemed to me to be somewhat thinner. Once the mate gripped me by the shoulder as the noises rose and fell again. They now seemed to be coming from a point broad on our beam. Every eye on the ship was straining into the mist, but with no result. Suddenly one of the men cried out, as something long and black slid past us into the fog astern. From it there rose four indistinct and ghostly towers, which resolved themselves into spars and ropes, and sails.

"A ship! It's a ship!" we cried excitedly. I turned to Mr. Gray; he, too, had seen something, and was staring aft into the wake. So ghostlike, unreal, and fleeting had been our glimpse of the stranger, that we were not sure that we had seen an honest, material ship, but thought that we had been vouchsafed a vision of some phantom vessel like the Flying Dutchman. Our sails gave a sudden flap, the clew irons flogging the bulwarks with hollow thumps. The mate glanced aloft.

"Wind's dropping," he growled savagely. "We shall never get out of this infernal place at this gait!"

Gradually the wind fell until it was a flat calm. No sound broke the deathlike silence save the rapid patter of the reef points, as she gently rose and fell on the light swell. Hours passed, and the watch was relieved and I then went below. At seven bells we were called again, and as I went along the deck to the galley, I noticed that the fog seemed thinner, and the air cooler. When eight bells were struck I relieved Hansard at coiling down the ropes. From him I learned that the steam had begun to clear about four bells, and that the temperature of the sea had fallen ten degrees.

In spite of the thinning mist, it was not until about a half an hour later that we were able to get a glimpse of the surrounding sea. It was still mottled with dark patches, but the bubbling and popping had ceased. As much of the surface of the ocean as could be seen had a peculiarly desolate aspect. Occasionally a wisp of steam would float up from the nearer sea, and roll undulatingly across its silent surface, until lost in the vagueness that still held the hidden horizon. Here and there columns of steam rose up in pillars, which gave me the impression that the sea was hot in patches. Crossing to the starboard side and looking over, I found that conditions there were similar to those to port. The desolate aspect of the sea filled me with an idea of chilliness, although the air was quite warm and muggy. From the break of the poop the mate called to me to get his glasses.

When I had done this, he took them from me and walked to the taffrail. Here he stood for some moments polishing them with his handkerchief. After a moment he raised them to his eyes, and peered long and intently into the mist astern. I stood for some time staring at the point on which the mate had focused his glasses. Presently something shadowy grew upon my vision. Steadily watching it, I distinctly saw the outlines of a ship take form in the fog.

"See!" I cried, but even as I spoke, a lifting wraith of mist disclosed to view a great four-masted bark lying becalmed with all sails set, within a few hundred yards of our stern. As though a curtain had been raised, and then allowed to fall, the fog once more settled down, hiding the strange bark from our sight. The mate was all excitement, striding with quick, jerky steps, up and down the poop, stopping every few moments to peer through his glasses at the point where the four-master had disappeared in the fog. Gradually, as the mists dispersed again, the vessel could be seen more plainly, and it was then that we got an inkling of the cause of the dreadful noises during the night.

For some time the mate watched her silently, and as he watched the conviction grew upon me that in spite of the mist, I could detect some sort of movement on board of her. After some time had passed, the doubt became a certainty, and I could also see a sort of splashing in the water alongside of her. Suddenly the mate put his glasses on top of the wheel box and told me to bring him the speaking trumpet. Running to the companionway, I secured the trumpet and was back at his side.

The mate raised it to his lips, and taking a deep breath, sent a hail across the water that should have awakened the dead. We waited tensely for a reply. A moment later a deep, hollow mutter came from the bark; higher and louder it swelled, until we realised that we were listening to the same sounds we had heard the night before. The mate stood aghast at this answer to his hail; in a voice barely more than a hushed whisper, he bade me call the Old Man. Attracted by the mate's hail and its unearthly reply, the watch had all come aft and were clustered in the mizzen rigging in order to see better.

After calling the captain, I returned to the poop, where I found the second and third mates talking with the chief. All were engaged in trying to pierce the clouds of mist that half hid our strange consort and to arrive at some explanation of the strange phenomena of the past few hours. A moment later the captain appeared carrying his telescope. The mate gave him a brief account of the state of affairs and handed him the trumpet. Giving me the telescope to hold, the captain hailed the shadowy bark. Breathlessly we all listened, when again, in answer to the Old Man's hail, the frightful sounds rose on the still morning air. The skipper lowered the trumpet and stood with an expression of astonished horror on his face.

"Lord!" he exclaimed. "What an ungodly row!"

At this, the third, who had been gazing through his binoculars, broke the silence.

"Look," he ejaculated. "There's a breeze coming up astern." At his words the captain looked up quickly, and we all watched the ruffling water.

"That packet yonder is bringing the breeze with her," said the skipper. "She'll be alongside in half an hour!"

Some moments passed, and the bank of fog had come to within a hundred yards of our taffrail. The strange vessel could be distinctly seen just inside the fringe of the driving mist wreaths. After a short puff, the wind died completely, but as we stared with hypnotic fascination, the water astern of the stranger ruffled again with a fresh catspaw. Seemingly with the flapping of her sails, she drew slowly up to us. As the leaden seconds passed, the big four-master approached us steadily. The light air had now reached us, and with a lazy lift of our sails, we, too, began to forge slowly through that weird sea. The bark was now within fifty yards of our stern, and she was steadily drawing nearer, seeming to be able to outfoot us with ease. As she came on she luffed sharply, and came up into the wind with her weather leeches shaking.

I looked towards her poop, thinking to discern the figure of the man at the wheel, but the mist coiled around her quarter, and objects on the after end of her became indistinguishable. With a rattle of chain sheets on her iron yards, she filled away again. We meanwhile had gone ahead, but it was soon evident that she was the better sailor, for she came up to us hand over fist. The wind rapidly freshened and the mist began to drift away before it, so that each moment her spars and cordage became more plainly visible. The skipper and the mates were watching her intently when an almost simultaneous exclamation of fear broke from them.

"My God!"

And well they might show signs of fear, for crawling about the bark's deck were the most horrible creatures I had ever seen. In spite of their unearthly strangeness there was something vaguely familiar about them. Then it came to me that the face that Stevenson and I had seen during he night belonged to one of them. Their bodies had something of the shape of a seal's, but of a dead, unhealthy white. The lower part of the body ended in a sort of double-curved tail on which they appeared to be able to shuffle about. In place of arms, they had two long, snaky feelers, at the ends of which were two very humanlike hands, which were equipped with talons instead of nails. Fearsome indeed were these parodies of human beings!

Their faces, which, like their tentacles, were black, were the most grotesquely human things about them, and the upper jaw closed into the lower, after the manner of the jaws of an octopus. I have seen men among certain tribes of natives who had faces uncommonly like theirs, but yet no native I had ever seen could have given me the extraordinary feeling of horror and revulsion I experienced towards these brutal-looking creatures.

"What devilish beasts!" burst out the captain in disgust.

With this remark he turned to the mates, and as he did so, the expressions on their faces told me that they had all realised what the presence of these bestial-looking brutes meant. If, as was doubtless the case, these creatures had boarded the bark and destroyed her crew, what would prevent them from doing the same with us? We were a smaller ship and had a smaller crew, and the more I thought of it the less I liked it.

We could now see the name on the bark's bow with the naked eye. It read Scottish Heath, while on her boats we could see the name bracketed with Glasgow, showing that she hailed from that port. It was a remarkable coincidence that she should have a slant from just the quarter in which yards were trimmed, as before we saw her she must have been drifting around with everything 'aback'. But now in this light air she was able to run along beside us with no one at her helm. But steering herself she was, and although at times she yawed wildly, she never got herself aback. As we gazed at her we noticed a sudden movement on board of her, and several of the creatures slid into the water.

"See! See! They've spotted us. They're coming for us!" cried the mate wildly.

It was only too true, scores of them were sliding into the sea, letting themselves down by means of their long tentacles. On they came, slipping by scores and hundreds into the water, and swimming towards us in droves. The ship was making about three knots, otherwise they would have caught us in a very few minutes. But they persevered, gaining slowly but surely, and drawing nearer and nearer. The long, tentacle-like arms rose out of the sea in hundreds, and the foremost ones were already within a score of yards of the ship before the Old Man bethought himself to shout to the mates to fetch up the half dozen cutlasses that comprised the ship's armoury. Then, turning to me, he ordered me to go down to his cabin and bring up the two revolvers out of the top drawer of the chart table, also a box of cartridges that was there.

When I returned with the weapons he loaded them and handed one to the mate. Meanwhile the pursuing creatures were coming steadily nearer, and soon half a dozen of the leaders were directly under our counter. Immediately the captain leaned over the rail and emptied his pistol into them, but without any apparent effect. He must have realised how puny and ineffectual his efforts were, for he did not reload his weapon.

Some dozens of the brutes had reached us, and as they did so, their tentacles rose into the air and caught our rail. I heard the third mate scream suddenly, and turning, I saw him dragged quickly to the rail, with a tentacle wrapped completely around him. Snatching a cutlass, the second mate hacked off the tentacle where it joined the body. A gout of blood splashed into the third mate's face, and he fell to the deck. A dozen more of those arms rose and wavered in the air, but they now seemed some yards astern of us. A rapidly widening patch of clear water appeared between us and the foremost of our pursuers, and we raised a wild shout of joy. The cause was soon apparent; for a fine fair wind had sprung up, and with the increase in its force, the Scottish Heath had got herself aback, while we were rapidly leaving the monsters behind us. The third mate rose to his feet with a dazed look, and as he did so something fell to the deck. I picked it up and found that it was the severed portion of the tentacle of the third's late adversary. With a grimace of disgust I tossed it into the sea, as I needed no reminder of that awful experience.

Three weeks later we anchored in San Francisco. There the captain made a full report of the affair to the authorities, with the result that a gunboat was despatched to investigate. Six weeks later she returned to report that she had been unable to find any signs, either of the ship herself or of the fearful creatures that had attacked her. And since then nothing, as far as I know, has ever been heard of the four-masted bark Scottish Heath, last seen by us in the possession of creatures that may rightly be called demons of the sea.

Whether she still floats, occupied by her hellish crew, or whether some storm has sent her to her last resting place beneath the waves is surely a matter of conjecture. Perchance on some dark, fog-bound night, a ship in that wilderness of waters may hear cries and sounds beyond those of the wailing of the winds. Then let them look to it, for it may be that the demons of the sea are near them.

If you enjoyed this, you might also like...
The Stone Ship, see page 365
The Boats of the 'Glen Carrig', see page 204

The Hog

Chapter I

WE HAD FINISHED dinner and Carnacki had drawn his big chair up to the fire, and started his pipe.

Jessop, Arkright, Taylor and I had each of us taken up our favourite positions, and waited for Carnacki to begin.

"What I'm going to tell you about happened in the next room," he said, after drawing at his pipe for a while. "It has been a terrible experience. Doctor Witton first brought the case to my notice. We'd been chatting over a pipe at the Club one night about an article in the Lancet, and Witton mentioned having just such a similar case in a man called Bains. I was interested at once. It was one of those cases of a gap or flaw in a man's protection barrier, I call it. A failure to be what I might term efficiently insulated – spiritually – from the outer monstrosities.

"From what I knew of Witton, I knew he'd be no use. You all know Witton. A decent sort, hard-headed, practical, stand-no-kind-of-nonsense sort of man, all right at his own job when that job's a fractured leg or a broken collarbone; but he'd never have made anything of the Bains case."

For a space Carnacki puffed meditatively at his pipe, and we waited for him to go on with his tale.

"I told Witton to send Bains to me," he resumed, "and the following Saturday he came up. A little sensitive man. I liked him as soon as I set eyes on him. After a bit, I got him to explain what was troubling him, and questioned him about what Doctor Witton had called his 'dreams'.

"'They're more than dreams,' he said, 'they're so real that they're actual experiences to me. They're simply horrible. And yet there's nothing very definite in them to tell you about. They generally come just as I am going off to sleep. I'm hardly over before suddenly I seem to have got down into some deep, vague place with some inexplicable and frightful horror all about me. I can never understand what it is, for I never see anything, only I always get a sudden knowledge like a warning that I have got down into some terrible place – a sort of hellplace I might call it, where I've no business ever to have wandered; and the warning is always insistent – even imperative – that I must get out, get out, or some enormous horror will come at me.'

"'Can't you pull yourself back?' I asked him. 'Can't you wake up?'

"'No,' he told me. 'That's just what I can't do, try as I will. I can't stop going along this labyrinth-of-hell as I call it to myself, towards some dreadful unknown Horror. The warning is repeated, ever so strongly – almost as if the live me of my waking moments was awake and aware. Something seems to warn me to wake up, that whatever I do I must wake, wake, and then my consciousness comes suddenly alive and I know that my body is there in the bed, but my essence or spirit is still down there in that hell, wherever it is, in a danger that is both unknown and inexpressible; but so overwhelming that my whole spirit seems sick with terror.'

"'I keep saying to myself all the time that I must wake up,' he continued, 'but it is as if my spirit is still down there, and as if my consciousness knows that some tremendous invisible Power is fighting against me. I know that if I do not wake then, I shall never wake up again, but go down deeper and deeper into some stupendous horror of soul destruction. So then I fight. My body lies in the bed there, and pulls. And the power down there in that labyrinth exerts itself too so that a feeling of despair, greater than any I have ever known on this earth, comes on me. I know that if I give way and cease to fight, and do not wake, then I shall pass out – out to that monstrous Horror which seems to be silently calling my soul to destruction.'

"'Then I make a final stupendous effort,' he continued, 'and my brain seems to fill my body like the ghost of my soul. I can even open my eyes and see with my brain, or consciousness, out of my own eyes. I can see the bedclothes, and I know just how I am lying in the bed; yet the real me is down in that hell in terrible danger. Can you get me?' he asked.

"'Perfectly,' I replied.

"'Well, you know,' he went on, 'I fight and fight. Down there in that great pit my very soul seems to shrink back from the call of some brooding horror that impels it silently a little further, always a little further round a visible corner, which if I once pass I know I shall never return again to this world. Desperately I fight brain and consciousness fighting together to help it. The agony is so great that I could scream were it not that I am rigid and frozen in the bed with fear.

"'Then, just when my strength seems almost gone, soul and body win, and blend slowly. And I lie there worn out with this terrible extraordinary fight. I have still a sense of a dreadful horror all about me, as if out of that horrible place some brooding monstrosity had followed me up, and hangs still and silent and invisible over me, threatening me there in my bed. Do I make it clear to you?' he asked. 'It's like some monstrous Presence.'

"'Yes,' I said. 'I follow you.'

"The man's forehead was actually covered with sweat, so keenly did he live again through the horrors he had experienced.

"After a while he continued:

"'Now comes the most curious part of the dream or whatever it is,' he said. 'There's always a sound I hear as I lie there exhausted in the bed. It comes while the bedroom is still full of the sort of atmosphere of monstrosity that seems to come up with me when I get out of that place. I hear the sound coming up out of that enormous depth, and it is always the noise of pigs – pigs grunting, you know. It's just simply dreadful. The dream is always the same. Sometimes I've had it every single night for a week, until I fight not to go to sleep; but, of course, I have to sleep sometimes. I think that's how a person might go mad, don't you?' he finished.

"I nodded, and looked at his sensitive face. Poor beggar! He had been through it, and no mistake.

"'Tell me some more,' I said. 'The grunting – what does it sound like exactly?'

"'It's just like pigs grunting,' he told me again. 'Only much more awful. There are grunts, and squeals and pighowls, like you hear when their food is being brought to them at a pig farm. You know those large pig farms where they keep hundreds of pigs.

All the grunts, squeals and howls blend into one brutal chaos of sound – only it isn't a chaos. It all blends in a queer horrible way. I've heard it. A sort of swinish clamouring melody that grunts and roars and shrieks in chunks of grunting sounds, all tied together with squealings and shot through with pig howls. I've sometimes thought there was a definite beat in it; for every now and again there comes a gargantuan GRUNT, breaking through the million pig-voiced roaring – a stupendous GRUNT that comes in with a beat. Can you understand me? It seems to shake everything... It's like a spiritual earthquake. The howling, squealing, grunting, rolling clamour of swinish noise coming up out of that place, and then the monstrous GRUNT rising up through it all, an ever-recurring beat out of the depth – the voice of the swine-mother of monstrosity beating up from below through that chorus of mad swine-hunger... It's no use! I can't explain it. No one ever could. It's just terrible! And I'm afraid you're saying to yourself that I'm in a bad way; that I want a change or a tonic; that I must buck up or I'll land myself in a madhouse. If only you could understand! Doctor Witton seemed to half understand, I thought; but I know he's only sent me to you as a sort of last hope. He thinks I'm booked for the asylum. I could tell it.'

"'Nonsense!' I said. 'Don't talk such rubbish. You're as sane as I am. Your ability to think clearly what you want to tell me, and then to transmit it to me so well that you compel my mental retina to see something of what you have seen, stands sponsor for your mental balance.'

"'I am going to investigate your case, and if it is what I suspect, one of those rare instances of a 'flaw' or 'gap' in your protective barrier (what I might call your spiritual insulation from the Outer Monstrosities) I've no doubt we can end the trouble. But we've got to go properly into the matter first, and there will certainly be danger in doing so.'

"'I'll risk it,' replied Bains. 'I can't go on like this any longer.'

"'Very well,' I told him. 'Go out now, and come back at five o'clock. I shall be ready for you then. And don't worry about your sanity. You're all right, and we'll soon make things safe for you again. Just keep cheerful and don't brood about it.'"

Chapter II

"I PUT in the whole afternoon preparing my experimenting room, across the landing there, for his case. When he returned at five o'clock I was ready for him and took him straight into the room.

"It gets dark now about six-thirty, as you know, and I had just nice time before it grew dusk to finish my arrangements. I prefer always to be ready before the dark comes.

"Bains touched my elbow as we walked into the room.

"'There's something I ought to have told you,' he said, looking rather sheepish. 'I've somehow felt a bit ashamed of it.'"

"'Out with it,' I replied.

"He hesitated a moment, then it came out with a jerk.

"'I told you about the grunting of the pigs,' he said. 'Well, I grunt too. I know it's horrible. When I lie there in bed and hear those sounds after I've come up, I just grunt back as if in reply. I can't stop myself. I just do it. Something makes me. I never told Doctor Witton that. I couldn't. I'm sure now you think me mad,' he concluded.

"He looked into my face, anxious and queerly ashamed.

"'It's only the natural sequence of the abnormal events, and I'm glad you told me,' I said, slapping him on the back. 'It follows logically on what you had already told me. I have had two cases that in some way resembled yours.'

"'What happened?' he asked me. 'Did they get better?'

"'One of them is alive and well today, Mr. Bains,' I replied. 'The other man lost his nerve, and fortunately for all concerned, he is dead.'

"I shut the door and locked it as I spoke, and Bains stared round, rather alarmed, I fancy, at my apparatus.

"'What are you going to do?' he asked. 'Will it be a dangerous experiment?'

"'Dangerous enough,' I answered, 'if you fail to follow my instructions absolutely in everything. We both run the risk of never leaving this room alive. Have I your word that I can depend on you to obey me whatever happens?'

"He stared round the room and then back at me.

"'Yes,' he replied. And, you know, I felt he would prove the right kind of stuff when the moment came.

"I began now to get things finally in train for the night's work. I told Bains to take off his coat and his boots. Then I dressed him entirely from head to foot in a single thick rubber combination-overall, with rubber gloves, and a helmet with ear-flaps of the same material attached.

"I dressed myself in a similar suit. Then I began on the next stage of the night's preparations.

"First I must tell you that the room measures thirty-nine feet by thirty-seven, and has a plain board floor over which is fitted a heavy, half-inch rubber covering.

"I had cleared the floor entirely, all but the exact centre where I had placed a glass-legged, upholstered table, a pile of vacuum tubes and batteries, and three pieces of special apparatus which my experiment required.

"'Now Bains,' I called, 'come and stand over here by this table. Don't move about. I've got to erect a protective 'barrier' round us, and on no account must either of us cross over it by even so much as a hand or foot, once it is built.'

"We went over to the middle of the room, and he stood by the glass-legged table while I began to fit the vacuum tubing together round us.

"I intended to use the new spectrum 'defence' which I have been perfecting lately. This, I must tell you, consists of seven glass vacuum circles with the red on the outside, and the colour circles lying inside it, in the order of orange, yellow, green, blue, indigo and violet.

"The room was still fairly light, but a slight quantity of dusk seemed to be already in the atmosphere, and I worked quickly.

"Suddenly, as I fitted the glass tubes together I was aware of some vague sense of nerve-strain, and glancing round at Bains who was standing there by the table I noticed him staring fixedly before him. He looked absolutely drowned in uncomfortable memories.

"'For goodness' sake stop thinking of those horrors,' I called out to him. 'I shall want you to think hard enough about them later; but in this specially constructed room it is better not to dwell on things of that kind till the barriers are up. Keep your mind on anything normal or superficial – the theatre will do – think about that last piece you saw at the Gaiety. I'll talk to you in a moment.'

"Twenty minutes later the 'barrier' was completed all round us, and I connected up the batteries. The room by this time was greying with the coming dusk, and the seven differently coloured circles shone out with extraordinary effect, sending out a cold glare.

"'By Jove!' cried Bains, 'that's very wonderful – very wonderful!'

"My other apparatus which I now began to arrange consisted of a specially made camera, a modified form of phonograph with ear-pieces instead of a horn, and a glass disc composed of many fathoms of glass vacuum tubes arranged in a special way. It had two wires leading to an electrode constructed to fit round the head.

"By the time I had looked over and fixed up these three things, night had practically come, and the darkened room shone most strangely in the curious upward glare of the seven vacuum tubes.

"'Now, Bains,' I said, 'I want you to lie on this table. Now put your hands down by your sides and lie quiet and think. You've just got two things to do,' I told him. 'One is to lie there and concentrate your thoughts on the details of the dream you are always having, and the other is not to move off this table whatever you see or hear, or whatever happens, unless I tell you. You understand, don't you?'

"'Yes,' he answered, 'I think you may rely on me not to make a fool of myself. I feel curiously safe with you somehow.'

"'I'm glad of that,' I replied. 'But I don't want you to minimise the possible danger too much. There may be horrible danger. Now, just let me fix this band on your head,' I added, as I adjusted the electrode. I gave him a few more instructions, telling him to concentrate his thoughts particularly upon the noises he heard just as he was waking, and I warned him again not to let himself fall asleep. 'Don't talk,' I said, 'and don't take any notice of me. If you find I disturb your concentration keep your eyes closed.'

"He lay back and I walked over to the glass disc, arranging the camera in front of it on its stand in such a way that the lens was opposite the centre of the disc.

"I had scarcely done this when a ripple of greenish light ran across the vacuum tubes of the disc. This vanished, and for maybe a minute there was complete darkness. Then the green light rippled once more across it – rippled and swung round, and began to dance in varying shades from a deep heavy green to a rank ugly shade; back and forward, back and forward.

"Every half second or so there shot across the varying greens a flicker of yellow, an ugly, heavy repulsive yellow, and then abruptly there came sweeping across the disc a great beat of muddy red. This died as quickly as it came, and gave place to the changing greens shot through by the unpleasant and ugly yellow hues. About every seventh second the disc was submerged, and the other colours momentarily blotted out by the great beat of heavy, muddy red which swept over everything.

"'He's concentrating on those sounds,' I said to myself, and I felt queerly excited as I hurried on with my operations. I threw a word over my shoulder to Bains.

"'Don't get scared, whatever happens,' I said. 'You're all right!'

"I proceeded now to operate my camera. It had a long roll of specially prepared paper ribbon in place of a film or plates. By turning the handle the roll passed through the machine exposing the ribbon.

"It took about five minutes to finish the roll, and during all that time the green lights predominated; but the dull heavy beat of muddy red never ceased to flow across the vacuum tubes of the disc at every seventh second. It was like a recurrent beat in some unheard and somehow displeasing melody.

"Lifting the exposed spool of paper ribbon out of the camera I laid it horizontally in the two 'rests' that I had arranged for it on my modified gramaphone. Where the paper had been acted upon by the varying coloured lights which had appeared on the disc, the prepared surface had risen in curious, irregular little waves.

"I unrolled about a foot of the ribbon and attached the loose end to an empty spool-roller (on the opposite side of the machine) which I had geared to the driving clockwork mechanism of the gramophone. Then I took the diaphragm and lowered it gently into place above the ribbon. Instead of the usual needle the diaphragm was fitted with a beautifully made metal-filament brush, about an inch broad, which just covered the whole breadth of the ribbon. This fine and fragile brush rested lightly on the prepared surface of the paper, and when I started the machine the ribbon began to pass under the brush, and as it passed, the delicate metal-filament 'bristles' followed every minute inequality of those tiny, irregular wave-like excrescences on the surface.

"I put the ear-pieces to my ears, and instantly I knew that I had succeeded in actually recording what Bains had heard in his sleep. In fact, I was even then hearing 'mentally' by means of his effort of memory. I was listening to what appeared to be the faint, far-off squealing and grunting of countless swine. It was extraordinary, and at the same time exquisitely horrible and vile. It frightened me, with a sense of my having come suddenly and unexpectedly too near to something foul and most abominably dangerous.

"So strong and imperative was this feeling that I twitched the ear-pieces out of my ears, and sat a while staring round the room trying to steady my sensations back to normality.

"The room looked strange and vague in the dull glow of light from the circles, and I had a feeling that a taint of monstrosity was all about me in the air. I remembered what Bains had told me of the feeling he'd always had after coming up out of 'that place' – as if some horrible atmosphere had followed him up and filled his bedroom. I understood him perfectly now – so much so that I had mentally used almost his exact phrase in explaining to myself what I felt.

"Turning round to speak to him I saw there was something curious about the centre of the 'defence'.

"Now, before I tell you fellows any more I must explain that there are certain, what I call 'focussing', qualities about this new 'defence' I've been trying.

"The Sigsand manuscript puts it something like this: 'Avoid diversities of colour; nor stand ye within the barrier of the colour lights; for in colour hath Satan a delight. Nor can he abide in the Deep if ye adventure against him armed with red purple. So be warned. Neither forget that in blue, which is God's colour in the Heavens, ye have safety.'

"You see, from that statement in the Sigsand manuscript I got my first notion for this new 'defence' of mine. I have aimed to make it a 'defence' and yet have 'focussing' or 'drawing' qualities such as the Sigsand hints at. I have experimented enormously, and I've proved that reds and purples – the two extreme colours of the spectrum – are fairly dangerous; so much so that I suspect they actually 'draw' or 'focus' the outside forces. Any action or 'meddling' on the part of the experimentalist is tremendously enhanced in its effect if the action is taken within barriers composed of these colours, in certain proportions and tints.

"In the same way blue is distinctly a 'general defence'. Yellow appears to be neutral, and green a wonderful protection within limits. Orange, as far as I can tell, is slightly attractive and indigo is dangerous by itself in a limited way, but in certain combinations with the other colours it becomes a very powerful 'defence'. I've not yet discovered a tenth of the possibilities of these circles of mine. It's a kind of colour organ upon which I seem to play a tune of colour combinations that can be either safe or infernal in its effects. You know I have a keyboard with a separate switch to each of the colour circles.

"Well, you fellows will understand now what I felt when I saw the curious appearance of the floor in the middle of the 'defence'. It looked exactly as if a circular shadow lay, not just on the floor, but a few inches above it. The shadow seemed to deepen and blacken at the centre even while I watched it. It appeared to be spreading from the centre outwardly, and all the time it grew darker.

"I was watchful, and not a little puzzled; for the combination of lights that I had switched on approximated a moderately safe 'general defence'. Understand, I had no intention of making a focus until I had learnt more. In fact, I meant that first investigation not to go beyond a tentative inquiry into the kind of thing I had got to deal with.

"I knelt down quickly and felt the floor with the palm of my hand, but it was quite normal to the feel, and that reassured me that there was no Saaaiti mischief abroad; for that is a form of danger which can involve, and make use of, the very material of the 'defence' itself. It can materialise out of everything except fire.

"As I knelt there I realised all at once that the legs of the table on which Bains lay were partly hidden in the ever blackening shadow, and my hands seemed to grow vague as I felt at the floor.

"I got up and stood away a couple of feet so as to see the phenomenon from a little distance. It struck me then that there was something different about the table itself. It seemed unaccountably lower.

"'It's the shadow hiding the legs,' I thought to myself. 'This promises to be interesting; but I'd better not let things go too far.'

"I called out to Bains to stop thinking so hard. 'Stop concentrating for a bit,' I said; but he never answered, and it occurred to me suddenly that the table appeared to be still lower.

"'Bains,' I shouted, 'stop thinking a moment.' Then in a flash I realised it. 'Wake up, man! Wake up!' I cried.

"He had fallen over asleep – the very last thing he should have done; for it increased the danger twofold. No wonder I had been getting such good results! The poor beggar was worn out with his sleepless nights. He neither moved nor spoke as I strode across to him.

"'Wake up!' I shouted again, shaking him by the shoulder.

"My voice echoed uncomfortably round the big empty room; and Bains lay like a dead man.

"As I shook him again I noticed that I appeared to be standing up to my knees in the circular shadow. It looked like the mouth of a pit. My legs, from the knees downwards, were vague. The floor under my feet felt solid and firm when I stamped on it; but all the same I had a feeling that things were going a bit too far, so striding across to the switchboard I switched on the 'full defence'.

"Stepping back quickly to the table I had a horrible and sickening shock. The table had sunk quite unmistakably. Its top was within a couple of feet of the floor, and the legs had that fore-shortened appearance that one sees when a stick is thrust into water. They looked vague and shadowy in the peculiar circle of dark shadows which had such an extraordinary resemblance to the black mouth of a pit. I could see only the top of the table plainly with Bains lying motionless on it; and the whole thing was going down, as I stared, into that black circle."

Chapter III

"**THERE WAS NOT** a moment to lose, and like a flash I caught Bains round his neck and body and lifted him clean up into my arms off the table. And as I lifted him he grunted like a great swine in my ear.

"The sound sent a thrill of horrible funk through me. It was just as though I held a hog in my arms instead of a human. I nearly dropped him. Then I held his face to the light and stared down at him. His eyes were half opened, and he was looking at me apparently as if he saw me perfectly.

"Then he grunted again. I could feel his small body quiver with the sound.

"I called out to him. 'Bains,' I said, 'can you hear me?'

"His eyes still gazed at me; and then, as we looked at each other, he grunted like a swine again.

"I let go one hand, and hit him across the cheek, a stinging slap.

"'Wake up, Bains!' I shouted. 'Wake up!' But I might have hit a corpse. He just stared up at me. And, suddenly I bent lower and looked into his eyes more closely. I never saw such a fixed, intelligent, mad horror as I saw there. It knocked out all my sudden disgust. Can you understand?

"I glanced round quickly at the table. It stood there at its normal height; and, indeed, it was in every way normal. The curious shadow that had somehow suggested to me the black mouth of the pit had vanished. I felt relieved; for it seemed to me that I had entirely broken up any possibility of a partial 'focus' by means of the full 'defence' which I had switched on.

"I laid Bains on the floor, and stood up to look round and consider what was best to do. I dared not step outside of the barriers, until any 'dangerous tensions' there might be in the room had been dissipated. Nor was it wise, even inside the full 'defence', to have him sleeping the kind of sleep he was in; not without certain preparations having been made first, which I had not made.

"I can tell you, I felt beastly anxious. I glanced down at Bains, and had a sudden fresh shock; for the peculiar circular shadow was forming all round him again, where he lay on the floor. His hands and face showed curiously vague, and distorted, as they might have looked through a few inches of faintly stained water. But his eyes were somehow clear to see. They were staring up, mute and terrible, at me, through that horrible darkening shadow.

"I stopped, and with one quick lift, tore him up off the floor into my arms, and for the third time he grunted like a swine, there in my arms. It was damnable.

"I stood up, in the barrier, holding Bains, and looked about the room again; then back at the floor. The shadow was still thick round about my feet, and I stepped quickly across to the other side of the table. I stared at the shadow, and saw that it had vanished; then I glanced down again at my feet, and had another shock; for the shadow was showing faintly again, all round where I stood.

"I moved a pace, and watched the shadow become invisible; and then, once more, like a slow stain, it began to grow about my feet.

"I moved again, a pace, and stared round the room, meditating a break for the door. And then, in that instant, I saw that this would be certainly impossible; for there was something indefinite in the atmosphere of the room – something that moved, circling slowly about the barrier.

"I glanced down at my feet, and saw that the shadow had grown thick about them. I stepped a pace to the right, and as it disappeared, I stared again round the big room and somehow it seemed tremendously big and unfamiliar. I wonder whether you can understand.

"As I stared I saw again the indefinite something that floated in the air of the room. I watched it steadily for maybe a minute. It went twice completely round the barrier in that time. And, suddenly, I saw it more distinctly. It looked like a small puff of black smoke.

"And then I had something else to think about; for all at once I was aware of an extraordinary feeling of vertigo, and in the same moment, a sense of sinking – I was sinking bodily. I literally sickened as I glanced down, for I saw in that moment that I had gone down, almost up to my thighs into what appeared to be actually the shadowy, but quite unmistakable, mouth of a pit. Do you understand? I was sinking down into this thing, with Bains in my arms.

"A feeling of furious anger came over me, and I swung my right boot forward with a fierce kick. I kicked nothing tangible, for I went clean through the side of the shadowy thing, and fetched up against the table, with a crash. I had come through something that made all my skin creep and tingle – an invisible, vague something which resembled an electric tension. I felt that if it had been stronger, I might not have been able to charge through as I had. I wonder if I make it clear to you?

"I whirled round, but the beastly thing had gone; yet even as I stood there by the table, the slow greying of a circular shadow began to form again about my feet.

"I stepped to the other side of the table, and leaned against it for a moment: for I was shaking from head to foot with a feeling of extraordinary horror upon me, that was in some way, different from any kind of horror I have ever felt. It was as if I had in that one moment been near something no human has any right to be near, for his soul's sake. And abruptly, I wondered whether I had not felt just one brief touch of the horror that the rigid Bains was even then enduring as I held him in my arms.

"Outside of the barrier there were now several of the curious little clouds. Each one looked exactly like a little puff of black smoke. They increased as I watched them, which I did for several minutes; but all the time as I watched, I kept moving from one part to another of the 'defence', so as to prevent the shadow forming round my feet again.

"Presently, I found that my constant changing of position had resolved into a slow monotonous walk round and round, inside the 'defence'; and all the time I had to carry the unnaturally rigid body of poor Bains.

"It began to tire me; for though he was small, his rigidity made him dreadfully awkward and tiring to hold, as you can understand; yet I could not think what else to do; for I had stopped shaking him, or trying to wake him, for the simple reason that he was as wide awake as I was mentally; though but physically inanimate, through one of those partial spiritual disassociations which he had tried to explain to me.

"Now I had previously switched out the red, orange, yellow and green circles, and had on the full defence of the blue end of the spectrum – I knew that one of the repelling vibrations of each of the three colours: blue, indigo and violet were beating out protectingly into space; yet they were proving insufficient, and I was in the position of having either to take some desperate action to stimulate Bains to an even greater effort of will than I judged him to be making, or else to risk experimenting with fresh combinations of the defensive colours.

"You see, as things were at that moment, the danger was increasing steadily; for plainly, from the appearance of the air of the room outside the barrier, there were some mighty dangerous tensions generating. While inside the danger was also increasing; the steady recurrence of the shadow proving that the 'defence' was insufficient.

"In short, I feared that Bains in his peculiar condition was literally a 'doorway' into the 'defence'; and unless I could wake him or find out the correct combinations of circles necessary to set up stronger repelling vibrations against that particular danger, there were very ugly possibilities ahead. I felt I had been incredibly rash not to have foreseen the possibility of Bains falling asleep under the hypnotic effect of deliberately paralleling the associations of sleep.

"Unless I could increase the repulsion of the barriers or wake him there was every likelihood of having to choose between a rush for the door – which the condition of the atmosphere outside the barrier showed to be practically impossible – or of throwing him outside the barrier, which, of course, was equally not possible.

"All this time I was walking round and round inside the barrier, when suddenly I saw a new development of the danger which threatened us. Right in the centre of the 'defence' the shadow had formed into an intensely black circle, about a foot wide.

"This increased as I looked at it. It was horrible to see it grow. It crept out in an ever widening circle till it was quite a yard across.

"Quickly I put Bains on the floor. A tremendous attempt was evidently going to be made by some outside force to enter the 'defence', and it was up to me to make a final effort to help Bains to 'wake up'. I took out my lancet, and pushed up his left coat sleeve.

"What I was going to do was a terrible risk, I knew, for there is no doubt that in some extraordinary fashion blood attracts.

"The Sigsand mentions it particularly in one passage which runs something like this: 'In blood there is the Voice which calleth through all space. Ye Monsters in ye Deep hear, and hearing, they lust. Likewise hath it a greater power to reclaim backward ye soul that doth wander foolish adrift from ye body in which it doth have natural abiding. But woe unto him that doth spill ye blood in ye deadly hour; for there will be surely Monsters that shall hear ye Blood Cry.'

"That risk I had to run. I knew that the blood would call to the outer forces; but equally I knew that it should call even more loudly to that portion of Bains' 'Essence' that was adrift from him, down in those depths.

"Before lancing him, I glanced at the shadow. It had spread out until the nearest edge was not more than two feet away from Bains' right shoulder; and the edge was creeping nearer, like the blackening edge of burning paper, even while I stared. The whole thing had a less shadowy, less ghostly appearance than at any time before. And it looked simply and literally like the black mouth of a pit.

"'Now, Bains,' I said, 'pull yourself together, man. Wake up!' And at the same time as I spoke to him, I used my lancet quickly but superficially.

"I watched the little red spot of blood well up, then trickle round his wrist and fall to the floor of the 'defence'. And in the moment that it fell the thing that I had feared happened. There was a sound like a low peal of thunder in the room, and curious deadly-looking flashes of light rippled here and there along the floor outside the barrier.

"Once more I called to him, trying to speak firmly and steadily as I saw that the horrible shadowy circle had spread across every inch of the floor space of the centre of the 'defence', making it appear as if both Bains and I were suspended above an unutterable black void – the black void that stared up at me out of the throat of that shadowy pit. And yet, all the time I could feel the floor solid under my knees as I knelt beside Bains holding his wrist.

"'Bains!' I called once more, trying not to shout madly at him. 'Bains, wake up! Wake up, man! Wake up!'"

"But he never moved, only stared up at me with eyes of quiet horror that seemed to be looking at me out of some dreadful eternity."

Chapter IV

"BY THIS TIME the shadow had blackened all around us, and I felt that strangely terrible vertigo coming over me again. Jumping to my feet I caught up Bains in my arms and stepped over the first of the protective circles – the violet, and stood between it and the indigo circle, holding Bains as close to me as possible so as to prevent any portion of his helpless body from protruding outside the indigo and blue circles.

"From the black shadowy mouth which now filled the whole of the centre of the 'defence' there came a faint sound – not near but seeming to come up at me out of unknown abysses. Very, very faint and lost it sounded, but I recognised it as unmistakably the infinitely remote murmur of countless swine.

"And that same moment Bains, as if answering the sound, grunted like a swine in my arms.

"There I stood between the glass vacuum tubes of the circles, gazing dizzily into that black shadowy pit-mouth, which seemed to drop sheer into hell from below my left elbow.

"Things had gone so utterly beyond all that I had thought of, and it had all somehow come about so gradually and yet so suddenly, that I was really a bit below my natural self. I felt mentally paralysed, and could think of nothing except that not twenty feet away was the door and the outer natural world; and here was I face to face with some unthought-of danger, and all adrift, what to do to avoid it.

"You fellows will understand this better when I tell you that the bluish glare from the three circles showed me that there were now hundreds and hundreds of those small smoke-like puffs of black cloud circling round and round outside the barrier in an unvarying, unending procession.

"And all the time I was holding the rigid body of Bains in my arms, trying not to give way to the loathing that got me each time he grunted. Every twenty or thirty seconds he grunted, as if in answer to the sounds which were almost too faint for my normal hearing. I can tell you, it was like holding something worse than a corpse in my arms, standing there balanced between physical death on the one side and soul destruction on the other.

"Abruptly, from out of the deep that lay so close that my elbow and shoulder overhung it, there came again a hint, marvellously faint murmur of swine, so utterly far away that the sound was as remote as a lost echo.

"Bains answered it with a pig-like squeal that set every fibre in me protesting in sheer human revolt, and I sweated coldly from head to foot. Pulling myself together I tried to pierce down into the mouth of the great shadow when, for the second time, a low peel of thunder sounded in the room, and every joint in my body seemed to jolt and burn.

"In turning to look down the pit I had allowed one of Bains' heels to protrude for a moment slightly beyond the blue circle, and a fraction of the 'tension' outside the barrier had evidently discharged through Bains and me. Had I been standing directly inside the 'defence' instead of being 'insulated' from it by the violet circle, then no doubt things might have been much more serious. As it was, I had, psychically, that dreadful soiled feeling which the healthy human always experiences when he comes too closely in contact with certain Outer Monstrosities. Do you fellows remember how I had just the same feeling when the Hand came too near me in the 'Gateway' case?

"The physical effects were sufficiently interesting to mention; for Bains' left boot had been ripped open, and the leg of his trousers was charred to the knee, while all around the leg were numbers of bluish marks in the form of irregular spirals.

"I stood there holding Bains, and shaking from head to foot. My head ached and each joint had a queer numbish feeling; but my physical pains were nothing compared with my mental distress. I felt that we were done! I had no room to turn or move for the space between the violet circle which was the innermost, and the blue circle which was the outermost of those in use was thirty-one inches, including the one inch of the indigo circle. So you see I was forced to stand there like an image, fearing each moment lest I should get another shock, and quite unable to think what to do.

"I daresay five minutes passed in this fashion. Bains had not grunted once since the 'tension' caught him, and for this I was just simply thankful; though at first I must confess I had feared for a moment that he was dead.

"No further sounds had come up out of the black mouth to my left, and I grew steady enough again to begin to look about me, and think a bit. I leant again so as to look directly down into the shadowy pit. The edge of the circular mouth was now quite defined, and had a curious solid look, as if it were formed out of some substance like black glass.

"Below the edge, I could trace the appearance of solidity for a considerable distance, though in a vague sort of way. The centre of this extraordinary phenomenon was simple and unmitigated blackness – an utter velvety blackness that seemed to soak the very light out of the room down into it. I could see nothing else, and if anything else came out of it except a complete silence, it was the atmosphere of frightening suggestion that was affecting me more and more every minute.

"I turned away slowly and carefully, so as not to run any risks of allowing either Bains or myself to expose any part of us over the blue circle. Then I saw that things outside of the blue circle had developed considerably; for the odd, black puffs of smoke-like cloud had increased enormously and blent into a great, gloomy, circular wall of tufted cloud, going round and round and round eternally, and hiding the rest of the room entirely from me.

"Perhaps a minute passed, while I stared at this thing; and then, you know, the room was shaken slightly. This shaking lasted for three or four seconds, and then passed; but it came again in about half a minute, and was repeated from time to time. There was a queer oscillating quality in the shaking, that made me think suddenly of that Jarvee Haunting case. You remember it?

"There came again the shaking, and a ripple of deadly light seemed to play round the outside of the barrier; and then, abruptly, the room was full of a strange roaring – a brutish enormous yelling, grunting storm of swine-sounds.

"They fell away into a complete silence, and the rigid Bains grunted twice in my arms, as if answering. Then the storm of swine noise came again, beating up in a gigantic riot of brute sound that roared through the room, piping, squealing, grunting, and howling. And as it sank with a steady declination, there came a single gargantuan grunt out of some dreadful throat of monstrousness, and in one beat, the crashing chorus of unknown millions of swine came thundering and raging through the room again.

"There was more in that sound than mere chaos – there was a mighty devilish rhythm in it. Suddenly, it swept down again into a multitudinous swinish whispering and minor gruntings of unthinkable millions; and then with a rolling deafening bellow of sound came the single vast grunt. And, as if lifted upon it the swine roar of the millions of the beasts beat up through the room again; and at every seventh second, as I knew well enough without the need of the watch on my wrist, came the single storm beat of the great grunt out of the throat of unknowable monstrosity – and in my arms, Bains, the human, grunted in time to the swine melody – a rigid grunting monster there in my two arms.

"I tell you from head to foot I shook and sweated. I believe I prayed; but if I did I don't know what I prayed. I have never before felt or endured just what I felt, standing there in that thirty-one-inch space, with that grunting thing in my arms, and the hell melody beating up out of the great Deeps: and to my right, 'tensions' that would have torn me into a bundle of blazing tattered flesh, if I had jumped out over the barriers.

"And then, with an effect like a clap of unexpected thunder, the vast storm of sound ceased; and the room was full of silence and an unimaginable horror.

"This silence continued. I want to say something which may sound a bit silly; but the silence seemed to trickle round the room. I don't know why I felt it like that; but my words give you just what I seemed to feel, as I stood there holding the softly grunting body of Bains.

"The circular, gloomy wall of dense black cloud enclosed the barrier as completely as ever, and moved round and round and round, with a slow, 'eternal' movement. And at the back of that black wall of circling cloud, a dead silence went trickling round the room, out of my sight. Do you understand at all…?

"It seemed to me to show very clearly the state of almost insane mental and psychic tension I was enduring… The way in which my brain insisted that the silence was trickling round the room, interests me enormously; for I was either in a state approximating a phase of madness, or else I was, psychically, tuned to some abnormal pitch of awaredness and sensitiveness in which silence had ceased to be an abstract quality, and had become to me a definite concrete element, much as (to use a stupidly crude illustration), the invisible moisture of the atmosphere becomes a visible and concrete element when it becomes deposited as water. I wonder whether this thought attracts you as it does me?

"And then, you know, a slow awareness grew in me of some further horror to come. This sensation or knowledge or whatever it should be named, was so strong that I had a sudden feeling of suffocation… I felt that I could bear no more; and that if anything else happened, I should just pull out my revolver and shoot Bains through the head, and then myself, and so end the whole dreadful business.

"This feeling, however, soon passed; and I felt stronger and more ready to face things again. Also, I had the first, though still indefinite, idea of a way in which to make things a bit safer; but I was too dazed to see how to 'shape' to help myself efficiently.

"And then a low, far-off whining stole up into the room, and I knew that the danger was coming. I leant slowly to my left, taking care not to let Bains' feet stick over the blue circle, and stared down into the blackness of the pit that dropped sheer into some Unknown, from under my left elbow.

"The whining died; but far down in the blackness, there was something – just a remote luminous spot. I stood in a grim silence for maybe ten long minutes, and looked down at the thing. It was increasing in size all the time, and had become much plainer to see; yet it was still lost in the far, tremendous Deep.

"Then, as I stood and looked, the low whining sound crept up to me again, and Bains, who had lain like a log in my arms all the time, answered it with a long animallike whine, that was somehow newly abominable.

"A very curious thing happened then; for all around the edge of the pit, that looked so peculiarly like black glass, there came a sudden, luminous glowing. It came and went oddly, smouldering queerly round and round the edge in an opposite direction to the circling of the wall of black, tufted cloud on the outside of the barrier.

"This peculiar glowing finally disappeared, and, abruptly, out of the tremendous Deep, I was conscious of a dreadful quality or 'atmosphere' of monstrousness that was coming up out of the pit. If I said there had been a sudden waft of it, this would very well describe the actuality of it; but the spiritual sickness of distress that it caused me to feel, I am simply stumped to explain to you. It was something that made me feel I should be soiled to the very core of me, if I did not beat it off from me with my will.

"I leant sharply away from the pit towards the outer of the burning circles. I meant to see that no part of my body should overhang the pit whilst that disgusting power was beating up out of the unknown depths.

"And thus it was, facing so rigidly away from the centre of the 'defence', I saw presently a fresh thing; for there was something, many things, I began to think, on the other side of the gloomy wall that moved everlastingly around the outside of the barrier.

"The first thing I noticed was a queer disturbance of the ever circling cloud-wall. This disturbance was within eighteen inches of the floor, and directly before me. There was a curious, 'puddling' action in the misty wall; as if something were meddling with it. The area of this peculiar little disturbance could not have been more than a foot across, and it did not remain opposite to me; but was taken round by the circling of the wall.

"When it came past me again, I noticed that it was bulging slightly inwards towards me: and as it moved away from me once more, I saw another similar disturbance, and then a third and a fourth, all in different parts of the slowly whirling black wall; and all of them were no more than about eighteen inches from the floor.

"When the first one came opposite me again, I saw that the slight bulge had grown into a very distinct protuberance towards me.

"All around the moving wall, there had now come these curious swellings. They continued to reach inwards, and to elongate; and all the time they kept in a constant movement.

"Suddenly, one of them broke, or opened, at the apex, and there protruded through, for an instant, the tip of a pallid, but unmistakable snout. It was gone at once, but I had seen the thing distinctly; and within a minute, I saw another one poke suddenly through the wall, to my right, and withdraw as quickly. I could not look at the base of the strange, black, moving circle about the barrier without seeing a swinish snout peep through momentarily, in this place or that.

"I stared at these things in a very peculiar state of mind. There was so great a weight of the abnormal about me, before and behind and every way, that to a certain extent it bred in me a sort of antidote to fear. Can you understand? It produced in me a temporary dazedness in which things and the horror of things became less real. I stared at them, as a child stares out from a fast train at a quickly passing night-landscape, oddly hit by the furnaces of unknown industries. I want you to try to understand.

"In my arms Bains lay quiet and rigid; and my arms and back ached until I was one dull ache in all my body; but I was only partly conscious of this when I roused momentarily from my psychic to my physical awareness, to shift him to another position, less intolerable temporarily to my tired arms and back.

"There was suddenly a fresh thing – a low but enormous, solitary grunt came rolling, vast and brutal into the room. It made the still body of Bains quiver against me, and he grunted thrice in return, with the voice of a young pig.

"High up in the moving wall of the barrier, I saw a fluffing out of the black tufted clouds; and a pig's hoof and leg, as far as the knuckle, came through and pawed a moment. This was about nine or ten feet above the floor. As it gradually disappeared I heard a low grunting from the other side of the veil of clouds which broke out suddenly into a diafaeon of brute-sound, grunting, squealing and swine-howling; all formed into a sound that was the essential melody of the brute – a grunting, squealing howling roar that rose, roar by roar, howl by howl and squeal by squeal to a crescendo of horrors – the bestial growths, longings, zests and acts of some grotto of hell... It is no use, I can't give it to you. I get dumb with the failure of my command over speech to tell you what that grunting, howling, roaring melody conveyed to me. It had in it something so inexplicably below the horizons of the soul in its monstrousness and fearfulness that the ordinary simple fear of death itself, with all its attendant agonies and terrors and sorrows, seemed like a thought of something peaceful and infinitely holy compared with the fear of those unknown elements in that dreadful roaring melody. And the sound was with me inside the room – there right in the room with me. Yet I seemed not to be aware of confining walls, but of echoing spaces of gargantuan corridors. Curious! I had in my mind those two words – gargantuan corridors.

"As the rolling chaos of swine melody beat itself away on every side, there came booming through it a single grunt, the single recurring grunt of the Hog; for I knew now that I was actually and without any doubt hearing the beat of monstrosity, the Hog.

"In the Sigsand the thing is described something like this: 'Ye Hogge which ye Almighty alone hath power upon. If in sleep or in ye hour of danger ye hear the voice of ye Hogge, cease ye to meddle. For ye Hogge doth be of ye outer Monstrous Ones, nor shall any human come nigh him nor continue meddling when ye hear his voice, for in ye earlier life upon the world did the Hogge have power, and shall again in ye end. And in that ye Hogge had once a power upon ye earth, so doth he crave sore to come again. And dreadful shall be ye harm to ye soul if ye continue to meddle, and to let ye beast come nigh. And I say unto all, if ye have brought this dire danger upon ye, have memory of ye cross, for of all sign hath ye Hogge a horror.'

"There's a lot more, but I can't remember it all and that is about the substance of it.

"There was I holding Bains who was all the time howling that dreadful grunt out with the voice of a swine. I wonder I didn't go mad. It was, I believe, the antidote of dazedness produced by the strain which helped me through each moment.

"A minute later, or perhaps five minutes, I had a sudden new sensation, like a warning cutting through my dulled feelings. I turned my head; but there was nothing behind me, and bending over to my left I seemed to be looking down into that black depth which fell away sheer under my left elbow. At that moment the roaring bellow of swine-noise ceased and I seemed to be staring down into miles of black aether at something that hung there – a pallid face floating far down and remote – a great swine face.

"And as I gazed I saw it grow bigger. A seemingly motionless, pallid swine-face rising upward out of the depth. And suddenly I realised that I was actually looking at the Hog."

Chapter V

"FOR PERHAPS a full minute I stared down through the darkness at that thing swimming like some far-off, deadwhite planet in the stupendous void. And then I simply woke up bang, as you might say, to the possession of my faculties. For just a certain over-degree of strain had brought about the dumbly helpful anaesthesia of dazedness, so this sudden overwhelming supreme fact of horror produced, in turn, its reaction from inertness to action. I passed in one moment from listlessness to a fierce efficiency.

"I knew that I had, through some accident, penetrated beyond all previous 'bounds', and that I stood where no human soul had any right to be, and that in but a few of the puny minutes of earth's time I might be dead.

"Whether Bains had passed beyond the 'lines of retraction' or not, I could not tell. I put him down carefully but quickly on his side, between the inner circles – that is, the violet circle and the indigo circle – where he lay grunting slowly. Feeling that the dreadful moment had come I drew out my automatic. It seemed best to make sure of our end before that thing in the depth came any nearer: for once Bains in his present condition came within what I might term the 'inductive forces' of the monster, he would cease to be human. There would happen, as in that case of Aster who stayed outside the pentacles in the Black Veil Case, what can only be described as a pathological, spiritual change – literally in other words, soul destruction.

"And then something seemed to be telling me not to shoot. This sounds perhaps a bit superstitious; but I meant to kill Bains in that moment, and what stopped me was a distinct message from the outside.

"I tell you, it sent a great thrill of hope through me, for I knew that the forces which govern the spinning of the outer circle were intervening. But the very fact of the intervention proved to me afresh the enormous spiritual peril into which we had stumbled; for that inscrutable Protective Force only intervenes between the human soul and the Outer Monstrosities.

"The moment I received that message I stood up like a flash and turned towards the pit, stepping over the violet circle slap into the mouth of darkness. I had to take the risk in order to get at the switch board which lay on the glass shelf under the table top in the centre. I could not shake free from the horror of the idea that I might fall down through that awful blackness. The floor felt solid enough under me; but I seemed to be walking on nothing above a black void, like an inverted starless night, with the face of the approaching Hog rising up from far down under my feet – a silent, incredible thing out of the abyss – a pallid, floating swine-face, framed in enormous blackness.

"Two quick, nervous strides took me to the table standing there in the centre with its glass legs apparently resting on nothing. I grabbed out the switch board, sliding out the vulcanite plate which carried the switch-control of the blue circle. The battery which fed this circle was the right-hand one of the row of seven, and each battery was marked with the letter of its circle painted on it, so that in an emergency I could select any particular battery in a moment.

"As I snatched up the B switch I had a grim enough warning of the unknown dangers that I was risking in that short journey of two steps; for that dreadful sense of vertigo returned suddenly and for one horrible moment I saw everything through a blurred medium as if I were trying to look through water.

"Below me, far away down between my feet I could see the Hog which, in some peculiar way, looked different – clearer and much nearer, and enormous. I felt it had got nearer to me all in a moment. And suddenly I had the impression I was descending bodily.

"I had a sense of a tremendous force being used to push me over the side of that pit, but with every shred of will power I had in me I hurled myself into the smoky appearance that hid everything and reached the violet circle where Bains lay in front of me.

"Here I crouched down on my heels, and with my two arms out before me I slipped the nails of each forefinger under the vulcanite base of the blue circle, which I lifted very gently so that when the base was far enough from the floor I could push the tips of my fingers underneath. I took care to keep from reaching farther under than the inner edge of the glowing tube which rested on the two-inch-broad foundation of vulcanite.

"Very slowly I stood upright, lifting the side of the blue circle with me. My feet were between the indigo and the violet circles, and only the blue circle between me and sudden death; for if it had snapped with the unusual strain I was putting upon it by lifting it like that, I knew that I should in all probability go west pretty quickly.

"So you fellows can imagine what I felt like. I was conscious of a disagreeable faint prickling that was strongest in the tips of my fingers and wrists, and the blue circle seemed to vibrate strangely as if minute particles of something were impinging upon it in countless millions. Along the shining glass tubes for a couple of feet on each side of my hands a queer haze of tiny sparks boiled and whirled in the form of an extraordinary halo.

"Stepping forward over the indigo circle I pushed the blue circle out against the slowly moving wall of black cloud causing a ripple of tiny pale flashes to curl in over the circle. These flashes ran along the vacuum tube until they came to the place where the blue circle crossed the indigo, and there they flicked off into space with sharp cracks of sound.

"As I advanced slowly and carefully with the blue circle a most extraordinary thing happened, for the moving wall of cloud gave from it in a great belly of shadow, and appeared to thin away from before it. Lowering my edge of the circle to the floor I stepped over Bains and right into the mouth of the pit, lifting the other side of the circle over the table. It creaked as if it were about to break in half as I lifted it, but eventually it came over safely.

"When I looked again into the depth of that shadow I saw below me the dreadful pallid head of the Hog floating in a circle of night. It struck me that it glowed very slightly – just a vague luminosity. And quite near – comparatively. No one could have judged distances in that black void.

"Picking up the edge of the blue circle again as I had done before, I took it out further till it was half clear of the indigo circle. Then I picked up Bains and carried him to that portion of the floor guarded by the part of the blue circle which was clear of the 'defence'. Then I lifted the circle and started to move it forward as quickly as I dared, shivering each time the joints squeaked as the whole fabric of it groaned with the strain I was putting upon it. And all the time the moving wall of tufted clouds gave from the edge of the blue circle, bellying away from it in a marvellous fashion as if blown by an unheard wind.

"From time to time little flashes of light had begun to flick in over the blue circle, and I began to wonder whether it would be able to hold out the 'tension' until I had dragged it clear of the defence.

"Once it was clear I hoped the abnormal stress would cease from about us, and concentrate chiefly around the 'defence' again, and the attractions of the negative 'tension'.

"Just then I heard a sharp tap behind me, and the blue circle jarred somewhat, having now ridden completely over the violet and indigo circles, and dropped clear on to the floor. The same instant there came a low rolling noise as of thunder, and a curious roaring. The black circling wall had thinned away from around us and the room showed clearly once more, yet nothing was to be seen except that now and then a peculiar bluish flicker of light would ripple across the floor.

"Turning to look at the 'defence' I noticed it was surrounded by the circling wall of black cloud, and looked strangely extraordinary seen from the outside. It resembled a slightly swaying squat funnel of whirling black mist reaching from the floor to the ceiling, and through it I could see glowing, sometimes vague and sometimes plain, the indigo and violet circles. And then as I watched, the whole room seemed suddenly filled with an awful presence which pressed upon me with a weight of horror that was the very essence of spiritual deathliness.

"Kneeling there in the blue circle by Bains, my initiative faculties stupefied and temporarily paralysed, I could form no further plan of escape, and indeed I seemed to care for nothing at the moment. I felt I had already escaped from immediate destruction and I was strung up to an amazing pitch of indifference to any minor horrors.

"Bains all this while had been quietly lying on his side. I rolled him over and looked closely at his eyes, taking care on account of his condition not to gaze into them; for if he had passed beyond the 'line of retraction' he would be dangerous. I mean, if the 'wandering' part of his essence had been assimilated by the Hog, then Bains would be spiritually accessible and might be even then no more than the outer form of the man, charged with radiation of the monstrous ego of the Hog, and therefore capable of what

I might term for want of a more exact phrase, a psychically infective force; such force being more readily transmitted through the eyes than any other way, and capable of producing a brain storm of an extremely dangerous character.

"I found Bains, however, with both eyes with an extraordinary distressed interned quality; not the eyeballs, remember, but a reflex action transmitted from the 'mental eye' to the physical eye, and giving to the physical eye an expression of thought instead of sight. I wonder whether I make this clear to you?

"Abruptly, from every part of the room there broke out the noise of those hoofs again, making the place echo with the sound as if a thousand swine had started suddenly from an absolute immobility into a mad charge. The whole riot of animal sound seemed to heave itself in one wave towards the oddly swaying and circling funnel of black cloud which rose from floor to ceiling around the violet and indigo circles.

"As the sounds ceased I saw something was rising up through the middle of the 'defence'. It rose with a slow steady movement. I saw it pale and huge through the swaying, whirling funnel of cloud – a monstrous pallid snout rising out of that unknowable abyss… It rose higher like a huge pale mound. Through a thinning of the cloud curtain I saw one small eye… I shall never see a pig's eye again without feeling something of what I felt then. A pig's eye with a sort of hell-light of vile understanding shining at the back of it."

Chapter VI

"AND THEN suddenly a dreadful terror came over me, for I saw the beginning of the end that I had been dreading all along – I saw through the slow whirl of the cloud curtains that the violet circle had begun to leave the floor. It was being taken up on the spread of the vast snout.

"Straining my eyes to see through the swaying funnel of clouds I saw that the violet circle had melted and was running down the pale sides of the snout in streams of violet-coloured fire. And as it melted there came a change in the atmosphere of the room. The black funnel shone with a dull gloomy red, and a heavy red glow filled the room.

"The change was such as one might experience if one had been looking through a protective glass at some light and the glass had been suddenly removed. But there was a further change that I realised directly through my feelings. It was as if the horrible presence in the room had come closer to my own soul. I wonder if I am making it at all clear to you. Before, it had oppressed me somewhat as a death on a very gloomy and dreary day beats down upon one's spirit. But now there was a savage menace, and the actual feeling of a foul thing close up against me. It was horrible, simply horrible.

"And then Bains moved. For the first time since he went to sleep the rigidity went out of him, and rolling suddenly over on to his stomach he fumbled up in a curious animallike fashion, on to his hands and feet. Then he charged straight across the blue circle towards the thing in the 'defence'.

"With a shriek I jumped to pull him back; but it was not my voice that stopped him. It was the blue circle. It made him give back from it as though some invisible hand had jerked him backwards. He threw up his head like a hog, squealing with the voice of a swine, and started off round the inside of the blue circle. Round and round it he went, twice attempting to bolt across it to the horror in that swaying funnel of cloud. Each time he was thrown back, and each time he squealed like a great swine, the sounds echoing round the room in a horrible fashion as though they came from somewhere a long way off.

"By this time I was fairly sure that Bains had indeed passed the 'line of retraction', and the knowledge brought a fresh and more hopeless horror and pity to me, and a grimmer fear for myself. I knew that if it were so, it was not Bains I had with me in the circle but a monster, and that for my own last chance of safety I should have to get him outside of the circle.

"He had ceased his tireless running round and round, and now lay on his side grunting continually and softly in a dismal kind of way. As the slowly whirling clouds thinned a little I saw again that pallid face with some clearness. It was still rising, but slowly, very slowly, and again a hope grew in me that it might be checked by the 'defence'. Quite plainly I saw that the horror was looking at Bains, and at that moment I saved my own life and soul by looking down. There, close to me on the floor was the thing that looked like Bains, its hands stretched out to grip my ankles. Another second, and I should have been tripped outwards. Do you realise what that would have meant?

"It was no time to hesitate. I simply jumped and came down crash with my knees on top of Bains. He lay quiet enough after a short struggle; but I took off my braces and lashed his hands up behind him. And I shivered with the very touch of him, as though I was touching something monstrous.

"By the time I had finished I noticed that the reddish glow in the room had deepened quite considerably, and the whole room was darker. The destruction of the violet circle had reduced the light perceptibly; but the darkness that I am speaking of was something more than that. It seemed as if something now had come into the atmosphere of the room – a sort of gloom, and in spite of the shining of the blue circle and the indigo circle inside the funnel of cloud, there was now more red light than anything else.

"Opposite me the huge, cloud-shrouded monster in the indigo circle appeared to be motionless. I could see its outline vaguely all the time, and only when the cloud funnel thinned could I see it plainly – a vast, snouted mound, faintly and whitely luminous, one gargantuan side turned towards me, and near the base of the slope a minute slit out of which shone one whitish eye.

"Presently through the thin gloomy red vapour I saw something that killed the hope in me, and gave me a horrible despair; for the indigo circle, the final barrier of the defence, was being slowly lifted into the air – the Hog had begun to rise higher. I could see its dreadful snout rising upwards out of the cloud. Slowly, very slowly, the snout rose up, and the indigo circle went up with it.

"In the dead stillness of that room I got a strange sense that all eternity was tense and utterly still as if certain powers knew of this horror I had brought into the world… And then I had an awareness of something coming… something from far, far away. It was as if some hidden unknown part of my brain knew it. Can you understand? There was somewhere in the heights of space a light that was coming near. I seemed to hear it coming. I could just see the body of Bains on the floor, huddled and shapeless and inert. Within the swaying veil of cloud the monster showed as a vast pale, faintly luminous mound, hugely snouted – an infernal hillock of monstrosity, pallid and deadly amid the redness that hung in the atmosphere of the room.

"Something told me that it was making a final effort against the help that was coming. I saw the indigo circle was now some inches from the floor, and every moment

I expected to see it flash into streams of indigo fire running down the pale slopes of the snout. I could see the circle beginning to move upward at a perceptible speed. The monster was triumphing.

"Out in some realm of space a low continuous thunder sounded. The thing in the great heights was coming fast, but it could never come in time. The thunder grew from a low, far mutter into a deep steady rolling of sound… It grew louder and louder, and as it grew I saw the indigo circle, now shining through the red gloom of the room, was a whole foot off the floor. I thought I saw a faint splutter of indigo light… The final circle of the barrier was beginning to melt.

"That instant the thunder of the thing in flight which my brain heard so plainly, rose into a crashing, a worldshaking bellow of speed, making the room rock and vibrate to an immensity of sound. A strange flash of blue flame ripped open the funnel of cloud momentarily from top to base, and I saw for one brief instant the pallid monstrosity of the Hog, stark and pale and dreadful.

"Then the sides of the funnel joined again hiding the thing from me as the funnel became submerged quickly into a dome of silent blue light – God's own colour! All at once it seemed the cloud had gone, and from floor to ceiling of the room, in awful majesty, like a living Presence, there appeared that dome of blue fire banded with three rings of green light at equal distances. There was no sound or movement, not even a flicker, nor could I see anything in the light: for looking into it was like looking into the cold blue of the skies. But I felt sure that there had come to our aid one of those inscrutable forces which govern the spinning of the outer circle, for the dome of blue light, banded with three green bands of silent fire, was the outward or visible sign of an enormous force, undoubtedly of a defensive nature.

"Through ten minutes of absolute silence I stood there in the blue circle watching the phenomenon. Minute by minute I saw the heavy repellent red driven out of the room as the place lightened quite noticeably. And as it lightened, the body of Bains began to resolve out of a shapeless length of shadow, detail by detail, until I could see the braces with which I had lashed his wrists together.

"And as I looked at him his body moved slightly, and in a weak but perfectly sane voice he said:

"'I've had it again! My God! I've had it again!'

"I knelt down quickly by his side and loosened the braces from his wrists, helping him to turn over and sit up. He gripped my arm a little crazily with both hands.

"'I went to sleep after all,' he said. 'And I've been down there again. My God! It nearly had me. I was down in that awful place and it seemed to be just round a great corner, and I was stopped from coming back. I seemed to have been fighting for ages and ages. I felt I was going mad. Mad! I've been nearly down into a hell. I could hear you calling down to me from some awful height. I could hear your voice echoing along yellow passages. They were yellow. I know they were. And I tried to come and I couldn't.'

"'Did you see me?' I asked him when he stopped, gasping.

"'No,' he answered, leaning his head against my shoulder. 'I tell you it nearly got me that time. I shall never dare go to sleep again as long as I live. Why didn't you wake me?'

"'I did,' I told him. 'I had you in my arms most of the time. You kept looking up into my eyes as if you knew I was there.'

"'I know,' he said. 'I remember now; but you seemed to be up at the top of a frightful hole, miles and miles up from me, and those horrors were grunting and squealing and howling, and trying to catch me and keep me down there. But I couldn't see anything – only the yellow walls of those passages. And all the time there was something round the corner.'

"'Anyway, you're safe enough now,' I told him. 'And I'll guarantee you shall be safe in the future.'

"The room had grown dark save for the light from the blue circle. The dome had disappeared, the whirling funnel of black cloud had gone, the Hog had gone, and the light had died out of the indigo circle. And the atmosphere of the room was safe and normal again as I proved by moving the switch, which was near me, so as to lessen the defensive power of the blue circle and enable me to 'feel' the outside tension. Then I turned to Bains.

"'Come along,' I said. 'We'll go and get something to eat, and have a rest.'

"But Bains was already sleeping like a tired child, his head pillowed on his hand. 'Poor little devil!' I said as I picked him up in my arms. 'Poor little devil!'

"I walked across to the main switchboard and threw over the current so as to throw the 'V' protective pulse out of the four walls and the door; then I carried Bains out into the sweet wholesome normality of everything. It seemed wonderful, coming out of that chamber of horrors, and it seemed wonderful still to see my bedroom door opposite, wide open, with the bed looking so soft and white as usual – so ordinary and human. Can you chaps understand?

"I carried Bains into the room and put him on the couch; and then it was I realised how much I'd been up against, for when I was getting myself a drink I dropped the bottle and had to get another.

"After I had made Bains drink a glass I laid him on the bed.

"'Now,' I said, 'look into my eyes fixedly. Do you hear me? You are going off to sleep safely and soundly, and if anything troubles you, obey me and wake up. Now, sleep – sleep – sleep!'

"I swept my hands down over his eyes half a dozen times, and he fell over like a child. I knew that if the danger came again he would obey my will and wake up. I intend to cure him, partly by hypnotic suggestion, partly by a certain electrical treatment which I am getting Doctor Witton to give him.

"That night I slept on the couch, and when I went to look at Bains in the morning I found him still sleeping, so leaving him there I went into the test room to examine results. I found them very surprising.

"Inside the room I had a queer feeling, as you can imagine. It was extraordinary to stand there in that curious bluish light from the 'treated' windows, and see the blue circle lying, still glowing, where I had left it; and further on, the 'defence', lying circle within circle, all 'out'; and in the centre the glass-legged table standing where a few hours before it had been submerged in the horrible monstrosity of the Hog. I tell you, it all seemed like a wild and horrible dream as I stood there and looked. I have carried out some curious tests in there before now, as you know, but I've never come nearer to a catastrophe.

"I left the door open so as not to feel shut in, and then I walked over to the 'defence'. I was intensely curious to see what had happened physically under the action of such a force as the Hog. I found unmistakable signs that proved the thing had been indeed a Saaitii manifestation, for there had been no psychic or physical illusion about the melting of the violet circle. There remained nothing of it except a ring of patches of melted glass. The gutta base had been fused entirely, but the floor and everything was intact. You see, the Saaitii forms can often attack and destroy, or even make use of, the very defensive material used against them.

"Stepping over the outer circle and looking closely at the indigo circle I saw that it was melted clean through in several places. Another fraction of time and the Hog would have been free to expand as an invisible mist of horror and destruction into the atmosphere of the world. And then, in that very moment of time, salvation had come. I wonder if you can get my feelings as I stood there staring down at the destroyed barrier."

Carnacki began to knock out his pipe which is always a sign that he has ended his tale, and is ready to answer any questions we may want to ask.

Taylor was first in. "Why didn't you use the Electric Pentacle as well as your new spectrum circles?" he asked.

"Because," replied Carnacki, "the pentacle is simply 'defensive' and I wished to have the power to make a 'focus' during the early part of the experiment, and then, at the critical moment, to change the combination of the colours so as to have a 'defence' against the results of the 'focus'. You follow me.

"You see," he went on, seeing we hadn't grasped his meaning, "there can be no 'focus' within a pentacle. It is just of a 'defensive' nature. Even if I had switched the current out of the electric pentacle I should still have had to contend with the peculiar and undoubtedly 'defensive' power that its form seems to exert, and this would have been sufficient to 'blur' the focus.

"In this new research work I'm doing, I'm bound to use a 'focus' and so the pentacle is barred. But I'm not sure it matters. I'm convinced this new spectrum 'defence' of mine will prove absolutely invulnerable when I've learnt how to use it; but it will take me some time. This last case has taught me something new. I had never thought of combining green with blue; but the three bands of green in the blue of that dome has set me thinking. If only I knew the right combinations! It's the combinations I've got to learn. You'll understand better the importance of these combinations when I remind you that green by itself is, in a very limited way, more deadly than red itself – and red is the danger colour of all."

"Tell us, Carnacki," I said, "what is the Hog? Can you? I mean what kind of monstrosity is it? Did you really see it, or was it all some horrible, dangerous kind of dream? How do you know it was one of the outer monsters? And what is the difference between that sort of danger and the sort of thing you saw in the Gateway of the Monster case? And what…?"

"Steady!" laughed Carnacki. "One at a time! I'll answer all your questions; but I don't think I'll take them quite in your order. For instance, speaking about actually seeing the Hog, I might say that, speaking generally, things seen of a 'ghostly' nature are not seen with the eyes; they are seen with the mental eye which has this psychic quality, not always developed to a useable state, in addition to its 'normal' duty of revealing to the brain what our physical eyes record.

"You will understand that when we see 'ghostly' things it is often the 'mental' eye performing simultaneously the duty of revealing to the brain what the physical eye sees as well as what it sees itself. The two sights blending their functions in such a fashion gives us the impression that we are actually seeing through our physical eyes the whole of the 'sight' that is being revealed to the brain.

"In this way we get an impression of seeing with our physical eyes both the material and the immaterial parts of an 'abnormal' scene; for each part being received and revealed to the brain by machinery suitable to the particular purpose appears to have equal value of reality that is, it appears to be equally material. Do you follow me?"

We nodded our assent, and Carnacki continued:

"In the same way, were anything to threaten our psychic body we should have the impression, generally speaking, that it was our physical body that had been threatened, because our psychic sensations and impressions would be super-imposed upon our physical, in the same way that our psychic and our physical sight are super-imposed.

"Our sensations would blend in such a way that it would be impossible to differentiate between what we felt physically and what we felt psychically. To explain better what I mean. A man may seem to himself, in a 'ghostly' adventure, to fall actually. That is, to be falling in a physical sense; but all the while it may be his psychic entity, or being – call it what you will – that is falling. But to his brain there is presented the sensation of falling all together. Do you get me?

"At the same time, please remember that the danger is none the less because it is his psychic body that falls. I am referring to the sensation I had of falling during the time of stepping across the mouth of that pit. My physical body could walk over it easily and feel the floor solid under me; but my psychic body was in very real danger of falling. Indeed, I may be said to have literally carried my psychic body over, held within me by the pull of my lifeforce. You see, to my psychic body the pit was as real and as actual as a coal pit would have been to my physical body. It was merely the pull of my life-force which prevented my psychic body from falling out of me, rather like a plummet, down through the everlasting depths in obedience to the giant pull of the monster.

"As you will remember, the pull of the Hog was too great for my life-force to withstand, and, psychically, I began to fall. Immediately on my brain was recorded a sensation identical with that which would have been recorded on it had my actual physical body been falling. It was a mad risk I took, but as you know, I had to take it to get to the switch and the battery. When I had that physical sense of falling and seemed to see the black misty sides of the pit all around me, it was my mental eye recording upon the brain what it was seeing. My psychic body had actually begun to fall and was really below the edge of the pit but still in contact with me. In other words my physical magnetic and psychic 'haloes' were still mingled. My physical body was still standing firmly upon the floor of the room, but if I had not each time by effort or will forced my physical body across to the side, my psychic body would have fallen completely out of 'contact' with me, and gone like some ghostly meteorite, obedient to the pull of the Hog.

"The curious sensation I had of forcing myself through an obstructing medium was not a physical sensation at all, as we understand that word, but rather the psychic sensation of forcing my entity to re-cross the 'gap' that had already formed between my falling psychic body now below the edge of the pit and my physical body standing on the floor of the room. And that 'gap' was full of a force that strove to prevent my body and soul from rejoining. It was a terrible experience. Do you remember how I could still see with my brain through the eyes of my psychic body, though it had already fallen some distance out of me? That is an extraordinary thing to remember.

"However, to get ahead, all 'ghostly' phenomena are extremely diffuse in a normal state. They become actively physically dangerous in all cases where they are concentrated. The best off-hand illustration I can think of is the all-familiar electricity – a force which, by the way, we are too prone to imagine we understand because we've named and harnessed it, to use a popular phrase. But we don't understand it at all! It is still a complete fundamental mystery. Well, electricity when diffused is an 'imagined and unpictured something', but when concentrated it is sudden death. Have you got me in that?

"Take, for instance, that explanation, as a very, very crude sort of illustration of what the Hog is. The Hog is one of those million-mile-long clouds of 'nebulosity' lying in the Outer Circle. It is because of this that I term those clouds of force the Outer Monsters.

"What they are exactly is a tremendous question to answer. I sometimes wonder whether Dodgson there realises just how impossible it is to answer some of his questions," and Carnacki laughed.

"But to make a brief attempt at it. There is around this planet, and presumably others, of course, circles of what I might call 'emanation'. This is an extremely light gas, or shall I say ether. Poor ether, it's been hard worked in its time!

"Go back one moment to your school-days, and bear in mind that at one time the earth was just a sphere of extremely hot gases. These gases condensed in the form of materials and other 'solid' matters; but there are some that are not yet solidified – air, for instance. Well, we have an earth-sphere of solid matter on which to stamp as solidly as we like; and round about that sphere there lies a ring of gases the constituents of which enter largely into all life, as we understand life – that is, air.

"But this is not the only circle of gas which is floating round us. There are, as I have been forced to conclude, larger and more attenuated 'gas' belts lying, zone on zone, far up and around us. These compose what I have called the inner circles. They are surrounded in turn by a circle or belt of what I have called, for want of a better word, 'emanations'.

"This circle which I have named the Outer Circle cannot lie less than a hundred thousand miles off the earth, and has a thickness which I have presumed to be anything between five and ten million miles. I believe, but I cannot prove, that it does not spin with the earth but in the opposite direction, for which a plausible cause might be found in the study of the theory upon which a certain electrical machine is constructed.

"I have reason to believe that the spinning of this, the Outer Circle, is disturbed from time to time through causes which are quite unknown to me, but which I believe are based in physical phenomena. Now, the Outer Circle is the psychic circle, yet it is also physical. To illustrate what I mean I must again instance electricity, and say that just as electricity discovered itself to us as something quite different from any of our previous conceptions of matter, so is the Psychic or Outer Circle different from any of our previous conceptions of matter. Yet it is none the less physical in its origin, and in the sense that electricity is physical, the Outer or Psychic Circle is physical in its constituents. Speaking pictorially it is, physically, to the Inner Circle what the Inner Circle is to the upper strata of the air, and what the air – as we know that intimate gas – is to the waters and the waters to the solid world. You get my line of suggestion?"

We all nodded, and Carnacki resumed.

"Well, now let me apply all this to what I am leading up to. I suggest that these million-mile-long clouds of monstrosity which float in the Psychic or Outer Circle, are bred of the elements of that circle. They are tremendous psychic forces, bred out of its elements just as an octopus or shark is bred out of the sea, or a tiger or any other physical force is bred out of the elements of its earth-and-air surroundings.

"To go further, a physical man is composed entirely from the constituents of earth and air, by which terms I include sunlight and water and 'condiments'! In other words without earth and air he could not *be*! Or to put it another way, earth and air breed within themselves the materials of the body and the brain, and therefore, presumably, the machine of intelligence.

"Now apply this line of thought to the Psychic or Outer Circle which though so attenuated that I may crudely presume it to be approximate to our conception of aether, yet contains all the elements for the production of certain phases of force and intelligence. But these elements are in a form as little like matter as the emanations of scent are like the scent itself. Equally, the force-and-intelligence-producing capacity of the Outer Circle no more approximates to the life-and-intelligence – producing capacity of the earth and air than the results of the Outer Circle constituents resemble the results of earth and air. I wonder whether I make it clear.

"And so it seems to me we have the conception of a huge psychic world, bred out of the physical, lying far outside of this world and completely encompassing it, except for the doorways about which I hope to tell you some other evening. This enormous psychic world of the Outer Circle 'breeds' – if I may use the term, its own psychic forces and intelligences, monstrous and otherwise, just as this world produces its own physical forces and intelligences – beings, animals, insects, etc., monstrous and otherwise.

"The monstrosities of the Outer Circle are malignant towards all that we consider most desirable, just in the same way a shark or a tiger may be considered malignant, in a physical way, to all that we consider desirable. They are predatory – as all positive force is predatory. They have desires regarding us which are incredibly more dreadful to our minds when comprehended than an intelligent sheep would consider our desires towards its own carcass. They plunder and destroy to satisfy lusts and hungers exactly as other forms of existence plunder and destroy to satisfy their lusts and hungers. And the desire of these monsters is chiefly, if not always, for the psychic entity of the human.

"But that's as much as I can tell you tonight. Some evening I want to tell you about the tremendous mystery of the Psychic Doorways. In the meantime, have I made things a bit clearer to you, Dodgson?"

"Yes, and no," I answered. "You've been a brick to make the attempt, but there are still about ten thousand other things I want to know."

Carnacki stood up. "Out you go!" he said using the recognised formula in friendly fashion. "Out you go! I want a sleep."

And shaking him by the hand we strolled out on to the quiet Embankment.

If you enjoyed this, you might also like…
The House on the Borderland, see page 303
The Baumoff Explosive, see page 384

Biographies

William Hope Hodgson
William Hope Hodgson (1877–1918) was born in Essex, England, but moved several times with his family, including living for some time in County Galway, Ireland – a setting that would later inspire *The House on the Borderland*. Hodgson made several unsuccessful attempts to run away to sea, until his uncle secured him some work in the Merchant Marine. This association with the ocean would unfold later in his many sea stories. After some initial rejections of his writing, Hodgson managed to become a full-time writer of both novels and short stories, which form a fantastic legacy of adventure, mystery and horror fiction.

Jonathan Newell
Foreword: William Hope Hodgson Horror Stories
Jonathan Newell is an instructor at Langara College in Vancouver, Canada. A specialist in weird and Gothic fiction, his scholarship focuses on the links between affect and ontology in works of supernatural horror. His first book, *A Century of Weird Fiction, 1832–1937: Disgust, Metaphysics, and the Aesthetics of Cosmic Horror* from the University of Wales Press, traces the twisted entanglement of revulsion, ecstasy, mysticism, and ontological speculation through the works of authors like Algernon Blackwood, H.P. Lovecraft, and William Hope Hodgson.

Sources

Carnacki Tales

The Gateway of the Monster
Originally Published in *The Idler*, January 1910

The House Among the Laurels
Originally Published in *The Idler*, February 1910

The Whistling Room
Originally Published in *The Idler*, March 1910

The Horse of the Invisible
Originally Published in *The Idler*, April 1910

The Searcher of the End House
Originally Published in *The Idler*, June 1910

The Thing Invisible
Originally Published in *The New Magazine*, January 1912

The Haunted 'Jarvee'
Originally Published in *The Premier Magazine*, March 1929

Dangers at Sea

A Tropical Horror
Originally Published in *The Grand Magazine*, June 1905

From the Tideless Sea: Part One
Originally Published in *Monthly Story Magazine*, April 1906

From the Tideless Sea: Part Two – Further News of the Homebird
Originally Published in *The Blue Book Magazine*, August 1907

The Mystery of the Derelict
Originally Published in *The Story-teller*, July 1907

Through the Vortex of a Cyclone
Originally Published in *Cornhill Magazine*, November 1907

The Shamraken Homeward-Bounder
Originally Published in *Putnam's Monthly*, April 1908

The Finding of the Graiken
Originally Published in *The Red Magazine*, February 1913

The Sea Horses
Originally Published in *The London Magazine*, March 1913

The Real Thing: 'S.O.S.'
Originally Published in *Cornhill Magazine*, January 1917

The Boats of the 'Glen Carrig'

The Boats of the 'Glen Carrig'
Originally Published by Chapman and Hall, London, 1907

The Weird and Strange

The Goddess of Death
Originally Published in *The Royal Magazine*, April 1904

The Voice in the Night
Originally Published in *Blue Book*, November 1907

The House on the Borderland
Originally Published by Chapman and Hall, London, 1908

Out of the Storm
Originally Published in *Putnam's Monthly*, February 1909

The Thing in the Weeds
Originally Published in *The Story-teller*, January 1912

The Derelict
Originally Published in *The Red Magazine*, December 1912

The Stone Ship
Originally Published in *The Red Magazine*, July 1914
(as 'The Mystery of the Ship in the Night')

The Baumoff Explosive
Originally Published in *Nash's Weekly*, Vol. 2, No. 2, 1919

Demons of the Sea
Originally Published in *Sea Stories*, 1923

The Hog
Originally Published in *Weird Tales*, January 1947

FLAME TREE PUBLISHING
Epic, Dark, Thrilling & Gothic
New & Classic Writing

Flame Tree's Gothic Fantasy books offer a carefully curated series of new titles, each with combinations of original and classic writing:

Chilling Horror • Chilling Ghost • Asian Ghost • Science Fiction • Murder Mayhem
Crime & Mystery • Swords & Steam • Dystopia Utopia • Supernatural Horror
Lost Worlds • Time Travel • Heroic Fantasy • Pirates & Ghosts • Agents & Spies
Endless Apocalypse • Alien Invasion • Robots & AI • Lost Souls • Haunted House
Cosy Crime • American Gothic • Urban Crime • Epic Fantasy • Detective Mysteries
Detective Thrillers • A Dying Planet • Footsteps in the Dark • Bodies in the Library
Strange Lands • Weird Horror • Lost Atlantis • Lovecraft Mythos • Terrifying Ghosts
Black Sci-Fi • Chilling Crime • Compelling Science Fiction • Christmas Gothic
First Peoples Shared Stories • Alternate History • Hidden Realms • African Ghost
Immigrant Sci-Fi • Spirits & Ghouls • Learning to be Human • Shadows on the Water

Also, new companion titles offer rich collections of classic fiction, myths and tales in the gothic fantasy tradition:

Charles Dickens Supernatural • George Orwell Visions of Dystopia • H.G. Wells
Sherlock Holmes • Edgar Allan Poe • Bram Stoker Horror • Mary Shelley Horror
Lovecraft • M.R. James Ghost Stories • Algernon Blackwood Horror Stories
Arthur Machen Horror Stories • William Hope Hodgson Horror Stories
Robert Louis Stevenson Collection • The Divine Comedy • The Age of Queen Victoria
Brothers Grimm Fairy Tales • Hans Christian Andersen Fairy Tales • Moby Dick
Alice's Adventures in Wonderland • King Arthur & The Knights of the Round Table
The Wonderful Wizard of Oz • Ramayana • The Odyssey and the Iliad • The Aeneid
Paradise Lost • The Decameron • One Thousand and One Arabian Nights
Persian Myths & Tales • African Myths & Tales • Celtic Myths & Tales
Greek Myths & Tales • Norse Myths & Tales • Chinese Myths & Tales • Japanese Myths & Tales
Native American Myths & Tales • Aztec Myths & Tales • Egyptian Myths & Tales
Irish Fairy Tales • Scottish Folk & Fairy Tales • Viking Folk & Fairy Tales
Heroes & Heroines Myths & Tales • Gods & Monsters Myths & Tales
Beasts & Creatures Myths & Tales • Witches, Wizards, Seers & Healers Myths & Tales

Available from all good bookstores, worldwide, and online at
flametreepublishing.com

See our new fiction imprint
FLAME TREE PRESS | FICTION WITHOUT FRONTIERS
New and original writing in Horror, Crime, SF and Fantasy

And join our monthly newsletter with offers and more stories:
FLAME TREE FICTION NEWSLETTER
flametreepress.com

GOTHIC FANTASY

For our books, calendars, blog
and latest special offers please see:
flametreepublishing.com